DOUBLE DOWN

THE
COMPLETE
SERIES

LISA PHILLIPS

Contents

Deadly Exposure

Book 1

Chapter 1

Norfolk, VA

Master Chief Bradley Harris did his best to disguise the limp in his stride. The man walking beside him was an old friend. Steve Preston led him down a wide hallway, gesturing as they went. "We have a gun range, workout room, a movie theater and a down room with bunks. A couple of the guys live out of town, so they sleep here if they don't have the time to get home. The warehouse on the north side is for mock-ups."

Bradley nodded. His SEAL team ran through mission scenarios set up to look like the building they'd be breaching. It was pretty standard operating procedure. But still, there was obviously money invested here. Not just a government budget at work. "It's quite the facility."

"My accountant would agree with you." Steve grinned. "He says I give him hernias."

Bradley chuckled. "It's impressive."

"The garage has four SUVs, two compact vehicles and a van. The plane is in a private hangar at Richmond. We sign each of them out as needed. Missions are dished out based on skill set, availability of team members, and the number of personnel the op requires."

"How many guys on the team?"

"Six, including me, plus one female operator. And my assistant, who handles all the paperwork."

This wasn't an interview, per se, but Steve had outlined the benefits packet. Bradley had weeks left in his service with the Navy. It was past time to start thinking about the rest of his life.

"How's the senator these days?"

Bradley glanced at Steve. The man hid his interest well, but Bradley had been answering questions about Rachel's availability and situation for longer than he cared to remember. "Good, as far as I know."

"Gonna see her while you're home?"

Bradley shrugged. "She wants me to come over later."

Steve nodded, something knowing in his eyes.

Had the man told Rachel that Bradley was in town? He wanted to believe his sister would just ask him, but figured her use of intelligence-gathering tactics wasn't unprecedented.

Would seeing her mean seeing Alexis? He figured not, since the two former best friends were estranged these days. He could stop by and have a late dinner with his sister—and not discuss Alexis.

"The team members on campus are in a meeting right now. Want me to introduce you?"

Bradley nodded. Steve led him down the hall and stopped by a door. Above it a red light was illuminated.

Steve opened the door into a six-by-six closet lined with hooks, a door on the other side. A TV screen mounted high on the wall had a list of six names—call signs probably—beside each of which was a score. It shifted constantly, the top two battling for number one. Half of the hooks held what looked like futuristic guns, along with various harnesses, vests and head lamps.

Steve tossed him a headlamp and Bradley realized it wasn't a headlamp at all. The strap was similar, but the circles on the front and back had a sensor in the middle. "Front and back of your head."

"Headshots?" Bradley realized then what the guns were for. He slipped the strap on his head.

Steve nodded, then handed him another, larger strap. Two sensors. "Heart—front and back."

Four spots to kill. Or, in this case, tag the victim.

Bradley tried to process what was happening, even as he tugged the larger strap onto his chest. This was some kind of icebreaker.

Steve did the same with his sensors. Was this just for fun or part of an unofficial "interview"? He wasn't sure if Steve, or anyone who worked for him, knew what regular people did for fun. And yet, this was exactly the kind of fun he was accustomed to as a SEAL. And these were definitely his kind of people.

Steve handed over a gun, then what looked like a knife. Bradley touched the blade and it retracted into the handle. His old friend lifted a finger. "One point for a kill shot, three for a knife strike."

"Hit the sensors?" Earn points. Win the game.

Steve nodded. "You're tagged, you're out."

Bradley swung the gun strap over his shoulder and tested the weight of the knife in his hand. Strike one of the four sensors? This was going to be fun.

Steve pressed a button on the wall beside another door, and spoke into it. "Two more coming in."

He shoved the door open. On the other side it was completely dark, the air full of smoke. Strobe lights flashed periodically in no pattern Bradley could detect.

His ankle smarted, but he wasn't being asked to run a marathon. "How many targets?"

Steve grinned. "All of them."

Then he disappeared into the smoke.

Bradley stood in the door and wondered what he'd gotten himself into. These people were the best of the best in private security operations. Was this what he wanted to do after he left the Navy?

Something moved in the dark.

Bradley chuckled, and then commenced hunting.

Two hours later he exited the building, sweat-soaked and grinning. Probably every day working here wouldn't be that much fun. But if this was how they blew off steam, he was all in.

Bradley pulled out the keys to his truck. He clicked the locks, but before he pulled the door open, he stopped. Glanced around.

Nothing amiss.

He headed across town to a burger joint he'd always loved. A milkshake was definitely in order.

At a stop light two miles from the hole-in-the-wall place, Bradley pulled up to the white line and waited for the light to turn green. He raised the volume on the radio and tapped his finger on the steering wheel in time to the beat.

Two doors slammed. He glanced out the back window of his truck. Men walked from the van behind him toward his truck, dressed in black fatigues and carrying rifles.

A woman screamed.

Someone honked their horn.

Bradley glanced at the light. Still red. Cross traffic was streaming by.

Guns raised.

He had a pistol in his glove box, but what would that solve?

Call the police? He left his phone in his back pocket. A passenger in one of the surrounding cars was likely already on the phone with emergency services.

The first gunman reached his window. Another on the passenger side. Bradley held the wheel. Looked at the light—still red. The gun raised, pointed at the glass beside his face.

Bradley hit the gas pedal.

Bullets grazed the sides of the bed as he sped away. A Buick driver honked. He swerved but still caught the front corner of the car.

Behind him the gunmen raced back to their van, determined to give chase. Bradley had grown up on these streets. He lost them quickly enough in a back alley, then retraced his route. All the while wondering who that was.

And whether they'd been sent to kidnap him.

Or kill him.

Chapter 2

Georgetown, VA

The door swung open and Alexis braced. Secret Service agent Alan Turner frowned with those bushy gray brows. He didn't have to say anything, not when that twist of his mustache conveyed plenty. He still didn't like her.

"She asked me to come." Why she said that, Alexis didn't know. She had nothing to explain to this man.

Alan stepped back, opening the door. She read what he didn't say in the line of his body. He was charged with Senator Rachel Harris's protection. And that meant, if necessary, he would take Alexis down. And here she thought they'd been friends.

Then again, she thought she'd been friends with all the agents on Rachel's detail—back when they'd spent their days side-by-side, serving the office of the senator. Doing their part for the country. Only months, but a lifetime ago now. Every day since, like a bad dream.

Alexis squared her shoulders. She clutched her purse tight against her side like a shield. Not the designer label she'd carried just a few months ago. No, this one was a knock off she'd bought for eight dollars at a thrift store. Like everything she owned now.

As she passed Alan, he muttered a dirty word.

From down the hall, a woman gasped. "Agent Turner. I expect better from you."

Alexis watched her friend emerge from the living room of her Georgetown brownstone home, shaking her head. Like it was possible for Rachel to be shocked. Striding toward them on four-inch heels even though she'd been home for hours. Her dress just as pristine as when she'd put it on that morning. "You do not speak to my friends that way."

Alexis didn't look back at Alan. She kept her focus on Rachel as he said, "My apologies, Senator Harris." But he didn't apologize to Alexis.

The Secret Service agent shut the front door and Rachel sighed. Alan had opted to go outside, rather than be in the house with Alexis. No doubt the rest of the agents felt the same way. Though, some would think she was there to harm Rachel. They'd stick close to make sure Alexis didn't do anything.

She was a pariah now. An outcast. Did she have that scarlet letter "A" on her chest? Maybe she should.

Rachel's gaze softened.

Don't.

She opened her arms, and tears filled her eyes.

Alexis walked into the embrace of the woman who'd ruined her.

"I'm sure he didn't mean it."

Alexis shook her head, an unladylike snort emerging from her throat.

Rachel cocked her head to one side. "Living room?"

Alexis sighed and followed her friend from the hall. They sat opposite each other. Rachel on a wingback chair, Alexis perched on a beautiful couch that was seriously uncomfortable. Kind of like shoes. The prettier they were, the more they hurt.

Didn't matter. She'd been uncomfortable for months now. Living the consequences of both their choices.

She set her purse on the floor, trying to figure out what Rachel had brought her here to say. Alexis wanted to demand the reason, but that never worked with Rachel. She would get to it in her own time, and no one was going to push her into it early. She was a senator.

An open bottle of red wine and two glasses sat on the low Victorian table. "Would you like a glass?" Rachel poured one, and offered it.

Alexis shook her head. "No, thank you."

"It's not like you'll be driving home."

The jab sliced through her, but Rachel hadn't meant it as a slight. It was a statement of fact, nothing more. Rachel rarely caught the implications of her words and she didn't bother too much with emotional subtext.

"I'd just rather not."

Rachel shrugged one slender shoulder and took a healthy sip. When she was done, she studied Alexis. "It's good to see you."

She nodded. "You, too."

"I've gone through six assistants in four months, Lex." Rachel chuckled. She shook her head so that her hair shifted around her face in waves. That four hundred dollar haircut was worth every penny. "They aren't as good as you. Not one of them is even close."

Alexis allowed herself a small smile at that. She had been a darn good assistant. "I'm sorry."

Though, she couldn't say what exactly she was sorry for. Not today, when they'd barely spoken in weeks. "What did you want to talk to me about?"

Rachel set her nearly empty wine glass down. "I thought I might need liquid courage, but that might've backfired." She touched her forehead with slender fingers, her grandmother's gold watch sliding down her forearm.

"That's okay." It wasn't like Alexis had anywhere to be.

Her purse buzzed. She slid her outdated iPhone out and looked at the cracked screen.

`Did she tell you what it's about yet?`

Alexis quickly replied.

`Not yet.`

It was sweet of him to be concerned. Lincoln had been one of the few friends who hadn't turned his back on her in the past six months. Ever since the story had broken over social media and both Rachel and Alexis realized what the fallout would be, everyone in their sphere had chosen a side.

Most had gone with Rachel, who'd valiantly tried to make it seem like not that big of a deal to her. To her credit, she'd tried to maintain the friendship they'd had. A friendship that had stretched from second grade, when Alexis's father was stationed in Virginia, all the way through college and Rachel's race for the Senate.

Years and years. Now all they had was awkwardness.

Why had she even come?

Rachel cleared her throat. "Lex..." She worked her bottom lip between her teeth.

"I think we're past the point of needing to be hesitant with each other. You can just say it, Rach."

Of course, then she'd have to listen to her own advice. Who knew what would come pouring out of her mouth if she started speaking the truth? Alexis didn't even want to know.

God, don't let me give in to my bitterness. He'd helped her hold her tongue for six months. To keep quiet instead of screaming the truth from the rooftops. She had no doubt in her mind that He could do that for her now.

The quiet time she'd had with the Lord through this season had been sweet and beautiful. But why had it come at such a high cost? She was trying to be okay with the fact He wanted this time with her. That God was going to use it to grow her through this uninterrupted time. She'd been stripped down. And while God hadn't caused it, He certainly wouldn't waste it, either.

Give me peace.

Rachel said, "I'm so glad you came. I know it's been hard for you, and you'll never know how truly sorry I am for that."

Alexis shook her head. "It wasn't your fault."

"But—"

"We agreed. We *both* made that choice. Don't backtrack now." She *needed* Rachel to stand firm. For both of them. Otherwise, it was all a waste. And Alexis would hate that more than anything else.

"I'm so—" Rachel's voice broke, and tears filled her eyes. "I shouldn't have let you do it."

Alexis fought her natural response, refusing to give in to the pull of her friend's emotions. That was a spiral Alexis didn't want to go down. They'd both been a mess at Rachel's parent's funeral. Ever since the moment Rachel cried, that switch was flipped in Alexis as well. Tears were inevitable. For years now, she'd loved this woman as a friend. And as the sister she'd never had. When Rachel hurt, Alexis did.

And when one of them was destroyed...

"We should have found another way."

"It's done." Alexis swallowed. "Please just let it be done."

"How is it going, finding a job?"

She shrugged, not wanting to talk about that. No one wanted to hire someone who'd been publicly shamed the way she had. The crucifixion she'd suffered online afterwards had driven Alexis into isolation, until Lincoln of all people had forced her to reconnect. She had no social media accounts these days, but still every meeting was a new experience for someone to laugh at her.

For once, she wanted to be invited in for an interview on the strength of her resume, and not just so whoever it was could ask her all the dirty secrets of her private life that had come to light.

Rachel swiped a manicured finger under one eye. "This is all my fault."

"It's for the best." The alternative being Rachel's career destroyed, and her reputation in tatters. Alexis would never have let that happen.

Instead, Rachel's integrity had taken a hit. Her stance on family values had been tarnished. Firing Alexis had been like slicing off an infected limb—at least according to the court of public opinion. The sentence—Alexis had been banished. Rachel had come out looking like the victim of an assistant with no moral compass.

Alexis would do it again. Even with everything that had happened, she would do it again every time. Anytime. For Rachel.

"I want to fix it. That's why I asked you to come." Rachel leaned over the table and set her hand on Alexis's. "I can't stand what's happened to you. And I want to make things right."

"No." How could she think that would be good? "You don't need to do that, Rachel. Not for me." *I'm not worth it.* She wanted to add those words, but knew they weren't true. Despite how she felt.

That was the old her talking. The child that had to prove herself to demanding parents who accepted nothing less than perfection.

Her father had publicly disowned her after it happened, completely cut her off. Alexis didn't even know what her mother thought. She wouldn't answer the phone so many times that Alexis had finally quit calling.

The parents she really needed right now, but couldn't have in her life? Rachel's.

Alexis said, "If you let the truth get out, people will know what really happened. The video will get air time all over again, and this will never be over. There's no point trying to change what happened. You can't fix my life now. We both made a choice, and as far as I'm concerned it was the right one."

Rachel just stared at her, tears in her eyes.

"If you try to explain, the fallout will be catastrophic."

"But you're hurting."

Alexis blinked back tears. She picked up her purse and stood. "It's for the best."

"Don't leave." Rachel jumped up and came around to take Alexis's arm. "Please. Lex. Stay and visit. I need your advice on an upcoming bill."

Alexis gritted her teeth. "Maybe another time would be better."

"Please. It won't take long. I just want to run some things by you, for old time's sake." Rachel's pleading face had convinced Alexis to help her many times. Things weren't much different now. Alexis still wanted to help her friend. But in order to do so, she'd have to bridge the chasm that now stretched between them.

"That's probably not a good idea."

Rachel let her go, and Alexis turned away. To the sideboard of framed photos. Pictures of Rachel, Alexis, and Rachel's brother Bradley. The three of them—a family. The distance now between her and Rachel was nothing compared to what Alexis and Bradley had done to each other. Another lifetime ago.

They'd barely spoken since. Rachel had known something was wrong, but not what had changed.

Alexis had genuinely liked Bradley, and still respected him. Who wouldn't respect a decorated Navy SEAL? But that didn't mean she was ever going to speak to him again. It was far too embarrassing.

"I'm going to tell Brad."

Alexis spun back. "Wha—"

"I am." Rachel lifted her chin. "He needs to know the truth. It's past time you two quit not speaking to each other and get back to the way things are supposed to be."

"Because you and I swore a blood oath?" Best friends forever. Soul sisters. Alexis was supposed to have married Bradley, so Rachel could be her children's Auntie.

Rachel's eyes warmed. "That hurt."

"It was one tiny needle. And it was your idea." Getting matching tattoos had been *way* worse.

"Still." Rachel looked a little green around the edges.

Alexis had to smile. This was the friend she remembered. No baggage, just the two of them. She didn't have any good memories in her life that didn't include Rachel. And Bradley.

Too bad that part of her life was done now. Gone like her reputation. Her job.

Her credibility.

She sighed, moving past the sideboard toward the hall. Didn't every family have problems? The three of them had been what Alexis had never found at home. And now it was all gone. Ruined, like the rest of her life. Though, admitting that out loud wouldn't be fair to Rachel.

There was no point dwelling on it further. She had to keep reminding herself that all this had happened for the best. A new chapter, because she'd done the right thing for her friend. That made it all the better.

"Lex."

She turned. "Please don't tell Brad." As much as she wanted him to know the truth—and to not look at her the way everyone else in the world did—it wasn't meant to be.

"He isn't seeing anyone right now."

"Rach."

Her friend enveloped her in a hug. Alexis sucked in a choppy breath, and hugged her back.

The crack of a gunshot echoed from another part of the house.

Rachel flinched and pulled out of the hug. "What was that?"

Alexis knew, but who wanted to contemplate that? "We should get out of the hall."

A Secret Service agent ran in. "Ma'am, let's get you—"

Another shot rang out. The red stain blossomed from his neck, and the man dropped to the floor.

Rachel screamed.

Beyond where the agent had stood was a man in a ski mask. Black clothes. Gas mask.

Alexis gripped her friend's hand, her feet seemingly frozen to the floor. Her brain unable to think about what they should do.

The man tossed a canister in their direction. It hit the tile in front of them and rolled over to where they stood.

Alexis shoved her friend towards the living room, through the cloud of gas.

Her eyes blurred. Stung. Her hip clipped a piece of furniture and she dropped to one knee. Cried out.

More gas clouded around her.

"Rachel."

Alexis could hear her friend moving, but couldn't see anything. She felt around, encountered the couch. The corner of the table. When her fingers found the soft material of Rachel's sweater, she grasped it. "Rach."

Her friend coughed. "Lex." Her voice croaked. "What—"

Rachel's sweater was yanked from Alexis's grip.

Rachel screamed, the sound moving away from Alexis. She scrambled forward to find her friend again, and her forehead cracked the end table. Something toppled on her. A vase. It smashed against the floor. She tried to get her balance and her hands landed on splintered glass.

Alexis hissed out a breath.

What was going on?

"Rachel!"

Two arms banded around her. The air expelled from her lungs and hot breath touched her ear. "Guess we'll see what you're made of now."

Alexis struggled as hard as she could, kicking her legs out and tugging at his arms with both hands. "Let me go!"

He chuckled.

"Enough."

The man stilled as a new voice entered the room.

Alexis tried to breathe, and could only cough. She kept up her struggle, trying to get free of whoever this was. Alan? She didn't know.

"You did your job, Turner."

"So gimme my money." Turner dropped her on the floor.

Alexis slammed onto the glass, ignored the slicing pain and scrambled away from him. Alan Turner had done this? Sure, he hated her, but where was Rachel? He'd never allow her to get hurt. And yet, it seemed he'd been paid to completely ignore his oath.

Alexis found the wall and huddled against it.

A gunshot rang out. She flinched and moved closer to the wall. Her eyes were streaming now, and she still couldn't make out much.

Who had been shot?

Footsteps crossed the room toward her.

Alexis looked around, trying to see through the swimming mist that was now her vision. "Rachel!"

No answer.

Two dark columns stopped in front of her.

Alexis looked up in time to see an arm swing toward her. It slammed into her temple, and everything went black.

Chapter 3

Bradley pulled over to the curb and stared at the scene playing out on his sister's street. His left eye still smarted from the blow he'd received in Steve's "game." He'd killed two of the Double Down guys, and gotten tagged in the eye by the female operator going for his forehead. But after he processed the fact she'd been taller than he was, he hadn't let her get him. Bradley had managed to slip away before she could regroup from his retaliation.

Now, cops and black and white cars with their lights flashing crowded the street. An ambulance was parked by the curb in front of his sister's apartment. The back doors were open, and inside a familiar figure sat receiving medical attention.

What was going on?

He grabbed the door handle and hopped out before he realized he hadn't shut off the engine. Alexis always made him act stupid. *Nothing has changed there.* He pulled the keys out and pocketed them, then made his way to her at a far more sedate pace. Where was Rachel? And why had Alexis come here on a night when his sister asked him to come over?

His ankle kicked back at him with every step. That pang of pain. He pulled back even more, slowing his pace. It was pure luck Rachel had caught him on two weeks of medical down-time between missions. Also, when he'd happened to be talking with Double Down Inc. about his plans for when he left the service.

He was OUTCONUS on missions all over the world close to three hundred days a year, but she'd called him this afternoon during his interview. *I have to tell you something.*

Bradley stepped up to the back of the ambulance, where an EMT held gauze against Alexis's temple. "Where's my sister?"

Her eyes lifted, and he watched like it was slow motion. Relief he was there. The realization that she wanted him there. Guilt. Frustration. He was pretty sure all that would be written over his face as well if he hadn't learned to keep it locked up tight. Who knew SEALs training would come handy in relationships?

Not that they had a relationship.

Anymore.

Underlying everything that Alexis's face broadcast loud and clear was one thing that beat out the rest: pure terror.

His stomach clenched. "Alexis, where's Rachel?"

"Sir!" A suited man strode over, not much older than him. The guy flashed a badge. FBI. "I'm Agent Walker."

"Master Chief Bradley Harris." Since they were doing titles.

He walked with the man over to the curb in front of his sister's house. Out of earshot of Alexis. Bradley said, "What's going on?"

"Approximately one hour ago, Senator Harris was abducted from her home. The Secret Service agents on your sister's detail were either incapacitated or killed."

He glanced over his shoulder at Alexis. And that haunted look in her eyes.

"She was in the house when it happened." The agent answered the question Bradley hadn't asked. "We're trying to ascertain if she had anything to do with what happened. So far she's been too shaken up to answer any questions. It can't be a coincidence, though. Your sister is abducted on the same night her disgraced former assistant is paying her a visit?"

It hit the tip of his tongue to tell the agent Alexis would never put Rachel in harm's way. That she would never do anything to harm her friend. But he didn't know that, did he? After everything that had happened, he had to face the fact he didn't know Alexis at all.

Maybe once upon a time he could've said that.

Bradley squeezed the back of his neck, and looked at his boots.

"Are you aware of anyone who might want to do something like this?"

He glanced up. "Abduct my sister? No. Who would do that?"

"No one she was up against, who might've had a grudge?"

"You'll have to ask her assistant that. I don't exactly keep close tabs." He realized how that sounded. "We're close, but I'm not in Virginia all that much and I'm not all up in her work." And it wasn't like he could tell her what he was doing. She didn't have the clearance.

"We're contacting her assistant, and I have agents already at her office looking through her files to see if any threats have been made," the agent said. "We're also going to talk to Ms. Calvert."

Alexis.

She'd been part of their lives for years. Bradley struggled to think of a memory of Rachel that didn't also have Alexis in it. At the time it had seemed so natural for their relationship to slip into more. Then came the awkwardness after, and wondering what Rachel was going to think. It had soured everything at a time when he'd been heading out for deployment. When he'd come back, Alexis had retreated into her head. She'd pushed him away and told him it was for the best. Bradley didn't want to believe it'd been because of him. But then, he'd always been good at denial.

"I'll talk to her." He swallowed, wondering if it would even help. "She's more likely to open up to me than someone with a badge."

"She has a grudge against cops?"

Bradley shook his head and just made his way to her, rather than get into all that with the agent. Alexis probably didn't want someone "official" wading through her business. It had already been splashed across social media and the news. He wondered how she'd even survived that when she'd always been such a private person.

Then again, if she hadn't wanted it exposed, then she shouldn't have done what she'd done. Right?

Bradley scratched the side of his head, trying to nail down the frustration so he didn't blow this conversation. He wanted to feel sorry for her that she'd gone through all that—having her private life blasted everywhere. But what was he supposed to think? She'd rejected him. It hardly even made sense to him that a woman like her would choose *that*. Over what they could have had? Made no sense.

The EMT had leaned close to her. Too close. The man's lips moved as he said something in her ear. She stiffened.

"Lex." He said the nickname before he even realized it.

Her attention shifted, latching onto him. A lifeline.

Bradley steeled himself against that need to rescue her. To be the one who saved her. He glanced at the EMT. "You done?"

Alexis scooted forward on the stretcher to the open door. "He's done." She shot the medic a look. The guy had said something to her she hadn't liked.

Alexis hit the mouth of the ambulance as he held his hand out. Helped her down. She blew out a breath. "Great timing as always."

"Except not, since I got here *after* Rachel was taken." He looked at his watch. "She didn't want me here until nine-thirty."

Alexis frowned. "She asked me to come at seven."

All this had happened in an hour and a half? Never mind the fact Rachel had invited them to come in the same night. Bradley couldn't make sense of this. Had she wanted to meet with them separately, or was his sister's plan for Alexis to still be at the house when Bradley showed up? She was a politician. He wouldn't put it past Rach to finagle a reconciliation.

Like that was going to work.

"Why'd she call you over?"

Alexis chewed her lip.

"Just tell me, okay? Whatever it is can't be worse than my sister being who-knows-where at the hands of a crazy person."

Tears filled her eyes. "She—"

Bradley waited, but that was all she gave him. "What?"

"He's going to hurt her." There was more she didn't say. But he couldn't ask about that right now.

Bradley got close. Forced her to focus on him only, and not anyone else. Or the fact that the special agent was listening to everything. "Who?"

Alexis sucked in a choppy breath. "I don't know."

The agent snorted. "You expect us to believe that? You're her closest friend. Or you *were*. So who would have taken her?"

A tear rolled down her face.

"Who?"

"I don't know who he is." The fear in her eyes, that pure unadulterated horror, washed over him. Bradley wanted to pull her into his arms and hold her tight. Keep her safe from all of it. But what he needed to do was help find Rachel. Alexis would be safe. She was scared, yes—but for her friend. Rachel was the one in danger right now.

"What can you tell the agent who's going to help them find her?"

Alexis shook her head, rubbing at her jaw with a shaky hand. That was a nasty injury on her temple. "I don't know."

The agent's tone dripped with sarcasm as he said, "We're supposed to believe—"

"*I don't know!*" She screamed the words at him.

"I should arrest you for conspiracy."

"Do it!"

Bradley wound an arm across the front of her body and pulled her back three steps. "Alexis. You need to calm down."

Her breath came in gasps as she deflated in his arms, her body bucking as she started to cry. Big, body-wracking sobs.

Bradley scooped her up into his arms and carried her to the front steps of Rachel's neighbor's house. He sat and held her on his lap as she cried, rubbing his hand up and down her back. She sucked in a breath. "He's—" Another breath. "Oh God, he'll—"

"Talk to me, Lex. Who?"

She shook her head.

"If you know something that will help them find her, you *have* to tell me." Otherwise he would let them arrest her. At least it meant they'd scare her into talking.

"She's probably so scared." A low moan escaped her throat.

He pulled her tighter against him.

Her body hitched and she started to pull away from him. He shook his head. "Lex." Tried to hold on tighter. Why was she always pushing him away?

She shoved out of his arms, her hand planted on the railing and she retched on the steps in front of him.

Bradley got up and pulled her hair back from her face. He looked at the agent. "Get her some water."

The agent didn't move. "Looks like all the signs of a guilty conscience if you ask me."

"No one is."

Alexis straightened. "My friend is out there—" She waved her hand at the city beyond this street. "—scared out of her mind, and probably fighting for her life. And you're being glib?" Bradley touched her shoulder, but she shrugged him off and squared her shoulders. "I want your superior here. I want an agent capable of acting like a professional."

"Good one." The agent sneered. "You of all people, lecturing me on acting like a professional?"

Alexis's whole body flinched.

The agent didn't seem to notice, or didn't care. "Excuse me while I go find your friend. And if I find out you had *anything* to do with this, you'll be in cuffs faster than you can say Snapchat."

She didn't back down until he'd walked away. Then she just…deflated again. Slumped against the railing like that was the extent of the fight she had in her.

Bradley studied her. She didn't have the guilty edge of someone who'd done what they set out to do. Or who'd been duped into it. She might know more than she was saying, but Alexis wasn't involved. He knew that. He knew her.

Or, at least, he *had*. He'd known her in every way a man could know a woman. But, was that any more than a college fling for her? A onetime, home-on-leave, fling for him. *Tell yourself that.* The fact she hadn't wanted to talk about it afterwards didn't stop him from making more of it than it was. He'd never considered himself a romantic, but there was something about him and Alexis that was just…right.

But that was years ago. Since then, he'd gotten saved, and he knew precisely what the Bible said about what they'd done. They'd known it was wrong as well. And while he didn't want to live with that guilt—and gave it to God daily—maybe there was more they had to do. A way they could reconcile things between them so he didn't feel like she'd trapped him—forever, in a way he'd never be able to get past her. And didn't think he ever would.

"You want me to give you a ride home?"

Tonight wasn't the night for that talk. It might've been why Rachel had called them both here, but he couldn't know that now. Not until he saw Alexis back to wherever she lived and hit the streets to find his sister.

With the help of Double Down.

Alexis nodded and pushed off the railing, clutching one arm across her stomach. He waited while she grabbed her purse, and spoke with one of the police officers. The man was aloof. Bradley could understand why, considering her public persona. The brush she'd been painted with on social media.

The guys on his SEAL team had peppered him with questions about her when it all came out. Bradley had been too shocked to do anything but tell them all to buzz off. None of their business. Even though the internet seemed to think it was *everyone's* business.

Still, the way her shoulders slumped and seemed to turn inward. The defeated look on her face. He had to rub a hand across his chest over that aching muscle that had never really let her go.

Bradley held the passenger door for her, and shut it after she'd climbed in. He rounded the F150 to his side. Sat in his seat, he asked for her address.

She gave him cross streets.

"You live above the Walgreens, or what?"

"You can drop me off there. It's fine."

"Do you need something for your head?"

She glanced at him as he pulled out. "I just want to go home. Can you *please* drop me off there without twenty questions? I'm exhausted, and—" Her voice broke.

Bradley heard her fighting back tears for the next two miles of Georgetown traffic. The area she'd directed him towards was run down. Where did she live? Certainly nowhere near the Virginia condo she'd been at before. That complex was high-end, and she'd been so happy the day they moved her in. This Alexis was…broken.

A consequence of her own making?

He wanted to listen to logic. All the evidence said her own actions had brought her low. But what was the truth? She'd been sweet. Honest. That post online was the opposite of everything he'd ever understood about her. Everything he'd loved about her.

He pulled over in front of the Walgreens.

She got out, then turned back. "If you…" She took a breath. "If you hear anything, will you call me?"

Bradley nodded. "You, too. Okay?"

She pressed her lips into a thin line and conceded with a nod.

"And I want you calling me if you need anything. Or if you think you're in danger. Got it?" She knew him. She knew he had to ask. No matter what had happened between them, Bradley would be there for her.

Alexis stared at him for a full minute, then finally said, "Thank you."

She shut the door. Bradley sat in silence until he couldn't hold his breath any longer. Then he inhaled. She'd looked at him like he was the best man she'd ever met. But it also seemed like she thought he just might be her *only* hope. And maybe he could be. He was a good guy. It made him feel kind of good about himself…until he realized it also meant she thought she was in trouble.

Serious trouble.

Bradley watched her move down the sidewalk—without going into the Walgreens—and turn a corner. He pulled onto the street and followed. Traffic slowed enough for him to see her enter a rundown apartment building behind the pharmacy. The parking lot was a mess of cracked concrete and weeds. Busted out windows. Boarded up doors.

This was where she was living?

Chapter 4

Minutes stretched into hours as the van drove. And drove. Each time Rachel thought they had arrived, the van simply set off again.

On her side in the back, Rachel lay still trying to fight off the groggy feeling. Her hands and feet were tied. A rancid cloth had been secured over her mouth so that she couldn't take a breath or swallow without tasting it. Black fabric— some kind of hood—had been pulled up over her face.

The needle mark in her arm where they'd doused her with whatever made her head swim, still ached.

Alexis. She didn't even know if her friend was okay.

This wasn't how she expected her night to have gone. Not by a long shot. And not like being kidnapped was one of the possibilities, but still. She'd had a plan, and this was what she'd gotten? She'd wanted to bring the truth to light once and for all so she could move on with her life.

She had to keep it together. *Stay calm. Survive.* She'd done it before, and she could do it again.

Bradley. He was in town. She knew he'd talked with Steve at Double Down today. Not that her brother had told her. She *was* a senator. She could find things out if she wanted—especially when Steve's assistant had called to ask what her brother's cell number was. Her feelings for Steve were one thing, the idea Bradley might go to work for him, another. It meant her brother would be home. She could run into Steve at a BBQ, or some other function. Both sent a rush of excitement running through her.

23

Alexis and Bradley were her family, and she wanted them to be happy. She could have gotten them back together. Everything she wanted had been so close she'd been almost able to grasp it. To clutch it in her grip and make sure nothing ever happened to any of them.

Not ever again.

Now look at yourself. Thinking about Steve brought up another set of spiraling thoughts she had to rein in. It wasn't worth thinking about him—or the fact he'd had his assistant call instead of calling himself. Like a chicken who couldn't speak to her himself.

Focus.

The van set off again, and her whole body rocked with the motion. A tear slid from her eye and ran into her hairline.

Survive.

Bradley was here. Her brother would find her.

Chapter 5

Alexis shut the door to her apartment and sank back against the door. Her knees threatened to buckle, but she locked them. The neighbors on one side were well into their nightly battle. Screaming at each other about this and that. Did it mean anything? Because mostly it seemed like habit. On the other side of her, loud heavy metal music threatened to drive her mad—if the arguing didn't.

She stumbled to her broken, ten dollar recliner and sank into the stale-smelling cushions. Her fingers drifted to her Bible on the end table she'd bought for college, which had been in storage. She probably should've thrown it away a long time ago. Now she was glad she hadn't. Bible on her lap, she grabbed her journal and pen. Clutched both to her chest.

Tried to breathe.

Tried not to think about Bradley. She couldn't handle that right now.

Tears threatened. Had they stopped? Rachel was gone. *Taken.* That madman had her, and there was nothing Alexis could do about it. She was nearly convinced he was responsible for the kidnapping as well, though logic didn't track. This had been a targeted attack that had bested the Secret Service.

Alan.

He'd betrayed them all, and Rachel was suffering for it.

How had he been able to live with himself? How were his wife and kids supposed to go on after it came out that he had betrayed the oath he had taken to protect those in his charge? She wasn't about to rob those innocents of his death benefits. He was dead, and there was no one to hold responsible anyway. No one to tell the FBI where Rachel was being held.

She squeezed her eyes shut. Was she hindering the FBI's ability to find Rachel?

The FBI and Secret Service would figure out Turner's connection to the kidnappers. Then the world would know what Alan had done. Rachel would be home safe, and things would go back to normal.

She thought back to the smells of that night, the gas in the air. In her throat. The sounds. The sharp crack that still rattled in her head. The EMT had seemed to think she might still be up for a good time even with the head injury. Why else would he proposition her in the back of the ambulance?

While his words had been grossly inappropriate, it was nothing new. It seemed like everyone in town knew her story, wanted to ask her about it, and some of them even wanted to star in the next chapter. Like she was going to let that happen when all of it had basically destroyed her. Personally. Professionally.

There was no coming back from it, and she probably needed to accept that fact. Even if they got Rachel back. Alexis wasn't ever going to be able to go back to the way things had been before everything went wrong.

She opened her Bible to the passage she'd read that morning, then laid open her journal and wrote, *Should I leave?* Maybe once Rachel was found, it was time to leave. Start over somewhere else. Make a new life for herself. Write a new chapter where no one knew—or just didn't care—who she was.

She continued writing, pouring all her fear and frustration out onto the page like David had done when he was running from Saul. Except it wasn't her in danger, it was Rachel. *Help her, please, Lord.* Emotion caught in her throat until she thought she would choke on it. The taste of the gas was still on her tongue. Alexis coughed at the scratchy sensation, and let the tears fall for her friend.

Then she read. Her lips moved as she took in each word, praying it calmed her heart as well as her mind. And as she read, it was like all the voices in her head were silenced as she soaked up the words. Here, in the pages of scripture, His presence shined on her fear to illuminate the dark places in her life. Washed it all to daylight. Warmth.

Thank You, Lord.

God had a plan. Even in this.

She didn't know what it was, and she prayed Rachel wouldn't suffer through it. She prayed this had nothing to do with the man who had torn both of their worlds apart. *Please don't let it be him who has her.* Rachel would never survive another encounter with that monster. Just the idea of it made Alexis want to be sick all over again. Just like she'd done in front of…

Bradley.

She couldn't be embarrassed. Not when he'd caught her up in his arms, and held her that way. No one had *ever* held her that way. And if anyone else had tried, she'd have found a way to politely remove herself from the situation. But then, Bradley wasn't anyone. He was everything she had ever wanted in life, and love. Nothing had changed there, except that he hated her now the way everyone else did. He looked at her with that same disapproving stare. Probably wondering what she was going to do next. How far she could be pushed.

He wouldn't do that. She knew that as surely as she knew the way he'd loved her. *Sorry, Lord.* That wasn't appropriate now. Still, she carried those sweet memories of the time they'd spent together in her heart. It might have been sin, but she treasured their time together. It was the warmest of memories, all of which included Bradley anyway. It wasn't like she was ever going to be able to escape him.

She kept reading and journaling until the knock at the door.

Alexis blinked and glanced at the time on the microwave. *11:37.*

Who was knocking?

She looked through the peep hole and blew out a breath. Lincoln. She pulled the door open and said, "Hey."

He nudged her out of the way and strode in, a red mark on his cheek.

"What happened?"

"I was about to ask you the same thing." He waved one hand around. "You're sitting here what…reading your Bible? You don't answer the phone? I thought something happened to you as well." And yet, there was none of the concern on his face that she'd seen in Bradley. Or was it just that she could recognize it easier in him than she could in Lincoln.

Alexis shut the door and held up both hands. "I'm sorry. I should have checked my phone." Even though that defeated the purpose of quiet time. Getting distracted by her phone didn't help her focus on the Lord.

He shot her a scathing look. Alexis had to remind herself that he was just a hot-head who was concerned about her. Lincoln had been a good friend when no one else in her life had stuck by her. She needed to focus on that. Not on the fact he didn't know how to temper his emotions.

"It's been a rough night," she said. "Rachel got kidnapped."

"I *know.*"

Alexis frowned. "Thank you for being concerned about me, and for coming here. How did you get hurt?"

"My neighbor's cat attacked me again." He leaned against her breakfast bar. "I should take that thing to a vet and have it put down, but it would probably tear me to shreds in the process."

"Sorry."

"You're saying that a lot. Which makes me wonder what all exactly you're trying to apologize for."

"What is that supposed to mean?"

"You tell me?"

Alexis turned away and tried to figure this out. Was he here to accuse her, instead of making sure she was all right as she'd thought?

Maybe there was another layer to what he was saying. Did he know Bradley was in town? How he could know that when she hadn't even known, was beyond her. Alexis had had no idea until Bradley walked up to the ambulance. It had been a wonderful surprise, and a terrible realization at the same time. Would there ever be an instance in her life when he could show up and it wouldn't birth conflicting feelings in her?

Lincoln might have feelings for her, or so she'd thought at one time, but she'd never given him any indication she was open to a relationship. What she needed was the friend he'd been to her the past few months.

Her life was far too complicated right now for anything more than that. She was trying to get a job. And not the pity offer Lincoln had given her to come and work with his father. The old man creeped her out. Lincoln might work for him, but she'd never gotten the impression he much liked his father. That wasn't the point, though. She wanted to get work on her own merit.

Dog walking and cleaning houses didn't pay all of her bills, though. Not in a town like this. Rachel had been helping her keep her head above water, but Alexis didn't like taking the money. She'd put as much of it as she could in her account for emergencies, mostly hoping she'd get a full time job and be able to give it back.

Lincoln slumped onto the couch and it groaned. Not because he was heavy. The man was six-two and slender, but muscled from doing martial arts since he was a kid. Some people might think he was attractive, she supposed. He just wasn't her type. Not for anything other than a friend. And she appreciated the way he'd stuck close for her. But there was only one man in her heart, and no one else she'd ever met even measured up.

"You're thinking about him again."

Alexis bit back another apology.

He stretched.

"Long day?" When he nodded, she said, "Coffee?" She only had a can of the cheap stuff. Put enough milk and sugar in and it tasted okay, though. Or she could pretend it did. She couldn't afford creamer.

He said, "Sure."

Alexis set up the coffee maker and when it began to trickle out, visited the bathroom to clean up a bit. She needed a shower, but settled for brushing her teeth quickly. Coffee and the taste of being sick didn't mesh, and the sensation threatened to bring more illness every time she swallowed. Her throat was still scratchy from the gas, and her hip smarted though she didn't look to see what the bruise was like.

However crummy she felt couldn't hold a candle to how Rachel must be feeling right now.

When she came out, Lincoln stood at the window by her desk, staring out at the street below. The coffee pot beeped, and she poured two cups. "One sugar, right?"

He wandered over. "You know I like that hazelnut stuff."

Alexis sighed, and put milk in both cups. "I—" What was the point in arguing, or telling him for the hundredth time that she didn't have the money for anything more than the basics.

The thoughts in her head swirled like a whirling dervish until all she could see was that fog. And taste the gas on her tongue. Until her fingers loosened the way they had when Rachel was pulled from her grasp.

The milk landed on the counter, sloshing over the rim.

"Watch it." Lincoln screwed the lid back on. "For someone so money-conscious, you don't mind wasting it, do you?"

She took the carton from him and placed it back in the fridge, then used an old rag to wipe the spill. "I wouldn't describe it as money-conscious. That implies I actually have two bills to rub together." If she did, she would be careful about how she spent them. Always had.

When she was little, they hadn't had much money. Her mom had married a businessman and things got better, but she never forgot those days of chipped plates and grilled cheese sandwiches night after night because that was all they could afford. Now her mother wouldn't even speak of those times. She'd called her step-father after everything went public. He'd hung up on her, after telling her to never call again. She was a disgrace now. He wouldn't even speak Alexis's name. As for her, she wanted to drop his and go back to her birth surname.

Lincoln touched her shoulder. "You're so sad."

"I'm worried about Rachel."

"You should be worried about yourself. I would be, living in a dump like this." He shuddered. "I'd be scared to close my eyes."

Like she wasn't? Good people lived in this building, and selfish ones. Just like any neighborhood. Didn't matter if the people who lived there were rich or poor. Money didn't make you a better person, it just revealed who you truly were. "I really think I should be alone right now."

He shook his head. "That's the last thing you need, babe."

Lincoln tugged her closer, his arms winding around her waist.

"I—"

He squeezed her middle. Too tight. "Enough talking, Alexis."

Chapter 6

"I know it's late, but call me back when you get this message. It's important." Bradley hung up, wondering if he should call the assistant at Double Down. Bradley wanted to scream out his frustration, but didn't, and not just because he was about to go through security to get into the FBI building. Steve hadn't mentioned to Bradley anything about dinner plans. Why wasn't he answering?

Bradley stowed his phone in a plastic bin to go through the scanner. He wanted Double Down's help on this. He needed the team, and was fully prepared to hire them if that was necessary. He didn't mind being a client, and would rather have the team with him as backup when he hunted the person behind this.

Job or not, he needed their skills.

"Thank you for coming, Mr. Harris." The agent was young and pale-faced, like they kept him in the office all the time instead of allowing him out into the field.

Bradley nodded to the special agent, and followed the guy down their office hallway. He'd never figured he'd get to see the inside of Washington D.C.'s FBI office, and yet here he was.

Rachel, where are you?

"If it helps me find my sister," he said, "I'm happy to go wherever."

Though, truthfully, he'd rather be out on the streets looking for her. Was there even a trail to find? The FBI weren't sharing if they had discovered anything that might indicate where she'd been taken. Or even what vehicle she'd been taken in.

When Steve called back, he'd get his boys to Rachel's house to do their own sweep. Get a lead they could follow. *God, we need to find her.* He realized what he'd said. *I need to find her.* He couldn't think of life in terms of him and Alexis—not when he didn't know her any longer. They weren't friends. Maybe estranged family members, in a weird way. But that was all.

The agent opened a door to a conference room and motioned for him to enter first. Not the same agent who had been rude to Alexis. This one was younger. A rookie, maybe. Bradley didn't mind answering questions for junior personnel, considering that meant all the senior agents were trying to find his sister. Even the rude one.

Having a bad attitude didn't mean the agent wasn't excellent at his job. If only Bradley had the patience to let them work. How could he? SEALs weren't the kind of men who sat around, waiting for a result. Orders were orders. And those orders meant action.

Green light: mission.

Now a senator was missing. Surely that meant all hands on deck, for the FBI and the Secret Service. So long as they didn't mind an injured Navy SEAL tagging along, adding his skills to the mix, that was fine by him. Because there was no way he wasn't going to be part of their investigation—and the operation where they rescued her.

The bare table and bland walls didn't exactly inspire him. So when asked, Bradley had to say, "No. There's no one I can think of who would want to do this." He debated how much to tell the man. They were going to dig into Rachel's life. Which, to an extent, meant digging into his. "We're set to inherit money soon. It was a trust set up by our parents in the event of their deaths."

Bradley swallowed, not wanting to let any emotion bleed into his voice. Emotions never helped, which was why he'd excelled at keeping things buttoned up. Unless it came to Rachel or Alexis, that was. The two women in his life—his sister and the woman he'd loved at one time—had always managed to get past his defenses. Which was probably why he'd pulled away from them lately. Being a SEAL had changed him, and left him with not a lot of time for a personal life. Sure, some of the guys had families, but Bradley had figured it was easier to keep his focus on point if he had no distractions at home.

There was time enough for that later.

Only problem was, later might be now.

"Anyone your sister was at odds with?"

Bradley shrugged. "She's a senator, of course there are people who hate her." It was the nature of the job, and something Rachel hadn't been quiet about. "She had a guy a few years back who got too close, but the Secret Service took care of it as far as I know. You can ask Alexis, though. She worked for Rachel then."

The agent frowned, then glanced down at his tablet. "Any boyfriend we should know about?"

He shrugged again, wanting to apologize for not knowing his sister better. He'd been wanting to reconnect with her during this visit. Would they get that chance? He didn't want to think about Rachel being killed, but he had to admit it was a possibility.

Bradley said, "I think there was someone she was interested in, but it didn't go anywhere. Again, you should probably ask Alexis. They're best friends and always have been, regardless of how they feel about each other now or what happened."

Even something as huge as Alexis being publicly disgraced, as well as destroyed on social media, couldn't have killed the bond between them. After all, Alexis had been there at the house. And that wasn't an indication to him that she had anything to do with it. More, it was proof that there were still feelings between them.

He'd always loved their connection, even as he bemoaned the fact their closeness had compounded what happened between him and Alexis. He didn't want to unpack all of it, but none of them had dealt well with the surprise—or Rachel's reaction.

Bradley scrubbed his hands down his face. Now wasn't the time to rehash all that. Maybe when he could sit both women down, they could talk it through. Then they could all move on.

Bradley's phone chimed. He opened his eyes and glanced at the screen. Not Steve calling back, it was an email. From an unknown sender.

Watch this if you want your sister back.

. . .

Lincoln's mouth started its descent toward her lips. Alexis moved her head out of the way before he could. "Lincoln." She pushed out of his arms. "Don't do that. Please."

He shook his head, making a disappointed noise. "Sorry if I can't help myself when you're basically teasing me into doing something about it."

"Doing something about *what?*"

"The tension between us, obviously." He looked at her like she was dense. "We both feel it. But no, you want to ignore it like you've ignored all my attempts to help you." He stepped back. "Well, you know what? I'm done. That's the last move I make to help you, Lex. I'm done."

"Lincoln!" What did kissing have to do with helping her? Like she should accept his advances just because he had been her friend?

He didn't turn back, or say anything else. The door slammed loud enough it rattled a photo hung on the wall.

Alexis set her hands on the counter and hung her head. What had he been thinking? She'd never given him the green light to kiss her before. They were *friends*, or so she'd thought. And she knew what disaster happened when friends took that turn. When it got romantic, and things were done that couldn't be taken back even if she wanted to. *Liar.* Okay, so she didn't want to take back anything she'd done with Bradley, even if it hadn't been right.

Lincoln, though? She'd never thought about making what they had physical. She didn't do that. Wasn't even attracted to him, anyway. And he'd thought he was helping?

A pounding fist hammered on the door.

She sighed. He would ask for forgiveness, and she wouldn't withhold it. That never helped. *God, let me understand.* The last thing she wanted was to lose one of the only friends she had left.

Alexis pulled open the door. "Its okay, Linc—"

Special Agent Walker stood there, gun drawn. He stepped into her space and continued in the apartment. "Alexis Calvert, you're under arrest for conspiracy to commit kidnapping and anything else I can think of that will get Rachel Harris back safely to her family."

"*I'm* her family."

Strong hands pulled her arms behind her back as more agents poured in her front door.

"Go through everything."

Her stomach dropped. "No—"

His gaze whipped back to her. "Something to hide? Something you might want to confess to?"

"I didn't do anything!" And God at least knew that was the honest truth. Even if the world believed something different. God, and Rachel. What did it matter the way everyone else looked at her? She had at least that to hold onto.

Agent Walker sneered. "I find that hard to believe. But don't worry, we'll get to the bottom of all of this. We'll figure out where you've stashed your friend."

Her stomach soured.

"I figure you're down on your luck. All that inheritance Rachel is about to get looks pretty good from a place like this." He motioned around the room with one finger, then jabbed it in her direction. "So you decided to stage a kidnapping. Put yourself in the scene, so we think you're just another victim. Wrong place, wrong time. Too bad you're not smart enough to cover your tracks."

I'm being framed. How could they think she'd do this to her oldest and best friend? Things had been strained recently. How could they not be? But there was no reason on earth she'd have betrayed Rachel like this.

"I didn't—" She choked. "I wouldn't!"

But he wasn't going to believe her, was he? This man was determined to think what everyone else did. The worst possible things a person could think. About *her.* When all she'd been trying to do was the right thing. It had even crossed her mind that it was the thing Bradley would have done.

If he'd known.

Rachel had never told him the truth. Now it would come out, and the truth would sting far more sharply than any lie ever had.

Alexis choked back another sob. The last thing she'd wanted was to cause Bradley pain, and now there was no way to stop that from happening.

"Bring the computer."

She squeezed her eyes shut.

"That's right," the agent said. "We know all about what you did."

Except there was just one problem with that.

He didn't know the half of it.

"Get her out of here. I can't even stand to look at her right now."

The agent who'd cuffed her hauled her out her door and walked her to the stairs while her neighbors looked on. Enjoying her misery.

She'd thought it wasn't possible to be brought any lower than she already was. *I was wrong.* God was going to stretch her farther. To ask this of her, after He had already asked her to endure so much.

For Rachel, she would do it. Gladly.

She would suffer whatever was necessary if it meant she could get her friend back safely.

Even the threat of losing Bradley. Which was going to happen, when he discovered the FBI thought she was involved in Rachel's kidnapping.

The agent stopped by an SUV and opened the back door.

She turned to him. "While Agent Walker is wasting time, going through my stuff, my friend is still out there. Everyone who should be looking for her is distracted, chasing *nothing.*"

"I figured you were a good actress, with that prim and proper thing going on." The corner of his mouth curled up. "But I didn't know you were this good; you actually sounded concerned for the Senator. Which is funny, considering you're the one who just sent the ransom video to her brother."

Chapter 7

Bradley gripped the edge of the conference table chair beside his knees, as he watched the video play on the laptop screen for the hundredth time. Even though his eyes were now burning, his coffee untouched. He'd heard the words when they told him the email came from Alexis's computer.

But he didn't believe it.

"The background is moving." He'd turned the sound down. Rachel's words, her broken voice, played in his head anyway. He didn't need to keep listening to it. He needed details—ones that would help them locate her.

The agent he'd been speaking with didn't look up from his own computer, a laptop which he'd brought in. "Curtain. A sheet, maybe. We're trying to figure it out."

"What about background noise?"

"Because you're going to hear a train, or a certain kind of bird that only lives in one part of town and get a location, Sherlock?"

Bradley glanced at the man. Maybe that *had* been what he was thinking, but apparently it didn't happen here. "Pardon me if I'm not an expert in kidnapping videos."

The agent sighed. "Sorry. There's nothing in the background. Whoever he is, he's good."

"What if it's a woman?"

"You think Alexis Calvert is responsible?"

That hadn't been what he was talking about at all, but the agent assumed otherwise. Especially now that they'd traced back the email to her computer. This could very well be the work of a woman as easily as a man, right? Just not Alexis. Or so he'd believed. He couldn't let his faith in her waver now.

Yes, she was hiding something. That much he knew just from talking to her outside Rachel's house. Her reaction had been mostly about what happened to her friend, but he knew her well enough to see more there. Just not what the FBI agents wanted to see. Because of the kidnapping? No way. She would never hurt Rachel. Except the fact that her public display of...*that* didn't exactly leave his sister unscathed.

Bradley sighed and moved to refill his coffee.

"You wanna tell me about this two million she said he wants?"

He topped his coffee with whole milk and turned, leaned his hips against the counter. This wasn't an interrogation. They needed this information.

"Neither of you has that kind of money."

"Not for another two days, no."

The agent's brow furrowed. "The inheritance you mentioned?"

"A trust our parents set up. When they passed away, it was kept for us until the day we turn thirty." He smiled. "Guess they figured we'd just waste it if we got it earlier."

And now the kidnapper wanted it.

"One million each." Bradley sipped his coffee.

It wasn't a ton of money, not by standards of wealth, but it was a life-changer. He wanted to be grateful for it. Truth was, with his parents gone he didn't really care all that much about dollars. He'd rather have them here. Even if it meant his mother was beside herself with worry about Rachel. His dad would be yelling at everyone to cover the fact he was scared out of his mind.

Bradley was barely holding it together as it was. The agents acted like this was just another day on the job, which he supposed it was, for them. If he had his parents here, Bradley doubted he would be holding himself together this well.

The agent said, "So the kidnapper is close enough to you to know about this inheritance. Knows precisely when you'll be getting it in order to coincide with handing it over in exchange for her."

That didn't mean it was Alexis. "Or he works at the law firm. Or knew our parents. They were popular in their sphere of business." He shrugged, even though his stomach was twisting. "You think figuring out who knows about the money will find her?"

It was a long shot from that to a location where she was being held. Still, they had to get a lead somehow.

No one had said as much to him, but he figured the FBI was running on next to nothing apart from this kick Agent Walker was on about Alexis. They were bringing her in right now so they could question her. All because the email had come from her computer. He figured she'd been hacked, but they would know that, wouldn't they? Was the misdirection just a way for the kidnapper to make sure the FBI was doing busywork?

The agent said, "We have to investigate every avenue. Never know which one will unearth the truth."

"And the meet?" It was set for two days from now. The day they were supposed to have hit the lawyer's office and signed all those papers. Not a coincidence, either.

"That's one of the avenues I—"

The second he saw Alexis being escorted down the hall, Bradley tuned out the rest. He set his cup on the table and moved to the door. Alexis had tear tracks on her dry face, what makeup she'd been wearing now smeared under her eyes. They marched her from the elevator down the hall while every agent in the room stared at her.

He didn't want to be as worried about her as he was about Rachel. He shouldn't be. But he couldn't help his sister, while Alexis might be able to—if she told the FBI what she was hiding. Both his girls were in trouble, just different kinds. That was the reality. Bradley was torn between them, trying to balance friendship with Alexis—or what remained of one—and his relationship with his sister.

What had Rachel wanted to tell him? And, why did it seem like it had something to do with Alexis? Maybe she'd wanted to make a change in her life. Or she'd met someone.

Bradley swung back around to the agent. "Does my sister have a boyfriend?"

"There's a guy." He flicked through screens. "It doesn't seem serious."

"Any indication he might want it to turn serious and she doesn't?"

The agent shook his head. "He isn't the pushy kind from what I've been able to find out."

"So we're not looking at him?"

"*We're* not looking at anyone. The FBI is investigating this case."

They didn't want his help? "What is the guy's name?"

"I can't tell you that."

Because they didn't want him paying the man a visit? He figured that was a waste of a perfectly good resource. "I want to listen to the interview with Alexis."

The agent sighed.

"We're not making any progress here, and I know Alexis better than anyone. I can give you guys insight."

"You said you haven't seen her in years."

His stomach clenched. "That stuff doesn't change."

The agent made a call, and Bradley was escorted to the viewing room. Probably so he was out of that agent's hair. Too bad for them he didn't care who he was annoying. He'd make them all crazy if it meant they found his sister faster. What did it matter if they did that just to get rid of him?

Bradley was more used to kicking down doors. Evade. Capture. Exfil. There was a mission, and that mission was undertaken until it was completed. Then they waited for the next mission. Simple, but not easy. There was a purity to it that didn't even touch this life stateside. It was hard to find people who understood the transition. Alexis was one of the ones who had made it easier. Made home worth coming to, just to see her smile.

She'd acted like he was this great hero every single time, even when the mission had gone wrong and he took his frustration out on her.

Then, in one night, they'd grown closer. The next morning Rachel had shown up and overreacted. Everything had fallen apart from there. He stared at Alexis through the glass. Did she regret what they'd done? She'd told Rachel it wasn't a big deal. That hurt, but he got why. Rachel didn't need to know the extent of the promises they'd made to each other in the dark.

Promises Alexis hadn't kept.

Bradley tried to see all that through the lens of what he believed now. The faith he had, and the fact God called him to live a holy life. Not out of obligation, but as worship. Gratitude for what God had done.

Alexis in his life wasn't a holy thing, but what if it could be? Maybe there was too much melted snow under the bridge to think about her and marriage in the same context. But why not dream big? Wasn't that the point of having faith in a big God?

"I already told you," Alexis pleaded with Agent Walker. "I have no idea what you're talking about."

"The ransom video was sent from your computer."

She blinked, and her mouth opened. No sound came out.

"She's surprised," an agent standing behind Bradley muttered.

"Could be faked." Another person.

"She isn't faking that." Bradley turned to stare at them both. "The woman can't keep a secret to save her life. She isn't capable of fake surprise."

"Then she's surprised she got caught." Bradley saw the guy's badge. An FBI shrink?

"No way. She didn't do this." He turned back to the window. They were probably sharing a look, but who cared? These people's opinions wouldn't change the truth.

Through the glass, Alexis shifted her hair back with a shaky hand. She looked exhausted. She was living in a dump. What was she doing for work these days?

He didn't want to soften toward her, but she had always lived in that part of him. The part he hadn't been able to toughen up. No matter what. This woman was what made him vulnerable. With her in his life, he'd felt like he could conquer anything. She was safe at home, so what was there to be scared about on a mission?

Alexis wiped a tear away. "My friend came over. I was out of the room for a minute. But he wouldn't do that. No way."

Snickers behind him made Bradley bite down on his molars. Alexis had a boyfriend? Here Bradley was defending her, and she was defending someone else?

"I don't think anyone came over," Agent Walker said. "I think you sent the ransom video yourself."

Alexis opened her mouth. Closed it. "I—" She cut herself off.

Bradley watched the thoughts play across her face. The woman had never known how to hide anything. Right now she didn't know what to say. She didn't know how to play this, whether to defend herself or argue with the agent. There was no subterfuge here, even with the FBI thinking she was part of it. Bradley was as convinced as he could be that Alexis hadn't done anything. And that wasn't blind feelings talking. He knew this woman. Just like he knew his sister.

If Rachel had brought Alexis to the house, and called Bradley to be there an hour and a half later, she had meant for them to all be there at the same time. Which meant whatever Rachel wanted to say had to do with Bradley and Alexis.

Agent Walker tossed a pen on the table between him and Alexis. "What's this mysterious friend's name, so we can verify he was at your house?"

"You mean, so you can tear into his life and terrify him with all this?"

"If he's innocent, what does he have to worry about?"

Alexis clutched her arms tighter around her middle.

"Or we can go through your phone and figure it out for ourselves. But saving us all that work..." Walker left off the implications of that.

Bradley didn't figure much was going to change the FBI's impression of Alexis. Least of all her giving them a name, when they already had her phone and computer. They probably already knew who her friend was.

Alexis shut her eyes for a second.

The shrink behind him said, "She's planning. Working out her next move."

Bradley bit down so hard he figured he was about to crack a tooth. Seriously, they couldn't just take her word for it? Alexis hadn't done anything to make the FBI believe she wasn't trustworthy...

That wasn't true.

He shut his own eyes. Her private life had been splashed across social media. Even with the outrageous public icons these days, it had still been a huge scandal for a Senator's assistant to act like that. She'd been branded. And not in a good way.

And he'd had his heart broken.

"Let's talk about you," Agent Walker said. "Assistant to a senator, nothing but success in front of you, and you throw it away. For what, a good time?"

Another video he couldn't get out of his head. But what did his sister's kidnapping have to do with Alexis's indiscretion? Surely the two weren't tied together. This was about money. Not what Alexis had done.

"It figures you're just like everyone else," Alexis said. "Fishing to find out if I'm up for a good time." She motioned to Agent Walker's wedding ring. "Things lacking at home?"

"Deflection," the shrink said.

Except that he'd heard that tone from Alexis before. It wasn't bitterness, or trying to get the attention off herself. It was pain. No, it was *anguish*.

Agent Walker didn't react. "Then your friend fires you, and you're left with nothing. No money, no life. No job. Can't get employment past menial labor."

"Cleaning houses is honest work."

"Until people find out who is cleaning their houses and they ask your boss to remove you. Scared they'll find their house in the next video, right? Or one of their paintings for sale on eBay."

"I'm not a thief."

"And yet you make regular cash deposits into your bank account that aren't part of your income. You're careful," Agent Walker said. "I'll give you that. Small amounts, couple hundred at a time. Different times of the day. Different branches." He leaned back in his chair. "You wanna tell me where that money came from?"

"Diff…" Alexis blinked.

"Where does the money come from, Alexis?"

She stared at the agent, her body still. "I know how this is going to sound, but the money comes from Rachel."

"Senator Harris was giving you money?"

Alexis shrugged one shoulder. "She wanted to help me out. It's a free country."

Because she felt guilty. The thought popped into his head, but he couldn't figure out why. Alexis didn't feel like she had anything to be ashamed of. Rachel had given her money—she'd helped her friend out. But there was another layer to it.

Just not the one Agent Walker seemed to think was there. "You mean you forced her to help you out."

"Rachel is my *friend.*" She chuckled, full of mirth. "And if you knew Senator Harris at all, you'd know that nobody forces Rachel to do anything."

"And yet you nearly destroyed her reputation with what you did."

Alexis looked like she was about to be sick. "I don't want to talk about this!"

"Too bad. Your friend took the hit, and you kept on keeping on. Getting paid. Living your life like nothing happened."

Alexis snorted, though it sounded more like she was about to start crying. "Have you seen my life?"

Bradley's stomach clenched. He'd seen her life. Rachel could have given her even more, but Alexis probably hadn't wanted it. Didn't want to be indebted to her friend.

At a time when she should have been begging to make amends.

None of this made sense to him.

Agent Walker said, "I guess that's what happens when you post that stuff."

"The original post came from a dummy account no one can trace," Alexis shot back at him. "Didn't you read the news reports? We didn't leak anything."

We?

Walker dismissed her words with a wave. "Why would I care?"

"Because then maybe you'd have an *inkling* of why I am *scared out of my mind* for my friend right now. She's been kidnapped and you're sitting here doing nothing." Alexis screamed the words at him. "This is a complete waste of time."

"You might think that." Walker's words were low, a dark tone. "But when I find the connection between you and the kidnapper, I'm going to nail you with everything I've got."

Bradley backed up from the window, his mind reeling.

"Doesn't look so innocent now, does she?"

He didn't care what the shrink thought. That wasn't even what he was thinking about. *Your friend took the hit.* It was a crazy idea, but in a weird way made total sense. Didn't explain everything. But maybe it gave him just enough. Just what he needed to begin to make sense of this.

First, they had to find Rachel.

Then, he was going to sit the girls down and make them meet with him.

Bradley turned to the shrink. He squared his shoulders, the same way he'd done with the guys on his team when those videos of Alexis came out. "She didn't do this."

He walked out of the viewing room, every stride making him more convinced he was right. They'd both lied to him, Rachel and Alexis, and he'd believed it. There had to be a reason, or he knew they'd have told him the truth. Instead, the girls had drawn a wedge between the three of them. He hadn't been able to help them, when that was exactly what he should have done. What he wanted to have done.

Now, with the FBI looking hard at Alexis, and his sister in the hands of greedy kidnappers, they were going to accept his help.

Whether they liked it or not.

He was here, and he was going to be here for them both.

Alexis was held for hours, during which time he kept calling Steve until the man picked up. And then he got the team activated. Finally the agent who'd been with him earlier came back in the conference room.

"She's been cleared to go." He said it with caution. As though he wasn't sure how Bradley was going to react. As if he'd do anything but make sure she got home okay.

"You guys didn't find anything incriminating on her phone?" Or, the FBI figured she was still part of it and they were going to follow Alexis hoping she would lead them to the kidnappers.

"Only the fact there was a text conversation between her and an unlabeled contact."

Bradley said, "What does that mean?"

The agent who'd been with him in the conference room said, "Whoever it is, their number is unregistered. So if she has a 'friend' who came over, she doesn't want anyone to know who it is." He shrugged. "Could be it's a code, but it also means we have nothing to hold her on."

"What about her computer?"

"Still going through it."

"There should be evidence the video was sent from it, right?"

"Should be."

The agent didn't tell him more after that. Bradley figured he'd been lucky they told him as much as they had.

Hours later, Alexis was escorted out of the interview room. Bradley crossed the office to meet them. When Walker saw him there he said, "She's free to go now, but I'm keeping an eye on her. Don't worry about that."

Bradley nodded. "I intend to do the same." He turned to her then, ignoring the shell-shocked look on her face. "In fact, why don't I give you a ride home?"

They walked to the elevator together, past agents filing in with boxes of belongings. Alexis's stuff?

She gasped. "They have my journals."

He tugged on her hand until they were alone in the elevator, not wanting her to break down in front of anyone else. She didn't need that. And he needed her to get to a place where she would start trusting him with the truth.

"They're going to find out everything." She whispered the words to the quiet of the elevator as they descended between floors.

Bradley figured the truth coming to light was a good thing, regardless of what fallout there might be. He turned so he faced her and ducked his head. "Lex." He waited until she made eye contact, then said, "Everything is going to be okay."

Her eyes widened. He saw it coming, but didn't move. She needed to do it.

Her palm cracked across his face. "How dare you!"

Chapter 8

The second the elevator opened, Alexis strode toward the glass doors that led outside. Agents, other people, security guards and staff—the lobby was full. She wanted to run, but what would that prove except to make her look like a guilty fool?

"Lex."

Ugh. Was he really going to do this? Bradley probably thought she was as guilty as the FBI did. She wanted to curl in a ball and cry for days. Even if he didn't, and he was actually trying to... She choked. Was Bradley trying to *help* her? He had to know there was nothing okay about this. Not one single thing. The FBI was too busy looking at her to even spare a second trying to find Rachel. Bradley probably figured cozying up to her would make her want to spill all her secrets to him.

Hah.

She pushed open the glass door and stepped out into the cold air. What time was it? The dark sky was covered in a layer of clouds, not that stars were usually visible. Maybe she should go somewhere she could see stars. Somewhere quiet, like Montana. Or Wyoming. A place with one area code for the whole state. Where her nearest neighbor was a mile away, and she could get a dog that would keep her company.

"Lex." His voice was entirely too close.

She spun to face him. "No."

That look. Ack. It got her every time when he trained that warmth and softness at her. Like they had a secret no one else knew.

"Don't." She couldn't handle that right now.

"The FBI will find Rachel. And if that doesn't happen before the time limit, I'll give the kidnappers all the money and get her back. I will."

Tears spilled over for the millionth time today. She swiped at the offending emotion. "One of the Secret Service agents was in on it. I remember he said he wanted his money, and the kidnapper killed him. I don't know who has Rachel, or where she is. Anything could be happening and I *can't help*."

"Lex." He groaned her name and pulled her into his arms.

Her cheek landed on his T-shirt, between the open sides of his jacket. How could anyone be this warm? He must burn up in desert countries. Under fire. Every day nothing but heart-pounding danger. A sob worked its way up.

"Always taking the world's weight on you." His chest moved like he'd laughed. "Protecting everyone, making sure everyone else is okay. Not even caring what happens to you in the process."

She pushed back. "What are you talking about?"

Bradley simply lifted one eyebrow.

"We need to get Rachel back." That was the focus here. Not…whatever he was talking about.

"I know. But the FBI has all the leads, and all the evidence. They're not telling me everything." He paused. "Did you know Rachel has a maybe boyfriend?"

Alexis shook her head. "Do you mean Steve?"

"I don't know," he said. "Do I?" It couldn't be the Steve he'd met with yesterday, could it? Surely the world wasn't that small.

She squeezed her eyes shut for a second, then said, "They're going to find out…everything."

He shook his head, a smile tugging on the corner of his mouth. "Doesn't matter. I'll be here, and when it's done I'll *still* be here."

"Brad." She bit her lip.

"Let's go, okay?" He let her go—hello, cold—and clasped her hand as he led her to his truck.

"I have to do something." She wracked her brain. "I can't just sit at home."

"It's the middle of the night."

She shot him a look. "And you'll be able to sleep when Rachel is…"

Bradley stopped at the passenger door. "Yeah, probably not."

"Then let's go."

He cocked a brow.

"I have somewhere I want to look." She climbed in and shut the door herself. Because she didn't always need his help, okay? When he climbed in, she said, "Can I look at your phone? I need a map. Mine doesn't do that, and the FBI has it anyway."

He swiped across the screen and handed it to her. "Folder in the middle."

She opened the maps app and found the hotel. Bile rose from her stomach to her throat.

"Where are we going?"

She handed it to him. "There."

"And where is this?"

God, am I actually going to have to tell him? "Somewhere she might be."

That was, if the same person from before was the one who'd kidnapped her now. If he wanted to re-create what had happened.

Alexis grabbed the water bottle in the console and sipped. She didn't care how old it was, she was going to throw up.

"This another one of your secrets, like that passel you were keeping from the FBI?"

"I don't know what you're talking about." *Liar.*

"I told them you couldn't keep a secret to save your life."

She rounded on him. "I guess you don't know me as well as you thought you did."

Except that wasn't true, was it? Bradley was the only person who'd broken through. Which was why the awkward scene of the morning after had been so heartbreaking. They'd been so young, and neither of them had really known how to handle something so huge. At the first hurdle, they'd stumbled. Caved to Rachel's overblown surprise and...walked away. She'd been happy for them in her own way. When she'd calmed down. But they'd left things between them to lie in a way that caused her to think about it—about what could've been—every day since.

Bradley huffed under his breath and drove. When he pulled up to the hotel, he said, "Am I coming inside with you, or you want to do this on your own?"

She definitely didn't want to do this alone.

"Let's go then." He cracked his door, and she glanced at his back as he got out.

How did he do that? It wasn't natural for him to be able to just...read her that way. Who did that?

Alexis followed him to the entrance, sickness sloshing in her stomach with every step. She wasn't going to eat for days at this rate. Maybe not until Rachel was back home. Safe, where she belonged.

Not suffering the whims of a sick madman.

Could it really have been Lincoln? He'd been the only one in her house with her during the time the ransom video was sent. But hackers put files in computers all the time. Right? It could've easily been planted and sent remotely, made to look like it was her. Just because she'd stepped out of the room didn't mean Lincoln was one of the kidnappers.

"What?" Bradley's hand on her arm waylaid her at the door.

She shook her head. "I'm just trying to figure this all out."

The FBI would find Lincoln's information in her phone. He'd texted to tell her he was coming over, after all. They'd question him. And if he was involved, then they would figure it out. Alexis didn't need to worry about his guilt. If he was part of the kidnapping, then that meant it had nothing to do with…what happened before. He'd been out of town during that weekend, anyway.

She shook her head. "I have so many thoughts spinning around up here I don't know which way is up."

"Trust that the FBI will find her."

She nodded, pretty sure she didn't look convinced.

"We'll get her back."

"Let's go inside." She didn't need him being sweet again, distracting her. Alexis needed to focus on this. Not on what should've been, wasn't, and likely would never be. That was fruitless. And it didn't get Rachel back.

Bradley apparently needed to realize that for himself. It was nice having him here in the meantime. She wasn't going to cry when he left. Not this time.

Alexis strode up to the front counter. "Is room one-thirteen open?"

The man's dark eyes widened below his turban. "It is you!"

Bradley's warmth hit her back. She wanted to lean into it, to rest there, but couldn't let herself have even that moment of peace. Not in this world she lived in now—the world where she was a harlot, condemned publicly for things people did in private every day.

They didn't know even half the truth of what had happened. But did anyone care? No.

Bradley's hand settled on her hip. "What's this?"

The motel employee spread his hands out, palms up. His name tag said Havi. "Thanks be to you! Business is booming, rooms are booked. Everyone wants to stay in the love motel! You the best thing that ever happened to me!"

Alexis couldn't even blink. She tried to speak, but all that came out was a squeak.

"So room one-thirteen is booked up, then?"

She was so grateful to Bradley just then, she could have collapsed in relief.

Havi lifted a huge iPhone from the desk and held it up. "I know! We take selfie!" He rushed to a door beside the counter.

Before he pushed through, Alexis fled the lobby. There was no way she was going to be part of this guy's marketing plan. No way, no how.

Bradley said something to the man, and joined her outside.

Alexis just walked. She read the room numbers, increasing from one-hundred one on up, and headed for where she figured one-thirteen would be.

"You aren't going to say anything about that?"

"What is there to say?" It was humiliating. But then, that was what she'd agreed to, wasn't it?

"Lex." He tugged on her elbow, but she shook him off.

"Don't. Please." It wasn't like she could tell him the truth, anyway.

She heard him sigh, but didn't turn back. Just tapped her knuckles on the door to one-thirteen. Loud enough she might wake a sleeping person, but not like, *This is the Police!* loud.

The door swung open. A man in boxer shorts and nothing else blinked at them. "What?"

Alexis looked past him to the room. Mussed bed sheets. A suitcase. Wallet and a phone on the table.

"Nothing. Sorry to disturb you."

She turned away and headed for Bradley's truck. Rachel wasn't here. She'd probably never been here. Maybe this had nothing to do with that. Just because the FBI kept bringing it up—like it was Alexis's motive for hurting her friend—didn't mean the two were related. The kidnapping was about money. It was about Rachel and Bradley's inheritance.

The second she grabbed the passenger handle, he was there, crowding her against the door. No, cocooning her in that warmth. Everything in her wanted to lean into his strength, but he thought the worst of her. What was the point? She would now and forever be tainted.

The last thing she wanted to be was the victim here. But it was so hard. *God, I didn't know it would be this hard.* She'd thought the whole thing through, but fast because there hadn't been much time. She and Rachel had figured out the best plan. Had she known it would be this bad, she'd have thought longer. But the outcome would've been the same, wouldn't it?

Which was why she had to stand fast.

Alexis steeled herself against the onslaught of that muscle memory. The instinctive reflex to lean in to Bradley. To let him take care of her when she had to do this herself.

"Talk to me, Lex."

She shook her head. "Step back."

"Lex. Talk. To. Me." Bradley gently turned her. She picked a spot on his shirt and stared at it, not willing to let him see all the feelings she was no doubt broadcasting on her face. He would know, and she couldn't let that happen to Rachel.

She said, "Back up. *Please.*" She could hardly even think when he was this close.

"This is where it happened."

Of course he'd figured it out. He was a smart guy, but this wasn't a complicated puzzle. She should have come alone, but with everything happening she didn't want to be by herself. She wasn't even the target. She shouldn't be this scared when Rachel was the one in so much danger.

Bradley touched her cheek. Her eyes lifted, a reflex she couldn't stop. Maybe she wanted him to find out. No matter the promise she'd made to her friend. Did part of her wish he knew? She squeezed her eyes shut. She couldn't go back on her word. Not even for him.

"You thought Rachel might be here?"

She nodded again, too choked up to speak.

"So you do think the two are related."

Alexis shrugged one shoulder.

"But she wasn't here," he said. "So do you have any other ideas?"

She opened her eyes then, and glanced around while she thought about it. "Someone who wants your money."

"That fact isn't widely known." A muscle in his jaw worked back and forth. "But it isn't a secret, either. Neither is it a secret that if one of us is incapacitated, the other gets control of the full two million."

"They did their homework."

He frowned. "They picked the weaker link and took her out of play. Targeted me for the ransom drop, and my desire to save my sister."

What was she supposed to say to that? Or was he just thinking aloud?

"I don't care about the money, Lex. I care about getting Rachel back, and nothing else."

"I know." She figured he was right about why the kidnappers had done things this way. Not that Rachel would have let him die to keep her money. No. But she'd have known Bradley could take care of himself. Maybe he wouldn't even have let himself get kidnapped in the first—

Van tires screeched. The door slid open, a roar of metal.

Bradley turned to face the danger, his own instinctive reflex.

Two men jumped out of the back of the van, one a passenger and the other from the driver's seat. Black clothes, black ski masks. They were tall, and built. Huge scary-looking guys. What on earth—

Bradley rushed them. The three collided like a wave breaking on shore, kicking and punching. Alexis wanted to cup her ears against the sick thuds. The fight was vicious like she'd never seen before in her life.

"Go!" Bradley yelled over his shoulder.

She couldn't move her legs.

"Lex, RUN!"

He wanted her to…

One of the men broke away from the fight and headed in her direction. Alexis dropped her purse on the ground and took off down the sidewalk.

Chapter 9

The next punch landed in Bradley's stomach. All the air in his lungs expelled in one gush. He sucked in a breath and rallied against the man who'd remained.

A punch to the throat. An elbow to the back shoulder.

The guy went down on one knee. He wavered but didn't go down completely, preparing to rally, and come at him again.

Bradley broke away to go after Alexis. One of the men had chased her, instead of sticking with him. He needed to know that she was safe.

"I call police!" The motel employee yelled from across the lot, in the direction of the office.

Bradley pressed all his speed into his feet like a sprinter when the starting gun goes off. Two steps later his leg caught, and he tripped. He turned and kicked the guy holding onto him with his free foot. Boot to the face. Broke the guy's nose. It wasn't pleasant, but this was life. And the world Bradley lived in.

Right now he didn't have his teammates with him. It was just him, and Alexis was in danger.

He cried out as he kicked again, beyond frustrated. Wanting to go after her, but waylaid. Bruises made themselves known all over. He pushed the pain aside, as he'd done for many injuries. Being a SEAL didn't make him immune to getting hurt. Usually he had weapons to fight back with. Not a Glock that was in his truck.

The assailant clipped Bradley's chin with his fist. Hard enough that stars sparked across his vision. He blinked through the sensation and hit back. Grasped the guy, and opted for wrestling. Gravel dug into his knees, and his left hip pressed painfully against the concrete, but Bradley put his weight behind the hold and incapacitated the man as fast as he could.

Sirens in the distance broke through the rush of adrenaline streamlining his thoughts. Good. They could take this guy off his hands while he went to find Alexis.

His assailant punched Bradley in the temple, then pushed with both hands while he fought to keep his hold. *Alexis.* Was she okay? These two guys hadn't pulled guns, which meant they thought they could overpower him and Alexis without them. This guy wasn't giving up. He was trying to knock Bradley out. Probably so he could stuff him in the van.

He wanted to get to Rachel. Was this the way God had provided?

The distracting thought was enough—the assailant landed another punch, then rolled Bradley to his back.

His head slammed on the concrete.

The sirens were louder now. Or was that the ringing in his brain?

He kicked at the man now trying to turn him, probably to secure his hands. Bradley needed a way to turn the tables back on him, get the man on the defensive instead of continuing to kidnap him. "You'll never get your money if you take me, too."

He would have brought it to them tomorrow, as requested. Why try to take him now? This could all be just a distraction. A way for them to get Alexis as well as Rachel. That had to be why there were two, right? Get them separated. Distract Bradley with a fight, while the other guy took her. *No.* He couldn't allow Alexis to be taken as well.

Or was Bradley simply not seeing the whole picture here?

He reached up and grabbed the guy's throat. "You're not taking her."

His assailant gritted his teeth and fought off Bradley's hold. It didn't matter who was on top, or who was on bottom. He wasn't going to allow them to take Alexis while he was still breathing.

"You're going to have to kill me."

If they did, that meant Rachel had full control over his half of the two million. Was this their plan? Get rid of him, then they had his sister to sign over control of the money.

Fire burst in his belly and he squeezed the man's throat even harder. No way he'd let them kill him and leave the girls with no one to protect them. He might not have done such a good job of that in recent years. He'd been busy protecting the country instead. Maybe he should rethink that.

But right now wasn't the time to make major life decisions.

His assailant's eyes rolled back in his head. Bradley threw him off and ignored the pain in his knee—probably way swollen by now. He hobbled down the sidewalk and saw the motel employee now holding a shotgun. He said, "Make sure the cops get that guy."

Two black and white vehicles pulled into the parking lot, lights and sirens going. Bradley didn't wait around for them to figure out what was going on.

He headed in the direction Alexis had run, not even having the first clue where to look for her. With the police sirens, he couldn't hear a fight going on. He glanced down the first alley, the deserted street that led to the back of the motel.

"Alexis!"

Where was she? He kept going, moving on some kind of instinct without any clue where it would lead him. "Alexis!"

He didn't see her assailant, either. Had the guy taken her?

He passed the next building, a rundown strip mall. Tattoo parlor, hole-in-the-wall BBQ place and two empty store-fronts. Past that was another deserted road. Dumpsters. "Alexis."

"Bradley." His name was a whimper he barely heard.

He found her crouched behind the trash bin, tears streaming down her face. All the fight went out of him, but he checked around just to make sure the man wasn't still here. Then he crouched, ignoring the fact his left knee didn't want to bend like this. He forced his weight to his right side. "Hey. You okay?"

She nodded and hiccupped a cough.

What was it about her that made him want to take on the world? When she looked at him with the pieces of her broken heart so visible behind her eyes, he wanted to become the softest thing on earth, just so she would never feel pain again.

"Come on." He held out his hand and helped her to her feet with all his weight balanced on one foot. "We should—"

Alexis slammed into his chest. Her arms wound around him and she squeezed like her life depended on it.

Bradley exhaled, then wrapped her up in his arms. "I told you everything is going to be okay." He'd meant it, despite her reaction to his words.

She didn't know what he'd done for his country, the things he was capable of. That was okay. Mostly, he didn't want her to know that. Alexis was all that softness in him, whether she knew it or not. She was his ability to be gentle, or peaceful. The opposite of this roiling mass of frustration and anger that seemed to live inside him all the time.

Maybe God had given her to him to be a source of peace in his life. Like a gift. Wasn't that what couples did for each other? He'd heard a married friend say they filled up where each other lacked. He'd dismissed it at the time, not being married himself. One of those unhelpful things married people said. Like being married was the ultimate achievement everyone should want to obtain.

His life hadn't unfolded like that.

Maybe because he'd met Alexis so young, and things had gone wrong. But still, he hadn't wanted anyone else. Not when no relationship could come close to the connection he'd felt with her. Now he thought that maybe—just maybe—he could believe it.

Alexis sniffed and leaned back. "Sorry. I'm trying not to get snot on your shirt."

"You think I care?" He studied her. "We should go talk to the cops." Though, he'd rather stay here and prolong this moment they seemed to be having. Alexis needed him, and she was finally admitting it instead of shutting him out.

Would she say it out loud? He figured she wouldn't. She probably didn't want to lean on him, even though she was. Likely she wouldn't want to admit she even needed his help.

"Okay." She squared her shoulders, still looking broken.

So cute. He wanted to whisk her away to a cabin in the middle of nowhere—via a pastor, two rings, and some vows—and protect her from anything else like this.

But he had to find his sister first.

And in the process he needed to answer the question of whether their two assailants had wanted her, or him. Or both of them.

He held her hand as they walked back to the motel. The cops had Bradley's assailant in their car, and were speaking with the motel employee.

"There she is!" The man waved at Alexis like he was president of her fan club. He probably was.

Two black SUVs pulled into the lot, and he felt Alexis tense. One of the officers strode over to them while the other remained with the motel employee.

"The two of you okay?"

Alexis nodded. Bradley said, "We're alive."

"I'll need your statements." He frowned at the FBI vehicles. "But if that's who I think it is, it's probably going to have to wait."

Bradley wanted to commiserate with the man, but the bleed off of adrenaline had him wanting to find a seat. Maybe put Alexis in his lap, and just sit. Hold her for a while.

She tugged her hand out of his.

He glanced at her and saw her chin lift. "Agent Walker."

She wanted to face the guy alone? That, or she was trying to protect him by not aligning them together. Too late. As far as Bradley was concerned, they were the home team. No one else. She didn't get it now, but there was no way he was going to let her pass him off. Not even for his own good. That was totally Alexis.

And the reason why one outlandish idea was starting to sound more and more plausible.

Walker came over, pulling out his phone as he walked.

"Did you find my sister, yet?"

The man looked up. "That investigation is ongoing, and when we do you'll be the first to know." He smiled, but it was borderline smirk. "Want to tell me what happened here?"

Bradley gave them a rundown of the attempted kidnapping.

Walker looked at Alexis. "And I suppose you're going to maintain that there's no correlation between Rachel Harris's kidnapping and what went on here?"

"I never said if there was or not. I have no idea, that's why we came here to check. Because we have to do *something*."

"Leave the investigation to the professionals."

Bradley said, "What are the professionals going to do now that it's evidenced our lives are in danger?"

"Protective custody. Until the ransom deadline."

"Great. Alexis and I can sit tight while you investigate." He liked the idea of her being safe. Enough to agree to them sequestering him in some safe house under guard. He'd bounce off the walls being cooped up like that, but it was about the result. Not the cost.

Walker said, "They were clearly after you so they can have control of all the money."

There was a lot to unpack there. Bradley started with, "They'll get it when I bring it to them to pay the ransom. Why try to kidnap me now?" He paused. "I actually think they were trying to distract me so they could take Alexis."

She gasped.

Walker shook his head. "There's no evidence to suggest that. Could be they wanted you, and the fact Alexis ran made it so the other guy got away. His buddy got arrested, and we'll talk to him, but the other one is still out there. He didn't take her." He motioned dismissively to Alexis.

"We could argue about this all day, or you could simply agree to put her in a safe house with me."

"We simply haven't ruled out Ms. Calvert's involvement enough to convince me you're not in as much danger in close quarters with her as you would be walking the streets alone. Navy SEAL or not." Walker shrugged one shoulder. "Your personal feelings aside, we aren't going to put you in that much risk."

Bradley could feel her stare. Because of Walker's comment about "feelings"? Could be. She should get used to the idea. And honestly, if she *didn't* know, he would be disappointed. After all they'd shared. All their history. How could she not know?

Then she turned to Walker. "I'm not going to put Bradley in danger. You think I'm involved in this, and I'm *not.*"

She'd barely finished before Bradley added, "She isn't."

They were a team.

Walker glanced between them, his attention settling on Alexis. "So you're the first completely honest person I've met in my life, then? You have no idea how many suspects tell me that—"

"Susp—" She sputtered.

"If you didn't want to hurt your friend, why did *you* leak the video from the hotel room?"

Bradley took a step back. The blow was only words, but he felt it. Alexis was the one who had posted it?

"I see you didn't know," Walker said. "What else hasn't she told you?"

"Lex." It wasn't a chastisement, or a question. He didn't know what it was. Nor did he know what to say.

She didn't meet his gaze.

Walker said, "It's my job to assume the worst. And I'll tell you, I'm usually right."

"You aren't this time." Her voice shook. She touched Bradley's arm and said, "Rachel knew. She knew everything."

He squeezed his eyes shut.

"Mr. Harris, if you want to be secured in a safe house we should leave soon."

He wanted to tell them to stick it. He wanted to rail, and defend Alexis. To spout more of that stuff about them being a team that he'd been thinking just a minute ago. Everything in him wanted to believe Alexis. To think the best of her. He'd even worked out an alternate scenario, where she'd protected the people she cared about, to satisfy his need to explain it.

But it wasn't true, was it? Otherwise she would have protected Bradley from the fallout of having all his buddies find out what kind of woman his best friend really was. That girl he was hung up on. Making him the world's biggest chump—and everyone knew it.

Still, if he went with the FBI, she could still be in danger. So he faced down Walker and said, "If I go to a safe house, so does she."

"Ms. Calvert can be taken into protective custody, but you aren't going together. That's my final offer."

"How do I know you aren't going to just stick her in a jail cell somewhere?"

"It's fine."

He swung around. "What?"

"Bradley, its fine." Alexis nodded. "I'll go. I don't care where they put me, even if it's jail."

"No—"

"I just want Rachel safe." She held onto both of his arms, just above his elbows. "And you're the one who can do that."

"Not if I'm locked up in a safe house."

"Only until tomorrow. Then you can go get her back."

She didn't care what happened to her, but he did. Bradley glanced at Walker. "Give us a minute."

Walker shrugged and turned away.

"I don't care what he thinks of me. Really, I—"

Bradley touched both her cheeks.

Then he kissed her.

Chapter 10

Alexis let herself into her apartment. The noise from the neighbors bled through the walls even though it was just before six in the morning. She couldn't remember ever being this tired in her life. So tired it brought tears to her eyes every time she thought of Bradley going with the FBI.

And after he'd kissed her like that.

She dumped her purse, not letting herself even think overly much about the fact that it had not been the kiss of a younger him. It'd been absolutely the kiss of a man. One who knew what he wanted, and was determined to get it. Thereafter he would no doubt make sure it remained safe for the rest of his life.

That kind of determination was palpable, and it had been present there in his kiss.

Foregoing the coffee that would keep her awake when she desperately needed sleep, Alexis grabbed her Bible and headed for her bed. There was so much guilt, she had to pray for forgiveness. But she was just too tired to go look for Rachel anywhere else. She slumped onto the bed covers fully clothed, and her Bible fell open to the middle.

She tipped it up so she could read the verse of Psalms it had opened to. She let the words wash over her like a wave, and swam in the waters of the passage. This whole situation did feel a lot like drowning. She didn't know how to swim to the surface of it. Rachel was gone, and there was next to nothing she could do about it—beyond thinking of places her friend might be.

When the reality was, she had no idea.

And what was that but the proverbial needle in a haystack of places that covered this entire city. If Rachel had even been kept locally. It had been hours since she was taken. They could have gotten her anywhere by now in a vehicle. Maybe even to another country. She was a high profile target, yes. But by the time the feds found her, who knew what condition she would be in?

Alexis turned her head and let the cool sheet soak up the drops of her tears.

She prayed to keep from thinking about what would've happened if Bradley had come with her. Or if she had gone with him. They would've been together right now, having to fight off the aftermath of the kiss. A little separation might scare her more than anything in the world right now, but it was for the best. The FBI didn't think she was in danger, but tell that to her stomach. It just couldn't settle when she thought about the danger she was in, or Rachel, or anything that had to do with Bradley.

She drifted off to a series of vibrant nightmares where she ran down the alley, stalked by some faceless killer. Before Bradley could show up to rescue her, she always woke up. Alone. Wondering if this could really be what God had called her to. She knew all about seasons, and every one being different. For her good. But that didn't mean this wasn't the hardest thing she'd ever gone through.

Around eleven-thirty in the morning, Alexis finally had the brainpower to put on a pot of coffee and take a shower, after which she felt vaguely human. If she was going to have any chance of finding Rachel, she needed to talk to her friend's newest assistant. Alexis had helped choose her replacement from the pool of candidates. Still, she had never met the man.

She found his number on the back of the receipt she'd been using as a book mark. She'd used the scratch paper to jot down thoughts about each candidate. She'd have more information if she still had the computer the FBI had taken, but this would do.

It would take them some time to leaf through her notebooks. Assuming they could read her handwriting. It was possible they might not. And thank goodness she didn't write her journal online, or they would already know everything.

Alexis shook her head even though she was alone. *You're seriously kidding yourself if you think everyone isn't going to find out the truth about what happened.* She figured from what had happened that Bradley was beginning to work it out. He was a smart man, and he was going to realize, even if she never said one word. It was just his way.

While he'd been gone, she had been able to convince herself he'd never find out. Now? There was no way to keep it from him. At least not for much longer.

After filling up a travel mug of coffee, she headed out to the office Rachel leased in a trendy building. It fit with her persona of the young millennial senator. Was the assistant even working today? She hadn't heard anything about him from the FBI, even though he should be a viable suspect. He had only been working for Rachel less than six months. He could be suspicious.

Whether or not he was in the office, Alexis was going to get some answers. Something Rachel had been working on recently could point to the kidnapper, as could anything suspicious in her financials or anyone who had been asking too many questions. It wasn't a secret that Rachel and Bradley were set to inherit a million each on their birthday in a few days. The twins' story had been published in newspapers and magazines around the time Rachel was elected. It could be that someone had bided their time and then taken her from her house, leaving Alexis to take all the blame.

She let herself in the office and knocked on the door as she moved into the waiting area. "Hello? Is anyone here?"

The assistant emerged from the senator's office with a frown on his face. "I hadn't thought you would show your face around here." *After what you did.* It wasn't said out loud, but it was implied.

Alexis was no stranger to this kind of reaction from people, so she just did what she did every other time. Shrugged it off. Said what she needed to say. "I wanted to talk to you, to see if I can help find Rachel."

"The FBI have already been here asking questions. Looking through all of Rachel's computer files.   "

"That doesn't mean you haven't thought of something since they left." And yes, she wanted to know what he had told them. But she couldn't act too pushy, or he would push back. "So what do you say? Want to help me try and figure out who did this to Rachel?"

He assessed her, probably just trying to decide if he thought she was guilty or not, then he seemed to make his decision. "There's nothing in recent business that's serious enough to warrant someone kidnapping her. I thought it was all about the money."

Alexis nodded. "I think Bradley is in danger as well. The kidnappers asked for both of their money, and the FBI have put him in police custody to keep him safe."

"Wow, I didn't know that."

"I think the police are keeping things close to the vest. What with this being a high profile story."

"Like I told the feds, I don't know much. I haven't been working here long enough. And Rachel doesn't let me in on everything. I know she's been having some issues with her cousin lately, and he's been showing up at weird times. But that's probably just family stuff."

The FBI had to be looking into that. It gave their cousin motive if he wanted the money Rachel and Bradley were set to inherit. Maybe he was mad that Rachel and Bradley were getting it while he got nothing. Maybe she should call him and find out just where his thinking lay on all this. Get a feel for where he was at.

Lincoln could be a bear sometimes when his back was up.

The assistant shrugged. "Sorry you didn't get what you came here for."

Alexis shook her head. "I appreciate you talking to me, I know it's weird. I'll let you get back to work." She pushed out of the office, praying yet again for Rachel to be safe. She could call Lincoln right now, but the FBI had taken her phone. Maybe she should go by his office. He was a marketing consultant at a small company that wasn't too far from here.

Walking to the Metro station was an exercise in surveillance. She had to use everything Bradley had ever told her about how to make sure somebody wasn't following you. Alexis was pretty sure there *was* somebody following her, though. Bradley's words about her being in danger kept coming back to her mind. About the fact he'd been distracted so that the kidnappers could try and take her.

That didn't make sense, did it? She wasn't the target here.

The Metro was quiet except for a few military personnel and government workers, along with the odd group of tourists. Her stomach rumbled, but she ignored it. Who cared about eating when Rachel was in so much trouble? She could even be dead by now for all Alexis knew.

Would they be burying her soon? Alexis would have to look Bradley in the eye and know she was at least partly responsible for what had happened. There was no way to consider any other option. She would just be hurt because she was kidding herself again. Living in denial and not reality, just because she didn't like this life she had now.

He wouldn't kiss her again after that. Alexis would have to live with the memory, hiding it away in her heart so that it kept her warm in all the lonely nights in all the years to come. Yes, that was a little melodramatic, but she was just that tired. Any other time she would've gone to a movie, or gone home and taken a nap. But that wasn't an option right now.

Lincoln wasn't even in his office. She left a message with his secretary to have him come by her house later tonight. After the way he'd left the last time, though, she wasn't sure if he would show up.

Still, the idea he might be involved with this was just crazy. The man was pushy, but that just made him good at marketing. Lincoln was the one who'd stood by her. The only one who hadn't shunned her after what happened. Even Bradley had never returned her call when she tried to explain to him what'd happened. She'd wanted him to know the truth. The truth she'd never even told Lincoln.

Making her way back to the Metro yet again, Alexis couldn't help thinking that she was wasting time. Wandering around the city with no idea who to talk to, or what to do. Even in police custody she'd have had something to do. She could have helped them get more information as to who could've done this. They would have considered it to be another interview of their suspect—her. She would've thought about it differently, though. Who cared if they arrested her, if it made Rachel safe?

Should she go and see the lawyer next? The man with executive power over Rachel and Bradley's parents' estate would surely have something to say about all this. He'd know who had been discontent with the outcome. Maybe even someone had filed a suit to get the wording changed. Could Lincoln have done that? Either Rachel or Lincoln himself would have told her. Wouldn't they? She considered Lincoln her friend. And yet, through all this, it seemed like it was Bradley who'd stayed with her. Until he couldn't anymore.

He was safe. That was all that mattered.

No matter that Alexis had no idea where to go next, other than home where she could sit around doing nothing. Just wondering about her friend. Just praying.

That should be enough, and it was. She just had to remember that, and stand on that firm foundation.

Emerging from the Metro station closest to her apartment, Alexis stepped off the escalator onto the sidewalk and headed for home. She purchased a few things from the corner store so she could at least make toast and eggs when she got home. The cashier nodded and handed over the receipt, along with her change. Alexis pocketed the coins and the paper and she stepped between the automatic doors.

The hair on the back of her neck prickled. That wasn't exactly what happened, but how else was she supposed to explain how it felt? She was pretty sure she had been followed this whole time. What was different now? The sensation of being watched wasn't in itself malicious. So what had her senses waking up and registering fear?

She headed for her apartment, wondering if she should have ducked back into the store and asked to use their phone. She didn't have a landline in her place, and the FBI still had her phone. She'd have to pray that somebody saw her being attacked, or saw someone trying to kidnap her, for the police to be called. Otherwise she would just be that suspect trying to distract everyone's attention by pretending to be in danger.

She headed up the stairs in her building, the walls of the place not making her feel more secure. She had never been safe in this home, or even felt that way. Even though she called it that. Home.

Home wasn't the place you lived. It was people who knew who you were to the very core of your being and still cared about you. Never mind the mess and the dysfunction. They just loved you anyway. She shut the door as a tear traced its way down her cheek. Rachel was that for her. At one point Bradley had been that. Now, she didn't even know.

And yet how could she be so selfish?

She stowed the groceries but didn't make anything to eat. That would've been selfish as well, when she didn't know if her friends were even alive.

She had just shut the fridge when someone banged on the front door.

Chapter 11

Bradley stood at the kitchen window of the safe house and clutched the phone to his ear. "Thank you, Selena. If you could have Marshall call me back when he gets in, that would be great."

He hung up and set the phone on the counter. Tried to figure out what else he was supposed to be doing. Calling the lawyer had been a bust. Marshall hadn't come into work yet today, and neither did he have any appointments. But Selena didn't think there should be any reason why he wouldn't show up to the office.

Should he be worried?

Bradley wandered through to where one of the agents sat at the dining table, setting up a workstation. "Someone probably needs to head to the lawyer's home. He never showed up to work today."

The guy blinked. "Huh?"

"My lawyer. The man who is going to release the money to me. He didn't show up for work."

"Oh," the man said. "I'm sure Walker knows that."

"Someone needs to check."

Bradley didn't want to be telling them how to do their jobs, but the man could be dead or in danger. Why not kidnap the lawyer as well, if they're trying to get their hands on the money? Who else knew what Marshall knew about how to obtain it from the account it was currently locked in? If it was Bradley, he would want to utilize every resource. Exhaust every avenue he could. If he was greedy enough to kidnap for money.

Instead, he was just scared for his sister and worried about Alexis. He'd been praying nonstop since they left her in the parking lot. Walker had promised him that the other agents would look out for her.

Was she in a safe house as well? Or were they making sure she was safe at home?

He didn't want to think this would last more than a few days. The ransom demand instructions had told him to bring the money tomorrow. But what if they never found Rachel? What if it was all just a ploy, and she was already dead? He wanted to have faith but things didn't always work out the way he wanted them to. Take him and Alexis for example. Nothing that had happened between them had been what he thought.

He remembered that morning, the perfect clarity of one of his worst days. Alexis had clammed up. Bradley hadn't known what to say. And Rachel had done her usual over-the-top, exuberant reaction. Between the three of them, they'd totally failed to communicate with each other. He and Alexis most of all. Regret that he hadn't just told her—explained he wanted what they had to be permanent—had eaten away at him every day since. And now all he wanted was for God to give him the chance to make things right. To have the relationship he and Alexis should've had from the beginning.

To be man and wife.

While the agent made calls, and yet more calls, Bradley paced the house. They'd assured him he couldn't be found here, but no security was completely foolproof. In fact, Alexis had been the one to tell him that one of the Secret Service agents on Rachel's detail played a part in her kidnapping. That meant the kidnappers had gotten to him and made him a deal he hadn't been able to refuse.

Tomorrow he would go out in public again, and try to make a deal of his own with the kidnappers. He would turn over the money in exchange for his sister's safety. The agents had said they would coach him on what to say, but Bradley figured he would fall back more on his SEAL training than anything they told him. Even if they were experts on this stuff.

Bradley was an expert on keeping his family safe.

He tried to imagine what it would be like having Alexis here. If they were married, she would've come with him. Then again, she would've never ended up in the situation that had destroyed her reputation. He would have kept her safe from herself, if she needed that. Having her here with him would at least have given him someone to talk to who was on his side. Not that the FBI was his enemy, but Alexis knew him. She knew the way he felt for his sister, and she would've sat with him to wait. She'd have spent this time with him making his day brighter. The way she had so many times before.

"Bradley?"

"In the den," he called out.

When the agent crossed the threshold, he saw it wasn't Walker, but one of his buddies. Agent Simons was older, and seemed to have a lighter touch. Dark skin furrowed on his forehead and he said, "Agent Peters said you wanted us to go by the lawyer's office?"

Bradley nodded.

"Why don't you tell me about him?" Simons motioned for him to sit, then took the chair across from him. "He was your father's lawyer, correct?"

"He was. I remember him at Thanksgiving a few times when I was growing up. I think he was separated from his wife at the time and came to spend the holidays with us. He seemed like a nice guy."

Simons nodded and used his index finger to type on his phone. "Have you been to see him recently?"

"I know he called and left a message about meeting with him ahead of the money being released. I assume he did the same with Rachel. He may have even planned for us to go together."

What this had to do with the kidnapping, he didn't know. Bradley said, "You can't think he was involved with this, can you? Marshall is an old friend of my father's. He would never do anything to hurt us, least of all for the money. If he wanted to do it, he'd have just found a way to transfer it out of the account while it looked like it was still there. Right?"

Simons scrunched up his nose for a second. "We have to look into every angle. Your sister's current assistant seems to be clean, but it could be someone else connected to you."

"Or it could be someone who worked at the bank and overheard. Or someone who saw the news report about our parents and wanted to cash in. Some people will do basically anything for payout, right?"

"That is true. And cynical for someone as young as you are." Simons gave him a wry smile. "We're going to find your sister, and make sure that money never leaves the account."

"Just worry about Rachel. The money doesn't mean anything to me, and if this kidnapper knew anything at all about me and the kind of man I am, he'd have just called me and asked for it."

"You don't think that's what the ransom video was?"

"I think scaring my sister half to death was pointless, considering I'd have just handed it over. And that's exactly what I'm going to do tomorrow."

"You gotta be careful, son. If you're too eager to hand over the money it could cost your sister her life."

"I'm not going to do anything that will put her safety in jeopardy. Which is why I need you to find her before I go to that meeting."

Simons nodded. "We're working on that."

"You guys keep saying that, but I'm not seeing a whole lot of results. Walker is focusing on Alexis for whatever reason he has in his head. That's not going to lead anywhere."

"You don't think it's significant the ransom video was sent from her computer?"

Bradley said, "Hackers can fake that stuff. Maybe they even rented the apartment next to hers and ghosted her computer. Who knows? I'm not a techie guy, but I figure it's not all that hard to do that stuff. Or to hire somebody who can do it for you."

Simons nodded, considering what he'd said. "If that's true, we'll figure it out. You just worry about your part in this."

Bradley got up. "I can do that. If you guys go check on the lawyer. There's no reason why anyone else should get hurt. It's the last thing Rachel or I want to happen. Or Alexis, for that matter."

Bradley didn't really care what it said about him that he kept bringing Alexis into this. That he was still just as convinced as he had been the first that she wasn't a part of this kidnapping. Sure, he had questions for her. He wanted to know the answer to a lot of things. But that didn't mean she was a kidnapper, or conspirator. Alexis had never cared about money that much. And she would never be a party to hurting Rachel.

Bradley went back to pacing while the agents did their thing on the phone and the computers. He prayed more. Paced. Prayed. Rachel was his twin. Wouldn't he know if she were dead? They'd both been hurt before, and neither had felt anything the way some twins did. Most of that stuff was myth, or unsubstantiated rumors. He'd never experienced more than the compulsion to pray for her, or Alexis. That was a recent thing, since he'd been saved. But he got the impression it was pretty normal for believers to get a sudden urge to lift someone up in prayer. He liked being part of that. Connected to them, even though he wasn't with them.

"He's not gonna like it, but you have to tell him."

Bradley turned to the agents. Simons saw immediately that Bradley had heard, and indicated to the other agent who turned in his chair.

"What?"

"I got a new report from the tech going through Alexis's computer."

He waited, bracing for whatever it was they seemed to think was going to rock him. If he was going to stand by her—for better or worse was the plan— then he had to keep his faith in her intact. It didn't matter what else had been planted by hackers, or what she'd done herself. Alexis was the woman he knew, and nothing was going to change that.

"She's been looking into the lawyer."

"Okay."

The agent sighed. "The whole thing paints a picture of someone entirely too caught up in your lives. Your sister has severed all connection with her, and yet Alexis still seems to be firmly in the business of your family. And that money."

"Did whoever you sent to the lawyer get there yet?"

The agent checked his phone. "I'm expecting them to call when they do."

"Then there's nothing else to say."

The agent's phone rang then, and Bradley listened.

"Really?" The agent blinked, then lifted his gaze to Simons. "Okay. Thank you." He hung up and turned to Bradley. "Looks like you were right. I'm sorry to say Marshall Phelps was found dead in his house this morning. They're estimating he was killed at least thirty-six hours ago."

"Before Rachel was taken."

The agent nodded.

"So whoever took her tried Marshall first, got nowhere, and put their plan B into place."

"Could be."

He was sick of them telling him all his ideas were possible. Like he was dealing in subjection. Bradley was trying to figure this out, that was all. Trying to nail down what this person was thinking. How desperate they were. How badly they wanted that money.

Then he'd know what they were willing to do to get it.

The agent turned away and clicked through windows on his computer. For a second it went gray-ish, though still with some color. Like an Instagram filter. Rachel?

"Hey." He moved to the man's shoulder and pointed. "Go back."

Because seriously, did the man have a video of Rachel on his computer? It wasn't one Bradley had ever seen before.

The agent flushed.

"Show him."

On Simons's order, the guy clicked back through until the image came up. Not Rachel actually, it was Alexis. Why had he thought it was Rachel? They didn't look so much the same to him, other than the matching tattoo on the backs of their shoulders. The same flower, just in different colors. They'd sworn up and down it was nothing but a college mistake—then they'd looked at each other and laughed.

"What is…"

Alexis moved, speaking with a man. "Is that her apartment?"

"It is."

"Does she know you installed cameras?" He glanced at the guy long enough to know the answer. "I guess not." He shook his head until the man turned, and he got a look at the guy's face. "Why is she talking to my cousin?"

He didn't even like Lincoln. Something about the guy had always seemed off, and not just because he had a father who epitomized the greedy old man persona he wore in public. He'd thought Lincoln was estranged from his dad. If he wasn't, Bradley couldn't think of anyone who might want to take their money more than those two.

Simons said, "Walker is outside. He's also listening to the feed."

"Is that even legal?"

The argument had gotten heated now. Lincoln looked like he was about to blow. As a kid, that meant massive tantrums. It didn't seem he'd grown out of that phase since. And why was a grown man having a hissy fit, anyway? Alexis didn't need that right now. And she didn't seem to be reacting well, either. Her shoulders were low, her body curled into itself.

Neither of the agents responded to his last comment. They might want to find Rachel as much as he did, but what was the point in Walker breaking the rules? They'd get her back, but not have evidence they could use for a conviction. The FBI couldn't make a case on a confession. And besides, Alexis didn't need to confess to something she hadn't done. How did they think bugging her apartment would lead them to Rachel?

Lincoln lifted his hand and slapped her across the face. Alexis's eyes widened on the screen and she touched her cheek.

"Send someone in," Bradley said. "She needs help."

"Walker will make that call."

Bradley leaned both palms on the desk facing Simons and said in a low voice, "Get him in there now. Before he really hurts her."

Bradley was miles away. Lincoln could kill her before he got there. Or he could kidnap her. Did he know the FBI was outside? What was he so mad about, and why couldn't Bradley hear the audio?

"Turn it up."

The other agent said, "Chill, okay? Getting worked up doesn't help your sister. We get that you care about this other girl, but Walker is on it."

"Call him and tell him to get. In. There. *Now.*"

Simons got up. "I will cuff you and stick you in the bedroom until tomorrow if you push me."

"Then tell Walker to help her."

Couldn't they see that she needed it?

Simons looked at his phone. "Walker is going to wait. He thinks if this Lincoln guy pushes her then she'll give up something."

"Or Lincoln is the one behind this."

"Why would you think that?"

"Because of his father." Did Bradley really think his uncle and cousin might be guilty? Was Lincoln the "friend" at her apartment when the video was sent? Had he betrayed their family for money, for his father? Bradley had no idea.

He pushed out a breath. "It's not like I have evidence, sitting in this safe house."

"Then let us do our jobs."

Chapter 12

"I need to stay, Lincoln." Alexis sighed. He was getting more and more pushy, the longer he was here. "I don't think it's a good idea for me to leave." The FBI didn't want her anywhere near this investigation. And she wanted them focused on finding Rachel, not proving her guilt.

"You'll be safer with me than shut up in this crap hole you call an apartment."

What was she supposed to say to that? "I just don't think—"

"That's your problem." His lips curled up on one side, but it didn't look like he was amused. "Thinking too much."

"I should stop thinking?"

"If you're making stupid decisions, yeah. I mean, the FBI thinks you're behind all this."

She regretted telling him that.

"You're letting it cloud your judgment. Acting like you have something to hide." He paused. "Do you have something to hide?"

First she was stupid for thinking, and now she was keeping secrets? Alexis pressed her lips together in a thin line. "Does it matter?" She never wanted him to know the truth.

"If it'll save Rachel's life, you should broadcast it from the rooftops."

She shook her head. "One has nothing to do with the other."

"Don't brush me off. I don't like it when people do that."

"I'm sorry." She knew how his father treated him—like nothing he did was ever good enough, or worth anything. But plenty of people had tough backgrounds. Why did he have to get so worked up about it all?

"No, you're not," he snapped. "Don't pretend."

That wasn't fair. "I'm just trying to explain why I should stay here."

He huffed again. "This is all your fault, you know. And I think maybe the FBI are right."

"I would never hurt Rachel!" Why did she keep having to tell people that? Wasn't it obvious that Rachel was her best friend, even now? They'd all bought the line that her "behavior" had been exposed finally, and Rachel had to brush her off as a liability. Did that have to change how Alexis treated her?

"But you did hurt Rachel, didn't you? And now she's been kidnapped."

"That doesn't have anything to do with me. For a second I actually thought it was you who did it when they told me the ransom video came from my computer. *You* were the one that was here when it was sent."

"So now you're going to push this all off on me."

"I'm not trying to hurt you. I—"

His open palm hit her.

Alexis took a step back and held her hand to her cheek. That seriously hurt. "What—" Never would she have thought Lincoln—of all people—would hit her. "Do you treat all your friends this way? Just snap, and suddenly slap them?"

"You think we're friends?"

"We aren't anymore. Not after that." She wanted to walk away, but this was her home. "You should leave. Now."

"I don't think Rachel wants that."

She gasped, her cheek still hot and stinging. She whispered, "So, you are involved."

He leaned close and said, "You would know." Lincoln's face had twisted, losing the façade of nice. She didn't even know people could actually do that. She'd been so blind. He said, "After all, this whole situation is on *you*. You're behind it all."

"What did I do?" She asked, took shocked to do anything but speak in a low voice. She sounded hurt, but couldn't help it.

He huffed. "I think you know."

She lifted both hands. "I have no clue why Rachel was kidnapped, except for her money. Where is she?" Alexis moved closer to him. "Tell me where she is."

If he told her, then she could let the FBI know. Or they could haul him in to questioning the way they'd done with her. Lincoln would tell them.

Where was her phone?

The FBI still had it. Why hadn't she gotten a landline? Right, she had no money for a landline. Did money matter when Rachel's life was in danger? There had to be something Alexis could do to help her friend.

"I mean it, Lincoln. Tell me where she is or…" She didn't know what.

His laugh was a low, dark chuckle. "I'm *so* scared, Lex."

"Don't call me that. You're the one who said we're not friends. So get out of my apartment." Then she could ask one of her neighbors to let her use their phone to get ahold of the FBI. Walker had to listen. He had to. Lincoln was part of this. "I said, get out."

He reached for her elbow. "You're coming with me."

She tried to step back, but he was faster than her. "No. I'm not. Let go of me!"

Why was he acting like this? Sure, he'd been pushy earlier, but this was way past that. She wanted to believe in her friend, but was he involved in Rachel's kidnapping? And now he was trying to take her as well. Was this really just for the money, or could it actually be about what had happened as well?

"Let's move."

"I don't have shoes on!" It wasn't the most important thing, but it was the first thing she thought of. He stalled, long enough for her to slip on some sneakers she kept laced up, then dragged her to the hall.

"Nice and easy." He left the door of her apartment open. "We're going to walk nice and easy past those feds outside."

There were feds outside?

"Not one peep from you. Two friends going out, no problem. You're going to do everything I say, or I make one phone call and Rachel gets a bullet between her eyes."

"Bradley won't give you anything if you kill her."

"He'll give me whatever I want. He doesn't have to know she's dead."

Alexis blinked away tears as they reached the base of the stairs and the empty lobby. Why was no one here? *God, please let someone see us.* The feds wouldn't let Lincoln take her with him, would they? They should have looked into him when they went through her phone. Why hadn't they?

He'd covered his tracks. That was the only explanation. And now he expected to get away with this.

"Why are you taking me?"

The truth was, she actually wanted to go to Rachel. To be with her friend. That would be the first thing in all this she'd be able to do that might help. Support her friend. Keep her from being so scared. With the added bonus that the FBI could follow her and Lincoln to where Rachel was being held.

Still, she had to know. Lincoln had a plan, and she wanted him to tell her what it was.

"Tell me why you're dragging me out here."

"You're gonna make things right." He squeezed her arm so hard she could feel the bruise forming. "And then I'm going to cut off your fingers until Rachel signs that paper."

Her friend wouldn't give up her money? "You don't need her signature. Bradley will give you all of it."

He pushed the front door open and said, "You still think this is just about the money?"

She looked around, trying to see where the FBI were.

"Act normal." He muttered a curse. "You're supposed to want to go with me, remember?"

"I should scream the whole street down."

"Rachel would die."

"Not if the feds got you before you could make that call—"

He grabbed her jaw, his palm over her mouth, and squeezed her mouth so hard those gathering tears fell.

"I see you get me." He let go and started walking again.

"I won't be leverage for you to hurt Rachel."

"Then I'll just kill you. Or give you to someone who will have fun with you, then they'll kill you."

"What kind of monster are you?"

"It's survival of the fittest. That's why I'm so sure you're going to die. You'll quickly outlive your usefulness, Alexis. In my world, being useful and making sure people owe you is how you stay alive."

"This is America."

"Maybe not the America you know."

She knew there was an underbelly to any society. Those who lived and died in the dark, killers or victims. It was easy to want to live above it all. To keep herself safe and protected from anything—or let Bradley do that for her. But how did knowing about it now help her situation?

Bradley. She wanted him to swoop in and rescue her, but he wasn't going to. He was safe with the FBI and she was going to Rachel. That was good. She'd see her friend. Hug her. Tell her they were going to get out of this, even though she didn't have the first clue how that was going to happen.

"FBI, freeze!"

Lincoln swung her around to face the approaching agents. Two of them, guns drawn.

Alexis lifted her hands. A reflex even before her brain spun with thoughts and questions. Lincoln's arm wrapped around her neck and the cold metal of a gun pressed against her head. "Don't come any closer or I'll kill her."

She couldn't think well enough to get out any words. All that emerged from her mouth was a strangled noise.

They stepped closer. "Drop the gun and let her go."

She figured they just didn't want her dead on a city street. Walker probably wouldn't have cared what happened to her—except the loss of a possible suspect. These guys didn't care anything about her. It wasn't shocking to them that she was about to die.

Or they were trained not to show any empathy. Maybe that was it...and why was she thinking about this?

"Lincoln, let me go and leave." She focused on one of the agents. "They'll let you go, right guys?"

He took a step back, hauling her with him. The pressure of his arm across her throat threatened to choke her. As it was, she could hardly swallow. The two agents moved toward them.

"Lincoln." She breathed. "Please, let go."

"Back off!" He yelled at the agents. "No one gets near me." He took another step back. Toward his car? What was he going to do? They had guns on him, but he probably figured they weren't going to fire if it meant they could hit her. She didn't want to be protected like that. She wanted to go to Rachel.

"Lex!" Bradley's voice.

He was here? She tried to look around, but Lincoln's hold on her kept her head only at one angle. "Bradley!"

He was going to try and save her.

"Let her go, Lincoln. Now!"

"Everyone just back up," one of the agents called out. "Give them some space."

"My finger's getting tired," Lincoln told them. "If you want her to live, you'll let me get in my car."

"That isn't happening." Bradley.

"Let him go," she argued. They could follow him to where Rachel was, right? Then Bradley would be able to get her back.

The whole ransom demand, and Bradley going to turn over the money in exchange for his sister, was all dissolving into ruins. Lincoln had to go—with or without her. He shouldn't have tried to take her, especially knowing the feds were outside. Why had he, except because of whatever personal grudge he had against her?

What was so desperate to warrant his actions? She didn't think she wanted to know, but she had to figure it out. A disagreement? A shot in the dark to complete the paperwork for the money?

She couldn't help thinking this might not just have to do with the money, but something else entirely. Lincoln seemed to think this was all on her. Like she was responsible for Rachel being kidnapped. How was that even possible when she had nothing to do with it?

Alexis prayed they'd find her friend, prayed the truth would come out. She swallowed. Maybe not all of it. There was enough fallout in her life without the public also knowing the story they'd been fed was wrong. But Lincoln—he needed to be seen for what he really was.

"Let me go, and *go*."

"Enough." The voice came from behind them.

Lincoln spun her and she saw Walker for a second, before he swung them back. Bile rose in her stomach as the dizziness spun her equilibrium.

"Drop the gun and put your hands on your head. You're not a killer, son. Don't make this any worse than it's gonna be."

Lincoln's heart raced in the wrist pressed against her throat. She was going to pass out in a second if she didn't get any air.

"Everyone, back off." The gun moved, then pressed harder against her head.

She winced, and more tears fell.

"There's nowhere to go now," Walker said. "You make one move except to lay down that weapon and we'll shoot. You don't wanna die, so this only ends one way. You let the woman go and set it on the ground." His voice was hard and full of authority. A man used to giving orders that were obeyed.

Alexis's gaze wouldn't settle. It just flicked over the scene, desperately grasping for a sight of someone who would give her hope. *Bradley.* Where was he? She needed him, but knew Rachel needed her family—Alexis or Bradley—even more than she. Her friend was all alone.

God, help her.

The tension in Lincoln's body had eased, even if only in a small part. Was he going to drop the gun? He exhaled, his breath warm on the back of her neck. He'd resigned himself to something. She wished she knew what that was.

His fingers moved on her shoulder and he grasped a handful of her shirt. Pulled her forward, away from his body. She swayed with the motion and nearly fell forward before she caught herself and stumbled.

Someone grabbed her. Bradley's scent enveloped her just as as her face landed against his chest. She took hold of the sides of his shirt, by his hips, and spun. "Lincoln."

This wasn't right. He was supposed to lay the gun down.

He still held it.

"Put it down!"

"Drop it!"

Lincoln's gaze came to her, and he lifted the weapon. Bradley sprang into action, moving her away from the crowd faster than her feet could move her.

Gunshots rang out.

She turned to look, but he pulled her face into his chest and said, "Don't."

Alexis shook her head. "He knows where Rachel is."

She turned and saw Lincoln lying on the pavement in a pool of blood. His eyes, dead. "He could have told us."

"It's too late now." Bradley's hold on her didn't let up. "He knew what was going to happen. He chose to die."

"Then Rachel is going to die, too."

Chapter 13

Bradley set the mug of tea on the table in front of Alexis. She sat, braiding her hair, her gaze out the window. Her thoughts a mile away. The big padded chair in the FBI conference room dwarfed her frame, making her look younger. As did the braids. That, and the shell-shocked look on her face didn't make him feel better.

"Lex?"

She winced and looked at him, then at the tea. She dropped the braid. He pulled a chair close to her while she blew on the tea and took a sip. "Thanks."

"It's nothing." He wished it was more.

After seeing her frightened panic, and Lincoln's arm across her throat, he still hadn't relaxed. He wanted to rage. Or punch something. He'd known what it felt like to be helpless before. Bradley didn't like it one bit.

"I'm trying not to be freaked out by you, but you're not making it easy."

Bradley leaned over and kissed her forehead. "Sorry." He needed to bleed off this anxiety and relax.

She shook her head. "You don't need to apologize. It's not your fault. I'm on edge as much as you are."

He took her hand and said, "Want to tell me about you and Lincoln?"

"Not really."

"Humor me." Because there had to be some kind of connection. Between their friendship and the fact Rachel had been kidnapped. "What's with you and my cousin?"

"You mean, what *was* with me and him." She sighed, and he knew he didn't need to respond to that. Just a symptom of the shock. Alexis had to state some things out loud, just to force her brain past that thought and onto the next one.

"I keep seeing him lying there." She winced, shook her head. "I don't even think he liked me, not really. I thought we were friends, but that was before he tried to…" Her voice trailed off.

Bradley stilled. "He tried to what?"

Alexis continued, not answering his question. "There was always something…off about him, but he was nice to me. He stayed my friend, even after everything came out… He was nice to me."

Now wasn't the time to ask her about that. He needed her to talk this out. To get past the fear.

"Yesterday he got pushy. Like he thought we should be…involved." She glanced up and saw whatever was on his face. Probably nothing good. "I turned him down. He didn't take it well. Then today, he kept saying all this was my fault. Like I'm the reason Rachel was kidnapped, and I was going to have to fix things. But what do I have to do with the money?"

Bradley shook his head. His parents had loved Alexis, but it wasn't like they'd put her in their will. If anything happened to both Bradley and Rachel, the money went to a charity. "Lincoln might've wanted the money for himself."

"Or his father does. I always thought it was odd that he didn't just keep the old man out of his life, but I guess some abused kids stick with what they know."

"Uncle Francis was horrible to him."

Alexis nodded. "He told me some stories, and I wondered if it didn't mess him up. But why go after the money? Did he, or they, really want it for themselves?"

"Could be they felt slighted when the will was read. Figured they deserved some of it." But that meant Lincoln had been working with his father to get the twins' inheritance.

"And to take Rachel just to get their hands on it?" Alexis frowned.

Why did that seem so cute to him? He wanted to kiss the crinkle between her eyebrows. He said, "The FBI are finding Uncle Francis. They're unpacking Lincoln's life so they can figure out to what extent he's involved."

"Like, if he's the mastermind, or just working on someone else's orders?"

Bradley nodded.

"What about you? Did they send you in here to find out if I'm involved as well?" She straightened in the chair. Bracing for a blow she thought was coming.

"I know you're not."

"Walker doesn't seem convinced. He glared at me the whole way here in the car."

"Lex, he's pissed someone got killed before he can get answers. He's determined to get to the bottom of this, even if it's just so he doesn't break his professional streak at finding kidnap victims."

"He seemed pretty determined to prove I was involved. He's probably looking for a link between Lincoln and me."

"Is there one?"

"We're friends. Texts. Phone calls. Emails. We're connected like that."

"When you were explaining there was a friend over during the time the ransom video was sent, you mentioned texts. The FBI didn't find anything but bland conversation with an unregistered phone."

"So Walker thinks I'm communicating in code with the kidnappers, that being Lincoln?" She glanced at the window. "Too bad he's dead, so Walker can't get it from the horse's mouth that when I said, 'I'll see you soon' that I actually meant *I'll see you soon.*"

"I know you're worried." Though, she didn't look worried. She looked more   scared. "But the truth will come out."

"Before or after the kidnappers find out Lincoln is dead and cut their losses? Shoot Rachel and move on to a less complicated target."

Bradley said, "I can't think about that. I'm barely holding myself together as it is. When I saw you on that screen and Lincoln slapped you I just… I lost it." He'd already told her they'd shown up because of the FBI surveillance. She hadn't taken it well.

And didn't do more than press her lips together now. "I'm sorry. You don't need my drama when you're worried about Rachel."

"That's not it. I'm worried, but you're here and I can help you. Or try, at least."

"That was what I wanted to do for Rachel. Be there."

He sat back in his chair. "You wanted him to take you?"

She shrugged. "For a minute there I figured it would be better than sitting here doing nothing. Or getting accused of being involved."

"When Walker asked you who was at your house, why didn't you give him Lincoln's name?" It came out a little shorter in tone than he'd have liked. "Trying to protect him?"

"At the time, yes. I didn't want someone I considered a friend being subjected to the same treatment I was. Do I wish I hadn't? Yeah. If it meant Rachel would have been found already."

The tears in her eyes were enough to wear him down. "You didn't know. He kept it from you, so how could you?"

"I knew something was wrong."

"But not this."

There was more she wasn't saying. He could see it in her eyes. "You can tell me anything, Lex. I want you to know that I'll never think less of you no matter what."

"Don't say that."

He read the truth on her face. She didn't want him to make it easier for her to say it. She wanted to keep her own confidence. Keep those walls between them, so she didn't have to brave the vulnerability of letting him in. Bradley had known her long enough he could see all that in her eyes as well.

"I really thought Lincoln was my friend."

He didn't tell her that he'd have set her straight, had she told him. He knew things about his cousin that would send her running.

"How am I supposed to trust anyone?"

"Even me?"

"You know what I mean," she said. "I'm going to doubt my judgment and always wonder if I'm being duped. Again."

He knew this was, at least in part, about her distracting him from the conversation they'd been having. But she didn't say anything without a reason. She really was worried.

He scooted his chair closer to her. "You can trust me, Lex. I promise you that I'm never going to do anything that will cause you to regret believing in me. And I'll never take your trust for granted."

He was going to protect her. He figured she thought she was protecting him—even if she was doing it by keeping her secrets. She was determined to keep hold of the one thing she still had left. The shreds of her honor. Alexis would never do anything but safeguard the people she loved. And she was about to get a healthy dose of what it meant for him to do the same for her.

He lifted halfway out of his chair and kissed her forehead again. "I'll be back."

When, he didn't know. But it was a promise he was going to keep. Alexis could be sure of that.

So long as she was here with the FBI, she was safe.

Bradley was going to get his sister back.

God, help this to work.

He nodded to an agent who noticed him walk toward the hallway. When the guy looked away, Bradley ducked into the stairwell. Two minutes later he strode out into the underground parking lot where he'd left his truck hours ago.

The FBI was going to know he'd left, but he didn't have time to worry about that. He had to do this—preferably faster than they could scramble to catch up to him.

They were likely also monitoring his cell phone, which he'd managed to retrieve from one of the agents who'd been on his security detail. He would get in trouble for this. But if it worked, he wasn't going to complain when they slapped him on the wrist. Alexis was safe, and he was going to make it so Rachel was as well.

Bradley pulled past the barrier. The guard station. Onto the street, where he headed south. He connected his phone to the truck's Bluetooth and called the number that had been communicating with Alexis. Lincoln's phone, the one the FBI had never found. Would it even be turned on? If they thought they could be tracked through it now, it might have been tossed.

The call rang through to a voicemail account for that number, a generic message. When the tone sounded, he gripped the wheel and said, "I want my sister. You want the money. It's time to end the games and just make the trade. We all get what we want, everyone walks away happy, and no one else gets hurt."

He was letting his vulnerability show. They'd know he had a weakness—the people he loved getting hurt—but Bradley was past caring. This needed to be done. Now.

"Pick the place and time, and I'm there."

Bradley ended the call and tossed the phone in the cup holder. He navigated D.C. traffic, weaving between lanes and making random turns. As soon as they contacted him—if they did—he would toss the phone out the window.

If the FBI caught up with him before then, so be it. He wasn't going to apologize for what he'd done. He was a SEAL, and SEALs didn't sit back while someone else took care of the people in their lives. They were front line. Battle-ready. This was a gamble, but if it really had been Lincoln and his father—Bradley's uncle—behind this, then it was a family issue.

And family was what it would take to resolve it.

The FBI didn't care about his sister the way he did. They only cared that it would be high-profile if they lost a kidnapped senator. They'd kept the whole thing under wraps so far. He was marginally impressed at the way they'd locked the whole situation up tight. No one even knew there were dead Secret Service agents and a missing civil servant.

Bradley needed someone at his back, though. So he made the call.

"Preston."

"It's Bradley. I got a problem."

"Your sister has been kidnapped, and you're headed to trade the money for her freedom."

Bradley's foot slipped off the gas. "How did you know that?"

"We've been working this since the 9-1-1 call went out from her house."

Relief washed over him. "I called you that night."

"I know. I had a team member get injured on an op and I was at the hospital most of the night. But I put a couple of the guys on it straight away."

Bradley said, "I could really use some backup on this."

"Two cars behind you. A red BMW."

"That's you?"

"One of my guys. Quartz." Steve said, "I realize now I should have put a man on the former assistant. That was my bad. We honestly didn't know there was a connection between you. Quartz said when she almost got shot…" He went quiet for a second. "Well, let's say we're now devoting resources to maintain her continued safety."

"I appreciate that." His insides were still chilled at the idea of Alexis getting hurt.

"Tell me when and where the meet is, and I'm there," Steve said. "Quartz will provide cover."

"Will do. Then I'm going dark. I have to keep the feds from barging in."

"Copy that."

"Thank you." Bradley swallowed down the rush of emotion.

"Anytime. You know that, right? No matter what you decide about the job, Double Down is here for you."

Bradley scrubbed his hand down his face. "I really appreciate that." He hung up and kept driving, not wanting to think on the tremble in his voice when he'd said that. Just the fact his friend was already pitching in meant a whole swath of the stress was gone now. He had backup.

He didn't get far before a text came through.

Gravelly point. One hour. No feds.

Bradley looked for the red BMW, but didn't see it. It was still there, though, he was sure. This Quartz person was just good at surveillance. He forwarded the message to Steve and got a reply back straight away.

I'll be there.

Bradley tossed the phone out a window, drove a mile down the street and pulled into a parking lot. He sat and thanked God for his friend being able to take his back on this. There was no way he wanted to face the kidnappers alone. Whether it was his uncle or not, he wasn't looking forward to the showdown this was going to be. And yes, he could have the FBI with him, regardless of what the message said. But they would want to take over. To run the operation and leave him with no say as to how it went down.

Bradley had planned missions. They might be professionals, but so was he, and he'd rescued kidnap victims the world over. This was what he did. And the fact this was looking like a family issue made him all the more sure he should be the one to face these guys down.

God, am I just trying to convince myself this is the right move? Truth was, even with all he'd seen and done he didn't think he'd ever been this scared in his life. Rachel could die. She could be dead already for all he knew.

The money. He couldn't say he didn't care at all about it. Truth was, those dollars were a part of his parents he wanted to share in. He could start his own business, or do some other good with it. If he didn't give it away to criminals.

But it wasn't worth more than Rachel's life.

He pulled into the parking lot at Gravelly Point just as an airplane flew overhead, landing at Ronald Reagan Washington National Airport. So low, the roar eclipsed everything and the truck windows shook. His life seemed out of control like that. Careening to whatever end this situation was going to have. Hopefully it would be nothing but a safe landing, not a fiery crash that involved the loss of life.

God, help me get Rachel back safely.

Steve parked beside him a couple of minutes later. Dressed much the same as when they'd walked through Steve's offices the day Rachel had been kidnapped. Bradley met him with a handshake.

Steve opened the trunk of his car and handed him a bullet-proof vest. Bradley looked at it, then at his friend. "Humor me."

"Fine." He put it on. "Thanks, I guess."

"We'll get her back. Without you getting hurt, yeah?" The intensity in Steve's eyes was one Bradley remembered well.

"One question."

"Shoot," Steve said.

"How'd you know a 9-1-1 call went out from Rachel's house?"

Steve's brow furrowed. "We monitor several properties. Relatives. Friends and family we want to make sure are safe."

"Who is she to you?"

Steve glanced aside. "Not nearly what I want her to be." He looked back at Bradley. "But that's her call."

Steve was the potential relationship in Rachel's life?

"When I got out of the hospital and caught up, feds were already crawling over the whole situation." He eyed Bradley. "The former assistant. That the girl you told me about?" *The one in the video.* Not said, but implied.

Bradley nodded.

Steve shook his head, then slapped Bradley on the shoulder. The back of his hand was covered with leathery scars. "Slow playing it. Overthinking everything, just like always."

"Unlike you?"

Steve's gaze sobered. "I'm thinking the tide may've just turned on that."

Bradley didn't have time to ask what on earth that meant. A black van pulled into the parking lot.

"That them?"

Bradley checked the weapon he'd stashed in the back of his belt. "Guess we'll find out."

Chapter 14

Minutes turned into half an hour while Alexis waited for Bradley to return. She sipped the tea he had brought her, and tried to reason with herself. She'd kept the secret for months now, a decision she and Rachel had made together. If she was going to break that confidence, even if it was only with Bradley and no one else, then she probably needed to talk to Rachel first.

And that meant Rachel had to be here, safe and sound.

Before that happened, she needed to focus and not get distracted by all that was Bradley. It was so tempting to just…fall into him. In love with him. Not that she'd ever *not* been in love with him, really. None of that had changed. Maybe it had actually grown.

But what did that mean for them? Life had thrown them back together, whether they wanted it or not. Did God plan for them to finally have a relationship?

For so long, she'd figured their night together nothing but sin. Something to be washed away. But even despite the truth of what God had done in her life, maybe He still had a plan for the two of them. Would God do that? She couldn't deny that Bradley had been everything she ever wanted, and still was. But everyone at church that she'd talked to had told her to let that be the past. To move on, because God wanted to do a "new" thing.

Then the video had come out, and they'd told her not to come back.

She was staring at the FBI cubicles when everything suddenly went wired. Four agents stood up from their desks simultaneously. One snapped up a phone, and another started yelling orders to the others. Alexis lifted out of the chair and wandered to the door. Had they found Rachel?

"Off the reservation…"

"Thinks he can do this."

The snippets of conversation didn't make any sense, until she realized Bradley was nowhere that she could see.

An agent stopped right in front of her. The frown on his face was accusatory.

She shook her head. "What?"

"You're telling me you had no idea he was going to do this?"

"Bradley?" When the agent told her what he had done, she realized it made perfect sense. "Of course he did. He wants to save his sister."

"At the expense of his own life?"

"If you're worried about that, go help him."

She wanted to do that very thing, but reality stalled her. She had no training except as an assistant. She would only get in the way of all these "professionals" running around with their guns and their operational plans. The best she could do was pray, the way she had been praying all the way through all of this. Maybe to some people that was redundant, but she figured it had saved her life many times. The only idea she'd had — that of going to the motel — had resulted in their nearly being kidnapped. And in Bradley being beaten up.

. . .

The two men who exited the van, Bradley had never met before. One wore sunglasses and the other squinted under the afternoon sun. Bradley used a finger to lift up the bill of his ball cap so they'd see his face. His, "I mean business" face.

"Where's my sister?"

Steve was behind him, close enough to touch Bradley's shoulder if he needed to. Despite their banter, his old friend held the same tension in his body as Bradley did.

The lead guy sauntered over. Or was that a limp? These two could be the ones from the motel. Were they affiliated with his uncle? Bradley wanted to know what part Lincoln had played in it. If these guys were just hired guns, out for their payday, that didn't bode well. They'd likely do whatever was necessary to get money—making them even more dangerous than his uncle or cousin. There was a chance he'd have been able to reason with family. These two, likely not.

"Do I have to say it again?"

"I get the money, I'll tell you where she is."

He shook his head. "That isn't the way this works. You bring her here. If she's unharmed, I'll sign the money over to you."

The man stopped, close enough Bradley could see the skin beside both eyes crinkle. Why would he be amused?

"I kept my part of the bargain," Bradley said. "Now it's up to you to do the same."

"Honor, and all that? I don't play that way. I get what I want, and we'll see what's leftover."

Steve moved. Bradley slapped his hand out so it collided with his friend's stomach. "Don't."

"That's right." The man smirked. "You put a leash on your dog before he learns who has the bigger bite."

"Make the call," Bradley said, done with this back and forth. "Get her here."

The guy reached back. Steve closed in.

Instead of a phone, the man pulled out a Glock.

Bradley pulled his out.

Then there were four guns, all aimed. Who would win this four-way stand off? "Easy." He didn't want a bloodbath.

"I said no feds." He fired before Bradley could see what he meant.

The bullet hit his vest.

Steve shoved into Bradley and set him flying. *Bang. Bang.* Pain slammed into his shoulder and he fired back. Two shots hit the man in front of him. The other assailant friend fled the scene while car brakes squealed. Then he heard boots on gravel, and shouted orders.

Bradley sat up to see where Steve was...

"Medic!"

Walker crouched beside Steve. "Ambulance is on its way."

Bradley looked at the wound on his shoulder. Just a graze. He ripped off the hem of his T-shirt and pressed it against the slice the bullet had left.

"That was an incredibly stupid thing to do."

"Brought the kidnappers out. Now we know who they are."

"These were hired guns." Walker glanced toward the entrance to the parking lot, then back at Bradley. "They aren't the ones behind this."

"So you know about my uncle?"

Walker frowned. "He isn't part of it."

"Of course he is. If Lincoln was in on it, then my uncle is the mastermind."

"Maybe that's how you think this is working, but that's not what we've managed to piece together so far."

Bradley shifted, wincing at the pain. "Then what have you got?"

"If you'd stuck around at the FBI office, you'd have heard. We were about to come and brief you when you ran off."

Bradley didn't want to talk about that. He glanced at his friend. Steve didn't look good. The bullet had nicked his hip, and he'd hit his head on the way down. Was he going to be okay?

"You'll be lucky if the man who hired these people doesn't have your sister killed because of this."

"If they do, they'll never get their money."

The ambulance pulled up, and EMTs got to work on Steve. Walker came over to where he was, and Bradley got up.

"I know you're just trying to save her, but there's more at work here that you know nothing about."

"And you're just now thinking you'll explain it to me?"

"We had to make sure Alexis was who she said. That she was completely clean. We couldn't risk it otherwise."

Alexis? "Where is she?"

Steve grunted and tried to sit up. Bradley knelt next to the EMT and put his hand on his friend's shoulder. "Easy, buddy."

Steve glanced at the paramedics, seemed to realize where he was, and blew out a breath. "Ouch."

"You hit your head on a rock, and got nicked."

"The guys are never gonna let me live this down," he said. "Until I tell them it was because I was saving your sorry butt."

"Tell them whatever. I'm just glad you're okay."

The EMT said, "Let's go. Get you checked out by the professionals."

Steve shook his head. Winced. "I'll get someone to pick me up. We have a doctor."

They did?

The EMT didn't look convinced.

"If I need a hospital, I'll go." Though, the look on Steve's face disagreed with him. Bradley knew how he felt about hospitals. They'd both spent more than enough time getting patched up—Steve more than anyone he knew. The guy was going to avoid that at all costs.

"You have to sign some paperwork," the EMT said. "So call your friend, because I'm sticking around until he gets here to make sure you're okay."

"Maybe *he* is a *she*," Steve said.

The EMT chuckled. "Whatever, man. Just make your call."

A car pulled into the lot. The driver stayed put while the passenger, a big man with sleeves of tattoos, a goatee and not much other hair, wandered over. Bradley thought he might recognize the man from his pseudo-interview, but wasn't sure.

Steve handed over his keys, and the man wandered over to Steve's SUV. Bradley walked with his friend to the passenger door and said, "Are you sure you're going to be okay?"

Steve held out his hand. "Worry about Rachel, okay?"

Bradley nodded.

"And if you need anything else, let me know. These feebs might talk a good game, but they mess things up and it'll be a tragedy."

One Bradley would never recover from.

"Just keep your eyes and ears open," Steve said. "And tell me if you need anything."

"I will." They shook hands, and Steve climbed in the car.

The ambulance left, and Bradley headed for his truck. He followed Walker back to the FBI office, wondering all the way there what on earth the man knew that he hadn't yet shared. And praying for Rachel. He didn't want to admit to himself that he'd made the wrong choice. He'd done what he thought was right for his sister with the knowledge he had.

Twenty minutes later, he reached the floor where he'd left Alexis.

When she saw him, her gaze darted to his shoulder. She gasped and ran to him.

He braced and she slammed into his chest, wrapped her arms around him. Then she leaned back and slapped his good shoulder.

"That's the second time you've done that."

"You got shot! I can't believe you!"

"I had backup." And he could have gotten Rachel back if those two guys had held up their end of the deal. What was the point in them shooting at him and Steve anyway? It hadn't been a diversion, just attempted murder. But why, when it meant they didn't get the money?

This hardly made any sense.

Walker wandered over and handed Bradley a first aid kit. Alexis snatched it for herself, then spun to the conference room. "Let's go, Harris."

Walker shot him a smirk and said, "I'll be there in a second."

Bradley followed Alexis to the chairs they'd been talking in not three hours ago. It seemed like much longer, and no doubt every minute dragged for Rachel. Not knowing when help was going to come for her. Subjected to who knew what.

"Sit."

Her voice was soft, beckoning him out of his spiraling thoughts and back to the present. "I just want her back."

She nodded. "I know." He sat, and she said, "I'm proud of you for trying. So proud."

"It didn't work, though, did it?" Saying he'd "tried his best" might work in grade school, but in his world it didn't matter how hard you tried. Not when failure got people killed.

She touched his wound with a wet cloth and he sucked in a breath.

Her brow furrowed. "It isn't bad."

"I know."

Walker trailed in, followed by another agent. They sat across the table, serious looks on both of their faces. Bradley didn't even want to ask what this was all about. Not when it was clearly big. And important.

"What is..?" Alexis's voice trailed off and the room was silent.

Bradley stuck a bandage on the gunshot he'd received, and Alexis taped it down. She said, "Do you want an Ibuprofen or something?"

He shook his head and turned to Walker. "Care to share?"

"I object to the insinuation that you wouldn't have gone off half-cocked if I'd have told you what I'm about to say earlier."

Maybe he would have, maybe not. "Guess we'll never know, will we."

Alexis put her hand over his tight fist.

Walker glanced between them, and said, "For the past three years, it has come to the FBI's attention that someone in Washington is blackmailing Senators, Representatives. Congressmen and women. It took a while to nail down the extent of the damage. Not too many of them were interested in having what they considered their private business revealed, even if only to us and not the public."

Alexis had gone solid beside him. Her hand slipped from his and he glanced at her. She was white as a sheet.

"What is it?"

"Rachel..." She didn't say any more.

Bradley didn't need her to.

Walker said, "We believe your sister became a target of this blackmailer."

"And now he's kidnapped her to get our inheritance money?"

"We believe that was his initial intention, yes. Money seems to be his end game." Walker cleared his throat. "But that isn't how it started."

Bradley glanced from the agent to Alexis.

"However, the actions of your sister and Alexis here made it so that the blackmailer's initial plan didn't work. He was forced to find a new tactic."

"Kidnapping."

Walker nodded.

Alexis shifted so her body was farther away from his.

"And he's done this to others?"

"A Senator from Wyoming killed herself. We looked into the case and found a video on her computer, buried in a series of subfolders. It would have destroyed her stance on honesty and family values if her husband, or the voting public, ever found out."

"Lincoln was right," Alexis breathed. "This is my fault."

Walker said, "We believe that when he contacted Rachel, she did something he never expected. Which is why he's resorted to this."

"My sister hasn't incriminated herself." He glanced at Alexis, who looked sick. "It's not like there's a video of her floating around the internet, right?"

Rachel had a wild streak and was entirely capable of getting herself into trouble, but that had been in college. And Alexis was *always* there to pull her back from the edge. To stop her from self-destructing.

Alexis swallowed. "She—"

Bradley laid his hand on hers the way she'd done for him. His heart sank as he realized what the girls had done. What had been an inkling before was so obvious now. They'd turned the tables on the blackmailer, and figured out a way to control the narrative.

He leaned back in his chair and pinned Alexis with his gaze. "The woman in the video. It wasn't you, was it? It was Rachel."

Chapter 15

Alexis shut her eyes against that stare of his. She nodded. She heard Bradley's exhale. The shift to finally knowing that it wasn't her in the video—it was his sister.

She opened her eyes. "I'm sorry." And she really was. It didn't make it better for him to know they'd lied. For him, it was probably worse.

He'd been able to push Alexis away. To nurse his hurt, but keep himself removed.

"Why didn't she tell me?" The pain in his voice echoed in his eyes.

Walker was listening to the whole thing, but if what he'd explained was true, then he had a right to know it all as well. If it wasn't just Rachel, but others as well who had been targeted, Alexis didn't know how to help them. She'd done what she could to save her friend from having both her career—so much more important than Alexis's—and her reputation from being destroyed.

"You know why."

"How could I?" He gave a slight shake of his head. Like he couldn't bear to move more than that. "None of this makes sense."

Agent Walker said, "Why don't you start from the beginning? Walk us through what happened."

Alexis took a breath and then swallowed. Not so much to figure out what she was going to say, as to brace herself for Bradley's confusion and hurt. Things were only going to get worse when he heard the whole story from start to finish.

"Rachel went to a benefit." She gave Agent Walker the date and location, a downtown D.C. hotel. "It was for a children's charity. The next morning, just after seven, she called me. She was in a motel across town with no idea how she got there."

"He drugged her." Bradley's tone was dark. Lethal.

"She figured out from the…discomfort…what had happened. I told her we'd go to the police, but she didn't want to report it." Alexis sucked in a breath. "I should have made her go, but she didn't want it on record when she didn't remember anything. It wasn't like she could identify who her attacker had been."

Alexis hadn't been able to sway her. And since it hadn't been her who was hurt, she'd let Rachel make the decision. "Even a couple of days later, when her head was clearer, she still refused to get it down on record. She didn't want to be seen as the victim." Alex shook her head, even though she understood. "I didn't agree with it. Silence isn't strength. I mean, sometimes it's the right thing, but not like this. Hiding it just because she didn't want anyone to know."

Walker nodded, like he knew. When he most definitely did not. He couldn't understand what that kind of vulnerability felt like.

"Then the video showed up in her email, along with a demand for two hundred thousand dollars. We knew it wouldn't stop there. Whoever it was would keep asking for money. He threatened to leak the video online. I contacted a friend of mine at the Pentagon and had her check into the email address, but we didn't get anywhere. We had no idea where it came from."

Bradley laid his hand on hers. She held on to his fingers, content to soak up the strength of his grip.

"So we did the only thing we could think of. We leaked the video ourselves and told everyone it was me."

Bradley exhaled.

"I know it was kind of a *nuclear* option. But we wanted to take the power back. To control what the public knew ourselves."

His eyes were fierce. "It *destroyed* you."

"You didn't see how she was after that email came through. It was eating away at her. She wasn't sleeping. She couldn't keep any food down. She couldn't even brush her teeth without gagging." Alexis glanced away. "So I talked to her about what options there were, so she could feel like she was in control again. When she agreed, I ended it. I turned the tables on that blackmailer, and we moved on with our lives."

Walker said, "What made you think people wouldn't realize it wasn't you?"

She glanced at Bradley. Part of her had wondered if he would realize it wasn't her, but if he had, he'd never said anything. "People see what they want to see. You can't tell the hair color is brown, not auburn. Not with it being almost black and white."

"Like a surveillance camera," Walker said. "And the tattoo?"

Bradley said, "Alexis and Rachel got matching tattoos in college."

The corners of her mouth curled up at the memory. "I couldn't believe how much it hurt. Like road rash. Afterward we decreed we'd never do it again." Her smile dropped. "How would we know it would actually come in handy?"

"What about the man in the video?"

She shrugged one shoulder. "We couldn't figure out who it was, not from just a shoulder and his legs. Dark hair. It's mussed in the video. We had no idea who he was."

Walker flipped open a paper folder, pulled out a sheet and placed it on her side of the table. A dossier. The man in the picture was handsome, and someone she immediately recognized.

"Rachel's new assistant."

"His real name is Aaron Jones. To cut a long and very colorful story short, he's essentially for hire and doesn't care what the job is. His specialty is date rape drugs, but he's not all that discerning about what he does."

Alexis swallowed back the bile. Bradley shot to his feet.

"Sit down, Mr. Harris."

He turned back, already at the door. "That scum bag—"

"I don't want to find Jones's body in the woods and have to ruin your life with a murder conviction, so do me a favor and *sit down*, Bradley. We have agents sitting on Jones, and we have for weeks. He can't even take a whizz and we don't know about it."

"Then bring him in. Question him."

"It's only supposition in this case. We have no physical evidence that ties this man to your sister."

"Then how do you know it was him?"

"Because we've seen this before."

Alexis said, "The Senator from Wyoming."

Walker nodded. Bradley sat again, no less tense than he'd been when he stormed to the door. That fire was always there. It was the best part of him, that need he felt to sacrifice himself to save his sister.

He had to know that. Maybe it would take a while, and she could tell him why she'd really done it. Eventually he would understand. But even if he got it, this would forever color what was between them. She'd lied. Covered up his sister's hurt. That big brother heart, his code of honor, might not ever recover from being set aside. And if he wanted nothing to do with her now, then she would let him go and make her own life. Far from here, where she wouldn't remember him too much. Somewhere she could live in solitude and pretend she would one day get over him.

Walker said, "The death of the Senator from Wyoming was ruled a suicide, but I wasn't convinced. I went back over the evidence, and I'm working on building a case for a murder charge. But if I can get evidence that ties Jones to this as well, then I'll be able to snap the trap shut."

Bradley leaned forward. "My sister has been kidnapped, and you're worried about your agenda?"

"Seems to me like nothing has changed since Agent Walker was accusing *me* of being behind the kidnapping," Alexis said. "And now Rachel has been a captive for two days, and you have...what? Nothing much by the look of it."

Walker let their words wash over him and didn't react. Alexis almost respected him for not firing back at them. He said, "Our priority here is making Rachel safe. Secondary to that is bringing this guy down. Do you want this happening to someone else?"

Bradley leaned back in his chair. "Of course we don't, but it's not someone else who was kidnapped. It was Rachel. And then they tried to get me—or Alexis. Lincoln tried to take Alexis with her. And after all that, two men shot at me and Steve. So how do we make sense of this mess and find Rachel?"

"Assuming the ransom drop is off, we're waiting to see if you're contacted again."

Alexis said, "You think they'll try to take Bradley now, to get his money too?"

"We aren't taking those chances, but the two of you have to work with us on this. Which means no running off on your own, trying to deal with these guys." Walker glanced at Bradley. "Or killing the only man involved in this so far that might actually know who the blackmailer is."

"And what about Lincoln? No one thought twice before you all shot him."

"That was unavoidable."

Alexis bit her lip. "What about Bradley and Rachel's uncle? If Lincoln was part of this, then his father could be the blackmailer, right?" She was so glad it hadn't been either of them who had drugged and attacked Rachel. That was beyond icky, when this situation was already bad enough. It was horrible enough thinking Rachel had been working with Aaron Jones as her assistant for *months*.

Bradley scratched a hand through his close-cropped hair. "I can't believe I'm even contemplating that my uncle could be a predator like this. A blackmailer and a thief. Not to mention hiring someone to do that to my sister?" He blew out a breath.

Alexis wanted to do something to comfort him, but nothing was enough. She had to face the fact she couldn't help.

Walker said, "We're looking into him. Running his financials. If there's something to be learned that we don't need a warrant to obtain, then we'll get it."

"And Rachel?" Alexis didn't know how on earth they were going to get her back when this was now even more complicated. It had seemed so hard to find her before. Now it was probably impossible. "She could be dead already, or he could have done worse to her than he did before."

Rachel could have been sold to someone who bought women. Or so many other scenarios too horrible to imagine. Alexis never wanted that world to touch the people she loved, but neither could she pretend it didn't exist. There was so much evil in this world. It would be easy to try and cocoon herself away from it out of self-preservation. But how would that help the victims? Those who were innocent, who couldn't fight for freedom but needed someone to fight for them.

Walker said, "I know. We're monitoring the dark web for any chatter that might indicate a transaction involving the Senator."

"But he wants the money, right?" Bradley said. "So he has to contact me again. Because with Rachel out of commission, he either has a shot at getting her to give up hers, or he has to get to me so he can get all two million."

"That's why we would like you to stay here where we know you're safe." The edge in the agent's tone was clear.

"Or I go out there, you guys watch my back and when he grabs me, you follow."

"We aren't going to use you as bait. We don't do that, even with Navy SEALs."

He didn't like it, but Alexis was glad. She didn't want him to get hurt, even if he didn't think he would because of his extensive training.

Walker continued. "We're going through Jones's life, as well as your uncle's. Between the two of them, we'll find a connection to whoever is masterminding these blackmailing operations."

"What about the original ransom drop…exchange." She didn't know what to call it. "What do we do about that? Or are we assuming he'll contact Bradley with further instructions?"

"I tossed my phone."

Walker said, "We know. But if he wants to find you, he'll figure out a way."

Alexis got up. She just couldn't sit any longer when nervous energy was building and building. "I want you to tell me he isn't hurting her. I want you to promise me that you're going to find her. Preferably right now. That she'll be okay." But he couldn't, could he?

Walker might've tried looking like he at least felt guilty. She'd take even false empathy about the fact he couldn't promise that this would turn out fine. Or even well. He wasn't able to control the outcome when all this time they'd been on the defense. Chasing behind what had already happened.

Alexis tapped her finger on her leg. They needed to turn things around. But how? Bradley had tried, and both he and his friend had been injured. It wasn't like she could go out and make any difference for Rachel.

"I hate feeling useless."

"It won't be long," Walker said. "That is something I can promise you."

Bradley watched her, while across the table Walker gathered his papers. What did he think? She'd given up her career for her friend, but that decision hadn't been a hardship. What came later had hurt, and she'd been working through it. God had been closer to her in the last few months than any other time since she first learned of Him.

"What are you thinking?"

Walker trailed out. She shrugged at Bradley's question, but said, "That this time, since I lost my job and pretty much all my friends…it's been some of the sweetest time with God that I've ever had." He smiled, so she continued, "I've had to depend on Him for everything, more than just all my peace and comfort."

"You could have called me. Told me," he said quietly. "But I know why you didn't. And I'm glad for you, Lex. You needed God, and He showed up."

She nodded. "He really did. I had no one else."

He motioned to the chair. "Sit. Please."

Why was he being so gentle? Alexis settled in the chair. "What is it?"

"I know now. Which means there's no reason you should be alone anymore." He took her hand. "I'm not going to let you do this by yourself. This is going to be a new season. For both of us."

"We should focus on Rachel now. That's what's important." She didn't want to talk about them. Not when it was inevitable that she'd let him down when she told him she was leaving town. Moving away to go live her life. He wasn't going to like keeping tabs on her from afar, but there was no way she could stay local when he'd only be looking after her out of obligation for what she'd done for Rachel. That was all that was between them, even with that kiss. Just a shared experience of stress, and not knowing what would happen. Their default—to cling to each other—was just reflex.

Nothing more.

Chapter 16

She was pushing him away again. Standing her ground, yes, but living behind that shield she'd erected to keep herself safe. The one he wasn't able to break through. Bradley respected her need to guard her heart, even as it completely infuriated him that she felt the need to do it. He was the last person she should be protecting herself from. Didn't she know that?

There was one other explanation he could think of—that Alexis actually thought *he* was the greatest threat she faced.

That had to mean her feelings were strong enough she'd felt like she needed to keep him from breaking her heart. As if he would. Bradley didn't know the future, but he did know he would never intentionally hurt her. Now really wasn't the time to try and convince her, though. He didn't know how long that would take. He didn't want to have half a conversation that would leave her unconvinced, and with possibly even more questions than she had now.

Retreating back behind that shield.

A tear fell down her cheek. Bradley's resolve broke and he gathered her in his arms. "What is it, love?"

He felt the hitch in her breath at his endearment. New territory for them, but he wanted to get them going those places. Forward. On to better things, whether that made them both vulnerable or not.

"I—" Her voice broke. "—I vetted him."

"Aaron Jones?"

She nodded against his chest. Bradley loosened his hold on her so he could look down at her face. "This isn't your fault, Lex. You couldn't have known what he was involved in."

"I left her with him. Alone, after what he did to her." She shuddered in his arms. "He could have done it again. Over and over."

Bradley wiped tears from both her cheeks with his thumbs. "He didn't. She'd have told you. If he'd drugged her again, she'd have known something was wrong."

He could hardly talk about this, considering it was his sister. How did anyone stand by and allow abuse like this to happen? He wanted to rage against the whole world, and the fact there were people in it who thought their own needs came before someone else's consent. Bradley wanted to line up everyone who'd ever hurt someone defenseless and show them what it was like to be vulnerable. To suffer because of another person's selfishness.

But that would only make him just as vindictive as them. Being the same as they were wasn't the goal, and it wasn't going to make the world better. He'd felt that urge to get vengeance time and again, facing enemies in battle who had no constraints on their actions. War was never a fair fight. He had to stay set apart from that "victory at any cost" mentality. The alternative would only mean he'd descended into the darkness they operated in.

Bradley wanted to live his life in the light.

Life stateside, with Alexis in his arms, was looking more and more appealing every second. When they got his sister back, he wanted to spend more time with her.

"This is all so wrong."

"But it isn't your fault, Lex. You couldn't have known this was bigger than one night, and more than just my sister. We just have to pray she's okay. That they find her before too much damage is done."

"Oh, God."

He hugged her again, sick to his stomach and completely agreeing with her. Powerless was not his thing. God needed to call him to arms. There had to be a way he could do something. But he'd tried, and it hadn't worked. Both he and Steve had been injured.

"We have to bring this sicko down so no one else gets hurt by him."

He needed to call Steve and make sure his friend was okay. If helping Bradley had cost the man time doing his job, that meant money had been lost. Steve would say it was okay, and he didn't care about the money. Bradley should open an account so he could be the man's client. Help him recoup his losses. Or, if he was making a move to be stateside permanently now, maybe he should just go ahead and outright ask the man if he got the job.

"Bradley. Alexis."

They turned to Walker, who didn't have a happy, "we found her" face. Bradley put his arm around Alexis. "What is it?"

"Preliminary forensics are back on the lawyer." Walker swallowed.

There was something in his gaze that Bradley knew wasn't going to be good. He turned Alexis to face him and said, "Can you go grab two coffees, or a tea and a coffee for me, or something?" Great, he was babbling.

She shot him a look. "You want me to get scarce so the men can talk?" She had on that *Seriously* face he thought was incredibly cute—and completely justified.

Bradley said, "Please." And he meant it. Because this was something he wanted to do for her. Yes, she was determined to stay strong through all of this. But he wanted to protect her from the full extent of it. She didn't have to endure quite so much today. She was strong, and she didn't need to prove it to him.

She lifted her chin. "I can handle this."

"I don't want you to have to."

"So you're going to take the blow for me?"

"If you'll let me, yes." He wasn't going to pretend what this was. She was a smart woman who had called him on the attempt to keep her out of it. "Will you, please?"

"For my own sanity, fine." She gave him a small smile of knowing he'd always liked. "I'll go refill our cups."

After she'd trailed out, Walker sighed. "That was a good idea. It's pretty gruesome."

Bradley said, "She'd handle it. There's no doubt she'd make herself deal. I just don't want her to have to."

"I get it."

"So, what happened?"

Walker sat on the edge of the table. "Before he was killed, your lawyer was tortured. It wasn't drawn out, but it was extremely painful."

"What did he give them?"

"You're assuming he succumbed?"

"Big city lawyer, but finances. Not criminal. Daddy was a lawyer. He didn't work out, he played golf on Sundays." Bradley shrugged. "He'd have let me intimidate him if I was that way inclined. So yeah, I think he gave them what they wanted."

"Likely he held out long enough for the torture to get seriously painful, so there's that." Walker looked at his file of papers. "We'll know more as the investigation continues. For now, we had a computer forensics specialist go through his devices. There was a file downloaded around the estimated time of death. It fits the window, if that's what he pointed them to."

"What was the file?"

"A document that allows the signatory to transfer funds to a third party."

"A bank form?"

Walker nodded. "Looks like they're going to try and have your sister sign over her money. Maybe you as well, probably through coercion."

Bradley strode to the conference room door and looked for Alexis. She was down the hall, chatting with a female agent. His stomach unclenched just a little.

Alexis was safe and not about to be used as leverage to force Rachel to give up her million dollars. It was Rachel he should worry about. And yet between the two women, his entire body was a mass of knots he needed to work out with a couple of hours at a punching bag.

"I put agents on the bank since the transfer will need to be done on site," Walker said. "If your sister shows up with anyone, we'll see."

Bradley nodded. He ran both hands down his face. Prayed. Took some deep breaths.

"We're also moving to locate Aaron Jones. A witness, a neighbor of your lawyer, places a slender man who fits his build leaving the scene around the time of his death. So we're bringing him in to question him in connection with the murder."

"Won't that let him know we're aware he's involved?"

Walker nodded. "I'm done treading lightly. We know this guy means business, and if Jones knows who he is then I want all the information he has. That's how we're going to shut him down and find Rachel."

Hopefully the order went a little differently than that, but Bradley would pray about that as well.

"Keep me posted." Bradley wanted to listen in on that conversation.

"Actually, I'd like to have you and Alexis go back to the safe house. It isn't that you're in the way here, but I want you contained so we can cut down on the variables of what's going to play out for the remainder of this investigation."

Which was basically getting them out of the way. Keeping them contained. Bradley wasn't mad, but he didn't have to like the idea either. He said, "Fine," mostly because Alexis would be with him. What was there to be mad about that? "But you find my sister."

Walker said, "I'll set up the transport."

"Can I make a phone call?" He motioned to the phone on the table.

Walker explained how to dial outside the office, then left. Bradley had just finished dialing when Alexis trailed back in with the drinks—and a wry smile on her face.

"Double Down Investigations, how may I direct your call?" The woman had a thick southern accent which, added to the fact she spoke extremely quickly, made all the words run together.

"Steve Preston, please. It's Bradley Harris."

"I'll see if he's done patching himself up after his escapade this morning. Not the first time he's been shot, and not the last. I don't know why I even bother—" The line muted for a good minute and hold music played.

Finally, Steve answered, "Bradley?"

"Yep. How are you?"

"I'd be better if my secretary didn't insist on giving me the third degree every time I get injured." He sighed. "I had my computer guy get into the building computer system where you're at. He got me everything those people have on all this. I'm not liking it, not in the slightest."

"Me either." Nor did Bradley like the fact Steve felt it necessary to hack the FBI.

"I'm looking into it. I'll let you—or them—know what I dig up."

Bradley gave him Alexis's number so Steve could get ahold of him. "Thanks."

"I should be saying that to you," Bradley said. "I appreciate this, Steve. And I appreciate your help this morning."

"I don't like being shot at. And I don't like a friend of mine being in danger. So let's work on getting her back."

"Thanks." Bradley hung up, not knowing that Steve and Rachel had been friends exactly. "Sometime soon, someone will need to explain to me what happened between Rachel and Steve Preston."

Her eyes widened. "That's who you called this morning?" When he nodded, she said, "Of course. That's perfect. He's exactly the kind of help we need. And, well…"

This was the part he wanted to know. "What is it?"

"She thought he might…have a crush on her. But then he went out of town, and it was weeks." Alexis shrugged. "He seemed nice. Really nice, actually. And I thought he might've really liked her." She paused. "He didn't get back from his operation until after…"

Bradley nodded, knowing what she was referring to.

"By then it was too late. She didn't want anything to do with anyone she didn't know well enough that she could ensure one hundred percent trust."

And yet, for Alexis, that had been Lincoln. She'd made a mistake trusting his cousin and now she was going to be gun-shy until she realized Bradley wasn't anywhere near that man's category.

He told her about Walker wanting them both at the safe house.

"We have to go?"

"Together, yeah." That was the part he liked best. "They're bringing Jones in."

She looked almost scared.

"Soon as they get us a ride, we're going to leave."

"I wish I could get some clothes. Take a shower." She rubbed her hand in her hair. "It's been a long day, and I feel awful being selfish about how I look. Or I how I feel."

"Rachel would understand. You've done so much for her, how would she begrudge you a shower?"

She shook her head, a sad smile on her face. "It wasn't that much. Rachel is a senator. She didn't want that all over the internet, and we weren't going to give him the money. That didn't leave us with many options."

"I would have helped you."

She bit her lip. "You'd have found him and killed him. Or never found him, and killed yourself with guilt because of it."

She knew him. He had to give her that. "One of these days I'm going to make it so you don't ever have to give that much. So you don't have to sacrifice that much for anything ever again."

"I *wanted* to do it."

"I know. That's what kills me. Because I know you'd do it a thousand times over, and I don't want you to ever have to do that." He touched both her shoulders.

"Harris." One of the agents he'd spoken with earlier said, "Let's go."

They followed him to the parking lot and climbed in the back of an SUV. Bradley didn't know what to say, so he held her hand as they pulled onto the street and headed to the safe house. Whether it was going to be the one he'd been at earlier, or a different one, he didn't know. Wherever it was, they would be together.

God, help Rachel. Keep her safe. Give her strength.

He could hardly stomach even thinking about what was happening to her. But what she was going through was far worse than his fear of the unknown. God knew. He was with her. Was Rachel trusting in Him? He knew she hadn't made the same commitment he had. Bradley tried to tell her what he'd discovered—that Alexis had been right all along.

The light turned green and the agent pulled away from the line.

A semi came out of nowhere and barreled toward them. It slammed into the driver's door and the back, on the side where Alexis sat. Before Bradley could react, the SUV spun through the intersection. Alexis screamed. The front windshield sprayed with blood from the driver. The agent in the front passenger seat whipped side to side like a rag doll. The way he and Alexis were doing.

His head slammed on the door frame and everything went black.

Chapter 17

Blood was everywhere. Her heartbeat thudded in her…face. Alexis touched her top lip and nearly screamed. Even that close to her nose, which was apparently broken, was too close. She sucked in a breath through her mouth. It was like suffocating, but she was still able to get air even as her sinuses and throat filled with blood.

She shoved at the airbag which had come out of the seat in front of her, the one she'd just slammed into, then looked around. Rotating her head made her bite back a scream. She twisted her whole body and saw Bradley, slumped against the door. Blood dripped from his face onto the shoulder of his shirt. Unconscious.

The agents in front were moaning. Alexis tried to think what to do. They'd been hit by a truck. Literally.

Her phone. She needed to call for help.

It was in her purse, by her feet. Alexis got her arms to respond and braced one hand against the airbag to feel around on the floor. *God, help me get someone here.* She wanted to believe a bystander had seen the accident and called the police. That they would show up any minute to help.

Her door swung open. What on earth? She glanced around, trying to figure out what was happening. Her brain was moving so slowly. A man grabbed her arm. She felt her butt slide across the seat, and he dragged her from the car.

"Take care of that."

Cold night air bit into her thin sweater. Who was he talking to? Her head swam and she tried to look around, see what he was talking about, but her eyes couldn't focus on anything.

Bang. Bang. Alexis's whole body jerked. The sound was like standing beside a firework right as it went off. "Wha…" He dragged her away.

She looked up and saw a mask.

Bang. Bang.

"Get the other guy, and let's go."

Bradley. Where was he? Was he awake yet? Maybe they'd killed him.

Had they killed the agents? Why couldn't she hear sirens? Surely the FBI knew they'd been hit. Now they were being kidnapped, just like Rachel.

"Brad…" She couldn't say more.

The man stopped, but momentum sent her careening into him. He let go and she slumped to the ground beside a van. The pavement gravel bit into her hands, and her head throbbed all the more.

She turned to the SUV. It looked like a great beast had stepped on it. The FBI agents were dead. Bradley…

A masked man hauled him over, his feet dragging on the ground. Was he dead, too? No. They wouldn't bring him if he was. They needed him alive.

Which meant they could kill her.

She scrambled away on all fours, got two feet maybe, and the man who'd dropped her slammed his boot into her stomach. Alexis crumpled to the ground. Her head slammed into the concrete, and she choked again on a mouthful of blood.

"Nice try."

He pulled her arm up, yanking her shoulder almost out of place. Alexis got her feet under her enough so she wasn't dragged like Bradley. She stumbled, and he tossed her in the direction of the inside of a black-paneled van. She landed face-first on Bradley, depositing some of her blood on his shirt. She liked that shirt.

Her arms were hauled up behind her, and plastic ties secured her hands behind her back. Stars pricked through her vision. The van door slid shut, and everything went dark. Except those blinking lights. She tried to breathe. Tried not to barf on her own blood.

Bradley moaned.

She shifted, tried to roll off him. "Brad…"

Where were they taking them? She'd wanted to go to Rachel, but not like this.

The van turned a corner, going way too fast. Alexis's body slid across the van and into something hard. With sharp edges. Bradley slammed into her and pushed her against it more. Breath expelled from her lungs in a whoosh.

"Bradley." He needed to wake up. Get off her, and out of the way.

The van turned another corner, going the other way. Her shoulders burned, pulled so tight behind her, but she scrambled with the momentum of the turn. She managed to get them farther across the van floor. If they turned again, she didn't want to be shoved against whatever that was.

Within minutes, they slowed. She heard a garage door roll up. Then a few more minutes, and they stopped altogether.

They hadn't gone far. Where, though? She didn't have to wait long to find out. The van door slid open to the inside of an empty garage. Not full of the organized—or completely disorganized—things that belonged to the garage of a house where people actually lived.

One of the masked men took a look at her, then waved a gun from her to the garage.

Alexis scooted to the edge and stood. She didn't have to pretend she didn't feel good, but she also wasn't going to go for belligerence. She would only end up with more bruises than she already had.

The man took a look at her nose and winced, like she was the grossest thing he'd ever seen.

She looked away, but lifted her chin. As if she even cared what he thought. Bradley was unconscious. "Where's Rachel?" It sounded like her nose was plugged. She wanted to demand they take her to her friend, but didn't think ordering them around was going to do much good. Especially not in this condition.

She was ready to see Rachel. Alexis could count on both hands and one foot the number of days they hadn't spoken to each other on the phone, if not in person, in the last…decade probably. Even with what had happened after the video. These men likely didn't understand that level of friendship—the kind that created a family she'd chosen for herself.

Or, maybe they did know.

And if they did, then she was likely here to have her life threatened to make Rachel, and probably Bradley as well, do what they said.

"Move." He shoved her forward, and she almost stumbled.

The floors were bare, the walls nothing but drywall with that mud stuff that builders used to cover the joins before they did that texture thing and then painted. So this house was still being built. Didn't that mean someone would be coming over to work on it? She glanced around, but saw only the one kidnapper behind her.

Where was the other one?

Were they both construction workers and this was one of their jobs? She didn't know if it was possible to hide kidnapping victims like that. But evidently it was possible, because they'd had Rachel here and no one had found her yet. Or they'd killed the person for being nosy and like…buried them under the patio. That was a construction thing to do, right? At least it seemed that way in mystery stories.

He prodded her in the back with the gun. "Right here."

She stopped by a closed door.

The gunman unlocked a padlock and slipped it free. "Inside."

Alexis looked over his shoulder, but the other man wasn't there. Nor was Bradley. Was he okay? Would they bring him here as well?

"*Now.*"

She turned the handle to find a room that looked like the rest of the house. Bare floor, bare walls. "Rachel."

He shoved her in, then slammed the door shut. She heard the padlock snap shut and moved across the room away from it. Rachel was curled on the floor in the corner, hands and feet both secured in the same ties she had on her wrists.

"Rachel." Alexis crouched, but couldn't touch her friend. Not with her hands behind her back like this. She tugged at the bonds. That only made them dig more into her skin. She lost her balance and her bottom slammed onto the floor. "Rach."

Alexis wanted to cry. Her friend was filthy, battered. Had she eaten? There were a couple of empty water bottles. The wrapper for a protein bar she'd liked before today, but would probably never be able to enjoy again, lay within arm's reach. Was there a toilet here?

Rachel flinched. Her eyes flickered open. She stared up at Alexis and dread washed over her face. "No." She took a breath. "No, no, no."

"Rachel." The word came out louder than she wanted, and her friend flinched. "It's okay. Bradley is here too. We're gonna get out of here."

How, she had no idea, but Rachel needed to believe it. She needed to have renewed hope and not descend into the lonely despair she'd probably been living in so far.

"They told me they were bringing you here." Rachel shook her head, shut her eyes. "I didn't want you to come."

"When there's nowhere else I'd rather be?" She looked around. "It's nicer than our first apartment." She tried to add levity. Probably wouldn't work, but now that she knew Rachel was alive, hope *had* swelled. For her. Yeah, they were tied up. And, what were those men doing to Bradley right now?

She had to believe God had done this. He hadn't left them all alone, He had brought them together.

Rachel exhaled, which might have been laughter, but that was probably only wishful thinking on Alexis's part. She pushed her bound hands against the floor and sat up. "You're here."

Alexis leaned in and set her cheek on Rachel's shoulder. Her friend laid her head on top of Alexis's for a second. It was as much of a hug as they could manage, but it worked. "Are you okay? I've been having nightmares of what they were doing to you."

Rachel's face was non-committal. "I'm alive, aren't I?"

Alexis told her that the FBI had linked this to the video, and that it was a larger investigation. "But that doesn't help us get out of here."

"They want the money, but I can't figure out how that's going to satisfy them."

Alexis shrugged. "Whoever they are, it can't be about just getting what they thought you owed them because we played off the video as me."

Rachel nodded. "That's what I've been thinking. I mean, kidnapping I get, but how did we go from blackmail to this? When they get what they want, won't I still be under their thumb? If we're all here now, they'll want to get the money. After that…"

"They'll kill us." Alexis didn't like this at all. "And whether they make it look like an accident or not won't matter, because we'll be dead."

"Or they'll kill me and Bradley, and you'll end up having to take the fall for it somehow."

Alexis said, "So, death or prison? That isn't much of a choice."

"It sucks as a five-year plan."

She wanted to smile, but couldn't. It was good that Rachel was finding reasons to be amused. Hope had flickered, and it hadn't gone out. She knew what miracles God could do. Would he rescue them even from this? Whether He did or not, she would still praise Him for what He'd done in her life. Fact was fact, and she'd been freed from her sin. If that freedom was in order that Alexis could start a ministry behind bars, incarcerated for something she hadn't done, so be it.

The FBI knew she wasn't involved, but even they weren't all powerful. Evil won every day. That was the world they lived in.

"We need to get out of here," Alexis said. "Find Bradley before they hurt him even more than he's already hurt."

"Says the woman bleeding all down her face." Rachel handed her a dusty fast food napkin.

Alexis wiped her nose.

"That needs looking at, or it'll be crooked forever." Rachel frowned. "Bradley could probably reset it."

Alexis ran her finger down her nose. Yep, it's bad. She winced. "Guess I won't win any beauty prizes."

"Yeah, cause it's all about your face." The corner of Rachel's mouth curled up. "Idiot."

Alexis chuckled. "If I'm so dumb, why did you copy from me on every economics test?"

"Just don't tell my constituents I did that, okay?"

"Pretty sure that's not the worst thing a politician's ever done. Besides, I'm saving it all for my memoirs. Seems like at this point I might have a bestseller on my hands."

Rachel leaned in. "Only because suspense sells. Then they'll read it and realize you're the best friend a woman could ever have. After that I'll never be able to get ahold of you, you'll be so popular."

"I'm getting dogs. Rottweilers. They can patrol my compound in the mountains so no one comes near me. I want to drink my tea and read my Bible in peace."

"That's fine," Rachel said. "Bradley can get around dogs. He'll probably do some ninja mind trick and make them harmless to only him so he can *invade your compound* whenever he wants."

"That actually sounds kind of gross." Alexis laughed.

"Don't worry. I'll make him put a ring on it."

"Did you seriously just quote Beyoncé to me?"

"She had a point."

"Yeah," Alexis said. "She really did."

Especially considering they'd already been there. Done that. Now that she knew what God had done, Alexis did want the whole 'marriage thing' if she was going to have a relationship again. Sure, she'd dated some. Nothing had stuck though. At the end of the day, Bradley was the one who'd always been there for her.

"I hope he's okay."

"Why don't you pray?" Rachel said. "That's what you do, right?"

Alexis frowned. She didn't want to get into that whole speech and everything Rachel was missing out on. Instead, she closed her eyes and prayed a simple prayer out loud that they would get out of there. That Bradley would be okay. That the FBI would find them.

The lock clanked against the door and it flung open.

Both of them turned to face it.

A gunman strode in. There were grazes on his knuckles and a gun in his hand. "Time to go for a drive."

Alexis moved in front of Rachel, blocking her with her body. It might not stop a bullet, but she wasn't going to let Rachel get shot.

"I'd love to get out of here." Rachel's voice rang with defiance. Because Alexis was there now? She wanted to be pleased at that, but couldn't help thinking this might not bode good things.

The gunman shook his head. "Not you."

Alexis looked at her friend, then at the gunman. "Me?" What was he going to do with her? She'd assumed she was nothing but leverage to get the brother and sister to do what the gunmen wanted.

"You fooled everyone into thinking you were her once. Now you can do it again," he said. "You're going to get dressed, and then we're going to the bank. Get ready to give the performance of your life. Because you're going to get me that money."

"And if I don't?"

"Then all of you are dead."

Chapter 18

Bradley's head thumped, his forehead pressed against the floor. He could hear the man who'd left down the hall now. Talking. With Alexis and Rachel? No gunshots—so far—meant they were still alive. He hoped.

His whole body hurt. The two men had kicked him in the stomach, the back, the ribs, the legs. Like it would take that much persuasion to get him to sign the paper saying Rachel could have his money. He'd played along, though, pretending he was being coerced. Like that money meant anything to him.

The girls' safety aside, the pop in his knee was what worried him. They hadn't known about his injury. And right now, Bradley couldn't say if he would be able to walk on it. That was going to be a problem. Just not one that would stop him from doing something.

The gunman still with him had a phone in his jeans pocket. The guy glanced back toward the door and the hall where the conversation was taking place. Bad move, allowing himself to be distracted. Loss of focus in a situation like this got you hurt. Or killed. Bradley kicked with his good leg and swiped the back of the man's knees. His legs buckled and he fell.

Bradley scrambled forward, praying the second man didn't come in, gun firing, having heard the sound of his friend go down. He didn't want to get shot for trying this. With the man momentarily fighting off surprise, Bradley punched him in the head and then grabbed the gun. The silencer muffled the shot to a pop. One the second gunman likely heard. Still, that couldn't be helped.

"Let's go." The gunman in the hall yelled.

"No. She isn't going with you!" Rachel's voice washed over him. But there was no time to absorb the relief. Not when he could have only seconds before the guy came back to check on his friend. He might simply leave and never even step in here, but Bradley couldn't take that chance. He had to do this.

The phone was locked, but he used the dead man's index finger to get into it. 9-1-1 was probably the fastest option to get someone here. He didn't dial emergency services though. He didn't need first responders walking into an unknown situation. Too much risk for one of them, or one of Bradley's family, to be hurt or killed. He didn't have time to explain what was happening here enough to get the right kind of help—SWAT. The gunman would simply open fire on them all, and kill the responding officers.

Not to mention the worst case scenario rippling around in Bradley's head. If this had been going on for years, it meant whoever was behind it could have someone in law enforcement. His call could get squashed, and then no one would come. The reality was, he didn't know who he could trust. So Bradley called the one person qualified to help that he had no doubt he could rely on.

He dialed the number for Steve's office, and then set the phone down on the floor. Whatever the receptionist heard—even if it were nothing on the other end—he prayed she'd know it wasn't just a mistaken call. That she would pass it on, and Steve would follow up. That he would call Walker. *Please, Lord.*

"It's fine!" Alexis used that *everyone calm down* voice of hers. But she was scared, too. He hated that she was scared. "I'm coming with you. Okay?"

Bradley scooted to the hall, and peered out. The gunman stepped back into view, pulling Alexis with him. Where was he taking her? Bradley could get a real call out if this guy left, but what was the use in getting help here for him and Rachel if Alexis was gone? And he couldn't be sure the man wouldn't get the word they were free somehow, and then kill her.

When the man turned his direction, Bradley ducked back in the room and held the gun ready. If the guy came in here, he'd have to shoot him. It was a risk to Alexis's life, but he'd be found out. The second man was dead.

And yet, the alternative was that Alexis be taken. Who knew where, with that man.

They passed the doorway and the gunman called out, "I'll be back."

Bradley shifted his good leg and then cried out. Pushed all the pain he felt into his voice and made it sound like the dead man was torturing him. It sounded horrible even to his own ears, and he heard Alexis try to come and help him.

The gunman chuckled. "Be glad I'm nicer than him."

"You aren't."

"Then I'm just more task oriented. Which means when you're done helping me, you'll be dead quicker. Happy now?"

Bradley scooted to look out the door again. Down the hall, Alexis was being pulled along by that man. She was out of her league, and it was going to get her killed. He lifted the gun and aimed. Put pressure on the trigger.

The gunman shifted Alexis closer to him and whispered something that made her whole body tense, the gun pressed to her ribs.

Bradley exhaled and let the trigger go. He couldn't shoot the man. Not when it meant the man might fire his own weapon on a reflex. Alexis would be killed, and he would never forgive himself if she was murdered because of something he did.

Right now what he needed to do was get the phone, get a real call out, and get to Rachel. She probably needed medical attention. He knew he did. His right knee was the size of a volleyball. Probably broken, and definitely not good for him to walk on.

He slid across the floor and saw a message on the phone's screen.

`Team en route.`

Whether the kidnappers would've seen that or not, didn't matter. Bradley had heard stories of Steve's team and what they could do. Anyone on the receiving end of their arrival should be scared. He was just relieved though. He texted back.

`All clear. Bring ambulance. Alexis gone.`

The rest he could explain when Steve got there, if the man didn't already have someone tasked to find Alexis after that.

"Rachel!" He crawled with his forearms, legs dragging behind him, out the door and down the hall. "Rachel, you there?"

"Bradley!"

They might not be okay, but that was the sweetest sound of freedom he'd ever heard. "I'm here! I'm coming in."

She looked up when he pulled himself in the room. "What…"

"Busted my knee." Her skirt was covered in dirt and dust, and her blouse was untucked. A bruise on her temple looked nasty, but was at least a day old. "You okay?"

"Alexis."

"I know." He knew *everything.*

And Rachel knew it. Tears filled her eyes, and she held up her hands. "Can you get me out of here?"

"I can get you free." He pulled the penknife out of his boot the kidnappers hadn't even checked for, and cut her wrists loose. Her feet. He helped rub some feeling back into her extremities. "If we're going to get out of here you might have to carry me, though." He smiled.

"She won't be doing that." Steve's voice rang through the room.

Rachel sucked in a breath. She was scared? Maybe not of Steve, given they had some kind of history. Or at least an attraction. But after the last few days—and months—she had a right to be wary of someone she didn't know that well.

Bradley shifted and got in her face, so she had to focus on him. "Look at me, Rach." When her gaze lifted to him, he said, "Let's get out of here. Together. Okay?"

She nodded. He put weight on his good leg, and they stood up. She slid her hand into his. "We have to help Alexis. He took her, and we have to get her back."

Speaking of, Bradley waved the phone at Steve, who didn't come and get it. "Maybe we can get the partner's phone number from this. Get a location."

Steve lifted one eyebrow. An arrogance Bradley figured could very well be justified if all those stories he'd heard were actually true. "Ambulance is outside." He looked like he wanted to offer to help. He'd probably pick up Rachel like a true hero. But Bradley could guess she might not want that. Though, they could both use some help.

In the end they hobbled out on their own, albeit slowly. One of the EMTs was female, and Rachel let her help her walk to the bus while he stood with Steve.

"You should go too, get that knee looked at."

The guy was probably right.

"And you can talk to her, see what she knows. We need all the intel we can get."

"Now you sound like the FBI." Bradley didn't smile.

"Speaking of…"

Two SUVs pulled up. A familiar sight at this point. Walker strode over. "Looks like I'm late to the party again."

"Rachel is good."

"And you?"

Bradley was standing on one leg. What did the man think? "One dead kidnapper inside. The other one took Alexis."

Rachel called out, "They're going to the bank. He wants her to pretend to be me so she can get the money for him."

Steve's reaction was palpable. "Pretend?"

Walker said, "Like she did with the video." When Steve said nothing, he added, "The video of Rachel, that they told everyone was Alexis."

"Walker." Bradley needed him to shut up, given the stricken look on Rachel's face. "Enough." He took a half step closer and looked between the two men. "Get Alexis back."

He left them to hash it out. Steve could figure out all this stuff with Rachel himself. When he did, he was likely going to be extremely pissed about what had happened. And determined to get in on the FBI investigation to shut down the entire blackmailing operation.

Bradley limped to the ambulance. He figured the kidnappers were hired guns, like the FBI had told him. But he had no way to do what needed to be done. Right now what he had to do was take care of his sister while they found Alexis. They were the ones with the skills and resources to do it. When they did, he would be right there.

First Alexis. Now Rachel. Soon, he'd be able to be with Alexis again. Then their lives could be where they were supposed to be.

He pulled himself into the ambulance.

"I'm fine." Rachel waved away the stethoscope. "Just tired, dirty and hungry. It's hardly serious. You should look at his knee."

Bradley had his knife out again. He cut the hem of his jeans, and then tore the material all the way up to his thigh. She might think her injuries were minimal, but he didn't discount the psychological impact of it. Not to mention that when they got to the hospital, he was going to have the doctor discretely ask her if she needed a rape kit done.

"Ye-ouch."

He didn't look up from the mess that was his knee. Not after he'd been thinking about her being hurt like that.

"You're not kidding." It was throbbing still. Was he going to need surgery to fix this? If he did, that meant weeks of recovery time. He'd already been thinking about life after the SEALs. Was this what God had planned to keep him here, available to the women? They'd been through so much—Alexis still—it wouldn't hurt them to have someone here to watch their backs now.

"Bradley."

She sounded so sad. He braced his good foot on the floor and lifted up to sit on the gurney beside her. Bradley gathered his sister in his arms.

She started to cry. "He took Alexis. He's probably hurting her."

He couldn't help it. Maybe it was the adrenaline, the fatigue. The pain, messing with his head. His body begun to shake with laughter, instead of the tears that should have fallen. "Two peas in a pod." He kept laughing.

The EMT looked at him like he was crazy.

"What?" Rachel leaned back and looked up at him.

"You and Alexis. Only worried about what the other one is suffering."

"Well, that's our biggest problem right now!"

"Two peas in a pod." Mad at him because he'd said something dumb. Angry because for some reason they thought weakness wasn't acceptable. Caring. So caring. They loved fiercely, and thrived because of it. He'd thrived because of it.

Steve wandered over, his gaze only on Rachel. "Hey."

"Hey." Her voice was soft.

"You okay?"

"I won't be okay until Alexis is safe."

Steve said, "Walker has men on the bank. The minute they show up, he'll swoop in and snatch them up. Alexis will be okay."

"But it won't be over."

Bradley said, "Because those men are just hired guns?"

Rachel sniffed. "Their boss isn't going to leave this alone. He's going to keep coming for us." Her voice shook. "For *me* until I give him what he wants."

"And what is that?" Steve's question was cold.

"I should never have let everyone believe it was Alexis. Now he's furious and on a rampage," Rachel shot back. "The loss of money is only part of it." She turned to Bradley. "We can't let him take it out on Alexis. She's already given him too much."

"Because you guys lied to everyone."

"I didn't want her to take the blame, but she said it was for the best. I knew what it would do to her."

Bradley's frustration bubbled over. "Then why did you let her do it?"

"Dude." Steve's single spoken word was a reprimand.

Rachel's face crumpled, but she didn't look at Steve. "I just wanted it to be over, but it isn't."

He pulled her into his arms, fighting the frustration of not being able to fix this for her. "I know. We can put it right."

"And it'll always be part of me. My history. My future," she said. "All of it. Stained with what he did to me. Even if you get her back and catch him. Whoever he is. It's not going to make it go away."

"I know." Bradley laid his hand on hers. "We'll get you some help."

"I don't want help. I want Alexis."

"We agree on that at least."

She huffed, a sound that might have been a laugh any other time.

Steve stood at the door of the ambulance in silence, his attention a hundred percent focused on Rachel.

Bradley said, "You heard the woman."

Steve held out his hand. "The phone."

Bradley handed over the kidnapper's cell. Steve lifted his chin and left.

"I've always thought he was cute."

Bradley said, "Personally I don't see it."

She shoved at his arm, a tiny smile curling her lips. "Will she really be okay?"

"She and I asked that question about you a hundred times, and here you are. So we do the same thing. We pray, and we work on getting her back."

Chapter 19

Alexis huddled as close as she could to the passenger door. They'd been so close. To the end, to being free. So close to the goal of finding Rachel, and all finally being safe. Now that was gone.

Bradley had tried, but this crazy gunman who drove like he was at NASCAR had taken her. She shut her eyes and tried to remember Bradley calling her, "Honey." Hugging her. That had only been a few hours ago. Why did it seem like forever?

The car turned a corner, and she had to grab the handle on the door to avoid leaning all the way over the center console. No more eyes closed. She would be sick. "Can you slow down?"

All the frustration she was feeling bled into her tone, but she didn't care if he wasn't going to listen. Or if she sounded whiney. He was probably going to kill her anyway. Then it was unlikely she would care. She'd be past all this hurt. Past the pain of her life being what it was. Sweet relief.

Not that she was eager to die. So much would be lost. Left behind, and left unrealized. But that was her reality, nonetheless.

God, please don't let anyone else get hurt. There had been enough hurt and pain so far. It was time for this all to be over.

The gunman laughed and pulled his ski mask off.

Alexis stared at him. "Aren't you worried I can ID you?"

He shot her a look. Probably in his forties, he was rough on the edges but traditionally handsome, in a way. "You'll be dead, so who are you gonna tell?"

Alexis didn't want to die. That might be the natural end of this situation, but she didn't want evil to win. Bradley filled her mind, then. A reflex. Her heart's desire, as much as she'd been suppressing it. She wanted to know what a life with him would be like.

"So you get this man his money and then what?" At least, her assumption was that it was a man who was the one blackmailing high profile people around D.C. It didn't seem like a woman would choose to victimize other women like this, but what did she know? She didn't like true crime TV shows.

Whoever it was, they had to have a powerfully good reason to do what they were doing. With every new victim they drew attention to themselves, risking each time that someone might go to the police instead of just paying up. Then they'd be implicated, and it would be all over.

Which meant, if they were clever, they were hiding behind layers of people, maybe even corporations or blind email accounts like the one she'd found. Layers of anonymity to keep their identity safe.

He turned another corner, then said, "I get that money. Then I do me. It's all about my life, my future."

"She and her brother, it's their money."

"Feds are all over that," he said. "Turns out all I needed was you and that broken nose of yours. Makes it harder to tell if it's you or Rachel." He smirked. "That was a good play, by the way. Pretending it was you in that video. Smart."

"What if I say no?" She lifted her chin, ignoring his approval of her personal choices. And her friendship. "I could jump out of the car now and run away."

"You want road rash, before that car behind us hits and kills you?" He shook his head. "You wanna go out like that, go ahead. Won't be me cleaning up the mess."

Okay, so no. She didn't especially want to do that. But still. "I don't want the blackmailer to get that money. Why do you work for someone like that?"

She could barely stomach what had been done to Rachel, it was so evil. Alexis didn't know if it was better or worse that her friend had been groggy and didn't remember it. Would the knowing be worse than simply wondering what had gone on? Alexis didn't know if she had a good answer to that.

The gunman snorted and glanced out the side window, then took another hair-pin turn. "So high and mighty. Too bad it's going to get you killed."

Alexis looked out the window on her side, hardly able to stomach much more of this. The guy cared about no one and nothing, except himself. She couldn't reason with a man like that. One who only valued getting paid. But what for? So he could spend it all however he liked, and then he'd need another job. More money.

She liked money as much as the next person. It certainly made life more comfortable. But in the last few months of being stripped of everything she'd had before, Alexis had been forced to face the fact that nothing truly valuable could be purchased. Family. Friendships. Affection. Everything she had with Bradley.

She wanted it. She wanted him

That dream of living a solitary life was still there. It might not be the hub of ministry God wanted her to be part of, like helping kids in need or people who are downtrodden, but it was what she wanted. To lick her wounds? Maybe. She'd been stripped so publicly, all over the internet. Why not rebuild her life quietly, away from all that? God couldn't begrudge her the desire to do that, could He?

He said, "You put your butt on the line to save your friends. I'll give you that."

She didn't turn from the window. "I'd have thought you would've kept them around. For leverage."

"I'll get what I want. Don't worry about my methods." She heard a tremor in his voice. He was worried?

"Who is he?"

The gunman swallowed.

"You're scared of him."

He huffed. "Don't matter. I'll be gone, and he won't find me."

"After you get paid?"

He said nothing.

"You're going to run." And leave his friend holding Rachel and Bradley to face the blackmailer. "You're going to keep the money for yourself and use it to escape, aren't you?"

"High and mighty. Just like I said."

"I can understand wanting to get away from someone like that."

The gunman huffed. "Yeah, he's *so evil*. There's a million of that guy in the world."

"Destroying others so he can profit?"

"Don't see what's so special about this guy." Still, that tremor was back.

"He's special enough you're scared."

His head whipped around so he could glare at her. He yelled, "I'm not scared."

Alexis lifted both hands. "Fine. Do your thing. Kill me, and take the money. Won't he just come after you, though?"

"Not if he wants what I know to stay a secret."

"So why don't you just testify against him?"

"Because he'll kill me."

Alexis shrugged. "Sorry, I'm just brainstorming. Trying to help you out of your jam, and maybe not get killed in the process."

"Like your life is so great." He pulled up at a stop light and looked her up and down. "You're kinda cute, though. Wanna come with me?"

"To a life on the run from a man you're scared of?" He was the scariest person she knew. At least right now. So who on earth was the man this guy was scared of? "No thank you."

Besides, Bradley wouldn't be there, and she was never going to trade what she had with him for this guy. Even if she wasn't scared of him, he still didn't hold a candle to that history. And yeah, she was derailing her whole "solitary healing" plan thing. Maybe Bradley liked cabins in the mountains and small towns.

Would he want to come with her?

Bradley seemed like he was interested, but wasn't he just going to go on mission again? He spent more time gone than he was here. Alexis could live the life of a military wife, even one gone on so many missions as the SEALs went on. But that wasn't exactly the full life she dreamed of. Plenty of people did their duty and spent buckets of time apart. It was hard, but they made it work.

The gunman shrugged. "Suit yourself."

She would. It was hardly a choice at all. God had put Bradley in her path years ago. They hadn't been ready for all that it was, all it turned out to be. They'd been immature. Hadn't dealt with it the right way. But they were different now. Mature—or at least more than they had been. He'd grown into the kind of man she could respect. In a way she'd never expected. He was *more* than her dream now. She hadn't even known how to dream that big. Would never have thought to ask for a man like him.

The idea that it had been God's plan all along floored her. Maybe God had given her everything she'd ever wanted—she just had to reach out and grab it. She realized now that it had been the pain, the time spent apart, the growth—as hard as that had been—and the choices, good and bad, that they'd made, which had made them into the people they were supposed to be. The kind of people with enough wisdom behind them to be able to handle it.

They weren't done. Far from it. They were still those same kids who'd succumbed to temptation. They still made dumb mistakes, and could be just as selfish as they'd ever been. And yet, without these years in between to bring them to now…would they even be here? It was a gift. Despite the struggle. Maybe the struggle was what had caused her to realize exactly how much of a gift it was. Because otherwise she'd have taken them being together for granted.

Now she knew just how precious it was. Alexis would treasure any time they spent with each other—even if it was only a few days a year.

The gunman pulled off the street into a pharmacy parking lot. "Bank's over there. Thirty minutes to closing, so you better hustle. Got me?"

He got out, and opened the trunk.

Just left her sitting there in the passenger seat while he rooted around in the back.

Alexis pulled the visor down and looked in the mirror. She couldn't see him. If she got out and ran, how long would it be before he noticed? Screaming would draw his attention along with everyone else. Could she get far enough someone would see her and she'd be able to get help? If this was the bank, there had to be a team of feds somewhere close by, waiting for them to show up. They didn't know they would only get this low-level player. Not the boss.

Alexis slowly pulled on the door handle. The click was barely audible, and she pushed the door open an inch at a time. She put one foot out, her heart pounding. As she lifted from the seat, she saw him out the corner of her eye.

Gun pointed right at her. A smirk on his face. "Get over here. You wanna try and run, I'll shoot you in the back, leave you to bleed out on the sidewalk, and then go get Rachel." He paused for a second. "After I put a bullet in the brother."

"His name is Bradley."

"Am I supposed to care?"

He was going to care when Bradley showed up to put a bullet in *him*.

Alexis walked to the trunk and saw there was a bundle of clothes inside. *God, please let Bradley come.* She didn't know what state they were in. Maybe she was alone here. But she had to pray.

"Put those on."

She unfolded the black trench coat, and shook it out. Dust puffed up and she coughed, hair falling over her face. Alexis used the hair tie she kept on her wrist for just in case to put her hair in a messy bun, the way Rachel did on her days off. The senator had been photographed plenty of times out on the town dressed like this.

Besides the coat and her hair, there was just one thing missing: the fact she wasn't Rachel at all.

"This goes under the coat."

She stared at the vest. Wires. Rectangular gray blocks that read C4.

She swallowed. "I—"

"You're taking too long." He swung it over her head and pressed down Velcro tabs on her sides. "All you gotta do is take that paper in and tell the bank manager to make the transaction. Account number's on there."

She couldn't think past what he'd put on her.

The gunman shoved aside a balled up length of rope and handed her oversized sunglasses that probably cost a dollar. Anyone who didn't know better—or who didn't look too closely—wouldn't know they weren't the real thing. Alexis had never really understood spending hundreds, sometimes thousands of dollars, on something she could get far cheaper at a department store. Or a thrift store.

Her mother had drummed into her the importance of labels, and projecting the right image, but Alexis had never understood it. No matter how hard her mom tried, she just couldn't see the point of trying to impress people who only cared how much money she'd spent on her outfit. One she couldn't wear again for fear they would see her in something "old."

She slipped the sunglasses on her nose and tried to think past the shooting pain going up through her sinuses. Her nose would be crooked for life.

A life that may not last too much longer.

He pulled out a small case and opened it, took out a tiny earbud and pushed it in her ear canal. She didn't even move.

He would…

He grabbed the trench coat and forced her arms into it. Fastened the buttons over the vest.

She didn't want this. She couldn't be responsible for the lives of everyone in the bank. That wasn't the plan. This was about the money, and her friends being safe now. Innocent people were never supposed to have been drawn into the blast radius of all that was happening.

He pulled out his phone and showed her the screen. Then waved it in the direction of the bank. "Off you go."

She didn't move.

"It's perfectly stable. Until you do anything I don't like. Say anything I don't like. Ask for a pen, so you can write a note. Nothing. No hand signals, or stupid attempts to ask for help. None of that."

She couldn't speak. Even to agree. Alexis gave him a tiny nod, while everything inside her screamed *No*.

"Get going. Do it right and this will be over in minutes."

That was what she was afraid of.

Alexis forced her legs to move. Forced herself to look both ways, and crossed the street. *Now would be a great time for me to get arrested for jay-walking.* But no, that wasn't the plan.

God, don't let anyone die.

She'd been prepared when it was just her at risk. Now there were countless others who could lose their lives if this went wrong.

Alexis pulled open the door and walked into the bank with a bomb strapped to her chest.

Chapter 20

From the rear seat of the SUV, Bradley watched Alexis cross the street. The desire to rush after her was so strong his entire body flinched in the seat.

"Hold."

He pulled his fingers back from the door handle. He couldn't hobble across the street fast enough to save her. Steve was the boss here. Bradley might be a Tier 1 Operator, but that didn't mean he could jump the gun and break from this team. From the plan.

More and more he wanted to be part of this life. Part of the fight stateside. Missions were one thing, and they had meaning, but Bradley wanted to be home. He wanted to fight on a different front now. The one that had Alexis in his house, his ring on her finger. *God, help me save her.* That dream was the best, but it wouldn't be reality if she didn't make it through this.

He'd had the doctor wrap his leg and give him a shot. Soon enough that would wear off, and he would be writhing in pain on the floor. But for now, it was all about Alexis.

"He got back in the car," one of the other team members said. "Tablet. Maybe a Surface."

Steve said, "You think he has access to bank security."

"You saw that move," Bradley reminded him about the earbud the guy stuck in her ear. "He's listening to everything she says."

"One wrong move and he's going to light up that whole bank."

115

A rock settled in Bradley's stomach. They'd all seen the gunman pull the vest on Alexis and strap her in. The idea that her life hung by such a delicate thread made him want to rage. Race after the man and put him down.

But Steve had said, "Hold."

And Bradley had to face the fact he'd get shot while he was still limping over there.

"Poor gal." He didn't know who said it.

Bradley gritted his teeth. Sympathy wasn't his strength. He'd rather rush in, aim his weapon, and get the result he needed. But there were too many players here to do anything other than a coordinated attack. One flash of movement to indicate someone was going after Alexis to get the vest off and this guy would probably blow up the whole bank.

He thought about her reaction and realized she'd fight whoever showed up to help her. "She'll make sure no one else gets hurt."

"How's she gonna do that?"

"By doing exactly what he told her," Bradley said. "She won't give him reason to detonate that vest. Alexis protects people. She won't rock the boat like that if she thinks someone will get hurt. That's why we have to end this guy *and* get to that vest. Before he can slip a finger on that phone and blow it."

If that happened, it didn't matter where Alexis was. Or how many people she was determined to protect. With a vest like that, anyone within fifteen feet of her would be hit by the blast. Ka-boom. Game over.

Bradley couldn't let that happen.

"Any word on this guy's background?" Steve had someone looking into the guy, and had found out he was ex-army. Whether he knew enough about explosives to make more than a basic vest was anyone's guess at this point.

Steve shook his head. "He has tech skills, though."

Bradley wasn't feeling much better, knowing the guy had the smarts to bug Alexis. And a backup plan to destroy everything if he didn't get his money.

"Got two feds headed our way."

Bradley turned to watch their approach down the sidewalk. Steve's vehicle was parked on the north side of the street, closer to the gunman than the bank. Alexis had crossed the street in front of their vehicle, headed for the bank. The two feds moved with purpose along the sidewalk on the south side of the street. Headed for the front glass doors of the bank.

His legs twitched. His fingers curled into fists. But Bradley held himself still while everything in him wanted to rush to her. To protect her—disable that vest, if he could, and get her safe.

"Should we intercept?" one of the guys asked.

"Terrence and Mint, head for the gunman. Bradley, you want the bank?"

"I want that remote," he said, already reaching for the door handle.

"Mint, you got the feds. Everyone kosher?"

A chorus of responses indicated in the affirmative.

"Execute."

They climbed out of the car simultaneously. Bradley kept to the building fronts on the north side of the street. He kept an eye on the gunman every step of the way and made sure he wasn't spotted. Sitting in the driver's seat of the car, the guy's attention was on the screen on his lap. Bradley got close enough to see the phone on the seat next to him.

Gun held in a loose grip, he limped swiftly enough and got the door open before the man realized what was happening. Bradley ducked in and reached for the phone. Too late. It was snatched up.

"Nice."

He slid into the seat, gun now aimed at the gunman. Forcing the pain in his knee out of his conscious thought. He wanted to shoot the guy in the face and be done with this, but the remote for the vest strapped to Alexis was now in his hand. If the guy dropped it, would it go off anyway? It was too much of a gamble to know whether he was right or wrong. And it would be too late for Alexis.

"You're done." Maybe he didn't know it yet, but he was. "This is over."

Past the gunman, out the driver's window, another of Steve's men held his gun on the man. The shot would come through the window, interfering with the aim, but it would still be true.

Bradley didn't have to look to know Mint had entered the bank. None of these men messed around. Despite no longer being active military, they were all professionals. They charged exorbitant prices, but they were also worth every penny.

"Hand me the phone. Nice and easy."

"And if my hand twitches? Your girl dies."

"She dies. You die." Bradley wanted at least that to be straight between them.

On screen he saw Alexis approach a closed door. The gunman didn't even look at it. Had he given up on getting the money? If he figured this was a lost cause then that meant he was considering his options of how this was going to go down.

There was no way for him to escape. Now it was all about exactly how much fallout there was going to be. If this guy figured he was going to die, he probably didn't care exactly how many he took with him—starting with Alexis.

"The phone. Now." Bradley held out his left hand, palm up. His right hand held steady aim on the gunman with one of Steve's Berettas. This close, the guy would be dead. No question. Could the guy hit that button fast enough?

The gunman set the phone in Bradley's hand, the gleam of something Bradley didn't like in his eyes.

A car engine revved. The roar was so loud it didn't surprise Bradley when two SUVs passed the front of the bank.

Gunfire split the relative calm of the street. That rat-tat-tat of automatic fire. *Alexis.* Bradley's body flinched, a reaction he couldn't control these days. The reflex to dive for cover was ingrained in him—and probably meant he should hang up his uniform. No one needed a Navy SEAL on the teams who reacted this way.

The gunman slammed the tablet computer into Bradley's face.

Bradley squeezed the trigger. A bullet shattered the glass from outside. The gunman cried out, clutching his leg.

Bradley shook off the surprise, as well as the impact of the electronic device shattering into his head and shoulder, in time to see the gunman slam his door into Terrence, one of Steve's men. The gun went off again.

Bradley ignored their scuffle, figuring Terrence could take care of himself against an injured man. He looked at the phone, and saw it was fingerprint protected.

"Don't let him get away."

Terrence didn't reply. He and the gunman wrestled for his weapon. It went off, and Terrence cried out.

Bradley stowed the phone in his back pocket and climbed over the driver's seat to provide Terrence backup. *Ouch.* He got his weapon aimed in time to see the gunman limp away and the former soldier on the ground, clutching his foot.

"Go."

Bradley didn't wait around, and neither did he need Terrence's order to head out after the gunman. He raced after the limping man, following to where he'd disappeared around a corner. Bradley went wide, just in case the man was hiding out of sight, ready to attack.

The alley was empty. A dead end. He wanted to turn back, to go to Alexis and make sure she was all right. Had she been shot? Had the men in those SUVs just shot up the bank and left, or had they gone inside afterwards and finished off all the bank employees and customers? Were the FBI there?

Bradley prayed as he searched behind a car parked in the alley. Around the dumpster. Found the gunman crouched on the far side of it. Eyes wide. Blood pooling around his leg. Not much worse off than Bradley, if he had to be honest about it.

"Shoot me," the man said through gritted teeth. "Just do it."

As if Bradley would give him the satisfaction of ending him like that. "Tell me who's running the blackmailing."

"No way." The guy jerked his head side to side. "He gets wind I told anyone and I'm still breathing, I won't get the chance to take my own life. He'll peel my skin off and display it as a warning to anyone else who thinks about talking."

Bradley frowned. There was no way—

"You think I'm joking? I've seen it, man. So if you aren't going to shoot me then I don't want it out there that I talked."

"We can get you in protective custody. But not if Alexis or anyone else dies." It turned his stomach even offering to keep this guy safe.

"Leave or kill me."

"You're coming in. I'm not gonna kill you when you know this guy's name."

"Which means if you arrest me, I'll be dead by end of day." The man's mouth pressed into a thin line. "He won't wanna run the risk of me talking."

"Doesn't trust you?"

"The man would kill his own mother if he thought she was goin' to do something he didn't like."

More and more it seemed like Alexis and Rachel had been caught up in something way out of any of their leagues. Bradley was actually worried the FBI even might not be able to handle this guy. If he was as bad as this man said, even Steve's team was jumping into a live volcano.

It had to be someone powerful. Private. Someone with money and resources at the center of what was going on in Washington. An insider, maybe even someone in government. Or in the White House.

What could any of them do if they didn't know who to trust? An investigation would go on record. Even Steve's company couldn't fly under the radar forever. Eventually the man behind the blackmailing would get wind of the fact he was being targeted. Investigated. It would take man hours. Surveillance. This guy could have an army behind him.

"Tell me who he is." Bradley wasn't going to murder the guy, but this was the best lead they'd had so far as to the man's identity.

"Give me the gun," the man said. "I'll tell you, then I kill myself."

"Or you'll kill me."

"Maybe I'll kill both of us," the guy said. His face was pale, his skin clammy.

"Or you'll bleed out in a dirty alley before we're done with this conversation." Bradley came at the guy from a different angle. "Who were those guys in the SUV's who shot up the bank?"

"Either way I'm good."

Bradley pulled out the phone—the bomb remote—to call Walker and get the FBI here to pick this guy up. If they weren't busy at the bank.

The gunman's eyes widened. "You brought the remote?"

"And now I'm gonna get the FBI here to arrest you. You can tell *them* who this guy is."

"Move too far away from the bomb with that remote…guess what happens?"

Ice cold filled him. Like jumping into a mountain lake in February. "It would've gone off." He'd have heard it. Bradley tilted his head to the mouth of the alley. "Get up. We're walking."

He called Walker while the gunman sat there, unmoving.

"Agent Walker."

"It's Bradley. I've got the kidnapper."

"And I've got four dead agents. Wanna tell me what on earth happened here? This was my operation, and you bring these yahoos to get in the way of my men?"

"Sounds like you could use the help," Bradley said. He was done waiting for the gunman to get up, so he lifted the sole of his boot over the wound. He gave the guy a pointed look, like he'd actually step on his wound. "Get up."

He dragged the man to his feet, helping some. He wasn't going to be mean about it. The gunman limped ahead of him. "I'm bringing the kidnapper to you."

"Great. Fabulous." Sarcasm dripped in his tone. "I'm pinned down. I've got carnage around me and shots are still flying. Don't get caught by a stray when you get here."

Terrence was gone from beside the car. Bradley grabbed the tablet computer and clicked the screen. He got the screen with the feds up and walked the man to Steve's team car, where one member of the team who'd been designated to remain stood.

Bradley couldn't remember his name. "Hey."

The man hopped out, got zip ties from the trunk and trussed up the gunman. Bradley had him sit in the back seat.

The team member beeped the locks and then said, "Copy that", though not to Bradley. He looked at his own tablet, "Two coming up in front." He was coordinating the fight for Steve?

Bradley wasn't going to get in the middle of an operational conversation. He flipped the tablet he'd gotten from the gunman so the guy could see what was on screen.

"Hold up." His gaze snagged, and he reached for the device. "I've got surveillance inside. I'm looking at two hallways and an office, as well as the main lobby." He paused. "No. I still don't have eyes on the woman, or Mint."

I still don't have eyes on the woman.

Alexis.

She was in the bank, unsecured, likely still strapped to that bomb. And very much in trouble.

Bradley raced for the bank. A side entrance the employees likely used to go out for smoke breaks.

Twenty-five feet from the building, there was a whomp that echoed through the air. It boomed toward him as a fireball erupted inside the bank.

Hot air slammed into Bradley, then the rush of flames. He flew backward and hit the concrete.

Everything went black.

Chapter 21

Alexis lay stunned on the floor of the manager's office. Her hip pressed into a sharp corner…the desk. She blinked and looked up at "Mint." Whatever kind of name that was, he hadn't felt the need to explain to her. Just told her he was a friend of Steve's, and then he was scanning the vest with his intense gaze. His face had dipped to look closely at the vest, giving her a view of the thinning hair on the crown of his face. He'd shaken his head, dislodging his thick black-rimmed glasses to slip down his nose a fraction. Mint yanked one wire.

Then he'd peeled the vest off and tossed it away. From the two of them and anyone else. Toward the approaching gunmen.

Boom.

The blast had blown them both back into the office. Had he known it would blow? Mint lay on the floor now, bleeding from a gash on his temple. She crawled to him and patted his shoulder.

The men in the bank lobby were rousing. She could hear voices. Orders called out to each other.

"Mint." She shook him harder.

Where was Bradley? Why hadn't he come in to help her? She wanted to believe he had a good reason. But not that he'd been hurt, or possibly even killed. Still, it stung that he wasn't here. Maybe Mint was Steve's explosives expert, but she needed more help than that.

She was still trapped in the bank with gunmen approaching. Mint wasn't waking up. Alexis found the gun, holstered on his hip. She slid it out.

Mint sucked in a breath and sat up. Halfway to sitting, his eyes flew open and saw her there with his gun in her hand.

"Easy."

His gaze zeroed in on her. "Could say the same."

"I know how to use it." Like Bradley would ever have been okay with her living on her own without being armed and knowing how to protect herself. His instinct to make sure those he cared about were safe was part of what she loved about him. He didn't smother her with his maleness. He trusted her to take care of herself. And he'd made sure that trust was warranted.

Mint took the gun and got to his feet. Alexis followed him to the door.

He glanced out and reached back at the same time to slide his phone from his back pocket. Unlocked it with his thumb as he brought it forward so that the screen was up. He hit two buttons and put it to his ear a second later.

"Yeah. All good. Holed up in the manager's office, but we've got some serious heat coming our way." Pause. "Got it." He stowed the phone.

Before Alexis could ask what the plan was, he grabbed her hand and headed out into the hallway. They raced to the end, past a break room and the restrooms. At the end was an EXIT door.

Bullets pinged off the wall. The floor.

Alexis screamed, running in a crouch. He tugged her hand to the left, then went right and ran into her. His arms snaked around her and he crowded her into a storage closet.

Shut the door.

Alexis stood wide-eyed as Mint scanned the shelves, loaded with bottles. Cleaning products. Vinegar.

He twisted the lid off one bottle, shoved a rag inside and lit the end with a lighter from his front pocket.

Mint pulled the door open, swung the bottle and then slammed the door before she heard it hit the tile of the hallway. The whoosh that followed was peppered with shouts.

Mint opened another bottle and did the same, the air now filling with the smell of chemicals.

This time when he opened the door, he fired two shots from his gun and then threw the bottle. Answering shots made her duck to the back of the storage closet.

There was nowhere to go.

He could throw lit bottles and fire his gun over and over again. Until he ran out of bullets. And cleaning supplies.

The door kicked in. Four men rushed the room, black fatigues. Helmets and face masks. For a second she thought they might actually be SWAT. But no indications on their uniform told her that. No badges were on display.

Alexis tensed up as Mint faced them. He lifted his weapon, but the closest man slammed the butt of his rifle into Mint's shoulder. He went down. The man kept hitting him over and over again until Alexis cried out, "Stop it!"

This wasn't just putting down a man facing you, armed and intent on deadly harm. They were enjoying this. Relishing the violence of what was happening.

Two hung back at the door. The man without the bloody rifle stalked toward her, a sneer curling his mouth. His friend closed in on the other side.

"Too bad he said no survivors."

She squeezed her eyes shut. They were going to kill the FBI agents. Bradley. Steve's team. Everyone still in the bank—most of the half-dozen customers had fled when she walked in. The security guard and all the employees.

The minute she entered the bank, she'd handed the manager the paper while they all stared at the vest on display. Pretty sure she was about to get fired upon as well as yelled at, she'd done exactly what the gunman asked of her. But where had playing it safe gotten her?

Mint had gotten her out of that vest, only to have it blow up anyway. Now he was down, and she was about to be executed.

She opened her eyes. Lifted her chin. She didn't want to die, but was ready if that was what was going to happen. They didn't need to know she was scared out of her mind. God had brought her through so many things, she knew she could do this.

Still, to stand here and wait was excruciating. There was no one left to protect. Nothing to do. Rachel was safe. Bradley wasn't here. She hadn't said goodbye to either of them, and never would be able to now. She'd done everything she could for her family—the two of them.

Alexis faced down the gun, waiting for the crack.

The end.

There was no use fighting it, since she would only end up being shot anyway. She couldn't take these guys down. Nothing left to do but let it happen.

A single tear tracked down her face.

A gun went off. The two men by the door went down. The third man spun. The one in front of her spun as well, and Bradley came through the door. *Crack.* The rap of each bullet was deafening in the tiny space. She sucked in a breath as the rifle guy dropped.

Bradley pressed a button on the chord of the earbuds he wore. "Clear. I've got her."

Her back pressed into the shelves, the metal lines biting horizontal across her back.

"Alexis." Soot and dirt covered his face. He limped two steps closer to her.

A sob worked its way up her throat. She coughed it out and nearly collapsed. Bradley caught her before she could go down. She said, "Mint."

"What?"

She motioned to the man lying on the floor. There was so much blood. "They hurt him."

Bradley held her elbows until she was steady. When she nodded, he crouched beside Steve's teammate. Pressed two fingers to the man's neck, then immediately grabbed the earbuds chord again. "Get an ambulance here. Back hall, storage room. Mint is down." He paused. "Beaten. Pulse is weak." Another pause. "Copy that."

Then he was coming back toward her. His eyes intense. That hitch in his stride. His hands brushed her shoulders. His fingers felt at her throat. Like he needed to feel her pulse as well.

"I'm here." She touched his sides. Felt the shift of muscle as each breath expanded his lungs. Then the exhale.

He nodded. "I thought you got caught in that blast."

Alexis whispered her fingers over his forehead, into his hair. "Looks to me like you're the one who got caught in it."

He didn't smile. Just stared into her eyes with so much intensity. Like he could hardly believe she was here. She was alive.

Maybe he just didn't know what to say. Maybe he didn't want her hanging on him.

Alexis dropped her hands and took a step back. She hit the shelves. "Ouch."

Bradley tugged her away from them, but with the bodies on the floor there wasn't far to go before they'd have to step over someone. The acrid smell of gunpowder and the recently deceased filled the room.

Alexis touched her roiling stomach. They couldn't leave Mint in here. The EMT's needed to hurry, before the worst happened.

"Lex."

She glanced over at him, but he didn't say anything else. Did he want her to say something? Was she supposed to thank him for killing these men for her? She didn't know the protocol in times like these.

Thankfully Steve entered, followed by the EMT's, who got to work on Mint. Steve shot Bradley a look, then said, "You okay, Alexis?"

She nodded, not entirely sure she could speak.

"Get her out of here, Harris."

Bradley followed the order, tugging on her hand. She'd been dragged around over and over today. Enough that she didn't want that to happen anymore. She pulled her hand from his. He glanced at her, but she folded her arms across her stomach and moved through the door.

She stepped over those bodies. Four men he'd killed—for her. Men intent on doing that very thing to her. After she'd been kidnapped and had a bomb strapped to her.

A bomb that had gone off.

She'd nearly been blown up.

The hall was empty, but bustling movement to her left caught her attention. The front of the building had been blown to pieces. Firefighters were spraying water on the pieces of furniture and debris that lay across the floor. The bodies.

She squeezed her eyes shut, remembering the look on the bank manager's face right before those gunmen had shot him.

Bradley said, "This way," and waited for her to step in his direction. He led her to the back entrance and held the door for her. They stepped into the sun, so glaring she had to lift a hand and shield her eyes.

"You've gone quiet."

She walked alongside him, mostly trying not to collapse on the ground. If he could walk, so could she.

There was so much destruction. So many times she'd thought he was dead. That she was dead. All those years, waiting for Rachel to call and tell her that he'd been killed in action. So sure she would never have what she'd always wanted. The future she wanted had been so close she felt as though she could touch it. Now…she didn't know. Didn't want to ask.

Before the end of the side street, he held an arm out in front of her and slowed to a stop. That would have been a gentle touch at any other time. Now he thought she didn't want him to touch her.

He looked…not frustrated, but the edge of it was there. He just didn't know what to do. "Please say something. Let me know you're okay."

She shivered, though the air held no chill. How she was still standing upright, Alexis didn't know. Surely any second now she would just crumple to the pavement—and all the fear, the relief—would come rushing out in one big wave.

But if he could stand, so would she.

Bradley stowed his gun in the back of his waistband and held his arms out, palms up. "What am I supposed to—"

Alexis took two steps. Her body slammed into his and she wrapped her arms around him, squeezing. Hard. Enough to keep them both standing. Enough to hold herself together. Enough she knew he could take it. That she could do this, and he'd accept it. That he would be strong for her when she had no strength left for herself.

The way he always had. And, God willing, always would.

But she couldn't say any of that. Not when she felt like she was going to choke every time she breathed. Not when she could hardly swallow, the lump was so big.

A second later his arms came around her, strong but not tight. He exhaled. Alexis tried to speak, but all that came out was a sob. It didn't stop, and she cried there in his arms while he spoke nonsense in her ear and held her.

Kept her standing when she knew she would fall.

Chapter 22

Two weeks later

The doors slid open and Bradley looked up. Instead of Alexis, who he'd been expecting to pick him up from the hospital, it was Rachel. "Where is she?"

Two Secret Service agents trailed behind Rachel into the hospital lobby. She huffed. "You can't be happy to see your sister?"

She would never know exactly *how* happy he was. Especially considering he had both women back in his life. The Navy had been by, and there was paperwork. He'd probably have to report back on base soon, but for right now he was home. The surgery on his knee was behind him. It was time to move on with his life.

And Bradley was ready.

Rachel rolled her eyes, more like a teen than a senator. "Fine. You want Alexis. But I convinced her to stay at the compound." Her face turned serious. "Because I need to talk to you."

The orderly rolled him outside to the curb where a town car sat idling. Maybe it was for the best that Alexis was at the compound. She was protected there. And she'd visited him after his surgery, then every day of his recuperation. So technically he'd seen her yesterday.

The blackmailer's identity was still unknown. He was still out there, and a threat to Bradley's family. He wanted an update direct from Steve on that whole situation.

Bradley slid himself into the car without help. His knee was wrapped and twice the size. Crutches lay on the floor of the town car for when they got to the compound. He wasn't looking forward to the healing process, but it was this or…nothing. As it was, he couldn't be a SEAL anymore. The alternative to surgery was being benched from doing anything in the security field for the rest of his life. As it was, he'd be on restricted duty.

Steve had offered him a job anyway.

Rachel got in the other side of the back seat. The Secret Service agents got in front, and the car set off. She looked over him, the close study only family could give you. "Okay?"

Bradley nodded. "They gave me pain meds." He'd bartered them down to the lowest dose, not wanting to lean too heavily on drugs. The flip side was it really hurt. "What did you want to talk to me about?"

Maybe that was a little short, but he needed to be distracted. He was far more tired, in pain—and okay yeah—grouchy, than he liked.

"I wanted to tell you in person that…" She paused. "Uncle Francis was found dead. The news reports and the police who I talked to all say it was suicide."

Bradley felt no loss over the man. He doubted Lincoln would have either, if he'd been alive still. "You don't think so?"

She shrugged. "Why would a man like that suddenly get a guilty conscience? I mean, you don't really know what's going on in someone's head, even if you're close to them. But he belittled everyone. He seemed to…enjoy it almost."

Bradley nodded. "So why would a narcissist suddenly up and decide to end his life?"

The alternative was murder. But surely the police would have found evidence of that during the investigation.

"Exactly," Rachel said. "Steve thinks he's a link in the chain, but not the mastermind. He actually believes Uncle Francis was killed by the blackmailer. Or one of his people. Though, we might never know the reason why." Rachel shrugged, her shoulders so thin.

Was she eating enough? She had seemed to be healing from her ordeal—both of them—as far as he could tell. He'd have to touch base with Alexis to know for sure, though. The two were closer than ever. And he counted himself blessed that both women had such character that they could forgive, move on in their relationship and love stronger than ever, even despite all that had gone on.

He said, "How are things with Steve?"

Rachel wrinkled her nose. She glanced at the window, and stared out at the streets going by. He let her have her quiet for a while. When she looked back at him, she smiled. "Alexis has been driving Mint *crazy*." She chuckled. "Fussing over him and hardly letting him out of her sight. When she wasn't visiting you, of course."

Bradley smiled. More over the fact that she spoke about Alexis and Steve's team members in the same context as thoughts of Steve. She was settling into life as part of the group instead of isolating herself, which she sometimes had a tendency to do. Although she was still clearly keeping Steve at arm's length.

Not for long, though. Bradley didn't think.

"She feels guilty he got hurt saving her." And Mint had been seriously hurt.

Rachel said, "It was funny when he had that concussion and he was yelling at her. Not that it was funny he had the concussion. But when he was yelling and slurring his words, she was ignoring him. Fluffing his pillow." She chuckled again, and Bradley was pleased she was enjoying life now.

The car pulled into the compound, and they climbed out. Bradley gritted his teeth and hopped to get the crutches under his arms and out of the way of the car door. This wasn't going to be fun.

The front door flew open, and Alexis ran out. "Tell me you're done talking!"

Rachel said, "I told him about Uncle Francis."

Alexis pulled up short before she slammed into him, and set her cool fingers on his biceps. Steve must have the air conditioning inside cranked. "Can I help you inside? Can I get you anything?"

Bradley said, "You can bring those lips a little closer over here."

She smiled wide, while Rachel groaned behind them. Alexis kissed him, enough for now but not so much they'd give everyone a show.

"Bye," Rachel said. "I'm leaving now because you guys are gross."

Bradley turned to her. "Call me later?"

Rachel nodded and got back in the car with her official escort.

The team assembled in a tiny room like a movie theater, but with huge recliners. Bradley tipped the chair back and the footrest up, and then tugged Alexis on his lap. She shifted so as not to touch his knee, and he kissed her arm below the sleeve of her shirt.

Steve stood up at the front, the screen black behind him. "Okay. Let's make this quick."

Someone in the row behind Bradley started making snoring noises. Everyone chuckled, while Steve frowned. "As I was saying, the FBI is attempting to gain information from the bomber. He isn't cooperating."

"They should let me have ten minutes with him," a female voice said.

Mint called out, "They don't want him missing any limbs."

"Like I'd leave a mark," the woman replied.

"Can we move this along?" Bradley said, laughing. "I need my favorite nurse to give me some T-L-C."

Steve frowned, while Alexis shifted on his lap.

"Easy."

She said, "I don't do sponge baths, you know."

Bradley figured that was negotiable. Especially considering his plans. All he needed was some time alone with her to plead his case to make this legal. Forever.

Steve said, "Perkins, give the brief about Aaron Jones."

A slender woman he would not like to meet in a dark alley strode to the front while Steve exited out a side door. Perkins frowned at the boss's retreat, cleared her throat and said, "Aaron Jones is still at large. The FBI can't find him, so we explained what we can do. They've given us everything they have on him, including his history, and we're opening a contract with them."

She glanced at her phone screen and swiped. "The second case we've opened since the bank is a missing person's case."

"I'll do it!" Mint shot up out of his seat. "Put me on the job." He all but begged for it.

Alexis frowned at him. "You're not well enough—"

Mint glared at her. "I'm sure you can find someone else to fuss over."

"Easy, bud." Bradley didn't want to have words with the man. But he would.

Steve walked back in just as Perkins said, "Mint can have the job."

"Yes!" He slumped back into his seat.

Perkins frowned. "You don't even know who you're supposed to find."

"Doesn't matter. I'm on it."

She frowned. "Emma Burroughs has been missing since the supposed suicide of Bradley and Rachel's uncle. We believe there's some significance that may prove useful to this investigation."

"And if she's dead?" Bradley asked.

Perkins shrugged, reminding him a little of Walker's official bearing. Did she have a federal agency in her past?

Steve walked over to Bradley and opened his fist. On his palm were two rings, a thicker black band and a smaller pink one. They weren't made of metal. Was it some kind of plastic, or silicone? "We use these when we're going on operation and posing as husband and wife."

Alexis shifted on his lap. Bradley winced at the tug. He set his hands on her hips and shifted her off him, then stood. "Why—"

Steve said, "If you think we're letting you take her up to your room for some…what did you call it?—T-L-C?—without these, then you're crazy." He glanced at Alexis. "We've gotten to know your girl over the past couple of weeks, and we like her."

"You think I'm going to disrespect her?" He winced, realizing they'd been down that road. Steve wasn't understanding where he was at now. "And what difference does it make if we have two rings?"

"A whole lot of difference, considering I'm a licensed pastor."

Bradley said, "Seriously?"

"Also an operation. But it's all legal."

"I'm so happy for you," Alexis said, her face deadpan. Uh-oh. "And why are we having this conversation, exactly?"

Bradley said, "Lex—"

"Maybe someone should actually ask me what I think about this," she said. "Because there are a whole lot of assumptions floating around in this conversation."

Bradley took the rings from Steve and put them in his pocket. Should he just do it? He was nervous now. More than he'd thought he would be. "Alexis, would you do me the honor of marrying me?"

"Because you don't want to be inappropriate when I'm helping you with your recovery?"

Someone snickered. Bradley ignored it. Trust her to get right to the point. "This isn't about convenience. It's about the fact that I've been in love with you for years."

Alexis pulled a section of hair over her shoulder and absently started braiding it. "I love you too. Of course I do."

"It's okay if you want to wait." It would probably kill him. And hello, did they need to get to know each other better? He didn't think so.

Alexis frowned, pushing the hair back over her shoulder. "You should probably call Rachel."

"Okay, that's good. You should talk to her."

"Because I'll need a dress, and she probably has one I can borrow."

Bradley felt his eyes widen. "She…"

"Plus, she should be here when we get married."

He hopped the one step away from the chair and crutches, and set his hand on her shoulder for balance. She frowned, then saw he was okay. He said, "You'll marry me?"

"Of course. It's not like I'm going to marry someone else."

Mint whooped. Even Perkins looked happy. Steve smiled at the floor. Since they were all occupied with their own reactions, Bradley swept her into his arms and kissed her, ignoring the pain in his knee.

In many ways, this was far from over. The blackmailer was still out there. They hadn't begun to unravel that web. But he and Alexis were together, finally. The way they should be.

The way they always had been.

Book 2

Deadly Secrets

Chapter 1

Four weeks ago. Richmond, Virginia.

Emma clutched the envelope. She sucked in a deep breath and pulled the side door open. Senator Sadler's house was huge, and in the four months since she'd come to work for him she'd never gotten used to it. She'd grown up in a historic Virginia house, but this was a modern mansion. *Keep thinking about the house.* Anything to distract her from what she had in the envelope.

And what it meant.

The house was quiet. No cars parked out front, but the Senator used the garage anyway. His staff had gone home for the night. It was the perfect time to have this talk. *Ambush is more like it.* She pushed the thought away. This was the most important talk of her life. The reason she had come to work for him.

Emma squared her shoulders and strode forward on her pumps. The watch her mother had given her slid down her forearm, the gold cool against her skin. She didn't like it, but her mother had insisted. And when her mother had posted about the gift on social media, her mother's fans had thought it was "wonderful," "inspiring," and "beautiful." So she hadn't exactly been able to argue—or stuff it in a drawer.

Another lie, on top of a life of lies. Duty. Doing what was expected of her.

She was only blowing the lid off her entire life now because she'd been forced into an even smaller corner. By an anonymous blackmailer who knew more about her than she did.

The light was on in the study where the Senator did most of his work, and the door was slightly ajar. A muffled noise came from inside. The Senator had tried to hide his grief since his son had been killed by federal agents just days ago. She didn't want to add to his distress, but she had to know the truth.

He wasn't a nice man. Hadn't been a good father to his son. The son had followed in his father's steps, making selfish decisions that hurt people.

Emma stepped up to the door of the study. She *had* to know the truth.

A whimper drifted to her. Emma peered around the door, trying to assess what she was getting herself into. A second man stood in the study, beside the Senator's chair.

Holding a gun.

She must have made a noise, because the man's head whipped around to her. *Aaron Jones.* The aide to a senator who had been kidnapped recently. It was all connected. Aaron Jones. Rachel Harris's kidnapping. Senator Sadler, and his son's death.

The senator moaned. Blood trickled from the corner of his mouth and his head lolled, his chin touching his chest. Emma gasped. "What are you doing?"

She reached for her phone, then remembered she'd left it in the car. She hadn't wanted any distractions when they talked. "Aaron, what's going on?" Was the man crazy?

He turned the gun to her. "Get in here."

She took a step back. "But..." He fired a shot at her. It hit the door frame. Emma screamed and ducked into the room. "Okay, okay." She tried to think. "Put the gun down, or something."

It was a ridiculous thing to say, but in the moment she couldn't focus enough to think this through. She had an accounting degree. She handled the Senator's personal and business finances. "Money. I can get you money." Surely he wouldn't begrudge giving up what was left of his wealth in order to save both their lives.

"No." The word dribbled from the senator's mouth. "You'll have to kill me."

If that happened, Aaron wouldn't get anything. Emma was the only one who knew how to access those funds. "I can give you whatever you want, just put the gun down."

Aaron sneered. "Come and take it from me."

She stared at him. It wasn't a challenge. He was actually asking her to get the gun from him? Emma wasn't sure it was a good idea, but she went anyway.

Hand outstretched for the gun, Aaron grabbed her arm. Then around her waist. "What..?" His arm pressed against her diaphragm and she tried to suck in a breath.

"Shut up." Aaron's hand wrapped around hers. His finger crushed hers against the trigger.

"Ow. What are you..?"

He moved their aim so the gun was pointed at the Senator. "It's easy," he said. "Just a simple murder/suicide to explain everything nicely."

"No." She struggled against him. "You can't—"

"I can." He pulled her finger against the trigger.

Emma shifted her arm. The shot went wide in the struggle, blowing a hole in the chair beside the senator's head. He cried out in that gruff voice of his. Not a nice man, and he certainly had some hinky business practices, but that was what made him a great politician. Just not the best father to Lincoln, or uncle to Bradley and Alexis. At least, as far as she'd been able to tell since coming to work there. He'd been gruff with her since she was hired.

Had he known her secret already?

She wanted to understand what the reason for his attitude was but hadn't managed to break through. That didn't mean she wanted him to be killed, though. And certainly not by her own hand.

"Stop!" She struggled with Aaron, trying to get her finger off the trigger. The gun went off again. She cried out at the pain, the pinch of skin between his finger and the gun. Her ears rang. It was like standing beside a firework when it went off. The room filled with the smell of gunpowder.

She stomped on Aaron's foot. He cried out. She did it again, using her heel. When she lifted her foot a third time, she scraped the pencil heel on his shin. He shifted against her and she elbowed him as best she could with her other arm.

The gun went off again. Another shot. This time it hit the senator in the chest. He grunted. She dropped the envelope. It landed on her left foot as everything dulled to single sensations. Trapped. *Can't breathe.* She'd just shot him. The senator. Her boss. He was more than that, but she couldn't think about that right now.

She struggled against Aaron's hold, forcing him to step back. She tried to move quicker, to slam him against the wall. Her foot caught the rug and she stumbled. They hit the credenza. Glass shattered. Aaron cried out.

His hold on her loosened.

Emma ran to the senator.

Aaron fired the gun. It hit the desk beside her, in front of the now dying man. The senator's eyes pleaded with her to help. But she couldn't. She grabbed the closest thing—a plastic file tray filled with a stack of papers.

She flung them at Aaron. Pages and pages floating through the air. She needed to get to her phone.

Not waiting around for him to recover from all that flying at his face, she dashed for her envelope and then the door. The gun went off. Before she even registered the sound, pain tore through the top of her arm. Emma cried out, slamming against the opposite wall in the hallway. She raced away, down the hall, gripping the envelope for dear life. As though it might protect her. Save her.

Another gunshot blasted.

She flinched and cried out, but no more pain came. Just the ice cold fire in her arm. She clutched at it, getting blood on the envelope. Tears tracked down her face. She could hear his footsteps behind her. She hurried to the side door, where she glanced back over her shoulder. He was coming!

She raced to her car and dived in, turning the key while she shifted her hips to get out of the awkward position she'd landed in.

Aaron appeared at the door.

She screamed and hit the gas by mistake. The car jerked forward and slammed into the house. He dived back inside. She shifted to reverse and hit the gas again, peeling out in a cloud of burned rubber and the sound of screaming tires.

Emma's bumper scraped the fountain in the center of the circular drive, and she roared down the driveway.

Two streets away she lifted her phone, and the blackmailer's email flashed on screen.

No one could help her now.

Chapter 2

Present day—somewhere in central Colorado

The inside of the diner smelled like bacon and cinnamon rolls. Mint's stomach rumbled, and a guy sitting in the first booth snorted as he walked by. Everyone else gave him some kind of reaction. They all saw him walk in. He sighed. Anonymity wasn't something he could count on. He stuck out, even with the wool cap and glasses.

Mint was dressed like most of the guys in here—jeans and a plaid flannel shirt. Dirty work boots. He pushed his glasses up his nose and settled into an empty booth, far too used to drawing attention by his sheer size. It wasn't like it bothered him. He needed the edge that made people give him a wide birth. They assumed he wasn't smart, that he was a dumb jock—also necessary. He cultivated the image because it played in his favor so often.

Don't come near. Don't underestimate.

It didn't take long for her to come over. Lime green waitress uniform, strawberry blond hair pulled back in a ponytail that made her look a few years younger than she actually was. The kind of subterfuge he used every day. A shift in appearance that played in her favor. She was a girl on the run trying to blend in and stay unnoticed.

Kind of like him.

She smiled, though her dark blue eyes remained guarded. "Coffee?" Her name tag read, "Ellie." Close enough she wouldn't trip over it too much, but nondescript enough she was able to hide here. But for how long? He'd found her. How long before the FBI did?

"Yeah." His voice sounded like a rusty door. He cleared his throat while she poured. "Thanks."

"Something to eat?"

He nodded. "I'll take the Lumberjack Breakfast."

She softened a fraction. "Good choice. I'll get that right out." She took his menu.

Mint watched Emma Burroughs, former senator's chief financial officer—now murder suspect on the run—walk away. Spine straight. Shoulders square. Chin up. Determined not to break.

Mint pulled out his phone and sent a text.

It's her.

Okay, so he'd been sent here to find out what she knew and to make sure she was protected—in the interest of the team's goals. Double Down wanted this blackmailer taken down. But he hadn't thought to find this affinity with her. A kindred spirit.

They were nothing alike.

And yet...

No, that wasn't why he was here.

Mint caught the gaze of the older man behind the counter. He might be wiping the surface, but all his attention was on Mint. Watching Mint watch Emma. Mint glanced at the salt shaker, and the plastic dessert menu perched between the ketchup and the hot sauce.

The man's handlebar mustache was mostly gray. His forearms corded. Hair was cut close to his scalp. Not a man unaccustomed to hard work. And it seemed Emma's newest boss cared enough about her to keep an eye on who in the diner took notice of her.

Good.

Mint scratched at the edge of his knit cap, wishing he could pull the thing off. If he did, the scar behind his ear would be in plain view when Emma came back over with his plate. He should've sat facing the other direction if he wanted that.

She carried the dish with her right arm. Intel said her left had taken the bullet. The sleeve went almost to her elbow, loose enough to cover what scar remained. Did it still hurt?

"It's hot," she said. "So be careful."

He glanced up at her and smiled. "Thanks again."

She blinked. Emma Burroughs, Ivy League degree and a high paying job. Impressive pedigree. Poise. Style. Her eyes lost some of that guardedness he'd seen before, and she smiled back. "Well, you're welcome. Again."

He held her gaze for as long as she let him and then reached for the salt. He paused right before he shook, then replaced the salt back on the table. He didn't need vices. Even if using the salt shaker wasn't exactly an addictive habit, he couldn't risk any of that. Strength had no foundation if the tiniest thing caused it to waver.

He rolled his shoulders, holding back the wince. His own recent injury had been more of an annoyance than anything else. Alexis had been saved, and even though she'd driven him crazy—causing him to jump on this assignment—he was glad they'd found her. All was well in the world of Bradley and Alexis. Mint was happy for them and had toasted their new life together along with everyone else.

And now he was here. A nice break, an engaging hunt for a missing woman who just might be able to tell them who the blackmailer was. The team at Double Down had their eyes on Senator Francis Sadler, until he'd been killed. Maybe Emma knew the real name of the person who had terrorized several people in various levels of government and private companies. Blackmail was a low game.

Mint was all in on the hunt for who was behind this.

Especially if it meant getting Emma Burroughs out from under FBI suspicion. She hadn't killed Senator Sadler. Though he figured it was likely he'd been killed because of his involvement with the blackmailer—there was no way his death was coincidental. From the look in her eyes he'd figure the FBI was right that she'd been there. She'd been hurt. She'd seen something she'd never in her life be able to unsee.

Mint had met murderers. He knew what evil looked like. He knew deception. Emma might be scared, but there was no way she was a killer.

He would bet both their lives on it.

Mint downed four cups of coffee and polished off the plate, but not the toast that came with it. He'd eaten so much toast when he was a kid, the only thing his perpetually drunk father had actually stocked the cupboard with. If he didn't see another slice of bread in his life it was too soon.

A sheriff's car pulled up outside, three spaces down from the truck he'd bought in Nebraska. Mint left cash on the table and hit the bathroom before he used the back hall to head out the side exit. He didn't need the sheriff noticing him as well, pegging him as exactly what he was—though he might not know why Mint was there—and asking way too many questions.

Ten minutes later, he pulled into the motel parking lot and headed to his room. Two doors down from Emma's.

The pool was dated, but clean. The owners were an older couple. Efficient and friendly, the kind of motel owners you'd find in a small town, fly-over state. Mint watched the parking lot through the blinds. The front desk didn't have an angle on these doors. The cameras weren't worth his worry. Only the one on the main entrance was even plugged in. The rest were just for show. He clocked the progress of the housekeeper, and when the timing was right, moved down to Emma's door.

He used his lock-pick kit and jimmied the door open in three seconds.

She was neat. Everything had been put away. Clothes folded. A small duffel lay at the bottom of the closet. He checked the safe, but found nothing. Whatever secrets Emma Burroughs held, she kept them well-hidden.

Between the mattress and box spring, he found two thousand dollars in twenties and her driver's license, both beside a bloody envelope. Crumpled, still sealed. He didn't have the tools on him to unseal it, and neither did he have the time.

Mint replaced her things, closed up the room, and headed back to his own. He stretched out on the bed with his clothes and boots still on and fell asleep in minutes.

Dark shapes twisted through his nightmares, images that rushed at him. His father's booming voice. That huge, clammy fist slamming into his face. His ribs. The smell of alcohol on his father's breath as he yelled about some infraction. Mint didn't even care anymore. What was the point when everything and anything he did was wrong?

He awoke to the feel of hot blood running down the side of his neck. Tried to swipe it away, and realized it was nothing but a memory.

Mint touched the stubble where his hair had been and traced the line of the scar behind his ear.

The room had gone dark, only the yellow glow of the parking lot street lamps to remind him where he was.

He exhaled, trying to calm his heart rate, and sat up.

Outside, someone screamed.

.   .   .

Emma stared at the dark figure in her room for a second before whoever it was ran at her, shoving her back. The elbow to her ribs took the breath out of her. He shoved her sideways and against the wall, and her head collided with the siding. Black spots blinked across her vision, then the lights of the parking lot. Her legs gave out, and she slid down to the cold concrete ground.

She blinked and looked up. Standing a ways down from her room was a familiar face, just one she couldn't place right now. He stared at her for second. Then he turned and ran.

Ran away.

Was he the man from her room, the one who'd just attacked her?

She sucked in a breath, and her head spun as she tried to figure out what was happening. Tried to breathe. Tried not to think about the senator, and the sound of a gun going off. Her arm still hurt from that night. She didn't know if she would ever forget the pain of being shot and having to patch it up herself because she was too scared to go to a hospital.

If she'd gone in, she would have gotten arrested for the senator's murder. A fact that had become even clearer in the days following. She'd been all over the local news coverage.

Had the blackmailer found her? Or Aaron Jones, the man who had killed the senator? This guy could be another associate of the blackmailer's. Had he sent an entire army after her?

Cold moved through her and she shivered, still sitting there on the floor.

"My goodness." The words were drawn out. A man's voice. He crouched in front of her, and she settled on that craggy face. The owner.

"I'm okay, Bill."

He frowned. Yeah, she didn't believe her either. He said, "Mary already called an ambulance. Can you stand?" He wore striped pajamas and slippers, an open robe over the top like a coat.

Emma struggled to her feet and sucked in a breath. She placed a hand over her ribs and winced. "Ouch."

Bill was frowning still.

Flashes of memory raced through her mind like a photo gallery. The senator's face. The feel of the trigger under her finger, the squeeze. The pain. Seeing his face on the front of a newspaper. Dead.

Hearing her name on a news report.

Wanted for questioning.

The sheriff's car pulled into the parking lot. Emma took half a step back.

Bill patted her shoulder. "The sheriff will take care of you. And I'll take a look at your door, see if you need new locks. Or a deadbolt. Okay?"

She nodded, though she hardly comprehended what he'd said. She watched the sheriff walk over for a few seconds, then turned and stepped inside her room. Flipped the light on.

The bed was rumpled. Clothes had been pulled out of the dresser. The mattress was square with the box spring. It hadn't been moved, which meant her savings—and her secrets—were safe. The person who'd come here wasn't a cop. But what did he want? It felt like Aaron Jones was toying with her.

First, she'd felt like she was being followed, and now this? What did he want?

The sheriff of this county was a different story. She'd never met him. Had no idea what to expect.

Her mind flashed again, overlaying a picture of that man right before he'd run. *The diner.* That was where she'd met him. He had come in and ordered breakfast this morning. It was a shame he was one of Jones's associates, because he'd had a nice smile. Obviously it was fake. Nothing but trying to feel her out, see what she knew.

Before they killed her.

Emma leaned against the open door and closed her eyes, trying to calm herself. Trying to figure out what on earth she was going to do next. This had all been about taking the power back. Confronting the senator over events long past.

Finding strength to do the right thing, and finally having control over her own life.

"Ms. Stevens?"

It took her a moment to remember that was the name she'd given Bill and his wife, Mary, when she'd booked the room. Emma opened her eyes. "You can call me Ellie, Sheriff." Like she was just another regular, everyday witness. A victim of a break-in.

"Would you like to sit?"

She nodded and made her way to the wood, upholstered chair. Kind of like a doctor's waiting room seat. If the appointment had been in 1967. It squeaked when she settled onto it. She shot the sheriff a smile, and he asked her what had happened. She told him about the man in her room, unable to keep the shake from her voice. He didn't need to know that it was about more than just tonight.

It was to her advantage that he hadn't yet had the occasion to run her photo through any database. The news report of the senator's death and her involvement hadn't spread nationwide. Yet. Another story had broken days later, and hers had been buried. No doubt people were looking for her—good and bad people.

"Ellie?"

She blinked and looked up. "I'm sorry?"

His eyes softened. "You might want to think about talking with someone. It's not a bad thing to seek out counsel, even if you don't think you need help per se." He gave her a soft smile and pulled out his wallet. "My wife is licensed." He handed her a business card. "I know firsthand that talking things out can help."

Emma's eyes widened. It was a particular kind of man who could admit he'd needed help in life. She could admit, at least to herself, that counseling may be worthwhile. But did she have the time for it? Emma hardly knew what would happen day to day, as had been evidenced by tonight.

Did she want to talk to someone?

Her mind flashed again, an image of that man. Not because she wanted to talk to him—even with that nice smile of his. "I saw someone."

The sheriff took half a step closer to her and nodded. He patted her shoulder. "I'm sure Bill and Mary can move you to another room if you'd like. Help you sleep better."

"No." She shook her head. "Outside. Right after he ran away. There was a man." She waved toward the sidewalk in front of the room and tried to get her brain to cooperate. "He was in the diner this morning."

"Was he the man inside your room?"

She didn't know. Not for sure. "He ran away right after I saw him."

"Any idea who he is?"

She shook her head. "He paid in cash, and he never told me his name. But he's new in town." Newer than *her*, at least.

"I'll talk to Patch. See if he can help me out."

Emma nodded. "Please." Her boss at the diner was a former biker—though, he'd never say "former" so she figured it was like being in the Marines that way—and he knew everything that happened in the diner. He'd even commented on the man who'd come in. The one she had seen tonight, outside her room.

Was he really an associate of Aaron's? Emma shivered. Either way didn't matter. They had found her. Which meant she had to move on, get out of town, keep running. Before they decided she wasn't needed anymore.

And they killed her.

Chapter 3

Mint pumped his arms and legs and chased after the guy fleeing from Emma's room. The man's body type matched the description of Aaron Jones that he'd been given, but he wouldn't know if it was that same man unless he got a look at the face. They'd been looking for Jones for weeks. Since he'd been implicated in the kidnapping of Senator Rachel Harris. Something the whole team took personally.

Double Down was fully invested in bringing down the blackmailer. And Aaron Jones was likely a party to whatever operation was in play.

Mint rounded a corner two seconds after Jones—if this really was him—and stopped. Turned around. Looked up and down the street.

Empty.

Not even the sound of a car engine, or footsteps fleeing. He even held his breath for a second just to be sure.

Aaron Jones was gone.

Mint wanted to kick the hubcap of the closest car, but denting private property wouldn't get rid of his frustrations. It would only add to them. Mint checked the whole area to make sure Jones wasn't simply hiding somewhere. When he was satisfied the man had given him the slip, Mint made his way back to the motel.

He approached from the opposite side and headed for his truck. He settled in the front seat but didn't start the engine. The sheriff's car was parked outside Emma's room. Was she all right? He didn't like the fear that had been in her eyes when she'd looked up at him.

Pain. Terror.

He didn't like that she felt those things. Not when he'd also known those, echoed down to the core of his being. And he hated those feelings. Had spent years trying to exorcise them by being as strong as he could. As fast. As lethal.

He wanted to help her, as much as it was unwise to see her as anything other than a witness. Mint wasn't there to make her feel better. He was only there to find out what she knew about the blackmailer who'd been involved with Senator Rachel Harris's kidnapping.

It had been a complicated situation, but Rachel Harris was all right now. And Alexis—her best friend who had taken the fall for her instead of bowing to the dictates of the blackmailer—was on her honeymoon with Mint's newest teammate, Bradley.

Mint's team consisted of six men and one woman. Mint had the feeling that the boss, Steve Preston, might have had a thing with Rachel at one point. But if they did, it wasn't public knowledge. Rachel and Bradley were siblings, twins in fact. And Alexis had been part of their tribe for years.

Mint had observed the whole thing from a distance, until Alexis had been shoved into a bank with a bomb strapped to her. Then he'd been pulled in, on the job as part of the operation. He'd injured his shoulder, and Alexis had insisted on taking care of him—out of guilt. Too bad her brand of "care" involved being all up in his space. Gushing about how she was *so thankful.*

An ambulance pulled into the parking lot. Dread moved through him and his fingers went to the door handle, before he even realized he'd made a move to get out. No. He didn't have the right to see if she was okay, and he never would.

Mint didn't want to consider what it was about her that caused this reaction in him. Dwelling on all that wasn't going to make his life easier.

Mint turned the brightness on his phone screen all the way down and called his boss. It was late on the east coast, but Steve never minded interruptions. That was the nature of their business.

His boss answered, "Preston."

"It's Mint."

"I have caller ID."

"My mother taught me it's polite to introduce yourself."

Steve was quiet for a second. "She really do that?"

"Of course not." She'd left before Mint could walk, and he didn't even remember her. Still, he didn't want to have a ridiculous conversation. "Jones was in her room tonight."

"He get anything?"

"No. There's an envelope under her bed, and he wasn't carrying it when he ran off."

"What envelope?"

Mint said, "Don't know. Didn't have time or the tools to get it open. But it's covered in blood, and she's keeping it with her run money and her driver's license."

"Not smart. Anyone could find that."

"Anyone?" Just because Mint had found it didn't mean "anyone" else would. His attention was half on the call and half on Emma. She sat in the ambulance now, and he was twisted in his seat trying to see her. The woman didn't want to be checked out, but was complying anyway.

"Mint."

He blinked. "Yeah?"

"I said, Perkins went through her bank accounts."

Perkins was their female team member. "She didn't find a transaction that might explain the envelope, but Emma Burroughs takes out cash a lot. Could be she paid for something with folding money. In which case, we'll never trace what it is."

"I can try a second time," Mint said. "Get into her room and see what's in there."

"It's your call, but don't wait too long to nail her down about what happened. We need to know what she knows about the blackmailer."

Mint wasn't actually convinced she knew the identity of the person who had blackmailed Bradley's sister. None of them were. Not really. Maybe she didn't even know a blackmailer existed, and she'd simply walked in on Jones and Senator Sadler having a showdown.

Mint said, "I actually have a feeling she'll run after this. He was in her room."

"Freaked her out."

He nodded, even though Steve couldn't see him. "At the least." He watched her climb gingerly out of the ambulance, one arm across her ribs. "Injured her trying to escape." His free hand curled into a fist, and he thought about slamming it into Aaron Jones's smug face.

The ambulance pulled away. She talked to the sheriff for a few more seconds, then shut her door. Mint waited, watching the room. He wasn't about to head back to his own and get drawn into this in a way that would handicap his ability to do his job here.

Sitting in his truck, watching, made this feel more like what it was. Business.

"She's our best lead right now."

"I know." Mint wasn't going to let the team down. Double Down, the private security and investigations business Steve ran, were professionals. Mint had been part of the team since he got out of the Army Rangers a few years back. He hadn't enjoyed that time in his life. It had been more about discovering who he was and making amends with himself for that. Still, the man the Rangers had crafted him to be was a man he respected. Maybe even liked.

Who he was now was more about using those skills on a local level, for a man he admired far more than any commanding officer he'd had. Steve had been to the edge of death and back. There was no one else he wanted to work for.

"I'll get what we need."

"I know you will, Mint." Steve's voice was filled with confidence. "And take care of Emma. That's the real reason I sent you on this mission, despite your being done with Alexis's cookies and brownies and cake because she was so grateful you saved her and didn't die." Steve chuckled. "But I know you won't let Emma down now."

Steve hung up. The unspoken words hung in the air even after the call ended. He watched from the truck, but Emma's light never turned off.

Mint wasn't the kind of man who let an innocent get caught in the crossfire. That might be noble, but it wasn't always the way the military wanted to operate. Sometimes there were casualties and that had been unacceptable as far as he was concerned.

That story went farther back in his history than Mint was prepared to travel. He needed to concentrate on the now, and not let the past breathe down the back of his neck. That never led anywhere good—not for him, or the people around him.

Half an hour before sunrise, Emma ducked out of her room, backpack over her shoulder.

She was running.

. . .

Emma walked across town to the diner, chin tucked in a scarf at her throat. Hands in her coat pockets even though she had gloves on. She wasn't sure where she would go after she got her last paycheck from Patch, but it had to be somewhere. Anywhere. A place she could disappear into the crowd once again, hoping Aaron Jones wouldn't find her.

She said, "Hi," to an older man she'd served a few times, who was walking on the street. It seemed a shame to leave this place. She'd come to like it here, especially the motel owners. And Patch.

The front still had the CLOSED sign out, so she went around back. There were only a few minutes until the diner opened for breakfast. Patch should be here.

Emma's shoulders clenched and she shivered. She glanced both ways, feeling like someone was watching her. Was it Aaron? She studied the area around her. Cars in the tiny lot behind the diner. The alley. The streets beyond. Then she went inside.

All she needed was her take for the last few days since payday, and then she could get lost. Surely Patch would understand her need to be away from here.

Okay, so there was no way he would understand.

"Are you just going to stand there, or are you going to come in?"

She nearly smiled at his gruff voice, but couldn't allow it. Emma stepped into the kitchen. Patch stood at the huge metal counter, taking a swig from a mug of coffee—what he called his "drug of choice."

"Hi."

"Not your day to work the early shift."

She swallowed. Nodded.

"Trouble found you?"

She stared at him.

"I can give you what I owe ya, but trouble is just gonna keep coming." He paused, looking at her with a knowing expression she'd never seen to this extent. "Am I right?"

"Yes."

"Will I be able to convince you to stay, Emma?"

She opened her mouth to tell him there was no way he would convince her to stick around and put everyone's lives in danger, not just hers. Then she realized he'd just used her real name. "You…"

"I don't run a diner cause I can't do nothin' else."

It took her a second to process what he'd said. "I don't think you're dumb. I would never."

"I know that, darlin'. It's why I like having you around, even knowing the trouble you'd bring with you."

"I can't stay."

He laid his cup down. "I know you think that. And if you gotta run, I got brothers all over who owe me favors. Could keep you safe. Hidden."

"Brothers?"

"The kind that ride bikes and wear leather."

Protection from bikers? That sounded scary, even while she figured it could potentially also prove her safest option.

"But for right now, Kerri didn't show up. I already called the motel twice. Didn't know you weren't there." He gave her a pointed look. "Need you to work the early shift." He was back to being the tough boss of a small town diner. "After that, I'll pay you, and you can decide what you want to do."

She stared at him, her mind going back and forth between the fact she'd faced down an intruder last night—and had bruised ribs to show for it—and how much she appreciated Patch taking a chance on her. Especially considering the trouble she had on her heels.

"How did you know I was in trouble?"

One bushy eyebrow rose. "I can smell it."

She frowned.

"That, and you asked me to pay you in cash. You have no references and no cell phone."

So, she wasn't super good at this "under the radar" stuff. It wasn't like she'd ever done it before.

He said, "Go flip the sign and get changed into your uniform. Make your choice later."

Apparently he was done talking. Time to work. Emma smiled to herself as she dumped her backpack in the office and quickly changed before she flipped the sign to open.

When she unlocked the front door, a dark figure filled the windows and cast shadows inside. She sucked in a breath. He opened the door before she could even think to bar it. By the time she grasped the wood, it was too late.

He was inside.

He looked down at her, far taller now that he was standing, not seated, at one of her tables. "I'll take some coffee," he said. "After that, we'll talk about me keeping Aaron Jones away from you long enough for my team to bring him down."

His team? She stepped back, not only because he was bigger than her and he'd crowded her into the diner by sheer force of his size. Without even touching her.

"I... you..." Her brain wouldn't even work.

"Pick a seat," Patch called out from across the rear counter, where he stood in the kitchen. "Coffee will be right up."

He turned away and slid into a booth.

It was enough for her to exhale. To fake a smile and welcome a couple more of the regulars, and get the big man his coffee. How had she walked into this? She was supposed to have left, but Patch was shorthanded. And now the man was here, talking about things no one was supposed to know.

Patch was watching.

Keeping Aaron Jones away from you.

Long enough for my team to bring him down.

Her mystery man wasn't working with Jones, and he wasn't working for the person behind Jones. Emma was glad to know this, but it wasn't like the knowledge allowed her to relax. Then again, the big man might be here, but he wasn't on her side. He couldn't protect her.

She wandered back to the rear counter to pick up her protector's breakfast—different from what he'd ordered yesterday. Patch was on the phone.

"When you get this, call me. Want to know you're okay, Kerri."

A sinking feeling moved through Emma's midsection. The other waitress was probably sick, laid up in bed and unable to get to the phone. Just because she wasn't here didn't mean Aaron Jones had done anything to her. This was only a coincidence of timing.

He hung up the phone and shot her a look. "Still can't get ahold of her. I called Barb, though. She's coming in early, so you can take off when she gets here."

"Okay." Emma appreciated him thinking of that. It was a weekday, so the diner wasn't going to be crammed. But it would still be busy.

She refilled a few coffee cups. The big man shot her a look, but she didn't offer him any more to drink. He could sit there until the end of time for all she cared. That was how much she didn't want to tell him anything. Just the idea of sharing what had happened that night made her want to be sick.

The FBI wasn't going to understand that she hadn't wanted to shoot him. She might not have hit him, but how could she prove it? It wasn't like her word meant anything. All they were going to see were her fingerprints on the gun. Her blood in the hallway. Her motive—or whatever they figured would've been her motive for doing it. What did it matter if it was true, or not?

Barb showed up. Emma told her she was going in the back for a break.

She had her backpack on and was headed out the fire exit before she even registered that she still wore her uniform. Flight mode had kicked in and there wasn't much she could do about it. She *needed* to run. What was the point in staying only for Aaron Jones to catch up?

But first, she needed to make sure Jones hadn't caught up somehow to Kerri and hurt her. Part of Emma didn't want to know. She forced herself to walk to the other waitress's house anyway. Praying it was nothing, that the girl just had the stomach flu or something.

When she found the front door open, she knew it wasn't nothing.

Then there was the blood. All over the hallway.

She shifted to step inside, to go search for conclusive news. A hand grabbed ahold of her backpack and used her grip on the straps to pull her back. She stumbled and fell against him before she managed to right herself.

The big man's dark eyes stared down at her. "Don't."

"But—"

"Don't say anything." He hauled her down the front walk. "Just get in the truck."

Chapter 4

"You killed her."

He watched blood drain from her face while frustration boiled up in him. "I didn't kill your friend." He sighed. "What are you even doing here?"

He tugged her away from the front door, but she yanked her backpack out of his grip. He could hold her in a way she'd never get out. He *could*. But he wouldn't do that.

She looked about as frustrated as he was. "I'm looking for Kerri."

"You were running."

"I came *here*, didn't I?"

And she'd done it with her backpack, which he guessed contained everything she needed to make a run for it. "I'm not chasing you across the country again. Not when you're risking your life to make a foolish move."

She gasped. "Foolish? Aaron Jones is going to kill me."

"Told you I'd protect you."

"I don't know you. I don't trust you."

"That's fair." He'd have said the same in her place. "But I'm telling you that you *can* trust me."

He watched her wait, expecting more. When he didn't say anything else, her eyebrows lifted. "That's it? I can trust you, so I should?"

"Do you need it to be complicated? Because we don't have time for that." He glanced over her shoulder at the hallway. He could smell the blood inside and could make out dark stains on the walls and hallway.

It was on the tip of his tongue to say, "Wait here," but knew she wouldn't. She'd split as soon as his back was turned. Instead, he tagged her hand in his and pulled her to the door. Ignored the sensation of her skin against his.

She stood to the side, facing the street, while he stared inside. Like holding his hand was nothing, which was good. It meant he could work on pushing away the feeling when it clearly didn't affect her.

There wasn't much else he could do when he didn't want either of them going in, contaminating what physical evidence had been left.

Was this Kerri person even dead? He didn't see a body. Might be worth walking around the back, peering in windows. Or maybe that would only lead to them stepping in footprints that could be the killer's. Aaron Jones needed to be stopped. If that meant jail, Mint wasn't going to get in the way of a sheriff's investigation that would put him there.

"Is she dead?" Emma's voice was soft.

Mint didn't want to soften toward it. But try telling that to his heart. He had to remember this was business. Emma Burroughs might be cute, but she was also nothing but a means to an end. There was a blackmailer hidden in Washington DC, and if they didn't figure out who it was then more people could die.

Emma was his ticket to Aaron Jones.

Aaron was their route straight to the blackmailer.

That was it.

Emma made a noise. Then she said, "I don't know your name."

"Mint."

"Like the flavor? Mint?"

He shrugged. "Call sign."

"Like in the military?" When he didn't confirm or deny, she said, "What's your real name?"

"Does it matter?" That was another step toward a connection with her. One that was decidedly *not* required in order for him to complete this mission.

"Okay, *Mint.*" She drew out his name, exaggerating it like she was making some kind of point. "Is Kerri in there?" Emma paused. "Is she dead?"

"I don't see a body, and I may not without looking around inside." He turned and started to tug her down the front walk of the house again. This time she actually moved with him. He didn't think she'd given up the fight, though. She was cleverer than that.

He said, "I'm not about to go in there and leave my footprints in the blood trail."

Emma said nothing, just shuffled down the sidewalk beside him. He headed for his truck. Halfway there, she shifted her arm. He felt her fingers touch his, and he shifted his hand away in a sharp movement.

For a second he thought she was going to hold his hand, but then she grasped his jacket sleeve instead. He glanced at her, but she kept her gaze forward. Refusing to make eye contact with him while she clung to him as though he was the one keeping her afloat in a choppy sea.

He clicked the locks and pulled the passenger door open.

She sat, but shoved one hand on the door before he could shut it. "We're just going to leave her there?"

He glanced at her. "I'll call it in. The sheriff will take care of her."

She bit her lip but pulled her leg in. He shut the door and called the sheriff's office, leaving an anonymous tip about the open door and the blood. If this other waitress from the diner had been killed, it was an awful coincidence. Had Aaron Jones come here last night, after he'd broken into Emma's motel room? If he had, he'd likely been hopped up on adrenaline. He could have snapped and killed a woman who'd invited him into his home.

Or, she could have been on the front step at just the wrong moment, and he'd forced his way in.

It could be a completely unrelated death. Done by someone Kerri knew, but for another reason.

He fired up the engine and drove, not really knowing where to go other than the motel. He headed for the town store instead, mostly so they could sit in the parking lot and talk. He hadn't eaten much of his breakfast before he realized she'd disappeared from the diner.

Patch had noticed as well, when Mint realized Emma had gone. The man's nod of approval when Mint had stood, intending to go after her, was interesting. And appreciated. Patch had figured out what kind of man Mint was, and Mint had done the same with the aging biker. And that was before the background check had come in yesterday. He didn't need Patch's approval now, but it was nice to know Emma had landed somewhere she had that kind of support.

The sheriff's car drove past them, headed in the opposite direction. Toward the house. Lights and sirens on.

Emma turned to watch it out the back window. "I want to hope she isn't dead. But that's probably futile, isn't it?"

Mint said, "Did you know her well?"

"We've worked together for a few weeks, but outside the diner we haven't really hung out that much." She rubbed the edge of her diner uniform. "And that's not the point, is it? Someone knew her. Someone loved this woman. Now she's dead."

"We don't know that for sure."

She huffed. And honestly, he agreed with the sentiment. "You saw the blood. What reason could Aaron Jones have for leaving her alive?"

"I could ask you what reason he would have for killing her," Mint offered. "It's close enough to the motel. Aaron Jones might have run this direction. But he also might not have."

She sat silently for a while. Mint glanced at her. Pale face, lips pressed together. He pulled into the parking lot of a drive-thru coffee shop and shifted to park. "I know you didn't kill the senator. Aaron Jones did, right?"

She nodded. Mint thought there might be more, but he didn't ask about it.

They could get to the part where she needed to tell him everything she knew about the senator and his dealings with other people in Washington. It was possible she knew who the blackmailer was.

Information. That's why he was here with her.

He'd been injured in the bank, helping the team get Alexis back from a crazy kidnapper. He didn't think Emma had escaped Aaron murdering the senator completely unscathed. He could see it in her eyes. That haunted look. The one he'd seen in the mirror so many times.

. . .

Emma sipped her coffee and studied the man in the driver's seat. "Mint" whose real name was apparently a closely guarded secret. Oddly enough, Mint actually suited him. She thought that probably there was a reason he'd been given that moniker. A reason she might like to know someday. Or in another life.

After all, this one wasn't likely to last very much longer.

Kerri. All that blood.

Emma shoved the drink in the cup holder and swallowed.

"Here." He twisted the cap off a water bottle and handed it to her. It was room temperature but helped keep the nausea down.

When she could speak, she said, "Thank you."

His phone beeped. Mint pulled it off the dash and turned it to see the screen. "The sheriff just called in to his office. Kerri has been listed as a missing person in extreme danger."

"What…" Emma didn't know what that meant, but it likely wasn't good.

"He thinks she was kidnapped. And judging by the amount of blood in her house, he thinks she's hurt," Mint said. "He'll be checking local hospitals, doctor's offices, the pharmacy and even veterinarian offices. Anywhere the kidnapper might take Kerri to get her medical attention."

None of that helped her feel any less sick.

"All of which means she's *not dead.*"

Okay, that helped. She nodded and took another sip of coffee. No sugar, just a latte. A good thing, considering a sugar bomb drink would have made her sick for sure. "So what now?"

"Good question. And the answer depends on you."

"Me?"

He glanced at her. From his look, she'd guess she wasn't going to like what he had to say.

"Whatever it is, just tell me."

Instead, he drove back to the motel. "Let's get inside."

She hopped out, glancing all around while she gripped the strap of her duffel and headed for her room.

Mint tugged on her arm, just above her left elbow. "This way—"

She couldn't hold it back that time. The angle, the tension. Emma sucked in a breath and tears filled her eyes at the pain. The spot Aaron Jones's bullet had sliced at her.

"What…" He asked it as a question even while he led her to a different room—not hers—with his hand on the small of her back.

When he shut the door he said, "Emma?"

"It hasn't really healed yet. It should have by now, right? I don't know why it still hurts." Like that was something to apologize for. And yes, she knew she was talking just for the sake of talking. Nerves and pain did that.

"Show me."

She dumped the duffel from her other shoulder and then lifted the sleeve of her work uniform. The clothes she'd changed into after Patch had convinced her to cover for Kerri, instead of leaving like she very much should have done.

The wound was still tender under the bandage. Hot, even. Though she didn't want to admit that to herself.

Mint didn't seem to think it was weird. His manner switched to all business as he tugged at the tape and unwound the bandage. Gone was the hesitancy in touching her. Now he was all efficiency.

When he pulled back the gauze, he let a breath loose. Almost a whistle. "Infected." He touched the back of his hand to the skin beside the wound. Red skin. "It's hot to the touch. Swollen. You need antibiotics." He sighed. "You probably should have gotten it cleaned and gotten stitches."

Emma tugged her arm away. "Sorry I didn't do a good enough job at fixing it up."

She'd done her best. But what bothered her the most right now was the hurt in his voice. What did she care what he thought? His opinion of her attempt to stay alive and get somewhere safe weren't the point right now.

She went to her duffel and sat cross-legged on the floor while she dug inside for fresh gauze and a new bandage. He thought she could get antibiotics? That kind of stuff only came with a prescription, and she wasn't about to draw attention to her flight from Aaron Jones by stealing it. She didn't even know how. She'd probably have gotten caught if she tried. After that, she'd be in jail. Yes, they had medical care there. She would have been given antibiotics in prison.

And then Aaron would probably have found her there, somehow. Jail for life, for murder. Or dead from an "incident." Did it matter?

"Emma."

She didn't turn around. Mint sighed. He sat on the edge of the bed, a few feet from her, and did something on his phone. Emma scooted so her back was against the dresser and fixed the fresh bandage over her wound.

"You aren't alone anymore, Emma."

She taped down the bandage and didn't look at him. As much as Mint might want to help her, for whatever his own reasons were, he couldn't fix this. He couldn't repair the damage that had already been done.

No one could.

His phone beeped. He checked the screen. "Antibiotics will be here in an hour."

She looked up then.

"Part of the service. I can better keep you from being killed by Aaron Jones if you're not feeling miserable and suffering at the same time."

"You need me ambulatory, that's it?"

He shrugged one shoulder, then folded his arms. All that did was draw attention to precisely how big—and well defined—his muscles were. Maybe that was his hesitancy with touch. Maybe he thought he would scare her, and so he tread cautiously. Only touched her when he had to. The long sleeve shirt he'd pushed up to his elbows might disguise how much definition he had, but it was still there. Eventually the truth came out.

Kind of like it would with her situation.

After that, she didn't figure he'd be so fired-up to protect her. Then again, it wasn't like he was doing it out of a sense of nobility. He was here for his own reasons.

His low, rumbling voice said, "That isn't a good look."

She glanced aside instead of answering him. She'd already given away too much.

"Eventually I'll need you to tell me all of it. But that doesn't have to happen right now."

His voice was deceptively soft. It probably worked wonders, charming a nice woman into believing he was gentle. That his roughness had soft edges. Or that the right woman could bring that out in him whenever she wanted.

It had been so long since she'd been in a relationship that Emma honestly didn't know what her type was. Mint wasn't it, though. His presence was far too overwhelming. It was like he eclipsed all the space around him. Like everything got sucked into his orbit.

Emma didn't want to be another casualty of that. She had enough going on right now. The last thing she needed was the added complication of the dance of getting to know someone. Wondering how deep they were in this, or if it was just a game. Being scared of how deep she was falling.

Once burned, and all that.

At least she didn't have to worry about it with Mint. He probably had that nice woman she'd imagined at home, waiting for him. He didn't wear a ring, but most people—who didn't have her mother in their lives—didn't care about that these days. Emma had a more traditional view of those things. But the fact was, Mint was probably committed to someone.

He got up from the bed and walked to the window.

"What?"

"You smell that? Like smoke?" He shifted, glancing around outside, then sucked in a breath. "The office is on fire."

Chapter 5

"Come on." He hauled her up by her good arm. "I have to go see what's going on, which means you're coming too."

Thankfully she didn't argue with him. Mint tucked his phone in the front pocket of his jeans and palmed his gun. She walked close behind him, out the door.

Aaron Jones had been busy, because none of this was a coincidence. There was no way a fire at the exact motel where Emma was staying, or a missing waitress whose hallway was covered with blood, didn't have anything to do with her.

He wanted to ask her more about that injury. He'd seen gunshot wounds before and knew from the FBI report that they figured she'd been tagged by a shot and hurt on her left arm. The gash was nasty, and it was for sure infected. He hadn't been lying about that. Gunshot wounds were notoriously dirty. Powder, dirt on the bullet. Not the cleanest things to come into contact with.

And now there was no time.

Mint wasn't going to allow Bill or Mary, or anyone else they worked with who might be in the office—or their attached residence—to get hurt. And he could guess neither would Emma. She wasn't feeling one hundred percent, but she kept pace with him. The woman might be scared, but she was going to push that aside and do what she had to.

They raced down the sidewalk. A guy, probably a trucker by the look of him, poked his head out of his room. Jeans, undone. No shirt. Round belly covered in enough hair it could be classified as fur. "Call 9-1-1."

They kept running.

Emma said, "What if…"

"Don't think about that," he told her. "There's no use. Let's just get in there and see what we can find."

Bill and Mary might be fine, or they might be already dead. Kerri could be in there, dead. Mint had no desire to see a burn victim, but this was the nature of what he did. You completed the mission, regardless of what that meant. And when it was done, you did what you had to do to get past it.

The front door of the office was shut. Mint tried the handle. Locked.

He elbowed the window and broke the glass, then opened it from the inside. Smoke poured out. Emma coughed. She didn't need to be here, didn't need to see this. But he had to keep her safe. If he lost her, he lost his shot at getting Aaron Jones to come to him.

Aaron was here, and people were getting hurt. He had to shut off his feelings about that or they would compromise his ability to complete the mission. Emma was his priority. And that fact didn't cancel out basic human decency.

"Anyone in here?" He yelled the question as loud as he could. "Bill? Mary?" Mint thought he heard a faint reply and fought through the smoke with Emma. There weren't flames in the office or behind the check-in desk. Just a whole lot of smoke. Where was the fire?

Emma grasped his hand tightly, keeping him grounded here.

A door marked PRIVATE, halfway down the hall, opened to a wall of flames. Mint coughed and lifted his T-shirt collar to cover his mouth. "Bill? Mary?"

The fire was a roar. He doubted anyone could hear him… until he heard a man call back. Bill.

Mint turned and pushed Emma back down the hall. "Go. Wait at the door. Tell the firefighters where I am." He wasn't trained at this, and he had nothing to fight the blaze with, but he went inside anyway. Skirted the edge, flames threatening to lick at him as he rounded a couch and nearly tripped over the coffee table. This was their residence. He made his way to Bill and hauled the man onto his shoulder. He looked around to try and find Mary, but couldn't see her.

Black spots threatened encroaching unconsciousness. His knees almost buckled, but he made his way back to the hall. Good idea or not, he had a shot at saving this man.

Mint made his way down the hall, back to the front office of the motel. He stepped through the front door, right as the fire truck pulled up. He laid the now-unconscious Bill down on the closest stretch of grass and looked around.

Emma was nowhere to be seen.

. . .

His hand covered her mouth. She wanted to bite him, but his fingers dug so tightly into her cheek she couldn't move her jaw. The gun pressed against her side, right below her ribs.

A muffled sound built in her throat.

Aaron Jones dragged her along so fast she nearly tripped. Around the building, scraping her arm against the side of the brick wall. She couldn't help but cough, the smell of smoke still in her lungs. The scratch of ash in her throat.

Where was Mint? What if he'd run into a problem helping Bill and Mary and was hurt? A tear trailed from her eye onto Aaron's hand. Had he saved them, or had he been a victim of the fire, too? Not that she thought Mint wouldn't be able to protect her. It was just that maybe, with what she'd done, this was the recompense she'd expected. Her finger had been on the gun when the first bullet went into the senator.

Aaron didn't slow. Just kept going, rounding another corner and then let go to slam her against the wall. Her head bounced off the brick, and the whimper escaped her throat. "Why?"

The gun pressed against her again, glancing off her ribs. One shot and she would be bleeding out. No one to help her. No one to even notice the shot, not with the sirens and the distraction of the fire. Dead in an alley with no one to see. No one to care. Except her mother, who would spin this tragedy and gain herself even more fans. Her father would continue on in his quiet way, keeping to himself.

Emma realized then that she had already resigned herself to this end. At least part of her had known her journey to try and be safe was futile. That she would end up here eventually, where Aaron would catch up with her.

The fire. Kerri. That wasn't what she'd expected.

"You didn't need to hurt them."

Aaron pushed in close, pressing the gun into her stomach. "Causing trouble, aren't you? All kinds of trouble."

She said nothing.

"No more," he said.

"What do you want?"

"Go back to Virginia, Emma. Bus. Plane. Hitchhike. Walk for all I care. But you go."

He wanted her to... "What?"

She blinked. He wasn't going to take her right now? He could kidnap her and kill her. Mint would never know where she was, until they found her bones buried in a shallow grave somewhere.

"You turn yourself in to the FBI and confess to the murder of Senator Sadler, or the waitress gets delivered to the diner, dead."

Another tear rolled down her face. All she'd tried to do was take the power back.

"You hear me?"

She said nothing, too scared to even nod. Finally she managed to croak out a question. "Why?" When she'd only been trying to do the right thing.

His grip tightened. "Turn yourself in."

"How do I know Kerri isn't dead already?"

Aaron wasn't exactly honest. She'd seen him do too much to ever believe that. Still, his bargaining chip might be nothing but a lie.

He laughed, a horrible sound that made her cringe. "Nice try. This is my deal, so I guess you'll just have to trust me." She must have made a face, because he laughed again. "Guess you aren't so scared of me now. Or you just don't think so much of me."

"Don't hurt her." Who knew what state Kerri was in? Or whether Bill and Mary were even alive.

"You want her to live, you do what I say. Turn yourself in."

"Oh—" Her voice hitched. "—kay."

"Soon as I hear you've done it, I'll let her go."

That, she wasn't so sure she believed. "Let her go now. I'll do it." Kerri could be dead before Emma managed to get herself to the closest FBI office.

She knew the feds were looking for her, at least as a witness to what happened. Her blood had been at the scene. If she showed up and told them that she'd killed him, would they charge her? The FBI couldn't base a case on a confession—she'd seen that on a cop show once and was mostly sure it was true—but would her story line up with what evidence they already had?

Aaron wasn't going to kill her. Not right now, at least. He needed her to turn herself in and take the rap for him. She tensed her stomach then. "Let me go, so I can *go*."

He hauled her by her injured arm, fingers pressing right on the wound. She stumbled. He slammed her against the wall, right by the corner, and pressed his body against hers. So hard against the bricks that she whimpered again.

She didn't want to be helpless. She wanted to be strong, but in the moment all she could think was, *Don't hurt me. Don't hurt me.* She couldn't think of any way to get him to leave her alone.

He twisted her so she was looking around the corner, at the firefighters. An ambulance. Mint glanced around, looking for something.

Looking for her.

"He can't help you. Not him or any of his friends. No one can. Not unless you want to be responsible for more death."

Emma shuddered.

The blow came before she even realized. Pain whipped through her skull and everything went black.

· · ·

Mint searched the parking lot first. Then both of their rooms. Then he widened the search, his stomach twisting increasingly into knots.

He found her in an alley, slumped against the wall. "Emma." He crouched and saw the blood trailing from her temple, down her cheek. She didn't wake.

Mint lifted her in his arms and carried her to the ambulance. He took each step with care, not wanting to stumble. His lungs burned from the smoke. He pushed aside the weakness and concentrated on getting her to the EMTs.

When he was close enough, Mint yelled, "I need help!"

She shifted then. "No." The word was a low moan.

"Don't worry. We'll get someone to see to you."

"No."

He ignored her protest and moved toward the back of the ambulance. But the doors shut, and it started to pull away slowly. Mint looked around.

"Don't."

He tucked his chin and looked down at her. "You need to see a doctor." Regardless of the fact the EMTs had just left, taking Bill or Mary—or both—to the hospital.

She shook her head. "Please. Don't."

The firefighters were busy. A few people milled around, watching what was going on. No one had heard him yell over all the noise.

The sheriff's vehicle pulled into the parking lot. Emma must have seen it because she shifted and buried her face against his shirt. "You have to get me out of here." He barely heard her. "Please."

Mint didn't like it, but he moved to his room and got her on the bed. He shut the door. "You need a doctor, Emma." His hands shook, his skin absorbing the sensation of her tight against him. She could so easily have been dead when he found her. Another victim of Aaron Jones.

She pushed off the covers and shifted to the edge. She swayed before her feet even touched the floor.

"What are you doing?"

"I have to go."

Mint shook his head. He wanted to crouch in front of her, have a soft conversation, but she looked like she'd push him away and make a run for it. He didn't want to end up on his butt on the carpet.

"What happened?"

She frowned at him.

"I'm sorry." He'd sounded short with her. Like this was her fault. "Tell me, Emma. Please."

"Aaron pointed a gun at me. He dragged me from the office to the alley."

Dread rolled through him. "Was he going to kill you? Which way did he go?"

She shook her head. "He said…" Her voice broke. She looked so small. Defeated.

Mint got a wash cloth and handed it to her. "Put this against your head." In the light of the room it didn't look too bad, but there was a good amount of blood. It would likely just need a regular bandage.

When she did as he asked, he leaned his hips back against the dresser. "Tell me what he said."

Mint listened, feeling his eyebrows rise as she told him. When she got to the part where she'd asked about Kerri, he said, "Good. Always ask for proof of life."

Her face twisted. "She's probably already dead." Emma looked like she wanted to curl up on the bed and cry. Then take a nap. But she pressed on. When she got to the end of her story, she said, "Are Bill and Mary okay?"

Mint folded his arms to keep from reaching for her. Comforting her. "Bill was out. I got him to the ambulance. The firefighters found Mary. It doesn't look good, but we won't know until the doctors check them both out."

She said nothing, just stared at him. Like Mint was supposed to figure out what she should do next. Like maybe he had answers to this colossal mess. He pulled his phone out. No messages. Not from Steve and not from the RV command center they had parked just outside of town.

Emma lifted off the bed and moved to zip up her duffel. She bent over the bag, hissed out a breath and collapsed to her knees.

Mint knelt by her and zipped up the bag. "Come on."

They could get out of here, and he'd figure out what to do next. He needed to pow-wow with his team members in town if they were going to have a shot at finding Kerri while he protected Emma. Then there was Aaron.

This was bigger than just Mint now. But that was why he'd joined Double Down. He could accomplish more as part of a team than he could alone.

She lifted up but took a step back. "Where? Are you going to drive me to Virginia?"

He shook his head. "Why would I do that?"

"I have to turn myself in. For Kerri."

The waitress was probably already dead. Mint didn't want to confirm for Emma that he thought the same thing.

"No one else is going to die because of me."

"Emma—"

"No! I don't want to hear you say it's going to be okay. It won't be. Not *ever*. I'm going to go to jail, and Kerri will be okay, and that's *it*."

He took a step toward her, but she twisted around him and headed for the door. Mint caught her arm. He loosened his grip before he would hurt her, then shifted her so her back was against the door. He felt her reach for the handle and grabbed it first. Kept his body close, but not touching. "Don't be stupid, Emma. You need me."

"No. What I need is for no one else to die because of me."

She'd said that once already. He said, "Tell me the rest of it." He knew she was holding back. They both were.

"Because I'm stupid?"

"Making bad choices doesn't mean you're dumb. We all do it, because we act without thinking. Without asking for help." He looked down at her, willing her to believe in him. For someone, for once in his life, to believe in him. "I'm standing right here, Emma. I want to help you. But you have to *let me in*."

Chapter 6

Emma lifted the duffel and slung it over her shoulder. Her head swam and she fought a rush of vertigo to stay upright. *Whoa*. Mint did nothing. He was back to not touching her. Not that she wanted him to try and help her. He'd done enough, calling her ideas "stupid." She knew he didn't mean she was dumb, even though she'd accused him of exactly that. Chin high, she strode to the door.

He wanted her to trust him, but that wouldn't save Kerri's life. Maybe he thought there was no point in her trying. That Kerri was already dead. But what kind of person would she be if she didn't at least try and save another person's life? This was her fault. Aaron had made her part of this—a product of bad timing, or more than that. Why did Mint care so much if she ended up in jail? He didn't need to worry about her future.

"Emma."

When she looked back at him to see what he wanted, he was looking down at his phone. Seriously? She was making a life-altering decision here, and he was distracted with technology?

She moved to the door and grabbed the handle. On the other side, stood the sheriff.

He frowned—apparently all the reaction he was going to show right now even though he was surprised. "I didn't expect to find you in here." The sheriff looked between her and Mint, a question in his eyes.

Emma said, "I was just leaving."

The sheriff held up his hand. "I'd like a minute of your time. I need a clear picture of what happened tonight."

"Are Bill and Mary okay?" Maybe he knew more about their conditions than Mint had.

"If you'll take a seat, this will only be a second."

She turned back to Mint, half-expecting him to object somehow. Make it so she could leave. He looked up, face pale. Eyes ringed by dark circles. He sighed, and it ended in a cough that shook his whole body.

Emma dumped her duffel and went to the bathroom. She unwrapped the provided plastic cup and filled it with tepid water from the tap. When she handed it to him, their fingers touched. He said nothing. Just took the cup and sipped.

The sheriff stood by the dresser. Emma sank into a padded chair, while Mint stayed in his seat on the edge of the bed. He looked like he should be taking a nap. She knew she felt the same way. They were both exhausted. Beat up. Injured and bruised. They'd been through the ringer today, even before the fire and her little conversation with Aaron Jones.

The sheriff had Mint show him an ID and, after that, called him "Davis." His real name?

Mint explained everything that happened from when they noticed the smoke to when he came out with Bill and the fire department was there. Hearing what he'd gone through humbled her. Despite the fact she could admit she had wanted him to come and save her, he'd been saving Bill. Making sure Mary was all right. He'd looked for her. She'd seen it.

And he *had* found her. She'd been roughed up but not hurt badly. Mint had sucked in smoke being a hero.

"If you're having problems breathing," the sheriff told him, "you should see a doctor."

Mint nodded. "I will."

The sheriff turned to Emma. "Anything you want to add, considering you stayed outside while Davis headed in? It'll help me have a more complete picture."

Emma tried to smile. Davis? Why did Mint seem to fit him so much better?

"That's a nasty gash on your head. How'd you get it?"

"Well," she started.

"My fault, I'm afraid." Mint cut her off successfully, then said, "I was a little unsteady. So when we were on our way back here, I stumbled her into the door frame."

The sheriff glanced at her.

Emma touched the bandage she'd put on and winced.

"I already made her promise to forgive me, but I figure I've got my work cut out for me with this one."

Emma blinked. Thankfully the sheriff had turned to Mint and wasn't looking at her. She bugged her eyes out at him, but he just sent her a smile back. The effect on his face was astonishing. Years bled away. Stress and fatigue disappeared. His lips curled up and he winked. "You did promise."

She'd done nothing of the sort.

"See what I mean?" Mint chuckled.

The sheriff did the same. "Yes, I do."

Okay, so maybe some of that emotion had bled onto her face.

The sheriff shook both their hands and headed for the door.

"Sheriff," she called out. Mint shot her a look, but she ignored him and turned to the law man.

The sheriff turned back. "Yes?"

"How is the search for Kerri going?"

"The missing waitress?" When Emma nodded, he said, "I can't really comment on an ongoing investigation—" She started to speak, but he held up his hand. "But I can say that, if you have any information at all that might help me find her, I would definitely appreciate it."

His face was grim. It was on the tip of her tongue to tell him about Aaron. Then a strong arm wrapped around her, and Mint pulled her against his side so that her cheek was pressed to his chest. His warmth was enormous. That was the only way she could think to describe it. Had she ever been that warm in her life?

"Thank you, Sheriff." He squeezed her shoulder while Emma fought the urge to pummel him. "We're both worried about Kerri. If we think we can help, we'll let you know."

The sheriff nodded. He glanced between them.

Emma managed a tiny smile.

Only then did the sheriff shut the door behind him.

Emma shoved Mint away from her. "He could have helped."

"He wouldn't have told you anything, and your information about Aaron wouldn't have done anything but confuse the man. He needs to follow the physical evidence for his best shot at finding Kerri in time to save her life."

"And you know this?"

He stared her down.

Emma pushed out a breath. Mint's phone beeped, taking his attention again. She'd left her phone in Virginia before she embarked on this desperate dash for freedom. Still, she'd never really enjoyed 24/7 access to the world, and the world to her. Most of the time she left the volume off and checked it when she was ready to engage. Her tiny rebellion against her mother's public persona.

"You really want to turn yourself in to the FBI?"

She turned back to him. "If it saves Kerri's life, yes."

"Okay."

. . .

As if he was going to let her turn herself in to the FBI. That was just ridiculous. And now that he knew the rest of the team in Colorado with him were actively looking for Kerri, he could focus better. Except for Perkins. His female team member was going to meet them. If Emma wanted to turn herself in to the FBI, he'd give her FBI to turn herself in to.

His head swam, but he fought the sensation and gripped the wheel as he drove. *Focus.* Emma was his priority. She was his part of the mission. Aaron would be found, and as a team they would find out what he knew about the blackmailer. Emma's knowledge—if she truly had some—was his to uncover.

And yes, part of that meant possibly using her as bait to catch Aaron.

"What's your plan?"

They raced down the highway to the next town. A neutral location where they could do this. And somewhere, Aaron could easily have followed them. Which he had, if that car that'd been tailing them the last twenty minutes really was who Mint thought it was.

"If you want me to trust you," Emma said with a short tone, "then you're going to have to start talking. Otherwise, I get out the next time you stop. I can make my own way to the FBI."

"I get that you want to save Kerri, and in order to do that you're trusting Aaron to keep his end of the bargain. But you're also trusting that he was actually telling the truth in the first place."

"I know that." She looked as happy about it as he was.

"So how about going to an FBI agent I trust. One that I know, who will do the right thing by you?"

"Why do I care if they 'do the right thing by me?'" She shrugged. "What difference is it going to make?"

"None, if Kerri is already dead." Mint changed lanes to let an Audi speed past him in the fast lane. "But we're talking about your future. You can turn yourself in if that's what you want, but you don't have to sacrifice your entire life as a martyr to Aaron Jones's demands."

There was something she hadn't told him. Mint was as sure of that as he was that if he ever saw his father again he would shoot the man. Certain things in life you didn't quibble about. Vengeance was one. Peace was another. And if Emma thought this would give her peace, he wasn't going to deny her the chance. But he would do his very best to change her mind.

A tear rolled down her cheek. She swiped it away. "I can't just do nothing."

"Is turning yourself in for a crime you didn't commit the answer?" He wanted her to be sure this was what she was prepared to do. "Because it's unlikely the charges will even stick if your lawyer can argue enough reasonable doubt that you didn't do it. So what does Aaron have to gain by forcing you into a messy legal battle that will last a while and then likely fizzle out. Except that it will leave you with a mark on your record, so to speak."

"And my mother's."

"Huh?"

She shook her head. "Nothing."

"So, what does the FBI possibly have that they can use to make their case?"

"Maybe you should ask your FBI agent friend that?"

"I'll do that." He'd have to email in to the office and get them to contact Agent Walker if he was going to find out what they had on Emma. Last he'd heard, though, was that they only wanted to talk to her. Still, what the FBI told the news to broadcast was likely different—spun to make Emma feel safe enough to show her face. After all, they'd told everyone Senator Francis Sadler had killed himself. To try and lull the blackmailer into a false sense of security?

They made a pit stop at a gas station, and he made a few calls. When Emma emerged from the restrooms he said, "My FBI contact is on her way. When she gets here, you can go with her to Virginia."

Hopefully he could lose the tail before Perkins got here.

They got back in the car, and he took her toward Colorado Springs. Not a long drive, but a good enough stretch of highway to see if the car was still behind them. Twenty minutes later it showed up again. The guy was good, but Mint was better.

Emma rubbed her hands over her knees.

"Nervous?"

She shrugged. "I just… Aaron said to go to Virginia and turn myself in. *Then* he would let Kerri go."

Mint bit down on his molars. Trusting Aaron, even if it meant the waitress lived, wasn't a good idea. "We have to assume he's watching us." Following them. "He'll know you met with an FBI agent. That you went with her."

Once Perkins had thoroughly questioned Emma, they would call agent Walker and figure out what would happen to her next.

Aaron needed to think Emma had turned herself in to the FBI. She needed to know she was doing what Aaron had asked of her. This was the way to do that. Because Mint was going to get the answers they needed out of Emma. He was going to help find Kerri. With his teammates. And he was going to bring down Aaron.

When Emma realized he'd deceived her, it wasn't going to go down well. But they didn't need to be friends when all this was said and done. She might pull on certain heart strings—if he let her, which he wasn't going to. He'd rather keep all those cut. Chopped up, the way his father had left them. She might forgive him when she considered everything she was keeping from him now.

Either way, he'd be gone.

Off to the next mission.

Personal ties weren't part of his life. He had the job and his friends on the team—such as they were when he engaged only the bare minimum. He respected them and that was enough. He was pretty sure that was reciprocated.

Emma and her big eyes, full of fear, couldn't be part of it.

Not if he was going to stay sane.

His phone beeped. He looked at the screen long enough to see that Perkins was in place and drove to the diner they'd agreed on. She'd been in the area, tasked with finding Kerri. Now they were going to switch places, forced into different roles. But that was the nature of the game.

Mint found the exit and pulled off the highway. He took a right and headed for the chain diner. A cookie-cutter match to all the others across the country.

Perkins stood leaning against a silver rental. Her blue jacket said FBI, and a badge hung from a chain around her neck. She was a striking woman a little older than him. Single, as far as he knew. Not interested in anything but doing her job, for reasons she didn't intend to share. They had that in common at least, and he respected it.

He lifted his chin as they approached. "Perkins."

She did the same, then held out her hand to Emma. "Special Agent Megan Perkins."

Megan? Mint tried to think if he'd ever heard her first name. He'd only ever used Perkins.

She narrowed her eyes at him. "I'll take it from here."

"Sure. Thanks."

Emma nodded. "We really appreciate this." She paused. "I just hope it gets back to Aaron, so he will let Kerri go."

Perkins motioned to the diner. "Why don't we get a cup of coffee, and you can tell me the whole story?"

Emma said, "Okay. Yes, that actually sounds good."

They moved toward the door. The window of Perkins's rental exploded in a shower of glass. A crack, like rifle fire, echoed off the building.

He yelled, "Get down!" And dove to the asphalt as bullets rained down.

Chapter 7

Emma's injured arm got squished under her torso, pinned against the asphalt. Perkins landed on top of her, pressing down hard enough that Emma bit her lip to keep from screaming.

"Stay down." Perkins's voice was short. Efficient, but she also seemed kind of mad. Even while she was covering Emma with her body. This woman would take a bullet for her? They didn't know each other, but maybe Perkins was exactly that type of person.

Time seemed to slow. The length between each shot that cracked across the parking lot growing longer. Every breath roared in her ears like the ocean. If Mint was going to dump her off on anyone and walk away, she was actually kind of glad it was this woman.

Perkins lifted up enough that it took the overwhelming pressure off Emma's arm. She tugged at Emma's other arm and said, "Up. Go to the restaurant and get inside. Keep your head down."

She didn't argue, just got her feet under her and started to move.

Perkins continued to cover her with her body, shielding her from bullets. Emma pushed at the front door of the restaurant.

A bullet hit the rental car and another window smashed.

Perkins shoved her inside and immediately pulled her phone out. "Mint?"

"I'm pinned down."

Emma heard his answer, even with the phone pressed to the other woman's ear. She also heard the stress in his voice.

"I'm coming to you," she said.

"No." His answer came fast. Too fast for Emma's liking. "Stay with Emma."

"Go help him." Emma motioned to the door. She *needed* Perkins to go out there and help him. To protect him the way she had protected Emma.

Perkins didn't move. She said, "Are you hurt?" to Mint.

The answer took too long. "Stay with Emma. I'll call and get our back-up on their way here."

"Fine." Perkins hung up. She moved immediately to the window and looked out.

"You aren't an FBI agent, are you?"

Perkins didn't turn around. Before Emma could say anything else, a man bustled up to them. He was shorter than Emma, maybe only barely five feet tall and had more red hair on his face than was on the top of his head. "Should I call the police?"

He directed his question to Perkins. She turned back from the window. "Tell them to keep it quiet. They show up, sirens blaring, it could scare him off, and we need this guy *caught*. Keep everyone away from the windows, and we'll have the situation locked down ASAP."

She certainly sounded like a federal agent.

"I'll get on that." He hurried away.

She didn't see a single head pop up above a table, and she could hear the muffled sounds of a baby crying.

Outside, shots were still being fired. But not at the restaurant.

"He's trying to kill Mint."

Perkins stopped her from going all the way to the window. "Will you stay here if I go assist?" She paused for a fraction of a second. "I'm not going if you're going to stick your neck out. Figuratively or literally."

Emma wanted to smile at that, but didn't. "Go help Mint. I won't move."

She had no desire to be face to face with Aaron Jones again. And as long as he was still firing—at Mint—then she figured he wasn't headed here to deliver another "message." Not to mention the fact she was about to fall over. Perkins needed to help Mint. That was her skillset.

Perkins was out the door before Emma realized. She caught a glimpse of the woman moving fast, on her phone again with her gun out in the other hand. Emma slid down the nearest wall and huddled in an alcove of the foyer.

For the first time in a long time, she wanted to pray. Not to the God her mother seemed to worship, a stifling being with no personality who expected perfection from His followers. No, Emma needed a rescuer. Mint needed a rescuer. She prayed for Perkins, that she would have the strength to help him, and that she would know what to do.

After a few minutes she realized the shooting had stopped. The door opened, and Mint strode in. His face was gray, even paler than it had been only hours ago.

She shot up and met him. "Come and sit down." She didn't comment that he looked like he was about to fall over.

"Your arm okay?" He slumped into a chair and winced.

"My arm?" She'd been pushing the pain away since it happened. What did that matter now? Her skin felt flushed, but apart from that and the nagging ache, she was all right. "Let's worry about you right now." That was the important thing. He'd been hurt.

"Just scratches." He pulled his hand away from his shoulder, but she didn't see anything. Until he turned. The shirt on the back of his shoulder was shredded. Blood stained the edges of the tears.

He twisted, trying to look over his shoulder, and sighed. Emma moved around to his back. "Let me look." She fingered the edges of his torn shirt and pulled it apart. Half a dozen places had been cut. "Looks like glass."

"From the car window."

Underneath and around the cuts were old scars. Warped skin, like he'd been burned. Pale white lines. Emma touched the edge of a prominent one and traced the line with the pad of her index finger.

Mint shot from the chair and paced away.

"Sorry. I didn't mean to hurt you."

He didn't answer her. Just strode to the window where he pulled out his phone and made a call. "Perkins, status." Like he was in charge, and she reported to him.

But Emma couldn't get those scars out of her mind. They weren't all war wounds. She'd volunteered at a children's hospital in college, reading stories to the kids. Keeping them company. Playing card games. She knew what abuse looked like.

His dark eyes turned to her. "Good." He hung up the phone.

She wasn't sure what exactly she should say. "I—"

He didn't let her get the words out. "Perkins is headed back. Jones got away."

Emma nodded. "Are you okay?"

He pinned her with a stare. "Are you?"

Touché.

What was that quote from that movie about being at an impasse? It fit here. They were both just stubborn enough to not admit they needed help.

"Perkins has your antibiotics."

Determined to help her get better. Did he have anyone in his life who would do the same for him? The way he'd held back from her. The way he was professional with Perkins. Telling her to stay with Emma…

She didn't think there was anyone who did that for him. And either he didn't think he needed it, or he wasn't prepared to allow it to happen. The phrase *kill them with kindness* came to mind. Was that how she was to break through to Mint, come at him with nothing but the softest of kindness?

And did she want to?

The man would be tough to crack...and apparently having stress and an injury made her think in nothing but analogies and metaphors. Mint might care about her and be determined to keep her safe—even if he wouldn't admit it to her. But would he accept her doing the same for him?

Emma figured she just might want to find out.

. . .

Mint figured he could stand for about five minutes, and then he was going to fall over. But he wasn't about to let Emma in on that little secret. Or anything else.

He couldn't get the feel of her touch out of his mind. He wanted to hold on to it, savor it. Even while he knew he couldn't admit he liked it. Or that he wanted more of it.

There was too much going on to even consider something with Emma. They lived in different cities, she was technically a client of Double Down—even if she didn't know it—and there were rules about making missions personal. And all that was before he got to his personal hang-ups. Or the possibility that Emma might succeed in her plan to get put in prison for murder to save the life of a woman she didn't know all that well, who might be in this situation because she'd gotten herself there.

Perkins shoved open the door, frustration lining her face. "Okay?"

He nodded. "You?"

"Thank you."

Mint glanced over and saw a redheaded man who looked like a gnome hand Emma a stack of first aid supplies. She came to him, a tentative look on her face. He didn't wait for her to ask, just sat so she could do what he couldn't do, because he couldn't reach that far. She stood behind him, Perkins in front.

"Jones got away?" he asked his teammate. He didn't want Perkins walking around to look at his wound. She would see what Emma had seen and then things would change. He didn't need his teammates looking at him with pity. Even if they called it compassion.

It was enough that Emma had seen. And maybe, just maybe, he'd wanted her to. He could admit that to himself at least. Then he shoved the idea aside and winced, since she'd slathered something cold and gooey over his cuts.

Perkins curled her lip. "I got the license plate on his car. I called it in."

"Any word from the others about Kerri?" He heard Emma's intake of breath at his question.

Perkins shook her head. "Not yet." But he knew that look.

His teammate didn't think much of Kerri's chance at a long life. If she did survive, she would be affected in a way that might never go away. And Emma would carry the guilt of that for the rest of her life. Mint understood. There were things in him that had been imprinted so deep, he would carry them forever. Things that couldn't be seen. Touched, with those soft fingers of hers.

She worked efficiently right now. Barely making contact skin to skin. She pressed tape over the gauze she'd placed on his cuts. They weren't bad but—like her gunshot wound—they would likely get infected if he just left them.

Two EMTs strode in the front door. Perkins glanced at the manager. "We should get out of here before the actual police show up."

Mint nodded.

"I'm done."

He turned to watch Emma carry two handfuls of wrappers to the nearest trash can. Perkins walked out the back fire exit with them. The sheriff was just walking in the front door when they moved around to the cars. Perkins's was barely drivable.

"I'll never get the deposit back on that now."

No one smiled.

Perkins collected her things, and they piled into Mint's car.

He turned on the engine and pulled out, asking his teammate, "Will your ID hold up when the sheriff runs whose car that is?"

"If it doesn't, then I took a job with the wrong private security firm."

Mint nodded, understanding exactly where she was coming from on that.

"I knew you weren't a real FBI agent," Emma said from the backseat. She left those words hanging in the air, and Perkins shifted in her seat to face their charge.

"We're here to keep you safe," his teammate said.

"By lying to me and putting Kerri's life at risk. Aaron Jones is going to kill her now."

Perkins continued as though she hadn't said anything, "And to find out who in Washington DC is blackmailing people with information *so* sensitive, one woman already took her life."

Emma said nothing.

"Do you know Senator Rachel Harris?" Perkins paused long enough that Mint figured Emma nodded. "A few weeks ago she was kidnapped. Her best friend, Alexis, was framed for it. Bradley Harris, Rachel's brother, worked with the FBI. Then they were taken as well, and Alexis got strapped with a bomb. A man who worked for the blackmailer was determined to get Bradley and Rachel's inheritance money."

Emma's voice was breathy when she said, "A bomb?"

Out the corner of his eye, Mint saw Perkins nod. "Mint was the one who saved Alexis."

He wouldn't exactly have put it that way.

Perkins continued, "Rachel is safe, and now Bradley and Alexis are married. But we still don't know who the blackmailer is. What we *do* know is that Aaron Jones works for him. We think he knows who the man is."

Emma stayed silent again for another moment. "A blackmailer?" Her voice was flat.

She knew. Mint could hear it in the tone. He said, "Who is it?"

"I don't know his name."

"Does Aaron know?"

"I don't know," Emma said. "I think Aaron works for him, but he's only here so I'll take the rap for the senator's death."

Perkins said, "He could be here under the blackmailer's authority. But Aaron could also be trying to save his own skin."

"Does that matter?" Emma asked, her tone short. "Kerri's life is what matters."

"Agreed," Mint said. But it was easier than finding her. They needed Aaron to lead them to where he was holding Kerri and that would take time. "He came out to shoot at us today—"

"He was shooting at *you*," Emma put in.

"Okay. He came to shoot at me—"

"Because he knew I wasn't going to the FBI. Before *I* even knew."

"Emma—"

"Don't, okay? You all have this plan, and you're on your mission to do whatever. But this is my life. It's Kerri's life. All you've done so far is jerk me around and lie to me. So pull over, because I'm getting out. I'm going to the *real* FBI, and I'm going to get Aaron to let Kerri go before she dies from whatever he did to her that left blood all over her house when he kidnapped her." She paused. He didn't turn around. He could hear her breath coming in great heaves.

He could tell her that was nothing but shock, but would it help? She wasn't likely going to accept much from him or give anything else to him. At least, not without some kind of exchange. Maybe if Kerri was already safe. If it was only Emma whose life was on the line.

"We're not stopping," Perkins said. "And we're not letting you out. If we're going to find Aaron Jones, have any hope of saving Kerri, and manage to bring this blackmailer to light, then Double Down needs your help, Emma. In return, you get a shot at a future that doesn't involve being in prison for murder."

"You think I care about that?"

"Everyone cares about that," Mint said, not at all happy with the fact she was still thinking about doing this. He needed Kerri found before Emma did something she couldn't take back.

Perkins shifted again, about to say something else. Her phone buzzed. She looked at the screen, then up at him. "We have a serious problem."

Chapter 8

"We have a lot of problems," Mint said. "You're gonna have to be specific."

Perkins shot him a look. In the back seat, Emma watched the interplay between the two colleagues. Perkins had ditched the FBI jacket and badge. Emma was pretty sure it was actually a crime to impersonate a federal agent. And she was still mad about the fact they'd lied to her. She'd thought they were taking her to turn herself in, in order to save Kerri, when they'd had a totally different plan.

She'd trusted them. In turn, they'd provided her with plenty of ammunition should she choose to go the route that would cause them a great deal of trouble with the authorities. Were they trusting her to not be that vindictive, or that she wouldn't lash back out of anger, or had they simply covered their proverbial butts in case of such an outcome? Emma didn't know which it was. She felt like she was floundering—in every aspect of this situation—and so far out of her depth right now she wanted to laugh. But the fact she could barely breathe with all the stuff swirling around her meant there was no way she would.

She shifted in the seat, huddling closer to the door. Her arm hurt, despite the medication Perkins had given her. Antibiotics took time, but the pain meds should be kicking in right about now. Was Kerri okay? Emma couldn't relax until she knew the other woman was all right. Or, at least, that she was being taken care of.

It was like being torn in a dozen different directions.

"Emma's face just hit national news," Perkins said, glancing back at her. "And the FBI has given up calling the senator's death a suicide. It's murder now."

Emma saw the glance out the corner of her eye, but didn't turn away from the window. She wanted to watch the world go by outside.

"The FBI are stepping up their search for her."

"As a murder suspect?" Mint asked. Maybe not because he wanted to know. Maybe he just wanted ammo to try and reassure her.

"Well, no." Perkins answered.

"That's grea—"

"But they're calling her a person of interest." Perkins's voice had a tone to it. "Everyone knows what that means."

Mint started to argue.

"They think I killed him," Emma said to the window.

Perkins said, "What did you do with the clothes you were wearing that night?"

"Tossed them in the trash at a rest stop in Nebraska."

"Good."

"It's not good." She turned to the other woman then. "I was there. My blood will be at the scene."

"Fleeing, because you were hurt, too."

She didn't want to absorb even the promise of hope in the other woman's eyes. "And when they find the gun with my prints on it?"

Perkins's eyes widened a fraction before she could squash the reaction.

"*Now* you get it," Emma said. "You get why the FBI wants to talk to me, whether they found the gun or not. I was there. Aaron was there. Shots were fired, and the Senator died." She choked on those last couple of words. Though, not for the reasons they would think. It was more than the fact he'd been her boss, and she'd been a party to his death.

More than Kerri.

More than Aaron Jones.

More than the truth that Senator Francis Sadler hadn't even been a good man.

She said, "So what does it matter that the FBI think I'm involved? I *was*. And I'd rather take my chances with them than with Aaron Jones when I have to explain everything. Even if they'll probably arrest me for murder, or being complicit in a murder, or something."

Mint sighed. Why he was so bothered by the idea of her going to jail, she didn't know. Except that it would put her out of reach to provide the information they wanted about the blackmailer... Something she didn't even want to *think* about right now.

"It will stop Aaron from hurting people."

"No," Mint said. "It won't." He didn't turn back, as he was still driving. "This guy has one play. To force you to confess by hurting someone you care about. Best friends or not, Aaron knows you don't want anything to happen to Kerri, so he's banking on you doing this."

"Well it's all messed up now. I didn't do it, and he knows."

Perkins said, "He had to have been following us. And somehow he knew I wasn't an FBI agent."

Mint shot her a look.

"Or not enough of one that he could tell."

Emma wasn't even sure she wanted them to explain that to her right now. She had enough swirling in her head already, she wasn't sure she could handle confusing, even if it was the truth.

"Why did he try and kill Mint?" She wasn't sure who she was asking, but needed to know. The last thing she wanted right now was another person hurt because of her. Mint had been injured, but it could easily have been so much worse.

Perkins said, "Because he wants you alone and vulnerable."

"The first answer is that he's a hothead and he's reacting. Going on instinct. Perkins's answer is the second," Mint clarified. "Aaron is flying by the seat of his pants. He still needs you to confess to that murder he committed, and if he can get that result, then he's willing to do almost anything. Other than that, who knows? He's tortured people before."

Emma turned back to the window. She tried to pray for Kerri, but the words wouldn't come. All she had was the silent cry of her heart, and she thanked the God she wanted to believe in so badly that it was enough. "He's going to kill her, isn't he?"

And he wouldn't do anything to minimize the pain.

For a couple of minutes neither of them spoke. Mint had to realize the subterfuge he'd undertaken to try and get her to talk with Perkins instead of a real FBI agent was what had caused this. If Kerri died by Aaron Jones's hand, responsibility could be placed on his shoulders. How had he justified that kind of gamble? He had to have known he was putting Kerri's life at risk. And still he'd done it.

A sour feeling rolled through her stomach.

Perkins said, "Two men we work with are looking for her."

That was something. But was it enough? She stared at the back of Mint's neck between the seat and the headrest. "Do you even care that she could die?"

Her voice had been quiet, but she was sure he heard her.

"You want me to grieve for a woman I don't know? People die every day. People die every minute. Should I shed a tear for each of them?"

She wanted to kick the back of the seat.

"I have my mission. It's you."

"Don't give me that. You were sending me with Perkins so she could get me to talk, right?"

"And then I was going to find Kerri."

She didn't let that penetrate. "Because finding her would lead you to Aaron."

"Do I want every part of this wrapped up? Yes," he said. "I'm not going to apologize for doing my job. And you don't get to judge that. Not when you don't know the first thing about me."

"Right back atcha." He wanted to judge her willingness to turn herself in to the FBI, but he didn't want her to give him back the same courtesy? He wanted the results he wanted, but he also didn't want this to get personal.

Fine.

It wouldn't get personal.

"Pull over. I'm getting out."

. . .

Mint kept driving.

"I want to get out."

He ignored her and stuck to his route on the highway. There was no way, after they'd all gotten shot at by Aaron, that he was going to let Emma go off on her own. Regardless of how she felt about him and his methods.

"Perkins call in," he said without taking his eyes off the road. "I want an update."

"On it." She didn't argue. She also knew he meant an update on the search for Kerri as well as Aaron.

Emma yelled, "Let me out of this car!"

Mint ignored her.

"Davis whatever your real name is, you pull this car over right now!"

His lips twitched. If he'd had a mom, she'd probably have spoken to him exactly like that. Too bad for Emma he hadn't. Which meant he'd never learned to respond to demands like that. His arms didn't even twitch on a reflex. Nothing but a flash of amusement that she thought might work—or was at least worth a try.

She didn't think too much of him. That was clear.

"Malone."

"What?"

"My real name," he said. "It's Davis Malone."

She'd pushed, and he was pushing back. She might have the strength in her to have faced all this so far, but that didn't mean she was going to push him over. He wasn't about to let her tread on him. Not when he was the one who had the skills to actually take care of her. That was a better solution by far than allowing her to put herself in even more danger.

It occurred to him that doing that in a controlled way—surveillance—while she did something benign like head to the diner for a shift, could draw out Aaron.

She would jump on that opportunity in a heartbeat. Which was probably why Mint dismissed it. That was a last-resort option, and in the meantime, they had other ways to work on clearing this up.

Emma's face had hit national news. Another snag to be dealt with. He didn't need the local sheriff getting in their business, regardless of whether the man thought he was "helping."

Whatever they were going to do, Mint figured it had to be clean, fast and effective.

Emma kicked the back of his seat and let out a frustrated sound. Letting him know that she was still there, and she was still mad.

Mint kept driving. Ten minutes later he pulled into the park where the company RV was hooked up to electricity. They didn't need the free Wi-Fi. They made their own hotspot that connected them to the main office in Virginia—and whatever else they needed access to.

He parked the car and got out, opening the back door for Emma. She had her arms folded across her chest. He reached over her and unbuckled her belt. The cuts on his back smarted, but he ignored them. It wasn't the first time he'd pushed pain to the back of his mind and determined to get on with what was in front of him. Probably wouldn't be the last time either.

"Let's go."

She stared at the RV, not a small amount of curiosity on her face. Eventually it won out, and she moved from the car into the vehicle. Inside was a bank of monitors and computers they'd replaced the queen beds with. The bunks were still used, when they needed sleep. The kitchen was still intact and fully functional.

He got to work cooking bacon in the oven, mostly so he could work while it browned and not have to worry about keeping an eye on it so much as if he had to flip it in a pan. "Perkins, get the camera set up."

The slender woman set her hand on her hip and shot Mint a pointed look. He said, "Please."

Perkins narrowed her eyes on him for a second, then moved through the RV, doing as he'd asked. Emma stood by the door. She stared at the inside like it was an alien planet. Finally, she looked at him. "You guys are criminals, aren't you? You think you're above the law, pretending to be federal agents." She included Perkins in her accusation.

Perkins straightened, the camera in her hand. "What arrangement I have with the Federal Bureau of Investigation is none of your business." She pulled the badge from her jacket pocket and set it on the table. "But, for the record, that badge is real." She turned away from Emma, giving the other woman her back, as she readied the camera on a tripod.

Something that might have been regret moved over Emma's face, but she shook it off and said, "What is the camera for?"

Mint slid the bacon in the oven. "We're going to record your statement for the FBI, and then we're going to forward it to our contact there." He waited for her judgement on that, but she apparently had none. "That way the FBI has all the information we can get them, and we can keep you safe here. Where you aren't exposed."

A frown crinkled her brow. "You think the FBI wouldn't protect me?"

"I think you're going to be protected here, where Aaron Jones has to go through me and Perkins. And where the blackmailer doesn't have the resources he would need to get to you and hurt you or kidnap you."

"Assuming it's a he."

Perkins straightened, turning slowly toward Emma so as not to spook her. Mint didn't react. "What makes you say that?"

Emma pressed her lips together.

"Tell me." He kept his voice soft. Neither he, nor Perkins, moved toward her. Letting her have her space but maintaining their positions between her and the door. She definitely looked like she was about to bolt at any second.

Tears filled her eyes, and she shook her head. "I don't know," she said, completely blowing him off. "I'm just saying."

Mint studied her. After a minute of letting her get increasingly more agitated, he said, "Ready to give your statement?"

She nodded. He knew she was worried about Kerri. She'd also faced down Aaron Jones and was feeling all the guilt of her finger on the trigger of the gun that'd killed the senator. And even though he wasn't sure he still had the full story on that, it was for the FBI to figure out.

Mint wasn't going to placate her. He needed her strength, which meant she needed to hang on a little longer. After that, she could fall apart all she wanted.

It occurred to him that it was possible he was only reacting like this because she'd obviously seen the scars on his back. Getting defensive to keep his emotions from being involved. And if that was what he needed in order to stay sane and not allow the specters of the past to swallow him up, then it was what he would do.

Mint's phone rang. He swiped to answer the call and said, "Malone."

Out the corner of his eye he saw Emma turn to him, but all his attention was taken up by what his teammate on the other end of the call said.

"I'll be right there." He hung up and said to Perkins, "Get the statement done. I'm going out."

She nodded. Didn't ask what he was going to do. "Sure thing, boss."

He wasn't her boss, but Mint didn't have time to quibble about that.

His teammates had found Kerri.

Chapter 9

Aaron crouched, making his way between trees to the house where he'd left the waitress. Carly, Kimmy. He couldn't remember her name. Didn't much care what it was.

Nothing but a means to an end. And that means had been satisfying. Somewhat. But now it was over.

He'd have to move up the timetable. The waitress would die—a statement for Emma. Aaron was serious. The man he worked for was serious.

She hadn't done what had been asked of her.

In more ways than one.

Movement by the house caught his attention, and he stopped. A man in a dark jacket moved toward the house, gun out. Creeping closer with intention. Aaron didn't move. He'd seen that man in the crosshairs of his rifle—knit cap and glasses. It really was a shame he hadn't managed to hit the big guy. Seemed he was intent on causing Aaron all kinds of trouble. Getting mixed up in business that was between Aaron and Emma Burroughs.

He and Emma had a connection. So strong, it was almost spiritual. They had held the gun together. Breathed together. Pulled that trigger together. A beautiful moment.

Two other men joined him. One went around the back. The interfering man hit the front door with the sole of his boot and went inside. Then, nothing.

Aaron didn't wait around for whatever they were going to do next. He'd been blown. Game over. Rage had him curling his fists. Blinded him enough he swayed into a tree and had to grit his teeth at the pain. Like taking a punch you didn't know was coming. Bested.

The cool breeze cut into him, ruffling his clothing. Making him aware he needed a shower. He smelled like smoke from the motel fire. Among other things. Gone were the days he'd been Rachel Harris's assistant, dressed to impress in Washington DC. Now he was in a nothing town in Colorado, crawling around the woods just to get stuff done. It was enough to make him cry. Or stab someone.

He needed some kind of release. If he let things bottle up like that inside him, it never ended well. He would explode—as his last psychotherapist had discovered.

He should have killed the waitress hours ago. Getting close enough to Emma to figure out what she was doing had been more important. In the end, he'd let the frustration over the appearance of this interfering guy get the better of him, and he'd started shooting.

Never mind that she'd been talking to a woman FBI agent. That wasn't what he'd told her to do. And it was far too coincidental that the guy'd had someone that close to this town only a few hours after he'd explained the plan to little Emma.

Aaron needed another way to secure her. And if the waitress wasn't enough incentive, then he would have to get more personal. Hit her where it would hurt more.

Soon as he got to his car, Aaron made the call.

It went straight through, no secretary. This was a burner phone the man kept on him at all times. He required immediate updates whenever the situation changed.

His voice was deep, his tone short. "Yes?"

Aaron gave him a rundown of the situation. He waited out through the swearing and reprimanding. Nothing he hadn't heard a hundred times before. Then he asked, "Should I find out who they are?"

"I want everything you know, and I want it *now*."

"Yes, sir."

"If they know anything about my operation, I need to know."

Aaron's stomach turned over. This man would drop him in a heartbeat—tossed aside in a way he knew he would never have another safety net. That was what his employer did when he was done with someone. If you were in, you were in for life. If you were out, it was because you were either dead, or dealt with in a way that meant you'd never breathe a single word about him to anyone. Because you no longer possessed the ability to speak.

Aaron never wanted to reach the day he was no longer useful. He said, "I'll find out who they are."

A pause. "You think I don't know who they are?"

"Well—" his brain froze. What was he supposed to say?

The light chuckle on the other end didn't reassure him. "It's only a matter of time before Double Down sinks their teeth in. The question is, whose flesh will be in the snap of their jaws? It's time for you to decide if you're going to live up to the promise of usefulness I saw in you."

"You can count on me."

"Clear up this mess. I want to know what they know and who they've talked to." He paused. "But *I'll* deal with Double Down."

"Yes, sir."

The call ended.

Aaron lowered the phone, his hand shaky. He wanted information on what Double Down—whoever they were—were up to? Aaron could do that. He could also snap his own trap shut on Emma Burroughs. If the man wanted results. If he wanted Aaron to prove his loyalty. Then Aaron was going to do exactly that.

And he would not fail.

Aaron knew the blackmailer wouldn't care about collateral damage, even if that meant Double Down lost some of their own. And even if *that* meant the company then stepped up their involvement.

He'd tried one tactic using Kerri. He could do the same with another person Emma cared about, hope for a better result.

Or he could make a statement she would in no way misconstrue.

Aaron drove to the edge of town and parked down the street from a tiny yellow house. A light was on in the kitchen, the man of the house home. The wife worked the late shift. The grandson—who they looked after—was at a friend's house.

A smile curled Aaron's lips.

Emma would fall in line, or she would pay the consequences.

Chapter 10

Mint walked down the hall at the hospital to the doorway where Perkins stood. She lifted her chin as he approached, and Mint slowed. He looked in the room. Kerri was unconscious, lying on the bed hooked up to machines. Emma sat beside her, holding the waitress's hand and talking too low for him to hear.

"How is she?"

"Lost a lot of blood," Perkins said. "They sewed up the cut on her abdomen. Other than that, two broken ribs and a lot of bruises. Defensive wounds on her hands and arms. Dehydrated and malnourished."

"She managed to fight back."

Perkins nodded. "Or at least attempted to defend herself." She sighed. "Please tell me you got this guy." She looked about ready to explode and punch something. Hopefully not him.

Mint said, "No sign of him."

"And no idea what he's going to do next."

"That's why we have her." He pointed to Emma in the room.

Perkins shot him a look for that comment. He knew how it sounded, but he wasn't going to take it back. Emma was talking. It wasn't like she could hear him.

"The guys are on the hunt for Aaron Jones. I'm going to sit down with the sheriff in an hour and explain our involvement." But he wanted to talk to Emma first. Get more from her about her involvement and why Aaron had targeted the senator in the first place.

Rachel and Bradley, the senator's niece and nephew, had originally thought that their uncle could be the blackmailer. Especially considering their cousin Lincoln's involvement with Bradley's wife, Alexis. They now knew he wasn't the blackmailer. This was bigger than any of them had thought. There was an epidemic spreading in Washington. Key people in government, business and finance were falling prey to the tactics of someone out for their own ends. Whoever the blackmailer was didn't care that some of his victims had committed suicide rather than have their secrets exposed to the wider world.

Double Down had decided to uncover this poison before it spread even further. And that meant Emma. It also meant Aaron. Mint was as convinced as he could be—without proof—that Aaron knew who the blackmailer was. Or at the least, that he had a direct line to whoever it was. The senator—Rachel and Bradley's uncle—had done something to warrant a death sentence. Mint figured the blackmailer wanted him gone, and so he'd sent Aaron in to do the deed. How Emma ended up caught in that sticky web, he didn't know. She could be involved just as easily as she could be an innocent bystander.

He wanted to believe she was innocent. But that kind of wishful thinking wasn't going to help him get to the truth. If she was connected to the blackmailer, then he had to divorce his feelings from the situation. They needed answers, not for him to make friends with her.

Which meant that Mint had to resist the urge to keep watching her as she sat with her friend.

Perkins said, "Want me to go help the guys?"

"Because you want out of babysitting duty?"

"Hey," she said, smiling, "I never said that." Then she leaned toward him, conspiratorially. "I actually kind of like Emma Burroughs." She paused, like maybe she shouldn't have admitted that. "She seems like good people."

Mint waved her away from the doorway, a couple of steps across the hall. "You don't think Emma might be a party to all this blackmail business?"

"No way." Perkins shook her head. "There's no way she'd be able to hide that."

"Okay." Had he just needed his colleague to confirm what he'd been thinking? It didn't mean they had any evidence. "Anything come of recording the statement for the FBI?"

Perkins said, "I got it sent to Walker. I'm waiting to hear back. The crux of it is, Emma showed up to talk to the senator and caught Aaron there. She got away by the skin of her teeth, actually. She was lucky."

"And the fact he's still chasing her?"

"Cleaning up loose ends, I'd guess. Especially considering he wants her to take the fall for the murder. Though," Perkins said, "she says the senator was alive when she left the room. She was in the hall when she heard another shot, not directed at her. I think that's the shot that killed him."

"So she can't testify that she saw Aaron Jones kill the senator, because she was fleeing the scene."

Perkins nodded.

"Darn. That would have wrapped it up nicely." Mint tapped his fingers against his leg while he thought it through. "So all we have is her word against his. All the evidence will say they were both there."

"And any gunshot residue on the clothes they were wearing will indicate they were both in the vicinity of a shot fired."

He chewed on that for a minute, then said, "You covered the murder in the statement for the FBI?"

Perkins nodded again.

"So we need her to tell us what she knows about the blackmailer."

"If she even knows anything."

Mint blew out a breath. "I'm banking on the fact she does. Even if Aaron Jones didn't get her there on purpose, she was in all of the senator's financial dealings. She might not have known exactly what she was looking at, but if we can ask the right questions she might be able to connect some of the dots together. Help us get closer to an answer."

Perkins nodded. "I'll go help the guys, you sit her down. I think having both of us there will put too much pressure on. Like we're ganging up on her."

"Okay. Keep me posted."

She wandered away down the hall, and he went back to the room where Emma sat with Kerri. He had less than an hour before the sheriff cleared up the scene where they'd found Kerri. Then the sheriff would be here, asking Mint a whole lot of questions he was going to have to be careful answering. Especially if he wanted to keep himself, his team, and Emma out from under suspicion. Now that Emma's face had gone national, it was only a matter of time before someone realized who she was.

His phone beeped. Mint checked the email and found a note from Steve, along with a link. Emma's mother, who was apparently a conservative radio talk show host, had apparently gone live on social media with a plea for her daughter to turn herself in to the authorities. So they could clear up what she called a "mistake." The woman was convinced it was nothing but a miscommunication, and that her daughter couldn't possibly be involved.

Mint wondered what planet she lived on, where the innocent were pure and righteous. Where everything was black and white. He, of all people, knew that even the most outwardly upright person could have the blackest soul.

And he had the scars to prove it.

The end of Steve's email had a quick note.

Did you find out what was in the envelope?

The envelope he'd seen. Of course. With everything that had happened, he'd forgotten about it.

He knocked on the door to get Emma's attention. When she turned to him her eyes were puffy, and she looked more exhausted than she had the last few days. The woman needed about a month of good nights' sleep. And if he could have gifted that to her right then, he would have done it. Even if it meant going against every procedure the company— and he— had in place.

"We need to talk."

. . .

The look on his face was something Emma wasn't sure she wanted to dwell on. Still, tell that to her exhausted, fragile heart. For some reason, being tired meant she had less of a handle on her emotions. Less ability to shore up her safeguards and keep herself from feeling so much. Because standing by Mint, even when they were just walking to the waiting area, made her feel safe. As much as she didn't want it, she'd acknowledged his strength. The fact that he protected her.

She sighed. He didn't care about her. She'd heard what he said, and she knew even before then that she was only a means to an end for Mint and his company. Double Down, Perkins had called it.

The woman was almost a female version of Mint. Both of them had so many walls up it was unlikely she'd be able to break through, even if she had years—and if she even wanted to. Emma wondered if the rest of the company was like that. Maybe it was a condition of their employment that they be guarded and brooding.

"Soda?"

Emma shook her head. They sat in a corner, and she leaned her head back against the wall.

"Sorry. I know you want to rest, but this is important."

She glanced at him. His gaze on her softened, making her wonder what he saw in her. It would take a strong woman who knew who she was to crack through all he'd built around himself. It would also take a concerted effort, and a good amount of time. He pretended to engage, but she wasn't convinced he actually felt anything. He was that guarded.

Effort and time. Neither of which Emma could handle right now. Not with all the craziness happening in her life.

"I know you went over everything regarding the senator's death with Perkins."

Her throat closed up, and she had to swallow past the sensation. Everything? It was good he thought that. Perkins, she wasn't so sure. Emma figured the woman knew there was stuff she was leaving out. Things which would come to light eventually.

The longer she could put that off, the better.

Everything that could've gone wrong, had. And she didn't exactly know how to fix it.

"Emma?"

She blinked. "Yes?"

"I asked you a question." When she said nothing, he sighed. "I want to know if there was a reason Aaron picked you. Were you there purely by coincidence, or are you more involved than that?"

"I went there to talk to the senator. That's when I found Aaron in his office with the gun."

"About a work thing?"

She said nothing.

"Not a work thing, then. So what did you go there, after hours, to talk with the senator about?"

Emma thought about the now bloody envelope in her backpack. It seemed so frivolous, so pointless now. "It's private. And personal."

"And if what's contained in that envelope is relevant?"

She gasped. "How do you know about...?" She sucked in a breath, trying to rein in her thoughts, then squared her shoulders. "I get to decide what I tell you. Do I care if it's relevant to your 'mission' here? No, not really. To be honest, it's just actually none of your business."

A shutter seemed to fall over his gaze and he shifted, withdrawing. "Fine."

Did he even know he reacted like that? He was protecting himself. But she doubted it was because she had the ability to hurt his feelings. They didn't know each other well enough for that.

"I've mentioned the blackmailer a few times already," he said, his face now completely blank in a way she decided she hated. "Do you know anything about that?"

Just like that? One simple question and a demand that she trust him, and she should just spill? Emma got up. "I've decided I do want a soda."

She strode to the vending machine, while she rooted in her backpack for her wallet and pulled out a couple of dollar bills. She opted for caffeine, but not sugar, since stressful circumstances weren't a good excuse to lose all of the basic principles that governed one's life, and winced when it tumbled out hard enough to shake it up.

"Emma."

The bubbles made her eyes water. That was her excuse.

"I need you to—"

"Trust you," she fired back. "Yeah, I know."

"I was going to say sit back down, but trust is good as well."

He knew. She should have known any reaction at all other than an outright lie was indication something was there. Something she hadn't told him about. And he was going to have to know. She would have to tell him, because if Double Down had even a shot at taking down the blackmailer that would make her life infinitely better.

Selfish, maybe. But the fact was that more was at stake here than just her freedom. Or the secret that she was guarding, the one she didn't want to *ever* come out. Could she risk doing nothing and let Double Down figure this out? There was no guarantee they would, or could, even do it. She didn't know them. Maybe they were new at this. Perkins and Mint both seemed professional enough, but even the FBI hadn't managed to figure this out.

She sat back in the same seat, and Mint took the one right beside her. She put the cap back on the soda and held it, tight enough the little grooves in the lid bit into the skin on her finger.

"Do you know who the blackmailer is?"

Emma shook her head.

"Does Aaron Jones work for him?"

She nodded. "Aaron is the one who comes to collect the payout. Cash only."

"What does he have on you?"

Tears pricked her eyes. "Not me."

His hand settled on her shoulder, fingers strong. The warmth under his palm was astounding. "He didn't find anything on you?"

She shrugged. "I've never done anything."

"Rachel Harris, she's a senator like her uncle, was drugged and then videoed."

Emma gasped. "The video of her assistant? That was *her* instead?"

Mint nodded. "I've met them both. That's exactly the kind of people they are, taking a hit like that so the other one can keep their reputation." He paused. "They didn't let this blackmailer tear them or their lives apart. They took the hit, kept their heads high, and carried on."

A single tear slipped down her cheek. Emma swiped it away. "It wasn't about me."

"So what does he have?"

"Okay, so in a roundabout way, it was about me. But not because I did anything." She blew out a breath. Was she really going to say it out loud? "It's why I kept working for him, way past when I wanted to quit. I needed to know the truth. Then the blackmailing switched from putting through paperwork, to the senator's money."

"You were siphoning funds from his accounts and giving it to the blackmailer?"

She shook her head. "It didn't get that far. I did the paperwork part, but when he asked for the senator's money, I said I wouldn't give it to him. I was going to talk to the senator. Explain. But I never got the chance."

"That's what you went there to talk to him about that night?"

She nodded. "And now he's dead because of me."

In more ways than one, she was responsible for his death. The man might not have been completely upstanding, or sometimes even very nice, but that wasn't the point. He was dead, and she might have been able to prevent it.

"What did the blackmailer know that involved both you and the senator?"

Emma swallowed.

The entrance door whooshed open and Patch stumbled in, blood trailing down his face. Shirt torn. Pants spattered with blood.

He took two steps and his legs gave out.

Chapter 11

Mint was two steps behind her as she rushed to Patch, now lying on the floor. The man looked to have been beaten nearly to the end of his life, and he'd put up a good defense. What state was the other guy in?

"Patch." She whimpered as she touched his shoulder, then his hand. "Patch, wake up."

An orderly rushed over, and someone called out for a bed. A doctor and two nurses lifted him to the gurney, and the doctor began giving orders. Emma matched them step-for-step as they ran down the hall.

She glanced back at him. Mint was behind her. When her worried gaze found his, he nodded.

They pushed Patch into an unoccupied bay, and the nurse grabbed the curtain. "Wait here please." She whipped the curtain closed.

Emma pulled up short. He stopped behind her and gave in to the temptation to put his arm around her shoulder. It felt almost...familiar. Like he'd done it hundreds of times before. As natural as her winding both arms around his waist and turning her face into his neck. Natural. Like she was meant to be there, in the shelter of his strength.

Where she should be.

Mint rubbed a hand between her shoulders. "He'll be okay."

"You don't know that." Her voice was muffled against his shirt collar. "But I appreciate you saying it."

His chest shook, but he didn't let loose the sound of laughter. Now wasn't the time and neither was this the place.

"Emma." The voice came from beyond the curtain. "No... No, quit it." Patch. "Get her in here."

She pulled from his arms. "Patch?"

The nurse pulled the curtain open, her face twisted with annoyance and confusion. "You're Emma?"

Mint let her step out of his arms. She said, "Yes."

"He won't let us treat him. Not until he speaks to you."

Emma shifted past the nurse and went to the bedside. The nurse gave Mint a scathing look. He stopped by the curtain and ignored her. There was no way he'd let Patch talk to Emma about what had happened to him without Mint hearing it firsthand. So far they were barely catching up to Aaron Jones. This could get them ahead of him, to a place where they might actually have a shot at capturing him. Plus, the sheriff would be here soon. Mint didn't need to wait on hearing what Patch said until after he'd talked with the local law.

Emma leaned close. "You should let the doctors give you something."

Patch frowned. His gray eyebrows crinkled together. "Said..." He swallowed like his mouth was dry. "This was about you."

"A man?"

Patch nodded.

She said, "Brown hair, slicked back. Mid-thirties. Thin and lanky."

Another nod.

"His name is Aaron."

"Tried to kill me." Patch puffed out his lips. "Tried."

"Did you hurt him?"

"Hope so."

Emma touched his shoulder. "Let the doctors take care of you."

Patch's gaze moved to Mint who understood what the older man was trying to say even without words. The intensity in his gaze communicated exactly how he felt about Emma. And the fact that Patch was now—if he wasn't before—seriously concerned about her.

"I got her." Mint nodded.

Patch closed his eyes. "Good."

"Emma. Let's step out so the doctor can work."

She didn't want to, but moved his way anyway. He walked with her into the hall. She was going to have to finish telling him about the blackmailer. Again, he hadn't gotten all of the information from her. So much was going on, it wasn't like they could take three hours out and get it all in the open.

But that was what they needed to do.

Right now, though, she was worried about her boss. And rightly so. Aaron Jones had come after Patch.

Mint had to start somewhere, so he said, "I can ask the sheriff to send someone to Patch's house." Though he assumed the hospital staff had already called the local law office. If he had already left for the hospital to get a statement, it was probably too late to ask him to search Patch's house. Could he send a deputy?

Emma's eyes widened. "Do you think Aaron's still there?"

"It's possible. Depends how badly Patch hurt him."

That got a reaction. A tiny curl of her lips. Not that she wanted someone hurt. She wasn't a vindictive person. But Aaron Jones had terrorized her, and he'd killed the senator. Who knew what else he'd done that they didn't even know about? It did feel good to know that Patch might have dished up some payback.

"Does that make me a horrible person?"

She had to have read it all on his face. Her thoughts had gone to the same place as his. He said, "No. He hurt you." He'd certainly dreamed enough of dishing out some of that to his father. But when he'd actually gone home, halfway intending to do that—though he hadn't wanted to admit that to himself—he'd found a wrinkled old drunk who hadn't even had the strength to get out of his armchair. What was the point? It wouldn't have made him feel better.

"Patch did that in self-defense. He was in the military."

When she frowned, he said, "We ran background on him. So when Aaron mentioned you, he'd have figured out Aaron was the reason you're here. The reason you look scared and lost. He fought back for *you*."

She didn't like that. Mint took her hand so she didn't get so far away she was out of reach. "I have to talk to the sheriff in a minute. Perkins is out looking for Aaron with the guys, so I'll need you to stay here and not leave. But I also don't want the sheriff seeing you." He let that sink in, wondering if she would acquiesce. "Your face hit national news, so it's only a matter of time before someone recognizes you and calls the FBI hotline. But the longer we can keep that from happening—and hopefully enlist the sheriff's help in the meantime—the better."

Emma stared up at him. Finally, she said, "Okay."

He wanted to know what the blackmailer had on her. She'd said it wasn't anything she'd done. So who's secret was she protecting? It had to be someone she cared about. Like when Alexis took the fall for Rachel, pretending to be the star in that raunchy video. Who was Emma prepared to go to prison for, taking the fall for a murder she didn't commit?

"I'm going to help you," he said, unable to hold the words back. "Whoever you're protecting, I'll do my best to keep their secret from getting out."

"You don't even know what it is," she said, frowning. "Or who it is."

"Doesn't matter. What matters is that you think their secret is worth keeping." Whether out of risk of embarrassment, or the threat of greater loss than just a reputation. Whatever the reason didn't make all that much difference. He needed Emma to trust him, and he would do whatever it took to protect her.

"Oh." She glanced aside, looking down the hallway.

He looked over as well and saw the sheriff making his way over. Mint said, "Stay close."

She squeezed his hand. "I will."

And then she slipped away.

. . .

Emma peered through the gap between the door and the frame. Mint stood completely casual, but looking for all the world like he was in complete control. Like he had all the authority when he was faced with the sheriff of this county. She would probably be far more nervous. He didn't look like anything at all bothered him. Just like any other day.

Mint lifted his hand and shook the sheriff's. Like two colleagues. What was Mint telling him?

"You gonna stare out that door all day?"

Emma whirled around to Patch. "You're awake."

His lips curled up. Face pale, except for the dark bruises already forming. A bandage had been placed on his temple. "Can't keep me down."

"And also can't abduct you. Or murder you. Apparently." She wanted it to sound light. Glib. But it didn't. The words came out far heavier than she intended.

"Darlin'." He waved her over.

She didn't look at his face. Didn't want to see that softening in his gaze she just knew would be there. If she saw it, then she would cave. Just give in to all his attempts to make things better for her. It was exactly the type of man he was.

"Sit."

When she didn't, he tugged her down to perch on the side of his bed. He kept his weathered hand on her arm.

"Tell me."

She shook her head.

"Kiddo." The word was almost sad. Like she'd disappointed him. But it wasn't the same disappointment she got from her mother every day. He wanted to help. That was all. The help Emma's mother wanted was more like advancing her career by being part of her social media marketing. Championing her mother's worldviews.

Most of the problem wasn't the fact she disagreed with her mother. Because on most things, she didn't. Emma was just far quieter in the way she lived her life. She didn't want all her personal thoughts and feelings to be posted all over the place for everyone to "like" or "comment" on.

He patted her arm. "At least tell me he's helping you."

Emma managed to nod. Then she said, "He has friends. A whole team."

"Good, because your mom's trending on Facebook."

She nearly choked. "What?"

Patch grinned, flashing her a row of crooked teeth that gave him character. "I've been following the story since my granddaughter shared it."

"You're on Facebook?" She couldn't believe it.

"How do you think I keep up with the kids? It's not like they call me to share what's going on." He chuckled. "Gotta go where the people are, darlin'."

"No thanks."

"No?"

She shook her head. "It's not like it's real. And the stuff that is, is so boring I really try to care…"

"I see."

"Now you're even more disappointed in me."

"Did I say that?"

"I can tell," she said.

"Huh."

"What?"

He said, "You sure you didn't miss your calling as a psychologist? Maybe you could'a helped me figure out why I can't stop drinking straight from the milk carton. I think it's because my mom didn't love me enough."

Emma shoved at his shoulder with zero strength. She didn't want to hurt him. "Fine. So you're not disappointed in me?"

"I didn't say that."

She frowned. "This conversation is making no sense."

"That's the beauty of relationships. It's supposed to be crazy, insane, beautiful and also make no sense whatsoever."

"So you're a biker and diner owner and dispenser of wisdom?"

"When you've lived the life I have, you learn a lot of things. One of which is that you keep those you care about close. Even if they drive you crazy." He gave her a pointed look. "Especially if your life is in danger, and they have the resources to keep you safe."

Was he seriously talking to her about Mint?

She started to back away, get up off the edge of the bed. Patch snagged her arm again. "No, no. Sit." He frowned. "You also don't run when things get hard."

Emma settled back on the covers beside his bed. "Way to go easy on me."

"Do you want easy?"

"Maybe?" Probably not. "At least I might want the choice."

The bed shifted with the force of his chuckle. "You don't want easy."

"I don't want a psycho chasing me."

"Your big guy will fix that."

"Seriously?" She'd had a plan. She'd been fully intending on just doing what Aaron Jones told her to do. That would end all this, right? At least *this*. Who knew what the blackmailer would do next—what he would find for her to do. Yes, she understood that what he had over her he'd have over her for the rest of her life.

Unless Mint and his team really could bring him down, expose his operation, but then he could still use it again and again to get her to do whatever he wanted. Even if that meant doing it from prison.

"Darlin'. Your mom—"

She shook her head. "My mom doesn't get anything. She never did, and maybe she never will." Emma paused to take a breath. "She has no clue what goes on in the real world, because she lives in this dream land where everything is the way she says it is."

"Some people need that."

"It's not real."

"And it isn't tempting," he said, "considering all that's swirling around you right now?"

Emma's skin crawled with the thought of being face to face with Aaron Jones again. She wanted to curl up and cry. To go see Kerri. To hug Mint again—which was crazy. She was exhausted, and her feelings were out of whack. That was all. She cared about Mint because he'd stood between her and bullets. He was a good man who had run into a burning motel office and saved Bill and Mary.

That was all.

Keep telling yourself that.

Emma sighed.

"Lot going on in that head of yours," Patch said. "Always was. Guess I know why now, considering he ambushed me in my kitchen and tried to stab me."

A tear rolled down the side of her face.

"It's nice you care, darlin'. Otherwise I'd have gotten stuck for no reason. Or a stupid one."

It was the way he said it. One second she was almost out-and-out crying, the next she burst into laughter. Still, tears rolled down her face.

He lifted his hand and squeezed the side of her neck.

"I'm really glad he didn't hurt you too badly," she said. "The world would be a poorer place without you in it."

"Darlin'."

She figured that was about the most she was going to get in terms of a thank you. She smiled at him, thanking God in her heart that Patch hadn't been killed—or kidnapped—by Aaron Jones. She genuinely didn't know what she would do if he was dead. The diner would never be the same. Nor this town. Or her.

Patch had become a mentor in the short time she'd known him.

And a friend.

"Knock, knock." A perky looking nurse stuck her head in. "Are you Ellie?"

It took Emma a second to realize that was the name she'd used when she showed up here. The name Patch knew was a fake.

She said, "Yes."

"Kerri is awake. She's asking for you."

Emma turned back to Patch. "I'll be back shortly." Hopefully she could avoid the sheriff in the hallway. It wasn't far to Kerri's room, and Patch could tell Mint where she'd gone.

She followed the nurse to the end of the hall, and they turned the corner.

"Right here."

This wasn't the right room. Had they moved Kerri? "Oh, but—"

The nurse said, "You should hurry."

Emma stepped into…the stairwell?

The door slammed behind her and echoed against the concrete stairs and walls.

"Took her long enough."

Emma spun around. Aaron Jones stood in front of her, a smug look on his face.

Holding a gun.

Chapter 12

Mint didn't bother smiling at the sheriff, who would know it was fake. "Unfortunately my client requires confidentiality." He didn't need the sheriff seeing Emma and realizing what this was—or arresting her.

"Of course they do." The man wasn't convinced. Mint was sort of surprised the sheriff hadn't put two and two together and gotten four. Yet. The man had talked with Emma at the motel. He'd also likely seen her face on the wires. News broadcast or otherwise. Or, the sheriff of this county just didn't watch TV and wasn't online all that much. The official notice of the FBI wanting to speak with Emma Burroughs may not have hit his desk yet. But anytime now he was going to connect the dots with national news and the woman he knew as the diner waitress, Ellie.

The sheriff said, "Anything you can give me on this waitress attack and the fire?"

"I can tell you they're all connected." Mint pulled out his phone and swiped to a picture of Aaron Jones. "This is the guy we're looking for."

The sheriff frowned at the picture. "And the woman you were with at the motel. Ellie, I think. From the diner."

Mint nodded. He'd concede that. "She's part of what the client wants from us. That guy has it in for her, and we're here to keep her safe while we find him."

"Good."

This guy was so far from the twisted machinations of a DC blackmailer that Mint would find it refreshing. If he wasn't completely astounded.

"I might look and sound like an old-time hick county sheriff, Mr. Malone. But that doesn't mean I operate the same way."

"Understood." Mint nodded. He'd given the sheriff his real name, his real ID, after the motel fire. As a gesture of good faith. It meant official record would be tied to Double Down, but they weren't trying to hide. Not even from the blackmailer.

That wasn't the point of what they were doing here. Plus, often it was easier to operate in plain sight than try to stay under the radar—under cover of darkness—and still be effective in their mission.

The sheriff's cell beeped. One of those old flip phones, completing the image of a man set in his ways who hadn't quite yet accepted the digital age. Mint didn't much appreciate the digital age either, but it was necessary for his job to have a smart phone. So long as that phone had been doctored by Double Down not to give away his location, or anything else he didn't want someone to know.

Two things happened then.

First, a nurse turned the corner at the end of the hall. Her face was smug, and she stuffed a wad of folded bills down the front of her scrubs top. He'd never understood women who stored personal items in their bras, but he also wasn't going to think too much about it.

Second, Patch opened the door to his room and hopped out holding one ankle off the ground as he looked around. He caught Mint's gaze. "Got a minute?"

Mint nodded.

The sheriff didn't object to his getting up, so he went over to the diner owner. "What's up?"

"Weird feeling. Something didn't sit right after that nurse said Kerri was awake. Can't shake the feeling."

Mint turned before he'd even finished talking and hurried after the nurse. His own injuries made it so he couldn't go all that fast, but this was a busy hospital. They probably had rules like they did back in school, about not running in the hall. "Hey!"

She glanced over her shoulder, saw him coming and let out a squeal.

"Where is she?"

"What? Who?"

"Don't play me. I invented that game." Mint folded his arms across his chest. Firstly it served the purpose of making her think he was less of a threat, but still reminding her he was huge. Secondly, it would keep him from giving in to the urge to throttle her. "Who paid you and what for?"

"Fine. It's just a prank." She rolled her eyes. "Big deal. The guy wanted to surprise his girl, so he had me bring her to the stairwell."

Mint leaned forward. "If he kills her, that's on you."

"What?"

She continued to sputter, but he didn't wait around to explain more. Mint yanked the handle on the stairwell door and had to make the decision—up or down. He chose down, considering Aaron likely still wanted Emma in DC taking the rap for the murder he'd committed.

He raced down the stairwell, praying she would be okay. That she wasn't dead, or hurt in a way she'd never recover. He had been all over the world. He'd seen what men could do to women, and sometimes it was worse than death. Praying was all the power he had, because there was nothing else he could do. Bradley and Steve both said it worked. Mint figured he didn't have anything else to lose. If God was real, then He could kick in now. When it counted.

He rushed out into the parking lot, and the first bullet sent him to the ground. It took a second to realize he'd reacted. He hadn't been shot.

"Mint!" She screamed his name, fear and terror in her voice.

He did a push up and got his feet under him. *Please, please, please.* It was like a mantra in his head. Or another prayer.

He raced after her and saw Aaron dragging Emma to a car.

Aaron lifted his arm and squeezed off another shot. Emma screamed and clapped her hands on her ears. But the damage would've already been done.

Mint dived behind an old Toyota and pulled his own weapon. He lifted up and fired a shot into Aaron's back tire.

Aaron moved to fire again.

Emma shoved at his arm.

Mint ducked, and the bullet hit the front of the car instead of the spot where his head had just been. Aaron wasn't a professional at this. But that didn't make him not a deadly threat. He was desperate and that meant unpredictable. Faced with Mint's military training, and the tactics Steve drilled into them, meant Mint didn't exactly know how this was going to go.

Emma screamed, part roar. He looked over the trunk of the Toyota and saw her wrestling him for the gun. Mint rounded the back of the car and made his way over, gun up.

"Back up, Aaron."

The stairwell door opened behind him, and Mint heard multiple sets of boots coming up behind him. More problems, or assistance?

"Put it down!"

"Drop the gun!"

The sheriff and another man. Security maybe.

Aaron sneered. He shifted his hold on Emma and got her in front of him.

"No. Let her go," Mint demanded. "She isn't your ticket out of here." He continued, hoping Aaron would do what he said, "So let her go, and lay your gun down. It's over, Aaron."

"It'll never be over," he said, now gripping Emma's neck in a way he could see wasn't good for her. "You think he'll stop coming? No one crosses him."

"Bradley and Rachel did. They're good now."

Aaron burst into humorless laughter. "Just a matter of time."

The sheriff moved into the corner of Mint's vision to his left. "Drop the gun, and let the lady go. Then put your hands on your head."

"I'm not going to *surrender*. I'll be dead before I hit whatever excuse you have for county lockup in this town."

. . .

Black spots had begun to invade her vision. Like a nightmare, she couldn't blink them away. Unconsciousness threatened to swallow her up. All she could see was Mint, a bunch of guns and sparking blackness.

Aaron's grip on her neck tightened. A whimper emerged from her throat. He was really going to use her as a hostage. And for what? He was hardly negotiating for them to let him go. The man seemed so sure of his fate. He'd hurt Kerri and Patch. He'd shot at Mint. People all over were looking for him.

It just made Emma so mad that he could think to cause so much damage and then…what? Get away with it? Wasn't that what he would be doing by resigning himself to death? What lay beyond wasn't exactly going to be a picnic for him.

She tried to shift in his grasp and kicked out with her foot. Around her they continued to shout, but she couldn't make out the words.

And then Aaron jerked once.

His body crumpled to the ground.

Before Emma could figure out what happened, Mint caught her in his arms. She knew it was him from the feel, and smell, of…his *shirt*. The warmth made her shudder, her face against the soft material over his shoulder.

He caught her up, lifting her into his arms. "Let's get you out of here. Have a doctor look at you."

A whimper escaped her throat. All the noise she could conjure up in that moment.

"No?" He almost chuckled. "I think you just took years off my life. If Perkins hadn't taken that shot, I would have, and it wouldn't have been nearly as neat. You're a very lucky woman. If I didn't know better, I'd say there was someone upstairs looking out for you."

A door slammed, and then his voice was echoing in the enclosed space. Emma opened her eyes. The stairwell. "I can walk."

"You can. Doesn't mean I'm going to let you." He paused. "I know I'm babbling right now, but like I said, you took years off my life. Give me this."

"Okay." She didn't exactly know what he meant. But if he wanted to carry her, who was she to argue? "Can we go?"

"You need to get seen by a doctor. If I can do that without the sheriff catching up to us, wanting to chat through what just happened, then I'm going to see to it."

"No." Exhaustion weighed on her until she could barely make out more than, "Go."

Mint sighed. She felt it move through his chest. He pushed through a door, and they were in the lobby area. Then he carried her outside and all the way across the parking lot. "Put me down, Mint."

His lips curled up. "I'm good. Almost there."

She wanted to roll her eyes, but that had taken the rest of her strength. She woke up in the backseat of his car with him driving, shifted and tried to stretch in the cramped space.

"You awake?"

"Yeah." The word was little more than a sigh.

"Give me a second. I'll pull over and you can get in front."

The rhythm of the car tires on the road was almost soothing. She said, "My dad took me on road trips." Where that thought came from, she didn't know.

"Mine took me to the local bar. I'd wait in the car while he got sloshed, and then he'd have me drive home. Didn't get caught doing it until the summer after my thirteenth birthday."

"Mint." She lifted her gaze high enough to see him shake his head.

"Don't, Em. I don't know why I told you that, and I don't wanna talk about it."

"'Kay."

He reached back, then glanced back for a second, and squeezed her arm. "Thanks." He pulled over at a gas station and got her some coffee. When he settled back in the front seat, her on the passenger side, she said, "What happened?"

"Perkins had a shot. She took it. Don't think the sheriff is too happy, but since she has federal credentials, he's going to have a hard time arguing with her. Even if it was a judgment call."

"Aaron is dead?"

He nodded. "One shot, one kill. I couldn't do it because there was too much risk of hitting you. She was behind you and to the side, so she had a clear shot of Aaron's head. It worked because you didn't move."

"Too busy passing out."

His brow furrowed. "You okay?"

She sipped the coffee rather than answer him. "This isn't over, is it?"

He stared at her rather than answer her question. Emma finished her coffee in the silence, concentrating on each muscle group and getting it to relax. Her hands shook through the release of adrenaline. She catalogued the new aches and pains she had. The wound in her arm, considerably less warm now that she was on antibiotics. But added to the bruises she was gaining with every passing hour, she didn't have a body part that wasn't sore.

Was Aaron Jones really dead? Part of her couldn't believe it.

"Convince me I shouldn't have taken you to a doctor back there." His voice was soft. Quiet. Like for once in his life, he might actually be unsure of himself.

"I'm..." she was going to say "okay" but that would be a lie. "I don't need a doctor. I need to cry for two hours and then nap for a week."

He started to smile.

"Oh, and a strawberry milkshake." She gave him a pointed look. "Great coffee chaser. Doesn't matter what time it is."

The smile turned into a chuckle. "This you in denial?"

"No. This is me enjoying a moment between the chaos, almost dying and running for my life. Realizing Kerri is safe, and Patch will be fine. Aaron is dead."

"You think the blackmailer will come after you now?"

"I don't know what he'll do."

"What does he have that he's holding over you? I need to understand the potential for fallout this could create."

She nodded. "You'll need to manage that as part of your mission."

He placed his hand over hers. "It's more than just the mission now. You know that, right?"

Emma thought about how it had felt, being held in his arms. How he'd told her that tiny snippet about his father—about his past.

He frowned and turned away. She'd taken too long. Emma bit her lip, then said, "Mint?" When he glanced at her then, she said, "I know." Putting all the feeling she didn't have words for in her gaze, praying he understood. The nascent attraction. How she felt, surrounded by his strength. All of it was something she didn't know how she was going to live without when this was over. When he got back to his life, and she got to work building a new one that would hopefully give her what seemed to be missing all this time.

She'd thought getting answers from the senator was what would've filled the part of her that had always seemed empty. Finally, she would know the truth. Then she'd have been able to move on.

Now? Emma couldn't help thinking that maybe life had brought her here instead—to Mint—for a reason.

He leaned closer. "I'm glad that you're all right."

"For now, at least." She felt her lips curl up.

"Let's plan on keeping it that way. Deal?"

She nodded, so tired.

Mint closed the distance between them. He was going to kiss her? At the last second he shifted his head, and his lips touched the corner of her mouth. Her cheek. She felt his intake of breath and shut her eyes at the sensation of his skin against hers. A tiny touch, but she felt it all the way to her bones.

How was she going to let him go?

Chapter 13

Mint parked by the RV and rounded the car before Emma opened her eyes. He pulled her door open and crouched. Touched her shoulder. "Hey."

She sucked in a breath and shifted as she blinked away the fog of fatigue. She looked around. "Oh."

Wishing she was somewhere else? Mint didn't know if that was disappointment or something else. Either way, they were here. He held out his hand. "Ready?"

She nodded, and he helped her inside. One of the guys—Drew—was on the computer with headphones. A video chat with one of the team members still in Virginia. He flicked two fingers in Mint's direction when they climbed the steps into the RV. Mint led Emma to the table, and she slid onto the bench seat. He made her a cup of tea, heavy on the honey, and set it in front of her.

She smiled up at him. "Thanks."

He slid in opposite her and grabbed his iPad, which he used to compose an email to the boss explaining what had happened. Steve was likely not going to be happy with the fact Aaron Jones was dead—if he didn't already know.

He gave her fifteen minutes to drink the tea and zone out. Collect herself. She'd been through more than one traumatizing event in the past few days, he wasn't about to push her farther than she'd already been shoved. The people she cared about who'd been hurt were all safe in the hospital, healing. The motel could be rebuilt. The diner would re-open when there was enough staff to do so.

What would happen to Emma was up to her.

"What now?"

The words were so soft he almost didn't hear them. Mint locked the screen on the iPad and put it on a shelf behind him. "We're waiting for the team to regroup. Until then you can just rest. Get something to eat, take a nap—"

She started to shake her head before he'd even finished. "I don't need you to coddle me. I'm fine. Tell me what's really happening."

Mint stared at her, mentally logging the fact he was going to have to work harder if he wanted to compartmentalize what she knew. Especially when each piece of information he gave her would add to her stress level. Then he said, "There's an FBI agent on the way."

She shot him a look. "A real one?"

He nodded. "Agent Walker. He's been our point person with the bureau since Rachel Harris was kidnapped. He saw your statement video, and he got on a plane straight away. He wants to speak with you about what happened to the senator, but he's also interested in the blackmailer."

Her face blanked. "Ah." She shifted her backpack closer and hugged it against her side. Protecting herself, using it as a shield. Or protecting what was inside.

"You had to know this would come out."

"I was doing what I thought I had to, but I was also going to find out the truth for myself. To do the right thing. That's why I went back to the senator's house that night. Only Aaron was there, so I never got the chance to ask him about it."

Mint leaned forward a little. Not that his colleague was listening, but he just needed to be closer to her for a second. "Whatever it is, no one is going to judge you. And we're also not going to be surprised. This is just another obstacle to overcome, like all the others."

Emma's eyes flashed. "You can say that because it doesn't affect you."

"Whatever the fallout, we'll deal." When she shot him another look, he went on. "Remember Rachel and Alexis? Their loyalty was stronger than the plan the blackmailer had. It was messy, but in the end they won out because they stuck together. That's in you, Emma. I know it is. Whoever you're protecting, I'm with you. We're going to figure this out, and I promise you now it's going to be okay."

He didn't know that. The truth was, he had no idea what the blackmailer had on her. Their computer tech hadn't been able to find anything in her past that even resembled a skeleton in a closet. The woman was as clean as a person came—and so far from him and his history that it was a little daunting even trying to be on the same team as her. If she found out everything he'd been through, and all he'd done, she would probably run screaming. And yet, she'd proven she had the courage to stick it out even when things got hard.

That protecting the people you loved was more important than career, or even freedom.

Mint's phone buzzed in his back pocket. He pulled it out and saw it was Perkins. He swiped the screen. "Malone."

Emma's lips curled into a small smile at hearing his last name.

He shot her a grin while Perkins said, "We got Aaron Jones's car and the place he's been staying. You want in?"

He said, "Yes," before he even thought through the implications of having to leave Emma at the RV while he joined Perkins in searching through Jones's belongings. Would they even find a link back to the blackmailer among his things? They could hope, but the chance was slim.

Perkins said, "Walker will be there in thirty minutes. I'll hang with Emma while he talks to her, make sure that's all good. You take point on the search."

"Sounds good." It sounded great. Perkins wanted to be here with Walker and Emma—for Walker, or for Emma? She could want to protect their witness. Or she could just want to be the person who stood between the FBI agent and their team business. Mint didn't know which it was, and he figured Perkins would categorically deny anything if he even asked her about it.

"See you soon." She hung up.

Emma's eyebrows lifted. She didn't ask him what the call was about. Probably didn't know if it was okay for her to do that, since she had no involvement in team business past what they'd already told her. A lot of women wouldn't have done that. He'd heard all kinds of stories from the other guys about wives and girlfriends who pestered them with questions until they caved, just to get the torture to stop. A woman who voluntarily allowed a man to keep his own confidence without assuming it was her business as well was a refreshing thing.

If this went farther than acquaintances, would that continue to be the case? Or was Emma the kind of person who suddenly sprouted a different personality when emotions came into play?

It was a risk. Was he willing to take it?

Mint hadn't met anyone in a long time he'd have even thought worth considering. Emma had proven she was strong. But could she handle all he would put on her, or would she buckle under the weight of it?

He said, "Perkins is headed here. She'll stay with you while you talk to Agent Walker. I have to head out for a while. Take a look at Aaron Jones's things. I'll be back though."

She nodded, biting her lips together. Not happy at the thought he wouldn't be here? He couldn't help the way that settled in him. The idea she wanted him close, at least while she dealt with hard things.

He put his hand over hers. "You'll do great."

And he would get an update from Perkins after. Because whatever it was, the information could potentially change everything they knew about Emma Burroughs.

He just hoped it would help them find the blackmailer.

. . .

There was definitely something going on between Walker and Perkins. Emma gave him a small smile as she watched Walker settle into the bench seat where Mint had sat. Before he left her. She wasn't going to be mad about that. Right now there was enough swirling in her head that she didn't have room for whether or not she was disappointed. Or how else she might feel about the fact Mint didn't want to stay and hear her story.

Maybe it was better that way. She might be able to get through this a little more easily if she didn't have to look at his face while she did it. And she definitely didn't want to see any kind of disappointment on his face. She hadn't even done anything.

And she wanted him to think she'd done the right thing. That she'd made the right choices like Rachel and Alexis.

Those two seemed to have impressed him. Which only made her wonder what he'd think when he found out just how connected Emma was to them— both, now that Bradley and Alexis were married.

Walker placed a digital voice recorder on the table between them and switched it on. He did some preliminary talking—who he was, who she was, and why they were there. Emma waited until he said, "Shall we start."

She nodded.

"Aloud, please. For the recorder."

"Yes."

He smiled. "Thank you."

The man was probably in his forties. His hair had thinned on the temples, and what was there had a silver tint. His suit was nice, but not so nice it would look weird for an FBI agent to be that well-dressed.

Along the RV, in the kitchen area, Perkins sipped her coffee. The woman was basically glaring at him over the rim of her mug while she did so. Emma had sensed a little…frostiness between them. She couldn't help wondering what, if anything, had gone on before now between the two of them.

But she couldn't dwell on that thought. Walker made her go over everything that had happened the night the senator died. Then he asked her about every day since then. When she explained a couple of the things Mint had done, his eyebrows lifted. Other than that, he didn't have any real reaction. The man was a professional. He wanted the job done, and he wasn't going to allow his emotional energy to be expended on something that had nothing to do with him. Except for the fact that it happened to be his job to connect the dots.

"Would you like to take a break or just carry on?"

Emma said, "I'm good with getting it all over with."

"Very well."

Perkins's eyes shone with something that looked a whole lot like pride.

"It was about three months ago. I got home from a movie that I'd gone to with a college friend of mine. There was a note that had been slipped under my door." She took a breath. "Inside the envelope was a photograph. It was old."

"What do you mean, old?"

"I figured it was taken around the seventies. Though I can't pinpoint an exact date. The paper itself was worn. But I'd never seen it before. It was…" She swallowed. "Indelicate." That was an understatement. And judging from the look that passed between Walker and Perkins, they caught what she implied.

Perkins started, "Do you—"

Walker held up a finger, stopping her. "We'll get to that. Ms. Burroughs, what happened after the picture showed up?"

"The next day I got an email. It told me that a reimbursement request was going to come in for one of the senator's staffers, and I was to approve it no matter what. No questions asked. Or the details of the photograph would be made public."

"Emma," Perkins said softly. "What was on the photo?"

She glanced up at the other woman. "Do you know who my mother is?"

"Conservative radio talk show host."

She nodded. "Family values. A republican bent."

"Honesty. Integrity."

Emma said, "I think it was around when she was in college, but she's never told me anything about having a 'wild' phase." No one wanted to learn that about their parent in a way that was that visual. And something she could never, ever unsee.

Perkins said, "And if it got out, she would lose all credibility. Regardless of the fact it happened decades ago."

"People don't care that everyone makes mistakes. They don't care that we're all human. They just want someone to make them feel better, and that person ends up getting crucified all over social media and the internet. Especially a public face like my mom. Maybe she only smoked pot one time and made one bad choice about who to spend an evening with."

It had certainly shed a new light on the fact there might be an underlying reason as to how particular her mom was about public appearance. Everything she said and did, what she wore, and how she got her hair done, was all about presenting the right front. Emma had often wondered why she couldn't just be herself. Wasn't that enough?

Maybe her mom didn't like who she was underneath all the superficial things. Or she was ashamed of what she'd done, and who she'd done it with.

Walker said, "So you approved the reimbursement request."

"I didn't want to," Emma said. "But I figured, 'what harm could it do?' Two weeks later there was another photo. Aaron Jones showed up the next day to tell me what he wanted me to do. That's when I knew it wasn't just a one-time thing." She didn't want to tell them this next part, but she figured she was going to have to if they wanted a full picture of what had happened.

She took a deep breath. "My mother had an affair with Senator Sadler. That photo had a date on it, and the date was significant enough that I stole the senator's toothbrush and had a DNA test done." She tugged the backpack closer and pulled out the bloody envelope. She'd never even gotten to tell him what she knew. Or to see his reaction. Would he have even been pleased?

He hadn't been a nice man. His son had been self-centered and gotten caught up between his cousin Bradley and Bradley's wife Alexis—and not in a good way.

She slid the paper out and showed it to Walker. "Senator Sadler was my father."

Perkins said, "Bradley and Rachel's uncle is your father?"

She nodded.

Walker said, "Do you think Sadler knew that when he hired you?"

Emma blinked. She hadn't even thought of that. "I—" She didn't even know how to answer, because she didn't know. Had Sadler known, all along, that she was the product of an affair he'd had years ago with Isabella Burroughs?

Perkins blew out a breath. "Emma, did you keep the pictures?"

"Yes. I put them all in a safety deposit box with a printout of the first email and everything else I knew."

Perkins set her mug down. "Emma, can Double Down have access to your safety deposit box?"

"Of course. Do you think it will help?"

"It's a long shot. If he's as good as he seems to be, he's covered all his tracks. But it's worth a try."

Chapter 14

Mint shut the glove box and stood up out of the car. "Nothing."

Craig slammed the door with far more force than was necessary. His teammate was a former Army MP officer. A military cop. He might be good at search and seizure, but anyone would be frustrated right now. He pulled a brown paper bag from the roof that he'd placed there. "I'll get this stuff sent in."

Mint nodded. They'd found a few personal items in the car, but what would that get them other than finding out if Aaron Jones was his real name? It could help. Then again, it might give them nothing but a tragic backstory they didn't want to know. He hoped it would provide a link back to the blackmailer.

If it did, then they could get Emma out of his target range.

His phone beeped. He read Perkins's summary of what Emma had told Agent Walker about the blackmailer. The senator was her biological father. He felt his eyebrows rise. All of this was about protecting her mother? That surprised him, at the same time it didn't really. She had no secrets in her past that could be exploited. And her loyalty to her mother was solid, even though he knew they didn't see eye to eye.

The blackmailer had used the only leverage he had on her, and then asked her to approve reimbursement requests? Something in the senator's business had been dirty. They needed to figure it out.

Double Down had suspected the senator of being the blackmailer at one point. Now it looked like the senator—who was Bradley and Rachel's uncle, though that relationship had been strained as well—had been linked to the blackmailer somehow. It tracked. But they were far from the point where they knew everything.

This was hardly over, even though Aaron Jones was dead. But hopefully they would get enough information that it might garner them an actual lead.

Mint turned and walked into the vacation rental Aaron had paid for with cash, under the name Jay Smith. Built around World War Two, it was totally off the beaten path. The cabinets were likely original. Carpets had been replaced, and tile laid down in the kitchen. Fresh paint.

Dishes piled up in the sink marred the attempt to freshen the place. It smelled vaguely of burned coffee, though how it was even possible to burn a pot of coffee, he didn't know. The bedroom wasn't in a much better state. The linens were half on the floor, half still on the bed, and only one pillow remained. A pile of clothes had been stacked up on the floor in the corner of the room. A tiny attached bathroom had towels on the floor, discarded there.

Aaron Jones badly needed a housekeeper. If he wasn't dead.

"Geez this guy is a slob."

"*Was* a slob," Mint told him.

"True. Suicide by cop." Craig shook his head.

"Gets him out from under suspicion and helps keep the blackmailer's identity a secret."

"Unless he wasn't all that forward-thinking, and he just didn't want to go to jail."

Mint shrugged. They would likely never gain insight into Aaron Jones's state of mind before he forced the sheriff to end his life.

He wandered the room, looking for more than just clothes or toiletries. He searched the drawers then pulled them out. Behind the third one, a phone had been taped to the back. Mint pulled the tape away and set the drawer down.

"Flip phone?" Craig said, crossing the distance between them. "People still use those?"

"I guess so. No Wi-Fi, probably, and maybe no GPS. Easier to stay under the radar, harder to track or trace."

"Yep. This guy knows what he's doing."

Mint flipped the phone open. He ran his thumb across the keys, headed for the power button. The phone screen flashed once, then went dark. "What…"

Instinct had him fling the phone away from him. Two feet from his head, flying across the room, the phone blew up. A localized explosion—couldn't pack that much plastic explosives in the case of a small phone anyway.

The flash of light was bright. The sound was what hit him.

Mint found himself on his back, staring up at the ceiling. His ears rang so loud the pain was blinding. He covered them with his hands, half expecting to find blood trailing down the sides of his face.

He rolled over and found Craig unconscious. Mint felt around his head and found a knot behind one ear. Knocked unconscious by the blast.

Smoke hung in the air.

He got his colleague outside where it was clearer and laid him down on the grass of the front lawn. Didn't want to stumble across anything else blowing up.

A phone that blew up. Who knew what tech it'd had in it? Something able to tell that it wasn't Aaron Jones holding the phone. It had looked completely normal. Smart phones these days could be unlocked with a fingerprint. Maybe he'd triggered the bomb with his thumb. Or Aaron had had to type in a code within a certain amount of time.

Which meant he'd had a direct line to the blackmailer.

It was far too coincidental for it to be anything else—or belong to anyone else. Even given the house was a rental. Aaron Jones definitely worked for the blackmailer. Whoever it was had their sights on Emma, and how she might be useful to him. Or her.

And they were playing for keeps.

Mint loaded Craig into the car, shut the door and drove away. He didn't need the sheriff crawling all over this. The man would likely find Aaron's car and the place he'd been staying eventually. Then he'd find out for himself that the man wasn't hiding anything that could be used to explain any of this. Mint had what he and Craig had collected.

On the drive he called his other colleague, the one who'd been at the RV. When he picked up, Mint said, "Phone exploded. Craig hit his head. I'm bringing him in."

"Copy that."

"I'm two minutes out."

When he pulled into the space behind Perkins's car and Agent Walker's rental, blocking them both in, the door flew open. Drew hopped out, heading straight for Craig, ready to put his field medic training into practice. Behind him, Emma jumped out of the RV.

"Mint!"

She ran to him. For a second he thought she might hug him, but instead she just clung to his arms while he told her what had happened.

"Oh no! I hope he'll be okay."

He squeezed her shoulder. "Get your backpack."

She frowned. Her mouth opened, but he didn't have time for questions. Even if they were valid. He said, "Now, please."

Emma did as he asked. Drew took Craig into the RV and, when Emma emerged with her backpack, Walker came out right behind her.

"Want to tell me what's going on, Mint?" The FBI agent looked less than impressed.

"Emma and I are getting out of here."

. . .

"We are?" She glanced between Mint and Walker, feeling like she was missing something. Did she need to tell Mint everything Walker had recorded her saying? Maybe that wasn't what this was about, but something else. "Did something happen to Craig that makes you think I'm in danger?"

"I don't want you where this guy, whoever it is, can get to you."

Okay, well, when he said it like that, it made her go all mushy. Perkins caught the look on her face and cracked a smile. Walker didn't seem to even notice. He was too busy glaring at Mint. "Then I'll get her in FBI protective custody."

"Except," Mint said, "the part about me getting her where he *can't* get to her."

"You think one of my people is going to give her up to this blackmailer?"

"I think he knows things, and he's prepared to use anything to get what he wants. And I think everyone can be bought for the right price."

She blurted out, "You do?" Before she could think to hold it back.

"I'm not even taking the chance." Mint's face was dark. Not scary, just very serious. "We're going off the grid where we can't be tracked. Or traced. And Double Down is going to get to the bottom of this."

They were going alone?

Mint glanced at her, a frown on his face. Exactly what type of girl did he think she was? They needed to discuss this if he thought she would just…disappear with him and get up to who-knew-what.

She knew how these things ended up. And she'd know he was only there to protect her. Her heart would soften, faced with his strength in such close proximity. The last thing she needed was to let her feelings get all wrapped up in him. Maybe he would even make a move just because she was there, and they were alone, and things would get messed up.

And as…nice as it might be, it wasn't like it was going to last. Mint was just doing his job. He wasn't thinking about long term relationships. Though, after all this, she was going to have to reassess some of her five and ten-year goals—and admit to herself that she did want a relationship. Not just a cat.

"I'm going to make sure you're safe," he said to her, then glanced at Perkins. "And Double Down is going to go through everything we've got. You can call me when you've figured out who it is."

Perkins's eyebrows rose. "You're abdicating?"

"No." He shook his head. "I'm prioritizing. And we need to keep Emma safe while we get a lead that will get us a result. If I'm trying to figure out the connection between Emma, Aaron and the blackmailer, then I'll be distracted when I should be focusing on her security."

It was kind of flattering. She wanted to know what it would be like to have a man like him *focused* on her. She shivered a little bit.

Then her thoughts went back to those pictures she'd seen of her mom. The two of them weren't the same kind of woman, but that didn't mean Emma had no vices. She knew where her weaknesses were, and she honestly regretted the fact she and her mom hadn't been able to talk the way she wanted. Emma should have been able to stand up for herself and tell her mom what she really wanted. Instead, her mom had dictated to her. She probably even thought Emma appreciated it.

Because Emma had never told her otherwise.

They should have been there for each other, the way a mom and daughter could be. Maybe she should have just talked to her mom, instead of jumping straight to the DNA test. Her mom had a reason for being the way she was. Maybe she just needed a friend who saw beneath the surface—the façade she wanted everyone to see—and appreciated her anyway.

Drew stuck his head out of the RV. "Craig is fine, in case anyone is wondering."

"Concussion?" Mint called back.

"Mild at most."

He nodded. "Thanks."

Perkins folded her arms. Walker didn't look much happier. Emma didn't know how to resolve the conflict happening between them. She'd been out of her depth since this whole thing started. But she was really glad Craig wasn't hurt too badly.

Mint motioned her toward his car. "Let's go."

They walked over there, Perkins and Walker lagging behind.

"I don't suppose I can convince you to at least let us tag along."

Mint shot Walker a look for that.

"Or let us know where you might be headed?"

Mint looked at Perkins. "Tell Steve I'm going up north. He'll know what that means." Then he patted his pocket. "I have my cell," he told Walker. "Perkins can get ahold of me."

Walker blanched. "Then you'll be traceable. That's not under the radar. That's exposing Emma to anyone who is looking for her."

Mint shook his head, but it was Perkins who said, "Special phones."

Walker lifted his arms and let them fall back to his sides.

Mint said, "I'm counting on you." He shifted his gaze from Perkins to the FBI agent. "Both of you. Find this guy."

Perkins said, "We will."

Mint's whole body jerked. His head whipped around and up, and he focused on the sky for a second.

Emma heard a whistling sound in the air before she saw anything.

Mint rushed for the RV. "Drew, get out of there!"

Perkins rushed after him.

Emma went to go as well, but Walker stopped her.

Something gray dropped out of the sky and hit the RV. The whole thing tore apart. Metal ripped as flames engulfed the entire thing. The sound was deafening, like the roar of an oncoming train.

She landed on her back before she even realized the sound had hit her. Walker landed on top of her. He shifted, shielding her torso and head from the explosion with his own body. She tried to suck in a full breath. It got stuck.

As soon as she managed to get a lungful of air, Emma screamed it out. "Mint!"

Perkins.

Craig and Drew had been *inside*.

Walker caught her chin. He looked down at her face and winced, then mouthed, *Stay here*. No way. She got up when he did, stumbling as she made her way to the flaming wreckage. She couldn't even hear anything. Just a loud buzzing and the feeling of way too much pressure pressing against her head. Like a nightmare sinus infection.

Walker caught up Perkins, lifting her into his arms. She was passed out, covered in cuts. Her clothes singed.

Emma raced to where she thought Mint might be and saw him a few feet away on his front. She didn't want to roll him over but did it anyway. A gash on his head. She patted his cheek, even though he might not appreciate her touching him. If his ears were anything like hers, he couldn't hear her talk anyway. When his eyelids fluttered, she smiled down at him.

Mint lifted his hand. His fingers slid into her hair, and his palm slid along her jaw. He tugged on her head, putting enough pressure into it so she moved closer. Then he touched his lips to hers. He let her go and sat up, swayed and put a hand down to stop the momentum that threatened to lay him flat again.

Beyond him she saw a figure dressed in black, headed their way.

For a second she thought it was help and lifted her hand to wave them over.

Then she saw the automatic weapon. The helmet. The others. Dressed like SWAT, or something similar, none of them had an indication of that on their clothes. No designation whatsoever.

"Mint."

He shoved at her even as he got to his feet. The balance wasn't there, but he moved her toward the car anyway. "Go." The word was muffled, but she understood enough when he said, "Run."

Chapter 15

Emma stumbled. Mint pushed all the pain and fatigue in his body down to a small corner of his mind, caught her around the waist and got them both moving. Perkins lay on the ground, Walker right beside her. The fed looked up, fear flashing on his face in the split second before he got his gun up and started firing.

Craig and Drew had both been in the RV. Now it was nothing but a burning pile of fiberglass and plastic—the debris from the explosion. There wasn't even time to search for their bodies.

Bullets exploded around them. Mint pulled Emma to a crouch behind the remnants of a picnic table. He winced when his knee hit the ground, but forced his thoughts away from the injuries he had sustained and pulled out his gun. He could feel the wet trailing down the side of his face. He lifted up to see over the edge and then ducked back down.

Three men, hired guns. Mercenaries probably. Or dirty cops. Feds. Their identities were a matter for later. The blackmailer had somehow managed to get a UAV retasked to American soil so that he could destroy the RV. Which meant both that he had the power to do that *and* that he knew where they were. Then he'd gotten these men to show up here immediately after.

To finish the job.

Whether that task meant killing Mint, or Emma, or the FBI agent with them, or all of them in one go—rendering Double Down practically destroyed and definitely scrambling to get a footing against this guy in the aftermath—Mint didn't know. And there wasn't time now to find out.

He lifted up again, fired one shot and downed the man to his left.

Two to go.

Walker kept firing. Drawing their attention his direction while he kept them from getting closer.

Mint fired off another shot, but missed. The man fired back. The bullet hit the wood right below his face. He ducked behind it, glanced long enough at Emma to see she was hunkered down and shifted to see Walker. He was totally exposed, covering Perkins with his body. Walker lifted up, firing. He took out the second man, leaving one for them to deal with.

Two friends down. Had the third man bailed, or was he hiding? Biding his time so he could personally take the rest of them out. After the job was done he would call the blackmailer and report in, saying that it was finished.

"Stay here." He waited until Emma made eye contact with him. "Do not move."

She nodded. No hesitation. She understood, and she wasn't going to argue.

Mint checked the area around her. He needed to cover her even while he checked the immediate area and went to make sure Perkins and Walker were all right. That led to him planting his knees beside his teammate—ouch—and scanning the area while he said, "How is she?"

"I'm fine." She didn't sound fine, she sounded mad.

Mint said, "Okay. Walker?" He made eye contact with the federal agent, then Perkins, for a second each.

Walker said, "He's still out there."

"I'll get him."

"Yes," Perkins said. "Get him." Still mad. Because she'd been caught in the blast, forcing Walker to cover her, and it dinged her pride?

Mint checked Emma again. So long as she was stuck there, and he could keep an eye on her—make sure the guy didn't sneak up behind her—she would be good. Physically, at least. Emotionally was another story.

He scanned again for the guy, but couldn't see him. Had he left? Not much of a help to someone who needed a job done if the hired help bailed when things got hairy. He'd never have been hired by Double Down. Which was likely why he was here, hired by the blackmailer.

"Emma?"

"Yeah?"

"Come over here and sit with Perkins."

She moved immediately. Mint covered her, making sure the missing man wasn't going to pop up and put a bullet in her. When she hit the ground beside him, he got up and began his perimeter search.

His phone rang in his pocket, but Mint ignored it. Even while his hands itched to pull it out. It was likely Steve, who had probably seen what happened. Or figured it out somehow.

With the immediate area cleared, he widened the search. They'd come from the northeast. Probably had a vehicle stashed there. Mint hadn't heard the approach because of the explosion, and his ears weren't all the way back to normal, but he also hadn't heard anyone leaving.

Mint rounded one of the vehicles, his ears pricking. But over what? He slowed, keeping an eye on the three people he was covering. Took two steps.

Gravel crunched under his feet.

A shift behind him brought his whole body around.

"Whoa." The sheriff lifted a hand. "Easy there. Wanna lower that?"

Mint blew out the breath he'd been holding. But he didn't allow the tension in his body to dissipate. He lowered the gun slightly, but by no means all the way. "There's a gunman possibly still hanging around."

"Copy that." The sheriff started to turn.

"And we need an ambulan—"

A shot rang out.

The sheriff's body jerked, and he dropped to the ground. Dead.

Mint ducked. "Down. Everyone down!" They were probably already taking cover, but he needed to say it.

"Mint!" Emma's cry rang in the air.

He crouch walked over to her. Walker had pulled Perkins behind his car so she was no longer exposed. He studied Emma's gaze, assessing her state in a few seconds. She was holding on, but she wouldn't be able to do that forever.

"Take Emma and go."

He turned to Walker. "What?"

"I'm good." The other man had his weapon out. He was trained.

"Me, too." Perkins's voice was far steadier now. "We're good, Mint. Take Emma. Get her safe."

Mint didn't stay much longer after that. And he didn't argue. He led her to the car.

A bullet pinged off the hood. Mint got the door open and slid across the seat to start the engine. Emma climbed in behind him.

He didn't want to leave Perkins or Walker. Didn't want to leave the RV wreckage when two of his coworkers were dead. Or the sheriff.

Tears blurred his vision. He coughed and willed the emotion away. Emma's hand touched his arm. He wanted to push her away, pretend he wasn't feeling anything. Ignore the softness of her touch. Stick with the tactic that he was strong enough, that nothing bothered him.

He shifted into the seat. "Stay down. We're getting out of here."

She got the door shut, and he pulled out.

Five minutes later, when he glanced in the rearview, his heart sank.

"What?" Emma looked back as well.

He gritted his teeth, then said, "We're being followed."

．　．　．

"Is there anything you want me to do?" She wanted to look back again, but how would that help? She was way out of her depth. Explosions and gunmen. Two guys that worked with Mint were dead, and they'd seemed like nice people. She'd wanted to get to know them. To learn those things about Mint that only coworkers knew. And that didn't even touch whatever family or friends they had, those who would be grieving the loss soon enough.

She sucked in a shuddering breath and tried to hold it together. Like Mint was doing.

"Mint."

He glanced at her, like she'd snapped him out of his thoughts. "What was that?"

"I asked if there's anything you want me to do."

"Oh, sorry." He thought for a second, then pulled out his cell phone and handed it to her. "Two-six, seven-five."

She unlocked his phone.

"Okay, Google." His voice was slightly louder now. "Call Steve."

She didn't even have to do anything, and the phone in her hand placed the call.

"Put it on speaker."

She nodded and pressed the button. The voice on the other end said, "Preston."

"It's Mint."

There was a quick pause, then the man said, "What happened?"

Emma shut her eyes while Mint relayed everything—and the fact that even now they had a tail on them. The last man. Biding his time, determined to finish the job he'd started.

She glanced out the back window again but couldn't see anything sinister. She didn't even know what she was looking for.

"He wants to cripple Double Down and stall out any hope we have of figuring out who he is," Steve said over the phone.

Mint replied, "Protecting himself and whatever he wants to do."

How on earth were they supposed to figure out what the blackmailer was up to? Emma figured he would probably expose the truth about her mother's past choices soon enough, if he hadn't already, and she just hadn't seen it because she didn't have a phone right now.

Small blessings in the middle of everything that was going on.

Kind of like being here with Mint. Even knowing their lives were on the line, she still felt a measure of safety just being around him. He'd given up working on their assignment to leave with her and keep her protected. But that had been before the RV exploded.

"So what's your plan?" Steve asked, his voice sad in a way she could tell he was holding back emotion. And she'd never even met the man.

Mint said, "Stick it out. Get him where I want him and force him to make a move. Then I'll take him out."

"I'd feel better if you had backup."

"The sheriff is down. Walker is with Perkins."

"I'm sending you an address. It's the closest airport. By the time you get there, I'll have a plane on the tarmac waiting to bring the two of you back to Virginia."

"You want us to come home?" Mint asked.

"We need to regroup, figure out our next move. You need to get off the ground in Colorado and head back here." Steve paused. "I'll talk to Walker and Perkins about clean up there."

She sucked in a breath. "He'll know." Emma had to say it. She knew it was true down to her bones, and nothing in her could deny it. Whatever move they made, the blackmailer would know.

Steve said, "I have people on the plane. When you pull in, they'll protect you. And I've covered your tracks as much as I can, chartering it using a shell company not linked to Double Down. Your names won't be listed on the manifest. Once you lose the guy behind you, you'll be home free."

She figured he'd only explained that because of everything that'd happened. Maybe all the stress and anxiety was there in her voice. He probably didn't explain himself to that extent normally. Still, she couldn't let go of the fear.

She said, "He sent that...thing."

Mint glanced at her. "It was a UAV."

She didn't exactly know what that was, but it kind of proved her point. "He'll *know*."

"You need to trust us." Mint squeezed her hand for a second, then moved it back to grip the wheel. "It'll be okay."

Emma shook her head. "There's a murderer right behind us. I'm not going to be okay."

She didn't even want to think about what Mint's intentions were with the guy. She'd seen far too much bloodshed. Were more people going to die? Even if they were bad, was she supposed to be happy about death? It wasn't ever going to make her feel better. Not even if it was them vs. her. She just wasn't built that way.

"Emma," Steve said, jogging her from her thoughts. "What did the blackmailer ask you to approve?"

It took her a second to realize he was talking about the reimbursement requests. "One of the senator's staff members had put a deposit down on the caterer for a charity fundraiser the senator was having." She thought over what day it was, realizing she'd already lost track. "It's this weekend, though it's likely been canceled now."

"Anything else?"

She thought for a second, then said, "The other reimbursement request was for the same event. For the cake decorator."

"Both food," Mint said. "And both related to this event."

"So what does a blackmailer want with a charity fundraiser?"

Emma couldn't figure out the answer to that.

"Emma can send you a link, get you all the info." Mint glanced at her, a question on his face.

She nodded. "I will."

Mint grabbed the phone. "Gotta go." He hung up, the car drifting to the center line for a second before he caught it. Then he took a turn at the last minute. Emma looked back to see a black truck do the same thing, with a screech of its tires. Mint drove a half mile and then pulled around the back of a closed down store. Not just shut, but permanently closed.

He pulled over, close to the wall so that she'd scrape brick if she opened her door. Boxing her in? Or cocooning her in that web of safety he wove around her.

Emma's hands shook as she rubbed down the legs of her dirty jeans. She didn't even want to think what her hair looked like right now… She shut that thought off. Not wanting to be *that* kind of woman, even as a distraction technique when the situation got really crazy. Her mom cared that much about her appearance, even when her life was out of control. Maybe especially during those times.

Emma needed to figure out what kind of woman she was going to be. Maybe she should already know that, but surely some people had to wait until their late twenties to discover the kind of person they were.

Mint said, "Head down. Don't get out, no matter what you hear."

She didn't meet his eyes, not wanting to see what was there. Or for him to see what was in hers. She was close to the edge. About to lose it. She knew herself well enough to know it was only a matter of time before she finally gave in to the stress and anxiety of everything that'd happened and ugly cry for, like, days.

He slipped out of the car.

The truck engine roared. Emma didn't turn back. She hunkered down in the seat, her breath coming fast now. He was going to kill that guy. She didn't want the man to kill her, but the idea that Mint was going to end someone's life, just to protect her. A sob rolled up her throat. She let it out, her body bucking. Tears rolled down her face. He was going to allow a black mark—the taking of another life—to be placed upon his soul.

For her.

The shot rang out. Her whole body jerked, and she gave in to the tears.

Mint opened the car door and got back in. "Em…"

She looked up. "I can't do this. I can't live this kind of life."

He started the engine and shifted to drive. The last thing she saw on his face before he turned away was a wash of something that looked an awful lot like disappointment.

Chapter 16

The warehouse was quiet when they pulled in, trailed by an SUV with two armed guards inside. Night had fallen, casting shadows in corners he'd rather have seen into. Too many places to hide. A couple of cars were parked in the lot, not much movement in the warehouse or around it. Lights were switched on behind the blinds—some on timers, some on because they needed to be. Mint had called ahead so Steve knew they were coming. He'd given his assistant the rest of the day off—or at least, Mint figured that was the case since Steve answered the phone himself.

Emma cracked her door before he even got around to it. She didn't look at him. She hadn't spoken one word to him the whole flight there.

The two armed guards got out of the vehicle behind them. Men Steve could call when he needed help. Not hired guns, just friends he would now owe a favor. For Mint. Men he knew couldn't be bought.

Mint nodded to both of them, and they all headed for the door where he punched in the code and let them inside.

"Kitchen's down there." He motioned to the hall. "Last door on the right."

The two men passed them and headed right for it.

Emma stood with her spine completely straight. So straight she was going to strain something soon enough.

"Malone." Steve strode toward them from the other direction. He angled right for Emma, hand held out. A warm smile for her. "Ms. Burroughs. I'm glad to see you made it here safely."

"Um…thanks." She glanced between them. "Steve, right?"

"Steve Preston." He was the consummate politician, all smiles and warmth. But Mint had seen that switch he made to lethal businessman. And he didn't mean a boardroom deal. Steve's dealings had more to do with his aim with the Sig he kept under his jacket. "Let's get some coffee, shall we?"

Emma nodded. "That would be great."

It was like Mint didn't even exist. They walked in front of him. Steve glanced over his shoulder toward Mint and frowned. Mint shrugged. Only Emma knew what was going on in her head. Apparently, the fact he'd shot the guy following them—a man who'd been a party to Craig and Drew's deaths—had been the last straw. Was she done with him now?

If Mint had left the guy alive, then he would've reported back to his boss. Mint had taken the phone off his body to see what Double Down could get from it. If Craig and Drew hadn't been killed, Mint would have had them question him. See if they could get information from him about who the blackmailer was. If the blackmailer hadn't covered all his tracks, they could have got something.

But now his teammates were dead. Mint couldn't gamble on the fact the blackmailer *might* have messed up. It had been far simpler to eliminate the threat to Emma. The blackmailer had taken from Double Down, so Double Down had taken from him. Mint didn't figure whoever it was would be all that cut up about hired mercenaries dying, but he had to know that Double Down was serious about this.

Deadly serious.

They filled mugs of coffee, and Steve walked Emma to the conference room. When they settled on chairs, Mint said, "Got an update on Perkins?"

"Doctors are looking at her. Walker stuck with her, though he called in his people on the RV bombing and the man you left on the highway. If there's anything to find, the FBI will find it. Walker has promised he'll keep me posted." Steve shrugged. "I'm hoping there will be at least *something* that will lead us to a possible identity for our blackmailer. But I'm by no means holding my breath."

Mint set his cup down. "Good."

"Can I…" Emma paused. "When is the senator's memorial?"

"Tomorrow morning."

The man had been killed four weeks ago. Was this a sign from God that she was here at the right time? Sadler had been buried. This was a small service for friends and family to remember him.

He said, "We're sending team members to be there, just in case something happens we need to know about. But other than having a presence there, we're going to leave it alone. Bradley and Rachel have agreed it's for the best that they steer clear, even though he's their uncle."

Emma nodded, though it didn't look like she agreed. It seemed her emotions were close to the surface. He could see she wanted to argue. But instead, she just sat back, looking spent. Like she had no energy and needed sleep. Which was pretty much exactly how he felt.

"What I'm concerned with is how this fundraiser relates to everything that's happened." Steve paused. "We have two days to figure out what the blackmailer considers to be so important he would get people he wanted in there."

Mint said, "The requisition requests were about the caterers." When Emma nodded, he went on. "Can you tell us more about that?"

"Okay." She didn't sound sure, but at least she made eye contact with him. If only for a brief second. "The vendor that I signed off on was a last minute bid. I don't know enough about caterers to know if this was a good decision or not. He wanted me to sign off, approve the choice, without even talking to the senator. Then the aide who had put it all through and set up the catering for the fundraiser was going to let the senator know about the decision." She frowned for a second. "I honestly don't think the senator cared who was hired for it. I think the whole fundraiser thing wasn't much more than a strategic move to convince people he was altruistic. He needed a feel-good."

Steve nodded. "Rachel and Bradley had a few things to say about their uncle and not much of it was good."

Emma winced. "He was always nice enough to me, I guess. Just like he had more important things on his mind. Even so, this fundraiser is a good thing. It will benefit the children's wing of the local hospital. What's not good about that?"

"Could be a front," Mint said before he realized it had been out loud. "The catering company could be a friend of a friend, someone doing a favor for someone else by getting them the job. Then again, it could also be something else entirely."

A ploy to discredit the senator. But he was dead now, so what would that do?

A way for someone else to take the credit for the senator's work.

A terrorist attack.

Unless they figured it out and, if needed, put a stop to it, Mint didn't know how they would get the answers they wanted. And yet, that wasn't his primary focus. As much as he was all in on this operation, what was foremost in his mind was having the chance to talk to Emma without the stress of everything happening hanging over their heads. He wanted…a lot of things. Most of which he wasn't going to consider, given the fact she would barely even look at him.

Would life really put her right in front of him, close enough to reach out and touch, and then snatch her out of reach again? He didn't like that idea one bit.

Steve, or Bradley, would tell him to pray. That if God didn't want him to have this—to have Emma in his life after all this was done—then Mint wasn't going to get the chance. Even though he'd been in the military, and he was under

Steve's authority now, Mint had never really submitted to anything. Not willing to relinquish the power over his life.

He'd fought way too long, and too hard, to get the freedom and independence he enjoyed now. Was he willing to give that up if it got him Emma's smile, pointed in his direction again?

. . .

Emma was racking her brain, trying to think up what the blackmailer wanted with the fundraiser. At the same time, she was considering the fact the senator's funeral was hours from now. Could she even go when people probably still considered her a suspect in his murder? Aaron was dead, but who knew if that information—and the fact he'd killed the man—had been disseminated?

"Emma?"

She blinked up at Steve. "Yes?"

Two chairs down from hers, Mint didn't move. She'd shut him out, and she knew that. Just as she knew there was no reality where she'd have done differently. He'd protected her, but it had cost both of them. Yes, he'd done the right thing. But Emma hadn't been able to handle it on top of everything else.

She wanted to be strong. But maybe she needed to face the fact she wasn't. And she was too tired to muster the energy to talk to him about any of it.

Steve smiled like she was his little sister who he was determined to make sure was all right. It was sweet, but the reality was she didn't know any of these people. They might be perfectly good-natured. And if she had the luxury of being wrong because they weren't, then she might be able to risk it. But she didn't have that luxury. Not now.

Which made her wonder if she ever had. Her activities and friends had both been curated by her mother. Her apartment. Her clothes. Had she made a single decision about her life that her mom didn't have a hand in? One. Getting that paternity test done.

And that had led to a man's death.

Steve said, "We'll find you a room where you can crash. Get you a shower and some fresh clothes." He checked his watch. "I'm expecting—"

The door flew open, and a young woman about Emma's same age filled the doorway. A handsome man stood right behind her, a frustrated look on his face.

"—Alexis anytime now."

This was Alexis? That meant right behind her was Bradley, brother to Rachel Harris the senator. Senator Francis Sadler had been their uncle.

That made them her cousins.

Right here, in front of her, was her cousin and his wife.

Emma stood. "Uh…"

The woman surged at her. That was the only way she could describe the rush, the flying braids. "Emma Burroughs. It's so nice to meet you."

Was it? Emma figured she wasn't lying. No one could fake that much excitement. She just didn't know what the reason for it was. Alexis went on, "We're so glad you're safe, aren't we, Bradley?"

He smiled and held out his hand. "Nice to meet you."

"You too." Emma let go as soon as he let her. His handshake was firm, but not one of those manly handshakes that felt like they'd broken every bone in your hand. That was good, at least.

"You can't believe how relieved we are. Mint said you were good but, seeing for ourselves, we can really believe that everything's going to be all right for you now. You're safe."

Emma nodded. "Right." She was pretty sure the exact opposite was on her face. This woman was a little premature, considering this was far from over. They didn't even know who the blackmailer was. Yet.

Steve said, "Alexis, maybe you could show Emma where she can sleep. Get her settled."

The woman beamed. "Of course." She wound her arm in Emma's and they were off. Emma glanced back before they turned the corner. Mint, Steve and Bradley stood in a huddle. Mint looked over at her. As if he'd sensed her attention on him.

He gave her a sad smile.

Emma's heart lurched as they headed down the hall. Alexis chattered away, as comfortable with Emma as she might be with an old, dear friend. This woman was completely happy. Her life was exactly as she wanted it to be, like she was living the dream.

Emma figured she might be the same way if it happened to her. She'd come out of her shell. Like someone who was completely sure, down to their soul, that they were absolutely loved.

"You look exhausted."

Emma nodded. "I really am." It wasn't feigned. And she figured it wasn't too rude to state the obvious. This woman, by all accounts, knew what she was feeling. She'd been through the ringer.

Alexis stared for long enough that Emma said, "What is it?"

"Just…" She paused and bit her lip. "Don't break his heart."

"Excuse me?"

"Mint. Please don't break his heart." Before Emma could give voice to her objection, Alexis continued, "I know he looks all tough and everything, but he's really sweet."

Sweet?

"He saved my life."

Emma just stared at the woman.

"Don't tell me you haven't noticed a soft side under that tough guy exterior. You know that's a front, right?"

"Mint is…" Emma wasn't going to say that. "You know what? That's between Mint and I, I think."

She was so tired she didn't have much of a filter right now, but she actually sounded like her mom. She winced, remembering everything her mom had said about Alexis after the news broke publicly—when Alexis had claimed a raunchy video was her, when in reality it was Senator Rachel Harris in the video.

She wasn't about to put Alexis in the same light her mother had. Or Rachel—the woman who had been drugged and victimized.

None of that had to do with the fact Rachel was Emma's cousin, either. It was just common decency to see that someone had been pulled into a situation they couldn't control and were trying to make the best of it.

Emma slumped onto the bed. Great. Sounding like her mom just made her a judgmental jerk. But she didn't want to think about her mom, because that would make her even more of a judgmental jerk. It was a slippery slope, made worse by the fact she was beyond exhausted.

Alexis's eyes filled with warmth.

"Sorry," Emma said, mostly meaning it. "You were trying to help your friend, and I didn't take it the right way."

Alexis shook her head. "You're right."

She was?

"It is between you and Mint." Alexis clapped, smiling like everything was perfectly fine. She pointed at a door on the other side of the room. "That's the bathroom. It's a jack-and-jill with the room next door, so lock both sides if you're going to take a shower, okay?"

Still being nice. Which made Emma feel more miserable, even though Alexis didn't seem to think anything was wrong. She nodded. "Thank you."

Alexis excused herself.

Emma flopped back on the bed. She didn't mean to fall asleep, but woke up hours later with the sun a low glow through the curtained window. Someone had taken off her shoes and covered her with a blanket.

She pushed it aside, not willing to think about who'd done that. She hadn't even locked the door before she gave in to the fatigue and crashed.

Emma selected a pair of pants and a nice blouse from the clothes folded neatly on a chair, underwear between the layers, and found all the usual supplies laid out in the bathroom. Even a toothbrush, still in its packet.

She felt a million times better when she was dressed, with her hair dried. Looking fresher than she'd felt in days.

She slipped on a pair of ballet flats from under the chair, then poked her head out into the hall and found no one. Not even a sound. Was everyone still asleep? She didn't really know what time it was. Her wanderings brought her to the kitchen, where she snagged a granola bar. When she turned around, she realized Mint was on the couch in the corner.

His chest rose and fell and even in sleep he looked…lethal.

There wasn't a better way to describe him. He wasn't a soft man. He was a warrior, a protector. Just being in the same room as him made her feel safer. Alexis might think there was a soft core in him and maybe that was true, but Emma *liked* the hardness of his exterior. It made him strong. And it made her wish that she could be like that, too.

Between them on the coffee table was a handful of change and a couple of bills. A phone. Car keys. Like he'd deposited the contents of his pockets there, pulled off his glasses and crashed.

Part of her wanted to stay. Wait for him to wake up so they could talk. The other part wanted her to run out the door. Escape. Flee. Get out of this place, just so they didn't have to keep bleeding money and resources just to keep her safe. So that Double Down didn't continue to get dragged into her business. Then they'd be able to focus on figuring this whole mess out, and finally uncover the blackmailer's identity.

With the added bonus that she wouldn't have to get into hard stuff with Mint. She didn't want to be a chicken, but it was easier than actually having to do the grunt work of figuring out their conflict. How did married people even do it, when it was so much easier to just walk away and not have to do the hard stuff?

Before she considered what she'd done, Emma had his car keys in her hand, and she was stepping outside.

She hit the unlock button on his keys. The beep made her jump. Why were they made to be so loud? She climbed in and started the car, getting settled. Refusing to think about what she was doing. Where she was going. The repercussions.

She just drove.

Chapter 17

Mint followed Bradley and Alexis up the front steps of the church where the memorial service was being held for Senator Sadler. Soon enough they were going to have to bury Craig and Drew.

The weight sat in his chest like a stone had taken up residence there. But he couldn't let it stall him.

This was about finding Emma.

He hadn't exactly been surprised when the tracking device installed on his car had led them here.

He tugged at the tie pulled too tight around his neck. How did guys wear these things, anyway? It was choking him. The sound of a delicate chuckle made him realize Alexis had caught his discomfort. She reached up and tweaked his tie. Finally he could swallow.

"Thanks."

After he'd been injured saving her from being blown up as a suicide bomber in a bank, she'd been acting like this. He lived with it because she meant well, and she was just glad they were all alive.

Bradley looked like he was about to laugh. At Mint's expense. If this wasn't a funeral he'd think about punching their newest teammate in his smug face. But Bradley knew how Mint felt about Alexis fussing over him like his big sister—or a mother hen. Mint knew just how to get rid of that look. "Your sister coming to this?"

Problem solved. Bradley's face shifted to the frustrated look probably also on Mint's face. Bradley said, "I left her a bunch of messages, but she never got back to me. I think Steve went to her apartment to check on her."

She'd moved out of her house after getting abducted from her own living room. If she was hiding out in this new place, that didn't mean anything good. Rachel was letting the fear get to her. And boy did Mint get what that was like. Fear swallowed you up. It was like being devoured by some great beast, and there was nothing you could do about it. Hopefully Steve would be able to snap her out of it.

Alexis said, "You look nice all dressed up. That alone is going to distract Emma from whatever she's doing here." On her face was all the hope in the world.

Mint didn't know how to have that much faith in life, or other people. "I know what she's doing here." And it wasn't anything good.

If she wanted to mourn the senator's passing, showing up at a public funeral full of public figures, high security and plenty of press wasn't the way to do it.

They'd gotten word from one of the security guards—a friend of a friend also in the private sector who used to be a Secret Service agent. It was a small community, private security, most of them former military. A guy Steve had known years ago on the job for the senator's funeral had called in to Double Down to let them know Emma Burroughs had shown up before the service.

They'd been on their way.

Bradley said, "We should get inside."

Mint motioned to Alexis with a tilt of his head. "I'll be fine. Thanks for fixing my tie."

She knew he was frustrated. Okay, he was pretty angry. Hard to protect someone when they took off. Thankfully she'd done it in a company car equipped with GPS. They'd tracked her all morning. And what did she think she was doing anyway? News had barely hit the wires that she was the principle witness in the senator's murder, and half the people who attended may not even have received word that she was no longer the FBI's prime suspect. Whatever game she was playing, the woman was taking an incredible risk.

For what? Saying goodbye to a man who, on all accounts, wasn't very nice.

His son, Lincoln Sadler had been a spoiled brat who'd nearly assaulted Alexis. He'd ended up being killed by federal agents. Dead because of his own selfish choices. For his refusal to give up Alexis and surrender. Bradley and his sister Rachel had never said anything good about the man. Only his constituents, who heard what he wanted them to, had anything good to say about him.

Hardly a legacy worth honoring, even if Emma was his daughter. But grief often didn't take into account the reality of who that person was. Loss had to be processed, no matter the circumstances. Sometimes the prevailing emotion left over afterwards was relief.

But had Emma stuck around so he could explain that to her? No. She hadn't.

Bradley and Alexis headed inside, leaving Mint standing on the front steps of the church by himself.

His father had dragged him to a pew every Sunday morning, after he'd drank himself stupid day after day through the week. Getting sloshed and screaming cuss words at Mint for whatever infraction he thought he had done. Steve and Bradley had both talked to Mint about their faith, but he'd only told the whole story to his boss. And while he figured it was taking the easy route to write off every Christian just because of the hypocritical behavior of one, actually confronting the dark places inside himself was a whole lot harder.

Emma was inside. That alone was what got him through the door. He wanted her to know he was here for her. That he would continue to protect her.

A slender woman brushed past him in fancy black shoes and a black dress that touched her knees. Black overcoat. Black purse. Her blonde hair had been perfectly styled. Makeup, too.

For a second he thought it might be Emma, but then he saw the face was at least twenty years older—though she'd done some work to hide that fact.

"Excuse me." Her voice was short, her tone like someone trying to choke back tears.

"My apologies." He held the door longer than necessary, continuing to study her.

Emma's mother.

Mint didn't know for sure, but he was pretty certain he was looking at Isabella Burroughs, the famous conservative talk radio host. She brushed past mourners gathered in the lobby and moved straight into the sanctuary. Mint followed. He stood against the back wall, blending in like he was one of the security guards. The woman sat four rows down, still in the back section. Perched on the edge of the row, like she wanted to be able to escape at any moment.

Mint watched while the service got underway. He scanned the back of heads for Emma while the senator's friends tried to tell stories of when he'd been altruistic, or the ways he'd bettered the country. There wasn't a lot of unique material, mostly just the same couple of stories told over and over.

And then she was there. Emma, walking to the podium.

A hush moved over the crowd. Cameras flashed. Her face was set, a polite smile he didn't believe one bit. She looked amazing, but then he'd followed her to the store where, with her stash of cash, she bought those clothes and purchased styling products to fix her hair. When she got to the memorial service, he'd rushed to change his own clothes.

Now he wished he'd stayed, jeans and T-shirt or not. He wished he'd forced her to face the fact he was still right there with her. To convince her that she wanted him to *always* be there.

Emma cleared her throat. "Many of you are probably surprised to see me here."

A murmur swept through the room. Several people pulled out cell phones and camera clicks filled the space.

"Yes, I was there the night the senator was ruthlessly killed by Aaron Jones." She swallowed. "I heard his final breaths. And my only regret was that I didn't get to share with him what I had learned just that morning." She paused, took a breath. "Senator Sadler and I shared more than just a passion for accurate accounting."

A chuckle broke out in a few places around the room.

"We shared a passion for helping the destitute in his community, raising support for those working every day to make the lives of women and children better. To provide support to fathers determined to leave a strong legacy. To those who might need an extra hand. To the homeless, and the sick. Because only by lifting each other up can we rise above hatred. Selfishness. Evil."

Mint figured most of the man's work in that area was due to his having a guilty conscience. Or making himself look good for the next election. But Emma had known the man personally. If she wanted to remember him in the best light, who was he to stop her?

"Kindness is the greatest virtue. And those who prey upon other people, who force them to commit atrocious acts, should be brought to justice."

Emma's voice broke. She took a step back and used a quiet moment to compose herself, while some applauded.

"Senator Sadler and I shared more than just the values we should all base our lives upon." She paused again.

Mint saw her mother perk up in her chair, glancing around. Why did she look nervous?

"I recently discovered that he was, in fact, my father."

Gasps echoed around the room.

"And I will cherish the memories of him that I now have. I will carry those with me always."

Emma's mother launched out of her chair and flew to the back doors, heels clicking as she went.

. . .

Emma forced herself not to react. She watched her mother rush to the back doors, where a man in a suit intercepted her. It took her a second to realize that the man was Mint.

He was here?

She hadn't even spotted him. And yet, why had she thought he wouldn't catch up with her? She'd felt eyes on her all day but hadn't been able to see anyone. It figured he would keep an eye out, and honestly it made her feel better knowing he was here now. He was listening.

This was the hardest thing she'd ever done.

A man in the front row got up, the senator's personal assistant. Beside where he'd sat was Senator Sadler's widow, now glaring daggers at her.

The man took her arm, the squeeze of his fingers far tighter than necessary. "Thank you, Ms. Burroughs." He tugged her back. She nearly tripped on the heel of her right shoe, but caught herself before she fell. "We appreciate your kind words about the senator."

His grip said anything but.

Emma made her way to the left aisle, and she kept her head high as she gathered her purse and made her way to the side door. Tears filled her eyes. Through the blur she managed to find the handle.

Cameras flashed. Voices drifted to her. No doubt this would be all over social media by the end of the day. The broadcast of her emotional confession that the senator was her father. A sob worked up her throat as she pulled the door open and moved into the side hallway.

"How nice."

She nearly slammed into the man.

The door clicked shut behind her, the sound echoing in the stone-walled hallway with its matching stone floor and arched ceiling.

His eyes narrowed in a gleam below dark brows. Styled hair. He smelled like expensive cologne. "Our *mutual friend* sends his regards."

She took a step back. In a second she realized, even with everything that was going on, who he was referring to. "What…" She sucked in a breath and straightened her shoulders. "Two of Double Down's team are dead. He's not going to get away with this."

Tears filled her eyes.

"Exposing the secret doesn't mean this ends." He grinned. Perfect teeth, a pretty cover to an ugly person beneath the surface. "We'll be in touch."

He disappeared. Emma slumped against the wall, and a tear rolled down her face, which was where Mint found her. One second all she could hear was the rush of her own breath in her ears. The next second, she caught his footsteps, and then his eyes stared down at her. Dark brown, light at the edges. So much darkness in the center, it was like she was being sucked down into it. And she wanted to fall in. To try and help him break free of it. But it wouldn't do any good for her to try and help someone as damaged as he was. It would be like two cripples trying to run a marathon.

"Emma." Frustration crinkled his brow. "Come on." Whatever he'd been about to say, he brushed it off and led her to another hallway off this one, where Bradley and Alexis stood with her mother.

Her mother flew at her, rage twisting her face. "I cannot believe that you—"

Mint shifted his body in front of Emma's and put his hand out. "Mrs. Burroughs, if you'd wait until we get somewhere private—"

Emma would prefer to do this—never. She said, "Mom, I know this affects you as well, and I'm sorry I aired something you didn't want to come out. You *never told me* that dad isn't actually my father."

"You ungrateful little—" She called Emma a name that made Alexis gasp.

"Don't catch your followers using that word. They won't like it." Emma didn't much care. The sheen had come off the rose, and now she saw her mom clearly for probably the first time in her life. "What you don't know is that there is more going on here. Senator Sadler was murdered, and I never got the chance to see if I could have some kind of relationship with him as my father. You took that away from me. But what you don't understand is that I had a reason for making that announcement."

She highly doubted her mother would see past her own outrage and what she saw as betrayal by Emma, to even understand that Emma had a serious problem. Her mom didn't care that the past few weeks had been the most terror-filled time in her life. Did her mom ask her how she was? Or why one bicep under her sweater was thicker than the other. Her infected arm was much better, but it was still really obvious.

"That *debacle* in there will go public." Her mom rummaged in her purse and pulled out a pink sparkly cell phone. "I have to call my assistant. And my publicist. We'll tell them you've been traumatized. Or—I know!—we'll tell them the FBI told you to say that." Her fingers flew across the screen. "Yes, that's good. The cops wanted you to say that. And, I'm sorry, but we'll have to say that you were going to take the blame for the senator's death before Patrick escorted you off the stage. Maybe you even put Aaron Jones up to it, or something like that. In collusion with him." She glanced at Bradley, then Alexis. "Is that the right word? Collusion?"

Alexis said, "I think you should leave now." Her voice was tight, her face set like stone.

It was like her mom didn't even notice. She breezed to the door and called back, "My assistant will call you and tell you what to say."

Emma noticed Alexis watch her mother leave.

This woman had faced down the blackmailer herself. She'd told the world a raunchy video of Rachel Harris was, in fact, her. She'd allowed it to discredit her, get her fired and blacklisted all across Washington. Alexis had stood up for her friend.

Emma hadn't stood up for anything. She'd told the world the senator was her father, but only to take away the blackmailer's power. Too much damage had been done. It hadn't been about saving anyone.

She couldn't even stand up to her own mother. The woman had forced her into the rhetoric her entire life, and Emma hadn't stood up to her. Not once. The past few weeks had been scary and lonely. She'd also learned more about herself than at any other time in her life.

Plus, she'd met Mint.

She glanced over at him.

A frown crinkled his brow and he said, "What?"

"Thank you."

"For what?"

Where did she even start? She shifted to face him and said, "For being here. Finding me in the hallway." She paused for a second, trying to figure out what to say. "There was a man here. He said there's going to be more. I didn't fix anything."

Mint's eyes hardened. "I was distracted by your mom, and he got to you?"

Emma pressed her lips together. She wasn't going to give him guilt when he'd been amazing the past few days. Still, she couldn't help asking, "What does he want?"

Chapter 18

Bradley had taken Alexis so she could be with Rachel. Steve's attempt to visit her had been unsuccessful; she'd refused to let him in. But if there was anyone who could get through to her, it would be her best friend and sister-in-law.

Which left Mint with Emma back at the warehouse. He didn't even know what to say to her. *Your mom is a piece of work.* Or how about, *You're crazy if you think that helped.* She'd tried to force the blackmailer's hand by revealing the information he held about her personal life. He knew she'd done it because it was what Alexis and Rachel had done, and it worked for them.

Steve sat at the conference table with his laptop open. The man's face was haggard. But then, they were planning services for two men on their team. Plus, his visit to Rachel hadn't succeeded.

Mint also sat, while Emma paced to the corner waiting for the kettle to boil. He said, "Any idea who that man was?"

Steve didn't look up. "I'm running our facial recognition software on the surveillance footage we got from security."

Mint said, "Good. Thanks."

"You can find out who it is?" Emma was still in her dress, though she'd taken off her heels, so she wandered over and stood beside him in bare feet. With her blond hair down around her shoulders, she looked far younger than she should.

Even though he tried to steel himself against all the feelings that welled up inside, she'd broken through. He needed to face the fact he had no safeguards against her. He said, "That's the plan."

"But it's not the blackmailer, right?" She glanced between him and Steve. "We're assuming he is just another minion, like Aaron Jones. Someone to be his public face. He said, 'our mutual friend'."

Mint nodded. He pushed out the chair beside him. "Sit." When she did, he said to Steve, "Do you have the profiles on everyone invited to the fundraiser?"

"In your email."

Mint grabbed his iPad from his locker. When he walked back into the conference room, Emma was chuckling at something Steve said. His boss's face was purposely blank, but the edge of sadness since he'd told them about Craig and Drew was still there. What had they been talking about?

He sat down. She lifted her chin. *Uh-oh.* He figured whatever this was, he probably wasn't going to like it.

"I'm going to the fundraiser."

"That's it?" he asked. "No lead in. No attempt to butter me up. Just a flat statement? There's a blackmailer out there with people willing to get in your face to threaten you, and you want to waltz out there *again* and put your neck on the line?"

She opened her mouth to speak, then closed it.

"Again."

"Do I have to say I'm sorry?"

He blinked. "That might help."

"You were there. You had my back."

"That doesn't mean you get to be reckless."

Mint looked down at his iPad and scrolled through the names of people invited. A few he knew. Some he'd never heard of. Doctors linked to the charity, and government staff. Wealthy businessmen and women. A Texas oil man. No one who really stuck out as vulnerable to a blackmailer looking for new targets, or who he could pinpoint as being the possible victim of some kind of attack.

They had to view this as possible terrorism. It wasn't as likely as other factors, perhaps, but it was on the list.

Mint mostly figured the blackmailer was after money, but probably also wanted to further his agenda.

His gaze snagged on one name. "Huh." He clicked on the bio and flicked his finger to send the page to the huge screen on the wall at the end of the room. Then he set the iPad down and walked over to scan the information so he could pace at the same time.

His iPad screen filled the wall.

"Who is that?" Emma came to stand beside him. "Brent Caulder." She read from the screen, where the name was listed above a picture of a fifty-something man who smiled at the camera, with clean-cut blond hair and a button-down shirt.

"Says here he's a researcher. A scientist in the field of auditory research, studying the effects of sound on the environment." He'd been flagged because of a note Steve's assistant had left tagged on the profile. "But his security clearance level is insane."

"What do you mean?"

Steve piped up from behind his laptop. "He means it's abnormally high."

"Kind of like yours," Mint said.

Steve chuckled. "That's need-to-know."

And Mint didn't need to know. Except when he did. Mint said, "How do we find out what he's working on?"

Steve got up. "Keep an eye on my laptop. I'll go make a call."

Mint nodded, but his boss was already walking out of the room.

"Do you think he's the target?"

He turned to Emma, still looking up at him with those dark blue eyes. If she was strong enough to face Aaron Jones and then go into a service full of people and tell them all—and the general public—her darkest secret, then she was stronger than she looked.

Strong enough to know when to stand.

She pulled at him, making him want to give her whatever she wanted. To believe she was strong enough even for this. Even when fear welled up in him. When it went against all logic and reason.

He liked her, but he didn't want to lose himself in the process. That just left a person empty when the relationship ended.

"Mint..." she sighed. "Can I call you, Davis?"

"No."

"Oh." She took a step back. "Sorry."

He caught her hand before she got too far away. "My father called me Davis when he screamed at me because I didn't cook dinner right. Or because someone was coming over, and I hadn't cleaned up. He screamed all kinds of things, names and insults. My name is no different. At least, in my head, it sounds no different. I don't want anything to do with it."

"Oh."

"You keep saying that." He tried to make light of it, but that didn't change the look on her face. One that was a whole lot like pity. "Em—"

She leaned over and hugged him. Her arms wrapped around his middle and she laid her head on his chest.

Mint stood still for a second, his mind blank, unable to figure out what he was supposed to do. Then reflex kicked in, and he wrapped his own arms around her.

A sob shuddered through her.

He shook his head. "So much emotion."

It didn't feel like pity, and it didn't make him feel worse accepting it. How was that? He'd assumed opening up would only add to the weight on him. How was it that it made him feel lighter?

She leaned back and slapped his shoulder, but it had no strength behind it. "You deserve it. Just blurting all that out, like you're telling me the weather forecast for tomorrow."

"I don't want you to know about him," he said honestly. "I don't want that staining you or what you think of me. Living with that for so long." He shook his head.

"When did you leave?"

"The minute I turned sixteen. I had a friend who'd moved from Indianapolis, where we lived, to Chicago. I took the money my father gave me to get groceries, and I bought a bus ticket instead. I lived with my friend until graduation, and then I joined the army."

A quiet moved over her. "I'm glad you had that friend. I could have used one of those. Someone like what Rachel and Alexis have."

He nodded.

"But I think I've realized that it doesn't matter what we came from or the mistakes we make now. It's what we do with it all that shows our character. I don't want to be someone forced into a box by my mother. Or dictated to by a blackmailer out for his own gains." She paused, then said, "I want to be someone you respect. Someone you consider worth having in your life. And that means going to the fundraiser."

There was a lot there he liked and a whole lot he didn't.

Mint lowered his arms and sat on the edge of the table. "Putting yourself in harm's way isn't the answer. I know you want to and that's enough."

"But it doesn't help find this man."

"Double Down will figure out who it is. Your job is to stay safe."

.   .   .

"I don't want to be hidden away and protected." Was he going to listen? Like, really listen and actually hear her?

"I know."

He thought he did, but the truth was they didn't know each other that well. Neither knew the extent of what drove the other. Only time would reveal that. Time, and getting to know each other.

"I want you to know me," she said. "And I want to find a new job. Maybe buy a house, because I've been renting for way too long. It's time to start the rest of my life."

Mint's lips twitched. "You jump around from conversation to conversation faster than I can keep up."

"Double Down has lost two people this week. Perkins is hurt."

"And Walker will help her. What's your point?"

She folded her arms. "That you need all the manpower you can get. Or, in this case, woman power."

"And I'm supposed to let you?"

"I'm not sure you're going to 'let' me do anything. It's not like I need your permission to step outside."

"You want to go to the fundraiser and put your life on the line."

"It's for a good cause."

"Not one that's worth your life."

He really wasn't going to budge on this? "You can't stop me."

Mint leaned toward her. "If you want protecting, then I'm afraid you're going to have to suffer the indignity of submitting to some of my dictates. Like, for one, not going off on your own without cover."

"Children." Bradley filled the doorway, his comment both a reprimand and a greeting.

Were they behaving like children? Emma was just trying to get Mint to see reason. She ignored Bradley and turned back to Mint. "I knew you were going to throw that back in my face. Well, you know what? The funeral turned out *fine*. So pardon me for wanting to honor my father."

He winced. "Nice for you."

She folded her arms. "And now I'm going to help you all figure this out."

"I'll take you," Bradley said, still in the doorway. The small smile on his face didn't reach his eyes—Double Down had lost too much for that. Still, was he getting amusement from the fact she was confronting Mint?

"No, you will not." Mint shook his head. "I'm not going to be forced into a corner and be distracted at the fundraiser. My focus will be split between protecting you and getting the job done."

Emma didn't like the sound of that. "That's what you think I'll be doing? Distracting you?" Maybe she didn't want him to answer that question. Her emotions were far too close to the surface right now. She would say something she didn't mean, and she would end up regretting it. She was trying to stand up for herself. He thought she was being a bully, making him do things her way?

She stood up then. "I need to go...lie down, or something." She edged toward the door without looking at Mint. Or Bradley.

"Let me know if you need anything," Bradley said quietly as she passed him.

Emma nodded and kept moving. She didn't want Mint to think she was bullying him. That was what her mom did, talking and talking and talking until she wore everyone down. They bent to her whim because it was easier than the backlash they would receive if they didn't do everything the way she wanted it done. Emma and her "father", the man she'd thought was her father all these years, had always simply given in. Or was that just his method of keeping the peace—and their secrets?

There was no way Emma wanted to follow in those footsteps. And yet, Mint's words revealed that was exactly what she'd been doing. Guilting him into what she wanted. Falling back on those ingrained skills she'd learned from years of watching her mother. Years of having that very thing done to her.

But it wasn't the only source of her power. Emma had to think on that for a moment and let it sink in. If she didn't want to be like her mom—and she absolutely did not—then she had to find a different way to operate.

Had she forced the situation by announcing to the funeral goers that the senator was her father? She'd been trying to do what Alexis had and take the power back. Had she railroaded the situation instead and ended up making it worse?

A tear rolled down her face. Life was such a mess. And it was hard. She didn't even know how she was going to move forward. It felt like she had nothing anymore. As though everything she knew and relied on, trusted in, had crumbled. Which made her wonder just how solid it had been in the first place.

Emma flopped back on the bed and let herself cry. She needed to release the emotion after the last few weeks. She was safe, but it wasn't like anything was fine. Far from it, in fact. She reached for a tissue from the box on the bedside table and saw the light on the phone base flashing. It was ringing, though the sound had evidently been turned off.

She blew her nose and sat up. The cordless phone was on its base, and she'd ignored it before now. Was it Mint, or one of the others, making sure she was okay? Maybe they just didn't want to deal with an emotional woman in person.

She picked it up and pressed the green button to answer the call. "Hello?"

"Look out the window." The voice was distorted, like a computer.

"What?"

Silence filled the line.

"Hello?"

She looked at the tiny screen, but the call was still connected. Emma shifted off the bed and went to the window.

The voice came back immediately. "In precisely two minutes, the man across the street in that tan van will slide the door open and point a rocket launcher at the Double Down warehouse. I'm sure you've seen the destruction I can wreak when I will it."

Authority rang in his voice, causing a cold to move through her. Emma shuddered.

"Walk out the north entrance now and get into the SUV. Or the three men in the building will burn."

"What?" Her voice was almost a wail. "Who are you? Why are you doing this?" There was no way Mint—or any of them—would let her leave. The building was secure. "They'll know if I just walk out."

"Security has been disabled."

He was in their computer system? How was that even possible? Emma tried to think. Should she just scream? She looked around for a way to write a note, or something.

"Failure to comply will result in four deaths."

The voice was void of any humanity. Was it really just a computer, or was the blackmailer some kind of sociopath who didn't care who got hurt? He'd caused so much distraction.

Mint would try to find her. After he thought she'd betrayed him, just like her mother screamed at her. He would think she'd tried to force his hand. Split his focus.

Another tear rolled down her face, just when she'd thought her tears all spent.

"One minute remaining," the voice said.

Emma dropped the phone. It smashed on the floor, the plastic cracked, and a couple of pieces flew across the thin carpet.

She looked out the window again, staring at the van. Was there really a man with a weapon in there? How did Double Down not know about it?

Could she take the risk?

Emma grabbed her purse and strode to the door. She prayed Mint would see the truth of what had happened and not hate her too much. If she went now, maybe she would meet the blackmailer. Maybe she would be able to end this, somehow.

She pushed against the bar on the exit door, praying an alarm would sound. But it didn't. She wanted one of them to stop her. Mint, Bradley, or Steve. Mostly Mint. Didn't one of them know?

Parked just beyond the alley was a black SUV.

The door closed behind her. The immediate ring of an alarm inside the building made her jump. The security system had gone off. Mint would know.

Across the lot, the back door to the SUV opened. A rustle of clothing behind her drew her attention. But not fast enough to stop the prick in her neck. A needle? Darkness swept her up, swallowing her like the cold ocean as she collapsed into thick arms. Emma felt herself being lifted.

And then there was nothing.

Chapter 19

Mint worked his way through the crowd. Evening dresses. Plenty of jewelry. Men in tailored suits. He glanced at shoes and saw nothing that would retail for less than five hundred. Most were in the thousands. He'd bought shoes for a mission in the Middle East once, infiltrating people for whom money—and appearance—was everything. Shopping for that had been more painful than the time he'd been captured in Nigeria.

The fundraiser was underway. People with too much money here to schmooze their way through the night, trying to one-up each other on how much they could give. Regardless of whether they actually cared about the kids the fundraiser would be helping.

Fear sat sour in his gut. Where was Emma? Why had she left like that? Was she okay? He wanted to be angry at her for the fact she'd exposed herself to danger again. But something about it just didn't sit right. Even with everything that had happened between them, he still didn't believe she'd just walked out. If she had, he'd have been able to find her. She would be here, doing what she had said she would—supporting her father's charitable efforts.

Mint was just glad he hadn't spotted her mother. Though, considering what had happened at the funeral, he figured Isabella Burroughs was somewhere trying to minimize the social media fallout of the big announcement—and the implication that she'd had an affair.

All this fuss over a man who, by all accounts, hadn't been a nice man. Or a good father. Or an uncle that Bradley and Rachel liked.

He, of all people, knew what happened when those in authority—those who were supposed to nurture and protect—became the kind of people who only tortured and terrorized. He was glad Emma hadn't grown up in the senator's house. Would he have broken her or twisted her with his mind games, the way he had with Lincoln?

When he found Emma and managed to get her back, maybe she would talk to him about it. He could convince her it was for the best.

Mint didn't want to dredge up the past. Not considering everything that would surface. It just wasn't worth reliving any of it, or even thinking about it again. He wanted to leave it buried and move on. Live his life now, not the life he'd had in the past—one full of humiliation and abuse. Otherwise, he'd never be truly free of it.

What he wanted was the chance to tell Emma that he liked her. That he was attracted to her, and how he wished he could spend more time—stress free, thank you—with her. Get to know each other better. See if maybe they'd been placed in each other's lives for a reason.

He didn't even know whether that was a thing. But, looking at what had happened between Bradley and Alexis, he thought that maybe it was possible. Some people were supposed to be with each other. As though maybe they'd been born to complement each other.

A weird vibe made the hair on the back of his neck stand up. He'd learned over the years to always pay attention to the feeling, so Mint stopped his forward progress through the crowd to see what was giving him this vibe. He'd been making a circuit of the room. Checking everywhere to make sure Emma wasn't here.

There.

He zeroed in on a woman standing at a table, flanked by two men in the uniform of wait staff. They didn't fit with the upper-class crowd. They looked more like hired goons, or bodyguards to some tough guy with enough money to buy the loyalty of unsavory thugs who would do anything because of the paycheck. Their outfits were no better than Halloween costumes, with guns clearly hidden under their aprons. The woman didn't fit with them. Her dress was a pale peach color, her hair up in a complicated knot. Her face was paler than her dress, and her fingers shook as she lifted her drink to take a sip. Not alcohol. Water.

The men were waiting. The woman was scared for her life.

"I caught that, too." The voice, belonging to Bradley, came through Mint's earpiece. "Wonder what that's about."

"Who is she?" Mint asked in a low voice so the people around him couldn't hear.

Steve was the one who replied, also over their comms. "Our survey says…Mrs. Brent Caulder. Doctor Elizabeth Caulder. Turns out they work the research lab together."

Mint kept walking, like he hadn't even noticed the men. He made his way to an empty corner of the room. On the way, he swiped a glass from a waiter. When he'd found a spot he could talk away from overhearing ears, he lifted the glass to his lips. Right before it touched, behind the disguise of the glass, he said, "So where is Mr. Caulder?"

He continued to scan the room.

"Got him," Bradley said. "At the bar, facing the room. Someone just dropped a phone behind him."

Mint found the man he'd seen on his iPad screen. Before Emma had left the room. Before the entire security system had gone haywire. Not even dark. A power outage, or some kind of brown-out would have explained that. Instead, the system had literally gone haywire. Someone had been messing with it big time. And they hadn't been able to figure out who before it suddenly stopped. Then the alarm at the end of the hall had gone off, indicating the fire exit had been opened. Security cameras outside hadn't come on for another minute, by which time there had been nothing to see.

And Emma had been gone.

They were way too understaffed to be able to cover all their angles. Two team members down and two out of town. The company could easily have been crippled and, as it was, they were running on little more than fumes left in a gas tank.

They needed to have two funerals as soon as they got the bodies—or what was left of them—back to Washington. Steve had already informed the families. It was time for the company to pull together so they could all move forward. Help the families do the same. Instead, they were here trying to figure out what the blackmailer wanted with Emma. And likely also Brent and Elizabeth Caulder.

Mint made his way to the bar.

If the blackmailer was watching, any move they made would be noticed. There was almost no way to make contact with either of them without being seen. But if the benefit was high enough, it would have to be done.

Mint asked the bartender for a soda water with lime and got a funny look. He stared the man down until the guy said, "Fine" and moved to pour it. Mint didn't much care what it said about him. What a bartender thought about Mint's dietary choices was hardly his biggest concern right now.

The phone rang.

Four feet to his left, Brent Caulder nearly jumped out of his skin. He spun around and swiped up the phone. Answered it with a shaky hand. "Hello?"

Brent Caulder's face paled. "Just don't hurt her."

. . .

The SUV pulled up outside the facility, and the driver threw it in park. Emma looked out the back window. Fences topped with barbed wire. No security guards that she could see, but they were there. Card swipe entrances to get in. Cameras. Sensors.

And finally, a keypad to a door inside that she was supposed to have the code for.

By the time she got there.

I don't like this.

The driver turned to her. "You know what to do."

She nodded, though it made her head swim. Whatever they'd stuck her with in that syringe had worn off, but not all the way. Could she walk confidently in a straight line? She was going to have to figure out how to fake that, or this wasn't going to work.

Emma tugged on the door handle, clutching the card they'd given her. Doctor Elizabeth Caulder's key card. Hopefully whoever was on security looked at their screens and realized it wasn't her. But Emma wasn't exactly hopeful. Not considering the man in the front seat—the one who'd confronted her in the hallway after her funeral speech—had a laptop open. The camera feeds for the facility were on his screen.

Had he hacked in? They'd managed to breach the security at Double Down, fool the system into seeing what they wanted it to see, and then set the alarms to ring when they wanted. Emma didn't think security guards at this medical research facility were going to see anything these men didn't want them to.

She paused, one leg out of the car, and turned to the two men. "You know who he is, don't you?" She had nothing to lose. Not at this point. What did it matter if they told her who the blackmailer was? Okay, that wasn't exactly true. Considering she would definitely lose the "something" that could be between her and Mint. All she had right now was the possibility, a hope that maybe they might have made something. Not now, though.

The driver smirked. "I hope you don't cross him, or you'll end up dead."

"Who is he?"

He chuckled. "You don't want to know." Then he twisted, pointed a gun at her. "Get moving or you'll have even more problems. Can't imagine it'll be easy to walk in there and carry out the device with a gunshot wound."

She already had one. Still, she wandered away and left the door open. Only for the sake of exercising the tiny bit of power she had, which wasn't much more than the power to kind of irritate them. She strode to the side entrance and swiped her card in the card reader. The gate clicked.

Crossing the forecourt made her breath hitch with every inhale. Yellow lights lit the place. Emma made no attempt to disguise the fact she was walking right through the middle of the open area, straight to the door they'd told her to use. If those guys back in the SUV were any good at this business, then she didn't need to bother hiding her entrance from anyone looking.

They could control security all they wanted, but what she prayed was that someone—anyone still there—would glance out a window at just the right moment and see her.

But it didn't happen.

She made it to the door without incident and stepped inside the medical research facility. The two men in the car also drilled into her the layout of the building. She had the card in one hand and, in the other, an old flip cell phone. They were going to call her and give her the code.

Did that mean they didn't have it?

Emma kept to the side of the hallway, a tiny piece of self-preservation flickering inside her. Like she could hide just by hugging the wall. Or manage to save herself. But her bravado had only gotten her so far.

The phone buzzed.

She flipped it open to see a text.

STOP.

Emma backtracked two steps and froze. Close enough to a door she could duck inside if she needed to. Wherever the door led to.

At the end of the hall, a security guard strode from left to right, not even glancing down the hall towards her. The man stared instead at the glowing screen of his cell phone as he walked. Keys jingled on his belt, tucked under the belly that strained buttons on his shirt.

Emma held her breath, scared to even exhale and make that much noise in the quiet. The man moved out of view. She blew out her breath as quietly as she could.

The phone buzzed again.

GO.

She set off, moving fast. All the way to the interior room they'd showed her on the map. Some kind of secret lab that only the top doctors—like Elizabeth Caulder and her husband—had access to. And only with a code.

How they were going to get it, Emma didn't know, but she prayed no one was going to die in the process. She figured the blackmailer had paid Aaron Jones to kill the senator. Or compelled him to do so in some way. Emma knew from Double Down that another woman, a victim of the blackmailer, had committed suicide.

He had cost people their lives through his actions. Emma didn't want to die. But more than that, she didn't want anyone else to, either. She was done being involved in so much death.

And so she prayed.

In the hallway of a medical research facility she'd broken into, she lifted the cry of her heart to the Father who always heard. The Father who had never deceived her.

As she walked, Emma glanced at the doorways. *Auditory research*. The next one said, *Frequency Studies*. All this had to do with sound? One said something about "resonance." She was an accountant, so she had no idea what it was all about except that it sounded interesting.

Patient Studies gave her pause. Was there someone inside she could ask for help? The SUV men had drilled into her how dangerous it would be to draw attention to herself. But wouldn't it be worth the risk to at least try? Maybe that was naïve thinking.

At the end of the hall she turned left. The overhead lights were more sporadic now, giving her the impression she was moving into some kind of secret area. Seriously, how obvious could they get? Emma pushed aside fear, and the temptation to look over her shoulder for the fiftieth time, and kept walking.

All the way to room 311.

The doctor's keycard got her inside where she was faced with a wall of glass windows. On the other side of the glass was a huge room that could have been a basketball court for all she knew. Except for the sign beside the door at the end of the viewing area where she stood.

Do not enter when red light is on.

Weapons testing in progress.

Auditory research, medical studies and…weapons testing? Her thoughts raced around and around as she tried to put all the pieces of the puzzle together in some semblance of order. A blackmailer. A place like this. Emma, caught in the middle. Others' lives in danger. Being pushed to take the blame for a murder.

The door she was supposed to get the code for was at the end. Lab 43. Highly protected by security in a building where weapons were being tested.

Emma took a step back, feeling like she'd been punched in the face. Did the blackmailer want her to steal some kind of weapon for him?

Like a bomb?

Was she going to be implicated in some kind of terrorist attack? Accused of killing hundreds of innocent people…or more?

Chapter 20

"Execute." The command from Steve came through Mint's earpiece.

Steve and Bradley took out the two men flanking Elizabeth Caulder. Mint waited while Brent realized what was happening and then said, "Let's go," in a low voice he hoped wasn't audible over the phone.

He ushered the man to a room off the main ballroom of the hotel. A quiet place that looked like a work area for professionals traveling. Or a meeting room.

He wasn't under any illusion that the blackmailer—or persons in his employ—weren't watching the whole thing. Whoever it was would likely know right away that they had intercepted the situation and resolved the danger. But the risk of exposure was worth it to secure Elizabeth Caulder and eliminate the threat against her that was being used to coerce her husband into doing the blackmailer's bidding.

Brent had the phone to his ear. He blanched, listening to the person on the other end. Mint waved for the phone, put it on speaker and laid it on the table.

"So nice of you to join us, Mr. Davis." The voice on the other end was distorted, probably male, and heavily disguised. There was no way to find out who it was without a sophisticated computer system.

"Where is Emma?"

Brent stood, listening, while the blackmailer said, "On an important assignment for me."

"Because you threatened her into doing it?" Mint balled his hands into fists. "You haven't tortured her enough so you thought you'd get your jollies doing it one more time?"

"My work is far more important than *jollies,* as you so call it." Disdain dripped from his words. Either he had a high position in life and so expected people to just defer to him on everything, or he was naturally completely condescending.

Either way, Mint figured the man believed this was the only way. But to do what? They had no idea what his endgame was.

Mint glanced at Brent Caulder. Did this man know? Hopefully Brent could shed some light on all this.

"Which brings us back to the point," the blackmailer said. "Mr. Caulder, the code if you please?"

"No." Caulder's chin lifted. "My wife is safe now. There's no way I'm letting you in my lab. Not now and not ever."

"Hmm. That presents a problem, doesn't it?" The blackmailer paused for a few seconds. "If you'll direct your attention to the phone on the table. A text just came in."

Mint's whole body jerked. The blackmailer couldn't just hear, he could *see them?* Mint had shut the door. There was no one else in the room with them.

He spun around and glanced at the walls. High up in one corner was a security camera.

"Smile. You're live."

Mint figured that was an expression, not that he was actually live on some website. Not that he cared. Who would watch a video of two guys staring at a phone? He snatched up the cell and swiped through to the text without ending the call. The number was unknown, the text—a photo. Emma.

"That's the lab," Caulder said, looking over his shoulder. "Or the hallway outside it, anyway."

The blackmailer's voice came through the line. "And so we move from one bargaining chip to another." He paused a second. "The code, or Mr. Davis's charge—who he hasn't been keeping close tabs on I might add—meets a disastrous end. Though, I'll let you pick, Mr. Davis. Death or life in prison."

"You hurt one single hair on her—"

Laughter rang out. When the blackmailer was done being amused, he said, "Perhaps if you care so much for her well-being, you wouldn't have allowed her to slip out from right under your nose. Twice, if I recall."

This man had been watching the entire time. The realization washed over Mint as he ran through the how and why of it all. They could unpack that later all they wanted. Right now there was a major problem to solve.

He said, "We're not going to allow you to leverage someone's life, and their future, for your own gain. Whatever you're trying to do, there's no way Emma would want that to happen. Whatever you have planned, it's not going to work."

Mint felt pretty good about that. Or at least, he wanted to. Inside, his stomach was roiling, and he wondered if he was about to lose his lunch all over the floor. With the blackmailer and a doctor he didn't know watching. That would probably amuse the blackmailer to no end.

The truth was, the man had a huge amount of leverage.

There was no way Mint wanted Emma to lose her freedom, her future, or her life. And he would do everything he could to make things okay again for her.

"Mr. Caulder?" the blackmailer said. "Your device, or this woman's life?"

Brent shifted.

Mint glanced at him. He wanted to shake his head, to tell Brent not to do it. Emma wouldn't want it. But despite what he'd said, Mint realized he didn't have it in him to convince someone else. Even though he wanted to.

Brent swallowed. "What difference does it make who is in danger? My wife, or a woman you care about?" He asked the question in a low voice, but not so low the blackmailer couldn't hear.

"She wouldn't want this."

"If he gets his hands on my device, he could destroy infrastructure. Entire buildings. Lives will be lost, if that's what he wants."

"So this guy is a terrorist?"

The blackmailer laughed again. "So quick to label everyone a terrorist. That's what's wrong with the world these days. Real terrorists are called religious extremists, and we're supposed to *tolerate* their beliefs. Anyone with an agenda is labeled a terrorist, even if their agenda is just to own a whole lot of guns."

Mint wanted to know why this scientific research doctor had made a device that could topple buildings and kill people. Whatever it was, why make it in the first place? Especially when it was vulnerable to being stolen by blackmailers.

"The code, Mr. Caulder."

Brent said, "If he takes it, you have to get it back."

"Don't let him get it," Mint said, torn between safeguarding national security and Emma's life.

"Tick. Tock."

Brent turned to the phone, as though he couldn't look Mint in the eye and give the blackmailer the code at the same time. It wasn't weakness. Not when lives were on the line. And it wasn't strength for Mint to allow Emma to be hurt, or die, just to keep some device safe. Mint didn't know what it was. He just knew he didn't like being forced to *make* the decision, the same way Emma wasn't going to like the outcome. No matter which he chose, it was going to cost all of them.

Mint ran his hands down his face while Brent listed off a series of numbers, letters and punctuation. Then said, "That's it."

The line went dead.

Mint said, "What is this device?"

Brent turned to him, defeat written all over his flushed face. "A sonic—"

The door slammed open. An armed man breached the doorway. Mint snapped into action, even before his eyes registered the man's weapon out, pointed at them. He slammed into Brent Caulder, and they both hit the ground.

Shots went off.

Mint pulled his gun, rolled to face the gunman and squeezed the trigger.

A bullet slammed into his chest.

. . .

Emma typed in the code. Her hand shook so badly she almost fumbled a couple of the numbers. But she managed to get it all in. She pressed enter and the light turned green, so she pulled on the door handle.

The door opened and with it came a whoosh of air, like the room had been pressurized. Sterilized, maybe, so dust didn't get in. Something like that.

In the center, on a table, was a silver thing that looked like some kind of weapon. Like one of those rocket launcher things they put on their shoulder and fired in movies. Or some sci-fi movie ray gun. She knew nothing about weapons or rockets. But she knew they were used to kill people.

What was this thing doing in a place dedicated to medical research?

The phone buzzed in her hand. It snapped her out of her thoughts so hard she almost dropped it.

Fifteen seconds.

She lifted the device…whatever it was. Heavier than it looked. Her arm muscles strained, but she figured she could carry it outside.

When she handed it off, would they let her go?

Emma couldn't help thinking she was going to her death. But was that preferable to going to jail because she got caught by security? Either way, it would cost the lives of other people. Lives she wasn't willing to risk. Her mom. The man she had always called "Dad", even though he wasn't her father. Mint. The rest of the team at Double Down.

The blackmailer had threatened to hurt them one by one. And where would he stop? If she didn't do this, there was no telling how many people would die.

Emma backtracked through the halls. On the way, she got two more texts to avoid the security guard. Fear was a tang in her mouth, like a metallic aftertaste. She clutched the weapon to her chest. Maybe she would inadvertently press a button and wind up killing herself when it went off. At least then she would no longer care.

But what would her life have counted for? Nothing but a whole bunch of mistakes and wasted time. She needed to get past this so she could finally build something good. She wanted to ask Mint what he thought about her ideas, because there had to be a way to put her skills to use that would benefit people's lives. Otherwise, she was just being selfish.

There was nothing wrong with wanting to earn enough to have a good life, but if she didn't give of her time and money to people in need, how could she say she believed loving others more than herself was the truth? Her mother talked—a lot. Emma wanted to *do* something.

The SUV was still parked in the same spot, but behind it a car had pulled up.

A suited man spoke with the two gunmen. He had silver hair and was probably in his sixties. Accustomed to giving instructions.

When she walked up, the man turned to her. "I'll take that."

She didn't move. It was like her arms didn't want to release the thing. The fear of what it would be used for was simply too great. Why had she been dragged into this? Certainly not because she was strong enough to put it all on the line and stand up to them.

She should just drop—

Emma let go and stepped back in one move.

The weapon fell to the ground with a thud. One of the men rushed forward. The other one who'd been in the SUV strode over.

She backed up, but he caught up to her. He punched her in the stomach.

Emma doubled over, coughing. It took a good few seconds before she could push the pain and breathlessness aside enough to straighten again.

The older man who'd shown up in the car was grinning at her. "Nice try." He turned to the one who'd picked up the device. "You can put that in my car."

"Yes, sir." The man did as asked. More like commanded.

Was this the blackmailer?

It was a shame the device hadn't gone off when it hit the ground. Hopefully it was broken now. Though nothing had fallen off with the impact.

Emma took another step back. Ready to run. The man's eyes gleamed. He shifted and pulled back one side of his suit jacket. On his belt was a badge. FBI. This guy was an *agent*? "Secure her and put her in my backseat. I'll get her booked for breaking into this facility."

"The weapon is in *your* car." Emma glanced between the three of them, trying to figure a way out. "It'll be obvious you stole it."

"No one's going to check."

"I'll tell them it's there!"

He chuckled and shook his head. "Gentlemen. I need to get back on schedule."

Emma turned and darted away. She got two steps before someone tackled her. They landed on the ground, and the weight of another person landing on her back drove all the air from her lungs in a whoosh. She cried out, struggling to get free.

Then she heard the rustle of clothing, but not from the man on top of her. The agent's voice came again, this time closer. "Take care of this."

She wriggled, pinned by the weight of her captor. Managed to see around him. The FBI agent moved away and headed for his car. He was leaving?

The man on her shifted his arm from under her. Emma had a split second to realize what was happening, and then both his hands were wrapped around her neck.

She kicked out with her legs, but his weight pinned her hips to the ground. Rocks bit into several places at her back. She got enough leverage to kick him and ended up expending breath and energy trying to get him off her.

She grabbed his wrists and tried to pull him off, but she had no strength.

Then there was no air left in her lungs. She choked, trying to draw breath. His fingers around her neck tightened.

A car started, and the sound of the engine moved away along with tires on gravel. Her vision swam. She let go of his wrists and felt around on the ground, knowing it was her last chance.

She was dying.

Chapter 21

Mint saw the fight leaving her, the second her body slumped against the ground. He dived out the front seat of the SUV, while the engine was still running. His feet touched the ground, already sprinting toward her.

Beyond Emma and the man *choking the life out of her* was another guy, watching. His gun came up.

Before Mint could lift his own weapon and fire first, a shot rang out from behind him. A red dot blossomed on the man's forehead and he hit the ground.

The man on Emma looked up. Didn't let go of her.

Mint dived.

He tackled the man's head and shoulders at full speed. They hit the ground, rolling end over end. He let go of his gun and grasped the man's head. In one short, sharp move he snapped the man's neck. *Crack.*

The man slumped. Mint planted one hand on the ground, finally acknowledging the pain in his chest where he'd been hit in the vest by a bullet. Then he pushed off and turned back to Emma. He scooted to her, his legs not quite moving as they should. He pushed aside the pain and stumbled to her side.

"Emma?" He touched the sides of her face. "Emma, talk to me." Dark bruises had already formed on her neck. Had he crushed her wind pipe? "He's gone. No one's gonna hurt you." Her chest moved, shallow breaths that jerked her torso. Like she was struggling. "Breathe, Em. Please."

"Mint?" Steve and Bradley stopped close to him. He didn't know which one spoke.

"She needs an ambulance."

"It's two minutes out."

Those two minutes felt like an hour. He watched while they stuck a tube down her throat and got her breathing normally. When they loaded her into the ambulance, he turned back to his boss.

"Go. We have this."

Mint nodded, and climbed in. Held her hand all the way to the hospital, where they were separated while she got checked out. Mint paced the waiting area. Twenty minutes later, the doors flew open and a familiar woman raced in, followed by a man moving at a more sedate pace.

Emma's mother.

She ran right to him and demanded, "How is she?"

Mint couldn't form any words.

The woman's hair was styled perfectly, not a hair out of place. Designer clothes. When her daughter went on the run—a situation caused in large part because of the secrets she'd kept—this woman had gone on the internet, calling for her to come home. Not because of her innocence, or the fact she'd been in danger. Because she needed to turn herself in.

Emma's mother had displayed more emotion in that two minute post than most people do in ten years. Now? Her eyes were completely dry.

The man behind her, dressed in a suit with his tie loosened and his top button undone, stepped forward. "Frank Burroughs."

"Davis Malone."

"Is Emma okay? They said there'd been some kind of attack."

"She was choked." Kidnapped. Chased. Shot. Lied to. Jerked around. Blackmailed. And how much of that had been after he'd entered the picture? Mint hadn't done a good job of protecting her, despite his intentions.

He sank into a chair and ran his hands down his face, unable to face Emma's parents. Unable to get the mental picture of her struggling to breathe out of his head.

"Well." Emma's mom huffed out the word. "I'll go speak to a nurse. I need to *see* my daughter."

A few seconds later Mint heard a rustle, and the seat beside him creaked. Not one near him. The one *beside* him.

He opened his eyes and looked over, the last few words of the prayer whispering from his lips. Emma's father—her mother's husband and the man she'd grown up calling "Dad"—was sitting beside him.

"Marines?"

"Army."

The man nodded. "Navy."

Mint glanced at the desk where Emma's mother was in heated discussion with the nurse.

"She means well."

He glanced at the man beside him.

"Likes things the way she likes them, sees the world the way she wants. Coping mechanism, her therapist said." He sighed. "We do what we need to so the people around us are happy. Doesn't always go perfectly, but we do our best."

Mint looked at his hands in his lap. Squeezed his fingers together.

"Did everything you could to help her. Still wasn't enough." The man's stare was a tactile thing. "Am I right?"

Mint nodded.

"I saw you at the memorial service. Got in my wife's face, stood between her and Emma, trying to protect her. Saw the kind of man you were then, knew I didn't have to step in. Someone telling my wife she needed to back down and think it through, instead of flying off the handle in a gut reaction?" He shook his head. "Not going to get in the way of that."

Because he didn't have the guts to do that himself? Mint wasn't sure what to say or think about any of it.

Emma's dad said, "She got hurt, but it wasn't your fault. You know that, right?"

No. Mint didn't know that.

"He came to me, first. Showed me pictures of my wife with that man." He shifted in the chair. "Knew it. Didn't want to believe it was true. Coping mechanism. Purging those demons out of her past, so they didn't rear their heads. It isn't right, but it is what she needs."

Mint couldn't look at Emma's mom. Not now. "It put Emma's life in danger."

"And that's on me. Because I refused, and he picked her instead."

"Do you know who he is?" Mint had to know. And he didn't want to talk about that other stuff. He had enough guilt to carry without adding this man's to it. They didn't need to share that. He wasn't going to be kindred spirits with anyone except Emma. And, coping mechanism or not, that was the way it was going to stay.

"Someone high up." Her dad paused. "He knew things. Deals I was involved in."

"But you pushed back."

"And Emma is the one who paid the price. Again."

A screeching voice cut into what Mint had been about to say. "I DEMAND TO SEE HER. NOW!"

Her dad let go of an expletive and got up. Mint was right behind him. Emma's mother stormed past the nurse and down the hall to a room. She elbowed an orderly and brushed off the nurse's attempts to stall her.

"Emma! Emma!" She barged in the room.

Her dad and Mint both followed.

"Honey—"

She rebuffed the dad as well.

Mint couldn't take his gaze off Emma. Tube still down her throat. Pale face, dark bruises. Eyes open and locked on his.

She'd never looked more beautiful.

And more overwhelmed.

The nurse said, "You *all* need to leave. Now."

Emma's hand shot up and she held it out. Mint moved, placing his hand in hers. She gripped his fingers.

"Emma, darling."

Emma turned her face away from her mother and shut her eyes. But not before a tear rolled down her face.

"You," the nurse pointed at her father, "and you," she motioned to Emma's mother, "out. Both of you."

Emma's mother sputtered. The nurse got them both past the door and then shut it in their faces.

Mint shifted so their faces were close. Emma made a sound. "Don't try to talk."

"Good idea," the nurse said, moving to the other side of the bed. "Let's get the tube out. Then you can have your heart-to-heart with the hot guy."

Mint stared at her.

"What? She was hurt. This is a hospital. You wouldn't *believe* the love stories I could tell you. Makes me believe again." She swiped an imaginary tear from beneath one eye.

Emma's body shifted as she stifled a laugh.

.   .   .

"One big deep breath, and then push it out."

Emma did as instructed, still holding onto Mint's hand. She didn't ever want to let go of him. The tube slid up her throat and out. She coughed even before it left her mouth. Then she coughed more, holding back the gag. She did not want to puke in front of Mint.

He stood beside her, holding the one hand she wouldn't let go of, the other rubbing up and down her back.

"You okay for a minute if I leave you with your guy?"

Emma nodded. "Yeah." The word was scratchy and barely audible, but the nurse nodded.

"I'll be back." She wiggled her eyebrows. "I want the scoop."

Mint's body stiffened. The nurse sauntered out. When the door shut behind her, he said, "I'll talk to her. Make sure she knows she doesn't tell *anyone* what she sees or hears in here. Or anything about your family."

Emma tugged on his hand. "Sit."

Mint shifted but didn't sit.

She tugged again. "Please."

He settled on the edge of the bed, because she gave him no other choice. And he didn't meet her gaze.

"Are you going to make me talk?"

He looked up then, surprised. "Hurts?"

She gave him a look like, *What do you think?*

He winced. "Sorry."

"Not your fault." But he didn't look like he believed her. Emma reached up and touched both sides of his face. She leaned close and mouthed, *Not your fault.*

He touched his forehead to hers, and shut his eyes. "You nearly died."

Emma stroked both sides of his face and into his hair. He groaned and touched a hand to his chest. After a minute or so of silence—who cared how long it was when Mint was with her?—he said, "No one has ever touched me like this."

She leaned back. Barely an inch. Just so she could look at his eyes.

"Not one single time in my life has anyone. Ever. Touched me like this." His gaze scanned her face. "How is it that you can be so strong—and so soft—at the same time?"

Tears filled her eyes. They were the sweetest words she'd ever heard in her life. But still, she shrugged. "I'm a woman," she whispered.

"Not just any woman," he whispered back. "*My* woman."

And then he sat back. Suddenly, like he didn't meant to say that. Or like he didn't know how she would react. Like it'd slipped out, and now he wondered if he should take it back.

"Mint—"

"I didn't protect you, and I should have." The pain that washed over his face was staggering.

"I didn't let you do it. I thought I could handle everything myself when I should have been trusting you to help me instead." She took a breath. "I was trying to make things better, and I made them worse. He has the device."

Mint nodded.

"He's an FBI agent."

Mint blinked. "Seriously?"

"Show me pictures, I'll tell you who he is."

"He tried to have you killed so you wouldn't say."

Emma had plenty to say.

"I love you." She didn't let him say anything, just forged ahead. "I know it's early, and we barely know each other, but I figure familiarity will come later. But it's like…I just saw you, and I *knew.*"

Finally, he breathed. Nodded. "Like everything clicked into place."

"Like it's finally right."

He nodded again. "I'm not leaving. Not ever. And I won't let you leave, either. We do this together. But one thing you're not going to worry about is that man getting his hands on you again. He won't hurt you. He won't ever get near you. Double Down will take care of him. He isn't even on your radar. You don't give him one single thought or second of worry."

She didn't know what to say. There was a lot there. She settled on smiling, appreciating his concern even though he chose to say it like that. She snapped straight and lifted her hand to salute him. "Yes, sir."

It was weak. She sounded awful. But she knew he got it when he smiled. "I'm laying my heart out, and she's giving me sass."

"Then maybe you shouldn't frame it so much like an order."

"It's a tactic and I'm trying it. Because if you think it's an order, then you might actually follow it."

She narrowed her eyes at him, unable to keep the smile from her face. "Thank you."

"For what?"

"Being here. Understanding. Saving me."

"Falling for you?"

She nodded. "That, too." She was all the way gone for him. And if he needed more from her—to win him over—she was okay with that. It would be a pleasure to do. Every bit of it. The mundane, everyday. The special and the romantic. She wasn't going to miss one single second of it.

She said, "So, what now?"

"Protection is number one. I'll call Steve and get it figured out."

She nodded. "Okay."

"You want to see your mom?"

Emma thought about it for a second. "Maybe later."

Mint touched her cheek. "Whatever you want."

She knew what she wanted. Emma touched his shoulders and leaned in. He met her halfway, touching his lips to hers.

"Have I said thank you?"

Mint's torso shook as he chuckled. "Not sure it's you that needs to be thanking me, but I'll take it."

"This isn't over, is it?"

"Now that you've seen him, we can get things rolling. Bring him down once and for all."

She said, "Before he uses that device." Mint nodded, his face now sober. She said, "He can kill a lot of people with it, right?"

"We find it, we find him."

Emma said, "You make that sound easy."

"Double Down is up to the task. Your job is to stay safe."

"Only if you're there."

He touched his lips to hers again. "I'll always be there."

Epilogue

Steve walked into the conference room first. Alexis followed him, trailed by Bradley. Then Rachel. Mint and Emma held hands as they entered. Since the hospital, Steve had rarely seen them when they hadn't been touching each other. Finally Perkins came in, along with Walker.

His assistant was at the gathering that had followed the funerals, helping with clean up.

Everyone wore black. Dresses, suits. Their expressions likely matched his. The past few weeks had been exhausting, and this was far from over. In the last couple of days he'd had their entire security system reformatted, not to mention a number of other upgrades.

Steve opened the file his assistant had left on his desk and took out the photograph. He walked to the wall where they'd pinned all the intel they'd gathered so far. He took the FBI agent's picture and tacked it to the top. "This is Special Agent Daniel Zimmerman. He works out of the Baltimore office, but he's in DC regularly."

Perkins shook her head. "I've never met him."

Walker glanced at her, then at Steve. "You honestly expect me to believe a senior field agent is in possession of a device that could kill people?"

Emma's haunted expression was enough of an answer. Still, Mint said, "Yes. We do. So either you're on board, or you leave now. Because we don't actually need your help to bring this guy down. We can use it, but we don't need it." Mint paused. "Zimmerman has done enough damage already. We don't need him doing more."

Walker blew out a breath and sat back. "It's hard to swallow, is all."

No one commiserated with him.

Perkins said, "So how do we find him?"

Steve studied her for a second. "You up to this?"

"Craig and Drew are dead. Bradley has Alexis and his sister to worry about. Mint needs to keep Emma safe." She paused a second. "So don't ask me if I'm up to this."

Walker shifted, looking at her. "You're going after this guy yourself?"

"I won't be on my own. Double Down is a team."

Walker didn't think much of that, judging by his expression. Steve wanted to tell the guy that they didn't need the help, but that would be a lie. He was entirely too torn by the fact Rachel wouldn't even speak to him. She'd barely allowed him to oversee security in her new place and hire the best he knew of to keep her safe. Nothing was going to get to her. No one would hurt her. Not again.

He'd been sick when he found out what happened to her.

For now though, she didn't want anything to do with him. Soon enough it would be time to snap her out of her funk and make her face the world again. Right now he had the time, and the resources, to give Perkins all the support she needed.

They were going to find this guy.

Mint said, "Anything you need, I'm there."

"Me, too." Bradley took Alexis's hand and held it. "This blackmailer needs to be brought down."

Walker sighed. "I'll go to the office, see what I can find out."

Perkins sat up straighter. She almost managed to disguise the pain that shifted throughout her body with the movement. "Don't put yourself out on our account."

"You think I'd put people's lives at risk because of my attitude?"

By all accounts, he'd done that exact thing when Rachel had been kidnapped. But it was looking now like he'd changed his mind on that, at least. Walker seemed like he was willing to set his feelings aside and do what needed to be done.

Perkins looked at Steve. The woman would be killer at poker. She betrayed not one thing she was feeling about Walker, or any of this. She said, "Good. Let's get this guy."

Book 3

Deadly Agenda

Chapter 1

Megan twisted the lock pick against the tumbler. She heard the click, pulled out the pick and twisted the handle. *Bingo.* With one quick glance over her shoulder, she headed in. Outside was dark, the street quiet and still—apart from the flash of light from a TV across the street. Upstairs window. Someone watching a show at two in the morning.

The door didn't open all the way. She shoved it far enough to get through, shifting back a pile of boots and shoes kicked off behind the door. Like the occupant didn't even use his own front door, except as a spot to discard clothing when he got home. Inside was musty. Like old laundry left wet in the washer for too long.

Cardboard boxes had been stacked on the left side all the way down the hall, with only a foot and a half gap to get into the living room. One couch. A coffee table stacked with pizza boxes and at least six remotes.

Megan stood in the hall to survey what she could see from this spot and waited for a minute before she stepped further in. No dog. That didn't rule out a cat. If he did have a pet, she didn't imagine it was faring too well in this mess.

The home's occupant, FBI Special Agent Daniel Zimmerman, was a Special Agent in Charge in Baltimore. Which basically meant he was a department head, or a manager. Zimmerman had stolen a sonic weapon from a research facility that had been involved in weapons testing a few days ago.

He was now on the run with a weapon that could topple buildings, killing everyone inside.

Megan trailed through rooms, ignoring the urge to hold her nose. The snap securing the holstered weapon on her hip was undone. She was going to leave it that way until she was back in her car and away from here.

Fear snaked up her spine, leaving a trail as it went. She shivered but kept walking. Bedroom. Bathroom. Thankfully the man hadn't felt the need to rent a house bigger than this tiny dump. He apparently preferred to sleep on a bare mattress and squeezed the toothpaste from the middle. Which made her wonder—was that because he'd recently gotten divorced, or was it the reason for it? Maybe she should pay the woman a visit and ask.

She'd think Zimmerman had moved in recently, except that the divorce had gone through six months ago, the lease had been signed months before that, and all the boxes were covered in a thick layer of dust.

Didn't care. Had better things to do. Only slept here, showered here, and occasionally ate in the kitchen.

Didn't have kids. Was reportedly a workaholic. Definitely the kind of boss that expected everyone who worked under him to be available 24/7, because that was the way he worked. Not many of his coworkers had good things to say about him.

But was he the blackmailer they'd been looking for?

Some of her team back at Double Down were convinced of it. Megan wasn't going to jump on that train without irrefutable proof. That just wasn't the way she worked.

Not now at least.

Once, a long time ago now, she'd been enthusiastic like that. Take-charge. Get the job done without fail no matter the consequences. Life had taken care of that. And for the past two years, since the darkest time in her life, she'd been a whole lot more cautious.

She trusted her boss at Double Down. Steve Preston ran the private security agency with a professionalism she'd never seen before. She'd certainly put him to the test before she took the job. He'd even joked at one point that it felt like she'd been interviewing him.

Which was *precisely* what had been happening.

Megan didn't trust. Not now, and certainly not when lives were on the line. She could take care of herself. She worked with the Double Down team because it gave her legitimacy and backup. But finding one FBI agent on the run? Megan didn't need help with that. She only needed a few days to look into his life so she could figure out where he would strike first.

Then she would take him down.

A dark figure moved outside, beyond the dining room at the rear of the house and out the window. Open blinds. Megan lowered the flaps of the box she'd been peeking inside—towels and other linens, musty from disuse.

She pulled her weapon free of its holster and backtracked to the hallway where she peered around the frame of the kitchen door. The figure didn't stop at the back door. He twisted the handle. Jiggled it. She waited.

A few seconds later the lock in the handle rotated.

He stepped inside.

She knew it was a man from his build, those wide shoulders. The confidence in his intention said he didn't think he was going to get caught. Then he paused, pulled a phone from the front pocket of his jeans and looked at the screen. It illuminated his features.

Not Zimmerman.

This man was younger, his face hardened by life and the world. Not a man she'd want to meet on a dark street. And also not one she needed to tangle with right now. She had what she'd come here for—a sense of Zimmerman's state of mind. Whatever this guy was here to do, he wasn't likely to strike gold among the boxed-up remains of Zimmerman's married life.

The man sent a text then slid his phone back in the pocket.

Megan needed the right moment to slip back out the front door, so she waited for him to move into another room so she could get out.

But he came in her direction.

She pressed her back against the wall and held her breath as he moved past her to the front door. Then she slipped into the kitchen, sidestepped behind the door, and peered through the gap. Not much light came in the front windows, but it was enough to see him open the door.

"It was unlocked."

"So." Another man entered, breathing heavy. He set something down. "Let's just get on with this."

"You don't think its weird the front door was unlocked?"

"I think I'm not going to care in a minute when the whole house is burning down, because I'll be long gone."

Megan took a step back. Purely self-preservation. Thankfully she didn't bump anything. That would have been disastrous. She turned for the back door.

"I thought it was weird, that's all," the first man said.

"Just get pouring."

Gasoline. She knew before she even smelled it. They were going to burn the house down.

The second man continued, "He doesn't want anything left behind. No loose ends."

"Does that include us?"

"It will if you don't shut up. I'll kill you and leave you here myself." He paused. "Now *get pouring.*"

Megan stared at the front door. They would see her. Fast enough to shoot? She'd have to get the door open which would give them a second or two to realize what was happening and then pull their guns.

One of the men was now headed into the kitchen. That cut off her route to the back door. She wasn't about to hang around in a burning house.

Megan darted around the kitchen door and down the hall to the front door, praying with every step that they were both headed the other way through the house.

She flung the front door open...

And slammed into another man.

. . .

It took Adrian a second to realize the person who'd rushed him was a woman. He grasped her arms, not sure yet whether he was supposed to arrest her or help her, when she spoke in a breathy voice, "Fire."

That was when his nose caught up with the rest of what was happening and at the same time, his brain registered the fact he'd found the woman he'd been here looking for.

Gasoline wafted from inside the house.

He turned. "Let's go."

"Read my mind," she said, moving past him. They trotted together down the front path. "Stay low. There are two guys in there."

He snagged her arm. "Two?"

When she nodded, he pulled his gun. There was no time for backup. He'd have to arrest them himself. With Megan's help, of course. "We can wait for them to come out and take them down." He slid his cell phone from the inside of his suit jacket, called 9-1-1 and asked for police and fire.

He couldn't tell them who he was. Not when this was an FBI agent's house, and he was a fellow FBI agent from a different office looking for the agent who lived here. The wrong person would be tipped off or this would get leaked to the media, and there would be widespread panic that an FBI agent had gone rogue—armed with a sonic weapon that could take down buildings.

When the dispatcher kept up with the conversation, Adrian said, "Gotta go," and hung up.

Megan turned and started to walk away, down the sidewalk. Adrian looked at the front door of the house. Still open. No one had come out. Had the person or persons inside not cared when a woman ran out?

"Megan." He caught up to her. "Back up. Let's go take these guys down."

She shook her head.

Adrian tugged on her arm.

She gave him a hard look and pulled her arm from his grasp. He backed up and held his hands up. "We can't leave them in there. They could hurt the firefighters, or cops. Whoever gets here first."

"They didn't hurt me."

"They could know where Zimmerman is. Or what he's up to."

She shook her head. "They're just minions."

"So you know for sure that they know nothing?" He shot her a look. "I thought you were better than that."

He stared down at her, black skinny jeans. Running shoes. Dark T-shirt under a black jacket. She'd pulled back her long blond hair into a ponytail.

The look on her face was…torn.

Adrian had the interesting urge to ask her how she was doing. But he swallowed it down and said, "I don't have backup. That means I need your help to take them both down."

They couldn't pass up the opportunity to get intel from whoever was about to burn down Zimmerman's house.

"No." She turned away. "They're minions. It'll be a waste of time."

"Fine. I'll go by myself."

She frowned over her shoulder. "And get killed?"

He shrugged. "They didn't kill you."

Adrian didn't wait for her answer. He couldn't let anyone get away with destroying possible evidence, especially not someone who might have key information that he needed. This was bigger than one fire. They needed everything they could get to find Zimmerman and stop him.

He glanced over his shoulder as he went back to the house. Megan stood still, watching him. It was dark, but in the streetlights he could see her face. Not properly, otherwise he'd never have thought she was scared. That wasn't her—a self-assured, professional woman. He must have read her wrong.

Adrian pulled his gun and made his way to the front door. Sirens in the distance meant cops would be here in a minute or so. He needed to stop these guys before the fire—

Flames whooshed through the house.

He stepped back at the rush of heat. When no one came out the front, Adrian went around the side through an open gate to the back door. At the rear corner of the house, two men ran at him. Headed away from here now that the deed was done.

"FBI. Hands up." It was as much of a reflex to say it as it was to bring his weapon up and brace his weight.

They barreled into him, running at full speed.

Adrian squeezed off a shot and landed on his back. The man grunted and then went limp, dead weight on top of him. His ears rang. Adrian shifted the man off him and turned to see the other one run away.

Then he was gone.

"Adrian!" Megan's voice was audible even over the ringing in his ears. She rushed over as he was climbing to his feet and gasped as she saw the dead guy.

"The other one?"

She shook her head. "He ran away before I could reach him."

"Didn't even stop for his friend." He pulled out his phone and snapped a picture of the dead man's face.

"Are you okay?" There it was again, that fear in her eyes laced in her voice as it trembled.

The police sirens got closer. The fire was bigger now.

"Let's go."

It grated him to do it but sticking around and explaining would take entirely too much time. Adrian was on assignment and his boss knew to cover him if anything was reported in about what he'd been up to.

Like firing a weapon.

Hopefully by the time regulation caught up to him, he'd have found Zimmerman.

He took Megan's hand, and they made it to the front of the house and the sidewalk before the cop car turned the corner. They headed down the street.

"Where are you parked?"

Would she disappear, and he'd have to find her *again*? He didn't like it. They would work much better as a team. But when he'd suggested it, she'd flat out turned him down.

She led him around the corner to a side-street and stopped near a vehicle.

"This your car?"

She nodded. "Later."

"Whoa." He held up his hands again, then got between her and the route she was taking around the car to leave. "Hold up. We should talk about this, go over our game plan."

She said nothing.

"We're both trying to find Zimmerman and stop him. Working together makes sense."

She lifted her chin. "I don't do partners."

Adrian tried not to let the fact she was seriously cute distract him. His ex-wife could attest that he wasn't good at relationships. "I know, on account of the fact you let me face both those guys by myself, and one got away. The other is a lost lead." Because he was dead.

She couldn't hide the wince. "I'll find Zimmerman. You don't have to worry about making sure the FBI saves face."

"You got this?"

She shrugged. "I usually do. Why would this be any different?"

Adrian squeezed the bridge of his nose. "Fine. I need *your* help. I'm flying solo on this. Maybe I'm the one who needs someone to kick ideas around with."

"So call Steve." Before he could object, she said, "Get my number."

"That's it?" he asked. "Get your number?"

She said nothing.

"What's so bad about teaming up?" Whatever reason there was, she adamantly refused to even let herself go there. Doesn't need anyone, doesn't need anything. So why did she still look scared? It hadn't gone away. And it hadn't been a mistake.

There was real fear in her eyes.

"Meg—"

"Get down!"

A gunshot echoed through the night.

He felt her body jerk as he grabbed for her and dived, and then they both hit the ground.

Chapter 2

The words "get down" had barely left her mouth before the sting of a bullet sliced across the outside of her hip, left side. Adrian hit the ground on his back because she'd tackled him. Her mother would be *so* proud of the life choices that led her here.

Like the gentleman he was, Adrian wrapped his arms around her and shifted her to the side between him and the car. So his body shielded her from bullets. Or, *more* anyway.

Megan bit back some choice words and sat up. She bent her legs and pulled out the keys to her car. Definitely time to go. She clicked the locks and reached above her head for the handle of the passenger door.

Adrian lifted up and fired twice over the hood of the car. Then he ducked back down, a frown on his face.

She said, "Watch out," and cracked the door open. Now she just had to get around it so she could climb in. Then, of course, she'd have to start it and drive away without getting shot through the window. First things first.

"Meg—"

She didn't even let him finish her name. She crab crawled around the door and started to climb in. *Ouch.*

"You're running away?"

She gritted her teeth. "Already been shot. Don't want to get hit again and end up a chalk outline on the street."

"You've—" He blew out a breath. "Megan, keep your head down." Then she could swear she heard him pass her and open the back door. But he wouldn't.

He *couldn't* have. Because that would mean he intended to stick with her, and that was the last thing she needed right now.

Megan glanced between the seats.

Yep, he was snaking into the backseat.

The glass of the rear door on the driver's side shattered. She screamed without realizing it, or even being able to control it. That happened sometimes. These days, at least. Adrian lifted up and shot through the now open window.

His FBI badge, tucked on his belt, caught light from somewhere and flashed.

"Get out of my car."

"You wanna go, then drive!" he yelled back. "He's used up a whole lot of shots. If he isn't out by now, he will be soon, but the cops will have heard it."

He shifted and that badge flashed again. Tears blurred her vision. Megan bit back what she wanted to say and heard police sirens. She had no intention of answering any questions from local law enforcement about what she was doing here. Or who she was.

Her life was way too complicated for that.

She twisted the key and heard the car engine turn over. Got herself as much in the seat as she could and glanced up for a second. She stuck the car in drive and hit the gas. Twisted the wheel. Megan waited until they were at the first corner before she sat up, stepped on the brake and turned the corner.

They were hardly home free. She'd have to keep watch on her mirrors for a tail, but they were at least out of immediate danger.

She glanced in her rearview but couldn't see Adrian's face. "I don't suppose you want to get on the horn with someone in the FBI and call off those cops?"

She heard him shift in his seat. "Are they behind us?"

"No, but they'll be wanting to know what that was." She waited for a second. When he said nothing, she said, "Well?"

"No."

Just one—infuriating—word. Megan wanted to roll her eyes, but she was way beyond being annoyed. "I never asked you to follow me there."

Silence.

"I got away fine. There was nothing in the house, anyway. And those guys were low level. Zimmerman must have sent them back to tie-up loose ends."

"Which, by definition," he said, "means there *was* something to find. Otherwise it wouldn't have needed to be destroyed."

At this point Megan wasn't even sure Zimmerman was more than a man with a plan and the means to cause major destruction. She wanted to pray for the wisdom to know if he was also the blackmailer who had been causing so many people serious hurt. But the words just wouldn't come out.

If she got honest with God, asking for what she needed, her failings would only be all the more obvious. She needed forgiveness before she could bring to Him her list of things she needed. There had been a wall between her and her Father in heaven since…

She couldn't think of that.

Not when it put a lump in her throat she had to swallow and cough to clear. "You okay?"

"No," she fired back. "I got shot."

"Pull over now," he yelled at her.

"No."

Adrian cried out in frustration. It was almost satisfying. Almost.

She turned a corner, biting her lip at the pain in her hip. It was a graze. That was all. No biggie. But it stung, and she just wasn't in the mood for verbal sparring she wouldn't win. She didn't fight when she couldn't bring her A-game. That wasn't how she did things.

"Megan." He sounded supremely frustrated.

When he didn't say anything else, she said, "It's a graze on my hip. It needs seeing to, but its fine."

"I don't believe you." His voice almost sounded sad. "And I don't trust you. I'm trying figure this out, so we can work together to find Zimmerman. Why are you so convinced that you need to do this by yourself?"

He'd been through FBI training, so he could read people. That was how he knew. But Megan didn't like it. She wanted to be able to hide her feelings, her fears. Apparently she was doing a poor job of it.

"I don't do partners."

"So you've said."

She gritted her teeth. "Maybe..." She had to swallow. "Maybe we could...share information, or something. Check in. Tell each other what we learn."

After all, why else would she have offered him her number?

He said nothing.

Megan kept talking just to fill the silence, even though she knew that was exactly what she was doing. "I might not want to be partners, and that's my business. I have my reasons, and I'm not about to explain them. But it doesn't mean we can't come to some kind of agreement."

She barely knew Adrian. She wasn't about to explain all her hang-ups to him. Especially not when he'd nearly arrested Alexis a short time ago. One look at Megan's new friend—her teammate Bradley's new wife—and anyone could see she'd never have been involved in a kidnapping. Especially when the victim was Bradley's own sister, and her best friend.

Which brought her thoughts back to the blackmailer.

The man behind all of this had torn lives apart. He'd hurt people. Killed two of the Double Down agents. That had rippled through the entire crew at Double Down. The latest people to be put under the spotlight were Mint and Emma, still laying low so the blackmailer couldn't get to Emma and try to leverage her into doing something else for him.

Daniel Zimmerman was going down. If it took her cooperating with Adrian Walker, FBI special agent, then fine. She could suck it up and do it. Otherwise lives were at stake, and she was actually risking innocents just to keep her independence.

No way.

"So what do you say, Walker? Do we have an agreement?"

. . .

He hadn't meant to snoop. She was hurt, so he'd been checking the duffel on the back seat for some kind of first aid kit or bandage, or something.

Adrian turned the badge over in his hand. An FBI badge.

Megan was an agent?

"Walker?"

"Yeah." It came out sounding like he was miles away. All he could do was stare at the badge in his hand. Leather folder, ID photo. Megan Perkins, Special Agent.

She sighed.

His brain spun. There were a few scenarios he could see being in play here. She was retired, but kept the badge. *Unlikely*. She was a current agent on assignment here. Maybe undercover with Double Down, investigating them for some reason. Could be they were up to something and she'd been tasked with figuring out how deep it went before the bureau swept in and arrested them all. But then why put her on the search for Zimmerman? That was a major conflict of interest. Not to mention she couldn't very well investigate Double Down if she was out looking for a crooked FBI agent.

Which left the possibility that she was the crooked agent. Maybe she was even working for the blackmailer...or she *was* the blackmailer.

Adrian blew out a breath.

"You okay back there?"

"Yeah," he said, aware he sounded like a dim whit. "Fine."

Was she dirty? There had to be a reason she'd been the one out looking for Zimmerman by herself. The one who wanted to walk away instead of facing those two men. The one who'd let a man go, after Adrian had faced them down and killed one. Was there a sinister reason why Megan had just wanted to leave and allow any evidence in the house to be destroyed?

Adrian had two choices now. Get out of the car and leave her, regroup, get backup and come back to sweep her up—meaning he'd be looking for not one, but *two* rogue FBI agents. And on the off chance she hadn't been playing him this whole time, he'd find out the truth of her situation from people he could trust.

The second option was that he could stick with her. Play this game she insisted on leading them through. See if she made contact with either Zimmerman *or* the blackmailer—or Zimmerman, the blackmailer.

Either way he had not only one FBI agent to find but another one to deal with as well.

Adrian slipped his phone from the inside pocket of his suit jacket and took a photo of the badge. Then he emailed it to his boss, Special Agent in Charge Hank Cromwell, who had assigned him to report back on what Double Down knew about the blackmailer.

They'd been chasing the blackmailer for months. And while they weren't all that convinced the blackmailer was an FBI agent from Baltimore based on evidence they had gathered so far, it was possible. If Daniel Zimmerman wasn't their suspect, then Adrian would put money on him knowing who it was.

Either way, when they found him they would also find the blackmailer.

"I'm gonna find a pharmacy and make a pit stop. I need supplies." He could hear the pain in her voice.

"Is it bad?"

"Well, I'm making a mess on the seat, that's for sure. It'll be a pain to get the blood out of the upholstery."

Adrian frowned. "I'll look up a pharmacy on my phone."

"I thought that's what you were doing a second ago."

The frown didn't let up. "I'll find the closest one so you can get what you need."

She didn't say anything. And he wasn't going to explain anything. They both had their secrets. They weren't friends, or partners. She herself had said she didn't "do partners"—whatever that meant. Maybe she'd been burned before. FBI agents worked with other agents, but they didn't have assigned partners. So what had happened to her?

Megan was a mystery he didn't have time to solve right now. Not when his job was to find Zimmerman.

"Take the next left," he said. "About a mile up there's a 24-hour store."

"Okay."

He directed her to the pharmacy and went inside himself. When he came out he half expected her to be gone. He'd probably have thought about ditching her in the same circumstances. The job always came before other people's feelings—especially when those people were professionals. Perfectly capable of taking care of themselves.

Megan was a strong woman. In the past couple of weeks he'd seen her get hurt in a gunfight and still carry on. That same day two of her Double Down teammates had been killed when their RV exploded—another incident related to this that his boss was looking into.

The blackmailer had retasked a UAV on American soil and used it to attempt to cripple Double Down.

Adrian felt for them. He'd seen the pain in Megan's eyes at the funerals for the two men and in the days since. He'd even been at the meeting where they'd ID'd Zimmerman. His emotions had been entirely too tied up in this whole thing and that had to stop. He needed to get his heart out of this, even though he just felt for them like anyone would. It wasn't about the situation. Or Megan.

He needed to get back to being a professional.

"Scoot over, and I'll drive," he said, tossing the bag on the back seat. There wasn't anything he could do about the stain on the driver's seat, so he ignored it as he drove them to the hotel where he'd booked himself in for the night. The kind of room with two queen beds. Would she mind sharing? It would be much easier to keep an eye on her when he could literally keep an eye on her. Not in a creepy way. He *was* capable of being a professional, thank you. Just because Megan was a beautiful woman didn't mean he couldn't control his basic instincts. Be a gentleman. If she agreed.

"A hotel?"

He nodded.

"I hadn't gotten around to booking a room." She studied it like it wasn't the same as every other chain hotel in America. "I'd probably have slept in my car, to be honest."

"This way you can clean up in an actual bathroom. Added bonus, you can sleep in a real bed."

She eyed him, but he got out of the car. She had a gun. He figured if he did lose his mind and actually try something, she'd just shoot him anyway.

When she got out, she said, "Can you grab my duffel from the back?"

Adrian did so. They used the side entrance, and he walked her up to his room. He set the duffel on the floor in the bathroom and she went in, locking the door behind her. He took the time to change into jeans and a T-shirt, figuring it would be at least a minute before she was done so he was safe.

His phone screen illuminated. He looked at the screen, which flashed to show the email from his boss. A reply to the report Adrian had sent in.

Bring her in.

Adrian frowned, then flipped his phone face down on the table. From behind the bathroom door, there was a loud thud. "Megan?"

He strode over and knocked. "Megan, you okay?"

Chapter 3

Megan blinked and opened her eyes, feeling vaguely human. She was lying on the bed. A quick shift told her the gunshot wound she'd received had been bandaged, and she was now wearing the jogging pants from her duffel. Same shirt she'd been wearing last night. So at least that was something.

Megan shifted to her elbows and looked around the room. Adrian's hotel room. He sat at the desk, working on his laptop. Back to her. The sheets on the other bed were rumpled. Something about the sight of that affected her more than she'd have liked. As though his being here made her feel...safe.

What was that about?

Megan took a minute to study him while he wasn't aware of it. Silver hair on his temples. Tall but slender, with long arms and legs. He probably had to have his shirts custom made. She wondered if he was muscled under that T-shirt and sweater he wore.

The guy was like every other FBI agent she'd known. Trained with. Worked with. They were all essentially cut from the same cloth. Follow the rules. Ask more questions than people wanted to answer. Discover the truth. Justice would be found.

Looking at him made her wonder how she'd managed to stray so far from that without realizing. She knew she'd lost her way. The fact she hadn't gone to church in two years made that plain to see. But when had she drifted from those basic tenets that had governed her life for so long? Not in one step. It seemed more like she'd moved, step-by-step from her core values.

Fidelity. Bravery. Integrity. The center of every FBI agent.

Now that they were so clearly right in front of her, embodied in all that was Adrian Walker, it made her realize just how off course she was.

"Coffee?"

Megan started. "What?"

He turned. He'd known she was awake but hadn't said anything until now. "Coffee?" He motioned to the half-empty pot on the counter with the pen he'd been using to write on a notepad. "We've got two hours until we have to be at the office in DC, so you have time to eat and get ready."

"DC?"

He nodded, his attention back on his computer now. "My boss said the sweep of Zimmerman's computer came in. We need to be briefed."

We?

She struggled to process what he'd just said.

"Okay," she paused. "Wait a second." This was going way too fast. "Did I pass out in the bathroom?"

"Yep."

"Did you break in and dress my wound, then change my pants?"

He shifted the chair around. Grabbed his coffee cup, took a sip. Shrugged. "You passed out. From seeing the blood, I guess? Or maybe you got light-headed?"

She wasn't going to tell him what the reason was. It was bad enough he'd been here for the experience.

"And you're not going to acknowledge the fact you saw my underwear?" Thankfully she'd been wearing one of her newer, nicer pairs. She didn't want to think about him seeing a ratty old pair that were supremely comfortable, but should probably be thrown away.

He shrugged. "I was married. Been divorced three years now. And for the record, that's no more skin than I'd see if you were at the beach in a bathing suit." He shot her a look. "Plus I was a little more concerned about the bloody wound than getting a look at your tan lines."

Megan pressed her lips together. Was she supposed to say thank you? That wasn't going to happen, even if he had helped her.

She recalled rousing in the middle of it, being on the bathroom floor. His frowning face, and the gloves on, tearing medical tape with his teeth. Had she felt then like she was in danger? No way. The crux of it was that whole FBI personality. She *knew* guys like him. And yes, there were some jerks in the bureau. They were regular guys, and some took things beyond the lines drawn by honor. Not Adrian, though. She'd known that about him.

"Feel better this morning?"

She had to concede that. "Yes, I do."

He got up and poured her a cup of coffee. She accepted it, still tucked under the covers. After she took a sip, and a few more of those sleep cobwebs dissipated, she said, "You were married?"

He nodded, settling back in the chair he'd pulled so it faced her. "Six years married. Three since then."

Was he going to tell her what happened? She'd never even come close to being engaged. What was the point? Her life hadn't been conducive to a heavy relationship. And the man she'd had feelings for...

Well, he was gone now, wasn't he? Too late to realize she'd loved him.

What was the point in doing that again when it had ended in a way she would never—not for one second of the rest of her life—forget holding him in her arms and watching him bleed out all over that cold floor?

Her head spun.

The mug swayed in her arm and some spilled on the comforter.

"Whoa." He got up and started over toward her.

Megan set the mug on the bedside table between the two queen beds. "I'm okay." She cleared her throat. She needed to think about something else. "What happened? If you don't mind me asking. Why did you get a divorce?"

He stood at the end of the bed. "I worked a lot. She didn't like the fact I was home late most nights, sometimes not home at all. She wanted someone who left work at work and came home clean of it. But that isn't how this job works."

Megan shook her head. "No. It isn't." Her experience with the bureau wasn't the same as his, but she knew that at least.

"She had an affair with a guy she worked with. Changed the locks." His expression seemed to freeze, like he didn't want to feel anything. "I came home after a particularly bad case. We'd taken down a ring of guys dealing in women—some of them teens and preteens. My stuff was all boxed up in front of the garage door, and the coworker had already moved in."

"Ouch."

"Yeah."

She could see pain and disappointment in his eyes. Even though it was three years ago, it was clearly still a wound he carried with him. Maybe he'd really loved her.

Megan got up and went to her duffel. She found some clothes that would work for an FBI office meeting and headed for the bathroom with the outfit bundled under her arm. She turned back at the door, coffee cup in her other hand. No sense in it getting cold when she could put it on the bathroom counter. "It okay if I use the bathroom?"

Adrian nodded. "I'll change out here." All business. Any traces of sadness or grief over the failure of his marriage was gone now.

Megan said, "Thanks."

She knew from the look he gave her that they were on the same page. That she was thanking him for more than just letting her take a turn with the bathroom.

"Oh," she called out before she shut the door, "Who is your boss?" Maybe she knew him. She took a sip of coffee and set her clothes on the counter.

"Hank Cromwell."

Megan swallowed a mouthful of coffee. "Okay." The word was strangled.

She shut the door to the bathroom and took a breath. Hank? The agent who had been one of her father's best friends?

This meeting was going to be *so* much fun.

Not.

.   .   .

Adrian flashed his badge to the security guards in the lobby of the DC FBI office. Then he turned to Megan, and waited.

She pulled the badge from her back pocket and handed it over.

The guard logged her name and other details and then passed it back. Access badges were given. So much procedure. But it kept them safe.

They made their way through security after a few minutes. Adrian had his weapon on him, but Megan had stowed hers in the car. It definitely made it simpler not to have to go through the rigmarole of getting her things looked at.

When he caught up to her, he asked her about it.

She shrugged. "I don't have a service weapon. Not anymore. And I'm not going to bring a Double Down gun into the FBI office."

"I'm not complaining." She didn't have a service weapon? She had a badge. What kind of agent was she?

He led her to the elevator and punched the button for the floor where his office was. She glanced over. "Didn't you arrest Alexis during that whole thing, when Rachel was kidnapped?"

Adrian winced. "In my defense, it made sense to think she was involved. And when it became clear she wasn't, we backed off. But we still kept her safe." In fact, he'd been there when she had nearly been killed by Lincoln Sadler, and they'd had to take him down.

Though, Bradley—Alexis's husband now—still looked at Adrian like the agent was going to pull out cuffs at any second. Which, of course, would result in Bradley tackling him to protect the people he loved.

Adrian respected him, and all of the team at Double Down, more than they would ever know. More than he would admit, anyway.

The elevator doors opened. He said, "It's this way."

"I know." She strode out. "I remember."

Adrian followed her, trying not to look like her entourage. "Are you going to explain that to me at some point?"

The look she sent him over her shoulder made him tense. Whatever the story was, it was huge. It had affected her career. Her life. Made her into this independent—and not really in a good way—woman who only wanted to work alone. Someone who skirted the line of legality, and got the result her way.

He nodded to a few of his coworkers and got a couple of pointed looks in return. Yes, he was back. No, he hadn't found Zimmerman. They probably needed a full meeting, so he could get updated and let them know what he'd learned.

Megan stopped at his boss's office. Adrian rapped his knuckles on the door twice. Adrian reached for the handle, expecting the usual, "Come in." But it never came.

Instead, the door opened. "That you, Meggie?"

Her face softened, and her mouth curled up into a genuine smile. "Hank."

Adrian stared while his hard-nosed boss hugged Megan. Like she was his long-lost daughter. Or granddaughter, given both their ages.

"It's so good to see you."

Hank leaned back. "Sure about that?"

She laughed. "Yes, I'm telling the truth."

"You always were a good liar. Got you out of trouble plenty of times." He stepped back.

She shook her head, but Adrian caught the look on her face when Hank turned away to his desk. "Got me *in* trouble plenty of times, too."

"Still does, by the sound of it." Hank waved to the chairs. "Sit. And shut the door would you, Agent Walker?"

"Yes sir." Adrian sat in the chair by Megan.

Hank's attention was all on her. A soft, fatherly gaze Adrian had never seen before. He could hardly believe he was seeing it now. And then his boss said, "It really is good to see you, Meg."

She pressed her lips together and smiled. "It's good to be seen."

Adrian figured that was the truth, despite her apparent ability to lie. Nothing about this woman made sense. She was an FBI agent. She didn't have a service weapon. In the weeks he'd known her, it was clear she worked for Double Down. Not the FBI. He wanted to ask what was going on, but was that too demanding? They seemed to be having some kind of moment. Adrian didn't want to intrude, or ruin it.

For the first time since he'd met her, only weeks ago, Megan actually looked relaxed. Not completely at ease. He didn't even know if that was possible. Still, she seemed comfortable. He didn't think it was the FBI office, so it had to be this man. His boss. She knew him, that much was clear. Had they worked together before?

His email hadn't been the first time he'd mentioned her in communications with his boss. It was, however, the first time he'd discovered her connection to the FBI. That was the catalyst for his boss asking them both to come in.

So was Hank going to explain?

Maybe he was going to tell Megan she should work with Adrian. That would help speed this along. Having her on his team and not out in front doing her own thing—with him feeling like he had to watch her back every step of the way.

"So." His boss started everything that way. Speech. Explanation. Didn't matter. Then he said, "We've gone over every inch of Zimmerman's computer. Work and home. All his online accounts, social media. Emails. Found some instant messages you're going to want to look through, Walker."

Adrian accepted the file his boss handed him across the desk.

"Speaks to his state of mind. And his sympathies toward a group of domestic extremists."

"Islamic?"

Hank shook his head. "Home grown, backwoods guys. Guns, Bibles, and freedom." He paused, his opinion of that clear. "They hate the government, no matter which side it's leaning toward right now."

Adrian didn't view the federal government as any kind of enemy of the American people. Some felt that way. And while he knew there were many flaws in the system, along with selfish people making important decisions for their own gain, he'd chosen to be part of it. To work every day to try and make it better. To not let men like Zimmerman take their anger out on innocent people.

Adrian said, "Any indication of where he might strike with the sonic weapon?"

"There's been chatter about the Republican convention in Denver next week. And a symposium of defense contractors in a couple of days, the location of which was *supposed* to be secret." Hank mashed his lips together, making his mustache twitch. "I'll keep you posted on both of those."

Megan said, "We'll know if he tries to fly the weapon into a city, right?"

Hank nodded. "It'd fit in a duffel, or large suitcase. But he'll know every avenue we're watching. He's been trained the same way we've been trained." Hank paused, his attention on Megan. "That's why we need someone who thinks outside of the FBI box."

"Me?" It was less of a question and more of a realization.

Hank nodded. "But there's another reason I think you're going to want to be all-in on this with us."

Adrian looked up from the papers he'd been studying over.

Megan's body had stilled. "What reason?"

Hank swallowed, looking unsure for the first time ever. "We found a link. Between Daniel Zimmerman and *El Cuervo*."

The Crow? Adrian's knowledge of Spanish wasn't much to speak of, but he thought he had that right. *El Cuervo* was reportedly a hitman for a Venezuelan drug cartel, an up-and-coming player, and he was high on the FBI's most wanted list. What did he have to do with—

Megan shoved her chair back and headed for the door, breathing hard.

"Sit down, Meggie."

Chapter 4

She turned back from the door, breathing hard. "Don't give this to me if it's nothing."

Hank's gaze softened the way her father's would have done. And it made all of this harder than it already should have been. Her dad had been gone for more than fifteen years, killed on the job as an FBI agent. A bust gone wrong, her dad had caught a bullet to the neck. Her mom had been used to living a single-parent life already, with Megan's dad being away so much. Still, losing her husband had hit her.

Being here in this office with Hank brought it all back. What she'd lost. What she would have had, as a legacy agent—her father being a special agent as well. He'd have supported her. And yet, without his death in the line of duty, would she have even become an agent? Maybe. Or maybe she'd have never even thought of it.

"Who is *El Cuervo*?"

She didn't want to look at Adrian. Not when she was like this, with her emotions far too close to the surface. Megan wanted to leave that part of her life behind, the way she'd left the FBI behind.

And kept the badge.

She figured it was Hank refusing to let her go, and twisting some arms to get it approved. Or maybe sliding paperwork through, under the radar. They didn't pay her. She didn't have the rights or authority an FBI agent possessed—at least, she hadn't attempted to exercise those rights. If she did, someone would probably notice and Hank would get into trouble.

Megan shook her head to chase away the errant thoughts. She had to focus, or Adrian would realize exactly how unhinged she was.

Hank was already frowning at her. "You want to tell him the story, or should I?"

"Why does he even need to know? So what if there's a link between Zimmerman and *El Cuervo?* It's probably only because one is an FBI agent and the other is a wanted criminal."

"They were communicating."

She lifted her chin. "We already know Zimmerman is dirty."

She knew she was arguing only as a delay tactic, because she'd rather run, but leaving would be too obvious. She also wanted actual proof before she jumped on this bandwagon and chased after Zimmerman for answers. "We're already trying to find SAC Zimmerman, what does it matter the reason? Our priority is bringing him in because of the sonic weapon and what he plans to do with it."

She glanced between them and let her gaze settle on Adrian. Wasn't he going to say something?

"Plus the fact he's been blackmailing people around Washington and terrorizing them for his own gain." Adrian studied her, then turned to Hank. "She's right. Unless this will help us locate Zimmerman, it's only an incidental connection."

She asked Hank, "Do you think Zimmerman has gone to *El Cuervo* for cover while he enacts whatever plan he has in place?" Then she realized another—possibly more deadly—scenario. "Or is he planning on selling the sonic weapon to the Venezuelans?"

A flash of disappointment moved over Hank's face. He sat back in his chair, the look disappearing almost as fast as it had come.

Because she hadn't wanted to talk in front of Adrian about what happened two years ago?

He said, "The chatter indicates the relationship was alive and well as far back as two years. Specifically in the weeks before…" He shot her a pointed look.

She didn't move a muscle. Didn't breathe. Didn't think, just said, "Before Special Agent Tennyson was killed?"

He nodded.

Megan was surprised she'd even been able to get her partner's last name out. "Was Zimmerman responsible for what happened?" Someone had burned her and Will, and it led to Will's death.

"Maybe you should find him, ask him that for yourself."

If Hank thought that would make her push harder to find Zimmerman, he was mistaken. The man was a traitor at best, a terrorist at the worst. She didn't need more drive than that to go out and find him.

"I will." She swallowed.

Adrian was watching the whole thing, glancing back and forth between them, but saying nothing. Just sitting there doing whatever he was doing. Her life wasn't that interesting. But would she be able to convince him of that? Probably not. She was an anomaly. That was all. Nothing but a mystery he needed to solve, having been trained extensively to spot inconsistencies, uncover hidden truths, and see things that were out of place.

Megan's whole life was out of place.

What special agent could ignore that?

Her phone rang in her jacket pocket, vibrating against her hip, but she ignored it.

Apparently Hank saw it. "Probably your mom."

Megan rolled her eyes. "Get me intel that will help me find Zimmerman. If you don't have it, then you're wasting my time here." She turned to the door, glancing back over her shoulder for a second. "It was good to see you, Hank."

Megan strode out through the bull pen to the hallway.

Hopefully he would need to talk more with Adrian, being the man's boss and all. That would give her some time to get out in front of Walker on the search for Zimmerman. She didn't need his help—or anyone else's—to bring down the rogue agent. Especially if he had something to do with Will's death.

She'd been looking for *El Cuervo* in her spare time since she signed on as one of Steve's team members at Double Down. Lately, she hadn't made much progress. Most of her leads had gone dry, given basically everyone who had been present—or who knew about that night—was either dead or in jail.

The ones in jail, two members of *El Cuervo*'s group, hadn't wanted to speak to her when she paid them a visit. They'd both died in prison fights less than a month later.

No one wanted her asking questions. Whoever was behind Will's death hadn't wanted her to find out the truth. And the FBI had told her to take some time. *Get her head together.* Whatever that meant.

But until she got answers, her head wasn't going to be "together." Was it? So she'd lived with the dissonance of it all for two years. Questions. No answers. Death. The end of her FBI career. Maybe Hank was only prolonging the inevitable, not doing her a favor by allowing her to keep her badge.

Sure, every so often he threw her the odd undercover assignment. Or a recon mission he didn't have an agent for. On occasion he needed someone off radar because it was sensitive.

Maybe she should just quit it all. Leave her badge on Hank's desk.

Give up Double Down.

Go back to her basement and the murder board she'd set up down there. Find a new lead.

Bring *El Cuervo* down.

Her phone rang again. She pulled it out and looked for a quiet place to answer. The caller ID said, *Double Down Inc.*

She slid to answer the call and said, "Hi, Mom."

"Megan." Her mom's voice was soft, which meant no one else was in the reception area of the office. Any other time she was all business. She treated Steve like he was her wayward son, and the other men like they were a bunch of rabble-rousers. Like, she'd *literally* used that phrase.

Megan said, "I thought we were packing up the office because of you-know-who." This wasn't an elaborate children's fantasy novel, but they did have a powerful enemy. One who was listening to everything.

"I have nothing to hide," her mom said. "I'm a professional, and Double Down is a professional company. We don't run from trouble."

Megan shut her eyes for a second, letting her mom's strength wash over her. Why couldn't she be more like that?

. . .

Adrian stared at the doorway Megan had just walked through, then he looked back at his boss. "I'm going to need more information than I have, sir."

Hank Cromwell, Special Agent in Charge and Adrian's boss, nodded. His thoughts seemed to be full of Megan still. Whatever all that was about, Adrian needed to know. There was more than a boss/employee relationship between Hank and Megan. The man seemed to have asserted himself into some kind of father figure role. And he'd called her *Meggie*. Which Adrian would have found hilarious—at any other time.

Not right now.

"*El Cuervo?*"

Adrian nodded. "Can you have support send me all the files? I'd like to look into Zimmerman's relationship with him."

Hank blew out a breath. "Can't believe he's had an agent on his payroll all this time. And we're only finding out about it because Zimmerman stole a sonic weapon." He shook his head. "If he hadn't exposed his real intentions, would we ever have known? He'd have been the Venezuelan's sleeper agent. And for how long?"

Not to mention, the damage the man might've done in the years since.

How much of that damage had affected Megan?

Adrian said, "What happened to her and this Agent Tennyson person?"

Hank was back to staring at the door. "Megan was undercover from early on in her career. Just had a way about her, it was noticed right away. Her being a legacy and all."

Megan had a parent who was an agent? Adrian had tried to find out about her background a few times. He hadn't managed to get any information past her job with Double Down, her current address, and the fact her mother worked for the company as Steve's assistant.

"Her father?"

"Perkins was killed in that Ceour d'Alene debacle." Hank let out a breath and shook his head. "Megan caught the bug. Decided she wanted to be an agent. I didn't want her undercover, but it was obvious that was what suited her."

Adrian nodded. He could see that from what he knew of her, and how he'd seen her be the past few weeks. She'd gone through the deaths of two of Double Down's team members, and while he knew for a fact she'd grieved, it was clear she had an incredible ability to compartmentalize. After all, she'd passed out in the bathroom at the hotel and rolled through the fact that he'd bandaged and dressed her in clean pants, only mildly thrown by the whole thing. He figured most of the reaction she'd had was due to the embarrassment of having passed out from blood loss in the first place.

She had strength. But he could also see that she'd suffered something, and it had shaken her to the core.

"Tennyson was her partner. Will was bent like her, but with a whole lot more wild." Hank shook his head again. "If anyone would've betrayed their oath, it was him. But psych evals all came back clean. Solid to the core, just had that renegade exterior. They figured it was a front. Like a part he played. So they stuck him undercover with Megan."

Hank blew out a breath and continued, "Thick as thieves, they were. Unstoppable. Closed so many cases they gained a reputation up and down the west coast. If they'd taken down *El Cuervo* like they'd planned, it would've gotten them both commendations, and they knew it." He paused. "Think that made them cocky. Will maybe more than Megan, at least. He probably pushed it, trying to get a result before it was time."

Undercover was a delicate balance of keeping the focus on the job, playing the part, and not being "made" as a fed. Adrian had done some undercover work but was more suited to the nuts and bolts after the crime had been committed, figuring out who was responsible and ensuring justice was brought.

If Megan had the skills for undercover, and it seemed that she did, then she would be a serious asset to finding and bringing down Zimmerman. She knew how to think like a criminal. How to talk like one. She likely had contacts in that world which would take Adrian weeks to establish.

He needed her. Which meant he had to convince her to team up with him.

First, though, he needed to know why she was so resistant to having a partner. And he figured it was wrapped up in this Tennyson person's story.

"What happened to her partner?" Adrian asked. Ready to get the answers he needed and get going after Megan. They were running out of time to find Zimmerman.

"*El Cuervo* found out who they were. Somehow. Had two of his guys pick up Will and Megan. Three days, no one knew where they were. Never found Will's body. Megan walked into the US embassy in Mexico City with torn up clothes, covered in blood. Didn't say a word until she got back here."

"Mexico City?"

Hank shrugged. "She only started talking when I showed up at the hospital in Bethesda and made her talk." Hank swallowed. "She said they killed Will in front of her. Bunch of lower level guys. Who knows what they did to her. She's never told anyone about it."

Adrian winced.

"Tossed her out of the van on the side of a highway. Took her a day to walk into Mexico City," Hank said. "She wouldn't tell me more than that."

"You think it was *El Cuervo?*"

Hank nodded. "She figured he was sending a message. Proof he's got someone on our payroll. She's never figured out who it is, and I know she's still looking into it."

"You think it's Zimmerman?" Adrian asked. "That he's the one who sold out her and her partner to the Venezuelans and got an agent killed?"

"And changed another agent's life irrevocably."

Adrian squeezed his eyes shut for a second. Megan had seemed like he didn't want to hear about the connection between Zimmerman and *El Cuervo.* Because she couldn't handle the news and had to compartmentalize it for later?

That was all the time Adrian gave himself to absorb everything that had happened to Megan in her career as an FBI agent. No wonder she didn't want to work with anyone else. She'd been there when her partner was killed. And even if there hadn't been anything romantic between them—which there very well could've been—there were likely deep feelings.

Undercover agents had to trust each other with everything. Not just to watch each other's back the way they did on operations. When you were undercover it was life and death. Every breath was dangerous.

And for Megan, it had ended in the worst possible way.

But she was still moving. Still fighting. He figured she organized her life in a way that meant she could cope. Set aside and process later. The woman had a job she needed to do, probably more than "wanted" to. And her mom was a close part of her life.

She was more than a mystery to him now.

Adrian got up. "Is that everything?"

Hank nodded. "I'll get you those files. You take care of my girl."

"Sir?"

"Megan Perkins is a priority here."

Adrian passed out of Hank's office at a stride, determined to catch up to Megan as fast as possible. They were going to take down Zimmerman, and Adrian was going to be with her every step of the way until that happened. Regardless of what SAC Cromwell had been attempting to imply with that comment.

Because she'd gone through enough. More than anyone—agent or no—should ever have to suffer. The FBI owed her.

And Adrian was going to pay that bill.

Chapter 5

Megan gripped the phone as she leaned against the counter in the break room, aware of several sets of eyes trained on her. She was an exception in the office, despite her relationship with Hank. It wasn't like she came around often.

"It just came through on Steve's email and the company account," her mom said.

"Huh?" She blinked and tuned into what her mom had been saying.

"Zimmerman stopped at a children's hospital in St Louis."

Megan's eyebrows lifted.

"He reportedly left a message with one of the patients, a boy with Leukemia." Her mom paused. "Very sad. The nurses sent the email through. Apparently the boy says Zimmerman was adamant."

"They mentioned him by name?" If this was legit, it was a serious breakthrough. But not because they'd gained a lead through hard work. No. Zimmerman had contacted them.

But why?

Her mom said, "I'll forward you the actual email."

"Don't do that." Megan saw Adrian in the doorway and frowned at the look on his face. He shook his head. She said to her mom, "Don't send it on. It could have a virus, or a worm. You can give away my location."

Her mom said, "Can't he just find your GPS because of this call?"

"Not if you're using the secure line."

"I am."

"Then we're covered. But read me the email anyway. Humor me. Yeah?" Megan waved Adrian over, and then put the phone on speaker.

"...trust your judgment. Of course." Her mom's voice came through so they could both hear it.

"Thanks, Mom."

"Here goes." Her mom paused. "It says, 'To Megan Perkins.' So he knows who you are. How, I don't know."

Adrian shifted. Megan didn't look at him. She didn't want to know what was on his face, considering she likely wouldn't be able to decipher it anyway. He probably had no clue why she'd wanted him to listen in on this call. He needed to piece all this together without her having to explain. Yes, her mom worked for Double Down. Receptionist since the day Megan was hired.

Now she could add the fact Daniel Zimmerman—a man she'd never met, and didn't know—had used her name. The logical explanation was that the blackmailer knew who she was.

Megan said, "What's the rest?"

"Are you sure—"

"Mom. Tear the bandage off quick."

"Well, it's not exactly bad news. More like informational."

"*Mom.*"

"Okay, fine." Her mom sighed. "This morning Daniel Zimmerman visited the oncology ward at the St. Louis children's hospital."

Adrian's body shifted, but he said nothing.

Megan waited.

"He left a message with one of our patients and asked that you retrieve it as soon as possible. Due to the patient's condition, we recommend that as well. Our department is not the place for whatever kind of arrangement you have established with this man, and the patient is in no condition to wait, though he insists on speaking to you himself." Her mom paused. "That's all of it."

Megan glanced up at Adrian then, asking her mom, "Can you get us—"

"The plane is at Potomac Airport. It's waiting for you, and the pilot already filed a flight plan for St. Louis."

"Take a look at the airports in and around St. Louis," Megan said. "See if Zimmerman took a flight out after he delivered this message."

"Will do. And...'us'? What's that about?" Her mom's tone switched to being entirely too hopeful. "Is Agent Walker with you? I've seen his picture." She whispered, "He's cute."

Megan shut her eyes. Her face flamed.

Adrian chuckled under his breath.

"Goodbye, Mom." She opened her eyes to end the call and stowed the phone back in her jacket.

How was she supposed to face Adrian now? He'd seen her with her pants off—thank you, Cross Fit. She kept in shape, so that was something at least. But now her mom thought he was "cute." Was it possible to die from embarrassment?

"Megan."

She grudgingly acknowledged his existence, still aware her cheeks were way too flushed.

"St. Louis?"

"I guess we have a plane to catch," she said. "If you'd like to come as well…" She let that go unfinished. Did he want an engraved invitation? He probably knew all about Will, which was why he now looked at her with that added bit of softness in his eyes. "I don't need your help," she reminded him. "But if we're both going to the same city next anyway, then it makes sense to take the same plane. Less gas. It's better for the environment." She lifted her chin.

"The environment?"

"Yes. Don't you care about the destruction of the planet?" It took all her undercover skills to keep a straight face despite the ridiculousness. Not of being eco-conscious, that wasn't what was ridiculous. Just using that for an excuse because she didn't want a partner, and that fact hadn't changed. But she couldn't ignore the fact that she'd gotten…used to him.

He'd been there through some insanity the past few days. Weeks.

They both wanted Zimmerman, the blackmailer, brought down.

They wanted the American people safeguarded from a rogue FBI agent with a deadly weapon.

She didn't have to explain why she did some things the FBI way. And she didn't have to explain why she didn't need his help. Once this was done, she wasn't going to have to see that sadness in his gaze anymore.

"Let's go." She breezed past him. The need to go see what Zimmerman had left with a sick child was like being overtaken by some body-snatching alien. She'd never felt so possessed. Zimmerman either was the blackmailer, or he knew who they were.

The past wasn't supposed to affect her this badly, but it was. Hearing that Zimmerman was connected to *El Cuervo* had done that. Was that why he'd sent her a message? And what did all this have to do with the blackmail scheme?

Hank stood at his office door. He stared across the bullpen at them coming out of the break room. She lifted a hand and waved. "Bye, Hank."

Several agents in the room blinked their surprise. They were trained not to give more than that away, and even that much was a slip. Still, she didn't blame them for reacting like that when she'd called their boss by his first name.

She jabbed at the button for the elevator, aware that Adrian had come to stand behind her. When she glanced at him, she saw he stared at his phone. Swiped. Tapped. Emails, probably. Updates. Reports. He hadn't had the chance to check in with his team, and now they were headed out into the field again.

Adrian's team—under Hank's direction—were after the blackmailer. That was why Adrian had been on her tail, determined to make a team with her. His involvement seemed so natural after he'd been there when two Double Down teammates had died.

Her heart tripped, but she pushed through the ache.

New day. Same old wound.

Thinking about Adrian was better than dwelling on *El Cuervo*. She hadn't exactly put the experience behind her, though she'd tried to make her mom believe that was true. Hank knew the real story, and he'd been helping her with information gathering.

Was Zimmerman really part of the Venezuelan's operation? And if he'd been part of it for years, that meant the Venezuelans had affected FBI operations for just as long. The virus would spread both ways, and there was no antidote. Good people had suffered. Justice had been subverted. And for what? So Zimmerman could get himself a payday?

The whole thing made her angrier than she'd been at the men who blew off Will's head right in front of her face.

"Megan." His voice was soft.

She glanced at Adrian. The doors to the elevator slid open on the ground floor. "Let's go." She swept out of the elevator car into the lobby. Tears blurred her vision, but she didn't let them fall. She'd shed too many already. To the point where she'd been determined to think her emotions had dried up. Evidently not.

She didn't want to yield. Not even to God, though that fact made her even sadder than she already was. Yielding meant she would soften, and that wasn't going to help her. Vulnerability was what had gotten her into this mess.

What she needed was to be strong. Secure. She had to find the strength within herself, despite the ways God had helped her. He'd been with her. He had sent help that meant she could get to the embassy. She knew she hadn't been alone. But she *had* been vulnerable.

And there was no way she was going to allow herself to slip back into that place again.

.   .   .

Adrian kept an eye on her the whole way to St. Louis. On Double Down's private plane, of all things. Actually, according to Megan, it was, "One of their planes." Like that was perfectly normal.

Maybe in the private sector, because it certainly wasn't true in the FBI.

Megan didn't say much beyond that one comment. She got on her phone for a while, checking email and such. Her comment to her mother that she shouldn't send over the email made him ask her if they thought the blackmailer was still in their computer system.

She'd said, "Can't be too careful."

The blackmailer had hacked the Double Down computer system and gotten Emma Burroughs, a victim of his, to leave the safety of their warehouse in order to gain control of her again. It was how the sonic weapon had been stolen by Zimmerman. Emma had broken into the facility while the blackmailer had coerced a scientist into giving him the door code to the secure lab. After that, Zimmerman had taken the sonic weapon and ordered Emma killed.

Thankfully, Mint—real name Davis Malone, and not a man Adrian wanted to meet in a dark alley—had saved her life. Now Emma and Megan's Double Down teammate were inseparable.

Good things that had come from bad. Kind of like Bradley and Alexis's marriage.

So why did that always seem to be true of everyone else's life? He only had to look at Megan's life to see the truth. Some people didn't get their happy endings, even as much as he might want that for her.

Adrian had sworn to himself that he would put his career first and then later see what the future might hold for him. After he'd established himself in his field. He knew he wasn't going to be an FBI agent forever. The hours, and the stress, were too much to hold onto it long-term. That meant one day he had to look past his tenure with the bureau. To relationships, and family.

Had Megan thought she was going to be an FBI agent for the twenty years it took before retirement was a possibility? Adrian didn't like to make assumptions about life—though wasn't that what he was doing by pushing the chance to have a relationship off until later?

If he'd assumed his first marriage would work, then he'd have been disappointed by the fact his wife cheated on him and then kicked him out. She'd made her choice. In response, he'd decided to focus on his career—the very thing she'd accused him of. So he had good focus, and it was even better since the divorce. He didn't know why that was bad. It wasn't like she hadn't known the job he did before they got married.

The plane landed, and they unbuckled their belts. When Megan reached for her duffel on the seat across the aisle, he said, "I'll get that. If you want."

She looked like she was about to argue, so he added, "Since you got shot yesterday, and all." He deftly took it from her before she could think to hold onto it. "I wouldn't want it to bump against your hip by accident. It's probably still sore."

He wasn't going to think about the fact he'd seen what he'd see if she was at the pool in a bathing suit. He might be a gentleman, but he was still a man. God had made him to appreciate the female form. It was a good thing, a blessing to be able to enjoy—in the right circumstances. Not that he thought he'd ever be able to have that with Megan.

If she didn't want a partner, she wasn't likely to let him in.

She'd had Will Tennyson, and he'd been killed. If she'd loved him as much as she trusted him as her partner, then Adrian figured she'd built those walls to hide behind for good reason. She'd been more than burned.

And wasn't that what he'd done, determining to save relationships for later? Who could say the next woman he fell for wouldn't object to his job the way Sandra had? He was saving himself from being hurt again by not even getting into a relationship until he was done with the FBI. Right? But maybe it was just another way of taking the easy route.

Megan was the one protecting herself from genuine trauma.

"Why are you looking at me like that?" She looked surprised she'd said it. "Never mind."

"No." He touched her elbow. "It's okay. And I'm sorry."

"For looking at me?"

"I'm not sure I'm going to apologize for admiring a beautiful woman," he said, purely to test the waters.

Her gaze softened, but he didn't get the smile he wanted. And she didn't blush. Maybe she'd been changed too much she didn't do that anymore.

"Not so bad looking yourself, champ."

He barked out a laugh. "I can't say it's ever been put like that before."

"Had a lot of admirers?" Now she looked like she was ready to punch someone. Good.

He said, "I guess you'll have to ask me some probing questions. Put those FBI investigative skills to good use and see what dark secrets I'm hiding in my past."

She rolled her eyes. "Please. A golden boy like you probably grew up wanting to be an FBI agent. A badge and a gun. Your mom cried when you graduated the academy, didn't she?"

"Didn't yours?"

She shook her head. "She didn't speak to me for a month."

Adrian didn't know what to say to that.

Megan lifted a smaller bag and slid it over her head so the strap went across her body. The bag rested against her good hip as she wandered to the door. "Your mom probably tells her friends all about you, so you get calls to fix people's parking tickets."

"I'm not a cop." That didn't mean it didn't happen exactly like that, though. "She knows that."

Megan chuckled. "Aced all your tests. Broke some records, maybe?" She studied him, so he nodded. She said, "Thought so. The G-man who closes all the cases."

"I'm waiting for the downside." When she glanced at him, he shot her a smile, then said, "I'm also unsure what this proves. Other than the fact you've figured out nothing about me that isn't plainly obvious."

"Your favorite color is red."

He frowned. "How did you know that?"

"And when you were married, you didn't wear your ring."

"It was too big." He'd always meant to go get it resized, but hadn't ever made time in his schedule. It just seemed like such an incidental thing when he had so much that was more important going on in his life.

She walked out of the plane and down the steps. Adrian followed. They made their way to the SUV parked close to the hangar.

The man leaning against the vehicle tossed Megan the keys. "Perkins."

"Hernandez." She turned and tossed the keys at Adrian. He caught them out of the air one-handed.

"You drive. I'll navigate."

The man by the SUV smirked. "Happy hunting."

Megan nodded her head, then tossed her bag on the back seat and left the door open so he could do the same.

"Friend of yours?"

Megan shrugged. "We contract out some things, on occasion." She got in the front passenger side.

Adrian went around to the driver's door and got in. She already had her phone loaded with directions to the hospital. He said, "You think he'll still be there when we show up?"

Megan buckled up, her attention out the window. "I doubt it. I figure he's long gone."

"On a flight out?"

She scrunched up her nose in a type of shrug. "I'd buy a beater car if I was him. Or steal one. But mom will be occupied with web searches and making phone calls, trying to find him regardless."

Things that wouldn't necessarily draw the blackmailer's attention. Or give anything away.

"Keeping her busy?"

Megan shrugged. "She wants to help."

And Megan had to balance allowing her to be part of her daughter's life with keeping her safe.

Adrian figured the blackmailer knew what they knew about Zimmerman regardless of Megan taking that precaution with the email. They had to assume as much. Which meant the blackmailer knew they were in St. Louis, and that they were headed for the hospital to retrieve whatever "message" had been left for them.

Adrian pulled out and headed for the exit. "You okay?"

She was looking out the window again. "Just can't shake the feeling someone is watching. And I *don't* like having a target on my back."

Chapter 6

"You think this might be a trap?" Adrian parked the car in an empty slot at the back of the hospital parking lot.

"I've learned the hard way to assume *everything* is a trap." Megan shoved the door open. The sun was bright, the air cool and crisp. She grabbed her jacket off the back seat, mostly so it would cover the gun on her hip. She wasn't here as an agent. Adrian needed to take the lead.

She was going to focus on their surroundings. Otherwise her thoughts would drag her down in the idea that Zimmerman had a relationship of some sort with *El Cuervo*.

Together they headed for the lobby and found the right floor. The nurse had given a room number for the sick child, but Megan wanted to talk to the woman who'd sent the email first. They needed details, along with whatever message was left for her. And the less they could bother a sick child, the better—as far as she was concerned.

Megan rapped her knuckles on the counter at the nurse's station. The woman looked up. "Help you?" She leaned her big body back in the chair.

Megan smiled. "We're looking for a nurse, Patricia Carlton."

"That's me."

Adrian pulled out his badge. "I'm Special Agent Walker, this is my associate, Megan Perkins. We need to ask you a few questions about the man who visited your patient."

The woman's countenance immediately fell. "José isn't doing well. He slipped into a coma about thirty minutes ago."

"He did?" Adrian's question came right when Megan opened her mouth to ask the same thing. The kid was in a coma? They needed to know if he'd conveyed the message to anyone—his mom, or one of the nurses—before he went unconscious. This would change their plan of action.

After the nurse nodded, Megan said, "Was anyone in the room around the time he slipped into the coma?"

"His mother was." The nurse glanced between Megan and Adrian. "She's been by his side for weeks."

Megan nodded. If they wanted to be completely sure, they'd need to look at surveillance. Make certain no one who shouldn't have been in the room had entered. She glanced at Adrian, who gave her a short nod. They were in agreement then. And he knew what she'd been asking.

It was possible the coma hadn't come naturally as a result of the illness. Someone could have forced the child's body into the coma. Hurt him, so he couldn't tell them anything.

"Did you see the man?" Adrian asked her.

The nurse shrugged. "He seemed familiar. Like maybe I've seen him somewhere before."

Maybe on the news? Zimmerman's face had been broadcast on TV and social media over the past day. If she'd been online at all, she'd likely seen his image.

"I can ask the mom if she'll speak with you."

Megan shrugged. "The last thing we want is to bother her at a time like this, but I'm afraid it's unavoidable." She didn't want to use the word "terrorist," but she would if she had to. "And if we could look at your surveillance footage that would be great."

If a verbal message had been given, they would probably never learn what it was.

"Let me check with José's mom," the nurse said, lifting out of the chair. "She might be ready for a break and willing to talk."

Megan thought for a second about the boy. About his life being in danger. They needed to put it out there—maybe on the Double Down server—that he'd slipped into the coma before he could tell anyone anything. Then the blackmailer would see it. Megan wanted to make sure he knew the child couldn't say anything, in the hopes the blackmailer would leave the boy alone. No sick child needed that, and it galled her that Zimmerman had dragged him into this in the first place. It was the last thing that should be on the rogue FBI agent's to-do list right now.

After the nurse moved out of earshot, Adrian said, "You should take point with the mom. I'll get with security about looking at their surveillance."

It wasn't an order, as such, but he also wasn't asking for her opinion. Adrian was a capable agent, calling the shots. She was a solo flyer. They were going to have conflicts, but right now wasn't the time to drag out their differences and start a fight. This relationship wasn't going to last forever, right? After they found

Zimmerman—and she got the answers she wanted—Adrian could take him in. She wouldn't have anything to do with a conviction.

All she wanted was peace.

"Megan?"

She realized she'd been zoning. "That's fine. If the mom wants to talk, I'll do it." One woman would be less intimidating to a distraught mother than a pair of federal agents. "You check and see if anyone came in or out of that room around the time the kid went into the coma. I want to know if he was hurt. Because if he was, that person should be brought before a judge and convicted."

Adrian reached out like he was going to touch her. He looked as though he wanted to say something. Before he could, the nurse said, "She's ready for you in the waiting area." The woman slipped back behind her desk. "And I'll call security, if one of you wants to talk to them."

"Thanks," Adrian said. He glanced once at her, and then he walked away.

Megan found the mother. A tiny Hispanic woman far younger than she'd imagined. The woman couldn't be more than late twenties at most. Puffy-eyed, she clutched a balled-up tissue while she sat in the waiting area the nurse had directed Megan to. "Can I get you some tea, Mrs...?"

"It's Sofía." She gave Megan a small, sad smile. "Sofía Gonzalez." Sofía sighed. "The nurse said you're with the FBI?"

Megan nodded. "How about that tea?"

Sofía shook her head. "I can't eat anything." She touched her stomach and made a face that might have been amusing at any other time. "But thank you." She had a slight accent, her long hair was disheveled, and she wore what were probably yesterday's clothes.

Megan figured she looked pretty put together given what she was going through. She sat across from the woman. "A man visited your son, is that right?"

She nodded. "I was downstairs getting some breakfast. When I came back up, José said a man had visited him. A white man, an FBI agent. That's what he said." She almost looked apologetic.

Megan shrugged, pulling out her phone. She pulled up a picture of Zimmerman and showed it to Sofía. "Have you seen this man around the hospital at all?"

Sofía frowned. "No. Is that him?"

"We can't be certain, but we think so."

"Why would a bad man visit my son?"

"I don't know," Megan answered, honestly. The idea Zimmerman had simply been there to deliver a message meant for Megan was bizarre, to say the least. "Did José say anything about what the man said to him?"

"Not much." Sofía shifted and pulled out something from the purse beside her hip. "But he said the man gave him this."

She opened her hand. Sitting in her palm was a thumb drive.

"May I have that?"

Sofía nodded.

Megan slipped the thumb drive in her pocket. Answers. This was all about answers. Could this be it? She'd been investigating *El Cuervo* for so long, trying to figure out his identity, trying to work out who had sold her and Will out. Was it Zimmerman?

The idea he would suddenly just hand her answers didn't make sense.

There had to be more going on here than she knew.

. . .

Adrian sat in the swivel chair and watched surveillance footage from the hallway outside the child's room. Hospital staff. Parents. They scanned through the recorded image, three hours of footage, before he saw the man they were looking for.

"Pause it, please."

The security guard clicked the mouse.

"That's him," Adrian said. "That's Zimmerman."

He opened his email and started a new message to SAC Cromwell, noting the time Zimmerman had shown up. He didn't send the email to Hank but instead set it on the desktop and left the message open, so he could insert the exact time the man left.

Zimmerman had entered the hospital room earlier that morning, almost six hours ago now. Adrian kept watching until he walked out of the room and then noted the time.

He'd stayed for seven minutes and then left. "What did they talk about that whole time?"

"Huh?"

Adrian shook his head. "Nothing. Just thinking aloud."

"My wife does that." The man huffed.

He ignored the man and studied the footage up until the time the boy went into a coma. No one went in or out of the room except authorized personnel. Which meant the likely scenario was that the kid's Leukemia had done that damage. He was deteriorating, that was all.

Adrian sent up a prayer for the kid. What else could he do? Nothing, except ask the One in control to give mercy in this situation.

Adrian wasn't all that good at mercy. Mostly he figured his role in life was to expect the best out of other people. After all, that was how he treated himself. If they didn't deliver, he simply readjusted his expectations so that the next time he knew what they *could* bring to the table.

He had yet to figure out Megan. One second she seemed eminently capable, and the next it was like she'd been paralyzed. Trauma, most likely. PTSD, probably. Like at Zimmerman's house when she'd avoided confronting those two men.

Then other times she seemed like she was dealing well, living her life. But maybe she'd never get over it. And maybe she never *should.* Life went on. She had however many days God gave her stretched out in front of her to enjoy. She didn't need to be mired in the past. But honoring the memory of a good man who'd been killed by bad people couldn't be a bad thing—so long as it didn't stop her from *living.*

His phone rang.

Adrian stood and said, "Thank you for your time."

The security guard nodded. "Sure thing, man."

He wandered out into the hall and answered his call. The ID said *Double Down* so it wasn't about Zimmerman being here. He hadn't even sent the email to Hank yet. He wanted to wait and see what Megan got from the mother.

"Walker."

"It's Steve."

"Hey." Steve Preston was Megan's boss, the owner/CEO of Double Down. And the only other time he'd called Adrian was the day the RV blew up in Colorado and two of their team members had died. Megan had been injured. Mint had been in a gunfight. Adrian had been the only one to answer his phone in the aftermath. "What's up?"

"Where's Megan?"

"Interviewing the kid's mom."

Steve sighed. "We know why he chose this child in particular. You need to find her, now."

Adrian started walking. "What's the connection?"

"The father. He's connected to *El Cuervo,* and not in any way that's good for Megan. We looked into him as much as we could in the short time frame, and we'll have more soon, but it's likely he was in Venezuela during the time Megan and her partner were taken. If he shows up, and she pegs him as being there two years ago—whether he was present when Will was killed or not—she's going to freak out."

Adrian crossed the threshold to the waiting area and saw Megan in quiet conversation with a young Hispanic woman. In Megan's hand was a flash drive. "I'll call you back. I think she got something from the mom."

Adrian hung up before Steve could reply. Then he looked both ways down the hall and at everyone in the room. He didn't see any Hispanic men. Maybe the wife didn't have contact with him. But it was in no way a coincidence that Zimmerman, who was himself connected with *El Cuervo,* had come to the son of an associate of the same man.

Trying to pull Megan into something that would throw her so deep into the past that she'd be unable to function? Adrian didn't like this, no matter what it was.

And how on earth did this have anything to do with their finding the blackmailer?

Megan glanced over. He tipped his head to the side, and she held up a finger. She spoke softly to the young woman, and then shook her head. Would she be this way with the woman if she already knew the child's father was part of the same Venezuelan organization that had almost destroyed her life?

She came over to him.

"Let's walk. I think we're done here."

She shot him a glance. "If you say so."

He headed for the elevator with her beside him. "Zimmerman was in the room for seven minutes."

"He gave the boy this flash drive."

Adrian wanted to reach for it, instinct probably. He safeguarded evidence. It was his job. But he fisted his hand instead, and she slipped it into the pocket of her jacket. He said, "What do you think is on it?"

"I don't know." She blew out a breath and shook her head. "A manifesto? A confession?"

He knew she wanted it to be more than that. She wanted an explanation as to Zimmerman's involvement in what had been done to her. Maybe something about the blackmailer as well. Adrian wanted to ask her what had happened, but it was too early for that. He also wanted to hug her, and promise she would always be safe. Likely she wouldn't want that, either. Would she ever?

"Soon as we get to a computer we can find out," she said. "Then maybe we'll know where he's going next."

"You think this is a cry for help, and he wants us to catch him?"

"Maybe." Adrian stepped out of the elevator first, into the lobby.

"Okay, tell me why you're in protective detail mode."

He glanced back, one arm out so he could put his hand on the small of her back. She lifted an eyebrow and stopped in the middle of the lobby. "Explain."

"I will," he said. "Once we're back in the car."

"Adrian."

A couple of people brushed past them, forcing him to take a step back to give them room. How rude. Adrian pressed his lips together, and when the crowd had thinned he moved closer to Megan. "We need to get that flash drive to a computer. And we need to get you somewhere you're not exposed."

She started walking. "There's more you're not telling me."

He nodded, then moved to hold the door open for her. "The boy's father is one of *El Cuervo*'s men. I don't want him seeing you if he does come, and I don't want you here longer than is necessary."

"Trying to protect me?" She glanced at him, then scanned the area around them. "How noble."

"It's not nobility," he said. "If you get hurt, or killed, I'll be spending a day doing paperwork instead of tracking down Zimmerman."

She snorted, but continued making her way to the car. "Sofía said he doesn't come around much. Can't handle seeing José like this."

Adrian nodded, and they got in without incident. He sent up a prayer of thanksgiving. It was that time of year, after all, when everyone was reminded to be thankful. He didn't want to be one of those people who only prayed when they needed something.

"Ready?" She looked at him expectantly.

"Just saying thanks that we got out of there, safe."

"I know what you mean. And I've been praying for that boy." He figured as much. Most of Double Down were Christians. It was nice to be around them, supported by people who believed what he did. His own work environment wasn't hostile toward what he believed, but it was expected that he leave his faith at home.

He didn't know where Megan stood on the faith issue, but he wanted to know. Would she share with him?

Megan ran her hands over the ends of her jacket. "What..." She dug in the pocket, then the other one. Then the inside pockets.

"You—"

She looked up, dread in her eyes. "The flash drive is gone."

Chapter 7

Megan threw the car door open and stalked back toward the hospital foyer. The guy that had bumped into her in the lobby. He had to have lifted the flash drive from her pocket.

She couldn't believe she'd been so dumb. Thieves were good, and the great ones could take things from you without you even noticing. Still, part of her had always thought she would notice it happening. Apparently not. She'd had all the answers, and now they were gone before she even had the chance to find out what Zimmerman wanted to tell her.

"Megan!" Adrian pulled to a stop beside her, breathing hard. Her breaths were coming fast as well. Evidently she'd pushed it to get across the street.

She kept going, scanning the ground in case she'd dropped it. Unlikely, but it was possible. Her hands curled into fists at her sides. "Whatever Zimmerman had to say is *gone*." But even as she said it, she realized she didn't want to give up. She wanted to find it somewhere.

Or find the thief.

An old man pulled open the front door of the hospital. He started to head inside, then halted and backed up half a step.

Two men walked out, Sofia between them. One held her arm. The other stood close to her side. Her face was pinched, her big brown eyes even darker in her paled face.

Megan put her hand out to Adrian. He stopped beside her. They both drew their weapons, but Megan held hers out of sight.

"Sofía!" Megan put on her happiest face, a wide smile, and waved with her free hand. She strode toward the younger woman. "How are you? It's so good to see you."

The men glanced aside at her, but continued to hustle the young woman out of the hospital. Sofia whimpered as they turned onto the sidewalk and headed for the street. Vehicle parked around the corner? They couldn't think that was less conspicuous than parking close.

"Hey!" Megan yelled again, like she was getting mad at being ignored. "Sofía!"

One of the men spun back, gun raised.

Both Megan and Adrian lifted their weapons.

He said, "FBI. Put it down. Let the woman go."

The other man continued to pull Sofia along while his friend faced off with them.

Beyond the gunman, Sofía started to struggle. "Megan!" She kicked at the man's shins, but he was bigger so her flat shoes had little impact on him. "They killed my son!"

Megan took two steps to the left. Adrian could take the first guy. She trained her gun on the man holding Sofía. "Let her go. Now." Then she said, "And give me back the flash drive."

Sofía whimpered against the man's hold, her energy to fight dissipating. She sagged. That was good. A limp victim was harder to control and harder to get her to whatever vehicle they had parked nearby.

"Put it down." Adrian's voice was strong and full of authority.

The man who'd turned back first shifted a tiny amount. Megan braced for the shots that would surely follow.

Then he turned and ran.

Cut and raced away, determined to get out of there.

Adrian ran after him, and the two of them bypassed the second man still holding Sofía. Megan used the momentary distraction to run at the man holding her. She couldn't see a weapon, but that didn't mean he wasn't hiding one where she couldn't see it. Where he'd have point blank aim on Sofía.

Sofía screamed. Megan barreled into the two of them, shoving so that she could put herself between Sofía and the man.

Security ran out of the hospital doors.

Megan shouldered the man into the ground, then put her weapon back into its holster. She grabbed the man's arms and pinned them behind his back. Then she turned to the security guards, holding their stun guns. "FBI."

She patted the man down, found his weapon in the back of his pants, and then pulled him to his feet. His hands weren't bound. She held his elbow while she moved two steps to the guards. "Secure this man."

"We called the cops."

She nodded. "Good." They would have handcuffs at least—better than the plastic ties the guards had. And they'd be able to take this guy in. Get Sofía's statement.

Megan needed to find Adrian and the other guy. She turned to go, and Sofía slammed into her. "Thank you. Oh, thank you so much."

Megan patted her back, not sure what else to do. "What happened?" The question was automatic, nothing but a reflex.

"They were in José's room. He coded and the nurses ran in. They dragged me to the elevator." She sucked in a breath, panting from the adrenaline of nearly being kidnapped.

Those two men tried to kill José?

Sofía whimpered and clutched Megan harder. "He's dead."

She didn't know what to say. Likely nothing would ever be all right for this woman. Not for a long time. Megan wanted to comfort her, even while she realized she didn't have time to stick around that long. And did she want to befriend the wife of a man who'd been part of the worst days of her life?

Megan was ready to get out of here.

See if Adrian needed backup.

Sofía ran her hands down her face. "I don't even know what to do. Though I guess I have to call Ernesto. And send an email to the man to tell him José has passed." Her lip quivered and her eyes filled with tears.

Megan shifted to face the younger woman, pushing aside her feelings about "Ernesto" and what Adrian had told her about José's father and his connection to all this. She said, "The man?"

Sofía sighed. "The one who is paying all our medical bills. He'll need to know."

Megan waved the young woman to a low brick wall. "Would you like to sit?" Sofía nodded and settled onto it. Megan sat beside her. She didn't want to burden the woman with questions. She'd just lost her son and then had almost been kidnapped.

As soon as Megan was done, she could let Sofía get back to the waves of emotion and thoughts that seemed to be barraging her. She said, "There's a man who pays your medical bills?"

This was all linked to the blackmailer. Megan didn't believe in coincidences. People were getting terrorized and pressured to do things or pay money…and Sofía's family was receiving it.

Perhaps her husband was more involved than Megan had known.

And if he was, then they had a clear link between *El Cuervo* and the blackmailer.

Sofía's face blanked. Megan was about to lose her to the fog of grief. "Ernesto said it would be taken care of."

A police car with flashing lights and sirens pulled up to the curb. The security guards walked the apprehended man over to them, and they stood in a huddle. One of the cops glanced at Megan and Sofía. Megan pulled her FBI badge out of her back pocket and waved it. The cop lifted his chin, then turned back to the security guard.

"Is there someone you can call?" She didn't want the woman to be alone right now. It wasn't good for her. And it wasn't safe.

Sofía nodded.

"The police will want your statement. Then you can go back inside." She would likely rather be with her son, saying goodbye. "Have the security guards go with you, I don't want you to be alone right now. Okay?"

Sofía nodded, her eyes glassy. She seemed almost dazed. Was everything catching up with her?

Movement down the sidewalk caught her attention. Megan stood. Adrian was making his way back to her. He shook his head.

The man had gotten away.

. . .

Adrian gripped the steering wheel, headed for the airport. Hank's voice came through the SUV's speakers. His boss said, "Security at the St. Louis airport caught Zimmerman checking in for a flight to Chicago half an hour ago."

"They're sure?"

"It's him," Hank said. "Duffel bag that could contain the sonic weapon."

Adrian wasn't convinced that meant Zimmerman had boarded the plane. He knew the FBI would be notified if he was caught on security camera. They were watching all airports, train and bus stations. Zimmerman wasn't dumb enough to make a mistake like that.

Unless he was trying to get caught.

Adrian couldn't shake the feeling that Zimmerman had made these moves on purpose. Leaving the flash drive for Megan—a flash drive that presumably had been on the person of the man he'd chased. All the way to that waiting van.

Megan had a better result with her guy, and she'd safeguarded Sofía. She was a good partner whether she wanted to admit it or not. It was Adrian who had let the side down.

And yes, he thought he was the weak link even though the van's driver had shot at him, and he'd been forced to dive to the ground. FBI didn't shoot at vehicles fleeing the scene—it was too easy to hit an innocent doing that. But he'd sure wanted to.

Megan hadn't asked him about the tear in his pants on his left knee. And he was pretty sure he had road rash on his elbow, but he was ignoring that.

"We'll keep an eye," the SAC said. "They have security scouring the footage to see where he went after he checked in. We'll find him."

Megan shifted in her seat. "Hank, can someone send me a picture of Sofía's husband?"

Silence.

Adrian listened while Hank blew out a breath into the phone. The SAC said, "You sure?"

"Yes." Megan's voice was hard, the word short. "She called him 'Ernesto,' but I want to know who he is. And my guess is the blackmailer is the man Sofía told me is paying their hospital bills. I want to know why there's a connection between the person behind all this and *El Cuervo.*"

Adrian glanced over, but she didn't meet his gaze. He looked back at the road. She'd fought this so far. Now she accepted the link, and it was costing her. How far would she bend before she broke?

Hank said, "Zimmerman is the blackmailer."

"I'm not convinced of that."

Adrian said, "Neither am I." Megan shifted. He saw it out the corner of his eye. Adrian continued, "I think Zimmerman knows who it is. But I don't think it's him." An idea had been floating around in his head the past few hours. "I actually think he used this connection to reveal the truth to Megan, but the blackmailer found out. Likely when we did." He was in Double Down's tech—their email and computer system. Maybe he was in the FBI's also—or he had a mole in their department feeding them information.

Megan said, "But we didn't get the flash drive." No accusation in her tone.

"So it didn't work," Adrian said. "Zimmerman gave it a shot, but it failed. Though maybe he won't know that unless we put it out there somehow. But either way, now he's back on plan. Doing the blackmailer's bidding is my guess."

"And what is that?" Megan sounded eminently frustrated.

Adrian glanced at her. He wanted to…squeeze her knee or something. Would that even help?

Hank said, "What I have from our profilers indicates Zimmerman is out to destroy the government he works for. That he's disillusioned and attempting to strike back because he's frustrated and angry."

Megan said, "Or he's frustrated and angry because the blackmailer is pulling his strings, and the one that's striking out is this mystery man whose identity we *still don't know.*" She balled her hands into fists on her knees and rubbed them up and down."

"Every time our computer people think they're close to uncovering something more in Zimmerman's computer, they realize there's another firewall…or a back door," Hank muttered. "My guess is he's giving them the runaround."

Adrian wondered about that. "Or he has someone else on his payroll. A hacker. Someone with the skills to breach Double Down's firewall and plant whatever he wants in Zimmerman's computer."

That meant he could get into their phones as well. And maybe even the FBI's system. He could even be listening right now.

There had to be a way they could use that to their advantage. Not the first time he'd had the thought about feeding the blackmailer misinformation. That had been in order to let the blackmailer know the sick child was no threat to him. But the blackmailer had the child killed. Maybe that was a mercy. In some states it was legal. But not without the mother's consent.

This was murder, pure and simple.

And one part of a big mess they had yet to unravel.

Megan said, "So if he's disillusioned and striking back at authority, whether he's the blackmailer or Zimmerman is simply following orders, where is he going to strike?"

Adrian had driven to the freeway, and he was heading in the direction of Chicago. It would take a few hours but if that was the flight Zimmerman had boarded, then Adrian wanted to be as close as possible.

Eventually he and Megan were going to have to stop and rest. The day was waning, and he wouldn't be able to drive through the night. He was already exhausted. And he figured Megan wasn't in a much better state than he was.

"That's the question." Hank wrapped up and ended the call.

Megan shifted in her seat. "All that for nothing?"

"The hospital?"

She nodded. "No flash drive. The cops have to interview the kidnapper but if the blackmailer had him come here to clean up, then I highly doubt he knows anything." She sighed. "This guy is too good to let something like that slip through the cracks. He probably has safeguards on his safeguards."

Adrian shifted his grip on the wheel. Cruise control was on, but he didn't want to lose focus. Especially not when he was this tired. One thing she'd said stuck with him, though. "Clean up."

"Huh?"

"Well, that's what those guys were doing burning Zimmerman's house down. They didn't want us to find anything there. Cleaning up all the blackmailer's loose ends."

"But we thought the blackmailer was Zimmerman," Megan said.

"Now that we think he isn't, we can surmise that the blackmailer is burning Zimmerman's life. To make him some kind of scapegoat. He has the sonic weapon, he's the obvious fall-guy. Recently divorced. Not doing well at work."

"So what does the blackmailer have on Zimmerman that forces him to do what he says and potentially destroy something, kill people?"

Adrian worked his jaw side to side in that way his mom had never liked. He could hear her reproof in his head, he'd heard it so many times. "Whatever it is, he tried to circumvent the blackmailer and get you a message."

Megan shook her head. "This makes no sense. It's not like we know each other. Why pick me?"

Before Adrian could suggest something, his phone rang again. Zimmerman could've picked Megan for several reasons. She was a kindred spirit to him. Or he felt like owed her. Or he wanted to hurt her, by dragging her in.

The call was from an agent he worked with. He tapped the SUV's dash screen. "Walker."

"Hey." The man's greeting was short. "Call just came over the wires. A think tank contracted by the government just exploded outside of Peoria, Illinois. We've got destruction and death. Emergency services just arrived on scene and the word is the place is a total mess. The whole building collapsed."

Chapter 8

Megan got out of the car, eyes glued to the utter destruction. She stared for a moment hardly able to process everything she was seeing. Finally, she managed to blow out a breath.

Adrian moved beside her and shut the door she'd left open. He waited, not saying anything.

"How many people are dead?"

"Two."

She turned. "Two?" One death was a tragedy, but she'd expected the number to be a whole lot higher than that.

Adrian shrugged, a concerned look in his eyes. "You want to wait in the car? I can check in with the agents here and get what we need and then come back. If you want."

Megan shook her head. "I'm good."

This might not be her job anymore, but that didn't mean these people couldn't use both of them. The agents, and the two that had been killed. She owed it to all of them to lend her skills to find out why Zimmerman had targeted this place.

Why the blackmailer had forced him to.

She was more convinced now than ever that the blackmailer had compelled Zimmerman to take the weapon and use it for his aims. "Did Hank say if they ever found Zimmerman's wife and kids?"

He'd said they weren't able to locate them. But that was, what, yesterday? She could hardly process the passing of hours with everything they'd been through.

Adrian pulled out his phone. "I'll ask."

She took a few steps and tried to assess where the FBI was at in their processing of all this. She didn't envy anyone the job of sifting through rubble while they prayed no more bodies showed up.

Adrian moved to her side again. He walked with her toward the FBI command center that had been set up. An RV—kind of like the Double Down one that had been destroyed by the blackmailer.

An agent stepped out. Older than them, probably late forties. Dark hair and eyes, Hispanic coloring. He glanced from her to Adrian and recognition flared in his eyes. "Walker, right?"

Adrian nodded. "This is my associate, Megan Perkins."

She shook the guy's hand.

"Agent Ramirez."

"Nice to meet you." She smiled as much as she could through the exhaustion.

Adrian said, "Can we assist?"

Ramirez said, "There isn't much to do here, but I do have a job if you're willing to lend a hand."

Adrian nodded. "I can put you in touch with the SAC at my office, and you can verify. This is connected to a case I'm working on, so we could use insight into what happened and why."

"I'm happy to brief you," Ramirez said. "And the job is interviewing Terrence Almonde, the man who's the money behind the think tank itself. That might help you get what you need."

Megan figured it would also get them out from under the feet of the team here, a group probably accustomed to working with each other. They didn't need agents they didn't know, verified or not, adding themselves to the mix and muddying things up. Procedure had to be followed. And when unknown elements were brought in, that gave the potential for things to be missed.

No one wanted that when there was a killer—a possible terrorist—to find.

He showed them inside the RV, and they sat on the couch across from a couple of padded chairs. No one asked for coffee, even though Megan could have seriously used a cup. Those two people who'd died would never get to enjoy simple things like that again. So now wasn't the time to worry about her stomach.

Ramirez pulled a tablet computer off a cluttered table top and swiped the screen. "One man carrying a bulky thing the witness said looked like some kind of sci-fi movie weapon fired at the building. Seconds later it began to disintegrate."

Megan felt her eyebrows raise. "It *disintegrated?*"

Ramirez nodded.

Adrian said, "The sonic weapon is tuned to the frequency specific to the material the building is made out of. In this case, the concrete on the exterior walls. The steel likely remained intact, but when the walls fell, the rest of it was compromised."

"Much of it is still intact, as you said, but the roof was concrete. It fell in, crushing everything. One of the men inside managed to call out. He was trapped." Ramirez paused. "He died before emergency services could dig their way to him. Ran out of air. The second deceased man was in the lobby."

Megan shook her head. "So it's specific to the building material."

Adrian nodded. "Which means he has to know how to recalibrate, or he'll have to carefully pick targets."

"Wouldn't a bomb have been so much easier?"

Ramirez shrugged. "This is destruction to a very specific target. The buildings around it were unaffected and still standing. They weren't damaged at all apart from debris and dust. If you want to be precise, then it's a good weapon to use."

"But it was experimental," she said. "So the blackmailer had to know it existed back when it was in a secret research lab."

"My office is looking at who knew about that facility," Adrian said. "But its more people than you'd think, given the government. Oversight committees. The Pentagon. Admin staff. It wasn't top secret. It was auditory research."

"But the weapon was high level clearance stuff, right?"

Adrian nodded. "The security guards even knew what was in there. Cleaning staff. There are a lot of people to interview, and we won't know if they're connected until we find another place in which their name comes up. There have to be multiple points of contact."

She knew that. Why he needed to explain it, she didn't know. Megan had gone through FBI training. She'd investigated crimes. She knew that someone could only be considered a suspect if their name came up more than once, and they were connected in more than one way to a crime. That was the kind of person who warranted more than basic scrutiny.

Someone with something to lose.

Adrian wrapped it up with Ramirez, getting the timeline of exactly how things had gone down.

Ramirez said, "I'll send you everything we have on the two victims."

They gave him their email addresses, and Megan pulled it up on her phone. She debated whether to send the information on to Steve. Was the blackmailer that deep in their system? He could have someone able to get past any kind of encryption they used working for him, even the kind the FBI employed. This whole thing was a delicate balance. Not letting the blackmailer know where they were at with the case, but keeping everyone in the loop.

She scrolled through the information on the two dead men—one on the janitorial staff, and the other was a former Army general, retired now. He had been part of the think tank's project.

"Do you know what they were working on?" she asked Ramirez.

The agent shook his head. "Maybe you guys can find that out when you speak to Almonde. Apparently, he's some kind of genius in biological research." Ramirez paused. "We have agents locating everyone else who was part of the think tank, including the staff. Trying to find out what we can from them. Why most of them weren't here this morning, and what they were working on."

Megan nodded. It was always a long process, unpacking a tragedy after the fact. Trying to understand who had perpetrated such an act—and why. If they knew who the target was, then they would be one step closer to figuring out the blackmailer's end game.

Because she didn't think the target had been concrete walls and a roof.

There was more going on here.

.   .   .

Adrian went first into the lobby of the building in downtown Chicago. The company was only two years old, a start-up that'd come almost out of nowhere to become the leading edge in technology with a biology interface. Literally, plugging people into computers. Though, much of it was still research.

He didn't think there would ever be a day where that was a good thing, no matter the applications for medical science. It mattered who was in charge and what their priorities were. And the man behind the think tank, the man who had started this business, was supposed to be a young free-thinker. A visionary.

Was he also someone who would push the boundaries of morality?

The receptionist looked up, still talking on her headset. "Yes, I will."

Adrian flashed his badge. Beside him, Megan did the same. They'd stopped for food and a fresh change of clothes. Megan had secured her hair in a ponytail, but still wore Converse sneakers with her skinny black pants and blouse. She looked like an office worker who'd left for the day and had to walk ten blocks home, so she'd changed her shoes to do so.

Or she'd forgotten dress shoes today.

Everything about her lived outside the tiny box he spent his life in. He was starting to enjoy the feeling of being challenged on literally everything he thought and did. Maybe she didn't even realize she was doing it. Still, he kind of admired that about her—the fact she was who she was, and she wasn't going to change or apologize for it.

Strength born out of a fire that had burned almost her entire life. A trial she may have yet to move past. One that made her who she was—a woman who wasn't about to back down.

A woman who might be scared, but still wanted to find a way to get those ghosts of the past out of her life. Once and for all.

The receptionist hung up. "Yes?"

He said, "Mr. Almonde is expecting us."

"If you'll come with me." The voice came out of right field, from a young man in a suit that only highlighted exactly how skinny he was. Tight haircut. Thin-framed glasses. He clutched an iPad to his tie. "It's this way."

His gaze brushed over both of them, dismissing them as irrelevant in one sweep. Then he turned and headed for the elevator.

Megan glanced at Adrian as they followed. She made a face, which threatened to make him laugh. He held it in.

They stepped into the elevator. The assistant jabbed the button for the penthouse and then jerked. Adrian realized he'd noticed Megan's shoes.

She grinned. "I have sixteen pairs, all different colors and designs. My nieces drew all over my white pair in colored marker. Permanent. Those are on my mantel at home." She motioned to her shoes. "These are my dress pair."

Adrian bit his lips together to keep from laughing.

The assistant huffed, then turned away from them. The doors beeped and slid open. He strode out into a luxurious hallway. Marble. Impressive paintings lined the halls. Tiny tables with vases and statues on them.

"I'm scared to swing my arms. What if I knock something over," Megan whispered. "Do you think they'll make me buy it?"

The assistant threw a set of double doors wide and said, "Two FBI agents are here to see you."

Seconds later he was gone, and they were standing alone in the foyer of the penthouse apartment. The entire wall opposite them was made up of floor to ceiling windows.

A young man wearing bicycle shorts and a tiny tank top strode in, a white towel over his shoulder. Curly hair was matted to his forehead with sweat that dampened his whole torso.

Adrian should have held out his hand, but didn't really want to.

Thankfully the man was undoing the Velcro on his bicycle gloves. He didn't offer a handshake either, but he clearly noticed Megan. His attention swept down to her shoes and then back up with far more appreciation than the assistant. And not in a way Adrian was all right with.

"I'm Special Agent Walker. This is Special Agent Perkins. We're here about what happened at the think tank building."

Terrence Almonde nodded, his face displaying appropriate empathy. And a smidge of respect at discovering she was in FBI agent.

Megan figured Adrian had introduced her that way purely for this reason.

"Terrible thing." Terrence moved to a row of cabinets on one wall and opened the one at the end. The inside housed a refrigerator. He pulled out a bottle of sparkling water and held it out. "Drink?"

They both shook their heads.

"I'd ask you to sit, but my housekeeper will tan my hide if I get sweat on the fabric." He paused, then lifted his eyebrows. "On second thought." He moved to the couch with a slight gallop in his step and sat down. Like a little kid who was going to eat that forbidden cookie out of the jar because the punishment was worth it.

Adrian just wanted to move this conversation along. "What was the think tank working on?"

"Ah, yes." He addressed Megan, who had perched on the edge of an armchair. Adrian stood beside the back corner of the seat. Almonde said, "Fantastically interesting. Genetic research." He shrugged. "It's what we do."

Okay, so that wasn't even a complete answer. "And what *specifically* was the think tank working on?" Adrian assumed they were solving some kind of problem. Get a bunch of people from different backgrounds together, all of them brilliant, to figure out a solution.

"Well, the science is still very cutting edge. But using DNA research, we've isolated genes specific to people groups around the world. They're working on the viability of using that to…aid the government in their fight against terrorism."

Megan chuckled, totally fake. "I'm afraid I got a C in biology. You're going to have to explain that a little more."

Adrian could see the guy was hedging. "I can assure you, we have the necessary security clearance."

Almonde waved his hand. "No, no. That's not it. Well, it's just all very unsavory really. Talking about," his voice shifted to a whisper and he leaned forward. *"Terrorism."* He made a *blech* sound and then said, "But one does what one can to fight that good fight, as it were."

"So they were using genetic research to target terrorists."

"Establishing the scientific basis, and moral implications, of targeting people groups who are known combatants."

"Like genocide?" Adrian said, very carefully. "But of our enemies."

Almonde blanched. "The effects would be contained and incredibly specific."

"But you're basically talking about killing people, wiping them out." Regardless of their intentions. They would end life purely due to DNA markers.

He said, "Enemies of America." Like Adrian was the one who didn't understand. "Anyway, it's only an idea. That's where the think tank came in."

The rest of the conversation didn't go much better. By the time they reached the elevator, Megan looked even more exhausted. Adrian knew how that felt. "That guy is a piece of work."

She nodded. "Okay, because I get that we're at war with ISIS, and we should use every method available—but that was nuts, right?"

He nodded as well. "So does the blackmailer want to end the research, hurt Almonde's business, or was he after one of the people who were killed today?"

Megan shrugged. They headed through the lobby and out to where he'd parked his car at the curb.

Seconds later, shots rang out.

The car windshield shattered. Megan screamed and fell to the ground.

Chapter 9

Megan grunted as she landed on the sidewalk, thankfully on her good side. Her hip was going to be bruised tomorrow. Another to add to the list of the injuries she'd gained over the past few weeks. She'd been doing pretty well so far. Healing.

She lifted her arm. Red and wet. Her head swam. She tried to sit up, but all she could do was lean awkwardly against the dirty car wheel. Two gunshot wounds? And both on the same side.

"Adrian." Her voice was barely audible.

Shots continued. Adrian was to her right, hunkered down. He lifted up. Fired three shots. Back down, behind cover. He looked at her then, his eyes full of thunder. *Not happy.* She understood that.

She should help.

Megan pulled her gun from the holster, thankful it was her left arm that had been injured. She started to shift around so she could fire. Pain ripped through her arm. She hissed out a breath, swallowing back bile.

"Stay down!" His voice was absolute command.

But he needed help.

She tried to shift again but only ended up with her back to Adrian and facing the street. People were hunkered down. Good. Her head swam, her vision blurring. She couldn't see a thing, let alone focus enough to figure out where the threat was and aim with any kind of precision. She blew out a breath and tried to steady herself. She was the wrong way around. If she leaned against the car now, she'd be leaning on her injured arm. That wouldn't do any good.

You've been shot again.

She pushed aside that unhelpful thought and got her legs bent under her so she could at least try to stand.

"I said, stay down!"

She gritted her teeth. Sirens could be heard in the distance. There was something to be said for being downtown, where police response was fast. She prayed no innocents had been hurt. They didn't need more deaths because of this guy's selfishness.

A car engine revved and then tires squealed as it sped away. A few more shots slammed against the building behind her. Megan ducked her head, even behind the cover of the car.

The sound dissipated, and she blew out a breath.

"Who's hurt?" Adrian's voice boomed over the near-silence of the aftermath. Like everyone was afraid to breathe.

A woman screamed a man's name, over and over.

Megan shut her eyes against the flood of wet. Her arm burned. She was alive and Adrian was okay.

Police showed up. EMTs. Megan waited while they treated those who'd been injured more badly than her.

Adrian didn't like it. "I'll drive you to the hospital."

She sucked in a clean breath of air. Enough to say, "I'll get blood all over the car seat. Again."

"I don't care."

She kind of didn't know why she was arguing. She did need to get to the hospital, and the ambulances were being loaded up. "Give me a jacket or something, to wrap it with."

When he pulled one from the trunk, she shifted her elbow away from her body. Swayed. Everything went dark for a second, and then Adrian's arm was around her waist.

"Okay?"

Megan nodded, unable to do anything else. "Wind it around my arm."

He frowned the entire time. And went way too slow.

"I'm fine." *Liar.*

He didn't even react, just finished up and pulled the door open. Helped her to the seat like she was an invalid. He even lifted her legs in.

She watched him talk to one of the officers and hand over his business card, and then he got in the driver's seat. She shut her eyes on the way to the hospital, not wanting to talk. Adrenaline just made her mad, and her heart was still racing. Her brain rushed to process the conversation with Almonde, everything at the think tank, and what had just happened in the parking lot. All past the pain in her arm.

The doctor jabbed her with a needle, and then it got better. She felt the pull of stitches. The slide of thread through her skin. Her brain snagged on that detail. As though it was important in the grand scheme. Or simpler to ponder over than everything else in her life. An interesting detail she wouldn't have otherwise paid attention to.

Adrian stood by the bed the whole time, hands on his hips. Jacket splayed wide. Fury on his face. She honestly hadn't known a man to do that before, but evidently extreme circumstances brought out reactions like that. Everyone knew putting hands on your hips was serious.

His gaze shifted to her face. "You're staring at me."

"You're stareworthy."

Adrian blinked. Beside her the doctor huffed out a quick laugh. Like he wasn't sure if he should think that was funny.

She glanced at the doctor. "Not that you're not. It's just..." She didn't even know what she was saying.

He shook his head. "Don't worry about me." Then aimed his bushy gray eyebrows at her wound again and twisted his mouth as he concentrated on the stitches.

She moved her head again to look at Adrian. She never would've thought she'd find herself attracted to another man. Not after what happened to Will. It was nice to know that part of her hadn't gone completely dormant when he'd been killed. But it didn't mean she was going to do anything about it.

If Adrian wanted a relationship with her, he would have to make the first move. Maybe she was old-school, but that was the way things were supposed to go. Or, so she'd always thought. It was how her dad had won over her mom. By making the effort to convince her she should take a chance on him.

If Adrian did that, she would kindly let him down gently. This was a one-woman show.

She didn't mean that in a mean, or self-absorbed way. It was just that life was a whole lot simpler if it stayed just her. The apostle Paul even said it was better to stay single—so you weren't distracted with having to please a spouse and take care of kids. Sure, they were *nice* distractions, and there wouldn't be this nagging loneliness all the time. But she only had to worry about herself.

See? Easier.

And it meant she could focus better on finding Zimmerman.

Adrian shifted and pulled his cell from the inside pocket of his jacket. "Gotta take this."

She nodded and watched him leave the room. He really was nice-looking. And a nice guy. Who was even like that anymore? So many men were sweet on the surface and toxic underneath. Women too, if she were honest. She'd spent enough time with Adrian the past few weeks to know his outward manner went all the way to the core.

He was genuine.

"Okay." The doctor secured the bandage down. "All done. I'll send the nurse in with instructions."

She nodded, her mind still mulling over Adrian being in her life. And then she was alone. The way things were supposed to be.

So why would she rather Adrian was back in here?

What was taking him so long anyway?

Okay, that was the meds. They'd given her something good for the pain. Maybe it was making her loopy.

She didn't need a man in her life. Not when she knew the reality of how much it burned when the person you cared about was taken from you. Even if he was a nice guy like Adrian.

. . .

Adrian paced the hall and clutched his phone, on the line with Hank. "Yes, both of them were South American. The same men who tried to abduct the boy's mother at the hospital."

It was too obvious of a connection to dismiss. Zimmerman had a connection to *El Cuervo*, and these men might have been the same nationality. Were they *El Cuervo*'s men? Traffic cams would hopefully get their images. Or they'd trace their identities from the vehicle details. The man the police had taken into custody at the hospital could talk.

One way or another they would figure out who they were.

"They really waited for you?"

Adrian said, "Yes," and had to bite back the urge to call him Hank. Megan was rubbing off on him. "Sir. They were in their car across the street when we exited Almonde's building. Pulled out of their parking space and opened fire."

He hadn't seen it. Witnesses at the scene had told the police what happened. Eventually those cops would show up here for their statements as well. Adrian was just thankful he and Megan were alive to give them.

Hank blew out a breath. "Glad you guys are okay."

"You and me both, sir."

"She's really all right?"

"It's a bad graze, but it's a graze." Kind of like her hip.

Adrian figured she'd downplay it, pretend she was still at full strength.

"Take care of her."

"Will do." He had every intention of making sure Megan stayed "okay" for the remainder of this manhunt for Zimmerman. And while they found the blackmailer. It was his part in this operation. "The link between Zimmerman, these South Americans, and *El Cuervo* is known. But what about the think tank? I don't believe it was a randomly chosen target."

"You think it's about *what* the think tank was working on?"

Adrian squeezed the bridge of his nose. "Genetic weapons aren't as far off as people think. Not with the strides science is making in that field. We can do incredible things with DNA splicing, and experimentation. Weaponizing it is never far off, no matter what the method."

Whatever breakthroughs science made, there were always people who wanted to use that to destroy their enemy.

Hank said, "You think Almonde is in on that? He funded the think tank. He had to know what they were doing."

"If you're asking whether I think he's patriotic or a threat, I have to say I don't know. He seems like a businessman. A visionary and an entrepreneur, just like the brochure says. But he was more interested in impressing Megan than showcasing the think tank's work. Maybe he just threw money at it to see what came of it. If they made a breakthrough, he could claim ownership and get the credit."

Hank made a "huh" sound. "So it was about one of the victims?"

"Pretty big lengths to go to in order to kill someone. Especially when it's easier to come up to them on the street and pull a trigger."

"Remind me not to get on your bad side."

Adrian figured it was more likely there would be a note made in his file that he needed a psych eval. "I just mean there are easier ways to kill someone than this elaborate plan."

"Unless it's all a smoke screen. Overcomplicating it so we're running in circles, trying to figure out what is going on."

Adrian nodded. The doctor passed him in the hall and lifted his chin. Adrian did the same. He was done with Megan already? Adrian needed to get back in there. He didn't want to leave her alone. And not only because he wondered, in the back of his mind, if maybe she'd bolt at some point. He just couldn't get a full grasp on her.

She was elusive.

He wasn't getting where he wanted to be. Which meant he wasn't fulfilling his duty to her. Hard to take care of someone who didn't want to be taken care of, but he'd been making it work so far.

He moved closer to the door to her room and saw a nurse head inside with a yellow paper. She was getting discharged. The woman needed a nap, but he figured he'd have to wait for her to pass out like the last time.

Not wanting his thoughts to return to that hotel bathroom—and the fear after he'd heard her collapse—he asked Hank, "Any updates on the think tank destruction?"

"The second body they found in the rubble." Hank was quiet for a moment, then he said, "Retired Army General Eric Thomas."

"Do you figure he was the target?" They for sure didn't have all the pieces of the puzzle they needed to answer that question. But Hank had resources.

There was no way to find Zimmerman unless they knew what the blackmailer's next target was, or where he was hiding. Adrian didn't figure the think tank was the end of it.

"Can't see how any other answer makes sense," Hank said.

"Anything else?" Adrian asked.

"Like Zimmerman's family? Can't find them anywhere. I sent crime scene techs to the house. They say there are indications the family might have been taken. It isn't obvious that they were kidnapped, but it's a possibility. In fact, it was so *not* obvious it was actually missed at first. Like someone cleaned up afterwards."

Adrian pinched the bridge of his nose. "They were abducted?" He'd heard "clean up" way too many times during this whole thing to pass over that as well. "The blackmailer took them, and then hid that fact. So is that the leverage he has over Zimmerman? He's holding the man's ex-wife and children hostage to force him to do his bidding?"

"It's definitely a possibility. Which confirms Megan's idea that Zimmerman tried to make contact with her for a reason. Maybe he was planning on telling her that he was under the blackmailer's thumb." Hank paused. "I passed the kidnapping over to a new group of agents. They're working that case."

"Okay, good. If we can find them then the blackmailer no longer has Zimmerman under his thumb."

Could Zimmerman really be nothing but a pawn in this whole thing? And his family dragged down into it as well? More innocent people suffering because of the whims of one man.

A blackmailer.

"I'll keep you posted." Hank ended the call.

Adrian stowed his phone away and went to give Megan the news about Zimmerman's family. Knowing the man had been coerced into destroying a building and killing three people didn't make it better. That hadn't been a noble act of sacrifice.

Adrian didn't know what he'd have done in that situation but figured the man had been right about trying to contact Megan.

He knocked but didn't wait long before he entered the room. Megan looked up from wiggling her foot back into her shoe.

"Good, you can help me with my laces."

Adrian pulled up a chair and set her foot in his lap. For some reason, Megan had been dragged in the middle of this. Zimmerman could have left that flash drive for anyone at the FBI. And yet, he'd specifically mentioned Megan. Like bringing her to meet the family of a man who'd hurt her so badly was a good thing. Or even that it was okay.

"There's some big thinking going on in there." She tapped the top of his head.

Adrian set her foot down and lifted the other one, along with her shoe. He slipped it on. "I'm just working through everything in my head." When her eyes weren't glassy, and her words weren't slurred, he would explain. "Feel like eating something?"

"Smoothie."

"And then I think you need a nap."

"Are you going to change my pants again?"

He chuckled again. "Thankfully, no. I don't have to do that."

Her brow crinkled, a note of humor in her eyes. "Okay." Whatever that meant.

Adrian stood, holding his hand out for her. "Ready?"

She hopped off the bed and nearly collapsed.

He caught her.

Chapter 10

If felt like she'd slept for three days, but the clock said it had only been sixteen hours. Still, Megan was more rested than she'd been for days. After all, she had enough brain power to calculate how long she'd been asleep. That meant something.

Adrian sat across the hotel room much like the last time she'd woken up. The covers of the other bed were rumpled again, like last time. So he'd gotten some rest, too.

The text came through while she showered.

She came out of the bathroom to brush the tangles from her wet hair while she booted up her computer. The message had come through to a burner phone she kept. A username. Then another text, the password.

When she'd first been hired on with Double Down, she'd been brought in on their security measures. It was serious if Steve thought they needed to go to the website they'd set up just for situations like this. For the purpose of a team meeting that could be kept off the radar. They would be secure—thanks to a friend she'd introduced to Steve who had a private security business. A computer whizz known only as "Remy."

Nothing was impenetrable, but this was about making it as hard as possible for the blackmailer to even know they were communicating with each other.

She waited while the video call connected, and three screens filled with an image. Emma with Mint beside her. Steve, in his office. Bradley—who'd chosen to keep Alexis out of this meeting. She was at Rachel's. Two of their team had been killed in Colorado a couple of weeks ago. Those windows were blank, and she had to bite her lip at the sight of them.

Adrian settled beside her. He rubbed a hand down her back. "Okay?"

She brushed off the grief and nodded.

"Arm hurt?"

"Dull, but whatever they gave me worked because it's manageable."

Steve's voice came over the call before his screen loaded. "That's good to know, Perkins."

She glanced at the screen. "Hi, guys."

"Okay, since everyone is here, we'll begin," Steve said. "Megan's injury was first on the list, so next is Sylvia."

Megan said, "Why, what's up with mom?"

Adrian shifted.

They both waited. Steve said, "Nothing's wrong." He lifted his fingers so they were huge on the screen. "Sorry. What I mean is, she's headed to a conference in a couple of days. So do we have her cancel and stick her in a safe house for the time being so the blackmailer doesn't target her?"

"Yes." Megan nodded. "Do that."

"Or," Steve said, dragging out the word. That meant this suggestion was his recommendation. "Do we let her go, send cover with her—with or without her knowledge—and let her keep her schedule?"

"Why does she need to go?"

Steve's gaze softened slightly. "Part of the conference is honoring fallen federal agents. They're going to have all the surviving spouses and some of their children come on stage."

"She told me she was going. But she didn't say anything about that."

Her mom knew Megan would never have gone for that. She hated the spotlight. Not to mention standing in front of all those people when she'd done nothing worth honoring was super awkward. No wonder her mom hadn't mentioned it.

Steve nodded. "So do we let her go?"

"Who would the cover be?"

He looked down at his paper. "Guy I used to know. Former Delta Force. The wife was CIA. Now they have kids. He's on retainer with Double Down."

"You trust him?"

"No doubt."

Megan didn't like it, but was it worth her mom complaining to the entire team and making all their lives miserable? "Let her go."

"Agreed," Bradley said. "I know those two as well, and they're solid."

Mint said, "Me too. On both counts."

"Okay." That made her feel better. Whoever this guy and his wife were, the Double Down team knew they were good.

And while she knew they weren't placating her, she couldn't help but think being a woman made them all want to take care of her. Good thing she was perfectly capable of taking care of herself.

"Next up is the think tank," Steve said. "We're looking into the backgrounds of the two who were killed, looking for something that might warrant someone retaliating against them."

"My office is doing the same," Adrian said. "Though my guess is the target was the Army general and not the janitor."

Steve nodded. "The general has a lot of top secret, redacted stuff in his file. Seems he was over a whole lot of clandestine operations. Some of them go back decades," Steve said. "If we're going to get a connection, we'll have to know what we're looking for."

"Whatever it is, has to be connected to South America."

Adrian's statement made her stiffen. He didn't glance at her, or acknowledge her reaction. Something she was glad for. The last thing she wanted was for the guys to think this was all getting to her. They'd yank her from the operation faster than she could dig her heels in.

Nothing they could do would remove her, or protect her, from this. She was right smack in the middle of all of it.

She said, "What about the others who were in Mexico?" Steve would know she was referring to the time she'd spent there when Will was killed and not anything else. "If Zimmerman went to the hospital because that kid's father was connected, then maybe he'll try again with a different one of the men who were in Mexico. Use one of them to send another message."

Steve said, "Good idea. I'll find out where they are."

If anyone could do it, it was Steve. "Thanks." She hardly wanted to end up face to face with any of them. But if it got them answers, she would do it.

Steve said, "Walker, do you have anything from the FBI about Zimmerman's family?"

"They're investigating the family's disappearance as a kidnapping. But considering the lengths gone in order to cover it up, I wonder if they'll find anything at all. None of these people have made a misstep. Only Zimmerman, trying to pass that flash drive to Megan. And the blackmailer got men there to intercept and steal it. They were pros. If it's the same people who took Zimmerman's wife and children, then it's going to be a hard task."

Steve took a second to absorb that. The man never reacted straight away. He thought things through, and his slowness infuriated Megan at times, but he was right.

Finally, Steve said, "He's killed a child already today."

Megan nodded, trying not to think of Sofía and José.

"I'll follow up with the FBI on that, if you want," Bradley offered. "Make sure we do everything to see they're found—no more victims."

Megan broke the seal on her prayer life and asked that they be found alive. She didn't want to see any more children killed because of this blackmailer.

On the screen, Mint nodded. Emma leaned against his shoulder, as though being right there was precisely where she wanted to be. Megan could appreciate that. It was nice having Adrian beside her.

Emma had talked to Megan about doing accounting for a nonprofit that helped victims of violence. It was a great idea, but they were all waiting until this was over before they made moves like that. Took different career paths. It was why Mint and Emma hadn't gotten engaged yet. Or so Megan figured.

Not wanting to make major life changes when the threat against them all was still very real.

Bradley's history with Alexis, and having known each other for years, meant he hadn't wanted to waste time. They'd gotten married weeks ago. Megan had always thought she wanted to make a fuss for her own wedding. After all, the idea was to only do it once. Right?

Someone chuckled. She focused on the screen and saw them all smiling.

"Yep," Bradley said, a smile on his face. "Drifting."

"I'm fine," Megan argued.

"Good." Steve nodded. "Because you'll be needed soon enough. I have a feeling that think tank was just the beginning of what he has planned."

. . .

Adrian stayed still while Megan bristled—mostly because he was trying *not* to bump up against her wound. He also seriously doubted she wanted him to coddle her when the men were acting protective. They probably thought nothing of it, but she was tense.

"I have an idea on that," Megan said. "My friend who set up this system. If anyone can figure out how all this is connected, it's her."

Mint said, "Can she hack top secret files?"

Bradley nodded. "Because Zimmerman could hit the next target before this 'contact' of yours figures it out."

"Maybe you should have a little faith in the people I know, okay?" Megan shrugged her good shoulder. "Aren't you always telling everyone to trust God?"

Bradley's eyes narrowed, but Adrian spotted a gleam of humor there. "Yes."

"Then don't make a stink when I want to try something," she said. "We need the help."

"It's a good idea," Steve said. "We know she's good, so why not call on her since we need all the resources we can get."

Megan shifted and smirked for a second before her face blanked. On the computer screen, Emma smiled.

Adrian didn't envy Steve his job. Seemed like it might be more like babysitting at times, or settling squabbles between siblings.

"Then I'll get on it." Megan shifted her finger to hover over the End Call button on the screen. "Talk soon?"

Everyone nodded. Megan tapped the screen on her laptop, then leaned back on the bed. An audible groan spilled from her mouth. Tears filled her eyes.

"Whoa, are you okay?"

"That hurt. *A lot*."

"Your arm."

She nodded. "And my hip from the other day. I think whatever you gave me last night wore off in the middle of the conversation." Her stomach rumbled.

He smiled and stood, looking for where he'd put his cell phone. "And evidently you need food."

Megan pursed her lips and blew out a breath. Then she touched her arm below the injury, cradling it to her. Face pale. Hair splayed out around her on the comforter.

"You really don't look well. Do you have a fever?" He wandered over and planted his hands on either side of her head. He leaned down toward her forehead to check for a fever.

Her head tilted up.

Did she think…?

"I'm not going to kiss you."

"Back up." Her face hardened.

Adrian stood. "I'm trying to check for a fever."

"With your face? What's wrong with just putting your hand on my forehead?"

"It's not as accurate." But he stepped back, realizing why she might be weirded out. "My mom always used to touch her lips to my forehead. It's more accurate," he repeated. "I wasn't making a move on you. Not when you're hurt."

She gave him a look he couldn't decipher. Did she want him to make a move on her if she wasn't hurt?

He moved away and grabbed the key card. "That isn't why we're in a hotel room."

"I know." She sounded mad, but he didn't know who she was mad at. Him. Herself. Both.

"I'll go get us some food." Surely there was a restaurant of some kind nearby.

"And coffee. Something with four hundred calories of dairy and sugar and four shots. No, six."

Adrian shot her a look.

"Unless you want me to continue being hangry."

"Will you be okay while I'm gone?"

Megan sat up and winced, then returned his look. "Are you sure you're here to find Zimmerman, not just to look after me while *I* try to find him?"

"That might be…part of it." And why not? She needed someone there with her.

Her eyes narrowed. "Get out."

"Megan."

"No." She bit the word out between clenched teeth. "Are you kidding me? I'm calling Hank." She rummaged around for her phone, though he could see it hurt her a lot. "I *don't* need babysitting."

"That's not what's happening."

"No? I don't believe you." She pushed out a breath. "Hank is going to answer to me."

Adrian took a step toward the door. "I'll be back in fifteen with food and that coffee."

At the last second before the door clicked shut, he could have sworn he heard the word, "Coward," spoken in a low voice.

From her, or from himself?

She'd said she was hangry, so what was the big deal in cutting out and leaving her to it? She wanted to be independent, she could protect herself. He wouldn't be long.

Fifteen minutes, in fact.

He juggled the bag and drink carrier with huge coffees for both of them, and got the door open. He half expected her to be cleared out and gone. Instead, she was looking out the window. Phone to her ear. Laughing.

Years. Stress. Pain. It all bled from her face in that few seconds she smiled wide and shared a moment of humor with the person she was on the phone with.

Adrian stared.

She shifted around, and he saw the gun in her other hand. She let the curtain fall back into place, and he set the food down on the desk. The knot that had collected around his heart eased.

"Okay." Megan moved to her computer. She hit a button on the phone and said, "You're on speaker. Adrian is back."

"Pull up a new browser tab and type this in." The voice was young. Female, low-toned. Rich. The woman rattled off a series of numbers and letters. Backslash, pound, asterisk. Enter. This had to have been the contact she'd mentioned to her Double Down teammates—the one who might be able to get them answers.

Megan said, "Done."

"Enter all the information on that page."

"Where?" Megan stared at the screen. "It just looks like a bunch of pictures of someone's vacation."

"Click between margaritas and whale watching."

"Okay, but…" Megan paused. "Oh. I see."

Adrian wandered over and looked at the screen. A window had popped up.

"Type everything in there. All the factors you have, and all the variables. I'll run the numbers and let you know what I come up with."

"And if the blackmailer gets ahold of this website?"

"He can try," the woman said.

"How about trying to predict where he might hit next?" Megan asked. "After the think tank collapsed, we need to get ahead of him."

"Without a pattern, there's no way to predict where this guy might target next," the woman said. "At least not without me figuring out the common underlying link first."

Adrian said, "Some of the information you're going to need is top secret covert black-ops stuff."

"Okay." Like that was no big deal.

"O-kay."

"Like I said," the woman continued. "I'll let you know what I come up with."

It seemed there was no doubt in her mind that she'd come up with *something*. The only question was what that something would be.

Megan said, "Thank you so much."

"No worries. My boyfriend went AWOL a few weeks ago. I've got the servers running overtime searching for him. Until I get a hit, I've got time."

Megan glanced up at Adrian, an "Eek" look on her face. He grinned, then handed over her coffee. She mouthed, *Thank you.* And then, *Sorry.*

He shook his head, then leaned down. Waited until she realized what he was doing. Adrian touched his lips to her forehead. She was warm, but not hot enough it could be a fever.

When he leaned back, he smiled. Shook his head again.

"Me-gan… Did I lose you?" the woman asked.

"Tunnel," Megan said, immediately.

She chuckled. "I know you're sitting in a hotel room. The restaurant next door has better waffles than you'll get downstairs."

"Bye, Remy." Megan hung up the phone, chuckling again. She took a sip of coffee. "Wow, that's good stuff." She looked up at him. "I'm sorry I snapped."

"I forgive you."

"I don't need looking after."

"Mm-hmm." He tore into the bag of food and pulled out a burrito. Bit into it.

"Not going to say anything else?"

He shook his head, then pointed to his full mouth as he chewed. Swallowed. Quickly took another bite.

Megan rolled her eyes. "That smells good. Where's mine?"

Chapter 11

She slung her bag over her good shoulder just as Adrian stepped out of the bathroom. His clothes were clean, his hair wet. He'd shaved.

She might like a little beard growth, but she could appreciate a clean-cut man.

"You're leaving?"

"Yes." It wasn't like they were going to stay here. Not after the phone call she'd just gotten.

"So you waited until I was in the shower to pack up?"

She made a face at that ridiculous idea. "If I did, I took too long since I'm still here." Hopefully he'd get the sarcasm. She'd taken another pill, but it had yet to kick in.

"Am I invited to go with you?"

"Only if you put your shoes on." Okay, that *might* have been too much sarcasm. Especially considering the way he glanced at her out the corner of his eye and moved to his suitcase. "I can't see that hanging around a crime scene with bare feet would be a good idea."

He straightened. "Crime scene?"

"Yeah. Hank called," she said. "The two shooters from downtown were found dead in their vehicle a few hours ago. We should go check it out."

"That's where you were going?"

"That's where *we're* going." She'd agreed to stay, hadn't she? Even though he'd basically admitted he was there to take care of her. As if she needed a nurse. Or a babysitter. She didn't want to find out later that Steve and Hank had made an arrangement for Adrian to stick with her for exactly those reasons. But if it happened, she wasn't exactly going to be surprised.

Though, she'd probably *act* surprised. Pretend she'd had no idea. Get mad at the injustice of it all. That would be satisfying. Especially if people were safe, and Zimmerman was in jail. If they had also exposed the blackmailer in this scenario, that would make things even better. All wrapped up, back to normal.

Not this weird limbo she was living in now, where there wasn't even time to find a laundry place and wash their clothes.

"If you say so." He sat on the bed to put his shoes on.

Megan cocked her hip. "What is that supposed to mean?"

He looked up. "Why are we fighting? Were you going to leave without me?"

"No. Of course not." Right now, at least. Who knew what might happen later?

"Then forget about it."

Just like that? When she was hangry she could be the queen of grudges. Too bad she hadn't had the emotional or head space recently to do more than sit around wanting to kill *El Cuervo*.

"I'm not sure what just happened on your face."

Megan shrugged. She turned to the food bag, swiped up all the wrappers and deposited them in the trash. She wasn't hangry anymore, so that meant she was only taking out her frustrations on him because he was here. That was all.

She needed to stop doing it, or she'd have to apologize again.

The drive to the crime scene didn't take long. They'd stayed at a hotel by the airport just in case they needed to make a quick exit to go after Zimmerman. Adrian parked around the corner from where Hank had told her the shooter's car had been found in a warehouse.

Two cop cars, one black and white and one that looked like a regular car except with a red light on the dash were parked in front of the warehouse, along with a Crime Scene van. Hopefully they hadn't removed all of the evidence yet. She wanted to get a good look at it.

They checked in with the officer at the edge of the tape, showing their badges. The cop said, "Detective Haralson is inside."

Adrian nodded. "Thanks."

Megan was better off hanging back. She didn't need to abuse the badge by pretending she had the authority to be here. She might technically still be an FBI agent, but she figured it was mostly just Hank trying to do her a favor. She didn't want to go back to being an investigative agent. Or undercover. She kept the badge because it was what her father would've wanted. He'd taught her to never give up, and she'd chosen this profession.

Regardless of the fact she was employed and paid by Double Down Inc, part of her would always be a fed. It didn't really sit right, though. She needed to hand her badge back to Hank. She didn't want to play both sides. If she kept going much longer she would get burned—or she would burn her friends.

Megan didn't want that to happen.

Adrian called out, "Detective Haralson?"

A gray haired man in jeans, a button down shirt and a suit jacket, no tie, looked up from the footwell of the car and spotted them. He removed his gloves and wandered over. "Help you?"

"Special Agent Walker. This is Special Agent Perkins."

"Not locals. How'd you end up here?"

Megan pointed to her arm. "Technically, I guess, we're the victims in this case."

Haralson's eyebrows lifted, crinkling his forehead. "Are you now? Gonna have to ask you to leave, in that case."

"We aren't interested in being part of your investigation." Adrian lifted his hands, palms out. "And we for sure aren't going to interfere. But we would like to know what you've learned. It's likely pertinent in some way to our search for Special Agent Zimmerman."

"This is about that?" the detective asked.

Adrian nodded. Megan did the same. She said, "We're hoping for something that might help us figure out where he's going. Where he might hit next."

"That's fair."

An interesting reaction, considering she'd just offered him the chance to assist in a national security matter. Maybe he was just jaded. Or he wanted to act like he wasn't bothered, for whatever reason. Megan didn't worry about it. She couldn't afford to expend extra energy on a guy they didn't know, who likely didn't factor into this.

But they did need his cooperation.

"I'll call your office and make sure you're approved first." He didn't ask if that was all right.

Adrian started to give the detective the number.

"You can just give me your boss's name. I'll get the number."

Adrian nodded. "All right. Special Agent in Charge Hank Cromwell."

"One minute." The detective wandered away a few paces and got on his phone.

"Wow," Adrian said. "Not a very trusting guy, is he."

"It's like he believes one of us might not be a real FBI agent?" She grinned. Adrian shook his head.

"Fine, it wasn't that funny."

He stared over at the car. "Inside looks pretty clean."

"Maybe they just had it detailed."

"Do you have an answer for everything?"

She shrugged. "Sometimes."

"That's fair, I guess."

She studied him, trying to figure out why he'd reacted the way he had to the idea of her leaving. Probably the fact he insisted on being there to take care of her. Not that he hadn't been nice about it. More of a gentleman than a lot of guys would've been in the same situation.

But was it because Hank had ordered him to do it? Or was he taking care of her because *he* wanted to do it? She tried not to care either way. It wasn't going to help her focus. But it didn't work.

She did care.

. . .

There wasn't time to ask her what she was thinking. Not again. Though Adrian wanted to know. Her face was soft. He didn't often see that look. Still, there was an edge to it he could only describe as…conflicted almost. Like she didn't like what she was feeling.

Adrian wanted to smooth that out for her. More than he probably should have, especially considering they were chasing a rogue FBI agent bent on destruction and the ending of life. Innocent or not, didn't matter.

The last thing he had time for right now was an attraction, no matter how drawn to Megan he might be.

"Looks like you're all set." The detective stowed his phone in his jeans pocket. "So I'll walk you through what we have, but then I have to get back to work."

Adrian nodded. The man was busy, and he didn't want to use up more time than necessary entertaining two feds.

"Two victims, both were shot in the head where they sat. From the bit of blood spatter that we found and the position of the bodies, we're thinking two shooters. Both of these guys were likely shot through open windows simultaneously."

Megan glanced at him, eyebrows raised. They followed the detective over to the car. Both doors were open, the bodies gone now. The detective said, "The car was cleaned."

"We noticed it looked like it had been recently detailed," Adrian said.

"Not just detailed." The detective waved them over to the driver's side and crouched. "The VIN number here and on the dash have been filed off. No plates, no papers in the glove box."

Megan waited for more.

The detective shrugged. "There's nothing on the two bodies. No phones, no wallets. I mean, we'll run their IDs and probably figure out who they are eventually. But whoever killed them wanted this process to be as slow as it possibly could be."

"Maybe they won't show up in IAFIS." Adrian mulled it over more, even after he'd said it. The FBI's database didn't have an ID for everyone they ran. If these guys were foreign nationals who were here illegally, they might not be in any US-based database. "Maybe this is a wild goose chase on purpose."

"The killers may even have assumed it would take longer before someone discovered their bodies and called it in." The detective shrugged. "We could be ahead of their anticipated timetable. That's why I'm going as fast as I can on this. If it was a turf war between foreign nationals, we might only have a limited time before someone hops a plane back home."

Adrian said, "Why do you favor the idea they're not American?"

"Couple of the tattoos." The detective pulled out his phone again. "We have a Sergeant in the department who was Army. He spent some time in South America. Says they were likely Venezuelan. Connected." He glanced at Megan. "Tattoos are often a resume of accomplishments. No need for references when your ink speaks for itself."

Megan nodded like this was news to her. "Thank you very much for your time. We really appreciate it."

"Sure." The detective wandered off, but kept an eye on them while they made their way out.

They headed for the car. Megan said, "So that confirms they were Venezuelan. Probably men brought into this by *El Cuervo*." She paused by the driver's door, even though he was the one with the keys. "I can't see our homegrown blackmailer hiring outside help. I prefer the idea they were outside his plan, and he cleaned them up. Maybe gone rogue."

"Like he cleaned up Zimmerman's house?"

She nodded and leaned back against the door. "He has people on his payroll. But I don't think it's the Venezuelans."

"Could be a loose arrangement, and they went off topic. Or they got the flash drive from us at the hospital. Now they were no longer needed."

Megan mashed her lips together. She was frustrated, but it kind of made her look cute. She cocked her head to the side. "Why are you looking at me like that?"

"If you don't want me to check your temperature again, don't ask that question." He lifted the keys and beeped the lock.

"We hardly have time for that."

"I didn't say it was high on our priority list."

She moved out of the way and rounded the car, sliding into the passenger seat. Adrian got in. He turned into a Chinese fast food drive-through, and they both got lunch. Then he pulled into a space in the parking lot with good visibility of the surrounding area. The last thing he needed was someone getting the jump on them. Or anyone in the restaurant overhearing their conversation.

There had been entirely too many surprises so far. And instances where Megan had been injured.

She stabbed at her honey shrimp, frowning while she ate. "Doesn't really make any sense, does it?"

"If there was something in that car that could potentially expose our blackmailer, and he made sure it was retrieved or gotten rid of, that means his intention is to remain in the shadows."

"So he doesn't want to get caught and possibly has more plans he doesn't want ruined."

Adrian nodded. "Right." He forked orange chicken into his mouth and thought for a minute or so. "If he's in this for the long haul, then we *really* have to find him. He can't go unchecked anymore. He's ruining lives."

And the last thing Adrian wanted was for Megan to have caught the blackmailer's eye, the way Rachel, Alexis and Emma had. She'd been through so much. He would hate to see her get even more hurt over this as well.

His phone rang. The sound came through the car speakers since the engine was still running. He pressed the button on the dash screen. "Walker."

"It's Agent Cromwell. Megan there with you?"

"I'm here, Hank," she said.

"Good. I just got word through a few back channels." He paused. Megan glanced at Adrian, as though he'd be able to explain it. Hank did that when he had something he didn't want to admit. Adrian shrugged. He didn't know what it was related to. Hank said, "We think *El Cuervo* just landed in the US."

"How?" Megan barked the word. "Who let him in the country?"

The authorities had his picture, so immigration would be alerted if he showed up. And the man would be immediately arrested.

Hank said, "He used diplomatic papers, and the word I got was that he was disguised. But my contact was sure it was him."

"Who?"

"*El Cuervo*," Hank said.

"No," Megan said. "Who is your contact?"

"I can't give you that information, Meg. You know that."

Adrian hadn't heard anyone call her "Meg," except for Hank. And he'd used "Meggie" in the office. One was a chastisement, the other likely designed to get her to relax, maybe get her a little annoyed by the father figure in her life.

Megan sighed. "I need to know if it's him. He can't move around unchecked."

"You can't kill him."

"Under the right circumstances," she said, "I absolutely could."

Hank said, "This isn't about revenge. It's about finding Zimmerman. I told you this because it can't be a coincidence."

Adrian figured he was right about that.

This was no coincidence.

Chapter 12

Megan climbed in the back of the SUV and slid across the seat, careful not to jostle her arm too much. Adrian entered behind her and settled on the opposite side. How many places would they fly to this week? She didn't even like flying.

"How was your trip?"

Her eyebrows lifted. Their contact here in Austin, Texas—was *Hank*?

He grinned. "You didn't think I'd let you have all the fun, did you?"

Megan shook her head. "No, sir. I did not."

Adrian shifted and held out his hand. They shook. "Sir."

"Walker."

"So what's the situation?" she asked.

Hank sat in the front passenger seat, the driver an agent she didn't know. Hank said, "El Cuervo entered this restaurant two hours ago. One of the local agents did a walk-through and he's reportedly still enjoying his carne asada."

"How do we know it's him?"

Megan was glad Adrian was the one who asked that question. She wanted to know the answer, but didn't think she could speak now without throwing up. The reality that *El Cuervo* was so close had settled on her. Inside her. Like a toxic cloud, or some kind of insidious poison.

Adrian reached over and touched her hand. Megan shifted her fingers and grabbed onto his. Her lifeline in the middle of this. She wanted to pray, the way she'd prayed all the way here that Remy would find the connection between everyone involved—a connection that would lead back to the blackmailer. Otherwise, they had little method of discovering who he was.

Now that she'd started praying, it almost felt like she couldn't stop.

The man behind all this was a master of technology. A master of disguising his own identity behind layer after layer of anonymity. Hiring people to operate on his behalf, folks happy to accept payment and never learn their employer's identity.

Uncovering his—or her, she supposed—identity was the key to all of it.

And one of the factors that remained an indisputable part of that, was the part *El Cuervo* played in all this. There was a connection. But how important was it?

Hank looked down at his lap. "We got a picture of him. Do you want to see it?"

Megan really did not. Though she'd only seen him once, and just from the side, he'd seemed an imposing man. Whether that was due to his reputation, or the fact she and Will had been his prisoners, she couldn't have said.

She swallowed, then reached with her free hand for the phone Hank held out. She looked at the screen. Dark gray suit. Dark hair. Thick, heavy brow. It was the same angle she'd seen him from before, and it wasn't completely in focus. Taken on the sly, moving fast, by someone who knew they would likely be killed if spotted.

"Was this the man who ordered Will's death?"

She nodded. "Yes."

Hank lifted a black radio. "All units be advised, suspect has been identified. Stand by."

Adrian squeezed her hand.

She said, "Are you going in there to pick him up, or will you wait until he leaves?"

"As much as I'd like to know what exactly he's waiting for," Hank said, "I'm inclined to interrupt his meal, and snatch him up. We may not get another chance."

She nodded, hoping he didn't ask her to join the operation. They likely had enough agents here. Maybe even local law enforcement backing them up. They didn't need her, right?

And yeah, she was a total chicken. Or it was straight fear. Though understandable given her trauma, she didn't like it. Megan had spent her life so far trying to live up to her dad's legacy. To honor his memory. Here she was, practically shaking, because a man was in a restaurant eating dinner that was no doubt better at home.

Where was her drive to kill him? Apparently when it came down to it, she was all bark and no bite.

Why was he here?

What was Hank waiting for?

Why had *El Cuervo* left her alive?

The question had been haunting her for years, and she had no more answers now than she did the day she walked into the American embassy in Mexico City, in ragged clothes and covered with Will's blood.

Megan felt the tears gather and squeezed her eyes shut.

"We move now." Hank's voice was solid. Sure. That father figure, determined to protect her. The way she remembered her dad doing when she'd fallen ice skating and broken her arm. He'd stayed up on the couch and watched movies all night with her because she'd been too uncomfortable to sleep with the cast.

"All units, green light. I repeat, green light."

The car door opened. Then another. Adrian didn't move, and neither did she.

Megan opened her eyes and saw the driver and Hank had both gotten out. Bullet proof vests. Weapons ready.

They made their way across the lot to the front door of the restaurant. Megan saw other agents head toward the side, to go around the back. They would get in position at all entrances and exits and make sure every way out was covered.

Then, when the signal was given, they would converge.

"You okay?"

She didn't turn back to Adrian. "Yes." Did he really want to stay here with her? "You can get a vest and go with them if you want. You don't have to sit with me." She didn't call it babysitting. He knew how she felt about him being here purely to "take care of her." That wasn't what this was. She needed his hand holding hers right now. They both knew it.

"I'm fine."

She knew that.

Megan smiled to the window at her own joke. She opened her mouth to offer him another chance to get in on the action, but a crack like a firework cut her off.

"What..." She tugged on the door handle on a reflex.

"I don't think—"

Another shot sounded. It didn't hit the car, though.

All the agents she could see ducked and ran for cover.

She tugged on the door handle. Nothing happened. She tugged again. It was locked. "Hank!" She called his name, and the sound echoed in the car.

Another shot came.

"They're shooting at the agents." That didn't make sense, but she couldn't think. All she could do was watch, and keep pulling on the handle. Hard enough it would break any moment.

The front.

Megan pulled herself up between the seats with her good hand and then got her legs over the center console.

Adrian pulled on her belt. "We're protected in here. Hank doesn't want you in the line of fire."

"I'm not just going to watch him die." The words left her mouth in a rush, her stomach sour. Her mouth filled with water, and a sick taste. "I won't do that again."

"Then draw your weapon," Adrian said. "We get out the passenger side, and we hunt the shooter."

Shots were still coming. Out there, in the glow of streetlights, they could see agents hunkered down all over. She climbed out the passenger door and kept her head low. Leaned against the SUV. When Adrian shut the door, she looked around him.

Found the muzzle flash.

"There." She pointed high on the building, then counted floors. "Eight. South-west corner."

"Stay low, and stay behind me."

Neither of them had vests. Hank and his people were sitting ducks until they flushed out the shooter.

El Cuervo knew they were waiting outside. That was the best explanation her harried mind could come up with right now.

And he'd sent someone to kill law enforcement, before they could take him in.

．　．　．

Adrian went first. Using cars and shadows for cover, they made their way to the building where she'd seen the muzzle flash. He'd seen it too, but the absolute terror on her face—and in her voice—was the thing he couldn't escape or ignore. Megan.

Would she have a day in her life anytime soon where she could live free of all this? Have peace. Not just the small amount she was willing to accept from God right now, but the peace that came from knowing the past was done. Knowing she wasn't responsible for the evil committed by sinful men.

Did she even want it?

Adrian ducked in the front door. An office. No security guard. Probably no surveillance cameras either. Maybe a cleaning crew.

He found the elevator and pressed the button for the eighth floor. Longest elevator ride of his life. When the door opened, they heard yet another crack of a shot being fired.

The shooter was determined. Everyone outside was pinned down, taking cover. Still they would watch the exits. And maybe *El Cuervo* didn't yet know what was happening outside. Perhaps there would still be the opportunity to catch him.

He prayed there would be.

Adrian wasn't going to assume the shooter hadn't heard the elevator ding on this floor. He hugged the wall, then motioned for Megan to stay behind him. She shook her head, that haunted look still in her eyes, then motioned for them both to go together.

Adrian moved. They didn't have time to argue, whatever the outcome would be. He wasn't going to win the battle to get her to take cover behind him. Realizing that might save them time, but it didn't make him feel better. He pushed his feelings aside as they cleared room after room on this floor. Where was the shooter?

Finally he found a room with the window open—some kind of kitchen, or break room. A round table had been dragged to the window. Spent shell casings littered the floor.

But the shooter was gone.

"He stopped firing, at least."

He nodded. She was right, and it was a good thing. "Let's check the stairs."

They cleared the rest of the rooms, in case the shooter was hiding there, and then found the stairs. In the dank stairwell, he stopped. Listened. Below them was the sound of someone taking the stairs at a rapid pace. That staccato patter of feet going faster than the brain said was wise.

Adrian set off down after the person. He stowed his weapon as he ran, figuring he had some time—but not much. He pulled out his phone, dialing with the hand he wasn't using to keep steady on the downward descent around corners, between floors.

"Cromwell."

"It's Walker." He huffed the words out, descending the stairs rapidly with Megan right behind him, keeping pace like they did this every day. She'd been hit by bullets *twice*. How was she not even out of breath? "Our shooter is about to exit the stairwell. Need agents there to cut him off."

"Copy that."

Adrian hung up, stowed his phone away and pulled his weapon again. They were on the third floor now. Were they too late? Had the shooter already gone outside?

He prayed they didn't lose him. That he and Megan, or other agents, would see the shooter and catch him.

At the exit door, he pushed the bar still running full speed and launched out into the night. Gun up. He spun both ways and ran right into agents sprinting around the corner.

"Did you see him?" One of them asked.

Adrian shook his head, thankful he didn't have to explain who he was. He glanced at Megan. "Let's go see if we can still catch him."

They took the opposite direction from the agents. The others would have seen the shooter, unless he'd gone this way.

Adrian rounded the corner, his breath coming in heaves. His side starting to hurt. "Think I need an uptick in my cardio."

Megan huffed out a laugh. They stopped and glanced both ways. Back street. No one around.

Didn't hear anything. Couldn't see anything.

"What..?"

He spun to Megan, and saw the look on her face, then immediately glanced the direction she was looking. A beat up old silver Ford pulled onto the street. Tires smoked as it screeched away. No license plate.

"Did you see him?" Adrian asked it even as he moved into the street to watch where it was going. "We can get an APB out. Have local law be on the lookout for the car."

He walked back over to her, ready to head back and get a situation report. Then he realized she stared at the car still. "Megan."

She jolted, then glanced at him. "Yes?"

"Explain."

Her face blanked. Trying to hide something.

"What is this? Did you see the shooter?" She had known he was in the car before the car even pulled out.

She sucked in a breath and lifted her chin. "I didn't see who it was." Then she turned away too fast. She set off, making long strides so he had to trot to catch up.

He didn't believe her.

What reason would she have for lying? He didn't know. But he did know she had looked straight at his face just then, and she'd lied her pretty little butt off.

Adrian followed her like a whipped puppy dog. He worked his jaw back and forth. He'd thought it was worth it to stick around, make sure she was safe. If Megan was going to lie to him, then maybe not.

His team was hard at work trying to locate Zimmerman and figure out where he would hit next. What was he doing? Babysitting Megan. He could see why she didn't like it. And he'd even thought he was doing them all a favor. Keeping her guarded, keeping up with what Double Down knew about the blackmailer and Zimmerman. Following up on leads.

Yes, his feelings had been involved. Part of him hoped that eventually she'd let her guard down. Talk to him about Will. Let him in. Maybe something would develop from that, maybe not.

He could hope.

Adrian was still frowning when they got back to the SUV. Hank glanced between them. "You guys okay?"

"Are *you* okay?" Adrian asked. "Was anyone hurt?" There should be ambulances here if anyone had been. Right?

Hank shook his head. "No, thank goodness. We dodged a bullet there. Literally."

A sniper who had missed? Maybe deliberately. "Could be it was a distraction," Adrian suggested.

"You think he pinned us down so *El Cuervo* could get away?"

Megan's body snapped taut. "He got away?"

Hank nodded. "Slipped out a side exit while the agents were occupied by the sniper. There was nothing they could do, but they followed as soon as they could. Didn't see a car, though. How'd you do with the sniper?"

Adrian glanced at Megan, letting her answer that question. Someone caught Hank's attention, and he glanced over.

"He got away as well," she said, her face blank.

Hank nodded. If Adrian hadn't been watching and hadn't caught her reaction, he might have bought it, too. But he'd seen the expression on Megan's face.

"So we have nothing?" Hank turned back to them, lifted his hands and let them fall to his sides. He moved to the other agents then.

Adrian didn't think they had *nothing*. What they had wasn't much.

The question was, what Megan planned to do with it.

Chapter 13

Adrian knew. Maybe not exactly what she'd seen—though he figured she got a glimpse of the shooter. What he didn't know, was who it was. He'd seen her surprise. He was a smart man. He'd either figure it out, or he would get her to tell him.

She trusted Adrian, but what she wanted right now was the time to process and plan. To figure out how she was going to manage this issue. If it came out the wrong way, this whole FBI investigation would tank. Or it would tangent in the wrong direction. They'd start looking at the wrong person.

And Double Down would be toast.

Hank strode away. She could feel Adrian's attention on her. Not staring. That was awkward. But the man had this ability to just *focus,* and he'd decided to focus on her.

She bristled and glanced at him. "Aren't you supposed to be finding Zimmerman?"

His eyebrows lifted, but he didn't say anything. "Care to share any new information you have in your possession? Information that possibly might help the cause?"

"I really hate people who do that." She blew out a breath and fought back the mad.

"Do what?"

"Flip everything back, so all of a sudden it's *your* fault. I had an ex who used to do that, and it's infuriating." She pointed at him. "You're the one not finding Zimmerman."

He was still staring—focused.

And now she was blathering. "Eventually you'll go back to your desk in DC, and you'll get some other case. I'll be a memory."

"A good one."

She narrowed her eyes. This whole conversation had veered into dangerous territory. "What's that supposed to mean?"

He lifted both hands, palms out. "Nothing, Megan." He blew out a breath. "Will you chill?"

"Did you just tell me to *chill?*"

"Yes, and apparently it was the wrong thing to say."

"You don't tell—"

He cut her off. "Is that your phone?"

She belatedly realized her phone was ringing. She dug it out of her jacket pocket. "It's the Double Down line."

She'd have preferred it to be Remy with an answer, but she would accept any distraction from this dangerous conversation with Adrian. He probably thought she was unstable. Maybe she was.

Adrian said, "So it's Steve?"

She stilled to keep from reacting and said, "Maybe."

Unfortunately, the lack of reaction was a reaction of its own. She didn't look up though. Didn't check to see what he'd seen, or hadn't. She swiped the screen. "Perkins."

"It's all over the police band that there was a shooting at your location involving a bunch of federal agents on an operation."

"Mom, I told you to stop listening to the police band whenever I'm on an op."

Adrian made a choking sound. When she glanced up she saw the humor in his eyes. Megan frowned at him, then focused back on her phone.

"...who knows where, and I have no idea what's going on."

"Did you GPS my phone?"

Adrian laughed out loud.

"Why else did we get on a family plan?"

Megan rolled her eyes. "Mom, I'm fine. Everyone's fine." She explained what had happened and how they'd chased the shooter, but he got away. It was mostly true.

"You're leaving something out," her mom said. "What is it?"

Megan didn't know how to answer that without saying too much in front of Adrian. "I'll email you the report."

There was a second of pause, then her mom said, "It had better all be in there. I mean it."

Megan nearly smiled, but didn't. "Not a problem." She figured if the blackmailer was in their system, then it didn't matter. He already knew who the shooter was. Megan needed someone she could totally count on to be in on this with her. She had few allies, but her mom being part of Double Down was one.

"Those two days you were gone were the worst days of my life."

Megan squeezed her eyes shut.

She felt Adrian step closer, and then his arm was around her waist and he hugged her into his warm body. Images from those days flashed in her mind. She managed to choke out, "I know."

"I love you. I'm glad you're all right," her mom said. "I'm leaving for my conference in the morning, so I'll be out of touch for a few hours."

"Okay, text me when you leave and when your plane lands. I want to know when you're at the hotel."

Her mom chuckled. "You sound like your father."

"Good." Megan swiped at the moisture under her eyes and tried to step back. Adrian's arm tightened a fraction, like he didn't want to let her go. She didn't fight it. He was warm and the night air was cold. That was all.

She said, "Love you, Mom," and then hung up. "She worries."

"Understandable." His gaze shifted as he took in her face. Assessing, but in a nice way. "You okay?"

"Sure. Why wouldn't I be?"

"You're lying."

"No, I'm not."

"And now you just lied again," he said.

Megan pressed her lips together. "Maybe it's none of your business." He saw entirely too much. "And you should just go find Zimmerman."

"Run along. Is that it?" he asked. "You've decided you're done with me, so I should go?"

She didn't say anything. It wouldn't be good if she did, and she figured she needed the practice at keeping her mouth shut sometimes. There was a whole lot of bizarre subtext happening here. She tried to figure out how it'd gotten so out of control.

"Dismissed." He let go of her. "I guess I'm figuring out how this is going to go, then."

"This—" She motioned between them with a flick of her finger back and forth. "—isn't going anywhere."

She couldn't let it. Not after she'd watched Will die. She'd failed him, and she had to live with that fact. There was no way she would allow someone else into her orbit to suffer the same fate. Especially not when there were multiple enemies in play.

They were circling, like sharks around their prey. And that prey was bleeding.

She had been for years.

Sticking with Adrian wasn't going to fix that. She couldn't use him as a crutch forever, just so she could feel stronger. That wasn't right. She needed to beat the fear over and over, every minute of every day. Choose bravery. Choose not to fear.

Choose life.

Adrian took a step back, his face blank in a way she hated. "Don't go anywhere. I need to talk to Special Agent Cromwell." He turned in the direction where Hank stood with a few of the local agents.

Megan watched him walk away, just to appreciate the way he moved. Trying not to think of the ways he'd helped her. Been there for her. Stuck around the last few days, so she wouldn't be alone.

She shook her head. That wasn't what he'd been doing. This had been about work. Protecting her in a way that meant he'd kept track of her progress and where Double Down was at this whole time.

Maybe it was for the best that she'd hurt his feelings. Adrian shouldn't get attached to her. This was a job.

Nothing more.

.   .   .

Adrian blew out a breath.

Hank said, "That bad?"

"She's hiding the identity of the shooter," he said. "She knows who it is."

Hank shook his head slowly. "Stay on that. If she trusts you as you say she's been starting to, then stick with it. It'll eat at her, and she'll need someone to confide in."

Adrian didn't like it. "I figure we'll get an answer faster by getting into her email. She's going to send her mom a report. If I was inclined to gamble, I would put money on the fact she'll tell her mom who it was."

"I agree." Hank pulled out his own phone. "I'll have that noted so we flag it when it comes through."

If there was any kind of tracking software in the Double Down system, they'd likely attribute the breach to the blackmailer. Megan didn't need to know the FBI was in there as well.

"There's more, though."

Adrian said, "What is it?"

"When *El Cuervo* slipped out of the restaurant, he left this behind." Hank lifted an evidence bag. Inside was a cell phone. "No password protection."

"So he didn't think it would fall into the wrong hands," Adrian said. "Or he doesn't care if it does. He *wants* us to see whatever is in there."

Hank said nothing.

"So what is in there?"

Hank shifted the phone, and the screen illuminated. "One thing."

A picture of Megan flashed on the screen.

"She's his target?" Adrian glanced back over his shoulder. Megan was typing on her phone, but he could tell she was aware of what was happening around her. She would never let herself get so distracted she'd be blindsided.

"Or they're working together."

"Megan and *El Cuervo*? That's nuts, Hank. You can't seriously believe that."

Hank's eyebrows lifted, but Adrian noticed there was a spark of something there.

"What I mean, sir," Adrian emphasized the word, "is that Megan was *destroyed* by what happened to her in Mexico. You of all people know that. I can't for one second believe she was part of it."

"Do we really know?" Hank asked. "I didn't get to this position by allowing my feelings to be blinded. Even by someone I've known over the years as well as Megan."

"So you've kept her close to find the truth about whether or not she was involved with him?" A sick feeling settled in Adrian's stomach. Had Hank just been using him all along? "Do you think she was in league with Zimmerman as well? He's a victim of the blackmailer."

"It's too coincidental. The blackmailer targets Zimmerman, who is connected to *El Cuervo*. And standing in the middle is Megan Perkins."

"If he turned her, she's given him nothing. She doesn't have access to privileged FBI information, so she can't be a mole. It was *you* who made it so she kept her badge, sir."

Hank said, "So you think she's an innocent victim in all this? Targeted by *El Cuervo*, she manages to escape when her partner is conveniently killed. Now Zimmerman is using her as the recipient of his 'message.' One we also conveniently never received."

Adrian folded his arms. "This isn't about Megan. It's about finding Zimmerman."

"And you still don't believe she's the key to all of this?" Hank shook the phone in front of his face. "*El Cuervo* wants us to know he's interested in her."

"Probably to unnerve her. He'll know we're working with her." It could all be a ploy to make them think she was working for the other side. But he knew Megan. She would never betray her friends, or her family, or the memory of her partner that way. Not even if she was being blackmailed. "If he's here to get her because she slipped out of his hands before, then it's more important now than ever that we make sure she stays safe."

Hank saw it. Adrian hadn't tried to hide it. He cared about Megan, and that wasn't going to be a secret. Not now. Not ever. He needed as much truth between them as possible.

And if Hank thought he could implicate her, he was going to have a fight on his hands.

"Either way," Adrian said, "I will be sticking with her."

"We're closing in on Zimmerman. The sighting of him headed for Chicago was legit."

"And now?" The think tank had been destroyed, and two people killed the last time he'd been seen.

"He was seen in Des Moines. We think he's headed west," Hank said. "As far as we can tell, we're about four hours behind him at this point."

"Good," Adrian said. It bothered him not to be on the front lines of the search. Local agents in each city were taking care of the leg work. "Keep me posted."

"Where will you take her?"

"We'll head northwest. That will at least get her out of the same city as *El Cuervo*."

Yes, he was essentially stringing her along. His intention was to be there to take Zimmerman down when the time came. But his orders were to stick with Megan. It had become personal, but the reality was that if he wanted to get ahead at the FBI, then he needed to follow them.

Now that they knew for sure she had a connection to the blackmailer, it was more important than ever that he stick with her. Get this done. Figure out Megan's connection to the blackmailer and the reason why she'd been repeatedly pulled in.

They needed to close the case. Preferably before he lost all focus because he'd spent far too much time with Megan.

After that, who knew?

Hank lifted his chin and then walked away. Adrian had been dismissed. Again.

He couldn't help feeling like the underling, which was exactly what he was. Hank acted one way with his staff, and a completely different way with Megan. And yet, under the surface, he was suspicious of her.

Adrian didn't know what to think. He knew what his gut said and what his heart wanted to believe. But following that could cost him the next step of his career—everything he'd been working on for years.

Long before Megan came into his life.

"Adrian!"

He turned to see her stride toward him, and called out, "What is it?"

"Phone." She waved for him to meet her, and they got into the SUV. Front seats this time. The keys were in the ignition.

"Okay, Remy," she said. "Tell Adrian what you just told me."

"I ran some calculations. Looked for links between everyone involved so far and tried to figure out the likelihood that all this was as a result of those connections. Then based on what I found, I did some digging. The kind an FBI agent isn't going to look past."

"I won't arrest you," he said. "Not if it gets us a result."

He wasn't about to lose the chance to get through this without it all going badly. They needed to find Zimmerman and the blackmailer, and he needed Megan to stick with him long enough for law enforcement to find *El Cuervo*. For whatever reason, the Venezuelan was interested in her.

"Oh, goodie."

"Remy." Megan said her name as a chastisement.

"Sorry. I'm just having trouble finding Shadrach and it's bothering me a lot. But this was a good distraction."

Adrian frowned at the idea that she thought this was some kind of intellectual exercise. They were talking about people's lives—and a potential terrorist threat.

Megan shook her head.

Remy said, "So the highest probability for a connection is that *El Cuervo* is linked to Zimmerman, which you know from his computer. What you don't know is that I found a link between the Venezuelan and Senator Sadler. And Bradley and Rachel's parents. *And* Megan's father. And a scientist named Brent Caulder, and Steve Preston. There are more people on the list, but those are the ones you know."

Megan stiffened at the mention of her boss. Hitting too close to home?

"It goes back to the eighties and a military operation in Venezuela."

"Was the FBI involved?"

"Yep. And the state department," Remy said. "I have a whole list of people who were part of this. Top of the list is General Eric Thomas, US Army retired."

"Sounds familiar," Adrian said.

Megan nodded. "The dead General from the think tank."

Remy continued, "So much of this stuff is redacted. It's going to take a whole lot more digging to get to the details of what actually happened. But what I know so far is that everyone who's been targeted by the blackmailer is linked by one common denominator. That operation in Venezuela."

Chapter 14

Megan could hardly believe Remy had found it—the answer they'd been looking for all along. She gripped the phone so hard it seemed like it would shatter in her hand at any moment.

Even Adrian looked like he couldn't quite believe what was happening.

Remy continued, "What I can tell you right now was that it was a black ops mission, and the signature on the authorization page is the general who died at that think tank bombing a couple of days ago." She paused. "It's connected, right?"

"Yes," Adrian told her. "It wasn't a bombing, despite the information that was released. It was a sonic weapon."

"I figured as much from the damage," Remy said. "It doesn't even look close to the kind of destruction an explosion would do."

He said, "Anyone else on there we should know about?"

Megan's stomach rolled over for the millionth time in the past few days. Remy said, "If we're looking at possible targets for who might be next, I have a couple of names as suggestions that I'll send over to Megan's phone. I'll list them in order of probability, as well as last known location."

"If you do that," Adrian said, "then won't the blackmailer know precisely what we know?"

"Not the way I send emails, he won't."

"This guy has breached security over and over throughout this whole thing."

"Sure. But now *I'm* in on it," Remy said.

Megan chuckled.

Remy said, "One of these days I'm going to run across something I can't crack, or someone who is better than me. When that happens I'll be sure to go back to bio-medical research."

Megan winced. "I'm not sure I'm okay with that idea." If the woman could hack anything, including genetics, it could lead to all kinds of breakthroughs, but that also meant she'd have a deadly virus or some brand new potential nerve agent on her hands. The federal agent in Megan wouldn't settle for that as a future possibility.

Remy chuckled. "Then pray it never happens."

Apparently done with their conversation, Adrian said, "So you'll send us those names over email?"

"Already done. Should be on your phone now, Megan."

She shifted the screen to check for notifications. "Yep, it came through."

"Alrighty. Stay safe."

The line went dead.

Adrian said, "I'm not sure I want to know how you met her."

Megan swiped through to the email. "Suffice it to say, she's saved my life more than once."

"Good."

Before she started reading, she said, "I didn't escape from *El Cuervo*'s guys. I was rescued. By the people Remy works with. Or for."

She'd never understood that distinction. Remy was part of a team the same way Megan was part of Double Down. Though, their team was comprised of an entirely different crop of people.

"Rescued?"

Megan nodded. "Somehow Steve knows them, and I knew *him* from an operation back in the day. When he heard I was missing, he made a call. It's why I chose Double Down." She paused. "Remy's team is so far under the radar, they don't even want anyone knowing they were there. Let alone what they were doing. So I made up the story of my escape."

"Wow." He shook his head. "That certainly answers a few questions."

"Concerned about the inconsistencies in my story?" She cocked her head to the side. "Sorry I'm not a better liar."

"I don't think it's necessary to be a good liar."

"It was when I was undercover." She shrugged, though it hurt to brush it off. "But considering how that turned out, maybe I wasn't as good at it as I thought."

Adrian nodded, his eyes distant like he was trying to solve a complex equation in his head. "Or this plan by the blackmailer has been in play for *years*." He shook his head. "There's a horrific thought."

"So my whole life has been nothing but someone else pulling strings? Making me do what he wants me to do, go where he wants me to go. For what?" she asked. "So he can get revenge for some clandestine operation my father was involved in? I was kidnapped two years ago. This can't have been going on that long."

"Revenge is a powerful motivator."

She certainly knew that from personal experience. He didn't need to tell her. If Megan ever found herself in the same room as *El Cuervo* again, she could prove exactly how powerful revenge was.

But that didn't mean Zimmerman and the Venezuelan had anything more to do with the blackmailer than the fact that Zimmerman's family had been targeted.

"I don't like that look on your face."

She folded her arms, then realized that just made her look defensive. Megan sighed and lowered them. What was the point in responding? She'd already given herself away.

The question was, what would Adrian do about it?

While he decided, Megan opened the email. "Two men are at the top of the list of Remy's potential targets. A captain and a rear admiral. Both navy. They were listed in the planning stages of the operation. Remy said they're both booked at the same hotel for this coming weekend."

"It's Friday morning," Adrian said. "You mean tonight?"

It was Friday already? Megan shook her head. The last few days had thrown her for a loop. "Yes."

Adrian made a face. "No, but yes?"

"No. Yes." She shook her head again. "Yes, tonight."

"I think you need a nap on the way there."

Megan blew out a breath. He wasn't wrong, but she wasn't about to admit to weakness. She wanted to trust Adrian. In a way, she already did. No question. And yet, at the back of her mind this thing just…niggled at her. Maybe that wasn't even the right word. Still, it was there. A tiny voice questioning whether everything was as she perceived it to be.

The same voice that had been there right before she and Will were captured. One she should have listened to.

If she had, would he still be alive?

If Will lived through that kidnapping the way she had, he'd be with her. Working to bring down Zimmerman.

But that meant she wouldn't be with Adrian.

Megan blew out a breath and ran her hands through her hair. She probably looked like she'd been dragged through a bush by her feet. *Been there.* Not something she wanted to repeat, but life was life.

She said, "What about Will?"

Adrian's look softened. "What about him?"

"Were we taken because we were on some list of the blackmailer's?" she asked, aloud. Not necessarily expecting him to be able to answer. "Or because our FBI cover had been blown?"

Adrian got on his phone. "I'll ask this Remy person."

Of course he had her number now. He'd probably memorized it off Megan's phone screen. Like it was that easy to contact Remy.

She said, "Maybe it had nothing to do with our trying to take down *El Cuervo* and everything to do with putting us in the path of this blackmailer. And then Will is killed—" She swallowed, but pulled herself together quick enough to say, "And I get...rescued. Which ruins their plans." She thought for a second. "Now it seems like I have a part in what's happening, all these years later. I don't get it."

In another scenario, would the blackmailer have forced her to get the sonic weapon from Emma and take it on a rampage? She could have been swallowed up by this, even more than she already was.

"Having a small part is a good thing, Meg." His eyes were soft still. She liked that look on him.

But a good thing? *Maybe.* She didn't like being the focus of some unknown entity playing God with all of their lives. Zimmerman could kill those two men—and more—before this was done.

She looked at the screen of her phone and kept reading.

"Adrian."

He glanced up from his phone, a frown still on his face. "What?"

"This conference in Denver."

He shifted to see what she was talking about.

"The place where these two men are booked, that Zimmerman supposedly wants to hit." She looked up. "It's where my mom is going."

.   .   .

Adrian braced, and asked the question, "Same place those two Navy guys are going to be?" She nodded. He said, "Then let's go," and waved toward the SUV.

They headed that direction, and he detoured for a second to check in with Hank and fill him in. When he got to the vehicle, he saw Megan in the front seat. He climbed in the passenger side.

"My turn to drive," she said, turning on the engine.

"Fine by me." His heart was still racing from hearing those shots ring out. That split second where he didn't know who was alive—and who was dead. Adrian had never liked those moments.

The FBI was all about regulation, procedure. Order. Then there were those times when it was pure chaos for a few minutes. The times that defined the rest of what they did and impacted the agents the most.

He tried to push away the adrenaline, even as it retreated. Get rid of the feelings of being flustered and out of control from his system as quickly as possible.

Get back to work.

The vehicle's GPS directed Megan to the airport. Did Double Down have a plane waiting? They'd done that before. The FBI could probably get them on a flight to Denver tonight.

Megan's phone buzzed in the cup holder. "Can you see who that is?"

"Sure." She gave him her passcode, and he unlocked her phone. "Text from Mint. He hasn't seen Steve." The phone buzzed again. "Bradley hasn't seen him either."

Megan pressed her lips together, then shifted them back and forth.

Adrian wanted to ask why she was trying to get ahold of her boss. He backed up to her messages and looked for the thread with Steve. She hadn't contacted him after she discovered Zimmerman's likely target. She'd done it before—after they'd chased the shooter.

Was the shooter Steve?

The implications of that set his brain to spinning. He reached for his own phone to inform Hank, then hesitated. What if it wasn't Steve who'd been the shooter? Megan might have just been trying to contact her boss so she could talk to him about who it had been.

Not Adrian.

No, she'd reached out to her boss.

The implications of that stung more than he liked. Hurt feelings were the last thing he needed right now, and weren't going to help them bring down Zimmerman before it cost innocent lives.

He needed to get over himself and focus on the work. Especially now he knew his feelings for Megan ran deeper than they should.

She tapped the wheel with her finger. "You think Zimmerman's going to use that sonic weapon on the whole building where the conference is? Or will he kill the two Navy officers some other way."

She was worried about her mother. Adrian set a hand on her shoulder for a second and gave her a short squeeze. "Hank is going to call the Denver FBI office. They'll get agents to the convention center to secure the place and look for Zimmerman. Between them and local police, they'll make sure people are safe." He paused, wanting to tell her there was nothing to worry about. That wasn't true, was it? "Zimmerman's picture will be everywhere. They can evacuate and do everything they can to keep everyone safe. They'll lock down those two guys."

Megan nodded. She knew the FBI was good at what it did. That was why so many terrorist attacks were thwarted. She had to trust.

He said, "The fact we know who we're looking for *and* where he's going puts us one step ahead of him."

"Unless he already set it off."

"Your mom is on her way there, right?"

She shot him a look. "Don't remind me."

"What I'm saying is that she didn't arrive yet, right?"

"Right."

Adrian nodded. "Then maybe Zimmerman is waiting until the right time. If we can redirect everyone before they get there and find those two guys, lock it down before the conference even kicks off tonight, then Zimmerman has no reason to set off that sonic weapon. Right?"

"Oh."

"So we're ahead of his game."

"That is right." She nodded. "Thanks."

"I'm not trying to get you to feel better. False hope isn't hope. But I'm trusting you'll see that we're on this, and we are ahead of Zimmerman. There's little reason why we can't stop this from happening."

"That's true." She reached over and squeezed his hand. "And hopefully while we get Zimmerman, Remy can use a process of elimination to figure out who the blackmailer is."

"You think it's *El Cuervo?*"

She shook her head. "No. But I think he might know who it is."

"Because the blackmailer had that shooter protect him."

"That doesn't necessarily indicate it's two different people. The reason why I don't think it's *El Cuervo* is because…" She swallowed.

"We don't have to talk about this, if you don't want."

"It's okay." She blew out a breath. "I met him, though it was only a few minutes. He has people to do his dirty work. But I know him. I know his type. And that man is not in anything for revenge, only money."

"Tell me about him."

"He's cold. Calculated. That's probably a cliché, but it's also true. He didn't get where he is in that cartel by being nice. He wears his money. Italian suit. Silk shirt. Gold watch, gold chain around his neck. Like he's trying to compensate for the scars on the side of his face by dressing as flashy as possible."

"Scars?"

"They look like burns. I don't know how far down below his collar they go, but the edge of one touches the bottom of his left ear."

Adrian said, "I don't know if the FBI knows that." Was it significant? He could pray it was, but that wouldn't make it so. What he needed to pray was that this might be a significant lead—and that Remy would find the connection. That she would uncover the blackmailer.

"They are minimal," Megan said. "Unless they're all under his shirt."

"It isn't on any of the photos of him that we have. Maybe Remy can look into his past and figure out where he got them." If those scars, and the life he'd led, caused *El Cuervo* to evolve into a calculated power and money hungry killer, it might be helpful to know the details. It could lead to a weakness they'd be able to exploit in order to find him.

Megan shifted in her seat. "Whoa."

"What is—"

Metal screeched against metal, and the SUV jerked forward. She hit the gas, and the engine revved as they pulled away. Adrian glanced out the back window. "Blue truck."

"I see it." She swerved between lanes, but it kept right on them. "Stay on the freeway, or get off?"

"Stay on." There was nothing around them. And who knew when the next exit was?

The truck came at them again.

Bumped them again.

A compact car in front of them braked. Megan gripped the wheel two-handed. The truck clipped their back left corner. She steered hard to the right to avoid the compact in front, and they spun out.

Over the rumble strip. Onto the dry brush at the side of the freeway.

Adrian's head whipped around, and he struggled to inhale against the inertia of spinning. Megan cried out, probably banged her arm on the door. But there was nothing he could do.

The SUV went down a shallow embankment and hit the berm on the other side. The airbags deployed.

Adrian shook off the impact and tried to get his bearings. He glanced over at Megan, slumped in her seat.

Lights flashed behind them. Headlights.

He reached for his gun.

They were coming.

Chapter 15

Megan's whole body hurt. She heard the moan that came from her own throat before she even realized she'd made a sound.

It hurt to breathe. *Adrian*. She looked over at him. Gun out, looking around. "What..?"

He started, then said, "Good. You're awake."

He didn't look hurt, just flushed. Adrenaline pumping again. The air in the SUV was thick with the smell of singed rubber. She coughed and almost passed out from the jolting pain it caused her body. Her arm and her hip, where she'd been grazed *twice* for goodness sake, stung like nobody's business. But they didn't hurt as much as her chest. It felt like she'd been sat on by an elephant.

"They're coming."

She shoved at the airbag and reached for the handle.

"Hold on. We do this together. Smart."

Megan reached around. "I need my gun."

She had to get to Denver. To her mom, and Zimmerman. Who was back there in that truck? If it was the shooter from the restaurant, then they were going to have a bigger problem than they already had. That had been a different car. But it could be him.

He grabbed her gun from the backseat and handed it to her. She checked to make sure it was ready to fire and flicked off the safety. "How many?"

"Three."

Outmanned and likely outgunned. This wasn't going to end well.

She found the button and rolled her window down, ready to point her gun out and take out whoever tried to come at her.

"Megan Perkins?" The voice that called out was thickly accented in a way that made her skin crawl. She had nothing against Venezuelans, but the sound of a voice like that lived in her nightmares in a way she wasn't ever going to escape.

What mattered was that it wasn't the shooter from the restaurant. She wouldn't have been able to handle someone she trusted betraying her like that—keeping her from being able to get to her mom.

"Get out of the truck, Megan," the voice called out again. "Come with us."

Her entire body chilled. She adjusted her grip on the gun. Tried to inject some life into her icy fingers.

"I can take the two on my side," Adrian said. "You take the one on yours."

Two? The second man would shoot him before he could take the guy out.

"No." She reached for the handle.

"Megan." He tugged on her arm, the one holding the gun.

She wasn't going to let him get hurt. "Stay here. I'm going, you get Zimmerman." It made her want to vomit just to say it, let alone the reality that she was going to actually do it. *Don't think about that.* The alternative was worse.

Adrian would be hurt. Probably even killed.

He needed to live.

"Meg."

She pushed the door open, then stuck her hand out so they could see she held nothing in it. No threat. *Don't hurt Adrian.* Fear blinded her. She couldn't even pray, the feeling was so all-consuming.

Adrian flung his own door open. *Bang.* He ducked against the onslaught of bullets from the gunmen. A split second later, he opened fire in return.

Bullets shattered the back window. She pulled her hand back in and tried to twist around in spite of the pain. Use the frame as cover, fire off a few shots of her own.

Time slowed in a way it always did when those moments between breaths meant the difference between life and death. Every pump of her heartbeat felt twice as fast, and yet slower than she thought possible. A strange dichotomy she didn't have time to mull over.

Not right now, at least.

Megan fired off two shots. The shooter on her side ducked behind a tree, then leaned out to squeeze his trigger. He held his gun one-handed. The front lifted as it discharged.

The driver's door window cracked, a bullet hole in the center. She ducked on reflex, even though it missed her by several inches.

If she died here, it was going to be all Adrian's fault. She'd been about to save his life—and the lives of many others. He'd forced this situation. And now it was going to get them both killed.

More shots rang out behind her. Adrian yelped. Megan gritted her teeth, then called out, "You okay?"

She watched the tree. Waited.

Adrian didn't reply.

Her shooter shifted a fraction, and she saw the opening she needed. Held her breath. Pushed aside the aches and pains she'd accumulated. Squeezed the trigger.

Her shot didn't go high. Or wide.

The shooter dropped to the ground.

Megan got out and turned to see Adrian's side. One versus one. He held his own. She ran to the shooter she'd hit and grabbed his gun. But he wasn't going to reach for it—he was dead.

She laid the gun by the back tire and made her way around the SUV. Adrian had dropped one guy, who moaned and clutched his shoulder. The other one had his back to her, his gun aimed at Adrian.

When the injured gunman's eyes met hers, she saw the flash of recognition. She shook her head. Not here to play, she didn't want him alerting his friend to her presence.

But apparently, he wasn't that smart.

The guy opened his mouth to yell to his friend. Megan didn't want to shoot him unless he posed a threat to her life, so she stepped out from behind cover and said, "Put the gun down."

Adrian lifted up, his own gun aimed at each of the two men in turn.

"I said, put it down." She took measured steps as she spoke, falling back on all that FBI training ingrained in her. "You don't wanna die. I don't want him to die. So drop it on the ground, and put your hands up." She'd circled all the way around the downed man and kicked his gun farther from his reach, even though he'd have had to scoot to grab it.

Adrian said, "You heard the lady. Put it down."

The standing shooter held his gun aimed at Adrian, and didn't move. Or say anything. She could only see the back of him, her own aim between his shoulder blades. She could shoot him, but not before he got his shot off—and Adrian was dead.

She couldn't see the intention in his eyes. Wouldn't be able to read the second when the situation changed, and he made his decision.

They needed to call this in. Get Hank here with agents to take these guys and question them—find out where *El Cuervo* was.

She took another step around the guy, so she'd at least be able to see Adrian's—

The gunman swung his arm around and shot his friend, the downed man. Before the guy had even fallen back to the ground, Adrian opened fire on the shooter. He hit the guy in his leg.

He crumpled, crying out.

Adrian yelled, "Don't!"

But his gun arm swung again. Adrian put another bullet in him. The shooter's bullet cut a hole through Adrian's pant leg a second before he slumped back to the ground. Dead.

He cried out and hopped back a step, uttering a couple of PG-rated expressions that made her want to laugh.

"You okay?"

He brushed off his leg and straightened. "I like these jeans."

Megan said, "They look better now." He needed a little distressed fabric in his life. It gave him character instead of him looking like a spit-polished G-Man. Which he was. But that didn't mean he couldn't branch out a little sometimes.

Adrian blew out a breath. "Are you okay?"

"Health-wise, yeah. But with you just forcing a gunfight?" She shook her head. "No way."

. . .

Adrian hung up the phone. Megan had her hand on her hip. He said, "You gonna put that gun away?"

"Maybe."

She kind of looked like she was thinking about shooting him with it. Why, he had no idea, considering he'd just saved her life—as well as kept her from being kidnapped.

"Hank is on his way."

"Good. He can clean up and we can get out of here." She pulled out her phone to glance at the screen. "We have two hours until my mom is going to land. I want to know where Zimmerman is before then, so I can call her and tell her it's all good for her conference."

Adrian stowed his own gun, then searched the dead man closest to him. Found a phone. A wallet. He looked at the driver's license and read the name aloud. "Lives in Austin."

"So, not Venezuelan. Or at least not right now."

"Or it's a fake." Though if it was, then it was a really good fabricated ID. He did the same with the other two while Megan watched, alternately switching which hip she had a hand on and sighing. Mad, but still uncomfortable. She probably needed another pain pill.

"Something you want to say?" He didn't look up from the last man. He could feel her stare on him like a laser aimed at the top of his head.

"You did that on purpose."

"Saved your life?"

"That isn't what I'm talking about, and you know it."

He straightened. "I do?"

The sound of car engines drew his attention. Three black SUVs pulled off the highway. She said, "You forced that gunfight." He turned back to Megan. She said, "Those guys would have left you alone."

"And kidnapped you," he said. "You think I was going to let that happen?"

"You *should* have." She huffed again. "That was dangerous, and stupid. Now we have zero shot at figuring out where *El Cuervo* is. You could have followed me." She waved at the dead men lying on the ground. "You could have left one of them alive for questioning."

Before he could reply, Hank called out, "Both of you okay?"

Adrian didn't take his gaze from Megan. "We aren't hurt." This time.

She pressed her lips together.

"Megan?" Hank said, closer now.

"I'm as fine as I was an hour ago."

Adrian figured that meant she was still irritated because of her injuries, in pain and lashing out at him because he was there.

"At least," she said, "until Adrian decided he wasn't going to let the situation ride, so he started a gunfight that lost us our lead."

Before Hank could say anything, Adrian said, "This could be completely unrelated. We're supposed to be catching up to Zimmerman, and you think getting kidnapped will help get us more information? We know where he's going. This little side trip would only have cost us time we don't have."

Megan's face hardened, and she took a step toward him. "You think I'm going to risk my mom's life on a whim? We know *El Cuervo* and the blackmailer are connected. I could have found out who it is!"

He took a step toward her. "You want to put yourself in that situation all over again? I guess last time wasn't so bad, if you're in such a rush to repeat it." She looked sick, but he kept going. She wasn't backing down, and neither would he. "It turns out you *still* don't care what happens to your partner because you're too busy doing your own thing. Again."

He watched that cut through her like a blade. He was not about to admit that it hurt him to see it. To know he'd done that to her.

"Special Agent Walker, go make yourself useful." Hank's voice was hard.

Megan didn't even blink.

Adrian wandered off mostly to clear his head. To do something physical, but also simple. His brain spun far too much to add more to what was swirling in there. She thought getting kidnapped was a good idea? That was just insane.

He'd saved both of them. But did she thank him? No, she didn't. Megan acted like he'd put them at a disadvantage.

Maybe she liked having her life in danger. Living on the edge like she was some kind of adrenaline junkie.

He didn't need that in his life. It wouldn't help them end the threat of Zimmerman and the stolen weapon, or ID the blackmailer. Why did she think it would? Had she really lost so much of her FBI training that she couldn't see the advantages in procedure and professionalism? Adrian wasn't going to let that drag him down. Not when he'd succeeded this far by following the rule book—the FBI plays they already knew would work.

Megan was just far too much of a maverick for this to work. Any of it.

Getting mad and blaming him? No.

One of the local agents stuck his hand out and introduced himself. "You look like you had a rough day."

Adrian shook his head, even though it was true on all counts. He shook the man's hand. "I need to get moving, get to the airport."

"Denver?"

Adrian nodded.

"Cromwell already alerted the Denver FBI office." Left unspoken was the fact this agent knew his job here was clean-up of this scene. Not racing somewhere else.

The agent said, "I'll need your gun."

Adrian cleared it and handed it over. He'd used it to kill one of the men here, so the gun was bagged as evidence. Fine by him, he'd be cleared. The only variable was whatever Megan said, which he could not control. He had to trust that she'd tell these agents the unbiased truth.

He didn't know what reason she'd have for saying otherwise, but he also wasn't entirely sure he could trust her.

He'd been with her to protect her. To be the FBI's eyes and ears, find out what she knew. See where Megan Perkins and her connection to all of this took them. It had been working, getting them to Remy—whoever that woman was, the agent looking into her hadn't come back with anything—and the link between all the people targeted by the blackmailer so far.

Maybe she would even be able to find the name of the blackmailer, something the FBI had yet to manage. And not for lack of trying.

He glanced back and saw Megan and Hank still in low conversation. She glanced at him. He held her gaze for a second and then looked at Hank. Shook her head.

Adrian turned away. He couldn't help with the scene here, considering he was the person who'd killed one of the men. All he could do was give his statement.

He told them what he could, and then checked his email. Learned Zimmerman hadn't been spotted at any airport or bus station.

Had *El Cuervo* really escaped the restaurant only to send men to pick up Megan the minute they were away from the other agents? It could mean that the whole restaurant scene was only to draw Megan out into the public.

Adrian tapped his phone against his leg while he thought it over.

A car engine revved.

He spun around to see Megan drive away in the SUV, alone in the vehicle. He started to run after her, realized it was futile, and headed for Special Agent Cromwell.

Hank stared after the vehicle.

"She left?"

His boss said, "Wants to go after her mom and make sure she's all right."

"So you just let her swing alone in the wind when *El Cuervo* is targeting her?" Adrian couldn't believe this. He'd seriously just let her go off alone, after telling Adrian to stick with her?

Hank's eyebrows lifted. "You have a job to do here, Agent Walker. I suggest you get back to it."

What on earth?

Something was off.

Chapter 16

Megan drove slower than she normally would have down the highway. She wasn't in a rush, and the idea was to be noticed. Not to escape.

She shifted her hands on the wheel. Squeezed the dense plastic—or whatever it was made of. Her hands were sweating. She wanted to squirm in the seat. Why was this harder than being tied to a chair and punched in the face over and over? They'd done that for a few minutes at a time over a period of hours.

Then they'd dragged out Will.

He'd cried out when he saw her face. After that, he said nothing. And she had to stare into his eyes while they demanded she tell them what she and Will had done with their money.

Now she figured that had been nothing but a ploy. An excuse to kill Will and torture her. Set her off her game so that she made a rash decision—a mistake.

She couldn't do that now. If *El Cuervo* was really after her, and she and Hank had agreed he would try again, then she was ready. Cool and calm.

Mostly.

He could come. Hank would be right behind him, along with Adrian and the rest of the FBI. Backup. The kind she hadn't had behind her in Mexico. Yes, she'd been nervous enough—it had to have transpired right then, or else she'd never have found the courage to do it. Bite the bullet. Take the reins. All those expressions that meant to climb in the car and head out. Alone. Not unprotected, but definitely exposed.

She doubted Adrian would appreciate the plan when Hank explained it. But how else would they finish this fast enough to get to Denver on time? Yeah, agents there were doing their job. But it was *her* mom. *Her* operation. *Her* hunt for Zimmerman, who had singled her out by trying to send *her* a message at that hospital.

And it would be *her* that would bring him down.

She just needed a distraction right now, so she could get her mind off the waiting. Megan pulled out her phone and used voice commands to call Steve. Would he even answer? She'd always felt like a bit of an outsider with Double Down. Though she'd have said that about Mint as well. He'd always been a lone wolf. Bradley was the new guy, so she didn't know him all that well. He was intense—exactly the way you'd think a Navy SEAL to be. Steve was the boss.

Maybe they were a group of loners. But they'd made it work.

Steve had been places and seen things she didn't even want to imagine. His former career had taken him all over the world as a covert agent for the CIA. These days he was private, no longer government, in both his business dealings as an operator in the security field and in his personal life.

Right before the phone went to voicemail, he finally picked up. "Yeah."

"It's Megan."

She figured he knew that. He had answered her call.

He sighed, loud enough the line crackled. "Megan." There was a wealth of emotion in that one word. Regret. A plea for help.

"You fired on a parking lot full of federal agents."

"No one was hurt, right?"

"Couple of bruises and a scraped elbow," she said. "That's not the point."

How was she supposed to be part of Double Down if this was what happened when her life became the mission? Steve had made it so *El Cuervo* could escape. That was probably the biggest betrayal of all.

He said, "Are you going to tell them?"

Megan gritted her teeth and stared at the road ahead. What was she supposed to say to that? Part of her was still loyal to the FBI, always would be. Her father had been an agent. It was what she'd wanted to do for years. Despite the fact it had gone so wrong, she had realized her definition of success. She'd been living it.

She said, "They'll find evidence." It didn't matter if she told them or not. With the investigative power of the FBI, there was no way they would not get some kind of lead that would point them in Steve's direction, eventually.

"I cleaned up."

"Adrian nearly caught you," she said. "He'd have seen you if I hadn't covered for you." Her instinct had been to protect him.

"Maybe you should've just told them."

Regret was a powerful thing. She wanted to believe he'd made a choice he could live with, a decision he could stand behind. She never wanted her friends, people she respected, to be forced into corners where they would do things they'd never normally do otherwise.

But maybe that was exactly what had happened to Steve.

"What does he have on you?"

Silence filled the line.

He said, "I wasn't going to hit anyone."

Regardless of what he'd been ordered to do, Steve had made sure the injuries were minimal. He'd fulfilled the task in a way no one got hurt. If he'd killed an agent—even one—the FBI would never have stopped hunting him. Steve's life would have been over.

"Maybe you could put in a good word for me with the bureau."

Megan said, "They won't accept it." Not from her. "But if we can prove he got to you, then there's a chance we can convince them you acted under duress." That was the only reasoning they would accept. And if it was the truth, all the better. Steve had a shot to get in the clear.

"Tell them I had to make a choice."

She said, "Tell them yourself."

"I can't. I have to go." He sounded distracted now.

"Steve—"

"Hold down the fort, Megan. Find Zimmerman."

"He's holding something over you," she said. "I know it."

"Tell Rachel…" His voice drifted away.

And then the line went dead.

Megan cried out in frustration. She tossed her phone in the direction of the passenger seat, changed lanes and took the next exit off the freeway. Steve was going to martyr himself for the company? All so Double Down didn't suffer when his career and reputation were completely destroyed?

She wanted to believe he'd safeguarded his past. That the things he'd done were redacted. Top Secret. They had to be hidden behind high layers of security clearance. He *had* been a spy, after all. So how had the blackmailer discovered some hidden truth?

Or was it something else entirely? Nothing to do with any operation, but an event in Steve's past. She didn't know enough about him to conclusively answer that. She wanted to call Adrian and talk it through with him. See what he thought. Adrian didn't know Steve all that well, but he could provide insight. Maybe use his FBI access and contacts to dig into her boss's life.

Because if it saved Steve, she was absolutely going to do it.

Megan pulled into a gas station and parked. She hung her head for a moment and prayed some more. What else was she supposed to do? She didn't know who the blackmailer had gotten to and who was safe. Even her boss—the man she had respected more than anyone except her father—was a victim of the blackmailer.

A vindictive enemy who had changed the course of her whole life.

And for what? Revenge. Money. Power. Maybe he was just sadistic, and this whole thing was nothing but a power play.

They were just pawns in some game.

Megan couldn't see her phone. It'd probably fallen between the seat and the floor. She grabbed the keys out and headed for the bathroom. Then she needed fuel—like an energy drink and a huge bag of chips. She needed to jump-start her brain so she could figure this out.

She hit the hallway to the bathroom and pushed the door open.

Someone crowded in behind her.

Arms banded around her waist. Pain tore through her arm.

She couldn't breathe.

. . .

Adrian followed Hank all the way to the gas station, after he'd borrowed an SUV from one of the other agents. Where on earth was the man going?

When he pulled off the highway and headed for a gas station, Adrian knew something was up.

Hank pulled in across the lot, in an out-of-the-way spot.

Right beside a fire exit door.

The SUV Adrian had been driving earlier was parked by the front doors of the gas station. Megan was here.

He headed inside, walked all the aisles, and then went to the restrooms area. A dank hallway with a wet floor sign at the far end. The exit door clicked shut.

Adrian picked up his pace.

He pushed out the door to the bright light of the day, weapon drawn. Something really wasn't right here.

Hank pulled a limp Megan to his SUV. He held her with one of her arms over his shoulder. Like she'd passed out, and he was "helping" her.

"Cromwell!" Adrian lifted his weapon as he strode over. Was he really going to do this? Would he shoot Hank if the man pushed him to it? He didn't know if he could. Let alone whether he actually believed his boss would push him to that point.

He turned, narrowed his eyes, and then the older man dumped Megan on the back seat. Before Adrian could say something, he saw the curl of Hank's lips.

Pain ricocheted through Adrian's head, emanating from one spot on the back.

The sidewalk lifted up and slammed into his face.

Everything went black.

How much later it was when he finally woke up, Adrian didn't know. His head hurt like he couldn't believe. His thoughts swam like the time he'd gotten a concussion playing football in high school.

He shifted enough to get his hands under him and pushed against the gritty concrete.

"You okay, man? That was some blow."

Adrian could only grunt.

"Might wanna take it easy, yeah?" The voice was older, and gravelly. "Should I call the cops?"

"FBI."

"You want me to call the FBI? Seems overkill, since you just fell or something." The older man paused. "You drunk?"

Adrian wanted to shake his head, but that was not a good idea right now. "I'm FBI." Those were all the words he could push out. Bile rose in his throat, and he managed to sit up. "Where did she go?"

"Lost your girl?" An older man crouched. Denim shirt. Gray stubble. "She do this to you?" He nodded for a few seconds. Or Adrian had blurry vision. Then he said, "I had a woman like that once. Kept me on my toes for sure."

Adrian tried to locate his weapon. Not on the ground. Not in his holster. Even his backup, the small caliber revolver he wore on his ankle, was gone. And his badge. His phone.

"Help me up."

The old man held out his hand, and Adrian clasped the man's wrist. He used as much of his own strength, not wanting to pull the man over onto the floor.

The world shifted when he was finally upright. Adrian waited for it to still, then reached up to touch the back of his head.

The older man grabbed his arm. "Your hands are dirty." He pulled a handkerchief from his back pocket. "This is cleaner than your fingers."

Gravel was still pressed into the skin of his hands. Adrian wiped them on his pants and took the cloth. He touched it to the back of his head and nearly dropped to the floor again. He shifted his legs, tried to get blood flowing around his body so he didn't pass out.

"Probably need an ambulance."

Adrian turned for the door of the gas station. He needed to make a call. Hank had taken Megan. Shoved her into his SUV before he took her...where?

And someone *else* had hit Adrian over the back of the head.

He turned back to the older man. "Did you see what happened?"

"Nah. Found you on the ground there." He waved to the asphalt.

Adrian needed security footage. And a first aid kit. He needed to know who he could trust, otherwise he wasn't going to get Megan back. Was her vehicle still here?

Was his?

He patted his pockets. Keys were still there, but they'd taken everything else.

Adrian stumbled to the entrance and went inside, right to the register, all the while trying to figure out what on earth had just happened. Hank had acted like a father figure in Megan's life. He'd called her "Meggie," and it seemed almost like he doted on her.

Until he suspected her of being part of all this—and not in a good way. Now he'd stuffed her in his SUV and driven off with her.

This *had* to be the work of the blackmailer. Or Hank was, for some reason, on *El Cuervo*'s side just like Zimmerman. Maybe he'd even betrayed Megan and her partner years ago while she was undercover. Or all of it was connected somehow, in some other way, which put Hank in the middle of everything.

Could *he* be the blackmailer?

The cashier was on the phone. "Looks like he might be okay." He hung up.

Adrian said, "A woman was just kidnapped out of the parking lot. I need witnesses, I need local cops here now to take statements, and I need a first aid kit. Not necessarily in that order."

The cashier's eyes widened.

The TV, hung high in the corner, interrupted whatever he'd been about to say.

"...breaking news story," the commentator said. The words ALERT flashed across the bottom of the screen. A local news show. "The FBI have just released a statement confirming that their missing agent, Daniel Zimmerman, is working in cohorts with another former agent. A woman who retired from the bureau due to medical issues, including mental instability."

A picture flashed on the screen. Zimmerman. Beside his picture was one of Megan. A bureau photographer had taken it years ago from the look of it. Definitely before Mexico. Shirt and blazer, neat hair pulled back. Minimal makeup.

She was working with Zimmerman?

Hank had taken her so the blackmailer could put it out on the wires that she was working with Zimmerman? Adrian had just suffered a head injury from someone working with Hank, who was clearly in cahoots with the blackmailer, but he could figure this much out at least. Yet more connections.

The blackmailer. Digging deep to make sure his plan came to fruition.

And Megan was going to take the blame, along with Zimmerman.

The idea that the blackmailer was Hank ran through his mind again. Adrian didn't want to believe it, but it was possible he supposed. Megan knew she was a target.

But they hadn't known just how deep the threat went.

"The FBI is now on the lookout for Daniel Zimmerman and Megan Perkins in connection with a missing weapon they may attempt to use. The two are considered armed and extremely dangerous. If you see them, call the number on the screen immediately. Do not approach them."

Chapter 17

Megan's cheek pressed against the carpeted floor of the SUV. Her head throbbed where Hank had shoved her in, and she'd clipped the door frame with her injured hip. *Hank.* She should be angry—so angry. She should be hurt by his betrayal. Inside, where that feeling was supposed to live there was nothing but…cold.

The sun flashed into view through the window. Megan winced and shut her eyes.

She could hear Hank breathing, each inhale coming rapidly as he drove wherever. To whoever. She had plenty of guesses. This whole thing had been a puzzle from start to finish. If she was going to maintain her sanity and not get dragged down into the crazy, then she had to hold back. Keep her defensive position intact. Not fall into all this, so she didn't end up dissolving into a ball of uncontrollable emotions.

She didn't need to do it. They didn't need to see it.

What she should do is figure out a way to get free of these bindings that had her arms locked behind her. Shoulders wrenched.

Hank swung around a corner. Megan's body swayed and her shoulder pressed against the seat. Against the bandage over her wound. She gritted her teeth to keep from screaming. Sweat rolled down her forehead. Megan stared at the back of Hank's chair. There was nothing she could do but lie here and wait for them to get wherever he was taking her.

Nothing but pray.

She'd needed God before, and she'd prayed then. Will had still died. But Megan had lived. And for what? This life certainly wasn't anything noble or great. She hadn't devoted herself to much of anything except survival and doing the best job she could for Steve.

She hadn't even gone after *El Cuervo*.

Because she knew, if she did, that he'd have destroyed her. Truth was, she never wanted to see *El Cuervo* again in her entire life. She knew that as well as she knew it was where Hank was taking her. Megan might have been looking for him but frankly, she hadn't found many leads. And maybe that was because she hadn't wanted to actually find much of anything.

Fear had held her back. It had kept her in a box of her own making.

If she'd gone after Will's killer, then she'd have destroyed the one thing God allowed to survive—her. She'd have thrown his gift of life back in his face.

And that was why she hadn't been able to do it.

Megan didn't know why she was saved when Will wasn't. She'd rather have lived in a world with him in it. Or for her to have died, and him to have lived. Will would've made the world a better place. After all, he'd done that for her.

Now she had Adrian in her life. The two men were so vastly different, she didn't even know where to begin comparing them, even if she'd wanted to.

Megan prayed.

Hank drove.

His phone rang. "Yeah." Pause. "I'm ten minutes out." Another pause. "Okay." He hung up, then said, "Not long now."

"You're taking me to *El Cuervo*?" The question filled her mouth with the taste of an acid that ate at her resolve. She'd tried to sound strong, but what was the point? Hank had done this, and he knew he'd won.

Hank said, "Nothing personal."

"He's got your life in a vice, right?" He'd know she was talking about the blackmailer. "So you'll hand me over, and say you had no choice."

"Coercion is a valid defense."

"I don't buy that. You're an agent." She'd had compassion for Steve, but there was none for Hank. "You know what we can do when we're faced with any kind of threat." She paused. "But you didn't choose that. You chose to bend and let him do this to you—get you to turn against me."

Then again, had he ever felt any loyalty toward her? Maybe it'd been nothing but a ruse to draw her in so he'd have exactly this opportunity.

"Does this have something to do with my father?" Remy seemed to think that was the connection.

All that talk of loyalty to her family because of the work Hank had done years ago with her dad might have been nothing but lies—keeping her close. For this.

She thought about it while he said nothing. Maybe he'd decided that he wanted to be there out of loyalty in the beginning. But anything after Mexico was suspect, and she didn't believe any of it was other than the blackmailer twisting his life for whatever scheme the puppet master had in mind.

"What does he have on you?" She asked the question out loud, even as she wondered again what the blackmailer had on Steve. "Did he kidnap Zimmerman's family? Is that what he does? Threaten the people closest to you to force you to do what he wants." But Hank didn't have a family.

She'd thought he considered her kind of like a daughter. Now she knew that couldn't be true. "What does he know that you don't want to get out?"

The question hung in the air. He was willing to sacrifice her for whatever it was. Maybe she didn't want to know. She might end up disappointed she was worth so little. She huffed out a breath—not anywhere near a laugh, but headed in that direction. The ability to be a little sardonic, especially at a time like this, helped shore up those defenses.

If she could focus on Hank, then she didn't have to think about—

The car slowed, and they pulled under the roof of a building. A warehouse. *El Cuervo.*

She tried to stay cold. Tried to keep her mind divorced from what was happening. Adrian…she couldn't think about him. Did he hate her for leaving? She had no idea what Hank had told him about her taking the car and going. Apparently not the truth, at least as far as she'd known it.

This was supposed to have been about baiting a trap for *El Cuervo.* Instead she was the target, and it was Hank who had snapped it shut. On her.

Lord… There were no words. Her eyes burned. Her nose stung.

The door opened and a man stood there. Megan didn't look at whoever it was. She just lay still on the floor behind the front seats.

He grabbed her foot and pulled her out. Her shoes slapped the floor. The man ducked his head and pulled her upper body over his shoulder. He stood, causing a grunt to rise in her throat. Her head swam along with the throb, upside down with all the blood pooling there.

He lumbered under the weight of her. Yes, she needed to quit her pizza habit. She didn't need the reminder, thank you very much. He shifted her again and deposited her on the concrete floor.

Megan blew out a breath and tried to relax every tense muscle. Her jaw screamed from being locked so tightly. Her shoulders were on fire. She took another moment to get some more breaths in her.

And then she looked up.

El Cuervo stood over her, dressed in the same suit. Did he have several in that color because he liked it so much? She pictured them lined up in his closet like uniforms. The scar peeked out his collar on the left side of his face, wrinkled skin from there to his ear. Burns—probably suffered years ago. Had that been instrumental in him becoming the man he was now?

Why did her mind keep coming back to his obvious injury?

"We meet again."

She'd pretended not to know Spanish the first time he spoke to her. Now she replied in English, just because she knew it would irritate him. "The pleasure is all yours, I'm sure."

. . .

Adrian buckled himself into the airplane seat. He'd gone right for Megan's SUV before anyone else got to it. First thing he'd done was try and look inside. The doors were locked. A check of the bathroom, the hallway, and the ground between the back door and where the SUV had been parked, yielded her car keys.

Inside the vehicle, he'd found her phone and purse. He'd taken the phone. It didn't matter that local cops would discover her ID and wallet, and likely her FBI badge, inside the SUV abandoned at the gas station.

Agents in DC at his office hadn't been able to locate the GPS on Hank's vehicle. They'd gotten nothing back but, "Error."

Adrian leaned his head back against the airplane seat and shut his eyes. His entire skull throbbed, but that was nothing compared with what Megan was likely going through. And she was being implicated as a terrorist along with Zimmerman. Two "rogue" FBI agents, supposedly acting on some prearranged plan. A stolen sonic weapon. Both of them knowledgeable about police and federal agency response times and high value targets.

It was a smart move to blame it on them.

Adrian decided then that the blackmailer really had taken Zimmerman's family. That had to be why no one had been able to find them. Now the blackmailer was leveraging their lives against Zimmerman's cooperation. Demanding he bring revenge on men who had wronged the blackmailer through a military operation undertaken years ago.

Years in which hatred and anger had festered and turned cancerous. Infecting the blackmailer.

Now the blackmailer was like patient zero with the virus being spread to unsuspecting people. His targets were suffering symptoms and passing it on. Forced to fight for him, so that more and more people were drawn in.

"You need to turn those off, sir."

Adrian opened his eyes. He glanced from the airline hostess to the phones he had in each hand on his lap. He turned off his, and then Megan's.

He'd tried her mom half a dozen times on the way to the airport. Calling out using her phone, while his rang on the passenger seat. Local FBI personnel trying to reach him, probably wondering what happened. Where Hank was.

No one had tried to call Megan's phone.

He tried to doze on the way to Denver. Mostly his head went around and around, whirling between worry over Megan to where she was, what Hank had done with her and where *El Cuervo* fit into all this. Not to mention how it related to the blackmailer. Did Remy know the answers?

All Adrian could do was head to the conference, find those two Navy guys, and make sure they were safe.

Protect Megan's mother, Sylvia, because that was what she would want him to do.

He knew *that* the same way he knew trying to find her was futile. Hank wouldn't leave his phone on so it could be hacked. He knew about GPS in their vehicles, so he'd disabled it. If he was part of *El Cuervo* being here in the US, or the blackmailer's business, he would need Megan alive. For now.

Adrian figured her time was limited. Dead or alive, she'd still be a scapegoat for them. Someone to blame all the destruction on. The target was those two Navy officers, so that was what he could focus on—stopping the blackmailer. That had been his job all along. He was supposed to have protected Megan, and he would do everything he could to stand up for her. To prove she was pulled into this against her will, just like the rest of them.

If he couldn't save her life—and he would do what he could on that—then he could at least keep her from being convicted.

It was the only thing that kept him from being overwhelmed right now— that, and the constant stream of prayer.

God had brought Megan into his life, because He knew she would need Adrian.

Help me to know what to do.

He had to focus on what he *could* do, rather than allow what he couldn't control to stall him. Double Down couldn't help. Not when he didn't know who to trust. The FBI was a long shot, except for the agents in his DC office. And that wouldn't last much longer. Soon enough they would find out that he wasn't working with Hank anymore.

Adrian prayed the Denver office hadn't been stained with whatever Hank had done. That his home office hadn't. That the agents in Austin were clear.

The plane landed. He grabbed his backpack and strode down the gangway, not even caring how much he'd paid for first class, just so he could be one of the first ones off the plane. He navigated to the arrivals area and saw two agents waiting for him.

He'd called ahead to the Denver office before boarding the plane, and asked to be met by agents. There was a chance Hank would circumvent Adrian's attempts to stop Zimmerman, but he had to risk it. He couldn't do this alone.

They clocked him about the same time he spotted them and headed over. Agents for the FBI just had a particular...professionalism about them.

For a split second, he wondered if they were going to arrest him. But then the first one stuck his hand out. "Walker?"

Adrian nodded. He shook both their hands and learned they were Peters and Bryant. "Good to meet you. Have you located the two Navy officers yet?"

Peters shook his head. "Who?"

"Retired Rear Admiral Frampton and Captain Charles St. Germaine. They're Zimmerman's targets."

Bryant said, "Zimmerman, the guy y'all are looking for over in DC?"

"He's in Denver for the big conference at the convention center this weekend."

They glanced at each other.

"You didn't know that." Adrian pinched the bridge of his nose. "You guys were supposed to have been informed. He said you had agents there, looking for Zimmerman and rounding up those two guys we know are targets."

"Who said?"

"My boss, SAC Cromwell."

Bryant shrugged. Like he'd never even heard of Hank. "Guess there's no time to waste, then." He waved Adrian to go with them. "We can call it in from the car."

Adrian left his own phone switched off. For now. He turned on Megan's phone and called her mother. Fear for Megan surged inside him. But he was miles away, doing the job he was supposed to have done with her.

Had he made the right choice?

"Hi honey," Sylvia Perkins answered. "I was just about to text. I've checked into my hotel."

"Good," he said. "Stay there."

"Excuse me, who are—"

"My name is Adrian Walker. Hank Cromwell gave Megan to *El Cuervo*."

No, he didn't know that for sure. But it was really the only explanation.

Adrian said, "I'm in Denver to stop Zimmerman. He's there at the convention center. Whatever you do, do *not* leave your hotel room."

"You think I'm going to sit here and do nothing while my daughter is in danger?"

"Ma'am—"

"I'm calling Remy."

"You know her?"

Megan's mother huffed. "Do we have time for that conversation, considering everything that is happening?"

"No, ma'am."

"Send me pictures of the two men you're looking for. I'll see if I can get word to them."

"Ma'am—"

"Call me that one more time, *Agent* Walker, and you and I will have a serious problem," she said. "You asked me not to leave the hotel room, right?"

"Yes, m—I did."

One of the agents with him grinned, then pointed to the passenger seat for Adrian to get in.

Megan's mother said, "So get me their pictures. I know people, and I can make calls just as well as anyone."

"Thank you. I could use anything you find out." Especially if she knew Remy.

"And as soon as you safeguard the two men, you can go get Megan."

"I will be doing exactly that."

First, he had to do his job. And for the first time in his life, it was the last thing Adrian wanted to do. Not to mention he had no clue where to even begin the search for Megan.

The only reassurance he had was the fact there were honest agents looking for her. As a potential terrorist, yes. But he would take it either way.

Hank had disgraced the FBI badge. Adrian would hand his in if it meant the difference between duty and being able to go after Megan. But if she knew he'd let people die, and let Zimmerman or the blackmailer succeed, she would never forgive him. Even when it put her life at risk.

Why else had she tried to leave him earlier, and go with *El Cuervo's* men?

Adrian had to take care of this first. And until the moment he knew Megan was all right, he was going to pray harder than he'd ever prayed that she could hold on.

Until he got there.

Chapter 18

The metal folding chair was hard against her back. Her breath puffed out in white clouds with every exhale. She might have been staring into those nightmarish eyes, so dark brown they looked black, but she had to think about anything and everything else.

"*Sí, hermano.*" He hung up the phone and those eyes narrowed into black slits.

"Who is he?"

El Cuervo said nothing.

"You just called him 'brother.' How do you know each other?"

He stood there as if she hadn't spoken. She needed him to tell her about the blackmailer, otherwise she'd have nothing.

Megan gritted her teeth, then said, "You're just going to kill me. Why not tell me who he is? What difference will it make?"

His lip twitched on one side. Great, so he enjoyed the thought of her being dead. Or was his pleasure in her own realization of it?

"You were supposed to kill me two years ago, right? Missed your chance."

"You have proven useful to him since."

She didn't react to that. "And now my time's up, right?"

"In death, you will also serve a purpose."

"Because my dad did something that wronged him? So he's taking it out on me, even though I was in elementary school at the time." And that was the reason Will was dead—because a parent of his had been a part of it.

Megan couldn't help wonder if Hank had put them together because he'd known even back then that their parents had been involved. Which meant he'd also had to have been under the blackmailer's thumb even then.

She looked back over her left shoulder. Could Hank be the blackmailer?

No. There were indications he'd been taking orders, and *El Cuervo* had been talking to someone on the phone. It had sounded like they were equals, though he'd received instructions. And called the man "brother."

Who was it?

Someone with computer skills. Someone with knowledge of redacted Top Secret missions. Someone old enough to have been affected by an event that took place decades ago—which narrowed it down, but not by a whole lot. He was at least her age, though likely older. And she also figured the blackmailer was connected. Like maybe he had a government job, or was military. Someone with the influence to be able to dig into Steve's background and put the screws to him.

"I want my money," Hank said.

She watched *El Cuervo* react. Cold. Calculating. His gaze flicked to land on Hank. She wanted to shiver. Sitting bound in the middle of four men—Hank, the Venezuelan, and two of his bodyguards—put her at a serious disadvantage.

One she remembered every second of every day and in all her nightmares as the worst, most fearful day of her life.

All she had to do was shut her eyes and she saw blood bloom across Will's chest. Watched his chair topple backward, him in it. Tied there, just like she was now. Just like she had been back on that day.

Powerless.

Emotion threatened to overwhelm her. But she *wasn't* going to break down, even if she wanted to just cry and be a girl surrounded by a bunch of thugs. They wanted her to do it. Wanted her to give up. To surrender to their strength.

And she wasn't going to.

No way.

She recited all the Bible verses about strength that she remembered. Said them all, one by one, in her head. It didn't matter what *El Cuervo* and Hank were talking about. How he'd betrayed her. How short the rest of her life was going to be. To die was gain, right?

She didn't want to leave her mom, not like this. She didn't like leaving with the blackmailer still free. Or not being able to see what might happen in her future with Adrian, void of a stressful situation.

Still, it wasn't like dying would be a bad thing—for her. She'd quite like to see what eternal glory might look like. No more pain. No more fear. Sign her up for that.

There was plenty to want to stay alive for, but she also knew God's plan might not be that she remained alive. He might want her life to be done here. It was His prerogative, and for the first time in her life, she was willing to surrender to Him. Because she trusted that God knew what was best—not what was easiest. And He would take care of the people she loved.

Megan prayed that the truth would be revealed, regardless of what happened to her. She prayed for everyone involved, all her friends. Her teammates. Her family. Adrian.

A single tear slipped from the corner of her eye and rolled down her cheek.

Regret and peace sat inside her like two things on opposite ends of a scale. The peace was overwhelming, a gift given to her by God, outweighing the regret. But that didn't mean regret wasn't still part of the balance.

The first gunshot caused a flinch in her body that nearly lifted her from the chair. Her ears rang.

Another shot blasted.

Then a third. A fourth. She lost count as sounds melded together and her ears rang, overwhelmed with the noise.

Bodies dropped to the ground.

El Cuervo.

Hank had shot him.

She turned back to the man who'd been her mentor. He lay bleeding, the gun inches from his fingers. Gasping.

The Venezuelan and his two bodyguards were dead.

She rose from the chair and fell to her knees. Stumbled over to him, hands bound behind her back, to lean over his face. "Hank." The word broke, and she sucked in a breath.

His body shuddered and he tried to speak.

"No. It's okay." She knew he couldn't talk. "You did the right thing." He'd killed her enemies. Ended the threat.

"So—rry."

She squeezed her eyes shut for a second. "I know."

Hank's breathing stopped, and she watched the flicker of light in his eyes die out as his heart gave in to the trauma. Then he was gone.

More tears rolled down her cheeks. She tried to move, but her hands were bound tight. It took a minute, but she found Hank's knife in his back pocket and cut herself free. *Ouch.* Blood welled on her wrist where she'd nicked the skin.

She moved to *El Cuervo* then and found his phone, which she used to dial Remy. She wanted to call Emergency services here, or Adrian.

"Mason Industries."

"That's a new one," Megan said.

"Oh, it's you. Thank goodness. I'm glad you called because I need to talk to you, and I only have a second. But first, are you okay?"

Megan looked at the carnage around her. "No. I'm not okay at all."

"You want me to call the boys? They're in India, but I can get them back here if you need help."

"There's no time," Megan said.

"Agreed. He breached my system, Meg. I have to go dark, but I wanted to give you something before I do."

"An airplane would be great."

"Done," Remy said. "You know the drill. But you won't be able to contact me. I got too close, and I'm being burned." She paused for a second, then said, "You'll be on your own."

Megan thought about all the people in her life. "No, I won't."

"I'm going to send everything I know to Special Agent Walker, including proof you have nothing to do with this."

"What?"

"Proof—so they can't keep blaming you for being in collusion with Zimmerman."

. . .

Adrian walked right behind them as agents Peters and Bryant escorted Rear Admiral Frampton (retired) and Captain St. Germaine to the waiting SUV. They'd even called in the local tactical team from their office. Plenty of guns watching.

Looking for Zimmerman.

Other agents and local cops plus state police were all over the place. The convention center had been evacuated, and people were still filing out.

It was over. But they hadn't found Zimmerman yet.

Adrian would be happy about it if he didn't have that niggling feeling this would only cause Zimmerman to go to the ground. He had to remind himself that lives had been saved today—on more than one front. Zimmerman could go somewhere else. Hit a new target. But they'd prevented an attack on innocent lives *today*. They had the two Navy officers. That meant a good shot to figure out where those might be. Information was what they needed right now; all the details they could get about what had happened. Adrian would add a whole lot of prayer, so that hopefully they could figure out the blackmailer's identity.

The SUV door shut. Bryant turned back and held out his hand. "We'll get them secured and talk with them. I've got your number and your email, so I'll keep you posted on what we learn."

Adrian nodded. He'd done all he could. He'd arguably saved the day, getting the convention center and the two men secured.

But why did he feel that niggling...whatever it was ...at the back of his mind? That it might not have been enough.

They still didn't know where Zimmerman was.

Megan was still being implicated.

"Thank you," he said anyway. "I appreciate it."

He couldn't discount the fact these two men might have been bought by the blackmailer, but he'd checked them out with their boss. The speed with which they'd called in the full force of the Denver FBI office had been impressive. These weren't lone wolves acting under duress.

They drove off, and he turned back. Considered calling Megan's mother again. Sylvia had been a lifeline during this, making calls to powerful people. He figured some of the FBI's arrival here had been due to her. The agents had been clear they were supposed to look for Zimmerman, and not Megan. Her mother likely had FBI contacts from her days as an agent's wife. But that was just speculation.

He pulled out Megan's phone, but there were no notifications.

His own had been quiet, as well. The agents at his office back in DC had confirmed that Hank's duty issued phone was turned off. Still no way to trace where he'd gone.

Where he'd taken Megan.

"Adrian!" A slender woman climbed out of a cab and raced toward him. It was like looking at Megan in thirty years. And the future was bright.

He met her halfway. "Mrs. Perkins?"

She nodded and made it all the way to stand in front of him. "Megan just called me. She's on her way here right now, in a private plane." The older woman held onto his biceps. "She's all right."

Relief swept through him. They'd talked more than once in the last few hours, and he figured it had slipped that he was worried about Megan. Maybe even that he cared about her.

He said, "That's great." Two words, so inadequate.

She grinned. "She sounded tired, but what's important is that she's all right."

Of course Megan had called her mother first. It made the most sense. He was here and busy, and she probably didn't want to bother him. Even if he *wanted* to be bothered. Especially by her.

Adrian blew out a breath. She was all right.

He'd made the right call. *Thank You, Lord.* Could this be the beginning of the end of this journey they'd all been on?

He said, "We're still looking for Zimmerman. This isn't over."

She nodded. "But our girl is safe."

Adrian wasn't sure he'd go that far just yet. He needed to see if Megan wanted to have that title in his life. She might not feel the same way about him that he did about her. But he prayed he would get the chance to find out soon.

Adrian looked at the glass front doors of the convention center, then at the surrounding area. Plenty of places for Zimmerman to hide with his sonic weapon, even with the police sweeping the area.

"We should head to the airport and meet her."

Adrian nodded before he looked at Megan's mother. "I'll let them know I'm leaving, but the SAC here doesn't need me. His team will take up the hunt for Zimmerman here."

Adrian was one man. It was the FBI as a whole that would bring him down. Right these wrongs.

Sylvia said, "You think he left?"

"When we gave the evacuation order, most likely. He probably saw us escort his two targets out of here, and now he'll have to check in with the blackmailer on what to do next."

She frowned. "Will he follow them and try to hurt them at the FBI office or in a safe house?"

Adrian said, "It's possible, and the agents will be watching for that. But he needs the exact frequency of the material a building is made out of if he wants to bring it down. It's not as easy as pointing and shooting."

"Okay." She nodded, but didn't look much relieved.

"If we can get Megan to the FBI office as well, then we can get her to give a statement. And I can tell them about Hank. We can get all this figured out and squared away."

"That would be good."

He was still convinced the truth, utilized by the law, was the way this would be resolved. Remy could find anything, apparently, but only when applied to the justice system would the blackmailer's plans be thwarted.

Adrian kept an eye on Megan's mother while he checked with the SAC on scene. He didn't need anything to happen to her on his watch. It was the guilt making him do it. Megan had gone off on her own. But he could have made sure she stayed safe, right? He could have caught up to her in time.

She was all right now—he hoped. But who knew what she'd gone through, or how she'd gotten out?

Adrian drove her mother toward the Denver airport, and into an alternative entrance. One for private parties and their private planes. Usually businesses the FBI would be interested in knowing about.

Megan's mother gasped. "Look."

A small plane was coming in to land. Much too fast.

Smoke poured out of the tail of the aircraft.

"Is that her plane?"

Adrian didn't know. He couldn't even speak to tell her mother that. His foot stuttered on the gas pedal, and the borrowed federal vehicle slowed. He couldn't watch the plane Megan might be on, crash right in front of him.

This had to have something to do with Zimmerman.

Adrian twisted in his seat to look around.

He drove past the hangar. Down the runway a man stood out in the open, a bulky object on his shoulder like a rocket launcher. Zimmerman. He'd exposed himself, on orders from the blackmailer, to bring down Megan's plane. All of it rolled through Adrian's mind, one realization after the other.

Adrian hit the gas and drove straight toward the man, standing out in the open.

Megan's mother gasped and grabbed the handle on the door.

"Hold on." He honked his horn. If it didn't get Zimmerman's attention, maybe he could alert emergency services. Or at least someone in the airport watching out the window. *Please God, let us be seen.*

He couldn't watch Megan die.

And while it wasn't the same as her witnessing Will's death, Adrian at least understood what losing his partner would be like. He knew he wouldn't survive it nearly as well as Megan had.

She needed to live.

Zimmerman didn't turn, despite the fact Adrian laid heavy on the horn. He just kept pointing the weapon at the airplane.

Adrian's speed hit sixty miles an hour, as he barreled right toward Zimmerman.

At the last second, the man turned. He saw Adrian coming and dived out of the way. Adrian clipped him with the car. The rogue agent flew through the air and landed on the runway with a thud. Megan's mother screamed. Adrian hit the brakes and turned the car around.

Behind them, the airplane's engines screamed as it headed for the runway.

It was going to crash.

Chapter 19

Megan swam in and out of consciousness. Kind of…disconnected from her body. Everything was soft and warm. It made her wonder if she was dead and maybe floating instead on some cloud. Until she heard the vague sounds of a hospital intercom. Beeping machines.

She blinked against florescent lights.

Too bright.

Soft pressure touched her forehead. "Get better soon. We need you."

The voice was familiar. She fought the pull of unconsciousness and blinked. Tried to focus. Finally managed to blink away the blur, just in time to see Steve dart out the door.

Her strength slipped away, like water down a drain, and she was out.

Megan came around the next time to the sound of low voices. Two people, a man and a woman, trying to keep the volume of their conversation down. She tried to speak and heard only a low moan emerge from her throat.

"Megan!" Her mom touched her hand.

She did the blinking thing again. There wasn't so much warmth this time, and her left leg didn't feel good at all. Nor did the rest of her.

But her mom was here. That made her smile.

Her mom's hand touched her cheek and she pressed a kiss to the other. "Honey."

"Hi." Her voice sounded awful.

"Oh, I'm so glad you're awake. The doctors were starting to get worried about when you were going to surface." Mom smiled. "It's so good to see those pretty blue eyes."

Megan didn't want to use up her energy, otherwise she would fall asleep again. Not like she had with… "Steve."

"He isn't here, but Adrian is."

Megan tried to shake her head. That wasn't what she meant. Steve had been in her room.

"He's actually in a lot of trouble." The voice was low. So warm and familiar. Adrian came into view at the side of the bed, his face a war between relief and something else. "The feds are looking for him in connection with the restaurant shooting."

She shut her eyes.

"But you knew that, didn't you? He was the one you saw fleeing the scene."

She opened her eyes. Nodded as much as she could.

"Hank?"

She said, "He shot… *El Cuervo*. For me."

Adrian said, "I got a report from the scene. Looks like he saved your life. But he was the one who put you in that situation in the first place." He paused, a frown across his forehead. "Time will tell what role the blackmailer played in that. The FBI has a lot to go through, between him and Zimmerman. Your part in all this. And finding Steve."

The blackmailer should've been found. This was going on entirely too long. Like a disease, now out of control. And it was spreading beyond the initially infected people. It was destroying even more lives now.

Megan took a deep breath and let it out. It hitched a few times as she tried to process everything, and her eyes filled with tears.

"That's enough for right now, I think," her mom said. "I'm going to go and find the doctor. Tell him you're awake."

Adrian shifted as well, and opened his mouth like he was going to say something. He was going to go, too? She didn't want to be alone.

Megan moved her hand and grasped his with as much strength as she could. "What?"

She didn't know what to say. Didn't know where to begin. This man had been with her through so much that she didn't want him to leave. But she also couldn't be that crazy, clingy woman who refused to let him go.

All she said was, "Adrian."

His face softened, and he leaned against the bed.

"What…?"

He finished for her. "What happened?"

She nodded.

"The plane you were in crashed." He looked down. Played with her fingers, while he said, "I won't ever forget watching it hit the ground. You were lucky to survive. One of the pilots didn't, and the other is in ICU."

She squeezed his fingers, and he looked at her. "Not lucky."

He nodded. "You know what I mean."

She should be dead.

"You have a concussion the doctors were worried about. Your left knee was shattered and they had to replace it. But all in all, you came out pretty amazingly intact." He paused. "Do you remember it?"

"No."

"They said that probably would happen. I guess it's a reaction to extreme trauma like that." He blew out a breath. "I wish I could forget it."

She moved her fingers across the back of his hand.

"Zimmerman is here, too."

Her whole body twitched. A wave of pain moved through her.

"No. Sorry. He's in ICU." He ducked his head, then lifted it. "I'm sorry. I guess I'm no good at this."

She wrinkled her nose. "You're doing fine."

"You have to say that."

Megan rolled her eyes as much as she could.

"You say plenty, for someone who doesn't have much strength to speak."

She smiled.

"I guess I learned your expressions."

They stared at each other for a while. Her body wanted to sleep, but she refused to look away.

"The doctor will be here soon. And I have to check in with the bureau." His mouth twisted in a wry smile. "I hit Zimmerman with my car, and they're not too happy. I guess I should have gotten out and arrested him, but I think your mom would have done it if I hadn't. Either way, it didn't stop the plane from crashing."

But he had saved lives. And Zimmerman had been caught. If he pulled through from his injuries, he'd be arrested. Right?

"Another thing we need to go through." Adrian ran a hand over his hair. "There's going to be a lot of unpacking on this. And maybe we still won't know who the blackmailer is, even when we tear this whole operation apart."

Remy hadn't given him the information? Megan tried to remember what account she'd have used to send that email. What had she gotten messages from before...

"Eckhart..." She paused to garner the strength to say, "Industries."

Adrian's head jerked back a fraction. "I got an email from them a couple of days ago with an attachment. I assumed it was a virus."

A couple of days ago?

Megan pushed aside that question and got to the important thing. "Remy."

"It was her?"

She nodded, just as the door opened. Her mom came back in, followed by an older man in a lab coat.

Adrian leaned down and touched her cheek with warm fingers. "I'm going to go look at what she sent me."

Megan nodded.

"Don't go anywhere, yeah?" He smiled, then touched his lips to her forehead. Kind of like Steve had done the first time she woke up. That soft pressure on her head. It better mean a whole lot more than that coming from Adrian.

He frowned. "What is that look about?"

Megan grasped his tie and pulled his face closer again. She tipped her face up, and he got the message.

Touched his lips to hers.

She heard her mom sigh.

Adrian said, "I'll be back soon."

. . .

The door clicked shut behind him and both Bradley and Mint approached. "Is she okay?"

"What did she say?"

Alexis and Emma were with them, looking as worried as their men sounded.

Adrian lifted both hands and took a breath. Being close to her, pretending there was nothing to worry about, had been harder than he'd thought it would be. And he'd thought it would be pretty hard.

Alexis put her hand on his arm. "Are you okay?"

He nodded to the woman he'd hauled into the FBI office for interrogation. The woman he had accused of being involved in her best friend's kidnapping.

Now that he knew her, and fully understood the scope of everything happening, there was no way he could believe she was capable of that. It was embarrassing to think he'd ever believed it.

Alexis's eyes softened. Bradley put his arm around her, and pulled his wife against his side.

Emma slipped her hand into Mint's, and Adrian noticed the ring on her left hand. They'd gotten engaged, even in the midst of everything swirling around them. No time to waste. Not when life was so short.

Adrian said, "She thinks Steve visited her. She said he was here, in her room."

"Someone would have seen him, wouldn't they?" Emma glanced around.

Mint shook his head. "If he didn't want to be seen, *no one* would have noticed."

"The feds are closing in on him," Adrian said. "Or, they think they are."

Alexis frowned. "And we're just going to stand here, doing nothing, pretending like our friend isn't being wrongly accused of being a blackmailer and a terrorist? We can't just lie down and let Steve take the fall for all of this. It's not right."

"Of course we're going to fight," Bradley said. "But if the real blackmailer thinks we're going to come at him, then he'll double his efforts to pin it all on Steve."

Adrian sighed. "I need to get to the Denver FBI office. Megan says Remy sent me something." Plus there were more debriefs to give. More details to go over. Every part of Hank Cromwell's life and career were being taken apart. The same was being done with Daniel Zimmerman. The FBI had been torn apart in the media, and the whole bureau was reeling.

If they took down the blackmailer, they could prove they still had the ability to bring justice.

Too bad they were looking at the wrong man.

Steve.

Alexis said, "We can stay with Megan until you get back."

He nodded. It would take some time but as soon as he got all the paperwork straightened out, and then turned in his badge and his gun, he'd be back.

When this was all over, maybe Steve would hire him on at Double Down. Because wherever Megan was, that was where Adrian wanted to be.

"That doesn't look good," Mint said, studying Adrian's face. "Then at the end, it got better."

Adrian wanted to laugh over the man psychoanalyzing him just from the look on his face, but there was no humor right now. Inside he felt the same cold since he'd seen the plane Megan was in, falling out of the sky.

He was lucky the bureau hadn't decided to bring charges against him for what he'd done to Zimmerman. Adrian had argued the timing. He'd had to act as quickly as possible, and he'd used what he had on hand. Still, he figured it was Megan's mother's pull that had smoothed out the repercussions.

The doctor came out of Megan's room and walked by them.

Emma said, "What can we do for Steve that will help him?"

"Not much," Bradley said. "I put a few kits of supplies—gun, money, etcetera—together. Left them in places I think he might go."

Mint nodded. "I put out some feelers to a few people I think he might contact."

"So we just wait?" Emma glanced between them.

Adrian said, "Steve knows what to do. He's not on the run, he's working. He'll find a way to clear his own name, and out the identity of the blackmailer."

"None of us managed to do it." Alexis looked near tears. "Why will Steve be able to?"

Bradley squeezed her shoulder. "Because we're going to pray, and we're going to trust God."

"But it's taking so long. Why can't this just be over?" She twisted to bury her face in her husband's jacket.

He rubbed a hand up and down her back. "We don't know why, but we know there is a reason. God has more he wants to do."

Alexis lifted her head. "With Rachel?"

Bradley shook his head. "What is it with you and the idea of Steve and Rachel?" The corners of his mouth curled up. "It's cute, how optimistic you are."

Alexis slapped at his shoulder. "Now isn't the time for that. This is serious."

He sobered. "I know."

Megan's mother touched Adrian's shoulder. "She's drowsy, but she's asking for you."

He nodded, then turned back to the group. "I'm available, whatever you need." The blackmailer had torn Megan's life apart, and Adrian wanted him exposed. He fully intended to see this through to the end. "Just give me a call."

Bradley and Mint both nodded. They shook hands. The women doled out cheek kisses, and then the four of them headed out down the hallway.

Adrian let himself into Megan's room. Her eyes were closed, her breath moving rhythmically.

"My mom looks tired," she said, not bothering to open her eyes. "Can you get her to go back to the hotel and take a nap?"

He leaned his hip against the bed. "I can try."

Her mouth twitched. "Now you feel my pain."

Adrian didn't. There was no way he could when she was lying beaten and bruised in a hospital bed, and he'd done…what? Hit Zimmerman with his car.

Closed the case.

Caught the rogue agent.

Averted a national disaster.

If he was lucky, the FBI would decide not to give him a commendation. That was the last thing he wanted, especially when more than a cursory look into his life would reveal the fact he was actively still searching for the blackmailer. Outside the FBI.

Too many people had been touched by the man behind all this. Adrian wasn't going to trust anyone outside Double Down until it was over.

"What?" She touched his hand.

Adrian leaned forward. He put his head on her shoulder, overwhelmed by all of this. "I'm sorry."

She curled her hand around the back of his neck. "You saved me, didn't you?"

He blew out a breath. "Please tell me what *El Cuervo* did." She still had the marks on her wrists from being bound. The doctor had told him there hadn't been any sexual assault, but he wanted her to tell him.

Her fingers flexed against his skin. "Tried to talk me to death."

He lifted his head, but only so he could see her eyes.

"I'm okay."

"Not because I saved you. Hank took you, and he's the one who killed *El Cuervo*. What did I do?"

"Your job." She shot him a look. "Or, how about, 'everything you could?' Which included saving my mother, and a whole lot of other people, and making sure Zimmerman didn't do something awful."

"They found his family."

She nodded slightly.

"The blackmailer had them killed." Adrian blew out a breath. "He had evidence planted there that makes it look like Steve is the one who did it."

Her mouth opened, but no sound came out.

"He's on the run."

She said, "We have to help him."

"We will." He leaned in and touched his forehead to hers. "I promise you, we will."

She kissed his cheek. Adrian turned his face, and their lips met. When he needed to catch his breath, he said, "I'm not sure I'll ever get tired of doing that."

She smiled. "We should keep doing it. Just to make sure you don't."

He chuckled then, and said, "Promise?"

"Only if you promise this is going somewhere good, and real. And maybe forever."

Adrian knew exactly what he was going to say. He straightened, then lifted his hand, palm out. "I, Adrian Jefferson Walker, do solemnly swear that I will support and defend this relationship from all enemies, foreign and domestic—"

Megan grinned, but he ignored it.

He didn't ignore the wince of discomfort on her face. But he did continue, "That I will bear true faith and allegiance to this relationship; that I take this obligation freely, without any mental reservation or purpose of evasion; and that I will well and faithfully discharge the duties of boyfriend, and later husband, on which I am about to enter." He paused. "So help me God."

She smiled wide, but not so wide he didn't see that she was in pain.

"You need rest."

"Only if you kiss me again. To seal the deal."

He did as she asked. Both of them were smiling.

Their lives weren't perfect, or safe. That didn't matter. God had brought them together, and He had charged Adrian with loving this woman. A woman so very worthy of the best kind of love he was capable of giving her.

Adrian fully intended to spend the rest of his life fulfilling his duty to keep her safe, and making sure she knew exactly how blessed he was to do it.

So help him God.

One Hour Later

Adrian didn't even take his coat off before he downloaded the email that had come from Remy onto a secure server. Megan's mysterious friend had found what they'd all been looking for these past weeks. Months, even.

She'd discovered who was behind all this.

He scanned down the pages and felt his eyes widen as he took all the information in. Not proof. This was a series of indications and ties, circumstantial. Remy had pulled it all together like a complicated algorithm that added up to one thing.

The only possible identity for the blackmailer.

A second later he tugged out a flash drive he'd transferred it onto. Turned around and walked out of the office. Once he was on the street, he pulled out his phone and called Bradley.

"Yeah?"

Adrian tried to breathe, but there was no air. He was going to have to hide this information until the time was right. "I know who the blackmailer is."

There was a second of silence, and then, "And?"

"This is worse than any of us imagined."

Book 4

Deadly Holidays

Chapter 1

Rachel slipped the cell phone into her purse. A phone that didn't belong to her. She walked through the first floor of the West Wing, headed for the correct office. Smiled to a couple of staffers. Ducked her head and kept going.

Just another day, another senator visiting a colleague in the government. Nothing abnormal about that. Though that depended on why he'd summoned her. And it had been a summons—no way to get out of it. He wanted to talk to her.

She nodded to the intern, then tapped on the door and waited.

"Come in."

Rachel took a breath and twisted the handle. She pasted a pleasant smile on her face and went inside. The blackmailer sat at his desk, an equally pleasant smile on his face. Both of them faking politeness in order to get this done. Have this meeting—whatever it was going to be about—and then get on with their individual plans.

Did he know that she knew who he really was?

Did he know she was going to *destroy* him?

"Please, have a seat."

Senator Rachel Harris left the door open and settled into a luxurious chair. Everything in the White House was like a museum. It was different here in the West Wing, looking a little more like a regular office. But not this office. All the furniture had been specifically selected to make a statement.

Power resided here.

Rachel slipped her hand into her purse and swiped the screen of the phone to initiate the program. If discovered, it would act like a regular phone. No trace of its true purpose in the operating system. The reason why she was here.

She placed her purse on the floor, and looked up at the vice president. "I have to admit, I was curious as to what you wanted to talk to me about."

Truth was, if he hadn't called her, she'd have fabricated a reason to meet with him in his office. Did he have some nefarious purpose for asking her here? Or was it a God-thing, like Alexis would've said? Her best friend was vocal about her beliefs. Rachel was inclined to agree but, with everything that had happened to her, could she really believe in a loving God? She'd been violated. Drugged. Sexually assaulted. Videoed.

The digital file had been used to try and blackmail her. But instead of rolling over, she and Alexis—her assistant at the time—had decided to leak the video themselves and tell everyone it was Alexis. Thanks to matching tattoos, the world had accepted that as the truth.

Until Rachel had been kidnapped by men working for the same blackmailer.

To say it had been an overwhelming last couple of months would be a serious understatement.

The VP's smile softened. "We'll get to that soon enough. First, I'd like to know how you're doing, Rachel. How are things?"

He seriously wanted to know how she was. This man had been in Venezuela as a young child, the son of missionaries in the village where an attack by US troops took place. He'd been eleven years old when his parents were killed as part of an operation involving a joint task force of military and federal agencies.

Now? They were almost certain he was the one who'd systematically ruined the lives of the adult offspring of everyone who had been a part of the operation—those on the team and those on the planning committee. And he'd had all those who had been present back then killed.

Blackmail and murder.

But they had no proof.

Now that Rachel had the wherewithal not to leap over the desk and claw his eyes out, she said, "I'm doing better." Knowing he wasn't going to accept "fine" as a good answer.

He employed his politician smile and said, "I'm so glad."

Yeah. She was sure. "Thank you. I know it's going to be a long road, but it doesn't stop me from wanting to get to the end already." She shot him a sardonic smile.

At the *end*, this man would be either dead or in jail.

All of her friends would be safe.

Happy.

Rachel would be able to move on with her life.

He nodded slowly. "Trust the process."

She didn't even know what to say to that, so she just nodded. Thankfully there was another tap on the open door, and someone came in. The VP's wife shut the door behind her, and swept over to Rachel on her four-inch pumps. Her blouse was silk. The suit she wore probably cost twice Rachel's, and hers had been an insane amount.

"My dear." She held out her hands and smiled.

"Mrs. Anderson." She returned the woman's smile and held her chilled hands. The woman needed a cup of tea.

"How are you, dear?"

It grated that *everyone* knew what had happened to her. It hadn't been much better back when the world thought it was Alexis, considering they all thought—and posted—horrible things about her best friend. She had been disgraced. Ruined and left destitute. Like this was olden times when they had to wear that scarlet letter. Rachel had helped as much as she could. She had been Alexis's employer as well as her best friend since grade school. Best assistant she'd ever had.

Now that it was Rachel who'd been the victim, she was pitied. Coddled. Treated like glass. She wanted to smash that glass with her fist and then scream so everyone could hear her.

She did *not* want to be treated like a victim.

"I'm good." Rachel slipped her hands out, ready to get on with an actual conversation. She sat and glanced once at the phone in her purse.

50% complete.

Mrs. Anderson sat in the chair beside her. Did she know? Did she have any idea the pain, destruction, and death that her husband had caused? Rachel wasn't sure. She wanted to say Mrs. Anderson had no clue. But Rachel had been given a hefty dose of what people hid beneath the surface of civility. Now, as much as she wanted to believe otherwise, she just didn't trust anyone.

Everyone had secrets. After all, she was only sitting here because that phone was being used to covertly access the VP's computer. Otherwise, she had nothing to say to these people. Unless they wanted to confess to multiple murders, coercion, blackmail, terrorism and everything else they'd done.

FBI special agent Adrian Walker and former agent Megan Perkins were busy listing out all the charges. Compiling what evidence they had. Taking statements.

There was nothing solid that tied everything that had happened back to this man across the desk, shuffling papers like he was looking for a specific one. If the phone got Remy into his computer, then their friend-of-a-friend genius hacker could get the proof.

The *only* reason she was here.

"Rachel, darling." Mrs. Anderson tried to take her hand, but Rachel didn't let her. The woman continued, "We have a project in mind, a 'mission' as it were. We think you just might be the perfect person to spearhead it. Given your…recent experience, I believe with all my heart you're going to see this meeting as a turning point in your life and in your healing."

Washington sincerity. That was what Alexis had called it. Altruism, but for a person's own gain. Where they looked lily-white, like they were the poster child for both humanitarianism *and* the little guy. All the while, underneath the press-release, was a different story altogether.

Maybe it was experience talking, or the distrust she couldn't seem to shake, but these days all Rachel saw was that "Washington sincerity." And she didn't believe one bit of it.

She smiled, not wanting to betray her true feelings. Everything was far closer to the surface. She'd been an expert at playing the game for years. Now was a different story. Experience had forced her to see the truth of wasting time with subterfuge. She *hated* fake. It made her want to vomit.

"William and I would like to start an organization. A charity, if you will. One that seeks to help women who have been exploited using social media. To aid victims in their recovery, and to educate teens on responsible internet use."

The VP nodded. "We would like you to be the face of the campaign."

Mrs. Anderson said, "To show people that strength and grace can come even in the darkest of circumstances."

Her husband took up the mantle. "That good can come from the pain you no doubt went through."

Rachel glanced between them, overwhelmed by the seamlessness in which they spoke. Either they were completely in sync—as married couples sometimes were. Or they had rehearsed this little speech. She didn't know which it was, but there was a reason it seemed like they were practically finishing each other's sentences.

"Well..." Rachel let the word hang while she compiled her thoughts.

Mrs. Anderson said, "Of course you don't have to answer now. Please take some time to think about it. We would be asking you to be more vocal about what happened to you. To share your experience with others in order to turn the tide of how social media is utilized. Hopefully we can expose even one person attempting to victimize someone online. Maybe even stop it before it happens." She smiled and her lip gloss glinted in the light.

Rachel nodded, like she was deep in thought. "It is a noble cause. A lot of good could come from it." She spoke slowly while she measured her words, mostly just drawing out the meeting so the phone could complete its remote hack of the VP's computer. "I'll have to think comprehensively about this. I agree it could do a lot of good in the world and in today's culture."

"As a member of the younger generation—" Mrs. Anderson's smile was brittle. "You're certainly the one that kids will listen to. An example they can relate to."

Rachel nodded. "I'm not sure I'm quite ready to be the main character in a cautionary tale," she said honestly. "I still have a long road to travel. But I will certainly think about what you've said."

She was ready to leave now. Ready enough she reached down for her purse to check the phone.

`78% complete.`

She'd asked Remy for that feature. Otherwise she'd never have known how close to completion the program was. Only a few minutes more and she'd be able to—

The door flung open. Mrs. Anderson let out a squeak. Rachel nearly jumped out of her chair. She dropped the phone back into her purse.

"Goodness me, Miles." Mrs. Anderson placed a hand high on her chest, displaying her perfect manicure. "Do you have to barge in? This is a private conversation."

"I'm sorry, sir," Miles, an intern in his 20s, said. "But the president is on the line." He didn't even acknowledge her or the VP's wife. "He says it's urgent."

She heard the rustle as Miles strode back to the door. Rachel's gaze was pointed toward the VP in time to catch the look on his face upon hearing the president was demanding his attention. For a second, a look of pure malice flitted across his face.

Then it was gone like it was never there, and he said, "Thank you, Miles. I'll take a coffee, please."

"Yes, sir."

That was Rachel's cue to leave. But the phone wasn't done.

She didn't move.

Mrs. Anderson lifted from her chair and trotted after the intern. "Miles, I don't want to hear you ever do that…" Her voice trailed off as she swept from the room in order to berate the intern.

Rachel wanted to roll her eyes. She would never speak to an intern like she was so far above them. Yes, that made her an anomaly in Washington DC. So sue her. She treated people with respect. It was the way she'd been raised.

After what had happened to her, she was more aware than ever of those secret scars. Ones everyone carried. You never knew what someone had been through—the pain they hid.

"Senator." The VP's voice was sharp.

She lifted her purse and glanced at the phone screen before she swung the strap over her shoulder and stood to face the vice president of the United States.

`83% complete.`

Why was it taking so long? She stood in front of the VP's desk. His hand was halfway to the phone, ready to take the president's "urgent" call. How was she supposed to delay this when he needed to get the phone?

She should reach over and touch his hand. Thank him for thinking of her as the face of this new opportunity.

It made her skin crawl just considering touching him. Bile rose in her throat, but she willed it to go back down. She wanted to lift her hand and slap him across his smug face. Scream to the world all the horrible things he'd done. But what would that get her? She needed proof.

Irrefutable, inarguable proof.

He lifted the phone, those assessing eyes on her. "Yes, Mr. President?"

She shut the door and left. Forced a polite expression as she walked out. Slightly vacant was good. She'd found that if people thought they were smarter than her, then they almost always gave away more than they'd intended, just to prove their superiority.

Rachel strode to the closest door and went outside. The December air was crisp, and she sucked in a deep lungful of it. Pushed it out as she waved to a security guard. Strode to the sidewalk, every step shoving off the feeling of being inside. Trapped. Locked in the mire of everything she had experienced. She'd explained the sensation to her psychologist, and the woman suggested Rachel get a dog so she could take it for walks.

Maybe a rescue dog. She needed something she could take care of and support. She also needed something capable of defending her.

Until then, she had to walk alone to the nearest coffee shop. Air and caffeine would do. For now.

She slipped out the phone.

`Operation incomplete.`

It grated that she'd failed in her mission. Unable to stomach doing what needed to be done in order to get them a result. She hadn't been strong enough. Not cut out for that kind of life, the way her friends and family were.

Bradley. Steve. Megan. Mint. Even Emma and Alexis. All of them had faced danger. They would have made sure the phone completed the hack.

Rachel hugged her suit jacket to her body. She clutched her purse under her arm, wishing she'd worn pants. Not that thin suit pants would be much warmer. The sidewalks had been salted. Air left her mouth in white puffs. Rachel wanted an extra hot mocha. Or maybe she should just Uber home and work in her jammies the rest of the day. Eat soup. Or hot noodles. Or noodle soup.

Something to take the bitter taste of failure from her mouth.

She ducked under scaffolding, and sidestepped a couple of suited men coming back from lunch probably. One sent her a sideways glance. A look she was familiar with now. One that meant he'd seen the video. He knew what she'd done under the influence of Rohypnol.

Everyone knew.

There was nowhere to run. Nowhere she could go where there wouldn't be someone who knew exactly what she'd been through. The add-on came on occasion. Instead of pity she would see the sideways glance that inquired whether she'd be interested in being that girl again.

Rachel lifted her chin and strode on. She headed for another chain coffee shop selling mediocre drinks at ridiculous prices. Maybe she should start a campaign for reasonably priced caffeine. Talk about an idea Americans could get behind. With the added bonus that everyone would be talking about her for a *good* reason this time.

She turned the corner onto a side street. Fear walked with quiet steps up her spine, but she pushed the sensation off. The man who'd victimized her was dead. Megan had killed him, making her Rachel's second best friend. Unofficially, of course.

The blackmailer could number the days that remained for him to walk free. She couldn't get scared every time—

Arms banded around her. Lifted her feet from the ground.

Hot breath against her neck.

She sucked in a breath to scream. He shifted his arm to her diaphragm. She choked on the exhale.

His voice was low. Gravel. "No screaming."

Chapter 2

Steve was on her tail. It was the last place in the world he should be right now, considering he was a fugitive. Not to mention wearing a knit cap to disguise his face and keep security cameras from seeing him was a dead giveaway in an ocean of suited government workers and tourists.

He'd been lying low, trying to figure all this out. Then Remy had contacted him. Rachel was going to the VP's office with a phone that would allow their hacker friend access to his computer.

Steve had hit the roof. He was so mad he stomped at a patch of ice on the sidewalk and nearly went flying. Caught himself. The motion of stopping jarred every muscle in his back and made him wince. Sleeping on a couch at his age was not helping. Still, fugitives could hardly be picky. It wasn't like he could get a hotel room.

As soon as he cleared his name and gave the FBI what they needed to convict this blackmailer, Steve was going on a beach vacation.

He rounded the corner and saw movement. Then nothing. He picked up his pace. Heard a muffled moan. *Rachel.*

Another corner, and they were in an alley. Steve saw the darkly dressed man, a knit cap pulled low over his ears. Heavy coat. Gloves. No visible weapon. Rachel was in his arms, her legs swinging back trying to kick him.

Ire rose, heating him from the inside out. He raced for them. Adrenaline energized his muscles as he pumped his arms and legs and prayed he didn't hit another patch of ice. The last thing he needed was to skid right past them.

At the last second he yelled, "Hey!"

The man swung around, and Steve spotted it—a knife, pointed at Rachel's midsection.

If he'd had a gun, he'd have shot the guy. Assuming he could've done it without endangering Rachel. *Not likely.* He didn't even like guns, though. In his line of work, they didn't factor overmuch. Force wasn't how you got a result.

Steve barreled into the two of them at full speed. The assailant hit the ground first. Steve landed on top, Rachel sandwiched between them. She let out a cry.

He got a hold of the man's wrist and squeezed. The assailant cried out as well, a throaty sound, but let go of the knife.

Steve tossed it aside.

He lifted off the man and pulled up Rachel in one move, so both of them stood together. He put her behind him. The assailant rolled away and came up on the balls of his feet. Steve saw his face. Realized who it was.

There was no time to process the why of it being *this* man. "Don't try it. This attempt failed."

"I don't get paid to abort." The throaty voice was familiar to him and brought with it a rush of memories. The house. Training. Missions.

Steve said, "Your call." Were they really going to do this?

The man pulled another knife. "Yes, it is."

"I won't let you hurt her."

"Yes?" Rachel's breathy voice came from behind him. "I need the police. Someone just tried to mug me."

The assailant's face twisted with malice. He threw the knife at Rachel. Steve dived in the same direction and turned. Rachel let out a squeak, as he grabbed her and spun. The knife glanced across the outside of the top of his arm.

Booted feet raced past him as the man fled the scene.

Steve hissed out a breath and glanced in the direction he'd gone. Disappeared.

"Yes, I'm here."

He looked over at her. Eyes wide, she clutched the phone to her cheek. When her gaze settled on him he saw the relief on her face. Something swelled he couldn't admit to. Or *wouldn't.* Not when he was a fugitive and her life was in danger.

She said into the phone, "The man ran off."

He could hear the person on the other end of her call, but couldn't tell what they were saying. Did she realize he'd have to go now as well? Her height put her level with his chin, and he weighed probably eighty pounds more than she did. That was all the assessing he was going to do. Any more put him in dangerous territory that also wasn't going to help him right now.

So she was everything he'd ever wanted in a woman, and he was a fugitive being hunted by every law office in the country. That wasn't likely to change. It meant Steve was everything she didn't need. And he would ruin her life if he tried to force their situation to be different somehow. Rachel and Steve were a one-time-maybe possibility that was now a never-could-be. That was life.

Steve needed to let it go. Let *her* go. But how could he, knowing she was in so much danger?

He said, "Hang up the phone," in a low voice.

She lowered it and pressed a button on the screen. "Good to know Remy's supersecret spy phone works to call 911, because I left mine in my office."

"Are you okay?"

She shook off whatever adrenaline remained and lifted her chin. "Of course."

He didn't buy it. "Liar."

Rachel shoved at his shoulder, a grin on her face. "Don't call me a liar."

He nearly smiled. "Don't lie, and I won't." She narrowed her eyes. He said, "I have to go."

"What? Why?"

"You called the cops. They can't find me." He was the top of America's most wanted right now. He shouldn't even be here. Let alone hang around and get taken in by the police. "I have to go."

"Oh." She actually looked sad.

"Did he hurt you?"

She shook her head.

"Where is your Secret Service detail, Rachel? You're a senator. You can't go walking around DC without protection."

"I didn't..." Her voice trailed off, and she said nothing more.

She didn't need them? Didn't want them? He didn't have the luxury of time to wait around while she figured out which it was. "Call Bradley." He started to back away.

"Wait!" She yelled it, probably louder than necessary. When he turned back, she said, "How did you know where I was?"

"Remy told me what you were doing." Too bad there was no time to talk about that. The hacker had gone dark, targeted by the blackmailer. She'd contacted him as a favor and then disappeared below the radar again. For Rachel. "What were you thinking, going in there like that? It was too risky."

"It could've ended this, and you'd have been able to come home." Her face was so sad he wanted to hug her. "It didn't work."

He wanted to believe home was with her. He hadn't realized how badly he wanted to believe that until he stood with her now.

"I won't ever be able to come home, Rach." Her gaze softened, but Steve couldn't let it affect him. "I'll always be stained by this, no matter what happens." She of all people should understand that. Her past went with her. It colored how people saw her. And while he hated that for her, it meant they actually shared at least one thing.

Being accused as the blackmailer, forced into a corner by the man himself and then set up, wasn't ever going to go away. The fact they now thought it was the vice president of the United States behind it all didn't make it better. In fact, it made it that much worse. No one was going to believe them. Not when the blackmailer had scared so many people into silence. The rest he'd killed or buried under scandals, so they had no credibility.

Rachel was a wild card. She'd withstood the scandal and was still here. No wonder he wanted her dead, too.

Steve wasn't going to skate out from under the charges. Even if they brought the blackmailer down, it would be he-said-he-said. Nothing more. The blackmailer was so good the evidence against Steve was compelling. The ensuing manhunt wasn't about to let up until he was either in handcuffs or a body bag.

His life would be forever stained by the past.

"Steve—" The sound of police sirens filled the air.

He located the knife and tucked it in his jacket. "Gotta go. I have dinner plans."

He didn't look back, not wanting to know—or see—how that affected her. He just walked and kept walking. Scanned the streets for the assailant. Committed the man's face, older now, to memory. Even if he located the man, would the blackmailer keep sending them after Rachel?

Would she ever be safe?

Then there was Double Down. Steve's private security firm was in tatters. The office was closed. His employees on hiatus. The blackmailer had infiltrated every part of the business, and Steve hadn't told any of them exactly how bad it was.

It took almost two hours to walk there—he didn't need his face on a Metro security camera—but he eventually reached the tiny apartment complex. Via a corner grocery store where he picked up the items on the list she'd given him along with three folded twenties. This part of Washington wasn't totally run down, but neither was it a huge step up from that. He lumbered up the steps, hauling the bags, and shifted them all to one hand so he could shove his key in the lock.

"I'm here."

Mrs. Cromwell looked up from the recliner, blanket on her lap. Tight, white perm cut close to her head. Her wrinkled cheeks lifted. "You get my soup?"

"Yes, ma'am." He resisted the urge to kick the door shut and used his hip instead. She'd called him on that last time. Made him wipe down the spot where his boot print had been with a wet rag.

He wandered to the kitchen, dumped the bags on the counter, and started putting things away. "You want bread or toast today?"

"Grilled cheese."

Steve glanced at her. Grilled cheese was good. It meant her stomach was recovering from that bout of flu she'd had last week. Not so much fun to clean up, though. "Coming right up."

She smiled, but didn't move her attention away from the TV. She loved *The Price is Right* so much he'd bought her a DVR, so she could watch one episode after another all day if she wanted. Didn't matter if she just repeated the same episodes in a row. She didn't mind.

Images filled his mind. That man and his knife and Rachel's face.

Steve hung his head for a second and blew out a breath before he pushed the images away. He couldn't even follow up and try to find out why the guy had been here or Steve would wind up exposing himself.

The bleed off of adrenaline made his arm smart. The slice he'd gotten from the knife he'd deflected away from Rachel stung. He found a rag under the sink and wet it, slapped it on his arm under the sleeve of his T-shirt, and turned so Mrs. Cromwell wouldn't see.

It had mostly stopped bleeding.

Two grilled cheese sandwiches for him, one for her. She had her soup and he heated some chili for himself. When she was settled with her tray, he plopped himself on the couch.

"Good day?"

He swallowed a bite of sandwich and said, "It was all right."

"That's good."

On the table was a pile of mail he'd brought in from her mailbox. Letters. Bills. Junk mail. Nothing from her sister, which she was waiting on. News about her niece's new grandbaby.

All addressed to, *Mrs. Elizabeth Cromwell.* The elderly mother of disgraced FBI agent Hank Cromwell. A man who had kidnapped Steve's friend and employee. He'd taken Megan back to the man who had terrorized her two years ago. There was nothing but white-hot rage in him. And if the man wasn't dead, Steve would have shot him himself. Who cared about the consequences?

Megan was fine now, but the fact it'd happened at a time when Steve hadn't been able to help find her, grated on him. Adrian, the man she had fallen in love with, had taken down another FBI agent and saved Megan's life. But in that moment when she was held captive, as reality and nightmare had collided, she'd had no one.

A man she had trusted betrayed her.

"Those are some heavy thoughts."

He glanced at Elizabeth. "Yes, ma'am." His voice was thick. He glanced at the wall. The blank spaces that showed where she'd hung pictures of her son at one time. The day he'd graduated from the FBI academy. When he'd received a commendation. Gotten married. The life he'd lived before he threw it all away because the vice president had found out about his gambling problem and leveraged that to cause Megan even more pain.

"Does it have to do with Hank?" Elizabeth knew it all. He'd explained what she hadn't read herself in the newspaper. Then he'd explained how he was part of all this.

Steve wanted to deny it wasn't all connected. Instead, he said, "Yes." Because she deserved honesty. And he *needed* it. "Just trying to figure out some stuff."

"Well then eat up. Brain food, I always call it."

He shared a smile with her.

"Sneaking out again tonight?"

Steve nearly choked on his chili. "Excuse me?"

"I might be old, but that just means I'm up plenty to use the ladies' room. Don't pretend you don't sneak in and out of this house at all hours of the day and night. I'm not senile." She also evidently didn't mind harboring a fugitive. She'd told him she was too old, they'd never put her in jail. And if they tried, she was going to pretend she'd lost her marbles.

It had taken some convincing, and she'd argued her case. In the end it was the fact she'd needed help. Hank was gone. Who else would assist her?

"No, you are not senile." She was entirely too astute. It was why he hadn't lied to her. Instead, the fact she'd so obviously needed help had turned his interview, and trying to get more information about Hank Cromwell and the blackmailer, into an offer of assistance.

She knew they were helping each other out equally. She'd even said it straight out.

"Yes, I'm going to sneak out tonight," he said. "A friend of mine is in danger. I need to make sure she's all right."

"A lady friend?"

Steve nodded.

"Well, then. Be the gallant hero." She grinned, two rows of neat false teeth. "Works every time."

Steve chuckled. He cleaned up, then helped her clean up and get ready for bed. He carried her to her room because it had made her chuckle the first time, and now it was just a thing.

"Tomorrow you'll need to get my Christmas tree out of the hall closet. Get it set up."

"Yes, ma'am."

Hopefully he would be here tomorrow. Alive and able to help her, instead of in jail for shooting at a parking lot full of FBI agents. What was the point in arguing he'd been under duress? Especially if they couldn't prove their claim of a blackmailer.

He thought on it all the way to Rachel's townhouse. She'd moved since her kidnapping, which he figured was reasonable since she'd been taken from her own living room.

Bradley's car was at the curb. He was glad that her twin brother and his wife Alexis—Rachel's best friend—could be with her after such a harrowing day.

Bradley worked for Double Down. Then there was Mint, who had found Emma and fallen in love with her. He was keeping her safe currently, tasked with retrieving what she'd put in a safe deposit box and ensuring she testify to the FBI.

Megan was the last member of Double Down. She was former FBI, and she'd hooked up with Adrian Walker who was an FBI agent investigating the blackmailer.

They'd lost two operatives to an explosion, which put them down to four. He'd fired Megan's mom from being his assistant and then sent her on an all-expenses paid vacation where the blackmailer would never find her. It was all such a convoluted mess that he didn't know where to even begin, or end, the train of thought before it crashed and burned.

Steve halted across the street. No point trying to talk to Rachel when she had her family there. He'd have to wait until they left.

A car engine drew his attention. It slowed as it passed the house. Not cops, not even unmarked.

Someone was watching her house.

Chapter 3

Rachel's brother squeezed her shoulder as he passed and headed for her kitchen. She dumped her purse on the floor beside her hall closet and went to the bathroom that was off her bedroom.

"Lex, you want tea?" Bradley called out to his new wife.

"Yes, please."

Rachel smiled to herself. So polite. She grabbed a change of clothes—yoga pants and a huge sweater that said, "Army." Bradley had been in the Navy, and a SEAL even, but she was an equal opportunity supporter. Everyone knew Senator Rachel Harris was one hundred fifty percent behind the military.

She washed up and changed, then tied her hair up in a messy knot before she headed back to the living room. Alexis and Bradley stood together at the stove, heads close. Talking quietly. The soft look on her brother's face wasn't lost on Rachel. He only ever did that with Alexis.

Now they looked so natural. Like they'd been married for thirty years—but without the part where two people eventually got on each other's nerves. They were *all* best friends. The three of them had been family for years, since before Rachel and Bradley's parents were killed. Now things had changed, and Rachel was sharing her best friend with her brother. That part wasn't lost on her either.

She was happy for them and still part of their tribe, but now Bradley and Alexis had something which had nothing to do with her. A fact she lamented, even while she accepted it was a good thing. They had a life now. They would have their own family.

Alexis spotted Rachel standing there, staring at them like a creeper. And yet, she smiled. That was just her way. Alexis was good. She was nice. Rachel was the one with the problem—in more ways than one.

She moved into the kitchen, pulled a glass out of her cupboard, and filled it at the refrigerator.

"Tea?"

She turned back to Alexis and sucked down the water while she shook her head.

Bradley wasn't buying it. "Are you sure you're okay?"

"Steve is the one I'm worried about. I think that knife cut him."

"I know. You kept telling the cops that."

She leaned back against the counter. "I wouldn't have had to keep repeating myself if they would just accept the fact he'd been there and saved my life. But noooo," she dragged the word out. "They insist he's this *criminal*. Like any of this is his fault."

"And aligning yourself with him?" Bradley raised his eyebrows.

Alexis stood quietly beside him. She knew how they could be with each other, and it was wise not to get in the middle of it. Instead, she turned to the kettle and poured two cups.

"You think I'm not going to tell anyone who will listen about how he's innocent of all of this." She lifted her palms and then let her hands fall back to her sides. "How can they think he did any of this?"

Alexis used her soft voice to say, "He did shoot at the agents outside that restaurant. He made it so that the bad guy could get away."

Bradley shot Rachel a look. "Exactly."

"And they don't think it's suspicious that the FBI have been investigating a blackmailer, and then Steve shoots *at* a bunch of agents and *doesn't hit a single one*? No one can look at that and not think he's under duress and doing whatever he can to keep everyone involved safe."

"Including himself?"

Okay, so *yes,* she wanted to know what the blackmailer had threatened him with. She asked her brother, "You know about his past. What might the vice president have on him?"

Bradley's jaw twitched. "I don't know much about his career before Double Down, only that he worked for the state department."

"What is that supposed to mean? I thought you knew him when you were a SEAL."

"It's complicated." He turned to the fridge and retrieved the milk. Stalling.

"Spit it out, Bradley. What do you know?"

Alexis said, "Is it a security clearance thing?" She glanced at Rachel, ever the peacemaker. "Maybe he *can't* tell you."

"He can tell me."

Bradley shook his head, then he took a sip of his tea.

"Quit stalling."

He moved, mug still in one hand. "I'm going to go outside and check the perimeter."

Rachel rolled her eyes. He trailed out and she said, "Will you talk to him?"

Alexis sipped her own tea. "I'm not being the go-between for my husband and my best friend."

"You're the one who decided it was a good idea to marry him."

"And you don't think it was a good idea?"

Rachel said, "You know that isn't what I meant."

"Do I?"

"Does it matter what I feel?" She placed her glass in the sink. "It's done, isn't it?" And they all had to live with the consequences.

"If I didn't know you, I'd be offended by that."

Rachel placed her hands on the counter and hung her head, trying as best she could to not fly off the handle. What she'd said was bad enough. Alexis didn't need the brunt of her frustration. Especially considering Bradley would go to bat for her now. The two of them, ganging up on her. The new "normal."

Too bad nothing about her life was normal.

She didn't know how to do this.

Where was Steve, anyway? She had the phone and no idea what to do with it since Remy hadn't contacted her. Was it all over? Failure. Nothing left to do?

"I know you're dealing with a lot—"

She swung around to face Alexis. "Why do you always have to be so *understanding?*"

"What else should I be?"

"Get mad. Be mad at me."

"I've been mad at you plenty."

Rachel rolled her eyes. "Yeah, like forever ago."

"Why should I be mad at you now? You've been through so much. I figure compassion is a whole lot easier, considering all you're dealing with." Alexis's face was soft and open. She was just so...nice. It was frustrating. Rachel wanted to fight with someone.

She said, "That right there is the problem. All that compassion. You pity me, and you're compensating by being *nicer.*"

Alexis started to laugh. "And apparently being nice is a bad thing. You'd rather I was a jerk to you?"

"Maybe," she yelled.

"Well I won't do it!" She might have sounded mad, but Alexis smiled.

"You're the worst best friend ever. I'm firing you." Rachel moved out of the kitchen to the sound of Alexis laughing. "I'm going to find someone else."

"You can try."

Rachel rolled her eyes and slumped down on the couch. "Where's a bad guy when you feel like punching someone?"

Alexis sat on the other side and set her mug on the coffee table. "I'm sure Steve is all right." She paused. "You said he walked away."

Rachel nodded.

"He's good at what he does."

"So is the blackmailer." And she'd had a chance to take him down, but she hadn't been able to do it.

"Steve will be fine."

. . .

"She defended you, you know." Bradley spoke to the dark yard.

Steve wanted to hang his head. He wanted to pretend he wasn't here watching. But Bradley knew the truth. Steve stood up from his crouch in the bushes and wandered out. Not so far that he'd be seen in the light that spilled from inside.

His arm stung, but he ignored it. Kind of like he ignored anything he didn't want to deal with. Like thinking shooting up that restaurant parking lot full of feds had been his only option.

"And she asked me who you were before Double Down."

Steve said, "You haven't told her?"

"I thought it would've come out in the news already, but they're still saying you worked for the state department overseas. Like diplomatic missions."

"Hey," Steve said. "I can be diplomatic."

"Sure, if they let you negotiate with a weapon."

"My results speak for themselves. And who is still around afterwards to complain?"

Bradley chuckled. The kind of macabre sense of humor shared by homicide detectives, FBI major crimes unit, former Navy SEALs...and ex-spies.

Steve sobered fast though. "Is she okay?"

"She's worried about you and scared of the blackmailer. She's covering it up by getting snippy with everyone."

"So...no? She's not okay?"

Bradley snorted. "Dude, you have a lot to figure out about women."

Steve would rather have had to only figure out one particular woman. He wanted to go inside and see for himself how she was. Maybe give her that hug.

But that ship had sailed, and the destination was Lonely Harbor. Men like him didn't get those chances. He'd thought Rachel might be his chance, but then she'd been drugged, assaulted, and kidnapped. Now there were dark shadows in her eyes that reminded him entirely too much of the reflection he saw every day in the mirror.

The sins of his past.

Rachel had that inside her. But his were because of what he'd done. Hers were because of what had been done *to* her. A pain he wasn't going to be able to erase. He would only drag her farther down…into his own darkness.

"Take care of her."

Bradley grabbed his arm before he could move away. "No. Don't do that. She needs your help. She's going after this blackmailer, and it scares me blind. After everything he's done to her, she just waltzes into his office?"

"If she isn't safe in the White House, where is she going to be safe?"

"It isn't like she can live there. And you're only proving my point—the moment she left, that guy tried to attack her."

"I don't think he was going to kidnap her," Steve said. "I think he was contracted to kill her."

"Any idea who he was?"

Steve pressed his lips together, then said, "He had training." What else was he supposed to say? He didn't have a picture of the man. He didn't even know the guy's real name.

"A mercenary?" Bradley blew out a breath. "I can't protect her from skilled professionals. There's no way to cover all the angles. And she wouldn't be any better off in FBI protective custody, or US Marshal witness security. He has people who can get to her no matter where she is."

"So what's the answer? I can't help, because you need her to maintain her high profile. If she's murdered now it will raise entirely too many questions. Ones he won't want answered."

"He'll blame it on you."

Steve thought for a second. "So I go elsewhere. Make it so I'm clearly in a different place. If she's hurt, then it can't be blamed on me."

Bradley shook his head. "You aren't seriously talking about letting her get hurt just so you have an avenue that covers your own butt, are you?"

"I'm just thinking it through. I can't leave town right now." Mrs. Cromwell needed help, at least until he could get assistance to come in. No one had called him back yet. "And we aren't going to be able to get evidence that it really is the vice president without me being here."

Bradley sighed. "I'm beginning to think this is a losing battle. What if he doesn't make a mistake? We won't have anything on him. He's too good. After all, he's managed to stay hidden for years."

"But right now, he wants his end to happen. He's on a timetable. The clock is going to run out."

"So what does he want so badly that he's pushing his agenda *now*?"

Steve said, "I haven't figured that out yet."

"You know you don't need to do this by yourself, right? The team is on it. Adrian and Megan are with the FBI gathering evidence and taking statements. Emma and Mint are going to collect what she had in her safe deposit box, and she's going to give a statement as well."

"It won't be enough."

"And Rachel."

Steve whipped his head around. "What about her?"

"She went to the VP's office to get into his computer. To get proof it's him."

"And?"

"She didn't manage to get it this time. But that doesn't mean she'll quit trying."

He sighed. "So far all we know is that the VP was in Venezuela as a kid, that he was the son of missionaries." Maybe he should pay his house a visit. Perhaps there was something there that could be used to convict him. "I should go."

"You're not listening to me. We're going to do this. Us. The team. Double Down."

"If anything happens to me," Steve said, "you should know, I left the company to you."

It seemed like Bradley was already running the show in his absence. The transition would take a little paperwork, and their lives could continue as they were.

The punch came out of nowhere. A solid right hook that knocked him to his back. He steadied himself in time to see Bradley rush at him.

He hit Steve with the force of a three-hundred pound linebacker. Steve blinked and saw stars. "Get off me."

"You think you're going to die? I'll kill you myself. After I kick your butt from here to Nebraska!"

They wrestled, rolling around on the snowy grass. Bradley got an uppercut in Steve's ribs. Steve retaliated by locking his friend up with his legs and arms, a wrestling move. But not regulation. It had a side of fighting dirty to it. He squeezed.

"Stop it!" Rachel's voice rang out.

"Get back inside, Rach. Please." That was Alexis.

Bradley dug his thumbs into a tendon that made Steve's right leg go numb. They rolled and Bradley's weight squashed the injury on Steve's arm. He moaned, unable to keep it in this time.

"Stop hurting each other!"

Bradley exhaled. Steve loosened his grip so his friend didn't pass out. Bradley rolled to his back on the grass beside him.

"Well?" Rachel demanded.

Steve wanted to ask, "What?" but didn't have the breath to do it.

"Do you feel better?" She asked it like it was a bad thing.

"Yes," Bradley said. "I do."

Steve found his breath. "Me too."

"Well you look like children. Get up!" Her demand rang across the yard. She started to yell again, but gunshots blasted.

The girls dropped, diving back inside. Bradley crouch ran after them. Instinct driving him to protect them. Good. They needed that when faced with something like this.

Steve pulled his gun and rolled away from the house. Found the flash of light indicating the muzzle blast. When he was clear of the shots, he headed for the source.

Chapter 4

"I'm Special Agent Adrian Walker." He pulled out the metal chair and sat. Motioned toward the woman leaning against the wall in the corner. "This is Megan Perkins. She's consulting with the FBI on this case."

Captain Charles St. Germaine—his mother was French—sat across the table. Street clothes, but pressed, despite living in FBI protective custody for the past three weeks. Pinched face, pale skin. Put him in a tailored suit and he'd fit perfectly in a board meeting—or at a dinner party with a cigarette in one hand.

On a Navy ship? Not so much. Despite his years of service, Adrian just didn't get that feel from this guy. He was at least fifteen years older than Adrian, who was himself pushing late thirties. Megan looked younger than she was, which had played in her favor as an undercover agent. Now she was in his life permanently, and Adrian had a ring burning a hole in his suitcase back at the hotel.

He'd promised himself he wouldn't ask her to marry him until this whole thing was resolved. She wasn't safe right now, and neither was he. The man behind those who had terrorized her was still out there. And that wasn't even their biggest problem right now.

Charles's expression turned bored. He stared at his fingernails.

"You were targeted by Daniel Zimmerman, along with Rear Admiral Frampton," Adrian said.

"And I've been stuck in protective custody ever since." He didn't lift his gaze, just kept looking at his nails.

"You'd rather be set loose where he can get to you again?"

"Zimmerman is dead." Charles glanced up then. He shifted his hand to point at Adrian. "Didn't you hit him with your car, or something?"

Adrian winced. It had been a split second decision, made before Zimmerman could bring down the plane Megan had been on. As it was, the aircraft had crashed. She was recovering still and used crutches most of the time—unless she was interviewing. It was why she leaned against the wall now. Though, he'd rather she sat.

Charles glanced between them.

"Why would he target you?" Adrian asked.

They knew the blackmailer wanted this man dead because of his involvement in an operation in Venezuela years ago. Besides the fact many people were killed, there wasn't much they knew about the secret mission. It was all classified. Some of the details had been uncovered, but there wasn't much not redacted past the code name given to the operation and the village where it happened.

A village the vice president had lived in with his missionary parents.

Which meant he'd been there.

It wasn't conclusive proof he was the blackmailer, but it was as close as they had come so far to finding the source of so much carnage and destruction. What else could it be but some kind of revenge plot?

Charles sniffed. "How would I know?"

"Because you were there, Mr. St. Germaine."

"Where?"

He insisted on playing it this way? "Venezuela in the eighties. Sebana to be precise. You must have been barely into your twenties, but we know that for some reason you were part of the planning for this mission. Maybe you didn't join the op. Your entire military record is sealed, Captain. I have no idea your skill set or area of expertise. But I'm guessing you weren't just the sous chef on the boat."

"They are ships."

"Whatever." Adrian flipped open a folder and turned a photo around. "This is Special Agent Zimmerman's wife and children. After they were found."

All three had been shot.

Charles had the decency to wince at least. Adrian said, "This happened as a result of that operation in Sebana. People were murdered. I don't know why but that much devastation does not go unnoticed, and yet no one even mentioned it. Until now. I'm asking *you* what happened back then. Why did the US undertake this mission on Venezuelan soil?"

He wanted to also demand the reason why someone would, so many years later, target those involved. Why they would also target the children of those people. He wanted to know what was so compelling that kids had been murdered. Why Megan and Rachel, and so many more, had been terrorized. But people like the blackmailer didn't care about the fallout—or who got caught in it.

The vice president—Adrian could hardly believe it was him behind all this—had suffered some kind of traumatic event, right? Years later he'd been triggered into taking that trauma out on those responsible. Adrian still didn't have a better answer than that as to why it was all happening *now*.

Most cases he'd investigated, Adrian didn't care why. But this had affected Megan in a way he could feel just by looking at her.

He wanted answers.

Charles leaned back in his chair, still bored. "The country was destabilizing. The economy was tanking, and people didn't like it. Used to be Venezuela was one of the richest countries in the world. Now?" He shrugged.

"And the mission?"

"Nothing that would cause someone to want me dead. Not that mission, anyway."

"We think someone who was there on that day is after revenge," Adrian said. "It would explain why he's targeting those present as well as those who helped plan the mission. It was a joint venture, right? More than one branch of the military and the CIA? Feds?"

Charles said, "Lot of operations I was involved in were. CIA contact, military boots on the ground as backup." He smiled, but the expression held nothing pleasant. "I have lived an interesting life."

"I figured that kind of cooperation was scared into the higher-ups of every government agency and the military after 9/11. Didn't know it happened even back then."

Charles shrugged. "Didn't say it was a friendly arrangement. Mostly one group show-boated because they thought they were better than everyone else."

"And then civilians get caught in the middle. Innocent people in the wrong place at the wrong time."

"What do I care? You guys will find him and, until then, I don't have to listen to my daughter whining about how I'm not a good enough grandpa. Like it's my fault the kid doesn't look like any of us."

Adrian said, "You aren't worried he might target her?"

"Do the world a favor."

He didn't react to that cold assessment. At least not outwardly. Inside, his stomach roiled. Who thought that about their own daughter and grandchild? Adrian needed to find them and make sure they were all right, not being used as some kind of leverage in this massive game. He wasn't certain Charles would care.

They'd only just uncovered the playing pieces, and he wasn't convinced they had all of them yet. What strategy the blackmailer utilized was another question entirely.

"What was the mission, Charles?"

He sneered. "Same as every other mission back then. Get the money, take out the opposition. Level the playing field."

Like that was supposed to make sense. "Who was the opposition in this case?"

"Cartel. It's always the cartel. Back then they were no better than feudal lords. Now it's worse since the economy tanked and the whole country is nothing but a giant cesspit." Charles brushed his hand across the table. "Don't know why you care so much."

"Maybe because innocent lives are in danger."

Charles shrugged. "Probably deserve it."

Adrian pointed to the photo. Zimmerman's family. "Did they deserve this?"

The man across the table was a decorated military officer. By all accounts a hero. How he had even passed psychological evaluation was anyone's guess.

"Maybe they did," Charles said. "How am I supposed to know?"

"Who is behind all this carnage?" Adrian was convinced now that Charles St. Germaine knew the identity of the man. "He tried to have you killed. Who is he?"

"Wasn't killed, was I?"

"Not for lack of him trying. He sent Zimmerman halfway across the country to destroy a building you'd have been in if I hadn't sent word your life was in danger."

"Yeah, heard about that. Another dirty FBI agent messing things up." He glanced at Megan, then back at Adrian. "I figure one is just a sign that all of them are the same. Infected."

"Not worried he'll try again?"

Charles said, "I've made my peace. Maybe you should call Frampton and tell him to make his."

Adrian folded the file shut and swept out the door, Megan right behind him. He said, "He doesn't leave until I'm done," to the Marshal standing beside the door. The man probably bristled at being given an order, but Adrian didn't wait around to see. He went straight to the desk of the closest agent by a phone.

"I want a real-time check on Rear Admiral Frampton. I think the blackmailer is going to go at him again, try and kill him."

"Okay." The agent snapped up his phone and dialed a number written on one of the papers on his desk. After a few seconds he said, "No answer."

He tried three different numbers, the agents on duty.

Adrian said, "Keep trying. Call local police if you have to and get them there."

There were both Marshals and FBI agents on detail protecting Frampton at the safe house where he'd been stashed. Not even Adrian knew the location. They were either already dead, or at the least, they'd been pinned down and were unable to answer the phone.

He turned back to the interview room where Charles sat.

Through the glass of the window Adrian watched the man's mouth turn up into a sick, humorless smile.

"Walker."

He turned back to the agent at the phone. "What is it?"

"I had local cops dispatched to the scene. There was a unit a mile away." His face was grim. As though he disliked the taste of what he was saying rolling off his tongue. "One of them answered the phone. He said it's nothing but carnage. They're all dead."

Megan slipped her hand into his.

"He's sending over pictures now. Says they were all shot twice, chest and head. Marshals, our agents and the Rear Admiral are all dead."

"Professional hits."

The agent nodded his agreement.

"He's not messing around anymore," Megan said. "He's serious about taking out anyone who knows about him."

Adrian squeezed her hand, but spoke to the agent, "If we get any evidence at all, it won't point to anyone local. Likely it'll be former military, maybe foreign."

The agent's eyebrows rose. "So how do we get evidence on this guy?"

Adrian had been forced to parse out information so far. If he said the words "vice president" he would get laughed out of this office—especially considering he had no proof. "The blackmailer has gone unchecked for this long because there has been little to no evidence on him, or anything he's done. We have to figure out the answer to that question so we can nail him."

The agent glanced over his shoulder at the captain, still in the interview room. A man who'd known this was going to happen. "But now we have someone connected to him in custody, right?"

Megan said, "He isn't going to give up the blackmailer's name, if he even knows it."

Adrian said, "I have an idea about that."

"Wha—"

He twisted to look over his shoulder at the marshal. He called out in an unmistakable, loud voice, "Cut that scum bag loose. I want him out of my sight."

. . .

"Wait until I open your door." Mint climbed out of the car he'd rented under an alias that couldn't be connected to anything. He rounded the car and checked every angle on the street, then all rooftops.

Only then did he open her door, one hand close to the gun strapped to his hip.

"You're doing it again."

Mint scanned the area. He continued to do it as he shut the door behind her. When she started toward the bank, he laid one hand on the small of her back.

"Malone."

Use of his real name was enough to catch his attention. Not his first name, which he'd told her his father used. "Yes, Emma?"

She ascended the huge marble steps to the front door of the bank. "Are you ever going to stop assuming a threat will, at any moment, spring from behind cover and take us out?"

"It'll take *you* out."

"Not if I dive at you and cover you."

Mint didn't even want to address the ridiculousness of that. Which one of them was trained former military anyway? "If you're asking whether I'm going to stop protecting you from potential danger, the answer is no."

"Even when this is done?" She stopped at the front door and glanced up at him.

"I'm thinking when we have kids I'll need to hire a team. And it'll be easier if we homeschool. Less variables."

She swung around, tipped up on the balls of her feet and kissed him, square on the lips. "I love you."

She didn't argue with him. Didn't make his life more difficult. She wanted to be part of the tactical decisions he made so that she could understand his motivations. What she *didn't* do was tell him his fears were silly, or try to convince him to figure out how to turn them off.

"Love you too." He glanced at her. The hand she'd placed on his cheek was her left. Her eyes strayed to it, as they often did these days when she pulled this exact move. Taking in the understated diamond on her left ring finger.

What followed was a softening of her gaze, the subtle shift of her lips. A fresh realization of exactly what that meant. To both of them.

But they were still out in the open. Exposed. He pulled the door open and ushered her in.

She shot him a smile. "Thank you, kind sir."

He followed her into the bank, a smile tugging on his own lips. Mint hadn't smiled all that much before she came into his life. There hadn't been reason to, so why bother expending the energy it took to even pretend to be happy? Now there was reason.

She was teaching him to enjoy his life. Because she was a part of it now, it actually worked. Hopefully he was teaching her to be more cautious. More aware of her surroundings. They would get to self-defense and weapons training soon enough.

The bank manager was summoned.

Emma said, "I'd like access to my safety deposit box, please."

The place she'd stashed all the communications she'd had from the blackmailer and everything else she'd thought relevant from that time. The files of recorded phone calls were with Aaron Jones. He was dead now, a patsy for the blackmailer. The financial records she kept were for a dead senator.

Pieces of this puzzle.

The manager checked her ID and confirmed she had the right passcode—which reassured Mint this place knew what they were doing. It was too easy to fake ID and steal a key.

He trailed her down hallways. Yes, he looked like a bodyguard, but did he care? She was alive. And she was going to stay that way until they were ninety-whatever and they died in their sleep at the same time. Corny, maybe. His life goal? Definitely. He didn't care what it said about him. Mint was private security, and she was the most important client he would have for the rest of his life.

The manager used his own key. Emma used hers. The manager slid the long rectangular box out, and then moved out of the room. "Take your time."

Emma watched over Mint's shoulder until the man was gone. He put his hand on her shoulder, just because she'd appreciate it. And because he could. Having her was like winning the best prize he could have—

"Mint."

He shook off the daze. She'd distracted him, and distractions were going to get her killed. He needed to focus. "What?"

Her eyebrows lifted.

He lowered his voice. "Sorry. What is it?"

"The box." She tipped it in his direction. "It's empty."

Chapter 5

Steve chased the shooter down the street. The man had jumped into the same car Steve had spotted earlier watching the house. Couldn't pass up the chance to kill all four of them? Whoever the guy was, he'd balked at the last minute. Apparently not prepared for the level of force that immediately retaliated back at him.

The car sped away. Steve slowed to a stop and hung his head, breathing hard. But why stop at all? It wasn't like he had business returning to the house. The cops would show up and he would only get arrested.

Steve pulled out his burner phone and texted Bradley.

Anyone hurt?

A few seconds later he got a reply.

Just bruises.

Steve stowed the phone and headed for Mrs. Cromwell's house. It was better than standing still on the sidewalk and wishing he could go back to Rachel. Make sure they were all okay. Bradley would be fussing over Alexis. He would take care of his sister as well, but Steve couldn't deny he wanted to be there.

Then again, he also wanted to walk right to the vice president's house and bang on the door. Finally have it out with the man. Would William Anderson call the cops when Steve showed up? Probably. He also had a contingent of Secret Service on site who would stop Steve before he even got close.

Lost cause.

They weren't going to let him punch the VP square in his smug face. As much as Steve wanted to do exactly that. Maybe more. Couldn't happen.

Then again, they claimed he was a threat. A killer. Why not make that real clear and just kill the guy? Make himself nothing but a self-fulfilling prophecy.

He'd certainly done enough awful things in his life, even if they weren't unlawful. He'd been an active CIA agent for years. Trained. He'd gone on missions precisely like the one responsible for the vice president's foray into blackmail and murder. Did that make either of them right? No. Life wasn't black and white, right or wrong. There were so many shades of gray. Good people did bad things and bad people did good.

Steve was only responsible for his own actions and reactions.

Instead of going back to Mrs. Cromwell, he walked all the way to the vice president's house. So much walking he was going to have sore legs tomorrow. But that was the way in Washington DC. You either drove everywhere and ended up stuck in traffic, or you walked.

Outside of the Secret Service's surveillance perimeter, Steve crouched. His watch said it was a little past midnight. His fingers were chilled, his nose going numb with the cold of December.

He waited there long enough to ascertain the Secret Service were sticking to a pattern he knew. Steve pulled a device out of his backpack, and turned it on. It would temporarily disable the heat sensors. He'd have to work around the security lights, but Mrs. Anderson didn't like them on all the time at night. They were often turned off altogether to prevent the flash from turning on because a squirrel crossed the sensor beam.

And how did he know that?

The person who'd been tasked with attempting to test the security set up at the VP's Washington residence was him.

One of Double Down's many physical security tests. And it seemed like they hadn't made many changes since then, despite the comprehensive report Steve had issued to the Secret Service about the security at the house, giving him intimate knowledge of the setup. Steve figured they should've tweaked at least something. Considering he was a fugitive.

Steve scaled the brick wall and used the cover of bushes and trees to make his way to the back of the shed. He checked that his device was still working, disabling the security cameras. Soon enough, whoever was on security would check. They would figure out what the problem was and sound the alarm.

He waited until the right break in rolling patrols and sprinted to the outside wall of the house. Steve used a lock pick kit to enter the French doors that led from the patio on the west side of the house into the vice president's study. So the man could look at the trees while he contemplated the fate of the country—or how to victimize more people.

The desktop was bare. Steve would only have seconds at most, so he went straight for the safe. A couple of jewelry boxes. A zippered pouch containing…probably a few hundred. File folders. He took pictures of the contents to look at later.

At the back was a leather bound book. A photo album. Steve flipped through the pictures and found they were of William Anderson's parents. Their mission where they'd preached the word of God in a small Venezuelan town.

Until that town was massacred.

They smiled for the camera. Small children surrounded them, all happy. William stood tall beside his father. On the other end of the row of four Anderson's was another boy, smaller than William. A younger brother?

That wasn't something that had come up in the background checks. Not the ones anyone had run on the VP's history. Steve took a photo with his phone. Could be relevant.

He kept flipping, aware that time was quickly running out. More photos of their family. The church people. William and another boy, a Venezuelan. Best friends? Steve took a few more pictures with the camera on his phone.

Two connections. People who knew everything about what the vice president had gone through? Confidants. Accomplices. One possibly his brother, the other a Venezuelan. Assuming they were still alive—though he'd never heard anything about a younger brother—and able, they could be in league with him. Or prepared to testify against him.

He stowed the belongings back in the safe and put everything back in its place. Was there really a brother out there, somewhere? The Venezuelan could have grown up to be *El Cuervo*. He was dead now, but Steve had been tasked with helping him escape that restaurant. Someone the blackmailer had wanted safeguarded.

Halfway to the patio door, he saw a flash of movement. Steve hugged the wall, out of sight. Not a roving patrol whiling away the night hours. This person moved with purpose. With intention. Who was it, and where were they going?

A scream rang out. Not from outside, this came from somewhere in the house. Yelling followed. Then the muffled shouts of multiple Secret Service agents. Steve stayed where he was. An escalation from "normal" to there being a situation would mean everyone was on alert now. He didn't need to rush this and end up being spotted trying to get off the property.

He moved in a steady pace to the patio door, intending to slip out. The door opened. Steve drew the curtain and ducked behind it in one move. The light flipped on inside the room. He took one slow breath and let it out silently.

Then he eased the handle down and moved outside.

Air blew in, a cool breeze that shifted the curtain.

"Freeze!"

Steve fired a couple of shots. He aimed high, so they'd hit the ceiling and not a person, and then he ran. Pumped his arms and legs and raced across the grass to the wall. He jumped, still running, and his trailing leg slammed the wall. He ignored the crack of pain and flipped his body over the wall.

He raced into the street a second before he realized those blinding lights coming at him were a car. The far corner glanced off his hip, spinning him around with the momentum. He landed on his backside in the street and rolled. But not before he caught a look at the driver.

Rachel.

A shot rang out.

The Secret Service agent who raced after him had jumped the wall.

Steve clambered to his feet and kept running. Mostly just trying to escape the mess that he'd made of his life.

. . .

Rachel blinked. Her foot slipped off the brake, and the Secret Service agent raced in front of the car. Too fast for her to do anything.

Could she have hit a fed on purpose? The way she'd hit Steve. Rachel touched her head to the steering wheel between her hands. What had she been thinking anyway, coming here? Apparently the same as Steve, except for the fact he'd wound up being chased by an armed agent. She only wanted to talk to William Anderson. Demand the reasoning behind the fact she'd been shot at tonight.

Her hip still hurt from when she'd flung Alexis to the floor.

Today was turning out to be a day for bruises. Enough to make her stiff tomorrow at the office. If she managed to make it back home tonight.

Rachel pressed the gas and drove into the vice president's property. She showed her ID. When the guard said it wasn't a good time she said, "Nonsense," and kept driving past him. Maybe he wouldn't shoot at her car. Or arrest her.

She'd discovered in the past few years that rather than attempt to persuade people she was in the right place—and that she knew what she was talking about—it was more effective to pretend you knew exactly where you were. "Fake it till you make it" was a valid option in Washington politics. Too bad it had spilled over to other parts of her life.

She parked away from the front door so she didn't block anyone important. It occurred to her that Steve could have hurt someone. She hoped not. She wanted to believe he wouldn't do something like that, but these were exigent circumstances. He'd been effectively pinned against a wall. Accused. Implicated. Some of it he'd actually done. Some of it he would take the blame for, simply because of who he'd been before she met him. She'd found out as much as her clearance level would allow, and had actually uncovered information on a couple of missions he'd been involved in as an officer for the CIA.

It had only made her prouder.

A ham-sized fist pounded on her window, jolting her out of her Steve-daze. "Ma'am."

She cracked the door and climbed out, shoving him out of the way with the door. "It's *Senator*, actually. Rachel Harris."

"Of course." Like that was obvious to him. Was she supposed to know who knew her and who didn't?

Before he could say anything else, she demanded, "What happened here tonight?"

If he knew much about her, as he seemed to think he did, he should know she was connected to Steve. A few reporters looking into this whole situation had uncovered the link to her and Bradley. Their story—parents killed, sister victimized and then kidnapped, brother part of the rescue—as well as Bradley's tale of long lost love with Alexis had all replayed over and over again in the media the past few weeks.

She was waiting for them to offer to turn her story into a made-for-TV movie.

"A woman was killed." The agent lifted his chin. "Sure you want to get involved in that?"

She blinked. "Killed by who?"

"The perpetrator hasn't been formally identified as yet."

He was going to brush her off with the "official" blurb? There probably wasn't even an investigation. Yet. And he was blowing her off?

Rachel said, "Was it Steve Perkins?"

"Why would you mention him, specifically?"

Rachel wasn't going to hide it. Not when it would come out. "I saw him running across the street. I actually hit him with my car, and then one of your agents ran after him."

The agent nodded.

"Who was killed? Did Steve do it?" She tried to sound concerned for the victim, but probably wasn't far from it being really obvious she would defend her friend. Why try to gloss over the truth? Most law enforcement personnel and feds, plus most of Washington, thought she was losing it, mentally. After all, they figured, how could she possibly heal from what had been done to her? They thought she had to be a pitiable victim for the rest of her life. Rather than actually have the chance to move on, find peace.

"Ma'am—"

She waved a hand. "Fine. You aren't going to help me." So much for finding out what had happened. Steve sure wasn't going to tell her. She didn't even know where he'd gone. Where he'd been staying.

Her eyes filled with tears just thinking about whether or not Steve had access to a safe place. "At least tell me whether or not it was the vice president's wife who was killed. Is Mrs. Anderson all right?" She moved closer and her voice hitched when she said, "I'd hate for anything to have happened to my friend."

Faced with a distraught woman, the Secret Service agent went into protective male mode. Worked every time. Especially lately, when people now knew what she'd been through. Yes, she was playing people who assumed she still should act like a victim. But it was effective.

"It wasn't Mrs. Anderson." He touched her elbow for a second, then let his hand drop back to his side. "Just between you and me…it was the housekeeper. She got up to get a snack, and someone stabbed her."

Rachel gasped. "Goodness me."

He nodded slowly. "It's a tragedy. Especially considering it was her daughter who found her. Both of them live on the east wing of the house. They were going to have a late-night snack after their movie ended. She's falling apart now."

Rachel couldn't imagine finding her mother like that. How old was the girl?

It had been bad enough hearing about her parent's deaths after the fact. They had gone on a trip, and their small plane was caught in bad weather. She'd been in college. Alexis had been her roommate at the time. Bradley was off on some SEALs training mission. The three of them had never been closer than when they were grieving.

Bradley and Alexis had even managed to set aside the weirdness between them. For a while, anyway.

Her phone buzzed against her hip. She pulled it from her pocket and looked at the screen. A text from a private number.

Tell me you aren't still there.

It immediately buzzed again.

Meet me at our diner. NOW.

He really didn't need to yell at her. What was wrong with asking nicely?

"That's why you can't stay here. This has to be an investigation, and we can't have any outside interferences." The agent had the decency to wince. "You'll have to leave, Senator."

"Of course. I understand." She got back in her car while he stared at her with raised eyebrows. Yeah, so maybe she was playing into the whole "unhinged" thing by acting erratically. But she really didn't want to be here, or part of a murder investigation.

Why would the housekeeper need to be killed?

She wanted to trust that Steve hadn't done it. So either it was completely unrelated to what was happening here—unlikely—or it had been done during a time he was in the house for a reason. In order to add more fuel to the fire? Make him look guiltier than he actually was, considering he hadn't killed anyone.

Yet.

At least she hoped he hadn't, and wouldn't have to either. Steve deserved better than that.

She maneuvered her car around the circular driveway. Two police cars and a coroner's van passed her on the street, headed for her house. When all of this had become her normal life, she didn't know. She'd wanted to do what she was good at *and* be able to make a difference in the world. Was that too much to ask?

What better way to help people than to be instrumental in turning the tide of the great government machine.

Somewhere along the way, she'd been dragged down into the petty taking of sides. Her attempt to be honorable was essentially ignored. Now her name meant nothing, and not because she'd done anything to drag it through the mud. She *had* been a victim. A fact the blackmailer was going to have to answer to.

When they finally managed to bring him down.

Chapter 6

Steve stood up out of the booth the minute she stepped inside. He waited by the table while she hurried over, her cheeks flushed. Not sure what to say, he opened his mouth anyway. She shook her head and didn't stop walking. Rachel collided with him. She wrapped her arms around his waist and laid her head on his collarbone.

Steve wanted to shut his eyes and savor the moment. He lowered his head so he could speak quietly, close to her ear. "You okay?"

She nodded, her arms tightened a fraction, and she let him go. "I should be asking you that. I hit you with—"

The waitress wandered over.

Steve shook his head. "I'm okay."

She poured them both decaf coffee, and he topped up Rachel's with cream. When the waitress was no longer within earshot, he said, "What happened at the house?"

"Nothing." She held the mug with both hands, probably to warm her fingers. Outside it looked like it was threatening to snow. "They said the housekeeper was killed."

"That's more than I know."

She blinked.

"Which you'd be able to guess, considering you'll know I didn't kill her." He measured his words. Then said, "Right?"

She lifted her hands, then placed her head in her palms. Steve let her have her moment. She looked exhausted. He didn't have any ill feeling toward her, not even frustration. They'd both been through some insane things.

Finally she lifted her head. "I know you didn't kill her. You would never hurt an innocent person."

He was glad she'd added that qualifier, though the label "innocent" was entirely subjective. In the right circumstances, he absolutely would kill. He would, and he had. Not the kind of thing a person kept tally of, but it wasn't a small number. Knowing that gave him a sense of control over his feelings. A detachment he needed to stay removed from the guilt.

Most of the time it worked.

"Bradley said there were bruises."

She shifted in her seat and winced. "I landed on my hip when I tugged Alexis to the floor."

Steve nodded. "I'm glad you're all right."

"The cops came, and we explained it had nothing to do with you." She sighed. "You'd think nothing even happened, for all the action they took. Except my house has bullet holes in the siding. No shooter. No one hurt. They didn't even write anything down. Bradley was *mad*."

Steve would have been as well.

"They basically insinuated I might've made the whole thing up, until Bradley yelled at them that he'd been there. Alexis managed to talk him off the cliff so he didn't get arrested for being belligerent with the cops, but they weren't happy." She blew out another breath. "None of us were. I told them to leave if they weren't going to do anything about it."

"How'd you end up at the VP's house?"

Her cheeks pinked. "How did *you*?"

He smiled. "I'm a fugitive. What's your excuse for heading there to snoop around?"

Her face washed with something that looked a whole lot like guilt. The good kind, from trying to do the right thing. Not the kind that either of them lived with every day, that soul-deep ache signifying the stain of sin. "I just want this to be done. Hacking his office computer for Remy didn't work. I was going to try his home." But she shivered then, and gave away her real feelings.

"I don't want you near him, Rach." He could see it made her sick to even think about being near the vice president. And why not? William Anderson had victimized her in the worst way.

He could hardly tell her to stay out of this.

Steve said, "It's clear he's targeting you. That guy who attacked you—"

She made a face like she didn't know who he was talking about.

"The man in the alley with the knife this morning."

She shook her head. "Was that seriously this morning?"

He said, "I know. But that man was there to kill you, not kidnap you. You're a target. I'd rather you laid low until this whole thing is done." When she started to argue, he lifted a hand. "One sec. Because you need to understand something." He paused. "I'm a whole lot more distracted not knowing where you are, and worrying about whether you're all right. I don't expect that to change, but I'd at least like to know that you're protected."

"I don't want the Secret Service up in my space all the time." She bit her lip. "I know it was just one guy who sold me out, but I can't separate him from the rest of the agents. If one can turn on me and something happens again, I don't know what I'll do."

He laid his hand on hers and said, "I know. Me either."

"I don't trust them. And I know that doesn't make logical sense, but I have to go with what I feel, until I can sort it all out." She paused. "I'm working on it."

"Good." He knew she was seeing a counselor, and he had thoroughly vetted the woman. "I can call some friends of mine, if you want. Ask them to come and stay with you. Make sure your space is secure, and that you're safe getting back and forth from where you need to be." He asked it like it was a question, but the truth was he already had them keeping an eye on her...and the rest of his team. As of this afternoon, he'd put it in place—after his heart almost stopped seeing her with a knife to her throat.

Steve didn't want to take any chances. Not with any of their lives.

She brushed her hair back. The woman was exhausted, and he was keeping her up.

"By the time you reach your bed, you'll probably sleep until dinner."

Her eyes lit, but she shook her head. "Too bad I have a meeting at eight in the morning. I'd have enjoyed working from home." She grinned.

In another life, he'd have taken her to a different restaurant—and not in the middle of the night. He'd have worn a suit, and maybe persuaded her to wear that blue dress from last Christmas. Things would have been a whole lot different without the blackmailer messing with their lives so thoroughly that he couldn't even imagine being more than a friend to her.

And how could he even have that much with her? This was probably all wishful thinking. Trying to fabricate a connection between them when it was the last thing either needed. The fact that she knew him would surely blow up in their faces. No one cared that they'd never been more than friends.

Not that he hadn't wanted it. Rachel was the dream that life would never let him have. There were too many reasons why they could never be closer than two friends supporting each other. And Steve didn't need Bradley to tell him what he already knew.

He didn't need his friend telling him to back off Rachel.

She lowered her cup. "Those are some seriously deep thoughts."

He was grateful she'd let him sit in silence, rather than force conversation. So many women chattered just to fill the silence. Steve enjoyed quiet, and the chance to think. Especially during a time like this.

He reached over and squeezed her hand. "I was just—"

His phone buzzed across the table. He'd laid it facedown. Not that doing so made it more polite.

She motioned to it. "See what it is. It's fine."

If circumstances had been anything else, Steve would have ignored it. This was the kind of woman you shut your phone off to spend time with. No distractions, full focus.

Maybe one day.

He flipped the phone over to see what had come in, since the buzzing had stopped now. Not a call. It was an email. The lock screen displayed the address as unknown@unknown.com.

He frowned, and swiped to see the message.

An address, and the specifications for a high-powered sniper rifle. A date—three days from now. A time, and place.

Target: the president.

Steve shot out of his chair.

"What—"

He said nothing, just strode to the back door of the restaurant. When he stepped outside, he started running.

The blackmailer had given Steve his task. The reason why Steve had been co-opted into this whole thing in the first place.

He was supposed to assassinate the president.

.   .   .

The next morning Rachel left her meeting and headed back to her office in the Rayburn building. She traveled in the tunnels that stretched under the street between her office and the Capitol building. It was old hat now. But seeing tourists, and their wonder, never got old.

She entered her office just before ten, and her intern glanced over from the computer.

"Morning." The smile was polite, but distracted.

Rachel started to remove her coat. "Anything interesting happen while I was gone?"

The young woman shook her head. Rachel didn't run a stuffy office like some senators did. She was fine with her people dressing down on occasion. Especially when interns like Ellayna walked all around the building giving tours. No point in wearing fancy shoes when they would be uncomfortable.

Rachel loved that people came all the way here from their homes just to see what they did. Her home state might be Virginia, and her parents' house that she and Bradley inherited was there, but DC was a cosmopolitan city. People wanted to get a look at how it all worked.

"Not that I'm going to tell you before I make you a cup of coffee." The intern got up. "You look a little…"

"Wrecked?" Rachel laughed and made her way through the tight winding hall back to her office. The other two women who worked for her were on the phones. She waved to both of them.

"I wasn't going to *say*." Ellayna dragged the word out, following her, and Rachel could hear the smile in her voice.

Rachel glanced back over her shoulder. "Honesty is always the best policy."

"What about, 'the truth hurts'?"

"I thought it was supposed to set you free?"

The intern shook her head. "I'm not sure I believe that. Sometimes it's better left uncovered because it's no one else's business."

Rachel was inclined to believe the same. God saw everything, so there was no point in trying to hide from Him, right? With people, it was an entirely different story.

She settled in her chair with a groan as the fatigue hit her. But was that the worst thing happening right now? Not hardly. She hadn't even asked how Steve was, and he had a knife wound! So selfish. Plus, she'd hit him with her car.

She was the worst friend ever.

Rachel ran her hands down her face. Sure, he'd ditched her in the diner and run off, but he didn't seem to have done it without good reason. She could hardly get mad at someone trying not to get captured. Trying to find evidence that would convict the man who'd destroyed her life.

Still.

No. She shook her head, even though she was alone now in her office. She wasn't going to think badly about Steve. She respected him way too much for that, and knew he never did anything without good reason.

Ellayna strolled in, carrying an extra-large size mug.

"You're a gem."

She set the cup down in front of Rachel.

"Seriously. I should give you a Christmas bonus."

The young woman laughed. "I won't say no."

Rachel shared a smile with her.

"I'll email you everything. There's nothing that won't wait five minutes. Or even long enough for a fifteen minute power nap." She headed for the door. "I'll make sure you get at least that much quiet time."

Rachel didn't have to smother the yawn. The door clicked shut, and she let it out in all its jaw-cracking, ear-popping glory.

She leaned back in her chair and ran through the details of the meeting she'd just come from. A legal pad in her drawer was a good place to make notes. Ellayna would be able to type them up for her. Rachel didn't love her computer.

Not since she'd first viewed the video of what happened to her on this very machine.

It made no sense that one event had changed her feelings about an inanimate object, but it was what it was. Her therapist was teaching her to accept her own feelings instead of dismissing them as inappropriate or misapplied. Or even just plain wrong. She had to work it through, and then get past them.

Her feelings for Steve, though? She didn't want to get past those. Seeing him, and having him hold her hand, had been more impactful to her than him saving her life on the street yesterday—even though that had been intense. When she'd sat across that diner table from him, it had made her wonder what could've happened between them had their lives not gone different directions.

Okay, so it was more like they'd been torn apart.

But whining at the unfairness of it all wasn't going to help. And it certainly wasn't going to fix the problem. *Any* of the problems she had right now.

Her dad had always told her to "buck up." Like pretending you were fine would fix what was wrong. But she knew what he meant. *Never let them see you break.* Well, it was too late for that.

She wanted to disappear from her life. Kind of the way Steve had done, but without the "wanted fugitive" part. Sooner or later the FBI and the Marshals hunting him would realize he'd never left DC, despite the trail he'd led them on away from here.

Rachel sipped her coffee and prayed. Couldn't hurt, right? Alexis, and now Bradley as well, always said it was the best thing to do. She wasn't going to tell them it did help her when her head got overwhelmed. Even if it was just ordering her thoughts as though she were communicating with someone else. Maybe God was real, and maybe He listened.

Her computer chimed. Rachel shook her mouse to see what was in the email from Ellayna. Tension knotted her muscles at the sight of new messages. But there was nothing from that address, the unknown@unknown.com she knew to be communication from the blackmailer.

She read through the email from Mrs. Anderson. The vice president's wife was surprised Rachel hadn't jumped on the opportunity they'd offered her to help victimized women. Considering what she'd been through, why wouldn't she? Rachel frowned. Was she supposed to always act and react the way other people expected her to? Because that was impossible.

The email from Ellayna was next.

`Senator Timmons wants to talk to you when you have a minute.`

The rest could wait. She knew what the Senator wanted, and he would accept nothing less than her immediate attention regarding his proposed bill. Rachel sucked down the rest of her coffee and decided this would be a whole lot better in person. Email just lacked the non-verbal communication that confirmed two people conveyed themselves clearly.

Plus, she was less likely to fall asleep at her desk if she was moving around.

She grabbed her suit jacket, slipped it back on, and pocketed her ID card. She swept past Ellayna and said, "I'm headed upstairs to Timmons's office."

"I'll hold down the fort."

Rachel nodded and hit the hallway. Before she was a senator, she'd never have imagined it involved this much walking. The talking—schmoozing—and the rest of it, yes. Walking? Not so much. She barely needed to work out, she got so many steps every day.

One floor up, she turned the corner for Senator Timmons's office and headed inside. The receptionist's desk, Ellayna's spot in Rachel's office, had a note on the top on a folded piece of paper that said, "Out to lunch. Back at 2pm."

Rachel frowned. Why would Timmons want to talk to her so much and then go to lunch? Were none of his staff here? She couldn't see anyone—

Out the corner of her eye, a bigger body rushed at her, nothing but a blur of movement.

She gasped, and he slammed her into the desktop. Office supplies went flying. The man tried to grab for her throat. Her arms came up on a reflex and blocked it. She didn't slam her head into his. That would hurt. She twisted and elbowed him in the face instead. Took a second to really look at him.

It was the same man from the alley. The man she got a feeling Steve might've known.

His fingers closed around her neck.

Rachel felt around on the desk with her hands. There had to be something she could use to...a letter opener.

Closing off all thought and any doubt over what she was about to do, Rachel swung it toward his body and slammed it into his ribs.

Chapter 7

Steve had called ahead. So when he ascended the stairs of the apartment building, Nicola already had the door open, watching for him. Her sculpted eyebrows lifted when she saw him.

Steve shook his head, passed her into the apartment and turned to face her. She closed the door and cocked a slender hip. "How did you know I wouldn't call the cops and have them waiting here for you this time?"

"I didn't." Because he trusted her? Maybe. Truth was, he didn't have many options left. And the ones he did have were quickly being pared down.

Nicola said, "Fine." She evidently wasn't going to waste time trying to convince him that he could trust her.

As a whole package she had drawn his attention three years ago when they'd first met. She played on her looks to get results in her work, work which garnered her the accolades hanging on her wall, alongside the picture of her with the Obamas, the one of her and the Canadian prime minister, and the one with the Dalai Lama.

She wore leggings he figured cost a couple of hundred dollars, along with an oversized sweater that hung loose on her slender frame. Aside from her looks and her work, there wasn't much to her. Something he'd found out after they had dated for a few months. She claimed their lack of things to talk about was due to being totally focused on her career.

Steve wasn't sure. But in a world of people who thought he was armed and dangerous, Nicola had seen a different side of him. He'd been a puzzle to her. She just hadn't wanted to lose that focus long enough to figure out the answers.

She trailed into the kitchen to where the coffee pot was trickling. "I haven't found anything on the men you served with under General Thomas, if that's what you're here about."

He shook his head and settled across the breakfast bar on a stool. The general had been the head of a task force Steve had worked with as part of his CIA career. Top Secret stuff, and nothing he was exactly proud of. The pinnacle of a career that didn't settle right with him.

Since starting Double Down, he'd actually been proud of the work he did. Now the company was in tatters and he was on the run. A fugitive.

The general had also been part of the Venezuela mission that had affected the VP enough to start this whole thing. Early in his career, he'd been on the team. Late in his career, when he'd aged into a grizzled old man with no patience for "young'uns," as he called the men he trained, Steve had crossed paths with him.

He'd learned a lot during that time and had the scars to prove it. What he didn't have was a way to speak to the man now. General Eric Thomas had been killed when a think tank was destroyed by a rogue FBI agent who had stolen a sonic weapon. Zimmerman had been blackmailed into doing it.

Now he was dead, and Steve had lost his chance to ask either of those men any questions, which had led him on a search to find the men he'd served with. Enter, Nicola. So far they had zip, except for the man Steve had seen try to kill Rachel. The blackmailer had gotten to them, the way he'd gotten to Steve.

She motioned to the coffee pot.

He shook his head. "Things have been escalated."

"They weren't bad enough already?"

Steve made a face. "I got an email. A mission."

She waited.

"You know the US/France summit on Monday?"

Nicola nodded. "I'm supposed to be there, reporting on it. Should be interesting."

His lips twitched. "I'm sure it will be, considering I'm supposed to kill the president of the United States."

She choked on the sip of coffee, lowered the cup and coughed. "You're…"

"He set me up with a gun." He stared at her. "I'm supposed to assassinate the president."

A fact he hadn't shared with Rachel. Yes, it felt strange telling it to Nicola now instead, but he was counting on her being more interested in work than her feelings. She wasn't going to get wrapped up in the emotion of him being trapped and hunted down by law enforcement. What he was hoping was that she would go public with everything he told her. That she would do what she did best—her job.

Rachel would give his heart what it needed. She would cry for him, support him and scream to everyone—if necessary—that he was innocent. Steve needed her in his corner because he loved her, and he wanted her behind him.

While he contemplated the fact that, yes, he did love Rachel, Nicola paced the kitchen. She blew out a breath. Started to say something. Shook her head and took up pacing again.

"I realize I've put you in danger just coming here…"

She waved away his concern. "I'm glad you did. This is big. Huge."

After all, he surmised, it was all about the story. He said, "I know who's behind it all."

"The blackmailer?"

He nodded. "I know who it is."

"Someone who wants the vice president to be sworn in as our commander in chief?"

Steve nodded again.

"Hmm."

He didn't know what that meant, but knew he'd given her a lot to think about. And she needed time to do just that. Would he have rather gone to Rachel? Sure. But what he needed was Nicola's ability to uncover answers—her authority to go public with the truth, married with her drive to be first but also one hundred percent accurate.

Whichever way this all shook out—and whether he was dead or in jail at the end of it, someone needed to know the truth.

Nicola had a voice.

"We could warn him, maybe," she said, like she was processing it all. "Or place an anonymous tip." She glanced at him. "You could refuse, but that will create a fallout you're not going to want."

He nodded. He'd kept her apprised of the blackmailer's activities thus far, at least what they could prove emphatically. She knew what happened to those who refused—like Zimmerman, whose family had been kidnapped and killed.

"You could miss."

He tipped his head to one side. "The fallout might still be the same, but I can probably set up contingencies for when that happens. Circumvent whatever he tries."

She said, "That's probably your best option."

"It isn't a good one, though. The people who have been coerced into taking shots at me and my friends are men I trained with." He'd only seen one face, but it made sense. "They've been doing exactly what you've suggested I do for the past couple of days. Not missing me, per se, but they've been warning me to be on my guard. If the blackmailer has them pinned down, it won't last much longer. They'll have to do some damage soon enough, or they'll suffer the same fallout."

"And we haven't been able to locate them." She frowned. "Though I didn't have a whole lot of time to look, and I had to keep it quiet."

Steve said, "The blackmailer probably has them moving around under the radar."

Nicola lifted a hand and scratched at her scalp, then ran her fingers through her hair. A light flickered. She dropped her hand back by her side.

The light settled high on her chest.

A single red dot over her heart.

"Gun!"

She'd been in war zones enough that the reaction was almost immediate. Nicola dropped to the ground at almost the same instant the glass of her kitchen window exploded.

He saw the shot hit her chest as she fell.

. . .

Rachel had been escorted by Secret Service to an out of the way room she hadn't even known existed. It looked like a police interrogation room, and she'd sat there for two hours before anyone showed up to speak to her. The one time she'd tried the door handle, she realized they'd locked her in.

The agent across the table was a man she'd seen before, but had never spoken to. Was he going to accuse her of being unhinged, like the other cops she'd given a statement to?

He settled in the chair. Didn't offer her a drink. Hadn't brought any papers with him. "I'm Agent Meeks."

"I'd like to say it's nice to meet you but…" She spread her fingers, palms up, on the table. There was blood on her hands. "I just killed a man in Senator Timms's office."

His face didn't change. No reaction at all to what she'd just said.

What he did was ask her about everything that led to her being in that office. She went all the way back to her meeting with the vice president yesterday morning and the attack afterwards—minus Steve's involvement.

Or the fact she'd met up with him later.

Her entire body felt like lead. It made her want to curl up on the floor and go to sleep. She was seriously dragging and had to rub the grit out of her eyes—without shifting her contacts out of place. Not an easy task when you were as tired as she was.

"I see."

"Yeah." She lost her Washington DC Senator thing for a moment. "You could say I've had a rough week." She didn't wait for him to ask his next question. "Do you have any idea who he was?"

"I haven't heard back on his identity yet."

Was that even the truth?

He said, "But he appears to have been military. Which begs the question—how did you managed to overpower him so quickly?"

She blew out a breath. "Instinct? My brother trained me in all kinds of hand-to-hand, and he signed me up for a gym years ago. Not one of those fitness places with treadmills and yoga classes. It's a dojo. I've been taking Krav Maga."

His gray eyebrows rose.

Rachel shrugged. "He wanted me to know how to protect myself."

Which probably cut Bradley up even more, considering it hadn't worked.

"The man was a professional who weighed nearly a hundred pounds more than you."

She said, "It isn't about brute force. I acted on instinct, grabbed the first thing my fingers found and used it against him. The alternative was to allow him to choke me to death before anyone found me."

He nodded slowly. "I see."

The door flung open and the vice president rushed in. Anderson looked enraged. "What is this, an interrogation?"

The agent sputtered.

"This woman was nearly *killed*," his voice rose. His face flushed and he moved to her, holding his hand out. "Let's get you some tea and somewhere comfortable to sit."

Her whole insides shrank, then her stomach flipped over. She was pretty sure she didn't manage to hold in all of her reaction. Rachel pushed the chair back and stood. She didn't take his hand. She walked past the vice president without giving the agent any more attention. He didn't need to see what was probably on her face.

And it wasn't just the residual terror of nearly being strangled.

The vice president's wife waited in the hall. She gasped when she saw Rachel. "Your throat!" She even reached out.

Rachel touched her own neck, not realizing until now how much it hurt. Her voice had sounded thick and scratchy. She turned away from Mrs. Anderson's grasp. They were going to have to accept her detachment.

Her strides were fast. She was aware of their eyes on her, plus those of a number of Secret Service agents. Security for the building. Office staff poking heads out of their rooms.

She wanted to run.

Kick off her pumps and tear out the front door of this building. Run to the Metro station around the corner and get lost somewhere, wander around. Find an airport. Fly to Tahiti.

Anywhere had to be better than here.

Ellayna rushed at her. "I'm so sorry." The agents around them closed in. "They think I set you up. That I knew what was going to happen when I sent you that email. I didn't know Senator Timmons was at lunch! How could I have known?"

Rachel didn't know what to say. The VP stepped in beside her. "Senator Harris has been through enough. Let's give her have some space, all right?"

Rachel turned to him. Why was he acting so deferential? It made no sense. This man was the blackmailer. He'd tormented and victimized her. Taken away all the power she'd had—power she was getting back, slowly but surely—and exposed her for all the world to see. She wanted to jump on him and scratch his eyes out until everyone saw him for the disgusting abomination that he really was.

He turned to the Secret Service. "I'll have my driver take her back to her house. You can contact her later if you require anything else."

He was going to kidnap her again?

One of Rachel's staffers shoved her purse and coat into her hands. She slipped it on before anyone could offer to assist, and she'd have slapped away the hands that did try to help her.

She was going to leave. But she first turned to the vice president and said, "I can make my own way home. But thank you for your offer."

"Nonsense." He fell into step with her. "I won't relax until I know you're home safe."

That was assuming, of course, that she *was* going to go home.

The VP walked with her to the exit doors and escorted her outside. His wife's shoes clipped on the floor behind them.

It didn't seem right for the sun to be that bright. She slid on her sunglasses and then dug out her gloves. The bite in the air made her breaths puff out in clouds in front of her. That would betray the fact she was almost panting.

Don't panic.

She needed refuge. A place to regroup, to get help.

"Right here." He waved her to a town car at the curb. A Secret Service agent stood beside it, another one in the driver's seat. A car was parked in front of it and another behind. Three-car convoy.

She wanted to run off down the street, but she would get where she needed to go faster in a car. One full of Secret Service agents.

She was supposed to trust them, right?

Rachel climbed in after Mrs. Anderson. As she settled in, she dug in her purse for her phone and found the voice recorder app. When the vice president had shut the door, and the three of them were closed in the back of the limo, she said, "I know you sent that man to kill me."

The car set off, and she shifted in the seat with the motion. Leather creaked. The vice president's wife gasped. "You think William did *what?*"

Rachel ignored the outburst and kept all her attention on him.

His face softened. "You've had a hard couple of days, and things in your life aren't optimal. I can understand how you might be mistaken, due to an extreme situation and stress."

"So you're going to dismiss my accusation and tell everyone I'm unhinged? After what you did to me?"

Mrs. Anderson glanced between them, mouth agape.

He said nothing.

"I will get the evidence I need to expose you. And you will pay for all the lives you've destroyed."

"Very well," he said, blank-faced. "I hope you're not too disappointed when you find nothing at all."

She looked out the window, saw where they were, and rapped on the partition between her and the agents in front. "You can let me out here," she called out.

The convoy pulled up in front of a building about halfway between the Capitol and the White House.

Rachel climbed out of the limo and strode into the FBI office.

Chapter 8

Nicola gasped for breath, flat on her back on her kitchen floor. Blood pooled around her. Steve grabbed her phone and dialed emergency services. He knelt in the blood and handed her the phone, mouthing, "Hold on."

She blinked and managed a short nod.

He grabbed the dishtowel and balled it up over the wound, then placed her free hand on it. The hand slipped away, but he replaced it.

He had to go.

She mouthed, "Go."

Steve took the stairs two-at-a-time down to the back door, the rear exit of the apartment building. As he raced to where he thought the sniper might have been set up, he prayed she would live. Faith was something that had enabled him to keep his sanity when the lines blurred between duty to country and morality.

In college, he'd been a youth pastor. The army and his subsequent operational career meant little time for ministry, but he'd made some of it work when he was home. Lately he'd been thinking about getting plugged in again at church.

Sweat beaded on his forehead as he ran, the moisture immediately chilling. He pumped his arms and legs, almost frantic. He couldn't stay with Nicola and make sure she was okay. What he could do was take down her killer.

Someone he figured was one of his old teammates. If he had to guess, he'd say it was Petey. Jerome was the one who'd tried to kill Rachel in the street. How many of the others were here, active?

A door opened on the adjacent building and a man strode out, looking both ways. A case in one hand.

Sniper rifle.

His eyes snagged on the blur of Steve as he barreled toward him. But there was no time for him to react before Steve slammed Petey against the side of the adjacent apartment building and smashed his fist into his former friend's face.

"I don't know what he has on you, and I *don't care*," Steve snarled. He planted his fist in Petey's face again. But the man didn't lift a hand to defend himself.

That was what took the fight out of Steve.

Sirens whirled behind him. The blue and red of emergency services lights shone in Petey's eyes. Steve said, "I should drag you over there, rifle and all, and turn you in."

Petey frowned. "If you wouldn't get arrested yourself."

Steve shoved him against the wall and then took half a step back. "She's probably going to die because of you. Bleed out on her kitchen floor. And for what?" Nothing but one man's greed and ambition.

Steve was over the whole revenge idea. He pretty much figured this was about grabbing as much power as the Vice President thought he could have.

"Dude—"

"Shut it." Steve couldn't handle conversation right now. He felt like screaming out all his frustration, right in Petey's face.

"I wouldn't've hit anything vital if you hadn't warned her."

Steve stared at him.

"I shoulda shot you. Done the world a favor."

This was what he had come to? Alone in an alley with a man who was supposed to have been his friend. He hung his head and sucked in breaths. Petey might kill him while Steve wasn't watching, but maybe that was for the best. Rachel didn't need him in her life. Seemed like he'd brought her nothing but trouble. Maybe he was even the link between her and the blackmailer. Why else target her?

Everyone else in their thirties and forties involved in this were the children of those who'd been part of that original mission.

Steve had nothing to do with it. Neither did Rachel. Except for his connection to the general.

Now the general was dead, and Steve's old team had been co-opted into this while his new team were all targets.

He straightened.

"You don't look so good."

Steve shoved him against the wall again, then stood back.

"Good as it was to see you," Petey said, a sardonic tone to his voice. "I'm gonna go now. Don't wanna be standing here when the cops decide to canvas the neighborhood looking for anything anomalous."

"Car?"

Petey pointed to the end of the building. "Around the corner. Need a ride?"

Steve had more questions, and he wasn't past the urge to kill the man, so he said, "Yes." He glanced once in the direction of Nicola's apartment. The broken window Petey had shot out. And then followed Petey. He got in the passenger side. When Petey pulled out of the parking lot, Steve said, "What does he have on you?"

Petey's fingers flexed on the wheel. "Too much."

"Family?"

He shook his head.

"So then what?"

Petey said nothing.

"I can't help you if you don't give me something."

"Doesn't matter."

"It does, or you'd have said no." Steve motioned with his hand.

He'd tried the same tactic Nicola had come up with—shoot to miss. The one Steve had toyed with himself. But was it going to work? There were entirely too many ways this could backfire on all of them. People would get hurt.

"Jerome was supposed to kill your girl this morning."

Steve shook his head. "That was yesterday." Jerome was the man who'd come at Rachel with the knife in that alley.

"Told me he was supposed to go to her office and take her out. He'd set it all up, passes and everything. So all Jerome had to do was get in like a tourist and kill her. But he had to do it barehanded 'cause of the metal detectors."

Not to mention the security guards. Steve pulled out his phone and sent Rachel a text. Was she all right?

"If he killed her, I'm going to hunt him down and put a bullet in his brain."

"And you'll do the same if your friend back there dies?"

Steve said, "Probably."

The world thought he was some kind of crazed killer, so why not prove them all right? He flipped the phone over and over on his thigh, waiting for her to reply. His stomach sank as the minutes ticked on.

Petey pulled over. "This is your stop."

Steve figured it was as good of a place as any, no matter that this was a residential street he didn't know. He grabbed the door handle. "Tell me something I can use to get us all out of this."

Petey thought for a second, then shrugged. "He had me pick up the weapon from Franklin. Might not be something you can use, but that's all I have. Everything else was untraceable."

The same place Steve had been instructed to pick up his own sniper rifle from. "You better start praying she lives—"

Petey cut him off. "Dude, you were always better at that stuff."

"Pray, Petey. Because this is going to take some serious divine intervention before it's over. We're going up against a man who thinks he's untouchable and so far we've sustained heavy losses." Petey probably didn't even know about the two Double Down teammates that had been killed. Or the lives affected so far.

Jerome. Petey. Was David part of this, too? Steve said, "Things are only going to get worse before they get better."

He climbed out of the car and started walking. Rachel still hadn't texted him back. Should he call her? His own former teammates were hunting her, trying to kill her. Nicola had been shot. Bradley had Alexis to worry about. Adrian and Megan were fighting an uphill battle trying to convince the rest of the FBI this threat was legitimate. Emma and Mint were trying to come up with evidence, and hadn't told him the results of their trip to her safety deposit box—which didn't mean anything good.

Could they actually survive this, or was it a pipe dream?

Like his shot at a future.

. . .

Rachel sat at the conference room table. Megan settled into the chair beside her. Two steaming mugs of tea sat on the table between them. Rachel sighed and took a sip of hers.

Megan huffed out a laugh that was barely above a whisper. She shot Rachel a wry smile. "I know, right?"

Rachel had to smile. The woman had been traumatized as part of her own kidnapping, back in the days when she'd been undercover with the FBI. Megan's connection with them was a little looser these days. She worked for Double Down and was dating Adrian.

Still, there was something elemental that connected Rachel and Megan.

They both knew what terror was.

They had survived some of the worst things a person could do to another person.

"Sitting beside him in the car..." Rachel shuddered. "I'm not sure I'll ever get to the place where I'm totally comfortable being close with anyone, apart from the few people I know really well."

Megan nodded. "I'm going to stick with Adrian, my Mom and Double Down." She shrugged. "The rest of the world can deal."

Rachel got updated on the navy officers, one now dead and the other at large. Under surveillance, because Adrian thought there was a chance that might lead them back to the blackmailer. She said, "Sounds like you've had about as much progress as I have getting conclusive evidence."

Megan nodded. "Adrian is hoping that following Captain St. Germaine will get us something to go on. The judge gave us a surveillance warrant for his phone and computer, so we're watching. We'll have to wait and see if the blackmailer reaches out, though the last person who heard directly from him—Aaron Jones—had an untraceable phone."

Megan was the one who had shot Jones, saving Emma from being kidnapped or killed. Jones hadn't ever shared the blackmailer's identity. If he'd known it.

"Seems like there's a lot going on, but not much happening in the way of results." Rachel set her mug down. "People keep trying to kill me."

"I know," Megan said quietly.

"I…" Her voice broke. "Killed a man this morning."

She squeezed her eyes shut.

"I'm not going to tell you that you had no choice. Or that it was you or him, and you were forced to make a horrible choice, even though that's true. I know what it feels like to take a life like that."

Rachel opened her eyes and looked at her friend. They hadn't even spent that much time together, but they were connected. She said, "My therapist is going to have a field day with this."

Megan grinned. "Tell me about it."

Rachel shifted in the chair. "I keep reaching for my phone without even thinking about it."

"Habit."

She nodded. "And not a good one. Maybe I need to turn the thing off and like, fast from it, or something."

"The tech guys should be done checking it soon."

Rachel leaned her head against the high back chair. She wanted to know for sure that she was safe from being spied on by the blackmailer. The FBI were going through every part of her phone, looking for an intruder. They had also dispatched an agent to do the same thing with her office computer and her home setup.

She would rather know if she was being watched. Or tracked. It would explain how hired killers kept finding her.

"Thanks," Rachel said. "I'd like to find out if Steve is okay."

"Worried about him?"

She nodded. "He's putting himself on the line."

"Not unusual for him," Megan said. "That's why he hasn't been caught yet. He was trained too well in escape and evasion. Especially in an urban setting. There are a million places to hide in the city."

Rachel nodded.

"He's probably more worried about you."

Maybe. Rachel wasn't sure if that was true, or not. "Yeah?"

Megan nodded. "I'm sure one of the main reasons he didn't leave town is because you're here."

Rachel saw something in her eyes. "What don't I know?"

Megan took a pause. While she measured her words? Rachel didn't like that she was thinking on what she was going to say. Why would Megan need to do that?

Megan said, "Steve has been keeping Bradley in the loop. But also, we've been watching the local news, to see if anything pops up on the police band."

"And?"

"A short time before you showed up here, a woman was shot in her apartment. Looks like a sniper hit."

"Who?"

"She's a reporter. Nicola Starns. She dated Steve a few years ago, and we think she was drawn into this." Megan paused again.

Rachel said it for her. "The cops investigating think Steve was the one who shot her?"

Megan nodded.

The fact that Nicola Starns had been special to Steve and a part of his life meant something. For how long they'd been together, Rachel wouldn't ever know unless she asked, which she wasn't going to do. Didn't matter. Ten minutes, or ten years, Steve wouldn't do that to someone he cared for.

She wanted to believe he cared for her too, but he'd never said anything about it. She knew he'd been interested in her. His pursuit of her before the video came out had made that clear. They were adults, and he made plain that he'd wanted to take her to dinner.

But then she'd been targeted by the blackmailer. After that she hadn't wanted to be around any man. Least of all one she cared for the way she cared for him.

Rachel shook off her morose thoughts. "The vice president is stacking up charges against Steve, trying to implicate him in so many things that no one will ever believe he's not guilty of at least *something*."

"The evidence is compelling."

"Well, it's wrong. Because he didn't do that. He wouldn't shoot someone he cared about. He didn't shoot those feds when you went to take down *El Cuervo*, right?" Megan couldn't argue against that. Especially not when she'd been there. Didn't she trust her boss? Or was she just playing it neutral, being a part of the FBI case now?

Megan sat back in her chair and sighed. "We're doing everything we can to prove it wasn't him, but unless we have evidence that ties the blackmailer to every single attack, then it doesn't provide reasonable doubt for Steve. He's been convicted in the court of public opinion already. Any jury would be swayed by what they've heard in the media and seen online. Everyone has an agenda. It's basically impossible to be impartial."

"You think he'll end up in jail?"

"I'm just saying it's bad." Megan leaned a little closer. "I want you to be realistic, Rachel. Because if anything else happens, and he's blamed for that as well, then this is going to get even harder."

"I don't care. He's innocent."

Maybe she sounded naïve. Or a little like a child digging in her heels. But Rachel was going to stick to her guns. Her office would be behind Steve—the man she knew him to be and not the man everyone believed he was.

She'd been trashed in the media. Alexis, too. The two of them had been sucked into the scandal surrounding her video. They had intentionally spun the narrative, knowing what it would do. She knew exactly how it felt to have people make up their minds about you and not be able to do anything to change it.

"You love him, don't you?"

Rachel turned to her friend. She opened her mouth to deny it, but didn't get the chance.

Adrian stuck his head in the door. "The agents following St. Germaine lost him."

Megan shot up out of her chair. "Are you kidding me?"

"I know," Adrian said. "He's gone."

Chapter 9

The fact the blackmailer knew the location of this house wasn't useful to Steve. At least, it wasn't more information than they'd known already.

So he was in their pasts and their computer systems. Did instructing Steve to come here actually mean something?

He climbed out of the car—a beater he'd purchased for five hundred in cash—and slammed the door. He was pretty sure the car hadn't been the property of the man who had sold it to him. Steve wasn't going to worry about that right now. On the list of his transgressions, it didn't rate all that high.

He was in West Virginia, not even two hours from Washington. His phone had buzzed the entire way there. Bradley wanting to know what was happening. Details about Nicola—alive, critical, and in surgery. Adrian had even called a few times, using a burner phone Steve had given to Megan. Asking where he was. Megan's message had been entirely in that cold tone of hers, the one she used when she wasn't happy.

Rachel had been attacked again. She'd killed the guy. They were going to try and figure out who the assailant was.

Steve didn't text back any names, though the list would have been limited to five, including Petey. His old team was in play, and one of them had tried to kill Rachel. Gotten close enough, according to Megan, to leave bruises on her throat.

He had his weapon out before he even registered it. Nothing but a reflex. The intention to kill had underlain his career for decades now. Cold moved through him, shutting off all feeling so that his emotions had no air time here. It was how he'd functioned for so long—in those days when he'd been a covert agent. No feeling.

He bent forward and squeezed his eyes shut.

Someone he had called friend had squeezed her throat, intending to crush her windpipe and stop her heart.

If she hadn't killed him—and he thanked God that she had saved herself—he would've killed the man himself.

Rachel was the only thing that broke through the resolve of his training.

He should be with her, protecting her. He wanted to be. But Rachel was entirely too well known to be flanked by a wanted felon twenty-four seven. It would only get both of them in trouble.

He needed to stick with this. Find the blackmailer.

That thought was what gave him the momentum to stride across the overgrown lawn to the house. To push aside the fear for *her* and complete this mission.

The place didn't look like it had been used in years. One of the front windows had been broken. Local kids messing around? The '*No Trespassing*' signs should have been warning enough. He circumvented the house and headed for the barn.

The door had been slid open and leaves collected inside. Still smelled the same. Didn't look the same, though. The floor was covered in debris. A small animal of some kind had wandered in, parked itself in one of the corners, and died.

Steve walked to the center of the room, stretched out his fingers, and then jumped. He grasped the beam above his head and pulled himself up. With his chin nearly touching the beam, he saw the spot where he had carved his initials. More letters flanked his—the initials of his teammates. Coupled letters spread all the way to the outer walls in both directions.

More than he'd thought.

Men and women who'd come here to be trained by the best. Formed into teams of covert operators. Steve had been twenty-two, and he'd figured being Army gave him at least some sway with the officer in charge of their training. That assumption had lasted about thirty seconds. Then Steve had been flat on his back, staring up at this very ceiling.

The officer he'd known during training had retired as a general and been killed at a think tank. In his life, that man had done more to prepare the people under his charge to perform covert operations than anyone else Steve had ever heard of. A man who, in his own younger days, had changed the course of one life to such a degree that it had been the catalyst for this whole thing.

That mission in Venezuela and whatever had really happened there. All the way to this place, where he'd trained operatives.

Steve turned away. Back to the reason he was here. Picking up a sniper rifle he was supposed to use to kill the president of the United States of America.

This whole thing was a delicate balance between saving the lives of people he cared for by playing along—and he had one particular person he cared about at the forefront of his mind—and figuring out how he was going to finish this without actually assassinating the president. He hadn't exactly figured out how to do that yet. But it didn't meant he wasn't going to work it out sooner or later. That, or one of his friends would come up with something.

Remy was AWOL, so that potential assist was out. She wouldn't have gone dark if she wasn't tied up in something serious. Or hadn't suffered a serious breach of her security.

Adrian and Megan.

Emma and Mint.

Bradley and Alexis.

Rachel.

Would one of them come up with something? The blackmailer would keep targeting Rachel. If Steve lost her, then he had nothing else in his life worth fighting to the death for. She was the only leverage the blackmailer had. And the fact he had uncovered that was interesting in itself, since it wasn't like there was an electronic record of his feelings.

If she was killed…

He didn't even want to think about that, but he had to. The fact was, he'd go dark. Off on a revenge spree with no care for collateral damage. Anyone who got in his way would be fair game. Steve would shoot the vice president, evidence or not.

No one was going to stop him.

Steve walked through the house, fighting the tide of decades old memories. He found the rifle tucked in the attic, right where the blackmailer said it would be. Steve flipped the latches on the case and looked at it. Blinked. This weapon? He fought the urge to say something he shouldn't. What on earth? This whole thing was a serious mind flip.

He'd used this rifle years ago. And he thought he'd retired it through the CIA. What was it doing here?

His phone buzzed in his pocket.

Steve drew it out. His chest tightened, wondering if it would be Rachel. He wasn't going to answer if it was. The same way he hadn't answered for any of his friends.

It wasn't though. The buzz had been a text.

`Further details will be forthcoming.`

Seriously? Steve sat back on his heels. This was insane. The blackmailer knew he was here, knew he had just collected the gun.

Steve rocked back and stumbled to his feet. He surveyed the corners of the upstairs hallway for cameras. Listening devices. Some kind of sensor.

Was the blackmailer watching?

The man had this phone number. Did the contact mean he had access to Steve's GPS, despite the fact Steve had disabled that function? He wanted to leave the phone, and the gun, go get Rachel and board a plane to…somewhere with no extradition arrangement with the US. Bradley wouldn't be happy if Steve essentially kidnapped his sister. But they would both be safe.

It wouldn't stop the blackmailer, though. He would only find a new target and the president's life would still be in danger.

His team would still be in danger.

Running wasn't the answer. As good of an idea as it looked to be.

Steve squeezed the phone so hard it almost broke. The blackmailer knew *everything*. And if Steve really did kill the president, it would only prove the truth about who Steve really was.

Something not even Rachel knew.

. . .

"How about this one?" Megan slid another page across the table.

Rachel stared down at the collection of six photographs. She pointed to the middle one, bottom row. "That's who held me at knifepoint in the alley."

So far she had identified two men out of the dozen or so pages Megan had shown her. "You aren't showing me pictures of just anyone, are you? There's a reason why you're choosing these. Why I've been able to pick out exactly who I saw."

Megan nodded. "The two men you pointed to were members of a team that Steve was part of. Special operations. A joint task force of men and women from the military and federal agencies retasked to other operations. It was run by the CIA, and we don't know much of what they did. But it wasn't peacekeeping. That much we can surmise."

Her mouth twisted in a wry smile, and she continued, "Most of it was classified. Adrian had to pull some serious strings with the agents looking for Steve. They caved and showed him what they know. But no one has all of the information. That much you can be sure of."

Rachel figured she could name at least one person who knew it all.

The blackmailer: Vice President Anderson.

"Would you like me to tell you what I know?"

Rachel shrugged. "It won't change how I view Steve Preston." Or how she felt about him. It didn't matter what he'd done. Who he had been.

She also didn't care if standing by him cost her her career. Her reputation. People already thought she was crazy. Rachel was still trying to decide if she was anything but annoyed by that. She couldn't change their opinion, the same way she couldn't change what had happened to her.

Megan shot her a look, like she didn't exactly agree with Rachel. So what if it was bad? She knew what the movies said about covert operatives. Real life wasn't going to be that far off—it might even be way worse. She could imagine plenty without the details.

"If Steve wants me to know where he's been and what he's done," Rachel said, "then he'll tell me himself."

Megan shook the papers into a stack.

Rachel said, "Would it change how *you* saw him if you found out he'd done some of the same things that were done to you?" Megan had been kidnapped and terrorized, her undercover FBI partner shot in front of her. But Rachel also knew how much she respected Steve.

She shifted in her chair and held the file folder of pages on her lap. "I know it's not a black and white thing, but he was working for us. You know, the US. Not that that makes assassination and kidnapping more righteous, like he was on the side of justice or anything."

"Too jaded?"

"I've seen the good and the bad in what missions are chosen. And I read the file. Steve has done some things that would make you want to put a panic room in your house and just live there."

"But he was a chaplain in the Army first, right?" Rachel took a second to figure out what she was trying to say. "So he went into this already possessing that honor he lives by now. I can't believe he'd have done it if it compromised who he already was." The person she knew now was a man at war with himself. Maybe he'd crossed a few lines, but he certainly hadn't given up his soul.

Megan shrugged one slender shoulder. "He's still my boss. I have a hard time believing in either pure good or pure evil. Not as far as God, because the spiritual world is different. But people? We're flesh. And unless we're walking in the Spirit, we make all kinds of irrational decisions. Bad choices. We hurt people."

Rachel nodded. "Alexis told me it's like having a battle going on inside you."

"And you can surrender to either side at any given moment," Megan said. "I've seen evil, and I've seen good. I try my best, and I believe Steve does as well. Whether that's to make up for what he did, or because it's who he wants to be, doesn't matter. What we do speaks to our character, and I trust what I know of his."

"That's exactly why I will stand by him. No matter what anyone—"

Bradley's voice rang across the room. "You're going to martyr yourself for Steve?"

She swung around in the chair to face him. "Why not?" Despite the thunder in his eyes, she continued, "He deserves loyalty, and that's exactly what I'm going to give him."

"Even if it destroys everything you have?"

"What do I have?" And the answer to his question was an unequivocal *yes*. "A public life in politics."

"One most people would envy."

"Why?"

Bradley blinked. "I don't know. They just would."

Not everyone wanted to be in politics, and that was fine. People should do what they love. But Rachel was losing her joy for her work. Maybe she was jaded, like Megan, because she'd seen too much. Experienced too much trauma.

What was it she'd said to Megan about her therapist? The woman was going to have a field day helping Rachel sort all this out.

Rachel waved a hand. "I'm not arguing with you."

"Good plan." Alexis wiggled between him and the doorframe. She stepped up onto her tiptoes and planted a kiss on Bradley's cheek. Then she came over and gave Rachel a hug.

Rachel shut her eyes and held on to her friend.

"You really stabbed him in the throat with a letter opener?" She leaned back.

Rachel shrugged.

"I guess my lessons paid off." Bradley poured himself a cup of coffee.

Rachel and Alexis shared a smile. His ego was big enough without her giving him the credit for anything.

"So what's the plan?" Alexis glanced at each of them in turn.

"I figure I'll stay here for...like, *ever*." Rachel slumped into the chair she'd been sitting in before her brother and his wife showed up. "I'm less likely to get attacked here. Plus I assume there are beds. Someone from my office could bring me clothes."

Megan smiled. "Protective custody."

"I'm not leaving the building. I'm staying right here." Why would she go anywhere, with anyone, when every time she did that someone came out of the woodwork to try and kill her? She shuddered. "Try to make me leave."

"No one is going to do that," Bradley said in a low voice that might've sounded threatening if she didn't know that his protective streak was all about her and Alexis.

"Agreed." Megan lifted her phone from the table and looked at the screen. "The tech looking at your cell phone has an update. He's on his way here."

A minute later, a wiry man with a tangled mess of overgrown hair on top of his head rapped on the door. "Senator Harris?" His face lit up.

"That's me."

"Wow. This is like...whoa." He waved his arms around but didn't seem to be holding her phone.

"You've been looking at my cell phone?"

His face fell. "I didn't see anything you wouldn't have been okay with. I was *very* discreet."

Was it worth explaining that she wasn't someone who kept sensitive anything on her phone? Yet another person who'd made up their own mind about what she did with her private life. She smiled. "Of course you were."

Ac ross the room, Bradley looked about ready to explode from his seat.

She said, "Did you find anything interesting on there, software or anything like that?"

"Actually, yeah." He ran a hand over his hair. "There's a worm. It's feeding back a record of everything you say and do on your cell phone to an IP address."

Megan stood. "Can you trace it? Get us a location?"

"I'm running the program now, but it's bouncing all over the place. Whoever he is, he's good."

"We know," Rachel said, mostly so he didn't feel too bad if it came up with nothing.

Bradley straightened to rest both fists on the tabletop. "Find out who it is."

"Uh." The tech stammered. "I can try."

"Then go do that."

He rushed out.

Rachel turned to her brother. "That was rude."

"Your fan club president needed to get back to work."

Alexis glanced at Rachel. They both sighed.

Bradley said, "What? What did I say?"

Chapter 10

Considering it had been Megan's idea, Rachel didn't have to do much convincing to allow the FBI to let her go off on her own. Wearing a wire. A team of feds all around her, disguised as regular folks, watching and waiting to see if there was another attempt on her life.

Rachel had made it seem like she was hemming and hawing, thinking it over. In reality, she'd been vacillating between fear that Megan was right and someone else would try to kill her, and wanting to jump at the chance for the FBI to catch one of these guys.

Now that she was minutes from walking out of the FBI office, she'd gone back to fear.

"Put this on." Bradley shoved a bulletproof vest at her. Like she was going to say no to that? Alexis smiled. Then he handed one to his wife as well. "You too."

Rachel's friend's amusement dissipated. "I'll be fine."

"You still wear the vest." He shifted closer to Alexis and fastened the straps for her. "You do what the agent says. Just go home and sit tight. Like normal."

She nodded. "Spaghetti or a stir fry?"

"What?"

"For dinner."

"Oh. Stir fry."

"Beef or chicken?"

Rachel chuckled. Bradley shot her a look. She said, "You guys. So domesticated."

Alexis smiled, "Your time will come."

Rachel shook her head, not even wanting to get into that. She turned to Adrian, off his phone now. "I'm ready." She pulled her coat on over the vest and slid her hair out of the collar.

Adrian nodded. "Okay."

Bradley snagged her elbow. "Be. Careful. I'll be right behind you, but I don't want to see you putting your neck out."

She knew he had to say it. These were dangerous times for all of them, and any one of their group could be targeted at any moment. There was really no way to escape the danger. Not even if she stayed here—which wasn't practical. Turning the tables on the blackmailer and doing something unpredictable might actually be what gained them a result.

"I will." She leaned up on her tiptoes and gave her brother a kiss on the cheek.

She was going out there, but he would be right behind her. And there was no one else she wanted to watch her back. Not just because he was her brother. Or the fact he'd been a Navy SEAL before he retired to work for Steve.

A minute later she left the FBI office. Vest on. Wire under her shirt so the FBI could record everything. She would be safe, no matter what fear—or logic—told her about what she was going to do.

Ten minutes later, she'd walked around two busy street corners full of holiday tourists braving the winter weather. No point in isolating herself so the FBI had to stay too far out of sight just to keep from being seen. There were agents on the sidewalk in front and behind her, keeping pace. Watching. Blending in.

A man walking the same direction shifted alongside her, too close. Trying to pass her? Rachel sidestepped, but he snagged her arm and pulled her to his side. She gasped. Ice immediately washed over her. Her body's own warning system of danger. Maybe her therapist was right, that she would be hypersensitive for a while before things went back to normal. Or maybe this was life now.

Danger.

Fear.

"Keep walking." His grip on her arm was tight enough, she'd likely end up with bruises.

A lump rose in her throat. She tried to speak, but could only choke out a noise that meant nothing but that she was scared. The FBI were close. She needed to remember that. To trust them. But trust in anyone didn't come easy.

"Nice and steady," he said. "Nothing to it."

She sucked in a choppy breath and glanced up at him. Stubble on the lower half of a craggy face she didn't recognize. He was probably late forties, or into his fifties—or hard living made him look older than he was. She should ask him a question. Get him to tell them something about the blackmailer, or why he was trying to kidnap her. But she couldn't think of where to start.

Rachel's heel clipped an uneven part of the sidewalk and she stumbled.

He dragged her back upright. "Eyes front."

She righted her stride, and they kept going, faster now. He tugged her around a corner. Toward one of those back street tourist parking lots that cost way too much.

Tires squealed.

He started to spin around. Agents jumped out from every angle. The cavalry was here. Rachel planted her right foot, twisted her hips and slammed her left fist into his stomach.

He doubled over coughing.

She backed up. Bradley caught her arm and dragged her behind him while the agents yelled, "Freeze!" and "Drop the weapon!"

It was all over in less than fifteen minutes. One of the blackmailer's men in custody. The FBI agents patted him down, emptied his pockets. Found a phone.

"No ID," one of them said.

Another put handcuffs on him.

"You okay?" Bradley asked.

"Yes, I'm fine." This was one of the better experiences, and yet she still seemed jittery like the other times. Adrenaline flowed through her, but she locked her knees to hold steady. The relief would come.

He touched her hands. "Adrenaline. Doesn't matter if nothing really happened. Your body reacted to the danger nonetheless."

They stood to the side while Adrian came over to the man. "Care to tell us your name? Or are you going to waste our time making us run your prints in the military's personnel database?"

The craggy man said nothing.

"Have it your way, then." Adrian grasped his elbow.

As they walked, the man said, "You could always ask Steve Preston who I am." He glanced over his shoulder and looked at Rachel. "After all, you guys are pretty friendly with him. Right?"

Bradley tugged on her arm. "Hang back with me. Let Adrian handle this."

She glanced at him and frowned. He said, "Most of them think Adrian has Megan close to him because she works for Steve. They think he's in the relationship to string her along until she can lead him to their fugitive."

Rachel started. "Seriously? I thought they were trying to help him figure all this out."

"That's the case he's building, no matter what they think. He intends to prove Steve is acting under duress just like Zimmerman did. The rest of the agents don't know it's what he's going to hand over to the judge at the end, when he has the evidence."

"Oh." Rachel thought for a second. "Isn't that dangerous, playing the line between two sides?" She'd seen Megan in the FBI office, participating almost like a real agent. And maybe because of her history, they gave her that respect. But, come to think of it, Megan hadn't been given any "official" duties. She'd just been there. Assisting where they could watch her.

"They think Steve will be in contact with her?"

Bradley nodded. "But he won't. Considering he's been meeting with you."

Rachel wasn't going to respond to that. She would only incriminate herself with her brother regarding her personal feelings for his boss. Feelings she'd managed to keep from him. Though, he'd likely figured it out now.

He got that look on his face. The one that meant he was about to tell her to be careful. "Rach—"

A shot rang out.

The craggy man fell to the ground. His body crumpled into a heap.

Bradley launched himself at her, and they both hit the ground.

. . .

Smoke wafted up from the barrel. Steve lifted it, clipped the legs back against the barrel and then took it apart so he could stow it back in the case.

He picked up the spent shell casing and looked around one more time to make sure he hadn't left any evidence.

And then he was gone.

He drove a few miles, then pulled over and sent the text.

It's done.

He'd killed Petey before his former teammate could tell the FBI anything about the blackmailer. The bureau wouldn't get anything from Petey's phone either. They should be able to guess that was a waste of time.

The message Steve had received, the instructions for him to kill the president, had disappeared from his phone already. Deleted. Erased. However it had been done, there was no way to trace it. Or even prove it had existed in the first place outside of his word. If Steve was to actually do it, there was no way to prove it wasn't him acting on his own.

He touched his forehead to the steering wheel and shut his eyes. An image of Rachel immediately filled his mind. He let it stay for a minute, indulging himself, even though it was a form of torture. The thing he wanted most. The thing he couldn't have.

His phone buzzed.

Confirm when final mission is complete.

Like he needed to be reminded that the summit was closing in fast? Adding in this additional mission evidently hadn't changed Steve's primary objective.

He'd never liked taking orders much, but put up with it for the sake of the Army. Mostly because he'd felt like he was serving God. With the CIA, he'd really been making a difference in the world. When it meant bad guys were dead or in jail at the end of the mission, that was easy to swallow. Occasionally the operation would be more of a gray area. Details got missed. Intelligence was faulty, or some analyst somewhere had made an assumption.

Steve had pulled a trigger. Or set a charge. Someone who shouldn't have died lost their life.

He wouldn't have been able to call himself a man if he didn't feel regret when life was taken for the wrong reason, and he was the one doing the taking.

Killing Petey might have been an order from the blackmailer. But seeing the man hauling Rachel along like that? No question. Steve hadn't even hesitated.

He drove around the city for a while. Well after dark he drove by Rachel's house. All the lights were out, but he didn't figure that was because she was sleeping. He tried Bradley and Alexis's house next. A tiny one-story place she'd had Bradley paint yellow. Bradley had even hung Christmas lights along eaves all the way across the front of the house.

The living room blinds were open slightly, so he could see the lit Christmas tree they'd decorated.

Life was happening. While his was destroyed, they were going to celebrate the season. His chest hurt just thinking about not filling that seat he'd promised to at their dinner table. Not sharing the Christmas meal with friends he'd considered family.

He left the phone in the car, parked three streets away. Checked for surveillance that would indicate the FBI was watching the house. He climbed the fence and landed on gravel behind it. Knocked on the guest room window.

Rachel pulled back the curtain, alarm on her face. The shock dissipated, and she smiled as she shoved up the window. "Why do I feel sixteen again?"

Steve said, "You had boys knock on your window at sixteen?"

"Uh…no comment."

"I think your constituents would have something to say about that."

Rachel rolled her eyes, and he finally saw she was wearing a sweatshirt that said NAVY.

"Seriously?" Surely she had one for the Army as well. Or should he get her one for Christmas?

"What?" She tried to look innocent, but there was a gleam of mischief in her eyes. "I support all the branches of our military."

"You stole that from Bradley."

"Maybe." She took half a step back. "Are you going to come in?"

"Actually, no." Steve leaned against the outside of the house. "It's better if I don't."

"Oh."

"Are you okay? Bradley landed pretty hard on you today."

She pressed her lips together. "So that was you. It's everyone's working theory."

Steve didn't argue. It was true, after all. "I have to keep up the pretense that I'm doing what he wants."

"Why? You could just walk away."

"That doesn't make Double Down safe." Or their friends. His family.

Her face shut down. "I see."

"Rach." He leaned in to the window and held out one hand. After a second, she placed hers in it. "My running doesn't make *you* safe."

"Oh." The word was soft.

"Are you okay?"

She sighed. "I'd like to live the kind of life where someone isn't asking me that every five minutes."

"You'll get there."

She studied his face for a second, then said, "I'd like for *us* to get there."

He loved that, but had to say, "I'm not sure that's ever going to happen. This whole thing has already gone way too far. I don't know that I'm ever going to be free. Especially knowing what he wants from me."

"What does he want?"

Steve shook his head.

"You need to tell me. Adrian can help you." She looked so earnest, it made him want to tell her. But then what would she think of him? Rachel said, "Trust me." As though it was the most important thing in the world to her.

He couldn't.

She knew it. She pulled her hand from his and let it fall to her side. "If you can't tell anyone, then no one can help you."

"Maybe that's for the best."

"I don't believe that." She shook her head, like she disagreed with herself. "I'm trying to believe trust really is the best thing. Especially when you know the people you have faith in won't ever let you down."

He wanted to be that man for her. The fact she believed in him enough to trust him, after what had happened to her, humbled him.

Too bad it would never happen.

"Can you do me a favor?"

She said, "What?"

"I'd like to know how Nicola is doing, but there's no way I can find out."

"Oh." Her face turned stony, but she said, "The last I heard was that she was in surgery, and that it wasn't looking good." She said it all with no inflection, as though she was giving a report on economic policy.

"Thank you."

"I can find out more. If I see you, I'll keep you posted."

He wanted to tell her that of course they would see each other. But how could he guarantee that? It wasn't even safe to be here now.

"Let you know that your girlfriend is all right."

"Rach—"

"Did you shoot her too?"

"No, I—"

"Because that's a reasonable question."

"Maybe it was a mistake to come here." He took a step back. "Take care, okay?"

She shrugged.

"Am I supposed to say something else?"

She shot him a look. The one women gave you when you were supposed to know what they were mad about. Steve fired back with the only ammunition he had. "If you hear a report that the president has been shot at. Assassination—or just an attempt—maybe you could do that trust thing you were talking about. At least give me the benefit of the doubt."

He ignored her gasp and turned away.

Bradley's voice drifted out to him as he moved away from the window. "Who are you talking to?"

"No one. Geez."

Steve heard the window slam down, and he raced away before anyone found him.

Chapter 11

Rachel stepped out of the elevator into the FBI office just after eight the next morning. Traffic moving through Washington DC had been horrendous, but Bradley insisted it was better for blending in. Especially while riding in a government car that looked like every other government car, equipped with GPS tracking and two armed guards.

She gripped the strap of her laptop bag, slung it over her shoulder, and moved down the aisle between cubicles. Bradley walked right behind her, Alexis beside him. Like they had nothing better to do than play bodyguard to her.

Rachel stopped and turned to them. "I'm here now. Thanks for dropping me off."

They'd gone all the way through security, getting passes to be up here. Surely they could have dropped her at the front door.

Bradley said, "Alexis is going to stay here today as well." He eyed her like he was trying to figure out what she was hiding. Alexis's study was a little less blatant, but it was still there. They'd probably worked out that she *had* been talking to someone out her window. Was she going to tell them who? No way.

Alexis spun around to face her husband. "I'm staying—?"

Rachel cut her off. "The FBI don't want to babysit us." They barely tolerated her being there, and only because she'd thrown around some "senator" weight. Mostly the agents treated her like she was about to have a total mental breakdown. She wasn't sure if she'd prefer they knew she was scared to do much of anything, or go anywhere, until people quit trying to kill her.

Adrian strode over before Bradley could say more. "Ready?" His focus was on her brother.

"Ready for what?" Rachel asked.

Alexis sighed.

Rachel glanced between the three of them. "Someone explain. Right now."

"It's nothing," Bradley said. "Geez." He shot her a look, payback for what she'd said to him last night. Then he wandered off with Adrian.

Rachel swung around to Alexis. Before she could say anything, Alexis said, "He knows you lied to him last night."

"And he's still mad."

Alexis nodded. "Was it Steve?"

All Rachel could think about were his parting words. She'd been trying to push it out of her mind all morning. But now there was no way to do that. It eclipsed everything.

That the president has been shot...

"What is it?"

Rachel shook her head. "I can't talk about it." Because if she did, that would make it more real. She wanted to believe it wasn't true. That it *couldn't* be true. But denial had never been her strong suit. She tended to get snippy instead, to cover the fact there was something she didn't want to talk about.

Like confronting Bradley. "What is he doing with the FBI?"

Alexis said, "Adrian called this morning. They found another signal in with ours yesterday—someone else listening in."

Rachel took a step back. "Is it... I..." She didn't even know what to say.

Alexis's face softened. "They're going to take care of it."

Rachel slipped her arm through her friend's and basically dragged her to the conference room. She shut the door, then dumped her laptop bag on the table.

Alexis winced.

Rachel said, "What do you mean, 'take care of it'?"

"Bradley is going with them, and they're going to trace the source of the signal. They're zeroing in on a location."

"Forgetting the issue of how that's even possible, because I wouldn't understand all the techno-babble anyway, isn't anyone concerned with *why* they are able to do this?"

"What do you mean?"

Rachel leaned against the edge of the table. "The blackmailer has someone in his employ who is a computer genius, right?"

Alexis nodded. "It's the only way he'd be able to get into Double Down's system. Not to mention all the other things he's managed to do and find out."

"So why do they think he would make a mistake now, at this point?"

"You think its trap?"

"They don't?"

"I should—" Alexis took a step toward the door.

It opened. Bradley stuck his head in. "We're heading out."

"Rachel thinks it's a trap."

She nodded. "Also why are they letting you go? You're not FBI."

"I made a call. Adrian confirmed with my former commanding officer from the Navy. I'm vouched for."

"So you get to play operator while we sit here wondering if you're walking into a trap?"

"I'll be fine." He dragged her over, then dragged his wife over and pulled them both against him.

Rachel's and Alexis's eyes met, squished in the hug. They shared a look. Alexis said, "You should just tell him."

Rachel pushed away from both of them and made a face. "Of course. Just put me on the spot, why don't you?"

"I swear," Alexis said, "You might be a US senator, but you act like we're still in junior high sometimes."

"It's satisfying." Rachel folded her arms. "And it keeps people guessing if they don't know how you're going to act."

Bradley adopted the same posture. "I have one minute before I leave. Start talking."

And tell him that Steve was supposed to assassinate the president? No way. At least, she was pretty sure that was what Steve had been insinuating. He hadn't spelled it out in so many words, but what else could that mean?

"It was Steve last night?"

She nodded in answer to his question.

"We'll talk more about this later."

"Okay, *Dad.*" Their father had literally said that exact phrase to her years ago.

"Considering who he was, I take that as the highest compliment." Bradley strode out, shutting the door behind them.

Alexis had tears in her eyes. She shook her head. "Can you guys even go an hour without bickering?"

"He started it."

Alexis gave her a pointed look.

Rachel slumped into a chair. "I have work to do."

Alexis said, "Need some help?"

Rachel eyed her former assistant. "Of course."

Alexis smiled, and sat beside her. "It's only a favor, naturally. You can't afford my going rate these days."

Rachel chuckled and entered the pin for her computer. "Married to my brother, I'm surprised he doesn't have you stay in the kitchen all day making him those huge meals he eats. I'm surprised you're not pregnant yet."

Alexis choked on the sip of water she'd been drinking from that water bottle she kept in her huge purse.

Rachel's eyebrows rose.

Alexis pressed the cap back on the bottle. "Um...how long do you have to wait before you can take the test?"

"Seriously?"

Alexis bit her lip. "Let's get the work done first, and then we can find out."

"Chicken."

Alexis shoved her shoulder.

They got some work done, but they were also seriously distracted. Conversations Rachel might've had with Ellayna today were nonexistent, so evidently she didn't have to worry about things being awkward. When she called in to her office she discovered the intern hadn't even shown up to work today.

Rachel found an agent she recognized and mentioned it. He told her he would make sure the young woman was safe. The last thing she wanted was for Ellayna to have been hurt because of everything swirling around Rachel.

A couple of hours later, the office erupted in noise. Six men strode out of the elevator, including Bradley and Adrian. In the middle of the huddle was a man. Maybe in his fifties, he wore dark clothes and handcuffs. Adrian and the other agents escorted him past the conference room windows and down the hall.

Bradley opened the door to them.

Rachel said, "Is that the hacker?"

He nodded. "We got him. But he's refusing to speak to anyone but you."

. . .

Across town in a hotel lobby, Steve leaned on a cane. His hair was liberally sprinkled with gray, and he wore slacks with the belt far higher than it had any reason to be. The blue shirt was buttoned all the way to his throat which was covered with a film to make it look like he had wrinkles. His whole face itched from the stuff. His bushy eyebrows felt far too large and heavy.

He blinked, which shifted the colored contacts. He ignored that annoying sensation and hobbled forward on the cane and scuffed brown shoes.

"Sir, this is a restricted area."

Steve looked up from his slightly hunched position and blinked at the Secret Service agent. Then he looked back, down the hall. He let out a, "huh" noise and then turned around, muttering. Not low enough the agent would be unable to hear.

He circled the ground floor of the hotel like he was totally lost. Clocked each of the Secret Service agents, and the plain-clothes local cops. The vice president was in a lunch meeting with someone whose name had been left off his calendar. He didn't figure the man was stupid enough to meet with anyone who could directly tie him to the blackmail. But whoever it was, Steve wanted to know.

Just enough time to look him in the eye. Tell him he wasn't going to shoot the president. Tell him not to touch *anyone* Steve cared about.

He wouldn't mind a minute alone with the man, but didn't figure that was going to happen. He couldn't deny he hadn't at least considered bringing the rifle the blackmailer had left at the house for him here. So he could shoot the vice president instead. The reasons for not following through with that idea were myriad, and he didn't need to go over them all in his mind again. He hadn't brought it, or any other weapon. That wasn't part of who this identity was, so it wasn't even a consideration.

But chief of the reasons he hadn't gone through with the idea, was the look on Rachel's face last night. The idea she would even think of him and the word "assassin" in the same context. Ever.

Even though he'd told her simply for the shock factor, he hadn't realized what affect her reaction would have on him.

Twelve minutes of wandering around, plus another sixteen reading a newspaper in the lobby to cover the fact he was watching the Secret Service movement, and then two agents shifted. One lifted his hand, sleeve close to his mouth. Said something low. A couple of others moved to a new position.

The vice president stepped out of the restaurant at the center of the hotel. Secret Service agents moved into formation around him, and they trailed through the lobby to a hallway. They would exit out a side door where the motorcade waited.

Steve watched the restaurant door.

A couple of minutes later, a man wandered out. Steve left the cane propped against the chair and tossed the newspaper on a nearby table. He followed the man out the front doors and stayed ten feet behind him for two blocks before the man turned a corner.

Steve turned the corner as well, but stopped almost short of completing the turn. The man he'd followed had his gun out.

"What are—" He started at the sight of an old man. "Why are you following me?"

"A better question is, why are you meeting with the VP in broad daylight?"

The man blanched. "Steve?"

"Hey, David. How are you?"

David Sanders blew out a breath. He ran one hand through his hair. "Dude." Like that was enough of an exclamation to cover everything.

Steve said, "I'm public enemy number one, and you're his lunch date?" He paused. "Petey and Jerome are both dead." He'd killed one, and Rachel the other.

David's face fell. "I know…" He shifted his weight from foot to foot. At least the gun stayed by his side and didn't come back up. It still concerned Steve. If this turned ugly, he had no way to defend himself. Dying would also solve a whole lot of problems, and not just for him.

It wouldn't get Rachel completely out of danger, but it would help.

He said, "He's using the house in West Virginia to pass weapons back and forth. We're dying, David. What's going on?"

"It's complicated."

"What was lunch about?"

"He just... I was supposed to, you know..."

"Assume I don't know."

David said, "I'm passing information back and forth. Making sure he knows what the situation is, and when he should be ready."

Back and forth between who?

Steve said, "You sold out. Those aren't the actions of someone whose whole family is being threatened." Less leverage meant the target was given a smaller job. More leverage—like Steve with his business and all the people he cared about—meant he was asked to kill the president. "He got to you, though. Like he got to Petey. And Jerome."

"And you?"

"I won't do what he wants."

David sniffed. "Then you'll lose everything." He made an explosion motion with his mouth and hands. "Gone."

"I'm not going to let that happen. I'm figuring out a way to bring him down, that's why I followed you. Because I need your help."

David took a step back.

"You wanna be his errand boy? We're the only ones left. Am I supposed to stand up to him alone?"

"I'm not interested in dying."

"So you'll make a deal and be his lap dog?"

David scrunched up his face. "I could kill you right now. Split, get out of town. Disappear. No opposition, no problems."

"Until he needs someone else to get the president in their crosshairs and pull the trigger, and you're the only one left alive."

He paled. "The pres—" His voice died.

"You see why I won't do it?"

"I guess some people wouldn't mind if he was dead. I can see why you'd think twice, but why d'you have to be so moral about it?"

Steve said, "You want me to explain the intricacies of why we have different tasks? Because I don't exactly understand it. Except that I'm a better sniper than you."

"And a more well-known scapegoat," David added. "Plus he gets to publicize the evils of private security contractors who think their skills mean they're above the law."

"Got the rhetoric down already?" Steve asked. "Then why did he try to kill my reporter friend? He could have fed her the line that he wanted out."

"Nicola would never have gone along with it."

"So all dissenters get dead?"

David shrugged. "Play your part, I'll play mine."

"I'm not going to shoot the president."

"Then he stops playing with your girl, and it's game over for her."

Rachel would be dead?

None of this had been even remotely a game. At every step the blackmailer had enacted his plan. This was no different, not when he wanted the president of the United States dead. Because the moment that happened, the vice president would become the commander in chief himself.

Steve didn't believe the vice president had been playing with Rachel. The blackmailer wanted her dead, and he'd hired trained operatives to do it. Members of Steve's own team.

Steve had figured the fact there was nothing obvious between him and Rachel meant she would be safe from his enemies. That the things he'd done in his life wouldn't make her a target.

"He knows everything." Fear shone in David's eyes. "Even what you never told anyone. So if you care even one bit about this woman, then do what he said. Because otherwise, she's dead. And he'll *still* get what he wants."

Chapter 12

It took an hour of debate with Bradley and coaching from both Megan and Adrian before Rachel actually entered the interview room.

The earpiece they'd given her so they could speak to her during the chat seemed to have been pushed too far into her ear. Rachel smoothed down that side of her hair, conscious of not touching it. The quicker she got this over with, the better she would feel.

Too bad this wasn't about her feelings.

Or her fear.

This was about finding out why a hacker wanted to talk to her. And how it would help them bring down the vice president.

Not that she could actually mention the VP specifically. That had been part of the coaching Adrian had given her. The other agents, including the special agent in charge, would be watching. None of them were aware Double Down had a suspect—and without proof they would not know. Rachel prayed quickly that she wasn't going to mess anything up. Adrian was walking a fine line. As the only federal agent among them, he had the most to lose if his coworkers found out he'd been playing both sides.

The older man looked up as she entered. Heavy jowls hung on the sides of his face, peppered with stubble. Dark jeans and a wool sweater with three buttons at his throat. A full head of dark hair frosted with gray.

Rachel shut the door behind her, not moving her gaze from him. She didn't want to give him her back, even if he was shackled to the table. Which was Bradley's idea.

She set the water bottle in front of him, close enough so that he could grab it. She pulled out the metal chair opposite him and sat back from the table. She didn't exactly want to be close to him. That part of Bradley's instructions she hadn't minded so much.

He stared at her.

There was something in his eyes she didn't want to think about. "Maybe you'd like to start." After all, this was basically an elaborate strategy game, like chess. Would he move a pawn first?

Was she the pawn?

When he said nothing, she said, "How about your name?"

The agents had taken his fingerprints when they processed him, but this would save them having to run his identity. Assuming he answered truthfully.

"I'm Rachel."

He shifted, a minute movement she almost didn't notice. Then his lips parted and his gravelly voice said, "Know that."

He held his body still. So much control. She had to do the same, or he'd know he was getting to her. Freaking her out.

"Would you like to tell me why you asked to speak to me?"

Maybe they could get this over with.

He said, "Figured I'd see you for myself. In person."

"Because my name is all over what he's asking you to do? Sending people messages and emails, giving out instructions. Orders to kill." He'd probably even seen the video of her—like everyone else. She wanted to shudder, but held her body still.

Was that what he meant—in person?

The glint in his eyes got to her. Rachel glanced at the wall behind his shoulder and exhaled, like this whole thing was boring her to tears. Which was a weird expression, when she thought about it. Why would she be so bored she'd start crying? Maybe fall asleep, but not cry. Bored to the point of snoring was probably more like it. But considering the rhyme there, maybe that was why it hadn't become a thing.

She glanced at him. "But now you're here. Caught."

He was older than she'd have thought a hacker would be. Wasn't that a younger person thing? Not someone born before the computer age hit every household in America.

So was he actually the hacker they were looking for or was he someone else entirely?

A voice spoke in her earpiece. "Rachel."

She didn't react.

The voice she assumed belonged to Adrian said, "He isn't in any US military database, or any branch of the government. We ran his photo through the DMV. There's nothing. Which means we have no idea who he is."

If they hadn't found his ID in any branch of service's database, that meant he couldn't possibly be part of Steve's team back when he'd worked for the CIA.

He wasn't part of it in any way, or his fingerprints would've come back with a result that gave them nothing but a reference number for a classified file they didn't have access to. Either way, there would have been some kind of record.

"Who are you?"

His lips curled into a smile. "No one." He laughed, the sound sharp against her ears. "That's why it's all so beautiful."

"Killing people is beautiful? Destroying lives by ruining people's reputations? A woman took her life, and you're sitting here laughing because you're 'so good' that you give the FBI the runaround?" She dropped her hands from the air quotes, no longer quite so nervous. "Why did you want to talk to me? Because I don't think it was just to gloat. You seem entirely too enamored with your own intelligence to not have something else going on."

A thought popped into her head.

"Are you stringing me along while you hack into the FBI's database somehow?"

His eyebrows rose. "I was searched. There's no electronics on me. It's all been seized."

"And brought here."

In her earpiece, Adrian said, "On it."

The hacker's mouth shifted.

"Is that what this is? A time-waste?" She paused for a second, then said, "What is his end game? What does he want?"

She needed him to spell out the fact the VP wanted to take the president's spot in the Oval office. Adrian's job would be a whole lot easier if the rest of the feds knew who the prime suspect was in all of this.

"It can't just be about revenge." She took a breath, aware she was—in part—speaking just to fill the silence. A nervous habit. "I don't buy that. I think he wants something."

"Power," the man whispered, his voice full of awe. "Money." His mouth shifted, and he flashed his teeth. "Isn't that what everyone wants?"

"And you get to share a piece of it?"

Something dark flickered in his eyes, and it made her entire body go cold. He'd asked to speak to *her*. It was a couple of seconds before he said, "If I want my share."

She jumped on that, ignoring the ickiness of this situation. Leaning forward, she said, "I don't believe you. I think he'll leave you behind, you'll be known as just the hacker he used to get the job done. Now he's on to bigger things. You'll be forgotten."

He fisted one hand and slammed it down on the table. "I won't."

Rachel jumped in her chair. She covered the reaction saying, "I think you know the truth."

His face twisted and he screamed, "He *won't*."

He knew that was a lie. Why else scream at her so loud? There was no need to face off with her if she was wrong. He'd just sit there, content he had the superior position. But he'd lost it. She'd turned the power back on him.

The question she had was, how to use it.

"I can help you." She let those words hang in the air. He needed to know she wasn't going to use her power against him, even the slim portion she had. "Tell me what you want, and I'll make it so you don't need him. He won't control you anymore."

He stretched his mouth wide and screamed at her, spit flying across the table.

Rachel got up and stepped back.

He slumped in the chair, breathing hard.

The door swung open. Bradley stuck his head in. "You're done."

Like this was her fault? She'd been getting somewhere. How was she to know this guy had a screw loose? Rachel smoothed down her skirt and glanced at the hacker—if that was who this was.

"Think about it." She pushed her chair back under the table. "My offer won't last forever."

. . .

"Two minutes."

Steve gripped the phone as he strode down the sidewalk. "Copy that."

At the street corner, traffic buzzed past. He hung back and waited for the vehicle Bradley had described to make its way along the street. Steve stepped up to the curb.

The big black SUV stopped but not before the painted white strips of the crosswalk, so Steve could cross in front of it. The vehicle came to a stop on the white, the passenger door right in front of him.

Steve opened the door and climbed in.

The whole thing took less than twenty seconds, then Bradley hit the gas and they set off. "Almost didn't recognize you in that old man getup. They teach you that stuff in spy school?"

Steve said, "Yes. Now tell me what gave it away." If there was something amiss, he needed to know.

Bradley shrugged one shoulder as he drove. "Nothing specific. If I wasn't waiting for you, maybe I'd have overlooked you."

But Bradley would probably have realized it later. Steve thought about that for a moment. If the feds looking for him saw this disguise, then they likely wouldn't realize it was him. At least not in time to act. The likelihood they would get an image of him from some camera and be able to figure his identity out later using a computer program? That was a whole different set of odds.

Steve dismissed that whole thing. "So what's happening?"

"Prisoner transfer."

He glanced over at his friend and saw the tension in his body.

"Rachel baited him." Bradley twisted his grip on the steering wheel. "Just sat there, cool as you like, and poked the bear."

Bradley was proud of her. At least, he was as proud as he was scared. His finger shook when he pointed to an armored vehicle a quarter mile in front of them, surrounded by black SUVs. The hacker was in there, being taken to holding at a federal prison? Steve's brain sparked with ideas—all of which were illegal.

Bradley continued, "He was obsessed with her before. Now?" Bradley blew out a breath and shook his head.

Steve said, "Obsessed?"

Bradley sighed.

"Explain."

"I can't pinpoint it."

"So your gut says what?" Steve asked.

"Something doesn't add up is all. Not just because he's older than me, and every computer geek I know is younger. Maybe that's stereotyping, but it's true, isn't it? And they all have this cousin in middle school they call when they get stuck. It's like a thing."

"But not with this guy?"

Bradley shook his head. "I can't put my finger on it. Maybe he's the most techy, old person ever, or he did what he needed just to get ahead. Stay at the top of the hacker game. What do I know? I'm a grunt with a gun."

He was a lot more than that, considering he'd been a Tier 1 operator before Steve hired him. "How is your knee?"

He'd had surgery a few weeks ago. Now he barely walked with a limp, though that didn't mean it wasn't still healing.

"Hurts." He glanced at Steve, then looked back at the road. "Don't tell Alexis."

Steve pressed his lips together, thinking about Rachel. It was inevitable. Despite the fact it was both redundant and pointless that his thoughts were full of her. Everything that needed to be said had already been said. Unless his life drastically changed, he wasn't going to ruin the career of the senator because she was tangled up with a fugitive. After all she'd been through, she didn't need that.

"Get anything?"

Steve heard the tone, as Bradley switched back to operational details. He told his friend about the meeting the VP had at the hotel, and the fact he'd followed his former teammate into that alley so they could talk.

Bradley glanced at him. "And then you just let him go?"

Steve shifted in his seat, as achy as the age his disguise pretended he was. Life on the run wasn't fun after your mid-twenties. "David is going to feed me whatever he gets, and I have his number. If you pass it to the FBI, maybe they can track him."

"So far we've come up empty on known associates."

Steve nodded. "We knew this wasn't going to be—" Brake lights lit up in front of them as traffic slowed to a stop. Buildings flanked them on both sides. "—easy."

Bradley said, "It's a choke point is what it is."

"Huh?"

"This whole street. It's—" Bradley didn't get the chance to finish.

The SUV to the right of the armored vehicle exploded. Both of them ducked in their seats. The reflex to a battle they'd seen many times over.

Men poured out of the buildings on either side, dressed in black and armed with high powered rifles. Skull masks covered their faces.

Bradley pulled a weapon from the backseat and flung his door open. Steve did the same on his side with the pistol under his jacket. Behind the cover of the doors, they fired off shots. One fell. Then another.

An agent up ahead lifted his weapon.

Gunmen took him down.

An older lady screamed. Steve spotted her, two cars in front of him. He ducked out from behind the door, then crouch-walked to the passenger side of her car. He opened the door and leaned in. "Come on!"

She blinked at him and closed her mouth. Her earrings swayed, but the screaming ceased. She clambered across the parking break toward him. He hauled her out, and they duck-walked their way back to the SUV. He gave her a little shove in the direction of two other people running away.

"Go with them."

In the distance, he heard sirens over the sound of gunfire. Smoke laced the air, thick with the scent of cordite. There was a limited amount of time he could stay here before cops descended, and he ran the risk of getting caught.

He turned back to the SUV. Got back in position.

Bradley ducked down, so his face was level with the door handle. "They're mowing down the agents."

Another vehicle exploded.

Steve yelled, "Rocket launcher!" He found the open window and pointed. "Up there."

Bradley nodded. "They're breaking him out."

There was no way they could let that happen.

"Ready?"

He didn't even need to explain the plan. Bradley said, "Go!"

They moved out from behind the doors. Strode between vehicles toward the armored truck. Steve reached a female agent pinned down with a gunshot to her leg. She lifted her weapon. A reflex.

"Stand down."

"Who are you?"

He decided to opt for truth. "Steve Preston." He was in an old man disguise. Maybe she wouldn't believe him.

She yelled, "Hey!"

He kept going and hoped she didn't shoot him in the back. More gunfire erupted from in front, this time at him. He'd lost sight of Bradley but heard the answering shots from his friend's gun. Steve took cover then took out two more of the gunmen. Hired. Not Steve's former team. The blackmailer had other people in his pocket—or just a lot of money. Enough to hire a black ops team to break out the hacker.

A mysterious hacker knew who he was and could even provide them with the evidence they needed.

Steve fired another shot, aware he was going to run out of bullets very soon. Two shots came back at him.

He ducked, then lifted back up.

The hacker strode out in the middle of a group of men. Steve caught a glimpse of his face. Not as old as Steve was pretending to be, but Bradley had been right. He wasn't your stereotypical hacker. This man had thinning gray hair and a craggy face.

More than that, Steve thought.

This man looked familiar. Steve had seen him somewhere before.

Chapter 13

The gunman at the rear glanced back. He shifted his weapon to fire.

Steve took cover.

Bullets clanged into the metal of the car beside him. He crawled back toward the SUV. "Bradley! Let's go!"

"Copy that!" His friend yelled back, but Steve couldn't see where he was.

Sirens were getting louder now. Time to leave.

He moved past the fallen agent. Blood now pooled on the concrete around her leg. He stowed his weapon then pulled his shirt open. Buttons skittered across the ground.

She gave him a look. "Nice moves hotshot. Too bad I'm going to have to arrest you." She lifted her weapon from the ground and pointed it at him one-handed.

Steve ignored her. He lifted her leg only enough to get the shirt under, then tied it around her leg and pulled the material tight.

She hissed.

Steve said, "Maybe next time."

He raced away. She didn't fire at his back. He'd have to send her a thank you note later, along with a box of cookies.

Steve climbed in the front passenger seat. Bradley jumped in the driver's door and said, "What are you thinking?"

"Cookies." He buckled up. "And hit the gas, or we'll never catch them."

The street was chaos. Bradley used the SUV to shift two vehicles apart enough they could slip between. Steve winced at the crunch of metal on metal.

Bradley turned the corner just as two black and white police cars tore down the road toward the scene. Plenty of agents down. A fugitive loose. A gunfight on a Washington DC street.

They would be busy for a long while. And as far as Steve had seen, no other agents had gone after the gunmen and their charge.

"Take the next left."

Bradley did as Steve ordered him to. They cut through a side street and came out on a parallel street, busy with cars. Bradley said, "We'll never catch them in this."

Steve wanted to believe it wasn't true. Still, he could hope. "I know him."

"The hacker? Who is he?"

"I don't know."

Bradley cut in front of a Mercedes and ignored the driver laying on his horn. "Talk it out. You might remember."

"I've seen him," Steve said aloud. "It was the turn of his head, that line of jaw. The gray hair." He tapped his fingers on his leg as Bradley sped down the street. "He looks like someone I've seen recently."

None of his teammates were old enough, and there wasn't one man from the Venezuela group that he hadn't spoken with—except, of course, those he'd heard were dead.

He kept his finger tapping, thinking through everywhere he'd been.

Nicola's apartment.

Rachel's house.

The VP's study.

He tried to remember details, but couldn't place anything. Bradley swerved and Steve grabbed the handlebar at the top of the door. "See them?"

"Nothing. But we don't know what car they're driving, right?"

Steve said, "Unless the FBI got it. Or they can look on traffic cameras."

He no longer had the clout to ask such a question. He was a fugitive. One who had stashed the sniper rifle he was supposed to use to kill the president in a safe place. Maybe he would just leave it there until after the summit. Or send it by courier to Adrian, c/o the FBI office. They could do all kinds of processing on it. But that was assuming the blackmailer had made a mistake and left evidence behind. Not likely.

Steve didn't figure they would find a fingerprint on the case. At least, not one that didn't belong to him.

Bradley tossed Steve his phone. "Call Mint first. I want to know where he is."

"So do I," Steve said, dialing the number.

No answer.

"Last I heard, he was going to the safety deposit box with Emma to retrieve what was in there."

Bradley nodded. "He hasn't called me since."

"If he got mixed up in something, he might have dumped his phone and gone dark." What about Emma? They would be together—but were they okay?

"Call Adrian."

Steve ignored the fact it was an order and did it. Good idea.

When he answered, Steve put him on speaker. Adrian said, "Kinda busy cleaning up a mess."

Steve held the phone out but didn't say anything.

Bradley said, "Not our fault."

"Yeah."

Steve didn't know how to interpret that. He wasn't happy, but he didn't blame them?

Bradley got in the left lane, his blinker on. "They were pros. A team of operators."

"Hired as a group."

"You can tell by the way they moved," Bradley said. "Totally in sync. No words or commands. They've done this before, in some shape or form."

"Okay, I'll run what we have against military databases. Thanks."

"No problem. One thing, though."

"What?"

Bradley said, "Can you send me a picture of the hacker? My friend here thinks he recognizes him from somewhere."

"Will do," Adrian said. "Keep me posted on that. It might help."

"I hope so." Bradley paused a second. "Let Alexis know we'll be back in a while."

"She left." Adrian's voice was distracted.

Bradley's face whipped around to the phone. "What?"

"Megan's with her. She took Alexis and Rachel to the hospital to check on that reporter who got shot."

Bradley took the left turn. As soon as there was a gap in oncoming traffic he flipped a U-turn. "Gotta go."

Steve hung up the phone, while Bradley muttered about his wife and sister.

. . .

Megan hung back. Rachel knocked on the door and cracked it, Alexis right behind her. The woman on the bed turned her head to see who was at the door. She clearly recognized Rachel.

"Is it okay if I come in?"

"Sure. I'm already bored of staring at the walls." Nicola spoke as though pained. Her face was pale, dark under her eyes.

"I won't stay long. I just wanted to make sure you're all right, so I can pass that information along to our mutual friend." She stepped into the room, but left the door open.

Alexis stayed in the doorway, Megan on duty in the hall. Their own personal protection detail. It was a risky move, but Megan had given them instructions they'd followed to minimize danger.

"If you're really not okay, I can leave."

Nicola said, "I'm not going to lie and say it doesn't hurt. But it's more discomfort than pain. They gave me some good stuff."

"Good." Rachel smiled at her. She'd heard of Nicola Starns and had read some of her work, but they'd never met. "I'm—"

"Senator Rachel Harris." She looked more curious than anything else. "Steve told me about the blackmail. He's kept me updated in case I can find information that might help clear his name."

"So you know he only acted under duress, firing at the FBI. He's been dragged into this even though it has nothing to do with him. It's all about a mission carried out by a colleague of his."

Nicola nodded. "The general who died at the think tank."

It was good she knew that. Even while it rubbed Rachel a little the wrong way that Nicola had talked to Steve. She had to remind herself that the two of them had a professional relationship these days. Nicola's career as a reporter made her the perfect person to advocate for Steve. No one else could.

Rachel would try. But even when she did, everyone wrote it off as the aftermath of trauma. Like she was losing her mind. "Have you been able to find out anything?"

Nicola shook her head, a tiny movement. "Steve's plan was to find other members of his team so that if he didn't go through with the *mission,* he could keep anyone else from going through with it. In case the blackmailer has a backup plan in place."

"Oh." Rachel had only just found out about the presidential assassination. It seemed like Nicola knew more than she did. Had Steve managed to find any members of his team?

"I'm going to call the Secret Service today. Let them know there might be an attempt on the president's life at the summit. I just can't sit back and not say anything. I would never forgive myself." Nicola paused. "Not if something happened."

Rachel tried to figure out why she hadn't thought of that. Instead she'd done nothing, which meant she was allowing an attempt on the president's life. She'd been convinced Steve was joking. And then, when she'd wondered if it was a real assignment from the blackmailer, she'd been sure he would never do it.

Was there someone else contracted by the blackmailer to take a shot at the president if Steve didn't do it?

She needed to talk to Steve. Make sure he had a plan in place. Of course he did, and okay, maybe it was the senator in her that needed to be kept abreast of the situation here. But that was who she was. Committees and meetings. So many meetings. Feeling like she was out of the loop on something this important wasn't fun.

"Adrian just called."

Rachel spun around. Megan stood beside Alexis in the doorway. The former FBI agent said, "The transport was attacked. The hacker was set free by a team of mercenaries."

Rachel yelled, "What?"

Nicola gasped, then groaned.

"Are you okay?" Alexis wandered over to speak to her in that low, soothing voice she had. "Do you want me to call a nurse?"

"I'm okay," Nicola said.

Rachel didn't believe her. "I think you should call for some protection to keep you safe while you're here."

Nicola bit her lip.

"Is there someone who can do that?"

Nicola shifted one shoulder. When she didn't elaborate, Megan said, "I can have the FBI send over an agent to sit at the door."

Rachel wondered if she'd have called Steve, if he hadn't been a fugitive at this present moment.

Nicola said, "Thank you."

Alexis backed up. Megan headed for the hall and spoke over her shoulder, "Two minutes." Her phone rang and she continued on her way out while she pulled it from her back pocket. "Perkins."

She disappeared into the hall. Alexis moved back over to the doorway but stayed inside.

Rachel turned to Nicola again. "We don't know each other." This was weird, but she didn't know how to say it other than to just say it. "But I'm glad you didn't end up as just another victim of this blackmailer."

Nicola's lips shifted, not precisely a smile. "Me too. Though I don't think I've ever felt worse."

"I'm sorry. I'll leave you to it." Rachel smiled her "senator" smile. "I just wanted to make sure you were all right."

"Nah," Nicola said, a gleam of humor in her eyes. "That isn't why you came. Not totally. You wanted to feel me out. See about me and Steve."

Rachel heard Alexis snort a tiny laugh but ignored it. She tried to sound as innocent as possible when she said, "There's a 'you and Steve'?" Like it was a perfectly reasonable question.

Nicola said, "A long time ago. He's a good man."

Rachel nodded. "He really is."

Something moved across Nicola's face. Rachel didn't know what it meant. The reporter said, "The tricky part is convincing *him* that that's true."

"Let's go," Megan called out from the door.

Rachel laid her hand on the reporter's for a second. "I'm glad you're all right." Would it be weird to ask if she wanted to hang out when she was better? Nicola beat her to it.

"Coffee, when I'm out of here? Or dinner?"

Rachel smiled. "That would be great."

Right now she needed as many friends as she could get. Even if this one was only just a potential friend at this point.

She waved and strode out.

"Feel better?" Alexis slid her arm into Rachel's as they walked.

"Yes." How had she known that?

"You always did like field trips."

Rachel chuckled as they turned toward the elevator.

"Stairs." Megan's tone left no room for arguments.

Rachel eyed her. Just a few weeks ago the woman had multiple broken bones. Rachel pulled open the door to the stairs. "How are you feeling, Megan?" There was a limp, but just like Bradley, Megan covered it well.

"Fine." Her full attention was on the environment around them as she watched for danger. Hand close to her holstered gun. The lines on the outside of her eyes were pronounced.

"You look like you need a nap."

"And you don't?"

Rachel smiled.

Alexis covered a yawn. "I seriously do."

Rachel's smile grew to laughter. "It's tiring trying to right wrongs."

"Don't I know it?" Megan smiled at her, and they proceeded to the bottom of the stairwell where they stood by the exit door. "Hold up. Our ride is almost here." She looked at her phone, but Rachel noticed she shifted her weight quickly to take the pressure off the knee that had been replaced.

Rachel didn't figure there would be many times like this before the summit—quiet moments where nothing was happening. She hadn't been expecting it to happen now, but it was nice that it had. They could pretend, for a minute, that they were three regular friends sharing a moment of humor. Then life would intrude upon them again.

The blackmailer.

An injured woman who fought for her life.

Their only lead into the blackmailer's activities? Out on the streets again.

"We have a ride?"

Megan nodded. "I think you'll like it. I know I'll enjoy listening to Bradley ask Alexis why she left the cover of the FBI office while he was gone."

Alexis groaned. "I feel nauseous."

Rachel pulled her in for a side hug. "I'll protect you."

Megan's phone screen flashed. "Let's go." She opened the door, where an SUV was parked outside with the engine running. An older gentleman stood holding the back door open.

Rachel did a double take. "Steve?"

He cracked a smile. It made his face look weird. "I guess it's not that good of a disguise."

They all got in. Bradley shot his wife a frosty look but pulled away from the curb. Alexis buckled her seatbelt. "Megan was protecting us." She motioned over her shoulder to the former FBI agent, sitting in the back row with her eyes closed.

Neither of them said much after that.

Rachel broke the silence. "Where are we going?"

Bradley's phone buzzed. He handed it to Steve.

"It's Adrian with that picture." Steve swiped the screen.

Rachel leaned forward so she could see as well. Steve glanced at her, and they shared a smile. He was okay. Right now, at least. And in the moment, couldn't that be enough?

He frowned, his attention on the screen. "I do know him."

"You—"

"The father," Steve said.

Bradley glanced over. "Whose father?"

"In the picture I found in the VP's safe. It was a family album, and all the pictures were from Venezuela. Probably before whatever happened." Steve paused. "The hacker looks like the vice president's father."

Rachel didn't want to disturb the flow of his thoughts, but she had to say, "Which means…"

"The only thing that makes sense, is if…the brother. Of course. He'd be the right age now. Mid-forties." Steve said, "The hacker is the vice president's younger brother."

Chapter 14

Alexis gasped. She reached over and grabbed Rachel's hand. Behind Rachel, Megan sat completely stoic in the back row.

Bradley, still driving, said, "Are you sure?"

"Not certain, no. All the information we got back about William Anderson said he had no brother. So where does the other boy come in to it?"

Steve glanced at her, but she didn't know what that look meant. She said, "If he's been hidden all this time somehow..." she let that trail off. "If they're behind all this, working together as brothers, then we need to expose it. Right?"

Steve nodded. "The mission is still the same."

"Unless the VP doesn't know anything," Alexis said. "And it's all the brother."

"But he's the hacker," Rachel said. "Not the mastermind."

Megan's clothes rustled as she shifted in her seat. "Could be he just wanted to get a look at all of us, so he got himself hauled in as the hacker. He might be behind it all—or maybe not— maybe they are in it together."

"How are we supposed to figure out which it is?" Rachel glanced between Megan and the two men in the front seat. "Can we do a DNA test and make sure you're right?" She didn't want Steve to think she didn't believe him. Rachel knew what it was like to have everyone distrust her and think of her as crazy. Now that she had killed someone—even if it had been self-defense—things were going to get even worse.

Steve stared out the front window.

Megan said, "We don't have the hacker's DNA. Just the print we ran that came up with nothing."

Rachel got on her phone. "Google says the vice president is an only child."

Steve shifted in his chair. "There was a brother in the photo I found in the vice president's safe."

"La-la-la-la—" Megan had her hands over her ears. "—don't say that where Adrian can hear you or he'll arrest you." She dropped her hands, but Rachel saw the gleam of humor in her eyes. "And don't tell me how you happened to have access to his safe, because I do *not* want to be an accomplice to this."

"Way to save your own skin, Perkins," Bradley shot from the front seat.

Alexis said, "She's not—"

"Yeah, I am. If Steve goes to jail—which we all know is a possibility right now—it's better if he doesn't drag the rest of us down with him," Megan said. "The less we know about what Steve has been doing, the better. It's why we're not actively hiding him."

"I thought that was just because of his spy skills?" Rachel said.

Alexis glanced around. "Steve was a spy?"

"Let's get back on topic, shall we," the man himself said. "Megan, I know you're between two sides here. You're loyal to Adrian, who has to be above board as an agent, and yet you're also loyal to Double Down. But since the company is no more, there's no being torn. You owe me nothing."

"If that were true," Megan said, "I wouldn't be protecting Rachel and sitting in this car with you."

"I appreciate that," Steve said. "Both of those." He paused. "And what all of you are doing for me. It means a lot to know I have friends standing behind me."

There was something in his voice she couldn't decipher. He sounded almost…sad. But she didn't think that was it. More, it was like he didn't expect them to be standing by him for much longer.

Rachel squeezed his shoulder. "Of course we're going to stand by you. Where else would we be?"

"She's right," Bradley said. Maybe he'd heard the same thing in Steve's voice. "You've given all of us focus, and the chance to use our skills. Double Down made a difference in all of our lives."

Rachel didn't know what it was like to be a veteran. She glanced at Megan. She also didn't know what it was like to be a former undercover FBI agent who had seen her partner killed. But she did know something about finding a place to belong. A place where she was valued because she *mattered*. And no, it wasn't in the senate that she'd found that. The senate was simply a place she went every day to wade through the sharks—to make a difference.

She'd found her place. With Alexis, and with Bradley. With Steve.

This was where she belonged.

At this point, she hardly even wanted to return to work and not just because she'd ended a life in that building. Who cared about all the posturing and policy when her friends were in danger, and the future of the presidency was at stake?

Surely there was something she could do in order to get this situation resolved. If she went to the president himself and explained what she knew, would he listen? She had no proof. The Secret Service weren't going to arrest the vice president without evidence. She would just get written off as having completely lost it. Trying to protect her friend, maybe. But definitely crazy.

Her credibility was at an all-time low. She didn't even want to know what was being said about her on the news, or on social media. She was trying not to even care. Rachel was actually sick of her personal life being discussed publicly. After being victimized, it seemed like everyone had an opinion. Whether that was how she should continue to play the victim, or that she should suddenly be this great "overcomer." Like Mrs. Anderson's opinion about Rachel and how she should've jumped into the role of spokesperson for their cause. Then there were the people who talked about how she probably deserved it.

Rachel was ready for a quiet life. Or at least some kind of change. She wanted her privacy back.

And she wanted Steve free and clear of all charges.

She wanted the VP and his brother stopped.

Alexis touched her hand. "You okay?"

Everyone quieted. Even Steve and Bradley stopped their conversation in the front seat. Rachel shrugged one shoulder. There *had* to be something she could do. Maybe she could approach the vice president's wife instead. Did Mrs. Anderson know what was going on? Surely she knew her husband had a secret brother, even if no one else was aware of that fact.

Rachel shifted in her seat.

"What?" Alexis asked. "What did you just figure out?"

"Nothing," Rachel lied.

"You're lying," Bradley said.

She gritted her teeth. "I have an idea, which I will discuss with Adrian."

"I expect to be informed."

Rachel ignored her brother's tone and kept thinking on it. Steve had to fight this battle his way. She was certain he would do that. But she didn't have to sit around doing nothing, did she?

Steve said, "And I expect you to remain under the cover of FBI or Secret Service protection at all times."

"You trust them now?"

He shrugged. "This is about the VP and his family, and the players here are all my old team. It's now only me and David, which has minimized the risk to you. But we're not completely out of the woods just yet."

"I'll be careful."

His lips twitched.

She said, "I promise."

"Make sure you keep that promise."

Because, when all this was over, he expected her to be there? That thought set her heart to racing. She wanted nothing more than to explore the promise of what she thought she could see in his eyes. Rachel didn't exactly enjoy being close to anyone, not after what she'd been through. But Steve, she trusted. He was a gentleman.

Yes, she would very much like to explore things with him.

"What about you?" She knew he was absolutely going to put his life at risk.

He glanced at Bradley. Her brother pulled the car to the curb and put the lever in park. Megan shifted in her seat. "Let's go, ladies."

"What?" Alexis glanced around. "We're leaving?"

"Time to get back to the FBI office."

. . .

"Probably should've dropped me off instead of the girls."

Bradley shrugged as he pulled away from the curb. "They have to walk two blocks on a street busy with sightseers. There's no way they'll make it without ending up in at least a few holiday selfies."

Steve's lips twitched. "You know about selfies?"

Bradley shot him a look. "I'm just saying it's hardly likely they'll be targeted in a crowd of people."

Steve could debate that but decided to focus on their stuff instead. "So what exactly do you think you're going to help me with?"

"You're taking this fight to him, right? Which means you need cover so you can confront the vice president about his brother and how this whole thing is masterminded."

He wasn't wrong, so Steve didn't bother arguing. "That's what I don't get. Did the brother really just allow himself to get found and arrested by the FBI just to have a face to face with Rachel?"

Bradley said, "A power trip. He wanted to be seen and to mess with Rachel. Plus, when the FBI finds out they had him, and then he got away, they're going to kick themselves."

"So he's just throwing his weight around. Doing it because he can." Steve thought. "We aren't thinking he's really the hacker, right?"

"He could be. But also just as likely not," Bradley said. "And that signal the FBI found was only because he *wanted* to be caught."

Steve nodded.

"So what's your plan?"

Steve tugged his cell phone out of his pocket and pulled up an app he'd used in the CIA. The one he'd bought now was the bootleg version—for people who wanted to keep track of merchandise they either weren't supposed to have, or shouldn't have been selling in the first place.

It loaded, giving him a GPS map location for David Sanders.

"Who'd you bug?"

"My teammate."

He tried to figure out if it bothered him that he and David were the only ones left alive. Not really. His loyalty was to Double Down's team members now. His old special ops spy team had parted ways years ago, with an understanding all of them had adhered to. He hadn't seen a single one of them, until the first one crawled out from the woodwork to attack Rachel.

Then she'd killed the second one who'd come after her.

Steve didn't want to think about the rage he'd feel if one of them had succeeded.

If he had to kill David, Steve would do it without hesitation.

He didn't much care whether they were being paid or acting under duress like Steve. If it came down to it, he would do what he had to in order to keep the people he cared about safe. After all, that was what he'd been doing for weeks now. Hiding out in Mrs. Cromwell's apartment where no one had found him.

He directed Bradley to the place where the blue dot sat, unmoving. "I think David is the fall back if I don't kill the president. I'm just hoping he has more information on the brother than what we know so far. He seems to have been working a different angle."

He had met publicly with the vice president. What if that had been to pass on instructions from the brother—or to get instructions *for* him? David might have been the go-between for two men who couldn't be seen together.

Bradley pulled over down the street, and they strapped on. Weapons visible, weapons hidden. They didn't know what they were walking into, so it didn't hurt to be more than prepared.

The location where the blue dot had stopped was a warehouse. At the side door, Steve gave his friend a series of hand signals. Bradley nodded. They went inside together and then separated so Bradley could find a high vantage point where he could provide cover. The place was a defunct textile factory. Rows and rows of tables. Industrial sewing machines. Where was David?

Steve checked the GPS again. He needed to be closer to the other end of the building, though it wasn't exact—just better than conventional cell phone GPS. He held his gun aimed low, ready to use it without assuming he was going to have to.

He moved close enough he could make out voices. More than one person was in the room with David. Could be the men the VP's brother had contracted to get him out of FBI custody. That had been a gamble, because it let the FBI know the strength of who they were up against. It had also cut the bureau's numbers, given the amount of agents either dead or injured. But the ones who were left? They were now more motivated than ever to find him.

It was a risk the FBI was going to ensure would wind up costing the VP's brother more than he ever wanted to pay.

Steve crept up to the door. The voices were louder now, but he still couldn't tell what they were saying. Until one yelled.

"Find it!"

Uh-oh. Had they discovered the fact one of their people had been low-jacked? Booted feet shuffled on the floor behind the door where Steve stood. He moved to the side and pressed his back against the wall. Two men walked out, dressed much like they had when they were breaking the "hacker" out of FBI custody. And shooting feds. They moved through the building like they were looking for something.

Steve shifted, willing to gamble since he didn't have much to lose. Were they going to kill him, before he could shoot the president? He placed a bet of his own and stepped into the room.

"Gentlemen."

He clocked three guys spread around the room. All three pointed their weapons at him. He knew immediately the one to his left was the team lead. In the center, David sat on a chair. His nose dripped blood, and one eye was swollen.

"I guess you won't be meeting the Vice President for lunch again anytime soon."

David said nothing. The team lead motioned with his gun. "Smart mouth for a guy who's going to go down for all of this," he said in heavily accented English. "Guess you didn't figure that out yet."

Venezuelan. Steve wanted to see their faces, but they all wore the same masks and head coverings they had on the street. Like even David wasn't supposed to see their faces. They wanted to walk away clean, no chance they'd be implicated as part of this. Determined to protect their identities no matter what.

A shuffling behind him brought Steve's attention around. The two who'd walked out came back in, dragging Bradley. One said in Spanish, "Look what we found."

They tossed him on the floor in the far corner. Bradley hit the wall and lay on his back. He kept his face passive, eyes on Steve. He'd probably let himself get "captured" just so he could be in the center of what was going on. Steve would've done the same thing.

Bradley blinked. Then blinked again. Steve watched the series of long and short blinks, already knowing what Bradley was suggesting.

Steve shook his head, a tiny movement. That was an awful idea.

The leader strode over to Bradley and pointed his gun at the former SEAL's face. He turned to Steve. Bradley motioned to the guy with a tip of his head. Yes, Steve knew Bradley could take the guy down, even from the floor. But that didn't get them what they wanted.

The gunman leader spoke. "Tomorrow is the summit. The president will die, or your friend here dies."

Steve made a face, like he was scared at the idea Bradley might die. It might have been more effective if Bradley hadn't been almost grinning. Steve had better acting skills than that.

Steve let his voice shake when he said, "Let him go."

"I think not. He stays here, and you go with your friend—" The gunman motioned to David with his head. "—to ensure the mission is completed."

"It's not exactly easy to kill the president of the United States, you know?"

"But you will do it, Mr. Super Spy. It is why you were chosen."

Steve looked at David. His former teammate gave him nothing, his face impassive and his eyes dark. He didn't like these guys, but he also wasn't objecting to any of this.

He glanced at Bradley again. His friend nodded.

"Okay." He said it more to Bradley than to the rest of them, but they took it however they wanted. "I'll do it."

Chapter 15

Three agents met them in the hallway, grim faces. One said, "Ms. Perkins." Then motioned for Megan to go with him. Another did the same with Alexis.

Rachel stood in the hallway, while the third moved closer to her. A forty-something agent who had buzzed his hair, so it wasn't so obvious he was balding. It didn't work. He reached out toward her.

Rachel took a step back, out of reach. "Please refrain from touching me."

He nodded. "If you'd come this way."

"May I ask what's going on?" Seemed like something serious given Adrian was nowhere to be found, and they were being separated. Questioned?

"Let's have a seat in here." He directed her to a small room with one table, two chairs and two way glass.

"Do I need a lawyer?"

"If you'd feel more comfortable. However, I assure you this is just an informal chat."

Because they couldn't arrest her for anything. Which meant they either had no evidence, just a theory, or they were still waiting for the warrant from a judge.

Rachel sat.

The agent took the seat opposite her.

"You aren't going to ask me if I'd like a cup of coffee?"

"Would you?"

"No."

His lips curled up at the corners.

Like he could've known that before she said anything. Rachel folded her arms. Not because she wanted to look belligerent, it was just freezing in here. Tea would have been good, but she needed to keep all her focus on what was happening here. Not be distracted by a yummy warm drink.

Did they know she'd been in the SUV with Steve? How could they, when he'd been in disguise?

So what did they know now that they hadn't known before Rachel went with Alexis and Megan to the hospital to talk with Nicola?

"How long have you known Steve Preston?"

"The fact that I know him isn't a secret, nor is it new information."

"Answer the question please, Ms. Harris."

"It's *Senator* Harris."

He sat silently for a second, then shifted in his seat to flip open his file. He turned a photo so she could see it. Black and white, but she got the image.

A dead guy, bullet hole in his forehead.

Next picture: two dead guys in an alley.

There were more.

Rachel steeled herself.

"These are all men Steve Preston has killed."

"I killed a man yesterday."

The agent stopped, mouth open. Rachel didn't want to gloat that she'd actually surprised him enough he lost control of his train of questioning, but she kind of wanted to. Maybe it was being so close to Double Down, all high-intensity operators, that had left her with this core of strength. Enough she could hold it together right now.

Maybe she would fall apart later, but that would be *later*. Right now she had to be strong. Stand up for her friends.

"If you're going to try and convince me that Steve Preston is some kind of murderer, I'll point out that he was working for the Central Intelligence Agency at the time. What he did prior to that and after his tenure as an intelligence officer, was also in service to this country. Mostly as a minister." She paused half a second, not long enough for him to speak, then said, "And everything he is doing now follows that same pattern. Regardless of what you've been told, or whatever the reason you're questioning me and my friends. And making accusations against my family."

She wasn't a politician for nothing.

The agent cleared his throat.

"And," she continued before he could say anything. "Whatever the reason you've decided to divide this family by showing me the worst of what a good man has done just to shake my faith in him, it's not going to work. Nor is telling anyone I've lost my mind, which seems to be the current rhetoric among law enforcement in this town."

As soon as they were done with this, Rachel intended to get back to her idea about reaching out to Mrs. Anderson. This conversation wouldn't help Steve. Doing her part against the blackmailer would.

With that thought, she realized this really was nothing but a time waster. Whatever—she assumed—the blackmailer had given to the FBI only made things worse for the Double Down team and everyone associated with them. But it was still just a tactic to slow them all down until the summit.

"What did he give you?"

The agent said, "Excuse me?"

"You got an email, or someone made an anonymous tip. Based on whatever you just learned, you decide to question each of us." Just the three of them, or the whole team? Rachel said, "Have you heard from Emma Burroughs and Mint?"

"Who?"

"Davis Malone."

"They were located by a team of our agents."

"Are they okay?" She hadn't heard from them in a couple of days, and everyone had been worried. "We were starting to get concerned."

"As far as I know they're fine, but I can check for you."

"So you've rounded them up like you rounded up the rest of us, right?" Rachel didn't like that. Emma had been a victim in all this as well, and Mint was only trying to keep her safe from the blackmailer so she wouldn't be a target again.

She said, "We aren't criminals, and you won't be able to make any charges stick. Which you know, or you'd be making arrests instead of fishing for information or new things to accuse Steve Preston of. Too bad for you and this expedition that you feel the need to try and drum up something; we aren't criminals. There is a blackmailer in Washington, which you know. You also can likely surmise that Steve is acting under duress the way Agent Zimmerman was when he went rogue."

"Is that right?"

"Anyone can put those two together and come out with a logical assumption," she said. "Even a senator."

He almost smiled at that. Almost.

"Why would we be hanging around the FBI office if we're behind all this? Seems like a strange way to protect someone who is hurting people, doesn't it? If Steve really was the blackmailer, then we'd probably be trying to cover it up. Not helping the FBI any way we can."

"Where did he go with your brother, Senator?"

"How should I know? I'm not either of their mother."

"Who is the blackmailer?"

She pressed her lips together.

"You know, don't you?"

"This is a conspiracy, Agent. The government is rotten to the core, and Steve is trying to stop it before it destroys the foundation of this country." She sat back in her chair. "I, for one, intend to do everything I can to help him."

"And if he does something you can't help him get past? If he incriminates himself in a serious crime, what then? You get dragged down as well and you lose everything."

It should have given her pause. That was his intention. But there just wasn't anything in her life that she cared for enough that she didn't want to lose. Except her family.

And that family included Steve.

She said, "If that happens, I'll still have everything important in my life."

. . .

David walked out of the warehouse first, followed by Steve, headed for a silver sedan parked at the far end of the building. At least, that was where Steve figured they were going. Halfway to the door, David turned around. Steve was ready.

David let go of whatever tether he'd been holding onto of his self-control.

Steve met his attack with a block. Then another block to the sneaky cross he tried to slam into Steve's side. Steve used a hook. David fell to one knee, coughing.

"Let's just go."

He climbed to his feet and pushed out a heavy breath. "You bugged me."

"You let him drag me into this, and you *knew* there was more for me to do. But you were fine with skating underneath everyone's radar like the snake you are."

"You think I have no skin in this?" David shot back. "I thought you were the better sniper, remember?"

He had said that. But Steve didn't need to be reminded of it. "So I get to have my friends shot right in front of me and others nearly killed. My business completely destroyed. And what? He threatens someone you care about?"

Steve did want to know about that. If he could safeguard whatever leverage the blackmailer had on David, then the guy would be less willing to do whatever he was told. "What does he have?"

David turned and lumbered toward the car.

"Dude. Just tell me what it is."

David pulled open the driver's door and got in. Steve climbed in the passenger side, then said, "Tell me what he's holding over you."

David blew out a breath. "I have no idea how he found out." He rubbed his hands down his face. "I was in Belize. There was this girl, a waitress. Mary. Mara. Something."

He didn't even remember her name?

"I drove her to this private beach. Secluded, you know? Things got...hot and heavy. She asked me to..."

Steve gritted his teeth. The story was about to get worse, and he probably didn't want to know what David was going to tell him. But he was going to have to listen anyway.

Long enough for David get to the point.

Steve's jaw dropped when David said it. He gaped. "You *killed* her?"

"It was an accident, okay? I took the boat out, and I dumped her over the side. No one was out there. So how does he know it even happened?"

David seemed more concerned that someone had discovered the murder than he was about the fact that his actions led to a death.

Steve closed his mouth. The man deserved whatever was happening, considering he'd been careless. There was no reasoning on earth that tolerated something like that.

David wasn't that far from the man who had victimized Rachel.

"I'm a horrible person, okay?" The sarcasm in David's tone detracted from the intention behind those words. There was no remorse in him. Just frustration that he'd been discovered.

"Yeah," Steve said. "You are."

"Fine. Be all judgy."

Steve glanced at the ceiling for a second. "That man they're holding back there?" He pointed out the back window at the rapidly retreating building. "He's the best man I've ever known. A good guy. A guy who deserves every good thing in his life, and yet he didn't find it until a few months ago. Now you've got him tied up with Venezuelans who won't hesitate to put a bullet in his brain and leave his wife a widow."

"This is my fault?"

"Yes."

"Like I'm that much different than you."

"I didn't say I was." Steve wouldn't have. Because the truth was, he was more like David than he was like Bradley. He hadn't exactly been lily-white in his life, despite being a chaplain. He'd done plenty of questionable things when they'd recruited him into spy work—and since then. But it was nothing like the traumatic experience that had been dished onto Rachel against her will.

He still had some honor.

"Tell me about the second man. The one who is the vice president's brother." That was the whole reason he'd sought out David today.

"You know about Harlem?"

"If that's his name, I guess. Anderson kept him a secret all these years?"

David visibly shuddered. "He's crazy. I know why Anderson never told anyone about him, because the guy is a psycho. Hidden away for years in some institution under guard."

And he was out now? Great. "He's the one running the show, or is the VP giving orders?"

"Who knows? Nearest I can figure is they both think they're in charge and neither one wants to back down from this."

"But the goal is for the VP to be the one in the president's seat?"

"How am I supposed to know?" David asked. "It wasn't like I sat him down on a couch and interviewed him like we're on a talk show."

"So you do your part and no one finds out you killed that girl?" He didn't care about the fallout at all?

David pulled up at a stop light and pressed his lips together. After a minute of silence, he said, "He had pictures of her. An autopsy. Said I strangled her to death."

Steve didn't have much sympathy for a man only trying to save his own skin. "How did he keep his brother a secret this whole time?"

David shrugged and set off again. "Institutionalized. But I guess he was kinda crazy before that. Then what those operatives did to his mother, and the Venezuelans tried to stop it?" He shook his head. "They were all slaughtered. It was a bloodbath."

"He told you?"

"Crazy eyes, man. Then he told me he's the one who killed their father."

"The vice president's brother killed his father?"

David nodded, and his adam's apple bobbed as he swallowed. "Doesn't matter now, though. It is what it is, and there's nothing we can do about it. Either you assassinate the president, or I do it. Then we walk away."

Steve didn't think it was anywhere near that simple. He had a ton more information than he'd known a short time ago, and still no way to prove it unless they could get evidence about the father's murder. That was something Adrian might be able to look into. But it wouldn't stop what was happening now.

Finding out what had really happened in Venezuela all those years ago could possibly put to rest the repercussions of those operative's actions. Everyone who'd been there was dead, except one Navy officer involved in the planning. And word from Adrian was that St. Germaine was now working for the blackmailer.

"Where is he?" Steve asked. "Where do you meet him?"

"Don't do that. It's suicide."

Steve reached for the revolver at his ankle. David saw, as he'd known the man would. He hadn't hidden it. Steve swung out his arm and hit the man in the diaphragm with the side of his fist.

David coughed.

"Pull over."

He did. Steve pulled the revolver. David said, "Going to shoot me?"

"I haven't decided yet."

He asked David again where he'd met the vice president's brother. When his former teammate told him, Steve grasped the back of his head and slammed his head into the steering wheel.

David slumped in the seat.

Steve tied him up, gagged him, and put him in the trunk of the car.

Chapter 16

The agent with Rachel led her back to the conference room. She frowned but went inside.

"...didn't know anything," Alexis was saying, her back to the door. She faced Adrian.

The agent shook his head. "I'm sorry. I don't know more than you do."

Megan was to the left. She leaned her hips against the sideboard where the coffee maker was, taking the weight off that leg again. The conference table stretched out to the right, down the middle of the room. On the far side, the blinds hung down in strips and muted the orange glow of sunset.

"What's going on?" Rachel moved toward her friend. She set her hand on Alexis's shoulder. Since Bradley wasn't here, Alexis needed all the support she could get.

"It's been hours. Where is Bradley?"

"With St—" Rachel turned back to the door. Open, but no one stood there listening. Still, she said, "You know who."

"He would have called by now." Alexis wrung her hands together. "I think something happened to him."

Rachel pulled her friend in for a hug, thinking of her brother. The connection between the three of them was strong. They'd been each other's whole family for years—even though Alexis's parents were still living. She didn't find love and acceptance with them. Alexis had found it with Rachel and Bradley.

Alexis reached up and wiped a tear from under her eye. "Sorry." She looked sheepish. "I can't seem to hold my emotions in right now."

"It's okay, Lex. You know he can take care of himself."

She nodded. Rachel's stomach knotted at the thought of what might've happened to both Bradley and Steve. She prayed they weren't hurt. Just as she prayed the FBI didn't find them before they accomplished whatever it was they were doing, which was surely an attempt to find the blackmailer.

She squeezed Alexis's shoulder and then asked Adrian, "Is there a laptop or computer I can use?"

"I can ask but something's definitely going on, so they may not allow even me to access a computer," he said. "They ushered us in here and told us to wait."

"Did they question you about everything as well?" She glanced around. Each of them nodded. "I think they're finally getting suspicious of us, even though we've been right here the whole time helping them as much as we can."

Adrian's attention shifted over her shoulder. Rachel turned to see what it was and gasped. Three agents escorted Emma and Mint down the hallway. Emma was pale, her arm through Mint's. Not just for her own sake. He looked like he could barely walk and had a bandage on his forehead.

The agent in front opened the conference room door. Emma walked Mint in, and the door was shut. The group closed in around them.

Rachel said, "What happened?"

Emma's eyes filled with tears. "One sec." She tugged him toward the closest seat. "You should sit down."

Mint turned around and sat on the edge of the table. Then he reached out his hand. Emma took hold of it, and he tugged her to stand by his side. "Tell them."

"After we didn't find anything at the bank, we immediately got the feeling we were being followed." Emma swallowed. "Mint got us away from them, but they found us at the cabin. Then the FBI agents showed up. They just rolled in, ready to take us into custody like we did something." She shook her head. "Mint kind of...lost it."

Rachel glanced at the windows between the conference room and the main office. One of the agents was rubbing his head. Another looked like he had a black eye. "Ah."

"That's not good," Adrian said. "I can try and persuade them not to bring charges, but if you bruised some egos, they aren't likely to drop the issue."

Mint shrugged one shoulder. "Mistakes were made on both sides. Somehow they had information on my history. And they knew all about Emma."

"They threatened to arrest *me*, if he didn't calm down," Emma said.

Megan groaned. Adrian stood beside her. Alexis took a seat on the far side of the table. Rachel leaned against the wall.

She said, "What are we going to do now? Do you think the blackmailer is purposely turning the FBI against all of us?" She turned to Adrian. "That isn't going to go well for you, is it?"

He shrugged. "Might have to kiss that promotion goodbye. Unless we can straighten this all out."

Rachel said, "If you get me something I can use to check my email, I can get on that. Or at least try."

"I'll ask." He moved toward the door. Two agents met him on the other side, and after a brief conversation, one shook his head.

"Ask them for a phone, then," Rachel called out. The frustration was growing, and it was hard to shove it back down. "They can listen in on my call if they want. But if I'm being held here, then I'm going to want my lawyer. And I'll need to place a call in to the Secret Service to advise them that the FBI are holding me." Her voice rose as she spoke, the irritation clear in her tone.

And who cared if she sounded like an entitled Washington paper-pusher? Certainly not Rachel. Especially if it got her what she wanted.

She could tangle up all kinds of bureaucratic red tape that would take months to get straightened out. If she and her friends were being held here, then their rights needed to be explained to them.

One of the agents moved in, past Adrian, and handed her a phone. "We will be listening."

"Ah," Rachel said, "So you do think we're all part of this blackmailer's plot, then?"

He lifted his chin.

"Certainly the first thing I'd do if I was trying to misdirect everyone would be to have someone drug and rape me and video it, then publish that video for all the world to see. You know—" She leaned forward, her voice dripping with disdain. "—just to throw suspicion off."

Alexis gasped.

The agent at least had the decency to wince. He knew exactly what had happened to her, just as everyone else here did. It wasn't a secret anymore. Her life was fully open for scrutiny. All that was left was for someone to publish a tell-all memoir.

Wouldn't that be delightful?

"Ma'am—"

Whatever he was going to say, Rachel didn't much care. She said, "Thank you for the phone." And turned away, fully dismissing him. Which he knew.

She heard him shut the door.

"Who are you going to call?" Megan asked.

Rachel turned to her.

"No." Alexis stood, fire in her eyes, interrupting the conversation Rachel had been about to have with Megan. The look on her face wasn't good.

"Lex—"

"Don't." Her best friend held up a hand. "We need to talk about that." She pointed at the door the agent disappeared out of.

"There's nothing to talk about." She dialed the number while she prayed the vice president's wife actually answered. That was new. Normally she wouldn't have thought to pray. But she appreciated the fact she'd thought to do it. At least she was progressing on something.

"What are you even doing?" Alexis asked. "Care to tell us who you're calling?"

Rachel listened to it ring. They would find out soon enough. But would it be in time to save Steve? Could she end this before what he'd said really happened, before word spread that there had been an attempt on the president's life?

She had to at least try.

. . .

Steve drove to where David said he'd met with the vice president's brother. He drove slowly past the old, rundown house. Brick wall topped with wrought iron. Overgrown driveway.

A thump from the trunk told him David was awake again. Mad enough to kick or punch out his frustration even though attempting to escape was pointless. Steve had disabled all the methods there were.

No way out.

Kind of like him, and this situation. He had to pray Bradley could figure out a way to free himself of those three armed Venezuelans. It wasn't impossible, but he would likely not manage it unscathed. And his knee injury meant Bradley would be taking measures to not reinjure it.

Whichever way Steve figured it, the situation was a long shot.

But that didn't mean he was going to kill the president. He would eat a bullet before he did that, no matter the fallout. He wasn't going to be the scapegoat. He glanced at the plans he'd been sent—pictures of vantage points and Secret Service routes—long enough to figure out what they were, and then deleted them.

The rifle was tucked away at the train station in the locker he used occasionally.

Steve parked on the next street and backtracked to the house while he watched for anyone. This time of evening, people were settling in. Dinner was done, or those who didn't eat until later were busy preparing it. He ducked his chin into the collar of his coat and made his way to the corner of the property where he climbed over the fence and landed on the other side.

Snow had collected up against the brick wall. His feet sank into it, the wet dampening his pant legs. Steve kicked the dust of snow from his shoes by tapping one heel against the other, one at a time, as he made his way toward the house.

It looked deserted, like no one had lived there in years. Whoever owned the house now had completely neglected it, so that it had definitely become *that house* in the neighborhood. The one kids rode their bikes past a little faster than they normally pedaled, just to clear it quicker.

Steve skirted the outside and found an open door at the back. Was the VP's brother even here? Would he find anything at all, or was this a giant waste of time? He would probably burn an hour of Bradley's life doing nothing and then go back to the car only to find out that David was gone. Or David would come to the house and shoot Steve.

He tried to think positively to come up with some good in this situation. Truth was God's domain, and Steve tried to recall His promises. All he could remember was that they *would* have trouble. *Check.* And that there were no guarantees except where God promised to give peace and grace. Forgiveness. Redemption.

He prayed over his friends, right there at the open door. It didn't matter if anyone saw him. This was important.

Then he asked for peace. Whatever he chose to do, Steve needed as much wisdom as he could get. And he needed the peace to know what the right thing to do was.

Feeling better than he had in weeks, Steve went inside the house. His heart ached for Rachel and what she'd gone through. As much as the knowledge that he couldn't help Bradley refused to settle.

He cleared the kitchen and dining room. The whole place was littered with leaves that had blown in. It smelled faintly of something he couldn't place.

He ascended the stairs and did the same search upstairs. Nothing. Not one single personal belonging. Not even a forgotten box in the attic. Floorboards had been removed from the main bathroom upstairs, and rats had chewed at the wires beneath.

Steve moved back downstairs. He resigned himself to the fact this had been a waste of time.

The shuffle of feet was the only warning before a solid weight barreled into him. They hit the floor, Steve on bottom. He couldn't stop the grunt that escaped his lips. He squeezed the trigger of the handgun, and the shot went into the ceiling. The sound was deafening and his ears rang.

David shifted to grasp Steve's neck, his hands still bound. He got a decent grip before Steve clocked him with the gun. David swayed and lost his grasp. But the weight of him kept Steve from taking a full breath. The gun flew out of his hand, and he realized he'd lost his own grip on it. His hands dropped, and he tried to lift them.

David spread his bound palms and grabbed Steve's neck again. "You are going to do this."

He squeezed tight. Bright spots flickered at the edges of Steve's vision. "Can't shoot…" He tried to breathe against the pressure on his throat. "Pres… If you…kill me."

David roared out his frustration. He lifted Steve's head in a punishing grip and slammed the back of it against the floor. But Steve didn't lose consciousness. Maybe he only directed Steve here for this.

"Did he even meet you here?"

David slammed his head down again.

His ears rang. His head pounded. Steve balled his fist and punched David's side. He never protected his flanks. Had always left them exposed and vulnerable. David's whole body clenched, his shoulder and knee drew together as he cried out.

Steve hit the other side.

Then he kicked David off him.

He looked around for the gun. Too far. David grabbed it first, lifted it with his bound hands and pointed it at Steve. "This was my house."

He fired the gun. Steve was already diving out of the way even before he spoke, but it wasn't fast enough. The gunshot echoed through the empty room. Hot fire slashed at his leg. Steve hit the dusty floor and rolled. He sucked in breath through his teeth.

He blinked and David stood over him, still holding the gun.

"Shoot me, and there's no one to blame for an assassination."

"Get up." David didn't even acknowledge Steve's words. "Guess who's going in the trunk now?"

Steve hobbled to the car. Blood made a wet trail down his left pant leg. David held the gun on him and opened the trunk. He motioned to it.

Steve climbed in. *Ouch.* He prayed someone glanced out their window, saw them and called the police. He wouldn't care if they came right now, and he was arrested. If someone could testify he was being abducted, that would help, right?

David slammed the lid down on the trunk. Steve groaned.

He got in the front—Steve heard the door open and close, and then the engine started.

Then he heard, "Yeah. It's me."

David was making a call.

"Kill the sailor."

Steve's heart sank. *Bradley.* All that, and it had been nothing but David making a power play. Directing Steve to a house David had lived in—and maybe still owned. This had nothing to do with the blackmailer. It had all been a lie. Subterfuge, the kind they'd both been trained in.

Steve wanted to scream out his frustration. Was he so far off his game that he'd fallen for it? He hated to even think that.

So much pride. Knowing he'd kept his honor through all of this meant nothing when his friends—and their families—had to pay the price for his mistakes.

Bradley was going to have to pay.

With his life.

Chapter 17

"Thank you so much for taking my call." Rachel leaned toward the base of the phone. She had the handset to her ear, but she had to focus. For some reason, that meant keeping her attention on the phone display and the buttons of this FBI nineties model phone. Not that there was time to think it through.

Mrs. Anderson said, "Of course, dear. I have a few minutes for you. Of course."

Rachel wanted to roll her eyes, but there were people watching. And listening. Agents, and techy people. They didn't need to know what she really thought of the vice president's wife.

She shifted in the rolling office chair. "I just wanted to touch base with you about your invitation to be the face of your endeavor."

"Oh!" The woman's tone was full of excitement. "That's so wonderful to hear."

Uh. Except, Rachel hadn't said she was going to do it. She just wanted to talk about it. Maybe Mrs. Anderson was one of those people who railroaded others by circumventing their own decisions and doing the deciding for them.

Rachel said, "I'd like to talk more about it and hear what your plans are. Perhaps we can meet up somewhere?"

"I'll speak with my assistant, and we'll put something on the calendar. Yes, I have so many ideas. There's such a need to reach out to people who've been victimized online."

"It certainly is timely, what with the suicide of the Senator from Wyoming. Such a terrible thing." The woman had been a victim of the blackmailer and taken her own life earlier this year.

"Yes." The VP's wife sounded like she swallowed. "It was terrible."

"Did you know her?" Rachel wondered if she'd been acquainted with the woman her husband and his brother victimized. Not exactly the same way they had with Rachel, but similarly enough. "Before she killed herself, I mean?"

"Possibly. When I saw the newspaper I realized she looked familiar, like I'd seen her around. Such a tragedy." There was no remorse in her tone. In fact, there was little feeling at all.

Rachel had no idea how to shift the conversation towards essentially implicating this woman's husband and brother-in-law as being responsible for it. She said, "Working to provide help and support for the victims, particularly the many who have been caught up in this blackmailing scheme, is something I would like to be part of. Not just because I'm one of them. The men who did this to me need to be stopped. The healing itself will take years."

She leaned back in the chair and wondered if the vice president's wife was going to pick up on what she'd said, or if the woman would just ignore it.

"The…men?"

Bingo. "The FBI believe there are two of them. One man organizing it, the other in the shadows. They believe he's hidden this man, his associate, for years. But I've seen him."

"You know who did that to you?"

"Yes," Rachel said. "And he sat across the table from me, taunting the feds, just for the power trip. Some of them think he came here just to speak to me, specifically. But I'm not so sure. Why do all of that and then have to hire gunmen to get you out?"

"Maybe you drew his attention somehow."

"How would I have done that?" Rachel asked. "I don't even know him."

"He knows you."

Rachel held herself very still. The vice president's wife couldn't see her. Rachel couldn't see the look on the other woman's face. All she could go on was the tone in her voice. "How would he know me? And what fault of that is mine? It isn't like I asked him to have Aaron Jones do that to me."

"No one asks him to do anything."

"So he's acting on his own, directing this whole situation." Rachel decided to throw caution out. "Trying to get your husband in the president's seat so he can be the man behind the throne, as it were? Is that it?"

The vice president's wife was quiet for so long Rachel wondered if she'd hung up. Then she said, "How am I supposed to know?" Rachel heard shuffling on the other end of the line, then a door closed. "After what he's done? And I'm supposed to ignore the fact I have no maid now?" She huffed. "Can I even live in the White House with no maid?"

Mrs. Anderson's question echoed on the line.

Rachel pinched the bridge of her nose. "Your husband's brother killed your maid?"

Mrs. Anderson let out a little gasp that had a squeak to it. There was a click, and dial tone.

"She hung up."

Rachel turned around in the chair and nodded to the agent. "She didn't answer the question either."

He nodded. Behind him, she could see Adrian replace the headphones he'd been using to listen in. He walked over and stood by the agent.

Rachel didn't need him to explain it to her. "I tried, but it wasn't enough."

Adrian nodded. "The agents looking into the maid's death can look more closely at the brother."

"But if there's no evidence he even exists, how are they going to find him? So far he hasn't left anything behind. We have no idea what his plan is, other than to sit back and wait for all this to unfold."

"It was a good try."

Rachel shoved the chair back and stood. It rolled and hit the desk. She blew out a breath in frustration. "It didn't help."

"Rachel—"

She waved him off. "It's fine. I tried. I'm just getting tired of trying to do something and getting nowhere. I don't like that he was here, and then he got away. It cost FBI agents their lives, and we still have no evidence that the brother even exists. Or that either of them is the blackmailer. How can we convince anyone of this conspiracy without proof of who is behind it?"

They were too good to be able to do all this without anyone knowing that they were the ones behind it.

The other agent nodded. "She's right. It'll be hard to prove they're responsible." He didn't even look all that convinced. "We need witness testimony. Electronic records. Taped conversations." He picked up the phone closest to him. "I'll find out what we need to get the Secret Service working on this with us. Maybe pull in his detail and interview them."

Finally. She looked at Adrian, but he didn't seem happy about this development. The FBI knew who Double Down's suspect was. "This is good, isn't it? They're looking at the vice president now."

He nodded, distracted. "There are so many variables. Investigating someone that high up takes finesse. There's procedure, and it'll be hard to do it without the vice president finding out. Which means his brother will know."

"And he'll disappear."

"Making it that much harder to find him."

Rachel groaned. "Steve is never going to be able to come home, is he?"

The phone she'd used to call Mrs. Anderson rang. Adrian answered it. Immediately his eyebrows rose, and he glanced at her.

"What?" She mouthed the word.

He said, "Yes. Thank you." And hung up. "Bradley is downstairs. They're sending him up."

"That's great." The look on his face didn't say it was great. "Isn't it?"

"Security says he's covered in blood."

Rachel brushed past him and went to the conference room. "Alexis!" Her friend met her at the door. Rachel set her hands on her friend's shoulders. She was just about to explain what Alexis should expect when she gasped. Rachel lowered her hands right as Alexis brushed past her. "Bradley."

Alexis stopped right in front of her husband, hands lifted like she wasn't sure she was supposed to touch him or not.

"Don't get this stuff all over you." He took one of her hands, his knuckles bloody. "I'm okay."

"You look like a wreck." Rachel had no problem stating the obvious. Plain for everyone looking at his bruised face, torn up arms, and bloody T-shirt. "What happened?"

Alexis shot her a frown over her shoulder. "Bradley needs to sit down, not be interrogated."

Bradley said, "I left an anonymous care package for the cops, and told them to call Adrian." He turned to the FBI agent Megan was in love with. "It likely won't be long before you get the call."

"You killed someone?" Adrian's voice was dark.

Rachel knew that was part of Bradley's life, and the work he'd done as a SEAL. She wasn't naïve. Still, she didn't exactly want the fact that he'd killed, and not just in the past, right up in her face.

Bradley shook his head. "More than a few broken bones, though. Maybe a concussion. I tied them up and called emergency services from one of their phones before I left." He nodded in Adrian's direction. "I put your name on one of the other phones."

Adrian nodded, then turned away with one of the other agents. Rachel recognized the flash of focus that jump-started a period of intense investigation. Though FBI agents rarely switched "off," they did frequently move between action and a kind of resting action. There wasn't a lazy one among them.

"Let's go sit," Alexis suggested.

"I just need to clean up," Bradley said. "But I'm guessing none of you can wait that long." His face split with a wide smile.

"Well ex-*cuse* us." Rachel set her hands on her hips.

Bradley took a step toward her, closing the distance, and whispered. "Steve will be all right."

They went into the conference room. Rachel tried to process what he'd said in order to make herself feel better about this situation. But it didn't work. There was next to nothing that could be said or done that would make her relax, or feel like this was over. Not when it was far from over.

She paced the length of the conference room while Bradley spoke.

"I'm not sure what happened between him and the guy he knew. David Sanders." He glanced at Mint, who got out his phone. "I think they were teammates like the others, and for some reason it's just the two of them left."

"To do what?" Alexis asked.

Rachel didn't enlighten her. She glanced around, trying not to make it obvious she knew—but also knowing she was so far past anything normal, they'd likely be able to figure it out. Sure enough, Bradley turned his assessing gaze at her. She shook her head.

They could talk about it together, but she wasn't going to do that in front of the whole group. Alexis, Mint, Emma, and Megan. Otherwise Steve would have told them himself.

Instead, he'd told her.

And not so she could feel better. No, he'd fired that statement about an assassination attempt at her to prove that he was somehow…stained. Not worthy of her time or attention. Her care.

It was like Nicola had said. He needed someone to convince him that he was a good person.

Rachel was trying her best to allow the team as a whole to combat the blackmailer. She was willing to do her part, but this situation had forced her to trust them all. Each had skills. A certain reach. Contacts. Steve was in the middle of it, and she had to believe he knew what he was doing. God was behind the scenes, working as He did. And He had given her these people for a reason.

That was what Alexis had told her.

Rachel only needed to trust that it was true.

These were the only people who didn't think of her as damaged for the rest of her life for what had happened to her. Or as a reason for them to assume she did something to warrant it, as some did. No, they'd cared for her. They supported her. They loved her. Steve was different, and what she wanted from him was different than what she got from everyone else.

Rachel had hardly been able to think about romance after what happened. Tenderness was difficult. Trust, even harder. But if there was a man who would treat her with both respect and kindness—and someone she was interested in treating her that way—then it was Steve.

Was that why God kept bringing them into each other's lives?

When they first met, there had been undeniable sparks. Since then, things had been more bad than good. She'd pushed him away. He'd let her, knowing what had happened to her and giving her time—part of that respect. Now it was he who needed her respect. He needed her to be safe, and to allow him to take care of this situation. It would be so easy to wade in and throw around her weight as a senator. But if Steve needed her to do that, then he would ask. It was more important for her to trust him now. To trust *his* skills. His honor.

Part of her believed that if he came into the FBI office, they could straighten out this whole thing. He wouldn't have to be a fugitive. But that would take her tricking him into surrendering himself, and she just couldn't do that to him.

Steve had proven he was the right man. And now, more than ever, Rachel was certain that he was the one who would take down the blackmailer.

She needed to keep from doing anything to jeopardize that.

"He's supposed to kill the president at the summit tomorrow."

Rachel whirled around. The atmosphere in the room went electric. "Bradley!"

Adrian's head whipped to her. "You *knew?*"

"Uh…" What was she supposed to say?

Bradley sat back in his chair, no remorse on his face. "You did know."

"It isn't like he's actually going to do it!" They all knew that, right? They were supposed to be his friends. Surely they didn't believe he could actually be coerced into this.

Emma shifted in her seat. Mint reached over and touched the back of her neck, his fingers tangled in her hair. They needed to get married soon—if they hadn't already done it while on the road. Whether it was a huge event with two hundred people or only a handful in a country church with the pastor, who cared? The intent was the same. If they were going to get closer, then Mint needed to make an honest woman of her.

Megan frowned, her attention on Adrian. When had he come back in, anyway? "I think you need to tell us what you know, Rachel."

"Why am I in the middle of this? It was a throw-away comment. It isn't like he's actually going to do it." Yes, she was repeating herself, but maybe they needed to hear it again. "Everyone the blackmailer could use as leverage in order to coerce him into doing something he would never in a million years do, is standing in this room. Or they're hidden so the blackmailer can never find them."

Megan's mother was gone on "vacation," and anyone else Steve cared about was here.

Bradley frowned. "That is true."

"It's probably why he told me to stay close." Plus he'd wanted her to have the protection of the FBI. It wasn't like she had anything to hide.

"And then the phone rang," Bradley said.

"What?" Was he trying to make sense or just processing out loud?

"And whoever was on the other end of the line told those guys to kill me."

"But you got away."

Bradley nodded. "Steve doesn't know that."

Realization dawned. Steve thought Bradley was dead, or at the least, still a captive. Was it enough to force him to go against everything he believed in?

Was Steve going to try and shoot the president?

Chapter 18

Steve's muscles burned. His head was back at such a weird angle that pain shot through his neck. He blinked against the blur of his vision and tried to shift. Lying on a floor.

Not the first time in his life he'd woken up not knowing where he was. And usually it didn't spell anything good.

He pushed himself up to sitting, his back against the wall. All he could see was sunlight streaming through a window. And a black figure.

A weapon fired. He flinched and the tang of cordite filled the air. He tried to breathe and had to cough. He lifted his head but it lolled forward instead. Then his whole body tipped sideways and he landed face first on scratchy carpet.

"Wha…"

His brain swam like the rest of his body. A warm floating sensation that had to have been drug induced. Concussions didn't feel like—

Someone stepped over him. Heavy, booted feet that narrowly missed his face.

"Hate to cut and run old friend."

David? What had he just done?

Steve managed to make a groaning noise from his throat but not much else. He was just barely able to think.

A shot.

His friend.

Drugged.

"Dave…"

A gloved hand patted his cheek. "Sorry. Can't have anyone knowing what I did."

David tugged on his hand. Steve felt the cold metal of a revolver press into his hand. *No.* His former friend shifted the gun...so it was pointed at Steve. Moving toward his chin.

He ignored the blur that meant he missed the look on David's face. Steve shifted his leg to kick the man away.

His leg didn't move.

Steve pushed against the gun. David's grip on his hand pinched the skin so hard a breath hissed out between Steve's lips.

He moaned again. "No..."

"Accept the inevitable," David said. "We all have to die sometime. I'm just sorry I told you now. But I've gotta say there were more than a few times I wanted to put a bullet in you. Now I've got the chance."

Steve kept pushing against the hand. But in his drug-induced state, there was no way he could put up enough of a fight against David.

He tried his free hand. It shifted.

Steve kept up the fight against the hand wrapped around his on the gun. With the other, he pulled at the knife he knew was on David's belt. Dragged it out of its sheath and across whatever it encountered.

He didn't have the wherewithal to figure out actually stabbing his friend. Just pushed with as much pressure as he could at this awkward angle and tried to keep from being shot in the process.

David cried out, mostly due to surprise. His hand let Steve's go and the gun toppled to the floor.

Steve blinked as much as he could. He could still see David's form and the sunlight shining in the window, but it was all clearer now. A black rifle on a stand. David's palm, covered in blood. He cried out in frustration. In the distance he heard sirens. Steve held up the knife, blade pointed out.

David got up and ran for the door.

Steve swam in and out of consciousness trying to figure out what on earth had just happened. David had used that sniper rifle. On the president? Were they at the summit?

He needed more information. Help. For this drug to get out of his system. He rolled over, tried to push himself to his feet and ended up falling back on his face.

He roused for a few seconds with hands jostling him.

Then again, hearing the sound of an ambulance siren.

Flashing lights moved over him. A bed. He was on a bed. Someone stuck a needle in his arm, and then he was out.

He woke up in a hospital bed, one hand cuffed to the rail. Like that was going to stop him if he wanted to leave.

He didn't know what day it was, and there was no clock to tell him the time. A doctor came in accompanied by two uniformed police officers. He didn't say one word to Steve. Sometime later, he actually saw a familiar face. The cop posted at his door let a man into the room. He was followed by two others. All three wore suits, ties. Badges were tucked away in breast pockets. Steve didn't need to see them to know all three of these guys were feds.

FBI, or Secret Service?

"The doctor said you were coherent." Adrian stood at the end of his bed. "You know who I am?"

A test, to see how well his brain was working? Steve could stall, get more time for himself so he could figure out what was happening. He didn't want to, though. He'd rather know what was going on here.

"Special Agent Adrian Walker, FBI."

Adrian motioned to the other guys. "Special Agent Franklin, Homeland Security. Special Agent Bryans, Secret Service."

Steve gave himself a second to contain his roiling thoughts, then said, "Who did David shoot?"

Homeland and Secret Service shifted, not liking what he said. Adrian was the one who spoke. "The vice president."

Steve frowned. He repeated it in his head while he tried to make sense of it. These guys didn't need to be privy to his thought processes, though likely they could read the confusion on his face.

"He's dead," Adrian said.

"David?"

Adrian shook his head. "The vice president."

Steve closed his mouth. Personal feelings about the man aside, it was a tragedy. The nation couldn't afford a loss like that. It shook people's confidence in law enforcement that they couldn't prevent such a thing.

One of the agents said, "Who is David?"

Steve shook his head. He tried to figure out where to start. How to explain who David was to him. "Killed a woman. In Mexico." He tried to contain his thoughts, and ended up saying, "Me too."

No, that wasn't what he meant.

The two feds he didn't know shared a look. Steve tried to figure out how to explain about the woman. The pistol David had tried to shoot him with—tried to make it look like Steve shot himself. Setting him up for the vice president's assassination.

"Kill me. Blame it on me." Steve shook his head. "Stabbed him, I think." He focused his attention on Adrian. "Blood."

"At the scene?"

Steve nodded, grateful this man understood what he meant.

"Techs are at the scene now. If there's evidence of another person present, then they'll find it," Adrian said. "We do need a complete statement from you, but not now. We have a lot of questions, and there are several things to clear up. The crux of the problem I have is that you were found at the scene, covered in gunshot residue. But you were drugged. Enough that it's unlikely you were able to make such a shot considering the state you were in."

He was giving Steve what he needed to make his defense. Steve had to base his argument on the fact he had a substance swimming through his blood. He needed to give the feds enough so they could prove David was there, and then convince them that his former teammate was the one who took the shot. Then there was the matter of Steve shooting at those feds in the restaurant parking lot.

This was going to be a lengthy process, with multiple fights to be won before he could go free.

And David was still out there. Along with the vice president's brother.

"Don't go anywhere," the Secret Service agent said. "I've seen your file. You won't like what happens if you try to leave."

Steve stared at him, but said nothing.

Adrian said, "I'll be back when you're feeling better. We'll get this ironed out."

He nodded and watched the men go.

The nurses acted like he was a killer who would lash out at them at any moment. The doctor wasn't much better. The cops at the door—he saw two before their shift changed and they were replaced by another two—weren't much friendlier.

Steve shifted in the bed and managed to sit up. There was no phone. A remote? Maybe he could get some news on TV…if there was one.

He sighed and leaned his head back on the pillow. The fog was almost completely gone now, and he was seriously ready for information. Or company. He wanted to know what was going on. If they were searching for David. If Rachel and the rest of his family were safe.

Hours ticked by. This was more than punishment and the worst kind of torture. Leaving him here with no update, no idea when the solitude was going to end. Sure, he'd been alone before. Solo missions. He'd even hiked Kilimanjaro on his own as a vacation. Steve enjoyed having the peace of only his own thoughts for comfort. Having to draw on his strength to get through.

Maybe it was the residue of whatever David had given him. Or the stress of the past few weeks. Not knowing what was going to happen.

He needed to check on Mrs. Cromwell.

At worst, he'd have to spend the rest of his life in jail. At best he'd lose his business. No one was going to hire the team whose leader shot at the FBI. The feds would tell everyone and he'd be blacklisted. If he hadn't already been completely destroyed in the media as public enemy number one.

He figured that now he felt at least somewhat of all Rachel had gone through. It wasn't the same, but he could certainly relate in part. He'd known all along that he wasn't good for her, but had been willing to set that aside. Now it was clear that his past was entirely too dark for him to deserve anything close to the happiness he knew she would bring to his life. Two damaged souls weren't going to be able to heal each other. And he would hate himself if he only made her feel worse. There was no way Steve would risk a relationship when it would most likely fail.

He drifted through a nap and dreamed about Rachel. Images that didn't help his resolve to do what was best for her. Especially not when he woke up with the taste of her kiss on his lips.

He tried to figure out what had woken him, then heard a knock at the door.

"Come in." He croaked the words out, his voice thick with sleep, and then cleared his throat.

The door cracked open and an older man stuck his head in.

Steve froze as the man entered. Suit. Tie. He flashed a badge, a real honest to goodness FBI badge. *Has to be fake.* The eyes, though. That alone would have told him this man was no special agent. The fact he'd seen the hacker's picture sealed it.

This was the vice president's brother.

Walking toward Steve, he stowed that badge back in his suit jacket. Steve didn't move until the hand came back out. No weapon. Was he going to kill Steve with his bare hands?

The older man cracked what was probably supposed to have been a smile. "Don't look so scared." He dragged a chair over to the bed.

Steve shook his head. "Then why come here?" He tried to remember the man's name, but couldn't. He should call out to the cops outside. But the blackmailer had flashed a badge to get in, so they weren't going to believe the man in handcuffs. Was it even worth trying? Or he could just hear the man out. Find out what he had to say.

He settled in the chair, a slight wince as he shifted his weight. "Bad hip. Has been since I was a kid."

"Venezuela?"

"They threw me off a roof. Fractured my pelvis." No anger, no fire. No inflection. He could have been talking about a static economy for all Steve knew.

"And now you've destroyed everyone who was there, or had anything to do with it." The man didn't look particularly upset about the fact his brother was dead. "Did David really kill the vice president?" It seemed weird to refer to William Anderson by his first name, so he stuck with the title.

The brother's lip twitched. A snarl. "Weasel. Shoulda known that sniveling piece of…" his voice descended into muttered insults. "Of course he double crossed me."

"Not everyone you blackmail is going to do what you ask." Steve had fired on the feds. Not killing anyone was a given, but the fact he hadn't even injured a single one was his personal rebellion. The only thing he could've done to save Rachel's life. Still, this man had sent Steve's own former team after her. "It isn't like there's any honor in you. I'm not sure you can expect it in those you're dealing with."

The brother said, "Where is he? Where would he go?"

He expected Steve to be able to answer that? "He's probably off for more revenge."

"Where?" The word exploded from his mouth. Loud enough it made Steve jump a little in the bed.

"South America." He lifted both hands, though the handcuffed one didn't go far, and then let them fall back onto the blanket that covered him. "He could come back here and try to finish the job of killing me. Or he'll disappear. Or come after you."

"That's it?" He didn't seem that impressed.

Or worried, considering Steve had just told him that coming here made them both targets.

"He could be anywhere. We aren't friends, and I'm not privy to his preferences or where he's been for the past few years," Steve said. "Don't you have ways of finding people?"

"I'm working on a considerably…scaled back operation right now."

"I'm not helping you." Even if this guy only wanted to kill the man who'd killed his brother. Steve said, "Not even if you're only planning to catch him so you can turn him in to the feds." He would rather David was free than this man get what he wanted. Not an honorable position, but it was what it was. He'd determined to at least be honest. Even if that honesty kept him from being with Rachel.

"So this was a waste of time." He winced again and shifted to get up out of the chair.

"Sorry I couldn't help you." Did this mean he was done terrorizing people? Done blackmailing and hacking, destroying lives?

The blackmailer said, "I will find him."

"I will find *you*." There was no way Steve could get out of here and not pursue this man until he caught him. That was, *if* they let him out.

The man snorted a laugh. "Enjoy prison, Mr. Preston."

"Because I defied you? Because everything didn't go as planned?"

"My brother is dead. Explain to me why I should 'do the right thing'? Wait—" He held up a hand. "Actually don't bother. Because I don't care."

"You aren't going to get away with this."

"Hard to catch a man who doesn't exist." He moved toward the door.

"David killed your brother because he knew what David did to that woman in Mexico, right? Same with trying to kill me."

The man stopped, but didn't turn back.

"He's not done."

"Worried about me?" He turned then. "No justice if I'm dead, right?" He looked like he couldn't care less if he was dead. No will to live. Nothing to fight for. So unlike the people whose lives he'd terrorized. People willing to do anything to keep the ones they loved safe.

"There will be justice," Steve said. "Even if it's just making sure everyone knows who you are, and what you did."

"Infamy it is, then." He smoothed down his tie. "When you write that bestseller about everything that's happened, maybe you could mention I have more hair than I really do. I'd like that."

The door clicked shut, and he was gone.

Chapter 19

Rachel twisted the handle and walked into her office at the Rayburn building. It was quiet inside, something she'd never enjoyed. The whole building had an echoey feel to it, in stark contrast to the Senate. This was a retreat. A place to recharge and get work done.

The nation was mourning the tragic death of the vice president. Not much would be accomplished in Washington today. Everyone was reeling, arranging for flowers and condolences to be sent to Mrs. Anderson. Which was only part of why Rachel was here.

"Senator Harris." Ellayna stood. She looked like she wanted to say something.

The last time they'd seen each other it had been when Ellayna realized her actions almost led to Rachel's death. And considering Rachel had just killed someone, they hadn't left things in a good place exactly.

Rachel unwound the scarf from around her neck and then took off her coat. When she'd hung that up, she removed her gloves. All to give Ellayna the chance to figure out what she wanted to say. She was putting the young woman on the spot. But it wasn't like Ellayna had to explain anything. The FBI would have charged her with something if she'd been an accomplice to the attempt on Rachel's life.

When Ellayna said nothing—though she stood there with her mouth open like she was ready to speak—Rachel said, "Coffee, please."

"Yes, ma'am."

Rachel strode down the hall. The girl would collect herself at some point, and then they could have a conversation in her office. She imagined there was a good amount of guilt, though all she'd done was pass on a message. Too bad it had been a message designed to lure Rachel to her death.

On the way down the hall, she checked in with the two other ladies who also worked there. Both would be headed off for their Christmas vacations soon.

It occurred to Rachel then that they might come back in the New Year to find Rachel had not returned. She was certain there would be another office for them to transfer to. Or her replacement would keep them on.

Rachel pulled her chair under the desk and booted up her computer. She ignored email and opened a new document, a letter she addressed to the Governor of Virginia. Mick would be sad about her resignation, but likely more irritated that she blindsided him.

Rachel just wanted a clean break. After everything, she planned to take some time to figure out what she wanted. Time to maybe talk with Steve, after he got out of the hospital. To wait out whatever happened with him. Time to decide if she wanted to air her side of the story in a book. Alexis was convinced it was a great idea, but writing all those chapters just seemed exhausting. And Rachel was tired.

So tired.

Ellayna tapped lightly on the door and entered with a cup of coffee. She set it on the desk. "I took the liberty of sending flowers to the vice president's widow, along with a note offering condolences from your office. I hope you don't mind."

"Thank you for doing that. I appreciate it." She lifted her cup and took a sip, then turned back to the computer. "That will be all."

Ellayna stood still in the corner of her vision and then quietly left the room. Rachel typed up her letter. All the while, her stomach threatened to bring breakfast back up. She'd had a single slice of toast, the only thing she could choke down.

Fear was like a blanket around her shoulders. But this was over, wasn't it? Steve was in the hospital, and Adrian had said they would get things cleared up. The vice president was dead, which was sad but also a relief. No more plot. His brother would be caught. She wasn't worried that the man would come after her. Why would he?

The phone rang. Rachel sloshed coffee on her desk, including her keyboard. She let out an irritated few words she probably shouldn't have said and snapped it up. "Senator Harris."

"It's Megan."

"Oh, hi." She leaned back in the seat and blew out a breath.

"Hi. Uh, Adrian wants you to head back over to the FBI office. He says we all need to meet."

She stared at the blinking cursor, halfway through her letter of resignation. "Right now?"

"If that's okay, yes. Do you need a ride? I can come and pick you up."

"I'll get there. See you in a minute." Rachel pressed the button on the base of the phone, then dialed Ellayna's extension to ask the intern to call her a cab.

The drive to the FBI office was less than five minutes, which she could have walked. But it was seriously cold outside, with fresh snow and everything. She didn't even know where her snow boots were. All the while her hair stood on end on the back of her neck. The skin of her arms prickled. She wrote it off as this lovely frigid winter weather, even being inside a warm cab. Add to that not knowing what Adrian was going to say, and she was nervous *and* cold.

It took her longer to get checked in and screened by security, then make her way upstairs than the entire car ride from her office. She still couldn't shake the feeling, though. Once this meeting was done, she would be able to move past the fear. The feeling of being watched everywhere she went.

She found the whole Double Down team—minus Steve—in the conference room. "Always the last one to the party." She laid her coat over the back of a chair.

No one smiled.

Adrian stepped into the room and shut the door. "This is actually good news, so you can all quit looking so sad."

Emma said, "Sorry. We've become accustomed to bad news." She leaned against Mint's shoulder.

Megan stood in the corner. Bradley and Alexis held hands and sat on the same side of the table as she. Rachel didn't want to waste time sitting. She said, "What is it?"

"The vice president's wife gave us permission to look at his personal computer," Adrian explained. "On it we found enough evidence to prove the VP was the blackmailer. It lists every victim, though none are ones we didn't know about. Which in itself is weird, considering I'd expect more than what we already know. But I'm going to take that as a win."

Rachel frowned. None of them said anything.

"It's enough to clear Steve of all charges, since it explains his coercion. He acted under duress and didn't hurt anyone."

"Really?" He was going to be free of everything and in the clear? Rachel's heart lifted. "That's great, right?"

Adrian nodded. "They're bringing him here from the hospital now, so he can make a statement. As long as that lines up with what we got from the computer, he'll be good."

"And the vice president goes down in history as a blackmailer."

Rachel turned to Bradley. "What?" Why did that statement he'd just made have a tone to it? And one she wasn't sure how to decipher.

"His brother is still out there." Bradley shrugged one shoulder. "He could have planted all that information so the FBI stopped looking for anyone else. He's still living in anonymity."

"The search for the escaped hacker is ongoing," Megan said.

Mint shook his head. "That sounds like a party line if ever I've heard one." Megan shot him a look. Mint said, "What if he's never found?"

She had nothing to say to that.

Adrian said, "What we need to focus on is the fact Steve is good. From here on out, it's just paperwork. He can go back to his life."

"And David?" They'd told her that he said the shooter was his teammate.

"Another ongoing search?" Mint said.

Emma shifted in her seat. Alexis did the same. Megan sighed.

Adrian said, "You've been privy to the internal aspects of this FBI investigation so far—"

"Because we were all possible accomplices," Mint said.

Adrian pushed away from the wall. "So was I, remember?"

"Guess we're all in the clear now," Bradley said. "A nicely wrapped package of information that's just enough to close the case."

"Exactly," Adrian said.

Rachel slumped down into the chair. "Because the VP's brother doesn't want anyone looking at him. But you are, because he came here as the hacker."

Adrian nodded.

Bradley said, "And he asked specifically to speak to *you*." Her brother shot her a look.

She glanced between them. "But if he's smart, then he'll be in the wind."

"He came to the hospital and talked to Steve."

She gaped at her brother.

"You don't go anywhere alone," Bradley said. "Not until I'm satisfied you're completely, one hundred percent safe."

She wanted to suggest that when Steve was cleared, he be tasked with keeping her safe. She would prefer that to any other scenario. And Steve would do it in a way she didn't feel like she was being smothered.

But it would also be completely obvious to everyone why she was asking.

She'd just about been convinced they were heading towards the end of this. Now Bradley wanted her under protection again. Still. Whichever it was, she didn't know. Couldn't muster the energy to figure it out.

It wasn't over.

Rachel groaned and buried her face in her hands.

. . .

The elevator doors opened. One agent led the way, and he followed. The other brought up the rear. He wasn't in cuffs, but neither did he have much choice about being here.

They led him through the office, past a bank of windows. One shoe caught on the floor and he nearly stumbled.

Beyond the glass, Mint stood. Then Bradley.

Alexis and Emma were in there.

Megan moved closer and stood beside Adrian.

Rachel sat closest to the door, head in her hands.

One of the agents said, "Come on."

But Steve didn't move. He just stood there and stared at his friends. His team. His family. There was no way he'd have guessed that seeing them again, knowing now he was so close to being free and clear, would feel like this.

He wanted to hug each one of the women. Shake the guys' hands, to which Bradley would laugh and pull him in for a hug. Rachel. He wanted to see her smile, not sitting in a chair looking so dejected. Was she all right? Had something else happened?

Adrian opened the door. He spoke to one of the agents. "Can we have a minute?"

Steve didn't know what to do, or say. He could argue he still wasn't a hundred percent since the drugs had left his system. Things were all out of whack. Maybe when he got his life back, then he'd feel normal again. But would routine even be that? People would always look at him with suspicion.

There was plenty still to do before this was over. They couldn't have a happy reunion when David—and the vice president's brother—were still out there. One, or both, wanted him out of the picture. Something didn't sit right with him. He just couldn't help but wonder if forcing David to run only meant the man would come back again.

He'd said no one could live that knew about what he'd done. Steve had remembered that part. The hacker/brother was another story. Would Harlem Anderson simply disappear, never to be heard from again?

Adrian glanced at him. "Want to say 'hi'?"

Steve nodded. Adrian moved back, so Steve stepped into the conference room. He didn't know what to do. Ended up rubbing his hands on the legs of his pants. Rachel stood, her face pale. He wanted to hug her. Would she let—

She rushed toward him and collided with him so hard he had to go back a step. Her arms wound around his middle, and he couldn't resist. He wrapped his around her, and laid his cheek on her hair. Closed his eyes.

"Are you okay?" Her voice was a whisper against his jacket.

I am now. But that might not last long. He had no idea what the future would bring. All he knew was that he didn't want her to be in danger. Especially not when it was because of him.

He rubbed a hand up and down her back. She stepped away from him and frowned. He shot her what he hoped was a reassuring smile and did the hugs/handshakes thing with everyone else, including the painful back-slapping from Bradley.

"I'm glad you guys are all right," he said to the group.

"And you will be as well, soon." Alexis smiled and took Bradley's hand. Steve nodded.

"What is it?"

Rachel's question made him clench down on his back teeth. *Should have left already.* Just excused himself and then got on with making that statement so the FBI would have everything on record.

"Steve."

He glanced at her and had to resist the urge to wince at her tone. "What?" What did she want him to say?

"Are you okay?"

"Things are still a little foggy." Even though it had been hours since he'd been given the meds to counteract what David had shot into him.

Rachel frowned. She didn't believe him. Which made sense, considering no one else did either.

"I should go make my statement."

"Maybe we can all go out to dinner later," Emma suggested. "Celebrate."

Rachel started to say something, probably agree like everyone else. Steve shook his head. That was a bad idea.

"Why not?"

He moved so his back was to the room, facing Rachel. "I don't think I can go to dinner." There was entirely too much hope in her eyes. Prolonging it meant it would grow, and then she'd be even more hurt. "I have to find David," Steve said. "Before David finds me to finish what he started when he shot the vice president."

"That's an ongoing FBI search." There was something in Mint's tone, but Steve had no time to figure out what it meant.

He shook his head. "I'm not going to sit around waiting for him to be found, wondering what havoc he's causing. Who else he's going to hurt."

"You're going after him?" That question came from Bradley.

Steve glanced over his shoulder. Nodded.

"Double Down will help, right?" Rachel said. "We'll all pitch in."

Steve turned back to her. Shook his head. If she was anywhere near him, she could get caught in the crossfire. He would never forgive himself if she was hurt, or she had to go through anymore. Considering what she'd been through so far, there was no way he would allow her to suffer anymore.

That meant being far away from him when David came back around. When the vice president's brother was uncovered from whatever rock he'd crawled beneath to hide.

"I have to go." He walked to the door and turned back. "It was good to see you guys. Take care."

He stepped out and rejoined the agents.

Rachel called out, "That's it? Take care?"

"What do you want me to say?"

She stared at him, all accusation. He could see the death of what she'd thought might be right there in her face. He watched that light go out.

"Goodbye, Rachel."

Chapter 20

Rachel tugged her coat back on. *Goodbye, Rachel.* She pressed her lips together and fastened the buttons, her fingers itching to go back out there, pull him around, and slap his face.

Goodbye, Rachel.

Like she meant nothing to him. Like he should mean nothing to her. *Ugh.*

"You're leaving?" Emma's voice was soft. Everything about the woman was just…lovely. In a way Rachel never was and couldn't ever hope to be. Mint should have been the totally wrong kind of man for her, but his hard edges and fierce warrior demeanor only accented Emma's gentleness. They balanced each other. Complemented each other.

Rachel didn't want to answer the question. She turned to Adrian instead. "Would you call the Secret Service for me? I'd like cover when I go home." She was exhausted. She felt exhausted and was sure she looked it as well.

Adrian's pointed stare saw far too much, but he nodded. When he left the room, Megan said, "You're going to run away?"

Rachel lifted her chin.

"You know he's just trying to protect you, right?"

A couple of them murmured in answer to Megan's question. Rachel didn't need to say it out loud. She'd have preferred to do this somewhere else, and not with everyone listening. Scratch that. She'd have preferred to do this never.

"He wants to keep you insulated from what's happening to him, so your career isn't put in jeopardy."

Rachel's thoughts jumped to that letter of resignation on her computer, the one she hadn't finished yet. She could redo it at home. Then she could get started figuring out what to do next. Big life changes might not be advisable in a situation like this. Maybe she should wait until life calmed down. But it was time to take charge.

She was done waiting for things to be perfect. Or better. Or even just calm.

Rachel stepped out into the hallway. Thankfully, wherever they'd been taking Steve, they were there already. She didn't want to see him.

Her eyes filled with tears. Rachel bit her lip, using the pain to distract herself. There was no way she was going to get emotional over a man. Not now. And least of all over Steve. Nothing had happened between them, not even a kiss. Certainly no promises had been made.

She needed to give up the idea there was going to be anything between them. He'd made that perfectly clear, and she needed to accept it.

Alexis found her in the hall. "Hey." She reached for Rachel, her face soft but knowing.

Rachel moved in for the hug. It was instinctual. They'd been on the same team. Family for years now. There was no one in the world Rachel was closer to than her brother and his wife—her best friend.

"It'll be fine."

Rachel snorted and stepped back from the hug. Alexis wasn't going to tell her Steve would surely see that he was mistaken and come back, asking for a chance.

They didn't lie to each other.

"Bradley is steaming though," Alexis said. "I think he might kick Steve's butt for doing that."

Rachel shook her head. "Tell him not to."

"You think he'll listen to me? You know what he gets like when he's worked up."

The man had a single-minded focus he'd possessed even before the Navy and SEAL training. Now it was a million times worse. *Thank you very much, Uncle Sam.* There was no stopping him when he had something to say. Or prove.

"You could try hitting him over the head and locking him in a closet," Rachel suggested.

Alexis burst out laughing. "I'm not sure how I feel about that, considering you think I'd even entertain that idea. Or that I'd actually be able to do it."

"It's really the only way to deal with him," Rachel said, totally deadpan. Straight-faced. "You and I both know that."

Bradley stepped to Alexis's side and tugged her under his shoulder. It would be cute he always wanted to be close to her friend—especially after so many years apart—if it wasn't also completely gross thinking about her brother and romance. "Why do I get the feeling there's nothing good about this conversation?"

Rachel glanced at Alexis, whose eyes went wide. They both laughed.

Adrian wandered over. "Two Secret Service agents, ones you know well, will be downstairs in five minutes."

"Thank you."

Bradley said, "Listen to them and do what they say. They're there to keep you safe."

"As opposed to the rest of the world, who are just out to get me?" Something flashed across his face. She ignored it and said, "I'm trying to work on getting past my distrust of everyone except the two of you. Don't make it worse."

The last group of Secret Service agents that had been assigned to protect her had a mole in it. She'd been kidnapped from her house a few months ago, before she'd moved to a new house. Not a time in her life she especially wanted to be reminded of now.

Bradley and Alexis had come for her then, and she'd been rescued. Steve's presence there afterwards, looking concerned, was something she didn't need to think about. She focused again on her family in front of her. "Thank you." She included them both in this. "I will be okay. It's time to ease up on the worry, because everything's going to be fine."

"We aren't out of danger."

"I know that David guy is still out there. And the vice president's brother. But neither of them has anything to do with me, right? So why would they come after me?" She paused a second, hoping Bradley realized that. "And I'll have world-class protection."

So long as neither of them betrayed her, or sold out to the blackmailer, she would be fine. And considering he wasn't even active anymore, she wasn't as worried as she would've been.

"I need eighteen hours of sleep and three weeks vacation."

Alexis chuckled. "I know how you feel."

"Hmm. That sounds like the makings of a plan to me." She ignored her brother's shift of his weight and asked her friend, "Hawaii, or Mexico?"

Alexis groaned. "Somewhere warm sounds amazing right now. It's freezing outside."

"Maybe I'll take both of you to a beach," Bradley said.

Rachel kissed his cheek. "If you wanna pay, I won't complain." They both had plenty of money they'd earned and a good inheritance from their parents, but that wasn't the point. If he wanted to treat them to a vacation, then she wasn't going to say no. Besides, she was about to be unemployed right?

They said their goodbyes and Rachel went down to the lobby to sign out and wait for the agents. Both were Secret Service personnel she'd met before and trusted. The wariness didn't leave, though. Maybe it never would.

But this feeling she was being watched? That she could do without. It stuck with her the whole way home and while they walked her to her front door. She unlocked it, and one of the agents walked through her house before she and the other one went inside.

She didn't even have time to change before there was a knock on the door. So much for rest. Rachel took the carafe from the coffee pot and went to the sink to fill it so the agents could have something hot to warm them and keep them awake.

Ellayna's voice drifted down the hall.

One of the agents replied.

"Its fine, Chuck," Rachel called out to him. Whatever Ellayna could want, she didn't know.

Rachel heard her intern step into the kitchen. She turned, holding the full pot of water in front of her. Ellayna was much too close.

Her eyes wide. Face flushed. She jabbed something sharp into Rachel's arm. "What…"

Rachel swung out, not even realizing what it was. The pot slammed into Ellayna's stomach, splashing water over her. She reared back with the force of the blow. The glass carafe smashed on the floor.

Rachel's world slowed and everything seemed to blur.

She glanced at her arm and saw the needle sticking out. Drugged? "Wha…"

Rachel slumped to the floor. Pain sliced through her palms as she hit the tile of her kitchen and the broken glass.

The last thing she heard before she lost consciousness were two gunshots.

. . .

Steve walked out the front door of the FBI office a couple of hours later, exhausted and parched from all the talking. Yes, he'd been giving a statement. But there was something about the way the FBI teased out information that was a whole lot like an interrogation.

They weren't even done.

He'd begged off so he could go get some rest among other things. Later he'd be back, happy to fill in the gaps of what they knew. Everyone wanted the focus on finding David and the VP's brother, so no one complained all that much.

He figured they would put two agents on his tail anyway, just in case he led them to the two men. Trust was relative. Especially in a situation like this.

Soon as he hit the street, a truck pulled up in front of him. The passenger window rolled down. Mint sat there; Bradley in the driver's seat. "Adrian said you were done," Mint told him.

Steve just stood there.

"Get in," Bradley called out. "Before they give me a ticket for illegally parking."

Steve figured that was flimsy at best, but he climbed in the back. Buckled up. Leaned his head back and closed his eyes. Exhaled.

"Where to, boss?"

Bradley was already driving down the street.

Steve gave him an address.

"That's where you've been staying?"

"No," Steve said. "But I do need to check something. One of you guys got a phone?"

Mint handed a cell back over his shoulder. Steve punched in the phone number and listened to it ring.

When she answered he said, "Hi, Mrs. Cromwell, it's Steve. Everything okay?"

"Steve?"

"Yes, Ma'am." Was she going to forget who he was? That would be embarrassing when his teammates sat in the front listening to everything.

"Will you be back soon? I need someone to help get my Christmas tree box off the shelf in the closet, remember?"

"I can definitely do that for you."

"Thank you. You're a good boy." Her voice drifted off, like she was half asleep.

"You're welcome. I'll see you tomorrow. Or—for sure at least soon."

"O-kay."

He hung up.

"Mrs. Cromwell?" Bradley asked. "As in, the Special Agent in Charge who kidnapped Megan and killed *El Cuervo*?"

"She's eighty-seven." He didn't want to explain more. How he came to be there, or the fact it'd been days since he saw her. Nor did he want to admit it had been mostly about having a safe place no one knew about—where he could regroup and actually get rest. "I'll get over there soon, make sure she's okay."

He didn't know when, but soon.

"Is that smoke?" Mint leaned forward to look out the front window into the night sky.

Steve shifted to see out as well. What was he even looking at?

Bradley pulled onto the street. "I'm guessing the address you wanted me to drive to is that house up there. The one on fire, with all the fire trucks outside."

Firefighters were all over the place. And residents from the street, watching everything. The whole structure was engulfed.

"That's David's house." Steve sat back in the seat. It was also the house where he'd drawn Steve to in order to kidnap him.

Bradley said, "You think he's going to target you?"

"I'm not going to sit around waiting for him to show up and try."

"Well he isn't here."

Steve didn't respond to that dumb statement. "Maybe the vice president's brother set the fire. I think David wants to kill him, too. Then everyone who knows about what he did will be dead."

He'd explained it all to the feds, including Adrian—who Steve had repeatedly given credit to for figuring things out. Now David had an even bigger problem.

The vice president's brother needed to be brought in, so he didn't simply pick up where they'd left off, terrorizing people.

David wanted to be free. And he was likely going to do the same, or worse, to another woman eventually. He needed to be found before that happened.

Both men were dangerous. "We can't just wait around for them to destroy each other and then swoop in and collect the victor to be prosecuted. We need to find them."

Mint said, "He'll try to draw one of you out first."

And they had no idea how to figure out which it would be. If the VP's brother had set David's house on fire, then who knew what message that was supposed to send. *I can find you.* Or, *I know all your hiding spots.* Whichever it was, Steve wasn't going to go to Mrs. Cromwell and put her in danger. She needed protecting, but he couldn't do it if that meant he led dangerous people to her doorstep.

Bradley said, "Where to now?"

"I don't know."

They'd both gone to ground, and if neither one lifted their head out of their respective hidey holes far enough for law enforcement or Steve to spot them, maybe they would never be found. If they disappeared and laid low, they could get away with this. Even despite the massive manhunt underway, there were still ways to flee the country.

Bradley's phone rang. He shifted in his seat, and said, "It's Adrian." He answered it. "Yeah."

He slammed his foot on the brake and pulled over to the side of the street, narrowly missing a parked car.

Steve sat forward.

Bradley hung up. He put the truck in drive and peeled out with a squeal of the tires, making a U-turn. "Rachel's Secret Service detail was supposed to check in with Adrian. They never did."

Steve's entire body went cold.

Bradley drove to her new house, the one she'd rented after she was kidnapped from her last house.

Before he even parked, Steve was out the back door and running up the front steps to the open front door.

A dead Secret Service agent lay in the hallway, gun drawn. In a pool of blood. Steve stepped around it, but there was almost no way to avoid it. "Rachel!"

He raced through the hallway, cleared the living room and then hit the kitchen area. Glass littered the floor, along with water. Blood had smeared on some of the shards, smudged on the floor.

Someone had been dragged out of here.

"I've got the other one," Mint said. "He's dead. Both of the Secret Service agents were shot."

Steve turned around to see his teammate, a dark look on his face. Bradley stood just behind him, looking sick.

Steve said, "She's gone."

Chapter 21

All three car doors slammed. Steve took the lead, and headed with Bradley and Mint to where Adrian stood with other agents on the banks of the Potomac.

Three hours.

That was how long she'd been gone.

It was almost the middle of the night now. All of them were exhausted. Rachel likely even more so. She hadn't looked well rested when he'd seen her in the FBI office. When he'd blown her off so he could finish this.

The fact David had been after him was small consolation. He tried to remind his own wayward thoughts that he genuinely was in danger. But it was too hard to reign it in when his mind insisted on coming up with every reason this was his fault.

His failure.

Steve stopped walking. He bent forward and sucked in breaths, hands to his thighs. Where was she? Was she okay? All the questions he could think of rolled through his thoughts, killing his ability to focus on the task at hand.

Three hours. That was how long she'd been in the hands of a crazy man. David, or the VP's brother, they didn't know. Did it matter?

Bradley set a hand on his shoulder. "If you fall apart, you're no help to me. I'll leave you here and go find her myself."

Steve straightened so fast Bradley didn't know what he was doing, until Steve shoved both hands against his friend's chest. Leave him here? There was no way Steve would allow Bradley to mosey off and save his sister by himself.

They needed each other. Bradley knew that. And this tough love business wasn't helping.

Steve said, "Don't get in my face. If I need a second, I'm going to take one. And then I'm going to focus."

Adrian walked over to stand beside Mint, who watched quietly.

Steve glanced at Mint, then Adrian, then at Bradley. "Tell me if it was one of your women that you wouldn't need a minute to collect yourself? Because you're all a bunch of robots? Well you're not. And I'd give you that minute."

"This isn't getting my sister back."

Did Bradley think he didn't know that? "You want me to hit you again?"

"That sissy-girl shove?" Bradley clipped Steve's shoulder as he passed him. A completely juvenile move Steve was going to ignore. Because *that* wasn't going to help them. "Why are we here, Walker? What does this have to do with Rachel being gone?"

Bradley stopped. He turned back to Steve, Mint, and Adrian. All the color drained from his face. "Wait. Don't tell me that's her."

"Just realized why we're here?" Steve asked. It was plain to see there was someone lying on the ground at the edge of the water. A body, surrounded by federal agents.

A woman. With dark hair.

Steve said, "We're all going to ignore your completely sexist remark about girls being sissies and should probably pray for Alexis since she has to live with you now." He took a breath and turned to Adrian. "Please tell us that isn't Rachel."

"It's not her," Adrian said in one quick breath. "I'm sorry you thought that." He glanced between them. "Any of you. I'm sorry you even thought for one second that was Rachel."

Bradley glanced at Steve, a certain knowing in his eyes. Steve didn't wait for an apology, given Bradley wasn't good at that stuff. He could cut the guy some slack, considering he hadn't even fully processed his reaction to seeing that woman lying on the ground—before he quit breathing for a second.

Bradley jumped on the weakness. The delay. Steve wasn't going to drag that out. He understood it. He turned to Adrian. "Who is she?"

"Ellayna Sanchez. She's Rachel's intern." Adrian started walking, and they all fell into step around him.

Megan stood with the agents close to the body, but not so close they ran the risk of stepping on evidence. The ground was covered in frost and the extra dusting of snow that had fallen in the last few hours, but the body was not. Which meant she hadn't been there all that long—not long enough for the weather to settle on her skin and clothes.

"One shot to the forehead," Megan said.

Mint shifted. "Just like the Secret Service agents."

Bradley moved close to Steve's side, like he thought Steve was a loose cannon about to completely dissolve. Or maybe Bradley was about to himself, and focusing on Steve meant he had something to keep him from falling into the downward spiral of what he thought *could* happen. What might have already happened.

Steve's mind came up with things that were a thousand times worse than what she'd already been through. *She doesn't need this.*

Bradley said, "David, or the Vice President's brother?"

"David," Steve answered. "A shot like that, one bullet and they're dead? It's military. At least someone with the training David has had. The Vice President's brother may or may not have computer skills. We haven't seen any kind of weapons training. Especially considering every shot was taken by someone he coerced into doing it. Or hired like that team of Venezuelans."

"So where did he take her?"

He looked over at Bradley. That had better be a rhetorical question. Steve didn't know where David would take Rachel. Why had he even grabbed her? This made no sense at all.

He wanted to rage and scream at all of them. Throw punches. Fire the weapon tucked in the back of his jeans that he wasn't going to tell Adrian or any of the other feds about, given he was in a legal gray area until the federal judge woke up tomorrow and made a ruling.

He didn't even know why they'd let him out. Why had they? They hadn't known Rachel would be taken. Two men were out there. Throwing a third, an unknown one, into the mix only made things more complicated. Especially when they could've kept him overnight without charges.

He glanced at Adrian and wondered if this man had pleaded Steve's case. Or if the feds had decided they'd catch him doing something, or they'd catch the men they were chasing because of him.

"So what does this tell us?" Mint asked. "Because there has to be a reason we're standing here—"

The end of his statement was cut off by the sound of a plane overhead. It roared above them, wheels down, and landed at Ronald Regan international airport.

Steve turned to Adrian. "The airport?"

"We think he dumped the intern—didn't need the extra body with him; she'd outlived her usefulness—and then took Rachel with him. Hopped on a plane."

"He could be anywhere by now," Bradley said.

Steve nodded. It was true. Now they had to widen their search grid to include…the whole world. He pinched the bridge of his nose.

Adrian said, "From her phone—which didn't have a passcode—we know he messaged her instructions for the grab. Told her where to meet him. We think from there they hit her house. Ellayna got him in, and he took out the Secret Service agents." He blew out a breath. "She probably didn't even know what she was getting involved in."

Or she did. Steve didn't much care what this Ellayna woman knew or didn't before she died. Nothing could change her fate. Not now. But Rachel's fate—they were going to do their level best to safeguard.

"She didn't need this."

Steve glanced over at Bradley. His friend wasn't talking about Ellayna, he was talking about Rachel. "I know." Everything she'd been through? She didn't need to be kidnapped *again*. To have God only knew what done to her *again*. It made Steve want to be sick just thinking about it. Same with Bradley by the look of it.

He reached out and set his hand on Bradley's shoulder where the tendon joined his neck. Steve squeezed, and leaned in so their faces were close. "We are going to find her."

"Good," Megan said from the other side of Adrian. "Let's go then. Double Down doesn't have much, but we still have a plane."

Steve dropped his hand from Bradley's neck. "And you know where he took her?"

"He wants to kill both you and the Vice President's brother, right?"

Steve nodded.

"So he's bringing the one thing you both want, and he's going to stick her in the middle of that showdown. After you guys are done fighting, he's going to kill whoever is left." She shrugged, but even in the dark he could see the sick look on her face. "He'll probably keep her as a souvenir. If she's still alive."

Mint brushed past them all. "Let's go!" He called it out, loud enough it could be construed as a yell.

Steve seconded that sentiment.

Megan followed them. "Don't you want to know where I think he took her?"

Steve pulled open the back door of the truck so she could get in. "Where?"

"The one place that links you all. The place where this all started for the vice president and his brother." She climbed in.

Adrian nudged Steve back before he could get in and sat in the middle seat beside his girlfriend. "Where this all started?" He buckled up.

Steve got in. "Venezuela? That's where you think David took Rachel?"

"It's a theory."

Adrian pulled out his phone. "I'll check with the agents I have running down all the private flights departing shortly after she was taken. We'll see if we get a hit on the flight plan."

It would confirm their theory. One step closer to finding her and getting her back.

Bradley drove like a man possessed. Steve was surprised no cop noticed and pulled them over. He held onto the door handle as they careened over to the airport and he prayed in a way he'd never prayed before. Rachel wasn't a believer, as far as he'd been able to tell. Not the way he was, or her family was.

But she certainly needed God right now.

. . .

Rachel's legs threatened to give out. Her hands were bound in front of her. Bad, but not the worst it could be. She just kept repeating that in her head. Bad, but not the worst it could be. Trying to trick—or convince—her brain into thinking this was okay.

He shoved her along, which was about all the touching he'd done. She wanted to land on her knees and take a second to thank the God everyone believed in that he hadn't raped her. Not yet, anyway.

She hadn't remembered the first time that had happened to her, as she'd been drugged. But she remembered how much she ached afterward. Rachel had no desire to go through any of that again.

A tear rolled down her face.

The trek from the car to wherever they were going was nothing but dusty dirt. Uneven ground. She stumbled over a root, or something. It was still dark. Vegetation was sparse. She wanted to ask him where they were, but conversation would remind him she was here. That he could interact with her.

He likely hadn't forgotten, since he was walking her to...wherever. But she didn't want to start a conversation. Not when she didn't know what it would end with. The more he left her to her own thoughts, the better.

Who'd ever have guessed she would have learned something from being kidnapped, repeatedly. Not her. But here she was. This was turning out to be her life.

Maybe her New Year's resolution should be to not get kidnapped anymore.

There was a good goal. Solid.

He shoved her again, this time with the barrel of his gun. Rachel gritted her teeth and had to bite back the urge to tell him she was walking as fast as she could. Climbing this hill that probably led nowhere, in whatever country they were in.

They crested a ridge and she gasped.

The valley below was...nothing. Dirt. Mounds of what probably used to be buildings. Maybe even a whole village.

"Whoa." She said the word under her breath.

To her disdain, he spoke to her. "Behold, the might of the American government."

She didn't turn to look or ask him what he meant.

David shoved her in the back so that she stumbled down the hill, before she managed to get her balance back. "This is where it all happened." He waved his hand to encompass the whole area. "Where America started a campaign to destabilize an entire country, just because these people had something we wanted."

Rachel glanced back at him. First he'd sounded like he was a bitter ex-operative with ties to nowhere. Now he sounded oddly proud of what they'd accomplished. Like he'd been a part of it.

"Venezuela was a thriving country with a strong economy. This village was probably a bustling community, full of people working and living with their families. Then a team comes through. Fire and destruction. Nothing left but ash and pain." David was quiet for a second, then he said, "The VP's brother told me the water in the river ran like it was blood for a week. And for what?"

He shook his head. Rachel glanced back at the scene in front and tried to imagine everything he'd said. Venezuelans. A mission, here where the vice president had grown up. Gunmen. The military. Death.

He said, "So we could get richer. Leave the rest of the world floundering, and we don't even care. Scrabbling for scraps. Destabilized, so cartels take over. People scared for their lives while Americans grow fat and lazy, hiding behind their border and their rules. People are dying."

"It's easy to make a stand for an ideology and preach to the whole world how you feel." She stared out at the first glances of the morning sunrise. "It's harder to take a hand and help someone out of the dirt."

"And which are you?"

She turned, then. "You know nothing about me, other than what you've read online. Or seen." He'd probably watched the video. He was probably like all the others.

Rachel turned away, unable to look at him. He shoved her on. Forced her to walk into the center of the destruction. Half walls, charred structures partly demolished. Beyond, he moved her to the river where trees grew. Tents had been raised, and shelters made with blankets strung between trees. Fishing boats were moored at a ramshackle pier.

The gunshots came out of nowhere.

She screamed and crouched. Lifted her hands to cover her head, before she looked back at him. David held the gun up. He fired into the air until his clip was spent.

People ran. Kids. Teens. Adults. Even an old man, helped by a younger one. Screaming. They rushed away, along the river bank. Some jumped into boats and rowed away.

Rachel wished she could go with them.

"Inside."

He shoved her into a dwelling. A one-room house, the walls made of boards and sheets of metal. Blankets covered the walls, decoration and protection from the elements. A spider ran across the floor. It was definitely a spider. It couldn't possibly be something worse.

She wasn't going to get bitten by a nasty creature.

That was enough to induce her to start praying to God. Whether He was really up there, or not, He was in charge of those things, right? He could keep them *away* from her.

David kicked out the back of her knees.

She yelped as they gave out and she hit the dirt, then rolled onto her hip. He left the "house." Someone's home. Rachel squeezed her eyes shut. These people didn't need their lives disturbed the way David was doing. He wasn't likely to leave anything but destruction in his wake.

Why had he brought her here? She didn't want to be the bait.

Rachel looked around, trying to distract her mind from falling into dark despair. It didn't work.

A worn leather book sat on the collection of blankets she figured was a bed. The words *La Santa Biblia* were written across the cover. Nearly worn completely away. Even here, where life was nothing like the existence she lived in Washington DC, people had God in their lives.

She wanted to know why they did that. Weren't they mad at God that they had so little? Maybe they thought they had everything they needed. What if they even pitied wealthy Christians in affluent countries? There were so many distractions. The person who lived here had a comparatively meager existence, but all that focus could be placed on things that were actually important.

Did Rachel need to experience what that kind of life felt like? She certainly knew what it was like to have everything taken away, even if it was only her reputation and her privacy. She'd thought she was going to die many times over the past few weeks.

She had things she wanted and didn't yet have.

Steve was top of that list.

A husband. A family of her own, not just the one Bradley and Alexis were going to make. That would be theirs. Rachel wanted to know what that would be like for *her*. She wanted to know what it felt like to be loved like that. Like she was the only person in the world for the one she loved.

Another tear escaped, but she refused to give in to it. She was not going to fear. She was going to trust that they would come for her. At least Bradley would. Steve…she hoped he would. But the truth was, she didn't know.

Help me.

The prayer sounded strange on her lips. Like a foreign language. At once, peace moved through her. She wanted more of that. *God. Help me.* She didn't know what else to say. All that sin Alexis had explained to her about weighed heavy on her shoulders, and she knew He wanted nothing to do with it.

And so she prayed that Jesus would clear her of the consequences of everything she'd done, and all that had been done to her. In all the ways she was dirty and stained, he had come to wash her clean.

Would He come for her even now?

David stuck his head back into the dwelling. The grin on his face made her stomach churn. "He's here."

Chapter 22

Steve crawled on his stomach to the edge of the ridge and lifted binoculars to his eyes. Mint and Bradley had positioned themselves away from him. They formed a grid that boxed David in and would allow them to tighten the noose. Steve didn't care if the man walked away from this or not. It only mattered that they got Rachel back. That she was alive to be able to heal.

Adrian shuffled up beside him.

Below, in the few dwellings that remained here after the destruction so long ago, there was little movement. People had scattered. One resident had told them about the gunman and the woman with him who'd been tied up. Which structure were they in?

Steve said, "Update?"

The fed settled flat beside him. "An agent took a look at Rachel's computer. There was a resignation letter on it, one we think Ellayna started typing to make it look like Rachel planned to leave."

Steve said, "She would never give it all up."

"I don't know," Adrian said. "Things have been crazy lately. Maybe she wanted to get out."

Steve didn't know, and couldn't without talking to her. If they got her out of this, then he'd find out. "Whatever they had planned, it didn't work. We weren't fooled."

The radio in Steve's ear crackled. A woman's voice. "I'm in position."

"Copy that," he replied to Megan.

Five of them. What was left of Double Down's team, plus Adrian who refused to let them go without him.

"I figured you'd have stuck with her instead of me," Steve said, considering Megan's recent injuries. "Babysitting me so you can report back to the FBI?"

"What if I am? You want to skirt the lines of legality being here, am I really going to make much difference? I'm hardly a restraining force."

Steve's hold on restraint was thinning with every minute Rachel was down there. The only things that had held him together all these years, through countless missions and top secret operations, were his honor and a loose hold on morals. Lately he'd come back to the closer relationship with God he'd had when he'd been a chaplain.

But with Rachel now in danger, his tenuous hold on restraint was being tested. His faith was being tested. He wanted to walk down there, gun raised, and just shoot his way through whatever obstacles he faced. And he'd have done it, if he didn't think David would put a bullet in Rachel's head. Too many variables made the operation a tricky one. David had been trained as Steve had—to eliminate those variables as soon as they grew too out of control.

The quickest way to do that would be to kill her.

"I'm here to help," Adrian said. "I know you don't trust me—"

Steve shook his head. "I just don't know you. But if Megan vouches for you, and I figure she does since you two are together, then that's good enough for me."

"So I get to stick by you just because I'm the unknown, then."

That worked for Steve. "My team functions well because we know each other. You, I've never been on an op with."

Adrian nodded. "That's fair. I'm just here to help get Rachel back. Saving her is what we all want. Especially after what she's been through."

"She didn't need this," Steve muttered as he stared at the dwellings and waited for some sign of movement. An indication as to what was happening.

"That's for sure." Adrian blew out a breath. "Praying for her on the plane was good. But I'm ready to do more now."

"I know what you mean."

Prayer had been all they were able to do on the plane. Hours of waiting, what else was there to focus on than giving it all up to God and asking Him for wisdom? It had helped them not feel useless, like they weren't doing anything.

Now it was time for action.

Steve keyed his radio. "Buckle up."

Mint replied, "Copy that. Ready."

Megan said, "Ready."

They all waited.

Steve said, "Bradley?"

He was ready to give the order to move. What was the former SEAL doing?

"Hold." Bradley's one word was clipped and even with that Steve could hear the frustration in his tone.

They all waited.

A minute later, Bradley's voice came over the comms. "Contact."

"Report." Steve was already scanning the area with his binoculars. He saw the man walking before Bradley replied.

"The vice president's brother. Coming in from the southwest."

"Copy that." Steve was watching him move. A confident stride, like he knew exactly where he was going. Blank face. No weapons visible, but his heavy coat could disguise a lot.

The vice president's brother stopped twenty feet from the dwellings.

He called out, "I'm here, Sanders!"

Bradley said, "I have a shot."

"Negative," Steve replied. "Do not take that shot." They probably all had an angle on the vice president's brother, given he was standing out in the open. Bradley was the only one with a high-powered rifle that could fire the round far enough to cross the distance and hit the man with any kind of accuracy. But he was too close to the structure, and Steve didn't want David retaliating by shooting Rachel.

Steve palmed his Sig and said, "Close in. Fifty feet, under cover."

Adrian followed, finding his own spot to hide behind. They didn't need to be seen.

The material covering an opening to one of the riverside dwellings shifted. David moved so Steve could actually see his body and not just his head in the doorway. Someone else would have a better angle, maybe even one where they'd be able to see his face.

"Bradley." It came out before he really thought about it.

His friend said, "No shot," frustration even more evident in his tone now.

David stuck a hand out, holding a weapon. He used it to wave the vice president's brother inside. He wanted a meeting? Steve had figured he would just shoot the man. It was what he'd wanted to do. David evidently had other plans.

If their theory tracked, he wanted both Steve and the vice president's brother dead. And then he was going to disappear where anyone looking for the assassin who'd killed the vice president would never find him.

The older man walked with a steady pace to the dwelling, then ducked his head to go inside. Why was he even here? Had the man really been lured by Rachel's having been captured? That meant he had some kind of draw to her.

Every way Steve spun that in his mind, it wasn't good. Who knew what the hacker/blackmailer wanted with her. Whatever it was, Steve wouldn't let it happen. No way. No how.

"We need eyes in there." He said it to himself, not airing his frustration over comms. They didn't all need to be sucked under by his feeling powerless. Especially Bradley. It was a tie as to who wanted Rachel back more. But then it wasn't a competition, either.

Steve heard raised voices, but couldn't make out what they said.

A shot rang out. Light flashed in the gaps between the fabric and boards that made up the structure.

A scream rang out. High and clear. A woman.

Rachel.

Steve got up and started running. "Move in. Now!"

. . .

Rachel sucked in a breath and touched her thigh, either side of the gunshot wound. Her head swam, and she swayed to the side before she caught herself. Put pressure on it, right? She could hardly see straight, let alone find something to push on the wound.

The thought made bile rise in her throat. She tried to think past the pain.

David had shot her.

The vice president's brother roared. He rushed toward the gunman and barreled into him. They hit the ground, shaking the entire house. Someone's home. And it was going to come down right on top of them.

Rachel shifted backwards so she could get as far away from them as possible. Black spots filled her vision and she gritted her teeth. She left a smear of blood. Had the bullet gone through her leg? Wasn't that important to know?

David and the vice president's brother rolled around on the floor.

Her back hit the wall, and she exhaled. It came out as a pained whimper that sounded horrible to her own ears. Where was everyone? She needed help. Bradley. Mint. Adrian. She would even take Steve, if he was willing to come.

Words tumbled from her mouth, a desperate prayer for help. She didn't want to promise God she would be one of His children just so He would get her out of here. But she wanted to. It was a temptation she wasn't sure she could withstand.

The two men rolled close enough they hit her leg. Rachel cried out. She heard something outside, but didn't know what it was. Help? The two men in here didn't seem to notice, so maybe she was just kidding herself. Filling the last moments of her life before she bled out onto the dirt in Venezuela with wishful thinking.

The gun went off.

Her whole body flinched, and she let out another cry. David's body went limp. The vice president's brother was still for a moment, and then he started to shove at David to get the dead man off him.

"Rachel!" The cry came from outside.

She knew that voice. "Steve!" He was here? Gratefulness rushed through her, and for a moment her leg didn't hurt so badly. She was going to be rescued.

The vice president's brother rolled to sit up. He lifted the gun and pointed it at the door. Before she could scream, "No," or warn them in some way, he pulled the trigger.

A barrage of shots. So many. Too many for her to count. She waited for the gun to click empty. It didn't. He shot holes in the material that covered the door.

The vice president's brother stopped firing.

Silence.

She wanted to scream. To call out and ask if Steve was alive. Surely he'd make some kind of noise if he was. Right?

A whimper crawled up her throat. *Steve.* Had he come all this way, to rescue her, only to die? Tears rolled down her face.

Harlem Anderson clambered to his feet and looked around. Figuring out what to do? Rachel opened her mouth to scream for help.

He pointed the gun at her. "Quiet."

She swallowed. The pain in her leg made her thoughts stutter until she couldn't string two things together.

From outside the call came. "This is the FBI." Adrian's voice rang out, though she could hear an edge of nervousness. "Come out with your hands up and surrender."

The vice president's brother climbed to his feet. He moved to the doorway and called out, "I'll kill her if you come near us!"

"There's no way you get out alive if you do that." Bradley.

Emotion rolled through her. Just a rush of feeling that overwhelmed Rachel.

They had come for her. God had brought them here.

Thank You.

Peace washed over her, despite the fact she was still in a hostage situation. She looked around, trying to figure out if there was a way to do something.

The Bible was great and all, and she would read it later, but it wouldn't help her against a crazy man with a gun. Right? She kept looking around. David's body wasn't something she wanted to look at. She forced herself to do it anyway.

Jacket. Cargo pants. She'd seen him stuff things in there. One pant leg was hiked up. Strapped to his ankle was a revolver.

Rachel had always been purposely neutral on the subject of gun control. Bradley had taught her how to use them to defend herself and made sure she had one at home. Now she wasn't so sure. She'd never used one on a person, only at the range.

Could she do it now, fire a gun with the intent to kill? It was easy to preach about her God-given rights—or government-given anyway—but this wasn't talk. This was action. Like when she'd stabbed that man, defending herself. When push came to shove, and she had to aim at something other than a paper target, could she do it?

Pushing aside the fear, she decided to trust what her brother had instilled in her. The drive to save the people she loved that had steered them all here. For her.

If she didn't do this, then the team could get hurt.

The people she cared about most.

Her family.

She shuffled herself across the floor, dragging her injured leg. Teeth gritted, she held back what she wanted to say. It was impossible to do so silently, but she also shouldn't let on what she was doing. Every breath she pushed out she used to shove the pain from the forefront of her mind. She got close enough to reach the gun strapped to David's ankle.

But the vice president's brother saw her.

She froze.

He figured out what she was doing. Started to lift his gun.

Rachel pulled the strap and tugged the revolver free. She swung it around, already firing. Two bullets punched holes in the wall. The third hit him. She kept firing.

He'd already pulled the trigger on David's other gun.

It hit her, dead center.

Her entire body jolted. Rachel blinked up at the ceiling. Tried to figure out what had happened. Several people were yelling. She was lying on her back. Her entire body a mass of pain. Damp under her fingers, warm and wet.

There was a rush of feet, and someone dropped to their knees beside her. Too close. She moaned, unable to keep the pain inside.

A heavy weight landed on her chest and pain tore through her again. He was pushing on her chest. "Why did you do that?" Bradley's face swam in front of her. "Why, Rach?"

She drifted in and out. "Help." They weren't the only ones who could save the day. She wasn't going to be a victim, not anymore.

Someone said, "He's down."

"She needs a chopper. *Now.*"

Rachel couldn't tell the voices apart. Consciousness was like trying to catch a snowflake. Cold. She was so cold. It moved through her with a shudder. Pain was like a knife. She was jostled and had to blink against the bright sun.

Wasn't it December in DC? She should be cold. Instead, sweat ran down her face.

"We're losing her!"

She didn't want him to sound so scared. "Steve."

"I'm here." Hands touched her face. "I'm right here, Rach."

"K." *Love you.* She did and whether he returned that feeling or not she didn't know. He'd never said anything. But she'd thought…

Rachel was lifted. Pain exploded everywhere.

The world went black.

Chapter 23

Three days. That was how long Rachel had been in and out of consciousness. Through a plane ride back to the naval hospital at Bethesda and two more surgeries after the rush of stabilizing her in Venezuela. The times she had been awake, she'd been so out of it on the meds they'd given her, that she made no sense.

Three days thinking about what she'd said. Wondering if it meant something more than a spur of the moment throw-away comment when she thought she was going to die.

Alexis walked into the waiting area. Steve stood as she approached, unable to get an update on how Rachel was from the look on her face.

The whole group huddled around. Megan and her mom, Adrian close by them. Mint and Emma. Bradley set aside his tiny paper cup of hospital coffee. "Lex?"

Alexis glanced at her husband, then at the rest of them. "She's awake."

Bradley made a move toward the doorway. Alexis held up her hand. "She's asking for Steve."

"I'm her brother."

Someone snorted.

Alexis shrugged, a guilty look on her face. "Sorry."

Bradley shot a nasty look at Steve, which he ignored. She really wanted to speak to him? He moved to where Alexis stood, between him and the door. He stopped beside her. "Is she okay?"

"She's coherent." Alexis made a face. "No more loopy Rachel, thank goodness."

He nodded. Made his way to the room. Secret Service agents flanked the door. She was out of danger, the threat neutralized, thanks to her. She'd killed Harlem Anderson. David was dead. Still, they took their job protecting her seriously, and he was grateful for their presence.

He'd had hardly any sleep worrying about her. Thankfully Megan's mother had offered to check on Mrs. Cromwell. How she found out about the SAC's family situation he didn't know, but someone had told her.

Steve tapped on the door.

"Come in."

Her voice was soft. He let himself in and closed the door behind him. Stood there, trying to figure out what he was supposed to do now.

"Are you going to stare at me all day?"

Steve didn't move. "How is it you look beautiful after getting shot only a few days ago?"

She smiled. Her skin was still a little pale. She usually had more color than this. But he hadn't lied. She did look beautiful. Rachel held out her hand. "Come here."

Love you.

He moved to her. Took her hand, which she used to tug him to sit on the side of the bed. "Your leg."

"Don't worry about it."

He frowned. She didn't let go of his hand, just held it tight in hers.

"You came to save me."

"Seems like you saved yourself." His whole world had flipped upside down hearing those gunshots. They hadn't been able to breach the dwelling until it stopped. A lifetime that stretched out in those few seconds before he ran in and saw all the blood.

Steve shut his eyes and sucked in a full, cleansing breath.

"It's over now."

He nodded, opened his eyes and looked at her. "You're all right."

"You aren't in jail."

Like that was even a factor. He didn't care. "You can go back to your life."

She made a face he didn't understand, then said, "Double Down is safe."

"For now," he said. "The blackmailer is dead." Along with everyone he'd worked with as an agent for the CIA. Not a great legacy, nothing but pain and death. Why was Steve the only one still standing, not dead or in jail?

"Was it the vice president, or his brother?"

"Both, from what Adrian has been able to figure out. The FBI found the motel room where the vice president's brother had been staying. Apparently there was quite the computer set-up, so they've concluded he was the hacker and computer genius, as well as part of masterminding the blackmailing scheme."

Steve sighed. "The vice president's wife claims she had no knowledge of what they were doing or planning. Who knows if the VP himself was the brains behind it, or if his brother orchestrated the whole thing? He isn't around to explain himself. Neither of them are. And that St. Germaine guy is still in the wind.

"What we do have is all kinds of people coming forward to share their stories. Seems like there were more victims than anyone knew about. People who didn't want to admit what they'd done, so they never told anyone they'd been targeted."

Rachel made a face. "Lucky me, mine got plastered all over everywhere."

She and Alexis had released the video of her themselves, something which had begun this whole thing for Double Down. He'd watched it, thinking like everyone else did that it had been Alexis. He'd felt for them both.

Now that he knew it was Rachel… Steve didn't want to view her as weak or a victim. Not when she'd proven to them all, and to the world, that she was strong.

"I'm proud of you."

She blinked.

"I mean that. Really."

"I know you wouldn't lie to me."

He shook his head. "No way I would do that. I respect you far too much to lead you on or tell you an untruth."

"Oh." Her face fell. "Right."

"That's why I was glad when Alexis said you wanted to speak to me. Because there are some things I'd like to say to you."

Her look turned cautious, as though she thought she might have to protect herself from getting hurt.

"I'm messing this up." He sighed. "Totally out of practice. In the sense that I've never actually done this before. Forty-three years, and I've never in my life told a woman that I love her."

Her jaw dropped.

"It's true."

"I—"

He waited for more, but she didn't say anything else. "I love you, Rachel."

Her hand squeezed his. A desperate grip that gave away exactly how much hope she had. He said, "I tried to give you space, even though I didn't want to. I hurt for you. I wanted to defend you. To be there for you. Then when I was contacted by the blackmailer, I wanted—more than anything else—to convince myself it was for the best to pull away from you. That not dragging you down into my guilt was the best thing. The right thing."

"You're a good man, Steve. The best kind."

"I'm not completely convinced of that. I've done some awful things. But who I am hasn't been totally overridden. I still want to do the right thing."

"And what is that?"

Steve looked down at their entwined fingers. Then he lifted his head. "I want to make an honest woman out of you. And I want you to make me happier than I ever could be by myself."

"I love you."

"I know." He smiled. "You told me that when you were bleeding out. I thought you were going to die—" His voice caught. He cleared his throat. "I'm so glad you're all right. I don't want to waste any time."

She stared at him, love in her eyes.

"Marry me."

She said, "I'm about to be unemployed."

"I have pieces of a business and no idea how I'm going to rebuild."

"Can I work for you?" She bit her lip. "I could be your public relations director."

"I probably need one of those, considering I was a fugitive just days ago."

"Steve?"

He let the smile fade away. "Yes?"

"It would be an honor to marry you." She paused. "Only…"

"What?"

"Are you going to kiss me at some point, or do I have to wait for the wedding?"

He felt the grin stretch across his face. "If we do that, the wedding is going to be tomorrow."

She shook her head, mischief in her eyes. "No way, buster. I'm not going to get married in the hospital."

"Next week, then."

"Next week is Christmas."

He leaned forward, using his free hand to touch a finger to her lips. "It can be your present. But you have to act surprised, okay?"

She smiled. "No one will fall for that."

He came so close that she felt the whisper of his lips on hers when he said, "I don't care."

. . .

Four days later, Rachel was released. She *itched* to get out of the hospital, so when they wheeled her out to the shoveled curb where the SUV waited, she had a smile on her face. Steve looked sick.

"This is insane. They should keep you longer than this."

"I'm fine." Okay, so that wasn't exactly true. "It's Christmas."

"Not quite yet." Bradley pulled the back door open. "Ready?"

"I'll help her." Steve closed the distance and held out his hands. Transferring to the car was painful, but she bit her lips together and didn't let on how much it hurt. He leaned in to buckle the seatbelt for her and whispered, "You aren't fooling anyone."

Rachel was so excited to be getting out of there, she whispered back. "Kiss me, then. It'll distract me from the pain."

Bradley got in the front seat, where Alexis sat beside him on the passenger side. "Are you guys going to be like this forever?"

"Yes."

Steve got in on the other side and took her hand. "I like that word." He grinned. "And I'm going to like, 'I do' even more."

Alexis giggled.

"Don't encourage them," Bradley told her. "It's only going to get worse."

Alexis leaned over the console and said something quiet to her brother. His eyes flashed with warmth. A secret they shared since they'd gotten married themselves.

Bradley shook his head, clearly exasperated with the whole thing.

Rachel didn't care.

"Alexis?"

Her friend turned in her seat. "I emailed your resignation letter to the Governor of Virginia. He called me this morning. He's sad that you've decided to leave the Senate, but he understands."

"Thank you."

Steve reached over and squeezed her hand. Rachel's leg was bandaged, so it was twice the size of the other one. Her entire torso hurt as well, but the bullet had missed everything vital. It could have been so much worse—a fact the nurses and doctors had exclaimed about over and over again.

"So where are we going now?" Rachel glanced at Steve. "Wherever it is, there will be cinnamon rolls, right? I was promised cinnamon rolls."

Bradley snorted. "You can take the girl out of the senate, but you can't take the senator out of the girl."

"Hey!" She needed something to throw at him.

Alexis laughed. Even Steve joined in. He fingered the diamond studded band he'd slid on her finger two days ago. Simple, unique. She loved it.

She was going to love her Christmas present even more.

Life wasn't going to be perfect. It might not even be easy. Her past was going to rise up on occasion, like the ghost of Christmas past sending ripples through the present. She'd explained that to Steve, wanting to warn him. She likely was going to have issues with trust and intimacy, even though her therapist had visited her in the hospital. She was never going to be "over" what had happened. But Steve had promised her that he would be there to help her get through it.

And she was going to trust him.

Bradley pulled into the parking lot of the Double Down warehouse.

"I thought we were going to my house?" She glanced around. Who was going to explain?

Steve said, "I saw your face when I mentioned you going home. I know you're excited to get out of the hospital, but I also know you didn't love your house."

"Which one?" she asked. "The one I was kidnapped out of, or the new one that I was also kidnapped out of?" No one laughed. Okay, so it hadn't been all that funny. Still. "Too soon?"

Alexis leaned forward, moaning. "Yes." Her voice was muffled, head in her hands. Bradley shot Rachel a look and rubbed his wife's back.

Steve said, "We made you up a room here, where we can *all* keep an eye on your recovery."

"Goodie."

He ignored her tone, and the look on her face. "And we brought over some of your things."

Oh. "Thank you."

"Stay there." He climbed out, came around and opened her door. "Come on. Let's get out of the cold."

She let him help her, because moving hurt. A lot. As they walked for the front door, very slowly, she looked up at the sky. "Where are we at on having a white Christmas?"

He chuckled. "I checked the forecast, as instructed." He pulled open the front door and a wave of warm air rushed out.

Rachel didn't go inside. "And?"

He leaned forward and touched his lips to hers in a quick kiss. "Looks like it'll be a white wedding."

Chapter 24

Emma shifted the cheese plate closer to the apples. Or should the bowl of nuts be in front? Would they be easier to reach that way?

Mint touched her hand with his. "Everything is perfect. Stop fussing."

She sighed. "I just want it to be right when Rachel gets here."

He didn't let go of her hand, but tugged her around so they were facing each other. He pulled her body against his and slid his other arm around her waist. He looked at her with the contented gaze of a man at peace, who had everything he wanted.

Or, at least, he *thought* he had everything he wanted. Mint didn't know what she'd gotten him for Christmas.

He kissed her. Emma forgot about the cheese. The apples. And the bowl of nuts.

"Um…you guys. They're here."

Mint shifted, and she glanced over. Megan chuckled, then added, "That looked like fun." She shot Adrian a look. He rubbed at his chin with his thumb and flushed. Emma found herself flushing also, completely embarrassed.

She glanced at Mint. They really needed to tell their friends the news.

The door opened. Steve and Rachel entered, followed by Bradley and Alexis. Rachel grinned. "You're all here."

"Merry Christmas!" Emma clapped. Mint pulled her against him.

Rachel leaned against Steve, looking very much like there was nowhere she would rather be. Clearly happy. She also looked like she needed to sit down. He led her to an armchair in the corner, beside the couch where Mrs. Cromwell sat with Megan's mom. Rachel started up a conversation with them, while Steve poured two cups of coffee.

The Christmas tree in the corner had a few presents scattered underneath. Small, carefully wrapped gifts.

Bradley said, "Anyone know what that rust bucket Jag is, sitting outside in the parking lot?"

Emma said nothing.

Most of the rest of them shook their heads and looked at each other to see whose it was. Mint strode to the window and pulled down two slats of the blinds. He stared out the window in silence.

Was he going to like it? This was their first Christmas together. She didn't want to mess it up.

"That's an E type. Looks like late sixties." He turned back, his gaze zeroed in on her.

Emma said, "Merry Christmas."

Bradley and Steve moved with long strides to the window to look out. Adrian joined them. The FBI agent looked out between the blinds. "Looks like a piece of junk."

"It isn't." Mint's voice was low and steady. Then he came away from the window and moved to her. "Did you buy me a car for Christmas?"

Emma pressed her lips together.

Bradley called over his shoulder, "Does the thing even run?"

"No," Emma said, not taking her eyes from the man she loved.

"That's not the point." Mint grinned, moving closer to her. His arms slid around her. He kissed her, shifting them both so she was bent back over his arm in a dip that took her breath away. Totally worth all the sleuthing, trying to figure out what he wanted. Turns out the answer to that was the "perfect" car, according to him. A project to tinker with.

When he straightened with her still in his arms, she touched his cheeks. "I love you."

Mint let go of her with one arm, but not the other. He clicked his fingers. "Bradley, get me that metallic green gift box. The little one."

Bradley huffed, but did as instructed and handed the box to Mint. He brought it between them so that she had to back up a fraction. Emma took the paper off and found a ring box.

"You guys are already engaged," Megan said, sounding slightly perturbed. Adrian tugged her to him so they could stand together.

Emma lifted the lid on the box.

Mint said, "Because I didn't get you one when we said our vows."

Two silver bands, one thin and small and the other wider and bigger, sat together in the box.

"Merry Christmas."

She kissed him while all their friends gasped and exclaimed.

"You guys got married!"

"Why didn't you tell us?"

Emma leaned back to find Steve standing beside them. He said, "Congratulations."

Rachel said, "When did you guys do this?"

"Couple of weeks ago," Mint said.

"We were together so much, in the car and then separate hotel rooms." Emma laughed. "It seems crazy to just do it for convenience sake, or so it was easier for Mint to protect me, but…" She felt her face flush again. Whatever their reason didn't change the fact she was right where she wanted to be.

Mint and Emma both put on their wedding bands, and he slid the engagement ring on her finger after it. They hugged all their friends, and everyone enjoyed their pre-Christmas dinner. The actual day was coming up soon enough. But why wait to celebrate? They were all safe.

Emma leaned against Mint. He glanced at her, and she shifted to look up in his eyes. She said, "I love you."

"I love you, too."

They kissed again.

"You guys are gross."

Megan's mother gasped. "Megan! I've seen you and Adrian act just as lovey-dovey as that." She started to laugh. "You're just jealous."

Megan pouted, a smile in her eyes.

"I guess that's my cue."

.   .   .

Megan frowned, watching as Adrian set his mug on the coffee table and moved to the Christmas tree. "What cue? What are you talking about?"

She saw her mother shift, out the corner of her eye, but ignored it. She'd much rather look at her boyfriend. Life might be in complete shambles, but there was something about him that gave her peace.

He stilled her. When Adrian wasn't there, the past crowded in. She got antsy and didn't know what to focus on. Maybe when Double Down was back up and running, and she was on missions again, then she'd have somewhere to direct her energy. But right now, there was just Adrian.

Strong. Calm. Steady.

She wouldn't be surprised if one day he was head of the whole FBI. Steve had given him all the credit for taking down the blackmailer, to the end that the president had called Adrian into his office to personally shake his hand.

Megan was the wild card. A renegade former FBI agent. She didn't fit the mold and even now preferred to work solo. The bureau would never let her team up with Adrian. She'd finally given up her FBI credentials just to smooth out all the ruffled feathers. She was a free agent. An operative of Double Down.

She was proud of all her friends and what they'd done, despite what each of them had been through, but this man was the man she loved. She wanted to be in his life any way she could be and hoped he felt the same way.

Adrian stood and held out a tiny wrapped package for her. Not a ring box, like Emma had gotten. This was long and thin.

She took it. "What..?" Was she supposed to know what this was? He stood in front of her in silence while she tore into the tape. No sense wasting any time getting to the good part.

Someone giggled. Her mother huffed. Megan ignored it. What was he...

Inside the tiny box was a square diamond mounted on a silver ring. From it looped a delicate silver chain. She knew nothing about jewelry other than the fact she liked certain things. Simple decoration. It had to be functional as well as beautiful. Just because something wasn't flashy, didn't make it less meaningful.

"I figured you wouldn't want to go on missions with it on your finger, so I had it put on a necklace." There was a note of nervousness in his voice.

Megan lifted it from the box and looped the chain over her fingers so the ring dangled down. It blurred as tears filled her eyes.

Adrian crouched. "I'm doing this wrong, aren't I?" He made a frustrated sound.

No one else spoke.

Megan shook her head. Words refused to form. She leaned close to him and pressed her lips to his. Tears rolled down her cheeks. She kept their faces close, noses touching, and leaned slightly against his face with her eyes closed.

"Megan." He whispered her name.

She turned her head slightly and kissed his cheek. Despite the fact they'd said they loved each other, she'd been wondering if they should have talked more than that about their relationship. But how did you start that conversation?

She wanted to get married. She wanted to have children with the man she loved. Bradley and Alexis had done it fast, but they'd known each other for years and didn't want to wait. Emma and Mint were engaged. Now they all knew the two had gotten married recently. Another case of not wanting to wait, not seeing the point in delaying the combining of their lives.

Megan wanted to get to know this man more. To build a life together on a strong foundation, like Bradley and Alexis had.

"I love you." She whispered it to him, there in front of all their friends.

"Will you marry me? Soon." He paused. "But not really soon, I want to give you time to actually plan it. Unlike these crazy people just getting hitched on a whim." He shook his head. "What is that about?"

Megan laughed.

Adrian took the ring from the chain. "Well?"

There was so much hope in his eyes. She loved it that she was the one who put it there. The possibility, the promise. It was a beautiful thing. "Yes, I'd love to marry you…in six to twelve months."

Everyone laughed. Her mother made a *Phew* sound and looked at the ceiling. "Thank You, Jesus." She glanced around then. "I love you all, but I'm going broke from these spur of the moment weddings—and Christmas."

Mrs. Cromwell lifted her glass. "Here, here."

Megan grinned. Adrian slid the ring on her finger and tugged on her hand until she stood. He kissed her again.

Mrs. Cromwell said, "Are we done with the big announcements, or is it time to eat?"

Everyone laughed. Bradley started toward the table of food, but Alexis caught his hand, stalling him. She said, "Well…" dragging the word out.

"You're already married!" Rachel laughed.

"Lex?" He didn't sound worried, but he had no idea why she hadn't let go of him yet.

Alexis bit her lip, looking up at her husband with a whole lot of what Megan felt for Adrian in her eyes.

"I'm pregnant."

Rachel gasped.

Bradley's legs looked like they gave out. He crumpled in front of her and landed on his good knee.

Alexis choked back a sob as he straightened, still on one knee.

"I… We…" It was like he didn't even know what to say.

A tear rolled down Megan's face. Adrian pulled her under his shoulder, fingering her ring with his free hand. She buried her face against his shirt and watched her friends.

Alexis nodded. In a soft voice, almost too quiet to hear she said, "We're having a baby, honey."

Rachel whooped loudly. Bradley hugged his wife's middle. Steve kissed Rachel. Emma and Mint spoke quietly to each other, whispering married people secrets.

Megan hugged her mother and gave Mrs. Cromwell a kiss on her cheek. It might seem weird to some that the elderly mother of the man who'd betrayed her, kidnapped her and then wound up saving her life would spend Christmas with them. But Megan had found forgiveness to be the most freeing thing in life. She might not have fully forgiven the men who turned her life around and killed her partner, yet. But inviting a lonely lady to be part of their family meant something to all of them.

It didn't matter what had gone on through the year.

Christmas was here.

Epilogue

Rachel faced the mirror, smoothing down the front of her dress. Megan's mother's Virginia house was beautiful, and she'd jumped at the chance to host an impromptu Christmas wedding.

The door opened behind her and she turned, unable to hide the wince.

Steve frowned as he entered. "That's what I was afraid of." He held up his hands, hiding her white wedding dress from his view. "I'm not looking at it until you convince me you're well enough to do this."

Rachel set one hand on her hip. "Oh, I'm doing this."

"Not good enough. You want me to send Bradley in here?"

"No!" She didn't need him playing big brother. Underneath the gruff and the complaining, she figured he was happy for her. He just also needed time to adjust to the fact she was getting married.

Rachel said, "It's too late now, anyway. We're already dressed, and the shrimp is going to get warm if we don't get on with it."

She looked down then. His suit was amazing. "You look so handsome."

Steve smoothed down his tie and smiled. He held out one hand, and she placed hers in it. He took her in, head to toe and then back up. "Wow."

"I forgot to get shoes."

"Go barefoot."

Rachel laughed, then groaned and laid a hand on her stomach.

"You aren't okay."

She shook her head, still holding his hand. "I want to do this. I might need a nap in a couple of hours, but I don't want to wait."

Maybe she was rushing just so the fear didn't take hold, but she was also trusting God that He would work it all out. They had the rest of their lives to figure out the little things. Rachel wanted to be in his arms, safe. Warm and comforted. Nothing denied, nothing but the two of them together in all the ways they could be.

New, beautiful memories to wash away the past.

He lifted his eyebrows. "Am I invited to this nap?"

She smiled. "Only after it's official."

"Good." He closed the distance between them. "I'm ready to start adding more tallies to the list of honorable things I've done in my life."

He crouched and lifted her into his arms.

"There's nothing wrong with my legs."

"I know." He strode to the door, carrying her.

"I can walk."

He said nothing.

"I love you."

He stopped in the hallway, short of where all their friends waited for them, and smiled down at her. "Merry Christmas."

Rachel smiled, happier than she'd ever been in her life. "Yes, it is."

DID YOU ENJOY THIS SERIES?

Would you consider leaving a review at the online store where you purchased it?

Reviews (good and bad) help prospective readers decide whether or not to click that "buy" button. I know I love to see what other people thought about a book.

Want to read more LISA PHILLIPS books?

Check out www.authorlisaphillips.com and sign up for the mailing list, where you'll be the first to hear about Lisa's newest books.

Also by Lisa Phillips

Denver FBI
- Target
- Bait
- Prey

WITSEC Town Series
- Sanctuary Lost
- Sanctuary Buried
- Sanctuary Breached
- Sanctuary Deceived
- Sanctuary Forever

Novellas
- Sanctuary Hidden
- A Sanctuary Christmas Tale

Double Down
- Deadly Exposure
- Deadly Secrets
- Deadly Agenda
- Deadly Holiday

Love Inspired Suspense
- Double Agent
- Star Witness
- Manhunt
- Easy Prey
- Sudden Recall
- Dead End
- Security Detail
- Homefront Defenders
- Yuletide Suspect
- Witness in Hiding
- Defense Breach
- Murder Mix-Up

Northwest Counter-Terrorism Taskforce
- First Wave
- Second Chance
- Third Hour
- Fourth Day
- Final Stand

Made in United States
Orlando, FL
05 February 2024

43295963R00339